T0066535

"The riveting conclusion to the Chaoswar Saga and
the Riftwar Cycle is satisfying in every way. . . .
In *Magician's End*, [Feist] has masterfully
brought the entire epic in a full circle."
Booklist

Praise for *A Crown Imperiled*

"Feist constantly amazes with his ability
to create great casts of characters."
SF Site

"With his storytelling mastery and ear for colorful
language and nuance, the author of numerous
books set in the dual worlds of Midkemia and
Kelewan here launches a series that takes his
fantasy universe into a whole new phase."
Library Journal

"Fast action, appealing characters, and a
splendid setting will delight readers of fantasy
and leave them eager for the next battle."
Kirkus Reviews

"Sheer readability."
San Francisco Chronicle

Praise for *A Kingdom Besieged*

"Feist has a command of language and a natural
talent for keeping the reader turning pages."
Chicago Sun-Times

"Feist's fans will look forward to
the saga's final episode."
Publishers Weekly

By Raymond E. Feist

The Chaoswar Saga
A KINGDOM BESIEGED
A CROWN IMPERILED
MAGICIAN'S END

The Demonwar Saga
RIDES A DREAD LEGION
AT THE GATES OF DARKNESS

The Darkwar Saga
FLIGHT OF THE NIGHTHAWKS
INTO A DARK REALM
WRATH OF A MAD GOD

Conclave of Shadows
TALON OF THE SILVER HAWK
KING OF FOXES
EXILE'S RETURN

Legends of the Riftwar
HONORED ENEMY (WITH WILLIAM R. FORSTCHEN)
MURDER IN LAMUT (WITH JOEL ROSENBERG)
JIMMY THE HAND (WITH S.M. STIRLING)

The Riftwar Legacy
KRONDOR: THE BETRAYAL
KRONDOR: THE ASSASSINS
KRONDOR: TEAR OF THE GODS

The Serpentwar Saga
SHADOW OF A DARK QUEEN
RISE OF A MERCHANT PRINCE
RAGE OF A DEMON KING
SHARDS OF A BROKEN CROWN

The Empire Trilogy
(WITH JANNY WURTS)
DAUGHTER OF THE EMPIRE
SERVANT OF THE EMPIRE
MISTRESS OF THE EMPIRE

ABIDE WITH ME

Abide with me; fast falls the eventide,
The darkness deepens; Lord, with me abide;
When other helpers fail, and comforts flee,
Help of the helpless, O abide with me.

*   *   *

I need Thy Presence every passing hour;
What but Thy grace can foil the tempter's power?
Who like Thyself my guide and stay can be?
Through cloud and sunshine, Lord, abide with me.

A. & M. 27

God Calling 2

A Companion Volume to
God Calling,
by Two Listeners,
Edited by A. J. Russell

BOOKS

Winchester, UK
Washington, USA

JOHN HUNT PUBLISHING

First published in 1950
First published by O-Books, 2009
O-Books is an imprint of John Hunt Publishing Ltd., 3 East St., Alresford,
Hampshire SO24 9EE, UK
office@jhpbooks.com
www.johnhuntpublishing.com
www.o-books.com

For distributor details and how to order please visit the 'Ordering' section on
our website.

Text copyright: A. J. Russell 2009

ISBN: 978 1 84694 273 0
978 1 84694 634 9 (ebook)

UK: Printed and bound by CPI Group (UK) Ltd, Croydon, CR0 4YY
US: Printed and bound by Thomson-Shore, 7300 West Joy Road, Dexter, MI 48130

We operate a distinctive and ethical publishing philosophy in all
areas of our business, from our global network of authors to
production and worldwide distribution.

THE REASON WHY

DURING the fifteen years that have passed since *God Calling* was born, more Messages have been received.

Now, in response to many requests for a companion-volume, and to mark the 212th thousand of *God Calling,* this new book, produced on the same lines, is launched.

Though, like *God Calling*, it makes no claim to throw new light on old truths, it is sent out with the prayer that it will be the means of showing readers more clearly what Christ may become to those who seek to know Him and to live with Him.

We know well that *God Calling* has been permitted to do this to a large number; very many have written to say so.

Others have said that the Messages have spoken comfort in sorrow, hope in despair, and brought courage and still more courage in the grey days of life. They have rejoiced with them that do rejoice, especially with many who love and laugh as they have counselled them to do.

By their insistence upon the simple teachings of Christ and His call to spiritual growth and progress, the Messages have unfailingly inspired readers without number to renewed effort through confident faith and trust.

Consequently again and again has come the question: " Though I have been reading them for years, why do the Messages seem always new?"

The answer is: They contain the story that is old and ever new, but they are *not* new; only the reader is NEW; year by passing year he or she is becoming the New Creature in Christ Jesus commanded by the New Testament.

And naturally so. Can anyone read these Messages day by day, strive to respond to their ceaseless promptings, without becoming renewed, or fail to realise therefrom an inner joy unknown before, the radiant joy of the Lord?

May many more be conscious of these experiences through the Messages and *Message* of *God at Eventide*.

For again it raises the age-old question and receives the same all-satisfying answer:

" Lord, to Whom shall we go. . . . Thou hast the words of eternal life?"

" *Learn of Me for I am meek and lowly in heart and ye shall find rest unto your souls.*"

JANUARY

All is Ready

WRITE for all things are now ready.

The world is waiting for My Message of Love, and Hope and Cheer. The very unrest of spirit is a sign. The turning from the husk of religion is a sign.

Man is no longer lulled by empty phrases and promises of a better life hereafter. He must *know* Me before he would wish to spend Eternity with Me. He must know Me here in the storm where he needs strength and rest.

He has been sleeping; now he has been shocked awake. Now he must find Me or fling defiance at Me or school himself into a denial, or indifference.

Reason and argument avail little. Only by the lives of My followers can man be helped; only by seeing Mine unmoved, at peace, joyful, in a world of sorrow, disillusionment and mistrust.

Your denial to-day will not be, "I know not the man." The world is indifferent as to whether you

profess Me or not. No, it will be your failure to present
Me in your life as I am—vital, sustaining, spirit-
renewing, your All.

Your Resolutions   **January 2**

IT is in union with Me that you receive strength to
carry out your good resolutions.

Contact with Me brings power for the work I wish
you to do, that work for which I know you to be most
suited and which you only can do, and do so well.

It is in contact with Me that you are endued with the
Grace that I alone can give, enabling you to minister
acceptably to those to whom I send you, and those
whom I bring to you.

Even among the distractions and manifold interests
of the world—live in My Presence, yet daily withdraw
yourself to be *alone* with Me.

Mutual Need   **January 3**

Abide in Me and I in you.

THIS year dwell much upon this stupendous Truth.
You need to abide in Me this year to share in the
Spirit-life of the Universe, in its creative power and
energy. Thus you are a part in God's whole.

But *I* must abide in you, for only so can I express My Love and Power and Truth through you interpreting them in deed, and look, and word.

In these words of Mine you have My two-fold nature. The Strong Protector! so Strong to shield; and offering you, My guest, all provision you need.

And then you have Me in My Humility, one with you, your close Companion, dwelling in you, and dependent on you. Think on these things.

Your Mandate   **January 4**

HERE in this evening hour I draw near to you—and listen. Tell Me of the Peace you know in Me; of the tender confidence in Me that has brought Peace and Safety into your life.

To-morrow you will go back into the world with My message of Eternal Life. Truths that you are only just beginning fully to grasp, that are bringing you Vision and Joy, you will pass to others, that they may be saved the wasted years that lie behind you. Turn to them as you would to one following you along a dangerous road and warn them against the pitfalls in their way.

Point out to them the beauties of *The Way*, the sunlit hills ahead, the sunset glories, the streams and flowers of My peaceful glades.

Direct their attention from earth's allures or mirages

to Me, your Companion of The Way. Tell them of your
Joy in Me. That is your mandate from High Heaven.

The Healing Hour   January 5

A S yet you can only dimly see what this evening-
time will mean for you.

For a while you shed earth's cares and frets, and
know the uplift of soul that comes through planned
Communion with Me.

You are renewed, and that renewing is your safeguard from mental and spiritual disintegration.

In this brief time you taste, in contact with Me,
something of My Resurrection Life. It is the glorified
Christ you know and to know Him is to partake too of
His Risen Life.

Thus health, physical, mental and spiritual, comes to
you and flows from you.

Land of Promise   January 6

I MAGINE the Hope of My Heart that day on the
mountain-side when I told My followers that to no
throne of earth I led them; old forms and negations that
had meant so much in the past were to be swept away;
motives and impulses were to be all-important.

By the thoughts of his heart was a man to be judged.

Prayer was like a son appealing to a father. Love was to be the foundation, the Golden Rule. Tribal, even racial, distinctions were to be ignored and the claims of the whole great family of God were to be met.

To such heights as they had never before scaled I led them, up to Peak-truths they had thought unscalable.

What hopes I had of them as their wonder turned to Vision and they responded to My Message.

What hopes I have to-day of each of you My Followers as you catch sight of your Land of Promise ahead.

Cleansing Light   January 7

I am the True Light that cometh into the world, and men love darkness rather than Light, because their deeds are evil.

TRULY not all men desire My Light. Not all men would welcome its clear shining.

Many shrink from its revelation, preferring the darkness that would hide their deeds, rather than the remorseless Light that would show the evil of which they are ashamed.

Pray for Light, rejoice to have it, welcome its revelation, and so, when in your lives it has done its searching, cleansing work, then bear it yourselves gladly, triumphantly, out into a world that needs so sorely the Light of the World.

Ways of Witness   **January 8**

I CALL upon you to make Me known—

> *By your unfailing trust in Me.*
> *By your joy, unrepressed by the difficulties of the way.*
> *By your tender concern for the weak and the wandering.*
> *By your acceptance of My Gift of Eternal Life.*
> *By your growth in Spiritual development, proof of that*
> *inner life, which alone can engender it.*

Make Me known, more and more, by your serenity, by unflinching adherence to Truth.

Make Me known by My Spirit within and round you, your conduct and speech ever bearing witness to the Power and the Wonder of My Presence.

So shall all men know that you are My disciple, and that your claim is never for the recognition of the self—but for Me, the Christ-in-you.

A Love-Home   **January 9**

HUSH earth's desires that you miss not My Footfall. It brings the strength of a warrior, and the eagerness of a Lover.

Let your heart thrill with the glad, "He comes." Forsake all thought but the thought of Me as I enter. Soul-rest and heart-comfort I bring. Forget all else.

Let Me lift the burden from your shoulders, My

burden, borne for you. Here in quiet, we will rest, while you are reinvigorated.

Poor dwelling, you feel, for the King of Kings. Yet I see your Home of Love as Love has made it. I come from locked doors, where youth is trying to live without Me; where old age, ever refusing to answer My pleading and knocking, now hears Me no more, and sits silent and alone.

Comfort Me, My children. Make of your hearts a Love-Home for the Man of Sorrows, still so often despised and rejected of men. Yet I would turn their sorrow into joy.

How Self Dies   January 10

HUSH your spirit still more in My Presence. Self dies, not by human combat, not necessarily by supplicatory prayer, but by the consciousness of My Presence, and of My Spirit-values. Thus self shrivels into lifelessness, into nothingness.

It is so necessary to dwell with Me, to draw so close to Me in an understanding as complete as it is possible for man to realize.

Do you not see now the need for the training and discipline I have enjoined on you? They are vital in that they attune your being to the consciousness of My Mind and Purpose. When this Mind is in you that is in Me you are able to penetrate the outer courts of the Temple, and in the very Holy of Holies to grasp the meaning that lay behind all I said and did and was.

Sacrifice all for this. Your work has to be inspired. Where can you find inspiration but in My Presence?

YOUR Good News   January 11

"**H**OW beautiful upon the mountains are the feet of those who bring glad tidings . . . that publish Peace." When you are weary think that yours are the feet of those who bring glad tidings.

This will rob your steps of weariness, will give a Joy and a spring to your walk.

"Bringeth glad tidings. Publisheth Peace." What a joyful mission. One of gladness and Peace. Never forget this, and the Joy of your message and mission will radiate from you gladdening and transforming.

Bright Shadows   January 12

He descended into Hell . . . He ascended into Heaven.

IT is good for man to know his Lord is ever with him through every danger, every change, every seeming chance. It is good to walk the dark waters with Me.

I did not make the darkness. It was no artist-design to create a darkness which should make My Light seem the greater radiance.

Wilfulness and sin have caused earth's shadows, but I am there to walk the dark places with you. So that even the darkest place may be illumined by the Light of the Sun of Righteousness.

Fight Evil Forces   January 13

YOU are going to be a mighty force against evil because you will be ever-increasingly the agent of Divine Power. Think, when this is so, how could you for one moment imagine that evil could leave you alone? It is to the advantage of evil to thwart you.

Think how those who care for you in the Unseen watch to see you conquer in My strength for My Glory.

The great battles of your world are fought in the Unseen. Fight there your battles and win. More than conquerors through Him Who loves you. Fight with the whole armour of God, ready prepared for you.

Victors through Me. Press on. Victory is in sight.

How Joy Comes   January 14

THE Joy that follows awareness of Guidance has ever been the upholding Joy of My followers.

It is the result of desiring My Will only, in every detail, and then the realization of the wonderful way I can act for you *when you leave the planning to Me.*

Truly all things, every detail in each day, do work together for good to those who love Me. My miracle-working power can become operative when there is no "kicking against the pricks," no thwarting of My Will.

Whether you walk here on earth, or are free from earth's limitations in My Heaven, it is Heaven to walk with Me. Man has sought to describe Heaven in terms of music and song. That is but his endeavour to express the ecstasy he knows on earth in Communion with Me, and to anticipate its magnified intensity in Heaven.

Where Danger Lies   January 15

I AM beside you—the eager Listener, so ready to hear your plea, so ready to say all that your heart needs.

Live more with Me apart, and so there will come an ever-increasing helpfulness to others.

Heart-poise, mental balance, spiritual strength, will be yours in ever more abundant measure. Never feel that you can help others unaided by Me, for therein lies danger.

Your self-importance is destructive of helpfulness, devitalising because *your* strength has such limitations. Mine is limitless.

Grow more dependent upon Me, yet more assured that you can do all things through Me.

The Foe Within   January 16

NEVER lose heart. Kill the proud self as you go on, for on that dead self you rise.

On ever with Me. Do not let earth's frets disturb you. Since you cannot follow Me and indulge self, at all costs turn self out directly its claims disturb; so only can you keep spiritual calm.

Not your circumstances but your *self* is the enemy. A man's foes are those of his own household.

Do others blame you falsely? I was reviled but I reviled not again.

Great Souls   January 17

I AM here. Realize My Presence. My love surrounds you; be filled with My Joy.

You are being truly guided though not until you are content to be led as little children do *you* really live fully in the Kingdom of Heaven.

Life with Me is of child-like simplicity. Simple souls are the great souls, for in simplicity there is majesty.

Joy of Meeting   January 18

SO many think of prayer as petition only. It IS petition. "In everything by prayer and supplication let your requests be made known unto Me."

But prayer is also a glad turning to meet Me for the joy of the meeting, for the rapture of My Presence.

Prayer, too, is preparation for to-morrow's return to those who need you, those to whom My love goes out from you.

Comfort and Joy January 19

I AM with you. I will help you. Through suffering to health, through sorrow to joy, through pain to ease, through night to day—you shall be led and comforted.

Without previous experience of dawn and day none could dream that the glorious dawn and fulness of day could follow the blackest night.

Regard this experience not as darkness but as dawn. The first faint glimmers of light are following the black night through which you have passed. The full day is not yet. But hail the DAWN with Me.

Now is the Victory January 20

I AM with you. I am delivering you. But look for deliverance not from circumstances alone, but deliverance from the self-ties that bind you to earth, and that hinder your entrance into that kingdom of service in which there is perfect freedom. All is well.

You shall rise to newness of Life. You cannot fail to rise as you free yourself from the toils and sins and failures that bind you to earth.

No past sins can enchain you. You look to Me and are saved. They are all forgiven. Conquer your faults with My Strength now, and nothing can prevent you from rising, nothing that is past.

Exceeding Great Reward   January 21

I am thy shield and thine exceeding great reward.

SHIELD from the storm of life. Shield from even the consequences of your own faults and failings. Shield from your weakness. Shield from worry. Shield from fear and sorrow. Shield from the world with its allure and temptations. Not only your shield, but your exceeding great reward.

Not the reward of perfection in your life, for that you could not win here. Not the reward of what you do, or of any merit in yourself. Only the result, or reward of your questing. The satisfaction of your hunger to find Me. Exceeding great reward.

Your reward is the same as that of the greatest saint who has ever lived. Given not as a trophy of victory, not as a recognition of virtue, but given because you are the seeker, and I, your Lord, am the Sought.

I Know All

I AM the sharer of the secrets of your life. How rich in blessing each experience may be if shared with Me alone.

How often, by much speaking and self-indulgent sharing with others, a jewel of rare beauty may be robbed of its priceless worth to your soul. A bud of Joy and sweet perfume too rashly forced to premature bloom will lose its purity and fragrance.

Even the sharing of past sins and failures may mean self for the time in the foreground, or vitality, so needed for the present, lost. Dwell in the Secret Place of the Most High.

Fear No Evil

I AM the Lord of your life, Guardian of your inmost being, the Christ of God. Sheltered in My Hidden Place no harm can befall you. Pray to know this.

Let this Truth become a part of your very consciousness, that where I am no evil can be, and that therefore when you abide in Me and I in you no evil can touch you.

Spiritual Truths take sometimes many years to learn, sometimes they come in a flash of sudden revelation.

Have You?   **January 24**

I AM teaching you, but not always Spiritual Truths
that gladden you.

Often, too often, there has to be the word of reproof
as I tell you of commands of Mine not obeyed, of
resolutions made when in contact with Me that you
have failed to keep, of work done for Me in no spirit of
Love and Joy, of failure to obtain supply because your
attitude (often not your heart) questioned My *unlimited*
supply.

I teach no easy lesson.

I choose no flower-bordered path in which to walk
with you, but take heart in that I *do* walk with you as
with Peter of old even when he had denied Me.

He had seen his sin. He went out and wept bitterly.

My Compensations   **January 25**

I AM listening. Picture Me, your Lord. Not as one
deaf to your entreaties, but rather as One straining
with an intensity of Love to catch the first faint cry from
one of His children.

Even in the case of those who love Me, how often do
I listen in vain for the spontaneous words of Love?

Do not cry to Me only when cares press and you are
weary. Speak to Me often. Share with Me all the little

happenings, all the frets, all the little glad things.

These not only draw us more closely to each other, but they are to Me compensations for the neglect I suffer from My world.

The Healing Life   January 26

I AM your Lord, trust Me in all. Never doubt My keeping Power. Behold Me, the Lord of your life. Gain strength from Me.

Remember that Healing, Divine Healing, is not so much a question of praying on your part, and of granting on Mine, as of living with Me, thinking of Me, sharing My Life. That contact makes you whole. Go forward gladly, go forward unafraid.

Help for All   January 27

I HAVE not promised My Help to the virtuous only. To the sinner who turns to Me, to the saint who lives with Me, to both alike My miracle-working Power is manifested.

Help, temporal as well as spiritual, truly I bestow, not as a reward of goodness but as a fulfilment of My pledge made to all who believe in Me.

But when one turns to Me I at once plan the rescue craved. If that one hearing My plan, learning of My

Purpose, should fail to do his appointed task in that plan, how can My healing of physical, spiritual or temporal disharmony be manifested?

Your Defender   **January 28**

I AM the Gift of God to man. Only so was it possible for man to know God the Father. Only so was it possible for man to know that he had ever an Advocate with God—the Sinless Christ.

There is always One Who understands your case, Whose appeal cannot fail to be heard. He has the right of Sonship. He has a right to plead for you.

If He can plead for offending man, undertaking full responsibility for him, what better Advocate could you have? He knows. He has seen the tears of sorrow, the heartache and temptation. He can plead as none other.

His own temptation was so real that, conqueror as He was, He can yet feel the tenderest pity for the vanquished. He knows how seeming fair evil can appear, and He can estimate the added burden of tainted blood, inherited weakness and sin.

He gave His only Begotten Son. This GREAT GIFT AM I, your Friend, your Companion. Leave all to Me, your Advocate, trained during My years on earth to plead, never for Myself, but for every one who rests his cause in My Hands.

Overcomers January 29

STUDY the "Overcomeths" in the Revelation to
My servant John, and you will see the tender
intimacy with Me promised as a result of overcoming.
To believe is not enough. To believe in Me does truly
involve the possession of Eternal Life, but that is a trust
to *use* as truly as the talent of My story.

It is not only a something to be *enjoyed.*

Eternal life is a refreshing, reforming, enriching,
uprooting, ennobling Power to be *employed* to the full
by those to whom I entrust it.

In this My servants so often fail, and so miss the
wonder of Communion with Me. Guard this Truth.

More Love January 30

I COME, a truly willing guest. Love always draws.
Remember that. Love is the magnetic Power of the
Universe. God is LOVE, the Power that draws all men
by various ways unto Himself.

Remember that your Love too, being of God, has the
same magnetic Power. Love, and you will draw to you
those whom you desire to help.

When you fail to do so, search your life. Love is
deficient. More love is necessary.

The Evening Call   **January 31**

SOFTLY at even, comes the footfall of your Master,
My day has been long and weary. Hearts that I
have yearned over and longed for still withstand Me.

I see the aged, desolate without Me. I see the
disappointment of men and women, who in Me would
find heart-satisfaction which others cannot give them. I
see youth crowding Me out of its work-filled, pleasure-
filled days. And yet I wait. I knock, I plead, I call,
unheard, unheeded, unwanted.

As I was the link between the Father and man, so
now must My followers be the links between man and
Me.

Human Love, material aid, human understanding
and friendship must bind those for whom I yearn.

Channels through which My help can flow to man
truly you must be, but also the means through which
man finds his groping way to Me.

" *O let me hear Thee speaking*
  In accents clear and still,
Above the storms of passion,
  The murmurs of self-will."

" *O speak to reassure me*
  To hasten, or control;
O speak, and make me listen,
  Thou Guardian of my soul!"

FEBRUARY

All Loves Excelling

SOFTLY I approach. Gently My Spirit speaks to your heart.

The mystery of man's communion with Me lies in the beauty and wonder of its aloneness. For the moment the world seems not to exist. Its noise and traffic seem hushed.

There is indeed wonder in that stillness. A faint glimpse is seen in the sudden realization of Love between two human beings. Surprise and wonder . . . the world is for them alone . . . no claim other than their love.

What wonder in the heart of man when he realizes the beauty, tenderness and closeness of Communion with Me!

My Wages

IF the world understands you, then you are speaking its language, actuated by its motives, living its life according to its standards. Will you have this?

Remember I said very clearly, "Ye cannot serve God and mammon." If you serve God, then, for your work, you should surely look to God for reward.

So many of My servants serve Me, and yet expect to receive the gratitude and praise, or at least the acknowledgement of the world. Why? You are not doing the work of the world. Why expect its pay?

Ambassadors All   February 3

IF you love Me, and long to serve others by showing them what I am like, you will assuredly do so.

Because self will disappear, be cast out.

When self has gone then those who see you will not see the self in you; only the ambassador of your King.

You have here in this seemingly narrow life of yours countless opportunities of overcoming self. Let this be your great task.

Wise Rest   February 4

REST should play a large part in the lives of My followers, for tiredness and physical strain can cause man to lose his consciousness of My presence.

Then the Light that banishes evil seems to be withdrawn—never by deliberate act of Mine, but as the result of man's attitude towards Me. Ponder on this.

The Aching Spirit
February 5

JUST as I said that those who hungered and thirsted after righteousness would be filled, so I say to you—none ever longed to know Me better and remained unsatisfied. Even with your imperfect knowledge, you are daily realizing how true this is.

Man dwells so much on material things that he fails to grasp the Spiritual Laws that never fail.

For all spirit-longing there is fulfilment. I soothe the aching spirit.

You think I answer your prayer. Yes, but the answer was *there*, awaiting the prayer.

You will see these simple Truths more and more as you live with Me; truths hidden from the wise but revealed to the little ones of the Kingdom.

True Humility
February 6

If I, your Lord and Master, have washed your feet, you ought also to wash one another's feet.

HOW My followers have misunderstood this. They interpret the required attitude to be one of service. In service there can be condescension, there can be a total lack of humility.

I sought to teach a lesson to those who would approach Me to partake of that wonderful Union with

Me, vouchsafed to those who worthily eat of My Flesh and drink of My Blood.

I desired to teach them that they must come to Me *in the Spirit of humility towards others*. No sense of superiority, especially Spiritual superiority. True humility. Learn this lesson in daily Companionship with Me. "For I am meek and lowly in heart."

The Way of Progress   February 7

IMPRESS upon all that growth is one of the laws of My Kingdom.

However long your span of life on earth, it can never be too long for growth and progress.

Be ever seeking My Will for you. Not a new religion, nor the right religion, but—My Will. Then all will be well and growth will follow.

Future All Unknown   February 8

PROBE not into the future. Prophecies are not for you. Be a humble follower in the crowd. Live with Me. Ponder My Words, My Teaching, My Actions.

Soon you will find that more and more opportunities of speaking of Me will present themselves. Do not make them. They will proceed from the pressure of inward growth, and not from outward stress.

All Will Be Well   **February 9**

IN humble anticipation—wait.

Wait as a servant anticipating orders. Wait as a lover eager to note a need, and to supply it.

Wait for My commands; wait for My Guidance; wait for My supply. All will come.

In such a life you may well be of good cheer. Can a life be dull when always there is that watchful expectancy, anticipation of glad surprise, that wonder of fulfilment, that Joy of full supply?

Your Power   **February 10**

IN your hands I have placed a wonderful force against evil. You cannot realize as yet the mighty weapon you wield.

Make known the Power of Prayer. A force so wonderful, so miracle-working, that when it is united with a will that seeks only My Will and with a Friendship with Me that calms, ennobles and enriches, then nothing can withstand its Power.

No Remorse   **February 11**

I SEEK to save you not only from falling into sin, but from the overwhelming remorse that follows the realization of sin.

I know that for frail man this is too great a burden. So when you let it overwhelm you, you nullify My saving Power.

I seek to save you from oppression and depression too. I bid you leave all to follow Me. That is, leave the sins and the failures of the past.

Out of the shadow into the sunlight of My Love and Salvation you must go.

See Me Everywhere Still   February 12

SEE Me in all your daily life.

See Me in the little happenings. Recognize me as the source of every act of kindness and Love.

Feel My Power with you when you face any task or danger. Know My consoling tenderness in every sorrow and disappointment.

I, the Master-Painter, can work into the picture colours of beauty, until you see the befitting background for the joy and ecstasy of the radiance I give.

Ever Secure   February 13

ABIDE secure in My Friendship.

A Friend who knows you through and through; knows all your pitiful attempts at living for Me, your many and tragic failures, your childish misunderstanding of Me and what I would do for you.

Your desire to serve Me, your clinging to Me in the dark hours of helplessness; your stumbling confidence in your efforts to walk alone—I know all.

I have seen your persistent blindness to My guidance; I have seen how you obstruct the answers to your own prayers; I have noted your easy acquiescence to those forces that oppose My loving purposes.

I know all this, and yet I say again: Abide with Me secure in My friendship.

Thanks for All   February 14

THANK Me for all the withholding as well as for the giving. Thank Me for sunshine and rain, for drought and springs of water, for sleep and wakefulness, for gain and loss. Thank Me for all.

Know beyond all doubt, all fear, that all is well. Cling to Me in moments of weakness. Cling still in moments of strength, imploring that you may never feel self-sufficient.

No evil shall befall you, rest in this knowledge.

Green Pastures   February 15

AFTER each salutary experience of life, each blow it may deal you, separate yourself from the world for a time. Walk in My Green Pastures, and wander with Me beside the Waters of Comfort, until your soul is restored.

This is necessary so that you may readjust yourself to life. For you are a new being; you have had a new experience. Learn a new lesson. Your Union with Me will be the closer for your experience.

This is the time when My Love can whisper new meanings to you, can make the Friendship between us a closer, more holy Union.

Come with your Lover into the stillness of My Green Pastures, and walk with Me beside hushed waters.

He Changeth Not　　　　　　　February 16

MARK My Changelessness.

If I am truly the same, yesterday, to-day, and for ever, then I am no God of moods as so often man portrays Me. Can you worship a God swayed this way and that at man's demand?

Dwell upon the thought of My Changelessness until you grasp the Truth that only as *man* changes and comes within the influence of My unchanging Law of Love can he realize and experience the Power and Love I have unchangingly for all mankind.

Practise Peace   **February 17**

PEACE must fill your hearts and lives, and then you will find that ills and difficulties and sorrows and changes leave you unmoved. Practise that steadfast immobility, no matter what may threaten.

This spirit of calm trust is the shield that turns aside the darts and stings of adversity. Practise it.

Then you must seek to abide at the heart of the Universe with Me, at the centre with Me. There alone is changelessness and calm, WITH ME.

The Perfect Pattern   **February 18**

See that thou make all things according to the pattern that was shown thee on the Mount.

OTHERWISE it would have been better not to have gone up the Mount at all? Take this lesson to heart. In your daily valley-life you must live out what you learn in the alone-time on heights with Me.

The Spirit-pattern is so glorious because it is made to fit your life, specially planned for you.

Obeying the command made Moses the good leader he became. This is the time, then, humbly to see your weakness, to adjust your life to the work of My Kingdom, to prepare to live in all things according to the pattern that was shown you on the Mount.

Youth Renewed February 19

THEY that wait upon the Lord shall renew their strength.

To discover the Pearl of Great Price is to renew your youth.

The Kingdom of Heaven is a kingdom of perennial youth.

The Secret of Joy February 20

SUCH rapture is yours. Count it all Joy to know Me, and to delight in Me. The secret of Joy is the longing to have My Will, and the gratification of that longing.

There is nothing in Heaven that transcends the Joy, the ecstasy, of loving and doing My Will. To a soul who realizes this wonder, Heaven is already attained, as far as mortal here can attain it. My Will for you is My joyous arranging for you.

The frustration of the Divine Plan is man's tragedy.

Wise as Serpents February 21

EACH servant of Mine should regard himself as an outpost for My Truths, where he must be prepared to receive My Messages, and to signal them on. This is work of great importance in My Kingdom.

Wherever you go make Me known. That was My Risen injunction, My Commission. Wherever you go establish outposts of My Empire, make contacts for Me. Make Me known to men—sometimes by speech, sometimes in silence.

Wonder-Work   February 22

ALL work with Me is wonder-work. God working in and through man. This should be the normal work of every Christian's day. For this I came to earth, to show man this could be.

For this I left the earth, so that this should be. Can life offer anything more for you than that you fulfil in yourselves My expectations for My disciples?

Satan frustrates My plan by whispering to My followers a mock humility, in which they trace not his evil hand—"They are too weak, too small, too unimportant to do much . . ."

Away with false humility, which limits not you but Me. Mine is the Power.

Conquering and to Conquer   February 23

ALWAYS seek some conquest, for spiritual growth requires it. In the natural world you see how necessary this striving is, and in the mental and spiritual worlds there must be struggle too.

So, as you go forward in your spiritual life, you will see always a fresh conquest demanding your effort.

Shun stagnation. Never be discouraged if always you see some fault requiring to be overcome, some obstacle to be surmounted.

Thus you go forth with Me conquering and to conquer.

Always Antagonism   February 24

And He passing through the midst of them.

FACE evil undaunted, and it will fall back, and let you pass on and do your work for Me.

The maddened crowd had sought to cast Me headlong, but they made way for Me, and through their midst I passed unhindered.

Do not be surprised to find antagonism where you meet evil, because you are a home of My Spirit, and it is My Spirit that arouses the antagonism. Go on your way so quietly, and trust in Me.

In My Strength My follower need not flinch, but, boldly facing evil, will overcome evil with good.

You follow the dauntless Christ.

The War Within   **February 25**

And he was dumb, because he believed not.

THERE is physical correspondence to faith and to doubt.

Especially is this so among those who would serve Me. For unlike others, they are not so controlled by the law of physical success or failure, but are under the direct control of the Laws of My Kingdom.

So, in many cases, you may note good health in one ignorant of Me, and ill-health in one of My followers, until he has learned the full control of the physical by the Spiritual. In his case the warring of physical and Spiritual may *cause* physical ill-health, or unrest.

So do not fret about the physical side, aim increasingly at control by My Spirit.

As from Me   **February 26**

TAKE every little kindness, every faithful service, every evidence of thought and of Love—as from Me.

As you, and those who live with and for Me, show loving-kindnesses to others, because you are actuated by My Spirit, so you draw contacts into the circle of My ever-widening Spirit influence.

This is unfailingly so. It is a spiritual law. Though no word of Me may be spoken, yet in this way souls *are* attracted until at length they find Me, the centre and inspiration of all.

Well did I urge My Followers to become fishers of men. No great oratory or personality is needed for this soul-rescue work. Just follow Me as little children.

My Tireless Search   February 27

SHARE with Me the tireless search for the lost, the ache of disappointment, the sublime courage, the tenderness of complete forgiveness. Share the Joys, the sorrows, the Love, the scorn.

I walk the lakeside still, and pause, as, to one and another, I utter the same call I uttered in Galilee, "Come and I will make you fishers of men."

The Simple Life   February 28

THE Gift of Eternal Life is a most precious one. Each one who receives it must demonstrate by Joy and Trust and radiancy of Spirit, expressed in being and in bearing, the quality of the Life he possesses.

The other life is existence—just not death.

Power and Joy must radiate from you. These are the expressions of Eternal Life. Life Eternal is to know the Father and Me, His Son, Whom He sent.

Simple and Direct   **February 29**

"GOD so Loved the world that He gave His only Begotten Son that whosoever believeth on Him should not perish but have everlasting (*i.e.*, Eternal) Life."

Directly that Life is possessed by a man, all that is not simple, child-like, has to go.

Not by complicated devices is My work accomplished.

My followers must be simple and direct, "Let your yea be yea and your nay be nay," I said.

Simplicity is forceful. Simplicity is great. It is a conquering Power.

UP-HILL
Does the road wind up-hill all the way?
    Yes, to the very end.
Will the journey take the whole long day?
    From morn to night, my friend.

C. G. Rossetti.

MARCH

Arise from Defeat

IT is not upon one battle alone that all depends, or there would be no hope for My failures.

You enter upon a long campaign when you enter My army. Is the battle lost? Acquaint yourself with the cause, discover your weakness, and with dauntless faith, go forth resolved this time to conquer.

No man can conquer who has not learned his weakness, not made ready for the next conflict, and who does not know and claim and trust My strength, always available when summoned, as you have already proved.

Complete in Me

A ROCK of Defence. A Joy to the saddened. A Rest to the weary. Calm to the ruffled.

A Companion of the sunlit glades. A Guide through the deserts of life. An Interpreter of experience. A Friend. A Saviour.

All these and many more would I be to you. Never a heart's need that I could not soothe and satisfy.

Search the ages. Many men have been many things to other hearts, but never one man to all men, never one man all to one man. This only the Maker of hearts could be.

Not only so, but in Me the soul finds its completion.

Shining Through   March 3

A S you grow like Me so My Love must reflect more and more through you Divinity and Majesty.

Sublime thought, yes, but you doubt if this can be. But God is Love, so God is Majesty. Thus gradually into the lives of those who follow Me there comes My Dignity and Majesty.

Have you not traced it in My closest friends?

To the Water's Edge   March 4

A S God was in the days of Moses, so is He to-day. Responsive to the prayer of faith. Still ready and willing to make a path through the Red Sea.

Have the faith of Moses, who never faltered in his trust, even with the sea before, the advancing host behind, and no visible way of escape. *To the very edge of the waters he led his People.*

His task was done, It was for God, his God, in whom he trusted, to act now. Moses waited for, and expected, that act. But to the edge he had to go.

How often man draws back, halts at the thought of the troubled sea ahead. To go further is useless, he says, and gives up.

Or he goes within sight of the sea, and pauses. He must go on, always as far as he can; he must do all his share. On—*to the Edge of the Sea.*

Learn from this a mighty lesson. Do all your work, and leave your salvation to God. To say it will be no good is not to go to the edge, and that is to miss the saving Power of God.

The waters shall be divided, and you shall walk through the midst of the sea on dry land. I have said it. I, the Lord. Have I not done this for so many in your own day? For you? Think on these things.

"Share, Share" March 5

I AM your Lord. Obey Me in all. You are being surely led into prosperity and true peace.

Let many share in your every gain. There must be no hoarding in the Christ-life. Not what you can gain, but what you can give. Keep your eyes fixed on Me. Seek to know My Will. Share. Share.

I am a Risen Lord. You cannot live with Me without partaking of My Risen Life. My Kingdom is sharing.

I must share all I have with My followers. So you, too, must share all that I give you—material and Spiritual Blessings—with others.

Your Circle Widens   March 6

A S the circle of your life widens you will feel ever more and more the need of Me. The need indeed to draw from My unfailing resources to gain the help and wisdom required to deal with these new contacts.

Do not refuse them, only let nothing idle or of little worth engross your attention.

As your circle is enlarged, your means to deal with it adequately must grow too.

This is My desire. Ever walk with Me. Learn of Me. Witness for Me, Glorify Me.

How Firm Your Foundation   March 7

A S one in a storm needs to dwell in quiet thought upon the firmness of the foundation of his home, so you need in dangers and difficulties of whatever kind to withdraw, and in quiet assurance dwell upon that foundation upon which the house of your life and character is built.

Rest your thoughts on this, on Me. Do not dwell on the channels through which My Help may be directed to you. To do so is indeed to feel at the mercy of wind and weather. You can draw no strength from such.

No, a sense of security can only come from relying on Me, the All-powerful, the Unchanging.

Security engenders Strength, then Peace, then Joy.

" Other foundations can no man lay."

New Life   **March 8**

ETERNAL Life gives a youthful resiliency.
Think of My parable of the wine-skins. Those who merely worship Me as a creed are like unto old wine-skins.

They cannot accept new truth, new life. It would destroy, not increase their faith.

Those who have My Gift of Eternal, youth-giving Life have the ever-expanding, revitalising, joy-quality of that Life.

The new wine poured so freely into new bottles. That bracing wine sustains the many who receive it.

Bear One Another's Burdens   **March 9**

DO not judge of another's capacity by your own.
If the burden another bears presses too heavily,

what matter that you could bear that load lightly?

You must learn of Me to judge of the sorrow or strain of another, not with a feeling of superiority, but with one of humble thankfulness.

Would not *your* burdens have seemed light to Me? But in so far as they pressed heavily upon you so did I judge of them.

That which tore your heart may seem light to another.

Truly I said—Judge not. Only to God can the heart of man be made plain.

Seek My Presence, not only that you may understand Me, but that you may gain the insight to understand more clearly My other children.

Turn It to Good   **March 10**

NEVER flinch. My standard-bearers must you ever be. Bear your standard high.

Life has its dangers and difficulties, but real as these seem, the moment you see in them a power of evil that will in response to your faith be forced to work in some way for your good, in that moment of recognition evil and danger cease to have any power over you.

This is a wonderful truth. Believe it. Rejoice in it.

Accept Your Task   March 11

TAKE life as a task; each step of it to be practised until it can be done perfectly, that is, with patience, with soul harmony, and rest.

Remember the Christ of the humble ways is with you. His "Well done, good and faithful servant," is spoken, not to the great of earth but to the humble bearer of pain and annoyance, to the patient worker in life's ways of service.

So even on the quietest day, and in the lowliest way, mighty opportunities are given you of serving the King of Kings. See that you welcome, and do not resent, these opportunities.

The Springs of Love   March 12

BE gentle to all.

Drink of the Living water, deep draughts from the inexhaustible wells, into which the very springs of Eternal Life flow from the Hills of God.

Think thoughts of Love and Beauty. Know no limit to all you can possess and be and do. Live in My Love; surrounded by It, blessed by It, shedding It bountifully on all about you, ever conscious of It being present with you.

You are here to reflect It.

Seek to see the good in all you meet—and in those of whom you hear.

You are Complete   March 13

BE happy in Me. Feel that your life is complete in Me. Know the Joy of a friendship in which those who love Me share.

Know a glad contentment in the security of your protected and guided life. Value the Power that Union with Me gives you.

The greatest power that money, fame or position of the world can give, still leaves the possessor but as a child beating helpless hands against an impregnable fortress, as compared with the Power of My Spirit, which can render a follower of Mine himself an invincible, an all-conquering force.

Your Weak Point   March 14

" Be not overcome of evil, but overcome evil with good."

THE instruments in your hand for good are invincible against evil, did you but use them.

Every evil you face boldly, in My Spirit, flees at once, ashamed. No evil can look good in the face. Teach to all—that good is stronger than evil. You must answer the challenge of evil.

This Spiritual warfare must be ceaselessly waged by My followers. Remember it is not where you are strongest that evil will attack you, but at your weak points. Hence the need to overcome. Be ready to see a weakness in yourself, and attack that until you are victor.

Guidance IS Guidance March 15

B E still before Me. How often in a crisis man rushes hither and thither. Rush is a sign of weakness. Quiet abiding is a sign of strength.

A few quiet actions, as you are led to do them, and all is accomplished wisely and rightly, more quickly and more effectually than could be done by those who rush and act feverishly.

Guidance IS Guidance, the being led, the being shown the way. Believe this.

Softly, across life's tumult, comes the gentle Voice, "Peace be still." The waves of difficulty will hear. They will fall back. There will be a great calm.

And then the Still Small Voice of Guidance.

Perfect Everything March 16

Be ye therefore perfect, even as your Father in Heaven.

T HAT was the aim I set before My disciples when I spoke to them on the Mount.

That is the aim I set before you and every follower of Mine to-day.

To *achieve* this you would be as God.

To *aim at less* would mean an unworthy standard.

To keep your gaze on this as your standard means that your eyes are fixed on the Heights of God, always directed above the difficulties and the lower aims and desires and standards of others round you.

The Real World   March 17

Blessed are they that hear My Voice.

DEAF to My Voice man can so often be. Live, My children, more in the Unseen World. There, in the contemplation of Me, your whole nature becomes sensitive to My faintest whisper.

I have told you, I tell you again, the Unseen World is the real world. Realize more and more as you go through this earth-life that this is only a material-plane parenthesis. The real paragraph, chapter, book of Life is the Spirit-Life.

This point of view will alter your idea of suffering, failure, and the work of life here. It will give you a new view of death. Birth begins the parenthesis, death closes it. Then back to real Life-History. Absorb this.

When you have done so, you will get that same idea

about the various periods of your earth-life. Times of struggle, defeat, joy, failure, work, rest, success— Treat them all as parts of a parenthesis in the one Eternal Life of *spiritual progress*.

Joy from Sorrow   March 18

I BIND up the broken hearts with the cords wherewith men scourged Me in the Judgement Hall; with the whips of scorn wherewith Men have mocked My Love and Divinity down the ages.

Symbol, this, of the way in which, out of seeming obstacles, stepping-stones can be fashioned, and, out of trials undreamt-of, blessings can be wrought.

Share My Life with its longings and tears, with its Joys unspeakable and its heartaches beyond human description.

Share My Joy.

Through the Archway   March 19

By the obedience of one shall many be made righteous.

OBEDIENCE is the keystone of your arch of worship. On it depend your Love and Power.

Through that archway shall many pass into My Holy Place. Once therein their questing souls will pass into

My Holy of Holies. Is it too much to ask of you obedience that this may be accomplished?

Do not fret that your life is lived in lowly places. It is not to be lived to impress this earth-plane, but to be so faithful and obedient that those for whom you desire much, shall have THAT much impressed upon them on the spirit-plane.

That much, and more, than you can desire for them.

First Place   March 20

I DO not promise My followers the world's ease and pleasures. I promise those Joys that the world can neither give nor take away.

I promise that heart-rest found with Me alone.

It does not mean that all the beauties and pleasures of the world must be renounced, but that they must be enjoyed only after the treasures and Joys of My Kingdom have been learned, appreciated and given first place.

Simplicity   March 21

B E content to do the simple things.
Never think that if you have not the cleverness of the world I cannot use your services.

Pure sparkling wine may be in a silver goblet or in a

simple glass, but, to the one who receives, it is the wine that matters, not the vessel, provided that be pure and clean.

It is My Truth that matters, not the person that utters it, provided the desire is there to deliver My Message for ME.

True simplicity is found only as you live in Me and act in My Strength; for only in our close companionship can real value be achieved.

Never accept the values of earth. Be content with simplicity.

Love's Overflow March 22

I DESIRE the love of man's heart in abundant measure.

Not because God would be adored for Himself and for His own gratification, but because I know that only as the love of man flows out to Me does man attain to his purest and best.

That rush of love, which follows the understanding and realization of My Love for man, sweetens and purifies his whole being.

"Thou shalt love thy neighbour as thyself." The love you give to your neighbour is the *overflow* of your love to Me.

No Personalities   **March 23**

DEAL with each difficulty as you must.
Then live above it. Say, "In Him I conquered."
The fight is ever between you and evil, never
between you and another. *Never make it a personal
matter.*

If you are fighting with the weapons of the world—
envy, resentment, anger—you cannot use those of My
Kingdom—Prayer, Love, Peace—which would give
you a God-given conquering strength.

It is the endeavour to call both God and mammon to
your aid that makes for lack of success. The world looks
on in scornful pity, and My followers themselves doubt
and wonder.

So often they do not see their own error, but
attribute to suffering for My Sake that which may not
be according to My Will.

If it Offends—   **March 24**

QUESTION yourself as to your weakness. What
caused your failure? To continue to bemoan
your folly is in itself a weakness. My followers must be
strong, not in themselves, but in Me.

The look at Self, however penitent, cannot give
strength.

Look unto Me, and, whatever the seeming sacrifice, be ruthless with what hindered or caused you to fall.

Sift Your Motives   March 25

WALK in My Ways. Follow the path I have bidden you tread.

Humble yourselves before Me, and keep My laws, so shall you have perfect peace.

I am with you to give you the needed strength. Go forward unafraid. Grow in Grace, and in the knowledge of Me, your Master and your Friend. Count all the learning of earth's wisest as nothing, compared with the wisdom that I, your Lord, would show you.

Love and learn. You have much, very much to do for My kingdom. So seek to become perfect. Sift your motives. All that is unworthy cast aside, uproot its inner growth.

You are freely forgiven. Forgive freely, largely, wonderfully.

Keep Step   March 26

GO forward, glad indeed.

Walk with Me until your faltering, flagging footsteps learn to keep in step with Me, and gain a firmness and a confidence unknown before.

Walk with Me until a gladsome rhythm reveals the conquest-spirit that you draw from Me, and your whole being thrills with the joy of being, doing and even suffering, with Me.

Thus, in loving Communion with Me, you learn to know My needs and My wishes for others.

"Here am I, Lord, send me" shows very surely a child-like eagerness, the eagerness of love, even the eagerness for adventure for My cause.

For in My Secret Service there is surely the thrill of *adventure*.

Spirits in Training March 27

GO on along the highway of the Kingdom until all that comes, that touches your outward lives and circumstances, has no power to ruffle your spirit-calm. Make it a delight so to train yourselves.

Why does man rebel at aught that should teach him poise of spirit, whilst in the physical world he welcomes severe exercise that would increase his powers?

The children of this world are surely wiser in their generation than the children of light. If My Children of Light gave to their spirit and character-training all the care that the children of this world give to the body—its feeding, its clothing, its wellbeing—how rapid would their spiritual progress be!

Yet how little does the body matter compared with the growth of the Spirit. "Fear not them that kill the body, but are not able to kill the soul."

In Eternity Now   March 28

HEIRS of God. Joint heirs with Me of Eternal Life, if so be that you suffer with Me, that we may also be glorified together.

Glory denotes perfection of character. This can only be learned as you allow discipline to play its part in your life, and also as you entrust your sinful past to Me.

Perfect through suffering. You cannot escape discipline, and be truly My disciple.

If you think that life is too short for all you have to do and to conquer, then remember that you have already entered upon ETERNITY.

The True Sign   March 29

HOW many believed on My Name after seeing the signs which I did?

Not for the signs, not for the water made wine, not for My miracles, will My true follower believe in Me.

No, for something deeper, seen only with the eyes of faith, realized only by a heart of love responding to My Heart of Love. Not of these must it be said, "I do not trust Myself unto them," as I said of those who saw My signs.

I must trust Myself and My Cause to My followers who see me with the eyes of faith. How else can I be loved and known?

They will meet Me, the outcast Saviour, when I am performing no mighty deeds, wandering unheeded and unacclaimed through dark and lonely ways, and they will pause, all other pursuit forgotten, and will yet turn and follow Me.

Follow because of some chord in them responsive to the yearning of My Heart for Man, who has shut Me out. Follow, too, because of that in Me which is responsive to the cry of man's hungering soul.

The Love of Your Life   March 30

I AM beside you. I am with you in all that you do. I control your thoughts, inspire your impulses, guide your footsteps.

> I strengthen you, body, mind and spirit.
> I am the link between you and those who are in the Unseen.
> I am the Love of your lives.
> Controller of your destinies.
> Guardian, advocate, provider, Friend.

Yes, love Me more and more. So will you not only enjoy to the full the treasures and pleasures of My

Kingdom, but increasingly those of Nature, My gift to My world.

The Wrong Voice   March 31

I AM the Great Teacher, so ready to explain the simplest lesson to the most ignorant.

It is not for you to seek everywhere explanations of Me and My Kingdom, its laws and its purposes.

Learn of Me. How often would I have spoken to some heart, but the voice of one too eager with explanations about Me crowded Me out.

When Andrew brought Simon to Me, *he* was silent to let his brother learn of *Me*.

The reason for this crowding out of My Voice by My disciples is their unwillingness to believe that I *do* speak to-day. So, thinking they worship a silent Christ, they seek to make amends by *their* much speaking.

" To Thee our morning song of praise,
To Thee our evening prayer we raise."

APRIL

The Time of Resurrection

SPRING brings its message of Hope.

Not only does it proclaim the Truth that Nature arises from her time of decay and darkness to a new life. But, My children, it surely speaks to the individual, to nations, to My world, that the time of decay and darkness for them too can pass, and that, from conflict and storm, disaster and sin, they can spring to a new and gladdening Resurrection-Life.

But Nature obeys My Laws. It is by her obedience that the quickening of new life is succeeded by the beauty of Risen Power.

So, only as man obeys My Will, and works according to My Divine Plan for him, can harmony follow chaos, peace follow war, and a reign of Love succeed one of conflict and carnage.

Resurrection Preparation

I AM the Master of the Universe. Accept My ordered Word. When you do this in joyful sincerity, you link yourself with all the creative forces of the Universe.

My Spirit can then be operative, first *in* you and then *through* you.

My followers forget that the scourging at the pillar, the Divine control (" He answered never a word "), and the Cross, man-rejected, man-forsaken, all these preceded the Resurrection.

Without these there could have been no Resurrection. These steps in Spirit-conquest had to be, before My all-powerful, Divine Spirit could be released to be for ever available for those who would hear My Call, and would will to walk in My Way.

See them Free April 3

IF I bore the sins of all in My agonised Heart in the Garden of Gethsemane and on Calvary, then, when you seek to punish others whom you despise, you punish and despise Me.

My throwing aside the grave-clothes, and My stepping out into that sunlit Garden on Easter Morn were symbolic of the freedom I had bought for My children, and which they would know in Me.

Are you seeking to bind the grave-clothes round Me? When you recognize a man's sins you must go further always and see him as free, the grave-clothes of sin and limitation cast aside; the stone, that shut out his Vision of Love and God, rolled away; he, a risen man, walking in My Strength, and conquering in My Power.

Sharing My Burden   April 4

REMEMBER the Truth that you are learning, even now, though dimly.

In Eternal Life there are no time-limits. So My sacrifice was for you to-day, this hour, as truly as ever it was for those who watched Me on Calvary.

I am the changeless One. The same yesterday and for ever. Sacrificing Myself to-day, rising to-day. You then, once you embrace Eternal Life, enter into My Suffering, and help to carry My Cross, as truly to-day as if you had walked beside Me to Calvary.

Redeemed   April 5

AGONY and heartache, pain and loneliness, such as no human being has ever known, were the price of your redemption.

Truly you are not your own.

You are bought with a price. You belong to Me.

You are Mine to use, Mine to love, Mine to provide for.

Man does not understand the infinite Love of the

Divine. Man teaches that as I bought him, so he has to serve, obey and live for Me.

He fails to understand that because he is Mine, bought by Me, it is My responsibility to supply his every need. His part is to realize My ownership, and to claim my Love and Power.

The Veil has Gone   April 6

And the veil of the Temple was rent in twain, from the top to the bottom.

THE veil, that had hidden God from the knowledge and sight of man, was at last removed.

I, God and man, had torn away the veil separating God the Father, and man, My brother. I came to reveal the Father to man, and I live, ever live, to make intercession to the Father for man. I am the Great Mediator between God and man, the Man, Christ JESUS.

Bear Reproach Gladly   April 7

REST unto your souls is found at My Feet. The place of rest is the place of humility.

When you rejoice to serve humbly, when you are content for men to think ill of you, when you can bear reproach and scorn gladly, then what can disturb the gladness of your soul, its rest?

No unrest can assail and hurt the soul that has not its spring in self. That self must be nailed to My Cross, that self must die before you can truly say—"I live, yet not I, but Christ liveth in me."

Stones Rolled Away   April 8

And they saw that the stone was rolled away.

HOW needless their questioning among themselves had been:—

"Who shall roll us away the stone?"

Wherever My followers go full of desire to do Me loving service, they shall find the stones of difficulty, of obstruction, rolled away.

They came, these faithful women, to the sepulchre, with the spices and ointments they had prepared.

Come, too, with your spices of Love to do Me service, and you shall find you have been anticipated. I am ever eager in Love to do you service.

The Life Glorious   April 9

If by the Spirit you mortify the flesh, you shall live.

THIS is a further progress-step in My Kingdom. The flesh must hold no pleasure for you that is not held in leash, always under subjection to the Spirit.

It was the utter subjection of the flesh that was

manifested in My Silence at the pillar, and in the face of the jibes and insults and blows. It was this complete subjection which meant a Risen Body.

Resurrection-faith is not a matter of belief in Me, and in My Power working a miracle, it is a faith in Me and My Power leading to entire subjection of the body.

The body completely under control of the Spirit *is* a Risen Body. See now the importance of self-discipline.

Break Free   April 10

I SENT no disciple to carry My Healing Power to the Syrophœnician woman's sick daughter, the centurion's servant, or to the ruler's son. My Word was all-sufficient.

All that I needed was the faith of the petitioner. Can you not realize that?

Learn to understand and to ask more of Me. If you do not, then others' bonds are your responsibility.

Loose your own body from all bonds. Remember the beam and the mote.

As the fault (the beam) is removed from your own eye, giving you the power to remove the mote from your brother's eye, so if you bring your body into subjection, discipline it wholly, you will be enabled to free your brother from bonds that bind him to ill-health.

Easter Gladness   **April 11**

L OVE and Laugh. To the world, sad faces and depressed spirits speak of a buried Christ. If you want to convince men that I am Risen, you must go through life with Easter gladness. You must prove by your lives that you are Risen with Me.

Men will not learn of My conquest over death by the arguments of theologians, but by the lives of My followers, My Risen followers. If you are still wearing the grave-clothes of gloom and depression, of fear and poverty, men will think of us as tomb-bound still.

No, live in the Spirit of the Garden on that Easter morning. For you, too, I will roll away the stone from the door of the supulchre. Walk unbound in the Garden with Me, in the Garden of Love, Joy, child-like, boundless Faith—the Garden of Delights.

Fair Delights   **April 12**

I T is My Pleasure that you wait before Me.

Companionship with Me, with its soul-rest, is all too often sacrificed for petition.

Be content awhile to be silent in My Presence. Draw in that Spiritual Power which will strengthen you to conquer the weaknesses you so deplore.

Life in Me is one of radiance.

Eternal Life is Life refreshed by Living Waters.

There is no stagnation in My Kingdom, in that place prepared for hearts that love Me.

It is a place of Fair Delights.

Claim what you will. It is yours.

Heaven's Almoner   April 13

IT may not be *your* need I am seeking to supply at a particular moment, but that of another through you.

Remember what I have told you before: it is empty vessels I fill, into open hands that I place My supply.

Too often My followers are so busy clutching their foolish possessions that they have no hands to receive the larger blessings, the needed gifts, I am waiting to pass to them, and through them, to others.

Help all to see the wonderful life that could open out before them. To be Heaven's almoner is the work to which I call each follower of Mine.

You Can Do This   April 14

I WILL give you rest.

My Gift truly, but the result of your trust.

Train yourself to trust so completely that no tremor even of doubt or fear can enter in.

No fear of the future, no cloud over the present, no shadow of the past.

When the absence of fear is the result of strength for the way gained by contact with Me, and of complete reliance upon My Tenderness and My Power, then you have *My Gift of Rest.*

The Sunlit Way   April 15

K NOW that your Source of joy is something changeless. The hopes of the world are but in material things and when these pass or change their joy fades, hope dies, only dark night remains.

Speak comfort to such. Tell of My Love surrounding you, that My protecting Power is yours. That I can never fail one who trusts in Me. That you can breathe in courage from My Presence as you breathe in air.

Tell the world—that for one who walks a cheerless road with Me, the bare hedge doth blossom as the rose, and life is bathed in sunlit joy.

Regain Dominion   April 16

Let them have dominion.

M AN has lost this dominion because he failed to be guided by My Spirit. He was never meant to function alone. Body, mind and spirit, he was created by My Father.

The senses were given him to link him to earth, and to create and maintain contact with the world around; but the spirit was definitely his link for guidance and instruction from the world of My Kingdom.

He is a lost soul until he links up in this way, just as a man blind, deaf and dumb would be in a world of sense. This was man's fall. He had this power and lost it.

New Beauties April 17

LIFE has so many lessons to teach you. You may not be able to travel through your material world. But for your spirit there are vast and beautiful realms in which you can be ever travelling and exploring; and, with ever-increasing capacity for enjoyment, discovering new beauties of Spiritual Truth.

God's Mosaic April 18

LIFE is a journey. The choice as to who shall be your conductor is your own. Once that choice is made, and you feel you have placed yourself in wise Hands, do not spoil your journey by frustrating the plans made for your comfort and happiness.

Rest content with the plans I have made for you. No

detail has been too small for My loving consideration. Know that your lives are being truly God-conducted, and so will bring you the greatest happiness and success.

The greater the trust you repose in Me the wider will be My scope for the plans I have made for you.

Life is a mosaic planned by God. Each God-directed thought, impulse, and action of yours is necessary to the carrying out of the perfect design.

That design is of exquisite workmanship.

Love-Controlled   April 19

LIVE in My Love.
Return to Me ever for refilling, that your soul may breathe in, and breathe out, Love, as your lungs breathe in, and breathe out, air.

There is nothing in you that creates Love, so how can you give it out unless you are receiving it?

All service, to be truly effective and of permanent value, must be wrought in Love. Where Love is, self cannot hold sway, and self nullifies the good in service.

See Me and My thought for you in all your daily life; so, conscious of My Love, you will absorb that Love, until it permeates your whole being, and inspires and illumines all you do and say.

The Joyous War   **April 20**

L IVE much a life apart with Me. In the world but
  not of it. You can do this even in a crowd,
provided self does not intrude.

It is a sign of progress that you cannot be indulging
thoughts of self and then turn to Me in complete
self-forgetfulness.

Your life must be one of intense service and
consecration. Your fight is not so much an active one in
the world, as one of active warfare on the unseen plane.
A war truly against principalities and powers. Never-
theless a joyous war.

"How Oft in the Conflict"   **April 21**

Lord, bid me come to Thee upon the waters.

" C OME."
       All that I did when on earth I do to-day in the
Spirit-realm.

My servant Paul realized this Truth when he spoke of
Me as the same yesterday, to-day, and for ever.

When the faintest fear of all that lies before you
disturbs you, when you are conscious of the loss of
Spirit-buoyancy, then you are looking at the waves and
feeling the wind is contrary.

Then you cry, "Lord, save me, I perish."

And My Hand will be outstretched to save you, as it saved My fearful, doubting Peter.

Light Comes   April 22

"LORD, show me Thyself" is a cry that never goes unanswered.

Not to physical vision comes the awareness, but to spiritual insight, as more and more you realize My Love, My Power and the manifold wonders of My character.

Its Humility, its Majesty, its Tenderness, its Sternness, its Justice, its Mercy, its Healing of sore wounds, and its consuming Fire.

Man turns to books, he studies theology, he seeks from other men the answer to life's riddles, but he does not come to Me.

Is there a problem?

Do not worry over its solution.

Seek Me. Live with Me. Talk to Me. Company with Me, daily, hourly. *Lo, suddenly you see.*

Words of Life   April 23

Lord Thy Word abideth and our footsteps guideth.

TREASURE My Words in your heart. They will meet your need *to-day* as surely as they met the needs of those to whom I spoke them when I was on earth for they were not spoken in time but in Eternity.

If My gift to man is Eternal Life, then the words inspired by that Life are eternal, appropriate to your needs to-day as they were then.

But the words and the guidance are not for all. They are for those who ACCEPT MY great gift of Eternal Life.

" And this is Life Eternal, that they might know Thee the only true God, and Jesus Christ, Whom Thou has sent."

"Lord Use Me, I Beseech Thee"   April 24

I WILL use you as you eliminate self and offer Me a consecrated personality, made in My Image.

There can be no limit to My power to use one such. Nothing is impossible to Me. My Love is limitless, My Tenderness is limitless, My Understanding is limitless.

Every attribute of the Godhead is complete, inexhaustible, in a way you can only dimly see.

Your Limitations   April 25

THE words I give you mark steps in Spiritual Progress.

There can be no limit to the Spirit Power you may possess as self is turned out and My Will welcomed.

But to those who yield themselves wholly to Me there *are* limitations as far as the material is concerned, as only what will assist Spiritual growth or manifestation is for these. Yet all your needs will be supplied.

Vain Toil   April 26

Master we have toiled all night and have taken nothing.

THERE will be nights of wearied anguish, when you toil and catch nothing.

There will be mornings of rapture when the result of your prayers and longings will be so great as to bring you to your knees with a humility born of a wonder of fulfilment—"the nets brake."

Share the loneliness with Me—the weariness, the dreariness, all with Me, as I share all with you.

Welcome Them   April 27

MORE and more I shall send into your life those whom you shall help. Have no fear. Do not doubt your wisdom to deal with them. It is My Wisdom that will help them, not any wisdom of yours.

Shower Love on all. Nothing will be too much that you can do for others. Delight in My Word, in My Love.

As you grow more conscious of that Love you will feel more and more the responsibility laid upon you to make that Great Love of My aching Heart known to those for whom I died, and for whom I ever live to make intercession.

Overshadowing Wings April 28

MY child you are tired with the burden and heat of the day.

Stay awhile and know that I abide with you, and know that I speak Peace unto your soul.

Dread nothing, fear nothing. Know that all is well. The day is far spent. The toil has been long, but evening rest with Me is sweet.

The gathering gloom of night will be to your heart but the *overshadowing wings* of the Eternal God.

Deep in your heart you feel the striving of wonderful Truths. Faint sense of the Glory to be revealed.

No Message, But— April 29

MY child, wait before Me.

You may receive no message, but in this waiting time, even if you are not conscious of being taught, you are being changed.

The eye of your soul will be focussed upon Me and the insight gained will be calming, remedial, strengthening.

My First Missionary   **April 30**

MY denunciations were for the self-satisfied.
For the sinner, who felt his failure and weakness, I had the tenderest pity. " Go, and sin no more," was My Word to the woman taken in adultery.

But what a Word of hope that was, revealing as it did the assurance that I trusted her not to fall into sin again. That I deemed her capable of a new life.

The Samaritan woman at Sychar's well I trusted with a secret that even My disciples had not shared fully with Me. She was one of My first missionaries.

I recognized the wealth of love in the offering of the woman who was a sinner. There was no public denunciation of her sin, no repulse of her love.

" *Holy Father, cheer our way*
With Thy love's perpetual ray;
Grant us every closing day,
Light at evening time."

MAY

Bounteous Giving   **May 1**

NOT what you can gain in any situation, but what
you can give must be your question. You follow
Me, of Whom it was said, "Even Christ pleased not
Himself." So love, so help, so serve.

Seek the weak and wandering. Care for all.

Realize My overflowing and overwhelming Bounty.
The stores of the Lord are inexhaustible. But to test
and prove My generosity fully you must be generous.

My lovers give with no niggard hands. A heart
overflowing with gratitude for what it has received
expends joyous gratitude in giving.

Peace Unto Your Souls   **May 2**

Peace I leave with you, My Peace give I unto you.

I KNEW that only in Peace could My work be done.
Only in Peace could My followers help souls to Me.
At all costs keep that Peace. If your heart-peace is

unruffled, then every thought is a mighty force for ME. Then every act is one of power.

Rely on My leading. Nothing is impossible to Me.

Unlimited expectancy yours. Unlimited power *Mine*.

Useless Activity   May 3

PREPARATION-time is so neglected by My followers. Consequently there is lack of power in work for Me.

To alter the laws of a country is no real remedy for ill. Men's hearts must be altered by contact with Me.

Remember the lessons I have taught you about useless activity. When most work cries out to be done, then it is truly the time—not to rush, but to Commune with Me and My Father.

Never feel strong in yourself. Know that only in My Strength can you accomplish all. No mountain of difficulty can then be insurmountable or immovable.

The Acceptable Gift   May 4

REST in My Love. Abide in Me.

Leave all to follow Me—your pride, your self-sufficiency, your fears of what others may think—All.

Have no fear. Go forth into the unknown with Me, fearful of nothing with so sure a convoy.

Just as a flower, given as an offering to a loved one so is your tribute of love to Me.

As Mary gave her Love-offering, spikenard very precious, so give to Me your love and understanding.

Dangerous Channels   May 5

" SAVIOUR, let me be a channel for Thy Mighty Power."

First you must be kept by that Mighty Power.

For it must be a consecreated life to be so used.

My Power passing through wrong channels would work harm. It could not be.

The alloy of the channel would poison the Spirit-flood.

The Fertile Glade   May 6

Seek and you shall find.

AS a mother hiding from her child puts herself in the way of being found, so with Me. So the finding of Me and of the treasures of My Kingdom may not always depend upon ardent intent securing attainment, but upon the mere setting out on the quest.

Is this a comfort to you?

When you set out upon a time of seeking I place Myself in your way, and the sometime arid path of prayer becomes a fertile glade in which you are surprised to find your search so soon over. Thus mutual Joy.

Clouds and Rain   May 7

S EE My goodness in the clouds and rain, as well as in the sunshine of life. Both express so wonderfully the goodness and love of your Lord.

Just as the shady glade, the cool riverside, the mountain-top, the blazing highway, all meet the varying needs of man.

The Dross and the Gold   May 8

S HARE your Joy with Me.

Tell Me of all that gladdens you throughout your day. I am near to hear. Feel that I alone share to the full your heart-thrills, because with Me no success of yours engenders regret nor is tinged with envy.

Is it not My Joy, My success, accomplished only in and through Me.

Share all with Me. The disappointment, not only in others but all too poignantly in yourself. Share your backward step as well as the one of progress.

Bring all to Me, and together, in tender Love, we can sift the dross from the gold.

Come back to Me, ever sure of a welcome, ever glad to feel My Presence in and round you.

Call Me Often   May 9

SPEAK My Name often during the day. It has the power to banish evil, and to summon Good.
JESUS.

In Me dwelleth all the fulness of the Godhead, so that when you call Me you call to your aid all there is of Good to need.

Talk to Me   May 10

TALK to Me about the world's misunderstanding of Me. Tell Me that your Love will seek to comfort Me for that. Tell Me your life shall be devoted to bringing about an understanding between Me and those you meet who love Me not.

As one who knows a prisoner has been wrongly convicted devotes a life-time to the vindication of that loved one's name, and counts all the trials and troubles, misunderstandings and hardships encountered in so doing, as nothing, so that his object is accomplished— let it be thus with you, longing to make Me known.

Bigger Demands   May 11

AS your faith in Me grows and your sphere of influence extends, your claims will be the grea- ter. Yet no real need of yours shall go unsatisfied.

You will make bigger demands, and ever more and more you will be trusting Me to supply the little wants. This trust will come as you realize My power more and more, and feel My Love, and know its tender watchfulness in every detail of your daily life.

"Rejoice, again I say, Rejoice."

With a loved human friend a big gift may be prized as proof of a big love, but great devotion is displayed even more in the anticipation of the little wants, in the solicitude shown in little ways.

Delight in My Love, so shown.

Lord of Joy   **May 12**

THE UNSPEAKABLE JOY offered Himself for joyful recognition.

This is a further stage of development.

You enter upon it when you realize that I was the expression in time of the Joy of all Eternity. That joy I offered to all who would see in My way the path of Joy, and who would hail Me, not only as the Man of Sorrows but as the Lord of Joy.

This truth becomes known to those only who give joyful recognition to this all-amazing, all-sustaining, all-revealing JOY.

Highways and Byways   May 13

THE way of Holiness differs for each of My followers as the character of each differs. My command for you is not necessarily My command for another.

My followers often forget this. Because I may have told them to take a certain road they are sure that you should be walking in the same way.

Heed them not. Remember, too, that a way of discipline for you may not be My will for another.

You Have Been Warned   May 14

FASTING is the starving out of self. It may not always be by food-abstinence. But it is an absolute essential of progress in the life with Me.

There is no standing still in the Christian life. If there is not progress there is retrogression.

I redeemed you. Bought you back from slavery to sin, of whatever kind.

So, when weakness overcomes you, and you yield to temptation, you make of My Redemption a mockery.

Grasp This Truth   May 15

TOO many hinder their work for Me by seeking to justify themselves. You are fighting for Christ the

King, not for yourself. The explaining or justifying must be for Me.

In any difficulty with another put yourself in his place and pray that his difficulty may be solved for him.

This will bring about a solution of yours, and help you to see better that for which you should pray.

The power to realize the needs of those you contact can only be acquired by absorbing sympathy and understanding from My Life. So, time for knowing Me must be increasingly dear and necessary to you.

Your task is to show the Power of My Spirit working through a life of yielded will, and the Joy that transforms the life when this is so.

Hungry Hearts   May 16

We would see Jesus.

THIS is still the cry of a hungry, dissatisfied, seeking world.

I look to My followers to satisfy that cry.

Reflect Me, that the seekers may see Me in you, and then go on to company with Me.

Rejoice at this as John rejoiced when he could point his disciples to Me with the brave and humble words, " He must increase, but I must decrease."

Go on in Faith and Joy and Love.

My Messenger Goes Before   **May 17**

WHEN you think of Me as your Rescuer, remember it is not only from sin, depression or despair.

It is from the difficulties of life also and from perplexity as to your path. I solve your problems. I provide the channel through which help will come.

I send My messenger to prepare your way before you. I train you so that you may be fitted for your next task, so that you may be worthy of My promised blessing. That Blessing which I long to shower on you.

The Healing Light   **May 18**

WHEREVER My followers go, *there* should be My Light surrounding them. The Light of the Sun of Righteousness.

Evil cannot live in that Light.

Man is only just learning that light banishes disease.

Every follower of Mine who is in close personal touch with Me is surrounded by this Light. Light Eternal. Light reflected by a consciousness of My Presence.

So whether he speak or not he must be the means of diffusing My Light wherever he goes.

The Ordered Life   **May 19**

YOU cannot be doing My work well and wielding a worthy influence unless all your life is ordered.

Let that be your aim and your achievement.

Secure this order and you will be able to do so much more in My service, and, without haste or unrest, reflect more the order and beauty of My Kingdom.

You need this discipline in your life.

Peace is the result of an ordered life lived with Me.

Prepare yourself for each task, for each occasion. Pray for those you will contact, your time with them.

This will save discord, and will enable the work and planning, in which you co-operate with them, to be fruitful for good.

Spirit Waves   **May 20**

YOU have been told to end all prayer upon a note of praise.

That note of praise is not only faith rising up through difficulties to greet Me. It is even more. It is the Soul's recognition that My Help is already on the way.

It is the echo in your heart of the sound borne on Spirit Waves.

It is given to those who love and trust Me to sense this approach.

So rejoice and be glad, for truly your redemption draweth nigh.

Soften the Soil May 21

IN My story of the Sower the hearts that lost the blessing, that held no good result, lost it because My servants had failed to prepare the ground.

They had failed to guard those they sought to influence, against the power of evil, and hardness of heart. They had failed to brace them to bear trouble and difficulty. They had failed to warn them against becoming too engrossed with having and getting.

The ground of the Sower had not been prepared. Much prayer must precede seed-sowing if the labour is not to be in vain.

So seek to prepare My way before Me. Then I, the Great Sower, will come. Harvest will indeed be great.

Christianity Has Not Failed May 22

MEN are trying to live the Christian Life in the Light and Teaching of My three years' Mission alone. That was never My Purpose.

I came to reveal My Father, to show the God-Spirit

working in man. I taught, not that man was only to attempt to copy the JESUS of Nazareth, but that man was also to be so possessed by My Spirit, the Spirit actuating all I did, that he would be inspired as I was.

Seek to follow Me by the Power of the In-dwelling Spirit which I bequeathed to you. This Spirit WILL guide you into all Truth.

I told My disciples that I could not tell them all but the Spirit would guide them. That is where My followers fail Me. Dwell more and more upon this Spirit-Guidance, promised to all, and so little claimed.

Getting and Giving   **May 23**

COME, My children, come and gladly claim. Come and take from Me. Come with outstretched hands to receive.

And keep nothing. Eagerly pass on My gifts so that I may again bless your emptiness and refill your vessels.

You begin to understand this Law of Supply.

Man does not realize that for the children of the Kingdom the law is not that which rules outside.

My followers must be channels through which My gifts can pass to others. You cannot obtain My supply and follow the way of the world.

No Separation   **May 24**

Come to Me.

AT first with reluctant footsteps, then, as our Friendship grows, ever more and more eagerly, until the magic of My Presence not only *calls* but *holds* you, and reluctantly you turn to earth's ways and duties again.

But, as time passes, even that reluctance passes too, as you know there is no separation, not even a temporary one, in such Companionship; because I go with you and My Words you carry ever in your heart.

New Temptations   **May 25**

YOU will find that as you grow in Grace evil forces are more ready to hinder your work and influence.

Walk warily, watchfully.

Always see that there is a new discipline to become a part of your armour, for as you progress new temptations will present themselves.

In rarified air there are subtle dangers unknown in the valley or on the lower sides of the mountain. Many a disciple fails because he is not aware of the mountain dangers.

A Day at a Time   May 26

THE problems of to-morrow cannot be solved without the experience of to-day.

There is a plan for your lives dependent upon the faithful work of each day. You frustrate that plan if you leave to-day's task incomplete, while you bestir and fret yourself over to-morrow's happenings.

You will never learn the Law of Supply if you do this, and the learning of that Law is the lesson for now.

Home of Content   May 27

CAN you not trust My supply?

All is yours. Could I plan your journey, your way of life, your work and not count the cost?

Can you not trust Me even as you would trust an earthly friend? Live in My Kingdom and then the supply of the Kingdom is yours.

I wish you to learn the Glory of a God-protected life.

No idle, fruitless rushing hither and thither.

Storms may rage, difficulties press hard, but you will know no harm . . . safe, protected and guided.

Love knows no fear.

Care for All   May 28

REALIZE My overflowing and overwhelming Bounty.

The stores of the Lord are inexhaustible, but to test My generosity to the full you must be generous.

My lovers give with no niggard hands.

Cares Cared For   May 29

Casting all your care upon Him, for He hath care of you.

HOW precious these words. Care, attention, and the Love which prompts them, are all indicated here, as also the most tender provision.

You are not told to put your worries away merely so that you may forget about them, but to cast them upon God. That is different: they will be dealt with.

Difficulties will be cleared away, mistakes rectified, weaknesses remedied, disease healed, problems solved.

See Clear   May 30

YOUR power to help your brother does not depend upon him: it is in your own hands. It is conditional upon your casting out the beam out of your own eye.

Attack not your brother's faults but your own. As you eradicate those you discover where your brother needs help, and you acquire the power to give him that help to conquer and to eradicate his faults.

Into My Likeness May 31

"CHANGED . . . from Glory to Glory." Changed from one character to another. Each change marking as it were a milestone on the Spiritual Highway.

The Beauty of the view you see in the distance is the realization of My character, My Glory, towards which with varying pace you are hourly progressing.

The way to secure better progress is to keep your gaze on your goal. Not on the road you traverse, assuredly not on the way by which you have come. Your goal is that Glory or Character that you see more and more clearly in Me, your Lord and Master.

"It doth not yet appear what you shall be, but know that when I shall appear (that is to you, to your sight, when you see Me), you shall be like Me, for you shall see Me as I *am*."

JUNE

Confidence June 1

CHARACTER-CHANGE comes by doing My Will in days when you see no Vision and hear no Voice.

Never leave the path of strict observance of all you were told to do when you saw Me and spoke to Me on the Mount. If you do you walk into serious danger.

These dull days are your practice days. Difficulties appear, failure seems inevitable. But all is necessary, so that you may learn to adapt your life to the teaching I have given you, may realize your own weakness, develop obedience and perseverance, without waiting for further instruction and inspiration.

Persevere with patience. I guide you still, for I am with you when you do not realize My Presence.

More faith will come through the confidence arising from experience.

Shake Free   **June 2**

Come unto Me . . . and I will give you rest.

R EST in the midst of work. Heart-rest in the
knowledge of My keeping Power.

Feel that rest stealing into your being. Incline your
ear and come unto Me, hear and your soul shall live.
Grow in strength, not overgrown by cares.

Let not the difficulties of life, like weeds, choke the
rest of your soul, choke and tether the soaring freedom
of your spirit.

Rise above these earth-bonds into newness of life,
abundant and victorious. Rise.

Praise For Everything   **June 3**

C ONFIDENCE must be the finishing chord of every
contact between you and Me. Joyful confidence.
You must end upon the Joy-note.

The union between a soul and Me is attained in its
beauty and complete satisfaction only when in every
incident that soul achieves praise.

Love and laugh and thank Me all the time.

Delve   **June 4**

C ONSIDER the Truths of My Kingdom as well
worth all search, all sacrifice. Dig down into the
soil. Dig when it means toil, fatigue.

Above and below the ever-present material you must look for My Hidden Treasure. It is not what you say, but what you perceive, that will influence other lives.

My Spirit will communicate this to you and also to those round you. So for their sakes delve.

Delve Further   June 5

EXAMINE yourself. Ask Me and I will show you what you are doing wrong—if only you will listen humbly and be unreservedly determined to do My Will.

True Joys   June 6

CONTINUE ye in My Love. Seek nothing for yourself, only what you can use for Me. Rely on Me for all. Be meek, not only towards Me but towards others. Love to serve. Have no fear. Seek to be true in all. Be full of Joy.

The world wants to see Joy, not in the thrills of worldly pleasures and dissipations, but in the beauty of Holiness. In the ecstasy of peaceful safety with Me. In that thrill of adventure My true followers know, in the satisfaction that self-conquest gives.

Let your world see that you are steadfast, immovable.

Lose Life's Sting
June 7

SUBMIT yourself entirely to My Control, My Kingship; then the sting is taken out of life's rebuffs.

Welcome each contact as of My planning. Be ready to widen your circle of influence at My wish. Do not let age or other limitations daunt you.

Trust Me. Can I not judge your fitness for the task I give you? Have not I a Love for your acquaintances as well as for you?

Do not question My decisions. All is planned in Love for all My children. Only self-will can hinder the carrying out of the Divinely-conceived plan.

Work gladly, knowing all needed wisdom shall be provided, also all needed material to do My Work.

Perennial Youth
June 8

COUNT all well lost, all other work well foregone, to rest apart with Me.

From these times you go out strengthened, glad, full of Life-giving Joy—My Joy that you can never find anywhere else but with Me, the Joy-giving Christ.

Let others sense this Joy. More than any words this will show them the priceless gain of life with Me.

You shall truly find that there is no age in My Kingdom, in My Companionship.

Set Apart   **June 9**

COUNT not these days as lost.

Y(u have, even in this seemingly narrow life,
countless opportunities for self-conquest. There is no
greater task than that.

I set apart those who greatly desire to reflect Me,
because there is danger that in the crowded ways, and
among others, self will gain the ascendancy.

For a time, until self is recognized and conquered,
you too must withdraw into the wilderness.

You are learning much, and I am your Teacher.

Come with Me into a desert place and rest awhile.

Do You Remember?   **June 10**

CULTIVATE the habit of thinking about Me. God
is everywhere. My Presence is always with you,
but recollection brings consciousness of that Presence
and closer friendship.

Deliberately recall some event in My life, some
teaching of Mine, some act of love. So will you impress
Me upon your character and life.

Your learning and accomplishments are valueless
without My Grace, which is sufficient for you. Leave
planning to Me. Leave Me to open or close the way.

Prepare yourself for all I am preparing for you.

Simple Obedience   June 11

Dear Lord, teach me to obey Thee in all things.

YOU are Mine, pledged to serve Me.

Every want of yours has been anticipated. Look back and see how each failure has been due to your not having obeyed implicitly the instructions I gave you in preparation for that task or trial.

Listening to My Voice implies obedience. I am a tender Lord of Love, but I am a Captain with whose words there must be no trifling.

You are a volunteer, no conscript, but if you expect the privileges of My Service you must render Me the obedience of that service.

The way of obedience may seem hard and dreary, but the security of My ordered life the untrained soul can never know. March in step with your Captain.

Spiritual Renewal   June 12

DEEP life-giving draughts of My Spirit are yours. Think of the aridness, the thirst, that is unquenched till the whole unsatisfied being is age-worn.

Can you help man in any better way than by proving to him that the cleansing waters of My Spirit have power to wash away all that hinders growth, and to satisfy to the full every thirst of your nature?

Conquest of Fear June 13

IT is not thinking about Me, but dwelling with Me that brings perfect fearlessness.

There can be no fear where I am. Fear was conquered when I conquered all Satanic power. If all My followers knew this, and affirmed it with absolute conviction, there would be no need of armed forces to combat evil.

The Soul Restored June 14

DO not sorrow if, after time with Me, you cannot repeat to yourself all the lessons you have learned. Enough that you have been with Me.

Do you need to know the history of plant or tree to enjoy the countryside? You have inhaled pure air and been refreshed with the beauty of the landscape. Enough for the day. So, too, you have been in My Presence and found rest unto your souls.

Down in the Valley June 15

DO not let doubt or fear assail or depress you because of this time of anguish and failure-sense through which you have passed. No, this had to be.

Useful work lies ahead of you. Before the onset of so

great a task My servant has usually to walk through the Valley of Humiliation, or in the wilderness.

If I, your Lord, before I began My Mission, had to have My forty days of temptation, how could you expect to go all unprepared to your great task?

You must taste anew the shame of unworthiness, of failure and of nothingness before you go forth with Me conquering and to conquer.

Down into Egypt   June 16

DOWN into Egypt, back into Galilee. These journeys were gladly undertaken. They meant no family upheaval, for was not the desire of that Family but to fulfil Divine Intent?

Upheavals come only when man is set on some particular way of life, and is called to forgo that.

When the fixed desire is to do the Father's Will, then there is no real change. The leaving of home, town, country is but as the putting off of a garment that has served its useful purpose.

Change is only Spiritual progress when the life is lived with Me, the Changeless One.

Bind Their Wounds   June 17

DRAW from Me not only the Strength you need for yourself, but all you need for the wounded ones to whom I shall lead you. Remember no man liveth to himself. You must have Strength for others.

They will come to you in ever-increasing numbers. Will you send them empty away? Draw from Me and you will not fail them.

Nearer to Thee   June 18

"LORD, show me Thyself," is a cry that never goes unanswered.

Not often to physical vision comes the awareness but to spiritual insight, as more and more you realize My Love, My Power, and the manifold wonders of My character—its humility, its Majesty, its tenderness, its sternness, justice, mercy, healing and consuming fire.

Draw nigh to Me, and I will draw nigh to you.

My Healing Power   June 19

WHEN life is difficult then relax completely; sleep or rest in conscious reliance on My Healing Power.

Endeavour that others may never see you anything but rested, strong, happy, joyful.

Before you meet seek renewal in My Secret Place.

Your tears and cares must be shared with Me alone.

My blessing be upon you.

Living Waters   **June 20**

DRINK of the water that I shall give you, and you shall never thirst.

I will lead you beside the waters of comfort.

I will give unto you living water.

Blessed are they that hunger and thirst after righteousness.

As the hart panteth after the water brooks so longeth my soul after Thee, O God.

This is the thirst that can never go unsatisfied.

Yours   **June 21**

APPEAL to Me often. Do not *implore* so much as *claim* My Help as your right.

It is yours in Friendship's name. Claim it with a mighty, impelling insistence. It is yours.

Not so much Mine to give you, as yours; but yours because it is included in the Great Gift of Myself that I gave you.

An All-embracing Gift, a Wonder Gift. Claim, accept, use it. All is well.

Right of Entry   **June 22**

DWELL with Me, and in doing so you admit those you love to the right of entry.

If their thoughts follow you as human friend and helper, they are drawn in thought, and later in love and longing, to Me with whom you live.

Each Need Supplied   June 23

INSTEAD of urging men to accept Me as this or that, first discover the need, and then represent Me as the supply.

A man may not feel his need of a Saviour. He wants a Friend. Reveal Me as the Great Friend. Another may not need guidance, only to be understood. Represent Me as the Understanding Christ.

Leave Me to satisfy each and every need as I do yours.

Zest in Service   June 24

YOUR will, your desire, must be to do My Will, wanting It, loving It, as a child hugging some treasure to its heart. So treasure My Will.

Find your delight in It. "Lord, what would'st Thou have me to do?" is no question of a sullen servant. It is the eager appeal of a friend, who views all life as a glorious adventure, with the enthusiasm of a youth permitted to share an explorer's quest.

Bring the unquenchable Zest into all you do.

Ladder of Joy June 25

YOU see in your lives cause for praise or prayer. You praise or pray. Your heart is lifted thereby into the Eternal, into My very Presence.

Thereafter the drudgery or commonplace or dreary waiting ceases to be the colourless something to be endured. It is the ladder, whereby you rise to Me.

You can then smile at it, welcome it. It is friend, not foe. So with everything in life. Its value for you must depend on whether it leads you nearer to Me.

So poverty or plenty, sickness or health, friendship or loneliness, sunshine or gloom, each may add to the Joy and Beauty of your lives.

Life's Furnace June 26

LIFE has its furnace for My children, into which they are plunged for the moulding.

At their request I watch and watch until I can see them reflect My Glory. Then comes the further shaping into My Likeness. But the metal from which that Likeness is fashioned must be indeed pure.

So often My children are impatient for the moulding, never thinking that the refining must come first.

To do My work there must be much refining.

Eternal Life   **June 27**

E TERNAL Life is a matter of VISION.
     Spiritual Vision is the result of knowledge which
engenders further knowledge.

"And this is Life Eternal . . . to know Thee the only
True God and Jesus Christ Whom Thou has sent."

Eternal Life.

Eternal in so far as the quality, the character of the
Life is concerned. Being of God it implies immortality.

It is My Gift of the Life that is Mine. Therefore it
must be Power-Life. This is your Life, to absorb, to live
in, and through.

"He that believeth—*hath* eternal life."

The Life Divine   **June 28**

A S you recognize My dealings with you, Eternal
     Life flows through your being in all Its sanc-
tifying, invigorating and remedial force.

Eternal Life is awareness of the things of Eternity.
Awareness of My Father and awareness of Me. Not
merely a knowledge of Our existence, even of our
God-head, but an awareness of Us in all.

As you become aware of Me, all for whom you care
are linked to Me, too. Yielding Me your service, you
draw, by the magnetic power of Love, all your dear
ones within the Divine-Life radius.

All One   June 29

EVERY man is your brother, every woman your sister, every child your child. You are to know no difference of race, colour or creed. One is your Father, and all ye are brethren.

This is the Unity I came to teach—Man united with God and His great family. Not man alone, seeking a oneness with God alone. See God the Father with His great world family, and, as you seek union with Him, it must mean for you attachment to His family, His other children.

He acknowledges all as His children, not all acknowledge Him as their Father.

Ponder this.

Immune From Evil   June 30

EVIL was conquered by Me, and to all who rely on Me there is immunity from it.

Turn evil aside with the darts I provide.

Rejoicing in tribulation is one dart.

Practising My Presence is another.

Self-emptying is another.

Claiming My Power over temptation is another.

You will find many of these darts as you tread My Way, and you will learn to use them adroitly, swiftly. Each is adapted to the need of the moment.

JULY

Out of the Unseen

Faith is the substance of things hoped for, the evidence of things not seen.

YOU do not yet see, nor will you see fully while you are on this earth, how faith, co-operating with Spiritual Power, actually calls into being that for which you hope.

Men speak of dreams come true. But you know them as answered prayers; manifestations of Spirit Force in the Unseen. So trust boundlessly.

Dangerous Power

DO you not see how necessary is your learning the method of Spirit-attack. There must be a certain root-faith in Me, or you could not trust yourself to perfect surrender to Me. But there must come to those who walk all the way with Me, a yielding of their wills and lives wholly to Me, or the greater faith that results would be a source of danger. It would drag you back to the material plane, instead of to Spiritual Heights.

For unless your will is *wholly* Mine, you will rely on this new God-given Power, and call into being that which is not for the furtherance of My Kingdom.

Hiding in Thee   July 3

FOLLOW Me, and whether it be in the storm, or along the dusty highroad, or over the places of stones, or in the cool glade or the meadow, or by the waters of comfort, then, with Me, in each experience there will be a place of refuge.

At times you seem to follow afar off. Then weary with the burden and the way, you stretch out a hand to touch the hem of My Garment.

Suddenly there is no dust, no weariness. You have found Me. My child, even if it seems unprofitable, continue your drudgery, whether it be of spiritual, mental or physical effort. Truly it serves its turn if it but lead you to seek help from Me.

Break Free   July 4

For by whom a man is overcome . . . he is the slave.

I CUT the bonds of sin which bound you to evil. With loving Hands I replaced each with my cords of Love, which bound you to Me, your Lord.

The power of evil is subtle. A cut cord, a snapped cord, would awaken your slumbering conscience, but strand by strand, so carefully, with gentleness cunningly acquired, evil works until a cord is free. Even then the work is slow, but oh, so sure, until presently the old bond I severed is binding you to evil, strand by strand.

Snap off these returning fetters. Satan hath desired to have you that he may sift you as wheat. He works with an efficiency My servants would do well to copy. He has marked you as one who will increasingly bring souls to Me.

My Family Circle   July 5

For whosoever shall do the Will of My Father, he is My brother and sister and mother.

YOU see how everything depends on the necessity of doing the Will of My Father.

Here is the intimacy of a new relationship. The only condition of this is the doing of My Father's Will. Then at once, into the inner Family Circle there is admission.

The plain way of discipline is the way of knowing My Will. That is the first requisite to the doing of it.

My Will for each day can only be revealed as each day comes, and until one revelation has been lived out, how can you expect to be made aware of the next?

Awareness of My Will is only achieved by obedience to that Will as it is made clear, and when THAT Will has been obeyed the veil, hiding My next desire, is lifted.

Listen Carefully   **July 6**

MY poor deaf world. What it misses in loving Words and Whispers.

I want to share so much with it. It will not listen.

"Wherefore do you spend money for that which is not bread and your labour for that which satisfieth not. Hearken diligently unto Me and eat that which is good and let your Soul delight itself . . ."

"He that willeth to do My Will—shall know."

Whose Voice would you hear? So many voices are about you that you may miss the Still Small Voice.

"This is My Beloved Son—Hear Him."

Love's Growth   **July 7**

LEARN from Nature the profusion of her gifts.

As you daily realize more and more the generosity of the Divine Giver, learn increasingly to give.

Love grows by giving.

You cannot give bountifully without being filled with a sense of giving yourself with the gift, and you cannot so give without Love passing from you to the one who receives.

You are conscious, not of yourself as generous, but of the Divine Giver as bounteous beyond all human words to express.

So Love flows *into* you, with an intensity that is both

humbling and exalting, as Love flows *from* you with your gift.

Remember Me   **July 8**

Give me a constant remembrance of Thee.

A SK what you will and it shall be done unto you. But only if the heart desires what the lips express. "The Lord looketh on the heart."

You will grow into the true attitude of remembrance of Me as you learn more and more to attribute all your blessings, all your guidance, to My increasing care: to the mind of your Master behind all, inspiring all, controlling all, the source of all your good.

Upheld   **July 9**

G O forward unafraid.
Face each difficulty, however great and seemingly unconquerable, as you go forward towards it.

The strength you will require from Me for that adventure into danger, as it may seem to you, will fortify you for its overcoming.

"Fear thou not, for I am with thee,

"Be not afraid, for I am thy God.

"I will strengthen thee, I will help thee,

"Yea, I will uphold thee with the right arm of My Righteousness."

Your Heart is Fixed   July 10

STILL go forward unafraid. The way will open as you
go.

It is fear that blocks My way for you. Have no fear.
Know that all is well.

No circumstances, no outward changes, can harm
you in any way. Each should prove a step of progress,
as long as your hearts are fixed, "trusting in the Lord."

I know no change.

More Doors will Open   July 11

GO on in faith and trust. The Way opens as you go.
In the Christian Life doors swing open as you
come to them, if so be that you have advanced to them
along the straight path of obedience.

As you started your journey, what would it have
profited had you worried about the closed door ahead?

In the Spirit-Life miracle-working Power operates
through natural human channels. As you have seen.

So this is the continuing lesson: Go steadily forward
in firm trust along the path of quiet obedience.

That is *your* work. *Mine* to cause the doors to swing
open, as you come to them, not before.

How often have I opened those doors for you in the
past? More will open. So trust, so hope, so love.

Your Order of Merit   **July 12**

GRACE is the distinctive mark I set upon My friends. It is no order of merit. It is the result of living with Me. It is even unobserved by those on whom I bestow it, but to those they meet who have eyes to see, it is apparent just as during My time on earth it was said, "They took knowledge of them that they had been with Jesus."

It may be the sign of My sustaining Power within a life. It may be the quiet strength of poise, the mark of self-conquest, some faint reflection of My character, or a mystic scent of the soul unfolding to My Love.

Harmonize   **July 13**

GROW daily, ever more and more, into My likeness. Do My Will as revealed to you, and leave the result to Me. If you are but My representative, then why concern yourself as to whether the action I have arranged for you is wise or not?

If your control of mind and body is not as progressive as that of your spirit, it is a hindrance. See to this. The three must work in unison; otherwise disharmony.

Beautiful though one instrument may be in an orchestra, with a beauty beyond that of any other, yet should it play its part ahead of those others, dis-harmony results; and so with you a sense of frustration and failure follows disharmony within.

Home of Creation   July 14

HAVE no fear. Wonders are unfolding ever more and more. You will be guided in all as you dwell in the Secret Place of the Most High.

Remember in that Secret Place was thought out all the wonders of the Universe. There all *your* wonder plans will be evolved. It is the home of Creation, and there you, too, share in Creative Power.

Home of Joy   July 15

HEART speaks to heart as you wait before Me. Love enkindles Love.

The air you breathe is Divine, life-giving, invigorating.

The place in which you rest is My Secret Place.

You do not come to ask Me of doctrine.

That is, as it were, the foundation of your Spiritual being; necessary, but once secure, you seek to fashion, with Me, its beautiful superstructure—the home of Peace and Joy where I come and commune with you.

Confidences July 16

HELP is always yours.

It comes so swiftly when you realize that *you* are insufficient to supply your need. But it comes the more potently as you grow to see that for each need the supply was already provided.

My followers so often act as if My supply came into being only through prayer for help.

Would any man in authority act thus in his business?

Learn of Me. I will teach you lovingly, patiently. My lessons are not of the schoolroom; they are fireside confidences.

Foretaste of Heaven July 17

I thank Thee, Lord, for the Joy Thou givest me and for Thy tender care of me.

GROW ever more and more conscious of this. Look upon all as under My Influence, and life will become increasingly full of Joy. This Joy no man taketh from you.

This is the foretaste of Heaven that will make your passing seem no death, and will mean that your spirit will be no stranger in the home of spirits but will be breathing an atmosphere familiar and dear.

Meek and Lowly   **July 18**

A S the world's great Teacher I taught not so much
by word as by the Living Word.

"Learn of Me" I said, adding that men should see in
Me meekness . . . and lowliness.

So that My disciples should take Me as their great
example, I epitomised My attitude towards My Father
in Heaven and towards His other Children as "Meek
and lowly."

Towards God the Father the meekness of a yielded
will; towards His other children lowliness, devoid of the
pride that sunders men, and prevents their humble
approach to God.

"Learn of Me—I am meek and lowly in heart." So
do you find rest unto your souls.

Wayside Meetings   **July 19**

I USE such simple things and casual moments to
reveal Myself to man. He can meet Me in the
common ways of Life—if he has but eyes to see and
ears to hear.

No great sign, nothing spectacular. In the seemingly
incidental along the road of life I meet with him and
reveal My Will, My Purpose, My Guidance.

No miles to walk, no long journey to travel, no strange language to learn, no state of ecstasy to be experienced first. Think on these things. Recall our many meetings by the wayside.

I Will Heal You   July 20

DO not recognize your illness. Each time you speak of it to others you stabilize it.

Ignore it as much as you can. Think more of Me, the Great Healer. Dwelling with Me you become whole.

Even My most faithful followers often err in not claiming of Me healing and perfection for every part of their being.

But to claim physical healing alone is a sign of living too much on the physical plane, and My Healing is of the Spirit.

Claim healing of spirit, mind and body. Then shall you, regardless of age, know wholeness.

Unconquerable   July 21

I WILL help you to conquer in the hour of temptation or difficulty. Cling to Me. Rest in My Love. Know that all is well.

Trials press, temptations assail, but remember, you

can be more than conquerors through Me. Lord of all, I am. Controller of all. Keeper, Lover, Guide, Friend.

Remember that when once your hearts have said with Peter, " Thou art the Christ, the Son of the Living God," then, upon that sure foundation of belief, I raise My House, My Holy of Holies.

The gates of hell, the adverse deeds and thoughts and criticisms of the world, cannot prevail against it. More than conquerors. Conquer in the little things. Conquer in My Strength and Power.

Lend a Hand   July 22

NOT once only in your lives, when I called you out to follow Me, but constantly—
Jesus calls.

In the busy day, in the crowded way, listen to the voice of your Lord and Lover calling. A call to stop and rest with Me awhile. A call to restrain your impatience, a reminder that in quietness and in confidence shall be your strength. A call to pause, to speak a word to one in trouble.

Perhaps to lend a hand.

Dear Name   July 23

THE murmuring of My Name in tender Love brings the unseen into the foreground of reality. It is like breathing on some surface, which brings into relief a lovely figure.

It is the Name before which evil shrinks away, shamed, powerless, defeated. Breathe it often. Not always in appeal. Sometimes in tender confidence, sometimes in Love's consciousness. Sometimes in triumphant ecstasy.

Christian Co-operators July 24

I HAVE always work to be done. So fit yourself for it by prayer, by contact with Me, by discipline.

Nothing is small in My sight. A simple task fittingly done may be the necessary unit in building a mighty edifice.

The bee knows nothing of its agency when fertilizing flowers for fruit-bearing.

Do not expect to see results.

The work may pass into other hands before any achievement is apparent. Enough that you are a worker with others and Me in My Vineyard.

Joy in Me July 25

JOY teaches. Joy cleans the smeared glass of your consciousness, and you see clearly.

You see Me clearly, and see more clearly the needs of those round you.

Perfect Yourself July 26

PERFECT as My Father in Heaven is perfect.

That means a life-struggle, an unending growth. Always as you progress, a greater perception of My Father. More struggle and growth. Above all a growing need of Me and My sustaining help.

I came to found a Kingdom of Progressive growth. Alas, how many of My followers think that all they have to do is to accept Me as Saviour. That is a first step only.

Heaven itself is no place of stagnation. It is indeed a place of progress. You will need Eternity to understand Eternal Mind.

Judge Not July 27

HUMAN nature is so complex. You can hardly, even in your most enlightened moments, tell what motive prompted this or that action of your own.

How, then, can you judge of another, of whose nature you have so little understanding? And to misjudge of what in another may have been prompted by the Spirit of God, is to misjudge God's Spirit.

Can any sin be greater than that? False judgment sent Me to the Cross!

Stupendous Truth   **July 28**

THE world can be overcome only by belief in Me, and in the knowledge that I am the Son of God. This is a stupendous Truth.

Use that as your lever for removing every mountain of difficulty and evil. Be cautious in all things and await My Guidance. Commune much with Me.

The truth of My God-head, of My All-Power, creative, redemptive, erosive of evil, must permeate your whole consciousness, and affect your attitude in every situation, toward every problem.

See the Lovable   **July 29**

DO not try to force yourself to love others. Come to Me. Learn to love Me more and more, to know Me more, and little by little you will see your fellow-man as I see him. Then you, too, will love him.

Not only with the Love of Me, which makes you desire to serve him, but you will see the lovable in him, and love that.

Real Influence   **July 30**

DO not let one single link of influence go. Cords of true love and interest must never be broken. They must always be used for ME. Pray for those to whom you are bound by particular ties, then you will be ready, should I desire your special help for them.

You must stand as a sinner with a sinner before you can save him. Even I had to hang between two thieves to save My world.

All in Order   July 31

He ordered my goings.

GUIDANCE first, but more than that, Divine order in your life, your home, all your affairs.

Order in all. Attain spiritual order first. The perfect calm which can be realized only by a soul that abides in My Secret Place.

Then the mental order of a mind which is stayed on Me, and has the sanity and poise of a mind so stayed.

Then truly must order manifest itself in your surroundings.

Each task will be entered upon with prayer, as a Divine Commission, and carried through without haste, in utter contentment.

AUGUST

Joy of Harvest August 1

He that reapeth receiveth wages and gathereth fruit unto life everlasting, that both he that reapeth and he that soweth may rejoice together.

DO you not see that if you are careless about the reaping you have prevented the harvest-joy of the sower?

If by your life and character you do not reap to the full that which they have sown, you are robbing them of the well-earned fruit of their labours.

Further learn this lesson. There are many of My workers and servants in different spheres of activity to whom you owe the seed of word or example or loving help that has influenced you.

It is a sacred trust. Use it fully.

Still Love and Laugh August 2

THIS has ever been My command to you. Love and Laugh. There is a quality about true Love to which laughter is attune.

The Love that does not pulse with joy (of which laughter is the outward sign) is but solicitude. The Joy of Heaven is consciousness of God's Love.

It was that Love that brought Me to your world.

Consciousness of that Love called forth your joy. Study My Words in the Upper Room—"Loved of My Father"; "I will love him"; "That your Joy might be full."

Love Lightens the Load   August 3

In due season you shall reap if you faint not.

THE way may seem long and dreary.

Sometimes My Heart of Love aches that I have to ask you to tread so long and so weary a way. Yet to each of My followers the road chosen is surely the one best suited to his feet.

But feet grow weary. Have you let Love smooth the toilsome way? We walk together.

Vision of Love   August 4

LOVE is the flower.

Love is the seed from which that flower germinates.

Love is the soil in which it is nourished and grows.

Love is the sun that draws it to fulfilment.

Love is the fragrance that flower gives out.

Love is the vision that sees its beauty, *and*

God is Love, all-knowing, all-understanding, from whom all Good proceeds.

Love in the Unlovely   **August 5**

L OVE to all must mark all you do if you own Me Lord, and if you would be a true follower of Me.

"His banner over me was Love." Those words express not only the loving Protection round you, but the banner under which you march as soldiers of Me, your Captain.

It serves to remind you of that for which you stand before the world. It is in Love's Name you march. In Love's Name you conquer. It is Love you are to take into the unlovely places of the world. It is the only equipment you need.

Deaf Ears   **August 6**

M AN cries for help. Man feels his need of Me. All unmindful that countless times I draw near unheard, pass on unnoticed, speak to deaf ears, touch brows fretted and wrinkled by earth's cares.

" The Christ is dead," man says.

Alive and longing, full of a living tenderness I passed his way to-day. He heeded not.

Man hears the storms, the wind, the earthquake, and his ears, still pulsing with the echoes he hears, no Still Small Voice. Oh, do not miss Me, My children.

Balm for All Ills   August 7

L OVE and care and pray. Never feel helpless to aid those you love. I am their help. As you obey Me and follow My teaching in your daily life, you will bring that help into operation.

So, if you desire to be used to save another, turn to your own life. As far as you can, make it all that it should be.

Let your influence for Me extend ever further and further. Let Love be your balm for all ills. The Power in which you will break down all barriers.

It stands, too, for the Name of the God you love and serve. So, with His banner floating o'er you, go on in glad confidence to victory. Your task to help, to strengthen, raise, heal. Only as you love will you do this.

No Hurt   **August 8**

He that overcometh shall not be hurt by the second death.

THE first death is the death to self, the result of overcoming, of self-conquest. This is gradual death.

When it is complete, the second death shall cause no hurt. For it is only the conquering Spirit sloughing away its human habitation for a better Life.

The courage My Martyrs showed was not only fearlessness engendered in time of persecution through faith in Me, and in My power to support and sustain. It was consequent on the overcoming of self already achieved. Self, having truly died, this second death had no hurt for them.

Theirs was then the Risen Life with Me.

Undivided   **August 9**

LIVE in My Peace.
There must be no divided life in this.

Peace in your heart. That heart-rest that comes from constant communion with Me, and from an undisturbed trust in Me.

Then Peace round you, where others are conscious of Me, and of that Peace as My Gift, and of the rest and strength and charm into which they are drawn.

Glad Surprise   **August 10**

L IVE so near to Me that you may never miss the opportunity of being used by Me. It is the prepared instrument, lying nearest to the Master Craftsman's Hand, that is seized to do the work.

So be very near Me, and you cannot fail to be much used. Remember that Love is the Great Interpreter, so that those who love you and are near to you are the ones you can help the most.

Do not pass them by for others, though your influence and helpfulness will gradually spread, in an ever widening circle. You will live in a spirit of glad surprise.

Absolute Honesty   **August 11**

L EARN to act slowly with sanctified caution. Precipitancy has no part in My Kingdom.

Be more deliberate in everything, with the deliberation that should characterize every soul, for it is one of the credentials of that Kingdom.

Lack of poise and dignity means lack of Spiritual Power, and this it must be your aim to possess.

Be truthful in all things, honest with an honesty that can be challenged by the world, and by the standards of My Kingdom, too.

Holy Revelry   **August 12**

LIVE with Me. Work with Me. Ever delight to do *My Holy Will*. Let *this* be the satisfaction of your lives. Revel in it.

Let the wonder of My care for you be so comforting that you may see no dullness in drudgery, in delay . . .

The Glory of My leading (the wonder of its intimacy) reveals such tender knowledge of you, past and future.

Let this reveal Me to you, and so daily increase your knowledge of Me.

The Road You Took   **August 13**

LOOK back at the way I have led you.

Say to yourself, " Is not my Lord as strong to-day as in the days that lie behind me? Did He not save me when human aid was powerless? Did He not keep His Promise, and protect and care for me? Can I, remembering that, doubt His Power now?"

So you will gain confidence and a firmer trust. As your faith is thus strengthened, My Power can operate more freely and fully on your behalf.

You are only beginning to realize My Wonders. You will see them unfold more and more as you go on. Bring Me into all you do, into every plan, every action.

Riches of His Grace   **August 14**

IT is for My followers to make My Word, the very
  Word of God, attractive.

My Word has to *dwell* in you richly. There must be
no stinting, no poverty, but an abundance of rich
supply.

Note the *dwell*. Nothing fitful, as I have told you.
Make its home there. Fittingly belong there. No
question of meagre or exhausted supply.

The Word of God grows in meaning, in intensity, for
you, as you bring it into operation.

Remember, too, the Word of God is that Word made
flesh, Who dwells with you, your Lord Jesus Christ.

My Image Restored   **August 15**

LOOK unto Me until your gaze becomes so intense
   that you absorb the Beauty of Holiness.

Then truly is the petty, unworthy self ousted from
your nature. Look to Me. Speak to Me. Think of Me.

So you become transformed by the renewing of your
mind. Other thoughts, other desires, other ways follow,
for you become transformed into My Likeness.

Thus you vindicate the ways of God with man—man
made in His Image, that Image marred, but I still had
trust in man; trust that man, seeing the God-Image in

Me, the man Christ Jesus, would aspire to rise again—into My Likeness.

Expectancy   August 16

IN all your work, your meetings with others, have ever the consciousness of My brooding Love surrounding you. Continue ye in My Love.

Meet Me at eventide with loving expectancy.

Premature Blessing   August 17

Give me strength to wait Thy time, accept Thy discipline.

ONLY your failure to do this can delay the answers to your many prayers.

The blessing you crave needs a trained, disciplined life, or it would work your ruin and bring upon you a world's criticism that could but harm the very cause, My cause, which you so ardently seek to serve.

Broken Bonds   August 18

Loose the fetters that bind me to earth and material things.

THEY shall be loosed. Even now your prayer is being answered. But you can only be completely released as you live with Me more and more.

Thought-freedom from self-claims comes by a process of substitution. For every claim of self, substitute

My claim. For every thought of fear or resentment substitute a thought of security in Me and of Joy in My Service. For every thought of limitation, of helplessness, substitute one of the Power of a Spirit-aided life.

Do this persistently. At first with deliberate effort, until it becomes an almost unconscious habit. The fetters will snap and gradually you will realize the wonder of your freedom.

Bounteous Giving   August 19

Lord I ask for Thine unlimited supply.

I GIVE with no niggard hand. See the Beauty in Nature, the profusion, the generosity. When I give you a work to do, a need of another's to meet, My supply knows no bounds.

You, too, must learn this Divine generosity, not only towards the lonely, the needy, whom you contact, but towards Me, your Lord.

Measure the wealth of Mary's gift by the offerings given to Me nowadays by those who profess their Love for Me. Ungenerous giving dwarfs the soul.

Glorious Opportunity   August 20

MAN'S life is no tragedy or comedy staged by a God of Whims.

It is man's glorious opportunity of regaining what

humanity lost—assisted by the One Who found the path-direct, and Who is ready at every point, and all along the way to supply man with the Life Eternal.

That Life Eternal which alone enables him to breathe, even here and now, the very air of Heaven, and to be inspired with the Spirit-Life in which I lived on earth; God made man.

Where to Find Me—Always   August 21

MAN so often seeks, and marvels that he does not find. Why? Because only along the path of simple obedience am I to be found.

I said, "I came not to do Mine own Will but the Will of Him that sent Me." I tread, as I always trod, the path of simple obedience. Along it shall I be found.

Man must be simply obedient to My Commands before his feet can come My way. Then, seeking, he truly finds Me. I said you must become as little children to enter the Kingdom of Heaven.

True Power   August 22

MANY are speaking ABOUT Me, and they marvel that their words have no force. They are not My Words, they are words about Me. Oh, how different.

The world is surfeited with words about Me.

The world needs to *see Me, not to hear of My Power, but to see it in action.* Not to hear of My Peace, but to see that it keeps My followers calm, unruffled and untroubled, no matter what the outward circumstances.

Not to *hear* of My Joy, but to *see* it, as from hidden depths of security, where true Power and Peace abide, it ripples to the surface of the life, and is revealed to those around.

Hunger for Righteousness   August 23

M ANY are wondering why their desire for righteousness is not satisfied according to My Promise. But that Promise was on condition that there should be hunger and thirst. If the Truths I have given have not been absorbed, there can be no real hunger for more.

So, when you miss the Joy-Light on your path, when the vision seems lost, and the Voice silent, then ask yourself, have you failed to live out the lessons that you were taught?

Live out My teaching in your lives, and then, hungry for more, come to Me, Bread of Life, Food of your souls.

Might and Majesty   **August 24**

Y OU see Me sometimes as the Man of Sorrows.
Behold Me, too, in the Majesty of My God-head.

Not always can man disregard My Wishes and break My Commands.

I view the desecration of My Image, I see the ruin of the kingdom of earth which was to have been the Kingdom of the Lord. I see passions let loose and innocence spoiled, and man clamouring for the mastery.

Then the Man of Sorrows walks a King with flashing eyes, as He sees the down-trodden, the oppressed, the persecuted and the persecutor, the tyrant and the weak.

How long shall I have the patience? HOW LONG?

House of the Spirit   **August 25**

" L EST perhaps you should let them slip "—" Hold fast that thou hast." Each Truth learned has to be cemented to your being by obedience.

Your soul-character is like a building. It IS a building (the Temple) in which the God-Spirit can make a Home.

Bricks lying on the ground separate are useless; placed together, united, they form a building. So obedience is the mortar by which Truths are retained and become a part of the being. Truths which would otherwise be lost.

So every Truth I give you must be lived out.

"I Die Daily"   August 26

I ENJOINED that if any man would follow Me he should deny himself and take up his cross.

The denial thus impressed upon My disciples as necessary was not a mere matter of discipline, of giving up, of going without.

It was a total repudiation of any claim the self might make, ignoring it, refusing to acknowledge it.

Not *once* was this to be done, but *daily;* there was to be a daily recrucifixion of any part of the self-life not already completely dead.

One Spirit-led Family   August 27

HAVE no fear. Wonders unfold.
In this Life or in the Larger Life, the lesson is the same—the absorption of My Spirit—living, thinking and acting in My Spirit, until others are forced to see and recognize its Power and claims.

Does this mean loneliness for My Follower? Nay, rather, though you, the human-self-you, has no recognition, the real you, transformed by My Spirit, shares in all that fulness of operation and resultant Joy.

You are no isolated being but one of a mighty Spirit-led family, partaker of all the family's well-being, co-operative in every act of each member, sharer of the blessing of each.

A foretaste this of Heaven's oneness and fulfilment.

Thread of Gold   August 28

L ET My Spirit of Calm enter your being, and direct you, filling you with Peace and Power. Find in each day that thread of gold that runs through all, and that links up all the simple tasks and words and interests and feelings into one whole.

Consciously hand the day back to Me at its close, leaving with Me all that is incomplete. It is Heaven's work to complete man's imperfect or unfinished task, when it has been of Heaven's ordering.

See the Joy of Life, and you, by that very act, increase it. Joy grows by man's consciousness of Joy.

Divine Extravagance   August 29

Let Christ be in you in all wealth of Wisdom.

I T is the niggard attitude of My followers that casts a slur upon My religion.

Dwell upon the Divine extravagance of terms used

by those who knew something of the wonder of My Kingdom—"The riches," "The wealth," "The fulness." There is no stint with God.

The only limit is set by the inability of My followers to take. Wealth of wisdom and unlimited Power to help others may be yours.

Stand Invincible   August 30

LIFE, earth-life, is a battle. A battle in which man will always be the loser unless he summon Eternal Life-Forces to his aid. Do this, and all that has the power to thwart you slinks back defeated.

Say, in the little as well as in the big things of life, "Nothing can harm, nothing can make me afraid. In Him I conquer." Stand invincible, face to the foes of life.

Heaven's Music   August 31

LIFT up your heart.
Lift it up—its love and its longings, leaving fears and faults behind.

Let your heart draw its strength and vitalising Joy and Confidence from Me, your Lord.

Let no vibration stir your being, that is not in harmony with the Eternal Music of My Kingdom.

SEPTEMBER

It is Enough **September 1**

L ISTEN and I will speak.
I seldom force an entrance through many voices
and distracting thoughts. There must be first the
coming apart, and then the stilling of all else, as you
wait in My Presence. Is it not enough that you are with
Me?

Let that sometimes suffice.

It is truly much that I *speak* to you. But unless My
Indwelling Spirit is yours, how can you carry out My
wishes, and live as I would have you live?

You Shall Hear **September 2**

L ISTEN to My Voice. Share all your joys and
sorrows and difficulties with Me, remembering
always that we share the work.

More and more souls will be sent to you to help. Be
ready, attuned to My slightest whisper. There is no lack
of help for My servants, but so often they are not in a
receptive mood.

Listen and you shall hear, is the continuation of "Ask, and you shall receive," "Seek, and ye shall find," "Knock, and it shall be opened unto you——"

Listen, and you shall hear.

Your Failures are Mine   September 3

Lord I present to Thee my failures. Only Thou couldst . . . repair the harm that I have wrought.

BECAUSE you are Mine I must identify Myself with all you are. I play the harmony of which you made such discord. I sound the hope in ears you had no charm of Love to woo from sin and failure.

I lead to happier ways those you misjudged, despised.

I take your failures, and because your desire is towards Me, and you know Me as Lord, these, your failures, it is My sacrificial task to bear, to reclaim.

Step up from your slough of failure in the robe of faith and love I give you.

Be strong to save as you have known salvation, strong in Me, your ever-conquering Lord.

We Walk Together   September 4

Lord I would walk with Thee.

SEE, I set My pace to yours as a loving parent does to that of his child.

So there must be much silence in our companionship, because you are not yet able to bear all the Wonder-Truth I long to impart.

But though words might find you unresponsive, you cannot fail to grow in My Presence, to grow in Grace, to grow in understanding.

So in that Rest I promised to those who come to Me, you do indeed gain the strength that comes from security in Love.

Love Leaps Forward   **September 5**

YOU must keep close to Me.

Faithfulness is not merely obeying the expressed commands of My Written Word. It is the intuitive knowing of My Wish, by close and intimate contact, from which has grown true understanding of Me.

Even with this knowing, faithfulness can only be possible when you are fortified with the Strength that Communion with Me gives.

If you know My slightest wish, and have absorbed from Me the Strength in which to carry it out, then Love leaps forward, responsive, rejoicing in the Lord.

No Pride   **September 6**

ARE you ready for training and discipline? Like my winter-trees, seemingly useless and impotent, to those who do not understand the enrooting in Me which keeps you steadfast amid storms and winter cold.

All through the dark months, when your beauty (your power to help and shield) has been sacrificed, you are yet drawing in strength and sustenance.

The time to help will come again, and you will have learned to have no personal pride in the beauty of your foliage and the restfulness of your shade.

You will use them for those who need them, but will give the glory to Me, your Lord.

"Lord, My Lord!" September 7

THE human heart craves a Leader, one whose will it delights to obey.

It craves a oneness of aim and achievement with a loved one. It craves to be understood.

It craves to reveal itself without reservations, and to gain only strength thereby.

To gain, too, an ever more intimate revelation of the heart of the loved one. Where can the heart of man find satisfaction as with Me?

Perfect Harmony September 8

NO discordant note mars your intercourse with Me, for only with Me can life be perfect harmony.

There may be much to regret on your part, failure, disloyalty, fear, sin.

In My Holy Presence all that is swept away by My Hand of Love. Only Love, Peace-bringing, Harmony-producing Love, remains. If you are to face the World and maintain your calm, you must take to the world, and your tasks in it, My Peace and Harmony.

Thy Heart's Desires   **September 9**

PAUSE upon the threshold of My House of plenty. Pause in awe and in the joy of Worship.

He shall give thee thine heart's desires. Give your desires themselves, conceived as they are in union with the Divine Spirit, *and* receive their fulfilment.

Know this, and let your heart sing with the joy of this Wonder of Supply.

Unruffled   **September 10**

PEACE. It is your task to keep this Peace in your hearts and lives. This is your work for Me. It is so all-important because if you lack it, then, as a channel, you are for the time useless.

Learn to sense the slightest ruffle on the surface of your lives. Learn to sense the smallest unrest in your heart-depths. Then back to Me until all is calm.

Think, some message may be undelivered, because I cannot use you. Some tender word unspoken, because self blocks your channel.

Only self can cause unrest, and My great Gift to My disciples was PEACE.

Lose this Desire   September 11

AGAIN I say, never judge another. That is one of My tasks I have never relegated to any follower.

Live with Me. So you will be enabled to see more of that inner self that I see in each one. Thus you will learn a humility that makes you lose desire to judge.

Oh, seek to love and understand all. Love them for My sake. They are Mine. As you live with Me, you will see how I yearn over them, and long for them. Seeing this, your love for Me must prevent your hurting Me by unkind criticism of those for whom I care.

Blame Not   September 12

NEVER seek to cast the blame on others.

If I bear your sins and those of others are you not casting your blame on Me?

If what is untoward is the result of your own fault or weakness, seek to remedy the cause by conquering the fault and overcoming the weakness.

If it has been caused by another, then apportion no blame, allow no thought of self to intrude to cause the slightest ruffle of your spirit-calm.

Safeguard the peace which I entrusted to you.

Cause of Sin   September 13

NO longer has sin any power over you unless of your own deliberate choice.

The surest way to safeguard yourself against any temptation to sin is to learn to love to do My Will, and to love to have that Will done, in all the little as well as in all the big things of your daily life.

So often man puzzles over this—If I have conquered sin, why is it then so powerful an enemy?

I conquered sin.

It has no power over any soul that does not want to sin. Then all that could lead to sin is desire.

I lay such stress on man's loving Me. If his love, his desire, is set on Me—he wills *only* to do My Will. Thus he is saved from sin.

Gifts for You   September 14

"NOT as the world giveth, give I unto you."

Not as the world giveth, but, oh, infinitely more richly, more abundantly, give I unto you.

The world expects a return, or gives only in return. Not so do I. My only stipulation is receive!

But to receive My Power, My Gifts, you must have room for them, and, full of self, there is no room for Me and My Gifts.

So all I desire of you is to be emptied of self, and to desire Me.

Bold in Prayer   September 15

MY child, there is no arrogance in your assertion when you say, "I will not let Thee go unless Thou bless me."

Have not I ever told you to claim big things. In so doing you obey Me.

You do right to wrestle boldly in prayer. There are times for demanding, for claiming.

Now is the time to claim. You are in no doubt about My Will. Claim its manifestations on earth.

Adoration   September 16

NEVER forget to adore. That is the most beautiful form of prayer. It includes all others.

If you adore, it implies that trust in Me and love for Me, without which all supplication fails to achieve its object. It implies thanksgiving, because adoration is born of repeated thanksgiving.

It also implies contrition.

Who could adore Me with a Joy-filled adoration, and not be conscious of unworthiness and of My forgiveness and blessing? Adoration is Love-filled reverence.

Leave Him to Me   September 17

IN My Kingdom judgment is not man's role. There is one Judge, and even He reserves His judgment until the last chapter of man's life is written, until all the evidence is secured, so anxious is He to discover some extenuating circumstances, or to wait until, by man's turning to Him and throwing himself upon His mercy, the position is altered, and the judge becomes the prisoner in the dock.

Then, God the Father, knowing His Beloved Son accepts responsibility for the deed (has in fact already received the punishment Himself), is bound to pardon the human sinner.

You then in judging (poor, weak, foolish, contemptuous arrogance), are judging not the sinner but Me.

You Can Help   September 18

MY followers were to save My world—by keeping My Commands, by close union with Me, and by the indwelling Power of My Spirit.

But they were to be a peculiar people. My religion which was to change men's lives, and was to be so revolutionary as to separate families and re-organize governments, has become a convention, tolerated where not appreciated.

Its Truths have been modified to suit men's desires. Its followers carry no flaming sword, they bear no Message of a Love so tender as to heal every wound, so scorching as to burn out every evil. My Cross is out-dated, My Loving Father but the First Cause.

Man delights in his self-sufficiency, and seeks to persuade himself that all is well. Can he deceive a loving, understanding Father, who knows that under all the boasting there lurks fear, longings, despair?

Can I leave man so? Can I offer him Calvary, and if he will have none of it, leave him to his fate? I know too well his need of Me. You can help Me.

Help Me   **September 19**

HELP Me to save your fellow-man, as dear to Me as you are.

Do you not care that he should pass Me by? *Do you not care that he should pass Me by?*

Do you not care that he is lonely, hungry, desparate and far from the fold?

Led by the Spirit **September 20**

L EARN to wait for spiritual Guidance, until its suggestion is as clear to your consciousness as any command of officer to soldier, of master to servant. This recognition distinguishes My true follower from the many who call Me "Lord, Lord," and do not the things that I say.

There are many who live according to the Principles I laid down when on earth, but who do not act under the impulse of My Spirit day by day.

"For as many as are led by the Spirit of God, they are the sons of God."

Barriers Burned Away **September 21**

M Y Light shall shine upon you. It shall illumine and cheer your way.

But it shall also penetrate the dark and secret places of your hearts, revealing perhaps some unrecognized sin, fault or failing.

Desire its radiance, not only for its comfort and guidance, but also for its revelation of all within you that is not wholly Mine.

I am the Sun of Righteousness. Rest in My Presence, not clamouring, not supplicating, but resting, until the impurities of your being are burnt out, the dross of your character refined away, and you can go on strengthened and purified to do My work.

I Am Forgiveness   September 22

My Lord, forgive me, I pray.

COULD I withhold forgiveness? I, who live ever to plead for My children, who told them that always when they pray they must forgive in their hearts?

I am God but I became man.

Perfect God and perfect man.

So human and yet so Divine.

Because I am Eternal—that I must *ever* be.

So see in Me all I enjoined My followers *they* must ever be and do. Could I withhold forgiveness?

Irritability Banished   September 23

CONSCIOUSNESS of My Presence imparts permanence and strength to all you do.

My Spirit, permeating every part of your being, drives out all selfish irritability, while fortifying all the weak parts and attuning your being to Heaven's Music.

To think of Heaven as a place where you sing praises to Me is right, but the singing is with your whole being, as My pulsing Joy flows through it.

All on the Altar   **September 24**

A BSOLUTE Love must decide all your actions. Fear nothing. Ride the storm.

Delight to do My Will.

Not only money affairs; lay all your letters, your work, all, upon My altar.

Make an offering of each day to Me for the answering of your prayers and for the salvation of My poor world.

Subdue every self-thought, utterly, entirely.

The Love that Satisfies   **September 25**

M Y Mercies are great to all who turn to Me, and to all who turn *from* Me.

How tenderly I yearn over these wayward ones. How I seek ever to save them from the hurts their very refusal of Me will bring upon them.

I long to save them from the hunger of loneliness that will follow their driving away the only love that will satisfy.

Storms May Rage   **September 26**

L IVE with Me, and words will not be necessary. You will know My Will.

The real necessity is your receptiveness.

That comes through self-discipline, that allows of spiritual progress into, and in, a Higher Life.

In that spirit realm you are conscious of My Will. You are one with Me. Truly, you may count all things well lost to win Christ.

I wish you to learn the Glory of a God-protected, guided life. No idle, fruitless rushing hither and thither. Storms may rage, difficulties may press hard, but you will know no harm. Safe, protected and guided.

My Striving Spirit   September 27

THERE is never a time when a man cannot turn repentant to Me and, craving My pardon, receive it.

But there is a time when I cease to be persistent in urging My follower to an action.

The human ear can hear a sound so often until it ceases to convey a meaning, to be heard with awareness.

So with the spirit-ear, unless the whole desire and effort is to carry out My plan, My servant may cease to hear, cease to be aware of My wish.

This is a grave spiritual danger, and I say unto you, watch and guard against it.

Your Only Way   **September 28**

THERE is a stage in Christian development at which My follower should have passed beyond that of general service and conformity to the rules I laid down for My disciples.

When he should be seeking to serve in some special way planned for that soul, and in the service that soul was destined for, which none other can so adequately do.

Think, the Salvation of My world, all planned, even to the minutest detail, but that work is not done through neglect, through failure, through indifference.

My way for you is not a path of general righteousness and obedience, but the actual road mapped out for you, in which you can best help My needy world.

Love Heals   **September 29**

YOU are asking to be used by Me to heal, but you are asking for the fruit before the root has become established, and the tree has grown to its stature.

With the elimination of self, and obedience to My Will, your Power in the Spirit world will naturally grow. Thus you will assuredly gain, in that world, the control that others seek to have on the material plane.

But you must forego all desire for control or recognition on that lower plane. As you cannot serve two masters, so neither can you operate on two planes.

Your Love must grow by dwelling with Me. It was My overflowing Love that healed.

The Future All Unknown   September 30

MY Word shall be a lamp unto your feet, and a light unto your path. No difficulty need appal you. You shall know in all things what to do, but remember that the light must go with you. It is to warn, comfort and cheer, not to reveal the future.

My servants do not need to know that. The true child spirit rejoices in the present, and has no fears, no thought beyond it. So must you live.

If I, your Lord, accompany you, shedding My radiance all round you, the future must always be dark, because as far as your acceptance of revelation, and your present development are concerned, I am not THERE.

But as the future of to-day becomes the present of to-morrow, then the same light and Guidance and Miracle-working Power will be yours. Rejoice evermore.

OCTOBER

Have Confidence

NOTHING happens to you that is not the answer to your prayers, the fulfilment of your desire to do, and have, in all, My Will.

So go forward into each day unafraid.

No Greater Joy

ON earth, or even in Heaven, there can be no greater joy than realizing that My Will is being accomplished in the little as well as in the big things.

Indeed, it can be *your* " meat " as I said it was *Mine*. It is the very sustenance of body, mind and spirit, that Trinity of being, symbolized in the Temple in the Outer Court, the Holy Place, and then in the very Holy of Holies, where man speaks with God and dwells with Him.

Into that Holy of Holies there can be no entrance except to sacrifice, to bring an offering of the physical and mental being, and, in Spirit, to identify the whole with that Supreme Sacrifice I offered for My World.

Constant Companion   **October 3**

Not unto us, O Lord . . . but unto Thy Name be Glory.

MY Name. I AM. Existent before all Worlds, changeless through Eternity, changeless in Time.

All I have ever been through the ages, I AM.

All that you ever crave I may be to you—I AM.

In a changing world you need to dwell much upon Me, your Master, the Jesus Christ of whom it was said—"The same yesterday, to-day and for ever."

Then it follows that with you to-day is The Lord of Creation, the Jesus of Nazareth, the Christ of the Cross, the Risen Saviour, the Ascended Lord. What a Companionship for the uncertain ways of a changing world.

Bright Reality   **October 4**

O Jesus make Thyself to me
A living, bright reality.

THEN will you show Me as a living bright reality? I died that I might live in you, My Followers, and you present Me to the world as a dead Christ.

"I am alive for evermore."

Though you may repeat those words they are not vibrant with Life, here and now. They speak but of My existence in another sphere, far removed from this earth and its joys and sorrows, achievement and stress.

Yet in all these daily things I would have My Spirit active in and through you.

How can man so misread My Teaching?

One With Me   October 5

ONE with the God of Creation.

One with the Jesus of Calvary.

One with the Risen Christ.

One with His Spirit operating in every corner of the Universe, energizing, renewing, controlling, all-powerful.

Could man ask more? Could thought rise higher?

Power-Seekers   October 6

HOW pitiful man's striving after power when God's Power, with all its mighty possibilities, is there for him did he but know how to obtain it.

To tell one such that this would only be possible for one who has entered My Kingdom of Heaven, might indeed arouse his curiosity.

But tell him the way into that Kingdom is one of self-effacement, obedience to, and love of, My Will, tell him that he must enter as a little child, that only by spiritual progress can he attain to man's true estate, and that the training might be long, the discipline hard—tell him this and he will turn empty away.

Yet in so doing he will renounce, all unknowing, the victor's prize, the life of peace, and power, and joy.

The Upward Way   October 7

ONLY with Me, and in My Strength, will you have Grace and Power to conquer the weakness, the evil, in yourself. Your character-garment is spoiled. Only by applying My Salvation can it become a wedding garment, fit robe in which to meet the Bridegroom.

The foundation-cleansing of the garment is belief in Me as your Saviour, your Redeemer. Thereafter to each fault and evil in your nature must be applied that evil-eradicating Power that can only come from relying on My Strength, and from living with Me, from loving Me, and loving to do My Will.

Mere general belief in Me as Redeemer and Saviour is insufficient. Set yourself now to walk steadily the upward way, strong in Me and in the power of My Might.

"Lord, Save Me"   October 8

I WILL, be thou clean.
Saved from all that tarnishes the purity of your soul.

Saved from harsh judgments.

Saved from disobedience to My Command.

Saved from all that offends My Justice, all that sins against My Love. I will, be thou clean.

Overcome Desire   October 9

THE listening ear—

Train the listening ear to hear Me.

The first step is to subdue earth's desires and to want only My Will.

Desire as a control must be overcome.

Then follows the turning within to speak with Me.

Then the listening ear.

Peter's Example   October 10

MY child, I will never fail you.

My Promise is not dependent upon *your* perfection, only upon your accepting My Will and striving ever to walk in it.

But, for your happiness, I give you Divine Assurance that though *you* may fail in achievement, if not in desire, *I* cannot plead human frailty, so *My Promises must be fulfilled.*

When I chose Peter *I* saw in him not only one who after failure and denial, would become a Power for Me in My Strength; I chose him that others, frail and weak, might take courage as they remembered My Love and forgiveness, and his subsequent spiritual progress.

All Clear   October 11

L OVE is the great power of understanding. Love explains all, makes all clear.

How *can* you understand Me unless you love Me? How can men see My purposes unless they love Me?

Love is indeed the fulfilling of the law. It is also the understanding of the law.

He that loveth is born of God, because he enters into a new life in God who is Love. Live in that Love.

Love it is that prepares the ground for My teaching, that softens the hardest heart, that disposes the most indifferent, that creates desire for My Kingdom.

Therefore love. Love Me first. Then love all, and so you link them to Me.

Eyes of the Spirit   October 12

Y OU have much to learn.

Life will not be long enough to learn all, but you are gaining that Spirit-Vision which replaces the eyes of your mortal body, when you enter into a life of fuller comprehension with My Father and Me.

Stories in the Bud October 13

L EARN a further lesson from the Two Debtors . . .
A lesson in forgiving others as you realize My
forgiveness of sins committed, lessons slowly learned,
faults and shortcomings so easily condoned, which
hinder your progress, and work for Me?

Can you show to others My patience to you.

Can you, too, give to others freely, while you claim
My unrestricted Bounty? Meditate on this.

A story of Mine is like a bud. Only to the Sun of
self-effacement and Spirit-Progress does it unfold.

Receptivity October 14

O NLY those in close touch with Me, inspired by My
Spirit, infected by My Love, impregnated with
My Strength, retain a resilience of being and receptivity
to new Truth.

The child heart that I enjoined upon My followers is
ever ready to be renewed, is ever responsive to all that
is prepared for " the new creature in Christ Jesus."

The Way of the Lord October 15

A LWAYS before My coming into a life there must
be a time of preparation. This is the work of
those who already know Me.

The preparation may differ in each individual case. The Baptist came with his thunder-note of repentance!

In many cases a loving hand of help may be needed before the ground is ready for Me, The Sower.

Prepare My Way:—by loving intercourse, by Spirited example, by tender help, by unflinching adherence to Truth and Justice, by ready self-sacrifice, and by much prayer. Prepare ye the Way of the Lord.

In Step   October 16

THIS means endeavouring to suit your steps to Mine. Yet know full well, with the trust that gives security, that I ever suit *My Steps* to your weakness.

Divine restraint springs ever from a tender understanding. With Me beside you, there is the hope, the assurance, that the day will come when My firm tread will be yours.

"Keep pace with us," the world says as it rushes by.

But there is One Who knows no feverish haste. He walks with you. Be not afraid.

See Clearly   October 17

THEN will you see clearly how to take out the grain of dust from your brother's eye. This is a promise.

You note the fault of another. You long to help.

You need the Spirit-inspired vision for this work.

That cannot be granted until all obstruction is removed. Obstructions are caused not by the sins of others but by your own sins and imperfections.

So look within. Seek to conquer those, and so to gain the Spiritual insight which will enable you to help your brother. My Promises are always kept.

Grace that Transfigures   October 18

MY Grace is sufficient for you, all-satisfying. Meditate upon this GRACE. Study what the Scriptures say of it. Learn to value it. Crave it as a gift from Me.

It can be the charm that transfigures all that without it might be sordid or dreary or monotonous. It is the leaven to the dough, the oil to the machine.

It is a priceless gift. Wait with bowed head and heart at that blessing. "*The Grace* of our Lord Jesus Christ."

A Royal Giver   October 19

YOU tell Me that your hearts are full of gratitude. I do not want from you gratitude as much as the joy of friendship. Realize that I love to give.

As the Scriptures say, "It is your Father's good pleasure to give you the Kingdom." I love to give. The Divine Nature is the Nature of a Royal Giver.

Have you ever thought of My Delight when you are

ready to receive? When you long to hear My Words
and to receive My Blessings?

Force October 20

MY Kingdom must be won by force, that is, by
effort. How can you reconcile this with My free
gift of Salvation?

My gift is free truly, and is not the reward of any
merit on the part of man. But just as God and mammon
cannot both be given the overlordship in any one life,
so My Kingdom, where I rule as King, cannot be
inhabited by one in whom self reigns.

Therefore the violence is that of discipline and
self-conquest, together with an intensity of longing for
My Kingdom, and tireless effort to know and do My
Will.

Absorb Good October 21

THE only way to eradicate evil is to absorb good.
This is My story of the seven other spirits.

This story was to illustrate the vast difference
between the Mosaic Law and My Law. The Pharisees
and the Elder Brother were the observers of the Mosaic
Law.

You have proved this in your own life. To pray that

you may resist temptation and conquer evil is in itself but useless.

Evil cannot live in My Presence. Live with Me. Absorb My Life, and evil will remain without.

A Noble House   October 22

THOUGH I was a Son yet learnt I obedience.

This was to teach My followers that allegiance to Me meant no immunity from discipline.

The house of your spirit is fashioned brick by brick—Love, Obedience, Truth. There is a plan, and each action of yours is a brick in its building.

Think. A misguided act, a neglected duty, or a failure to carry out My wishes, would mean not only a missing brick but a faulty edifice.

How many an otherwise noble character is spoilt thus. Build now for eternity.

Passing Understanding   October 23

The Peace of God that passeth all understanding.

THAT Peace both fills and encircles the soul that trusts in Me. It is born of a long faith-experience that is permeated through and through with the consciousness of the never-failing Love of a Father.

A Father Who supplies and protects, not alone

because of His obligations of Fatherhood, but because of a longing, intense, enduring Love, that delights to protect and supply, and that cannot be denied.

A Special Message   October 24

PEACE has, for every true disciple, a special meaning and message. It is endeared to him by association. It was the parting gift of his Lord to His followers, bequeathed through them to followers of each succeeding generation. It is not the peace of indifference, of sloth: *that* is mere acquiescence.

No, the Peace I left to My own is vital and strong. It can exist only in the heart of one who lives with Me. It derives from Me that Eternal Life which is Mine, and which makes the Gift ever full of an imperishable beauty, and instinct with Life indeed.

Fulness of Joy   October 25

THERE is a Joy of My Kingdom that My followers may know, and that no shadow of the world's pessimism can endanger. It resists all cramping of outward, soulless convention.

Too often My followers fail to see how full of Joy I could be. They see Me, the JESUS who beheld the city and wept over it, Who was so touched by the suffering all round Me, and they fail to realize how filled with Joy

I could be at the response to My Call.

No shadow of the Cross could darken that Joy. I was as a bridegroom among the friends he had chosen to share his wedding joys.

As such I refused to consider the implied reproof of the Pharisees. We were a band filled with desire to save a world, we were full of hope and enthusiasm. Our Spirits could not be compressed into the outworn bottles of mere pharisaic convention. Ponder this, and recognize your Master Who bids you Love and Laugh.

Love is Duty-Free   October 26

HOW human, how earth-bound, are the thoughts man has of God. He judges of Me and My Father by his own frail impulses and feelings.

There is in Divine Love no compulsion of duty from the loved one to the Lover.

Love draws, certainly, and then love longs to serve and to express one's love.

But no question of duty in return for Love.

Mysteries   October 27

THERE is only one road that leads to the solving of mysteries, the road of obedience and Love.

But in perfect Love there is no curiosity, only a certainty that when the time has come all will be clear, and that until that time there is no desire to know anything that the Beloved has not chosen to reveal.

Does it matter if no mystery is made plain down here? If you have Me, then in Me you have all. Continue ye in My Love.

Growing Young   October 28

THERE will never be a time when you will have conquered all of self. As you mount higher and higher, you will see more and more clearly the errors and shortcomings of your character and life.

That is as it should be. Progress means youth. Arrested growth means stagnation. Lack of progress and failure to conquer mean—old age.

In Eternal Life there can be no old age. Eternal Life is Youth-Life, full and abundant Life. "And this is Life Eternal that they may know Thee, the only True God, and JESUS Christ, Whom Thou hast sent."

Little Difficulties   October 29

THE secret of true discipleship is service in little things. So rarely do Mine understand this.

They are ready to die for Me, but not to live for Me, in all the small details of this life.

Is not this the way of men, so often, towards those they love in the world? They are so ready to make the big sacrifices, but not the little ones.

Guard against this in service for Me. Suffer little hardships gladly, overcome little proud impulses, little selfishnesses, and little difficulties. Serve Me in the little things. Be My servants of the little ways.

Rest in My Love   October 30

AGAIN I would stress that the service of My followers must be ever one of Love, not of duty. Temptations can so easily overcome a resolution based on fear, on duty, but against Love temptation has no power. Live in My Spirit, rest in My Love.

Remember, if you look to Me for everything, and trust Me for everything, and I do not send the full measure you ask, it must not be thought that it is necessarily some sin or weakness that is hindering My Help from flowing into and through you.

In some cases this may be so, but it may be simply My restraining Hand laid on you as I whisper, "Rest, step aside with Me. Come apart and rest awhile."

And Seek No Surplus   October 31

I WOULD impress upon you again that only as you are channels can I make your supply plentiful and constant.

If you keep all you need, and then intend of your surplus to give to Me and Mine, there will be no surplus. I have promised to supply your need, so that as you impoverish yourselves, I repair that loss. Try and grasp that Truth in all its fulness.

NOVEMBER

Joy in November

These things have I spoken . . . that your Joy may be full.

THE hallmark of a true follower of Mine is Joy. Not a surface pleasure at life's happenings, a something that is reflected from without, but a welling up from within of that happiness that can only come from a heart at peace, secure in its friendship with Me.

Joy, strong and calm, attracts men to Me.

How many who claim Me Lord reflect a dull Christ, and wonder that the world turns rather to the glitter and tinsel of that world's pleasures.

Truly My followers deny Me in so doing. I am a Glorified Christ. A Christ of Triumphant Conquest.

Alas! My followers point too often to the grave-clothes of the tomb. Still learn to love and laugh.

Your Store of Wealth

THE stored wealth of the Spirit of Jesus Christ. The giving out of that Spirit-wealth.

The Supply of the Spirit of Jesus Christ.

This, My Spirit, must be absorbed, not in a moment of emergency, but in the quiet alone-times, so that from this store all help and strength can be supplied.

The mistake My followers often make is that they rely upon this supply being ready for them to claim from Me at need, when the claim should have been made before, and My Spirit in all its fulness have already become a part of them.

My Spirit is not a Spirit of Rescue alone. It is both Builder and Strength, making of My follower that strong soldier ready for the emergency or strong to avoid it, as the need of My Kingdom may demand.

Up in the Heights   November 3

THE Sunlight on the Hills of God lures men to seek His Mountain Heights.

Get away from valley prejudices and fears on to the sunlit slopes with Me. Gently at first I will lead, so gently; then, as you gain strength, we will leave, together, the grassy slopes for the rugged Mountain Heights, where fresh visions are spread out before you, and where I can teach you My Secrets of those Heights.

Life holds in store more wonderful possibilities than you can sense as yet, and ever, more and more, as you go on, will further possibilities reveal themselves.

The Life Beautiful
November 4

The Wonder of a life with Thee, dear Lord.

IN the Spirit realm Truths reveal themselves in the same varied wonders of colour as Nature her beauties.

Experiences, Guidance, Revelation of Truth, these are all, as it were, the flashing of glorious colour-harmonies upon your inner sight, provoking such a wealth of joy, such a thrill of ecstasy as is beyond mortal tongue to describe.

That joy is no shimmering beauty of the surface, but strength-giving and comforting. It furnishes the very foundation-altar upon which your life yields itself in sacrifice to Me, and from which your prayers ascend.

Wine of Life
November 5

They have no wine.

SOMETHING is lacking at the feast of life.

I only can supply that wonderful Life element that the world lacks. The Joy, the sparkle is Mine to give.

Yours to feel the lack, the soullessness. Yours to say—"They have no wine."

"Whatsoever He saith unto you, do it."

Your task to fill the water-pots with water.

Your Garden of Life

November 6

THINK of Me to-night as the Great Gardener, tending and caring for you as a gardener does for his garden.

Pruning here, protecting from frost there, planting, transplanting. Sowing the seed of this or that truth, safeguarding it with the rich earth, sending My rain and sun to help in its growth, watching so tenderly as it responds to My care.

Lovingly anxious when its first eager green appears. Full of joy at the sight of bud, and when the beauty of flower is seen. The seed and fruit of His pastures.

The Great Gardener. Let Me share with you the tending of your garden of life.

Lost Opportunities

November 7

THINK of one who has wrought great evil in the world or in your own life. Then remember there may have been the time when a simple act of obedience to Me, by one who crossed his path, might have corrected and shown him his wrong before evil mastered him.

Many a sin unconquered, an evil occurrence, could well be traced back to a lack of obedience, perhaps in years long past, of one who professed to serve Me.

Remember this in speaking to those who judge Me by the evil they feel I permit in the world. For yourself now, dwell not on the past, but dwell more with Me, that in future there be no sins of omission or commission.

Your Life-line   November 8

THINK of the strong life-line of Faith and Power. This I have told you is your line of rescue.

It means constant communication between us.

You pray for Faith. I give you Faith. This enables you to test the Power I give, as your Faith goes back to me in ever-increasing strength. My Power and your Faith ever interchanging. The one calling forth the other, each dependent upon the other, until *My Faith* in *you* is justified indeed by the Power you exercise.

The Glowing Heart   November 9

THINK of the Walk to Emmaus, think of the feast of Revelation that followed, of the understanding Friendship that was the result. How much I, their Lord, their Risen Lord, had explained to My two disciples during that walk. So much that was mystery to them became clear as we went along the way.

Yet not as their Master did I become known, until in the Breaking of Bread I revealed Myself. In speaking of Me afterwards they said, "Did not our hearts burn within us when He talked with us by the way."

So do not fret if all that I can be to you is not yet revealed. Walk with Me, talk with Me, invite Me to be your guest, and leave to Me My moment of self-Revelation. I want each day to be a walk with Me.

Do you not feel, even now, your hearts burn within you, as if with the glow of anticipation?

Rest for the Weary   **November 10**

THIS weariness must compel you to sink back, a tired child, to rest in My Love. *There* remain, until that Love so permeates your being that you are supported by it, and, so strengthened, arise.

Until you feel that this is so, remain inactive, conscious of My Presence. Yours is a big work, and you must refresh yourself and only approach it again after periods of repose.

The activity on the Spirit-plane is so great, so wonderful, that but for the times of enforced rest and prayer, you would be stirred to an emotional activity on the physical plane that defeats My ends.

The Peace of God

THE Peace of God lies deeper than all knowledge of earth's wisest. In that quiet realm of the Spirit, where dwell all who are controlled by *My* Spirit, there can all secrets be revealed, all Hidden-Kingdom-Truths be shown and learned.

Live there, and *Truth* deeper than all *knowledge* shall be revealed to you.

Their lines are gone out into all the earth—so travels the influence, ever-widening, of those who live near to Me.

Take time to be with Me. Count all things but loss, so that you may have Me.

Heaven's Music

TO glorify Me is to reflect, in praise, My character in your lives. To mount up with wings as eagles, higher and higher, to soar ever nearer to Me.

To praise Me is to sing, to let your hearts thrill. To glorify Me is to express exactly the same, but through the medium of your whole beings, your whole lives. When I say, "Rejoice, Rejoice," I am training you to express this in your whole natures.

That is the Music of Heaven, the glorifying Me, through sanctified lives and devoted hearts of Love.

A Lonely Road

TO Me each one of My children is an individual with varying characteristics and varying needs. To one and all, the way to the highest must be a lonely road, as far as human help and understanding are concerned.

None other can feel the same needs and desires, or explain the inner self in the same way. That is why man needs Divine Companionship. The Companionship that alone can understand each heart and need.

Joy is Yours

THE future is not your concern, that is Mine. The past you have handed back to Me, and you have no right to dwell on that.

Only the present is My gift to you, and of that only each day as it comes. But, if into that day you crowd past sorrows and resentments and failures, as well as the possible anxieties of the years that may be left to you here—what brain and spirit could bear that strain.

For this I never promised My Spirit and Comfort and Help.

Sharing with Me

NOT by life's difficulties and trials are you trained and taught as much as by the times of withdrawal to be alone with Me.

Difficulties and trials alone are not remedial, are not of spiritual value.

That value is only gained by contact with Me. Joy shared with Me, or sorrow and difficulty shared with Me, both can prove of great spiritual value, but that is gained by the *sharing with Me*. Share all with Me.

Remember in true friendship sharing is mutual, so as you share with Me, do I in ever-increasing measure share with you—My Love, My Grace, My Joy, My Secrets, My Power. My Manifold Blessings.

All are Worthy   November 16

TREAT all as those about whom I care.

You would visit the poor, the sick or those in prison, knowing full well I would see it as done unto Me.

I want you now to go still further along the way of My Kingdom. You contact many who are not poor, not sick, not in prison.

They may be opposed to you. They may disregard much that you consider of value, they may not seem to need your help. Can you treat these, too, as you would wish to treat Me? They may be in need greater than the others you long to aid.

To you their aims may seem unworthy, their self-seeking may antagonize you. When I said " Judge not," was I not including them too?

Can you limit My words to suit your own inclinations?

This is not an easy task I set you, but your way is the Way of Obedience. I did not suggest to My followers one they could take or not as they willed. My "Judge not" was imperative, and a new *commandment* I gave unto them that they should love.

For those who do not yet name Me Lord, Love is the only magnet that will draw them to Me.

Be true, be strong, be loving.

Union with God   November 17

TRUE religion is that which binds the soul to God, and supplicatory prayer binds the soul less than any other form of approach.

It is necessary, how necessary, but how often it can fail to bind truly. Meditation and Communion are of infinitely more value.

Meditation is man's line thrown out. It links the soul to God. Communion is God's line thrown out. It draws and unites the soul to Him.

Joy and Courage   November 18

TRUST in Me. Do more than trust. Joy in Me. If you really trust, you cannot fail to Joy. The wonder of My Care, Protection and Provision is so transcendingly beautiful, as your trust reveals it to you, that your whole heart *must* sing with the Joy of it.

It is that Joy that will, and does, renew your youth. That source of your Joy and Courage.

Truly did I not know what I was enjoining when I said, "Love and Laugh." But—your attitude must be right, not only with Me, but with those around you.

Check Up   **November 19**

TURN out all of your self that would rebel against My sway. Know no other rule.

Check your actions and motives habitually. Those that are actuated by self-esteem or self-pity—condemn.

Discipline yourself ruthlessly rather than let self gain any ascendancy. Your aim is to oust it, and to serve and follow Me only.

Watchful Expectancy   **November 20**

WAIT before Me, in humble, silent anticipation. Wait in entire and childlike obedience. Wait as a servant anticipating his master's orders and wants.

Wait as a lover eager to note the first suggestion of a need, and to hasten to supply it. Wait for My orders and commands. Wait for My Guidance, My Supply.

Well, indeed, in such a life may you be of good cheer. Can a life be dull and dreary when always there is that watchful expectancy, always that anticipation of glad surprise, always wonder of fulfilment, Joy of supply?

Be Glad in the Lord   November 21

WAIT before Me with a song of praise in your hearts. Sing unto Me a new song. There will always be something in each day for which to thank Me.

Acknowledge every little happening as a revelation of My Love and thought for you. Praise has the power to wash away the bitterness of life. Be glad in the Lord.

Rejoice evermore. Great is the heart's "Thank You." As you learn to thank Me more and more you will more and more see Me in the little happenings, and increasingly see much about which to rejoice. Praise and thanksgiving are the preservers of youth.

The Look of the Lover   November 22

HOW few *wait* on Me.
     Many pray to Me.
They come into My Presence feverish with wants and distress, but few wait there for that calm and strength that contact with Me would give.

Look unto Me and be ye saved. But the look was not meant to be a hurried glance. It was to be the look into My face of the lover beholding the Beloved.

When Misunderstood   November 23

WAIT upon Me.

Wait until My strength has filled your being, and you are no longer weak, petty, "misunderstood."

Rise above any fret as to how others may judge you. Leave Me to explain what I will of you and your actions.

Would you seek to follow a Christ Who had wasted His God-power on fruitless explanations?

So with you. Leave Me to vindicate you, and to be your Advocate, or trust My silence in this as in all else.

Eternal Calm   November 24

REMEMBER that you live in Eternity, not time. Let there be no rush to do this or that.

It follows that for each task Eternity is yours.

How often, and how sadly, impotent haste has hindered not hastened the work of My Kingdom.

Live more quietly, bathed in the calm of Eternity. Feel this before you leave My Presence.

No fevered haste to work My Will. You must go forth in God's Great Calm.

There was no haste in His Creative Plan. Do you not feel the Strength of Calmness that lies behind God's work in Nature? Rest and know.

Green Pastures
November 25

WALK in My Pastures. The eye will be rested and the spirit restored by the soft green of their verdure. The ear soothed and then enchanted, by the sound of My Waters of Comfort.

No stones will impede your progress.

The soft haze over all will speak of unrevealed mysteries, while the wonder of life about you will tell of My ever-active, creative and protective Power, and you will be filled with a content that will merge into a strange yearning for a spirit-oneness with Me.

Then—you will know I am there.

Complete Obedience
November 26

WALK in My Way.

My Way is that of *doing*, not only of *accepting*, the Father's Will.

Submitting to that Will, however gladly you may do so, is not enough.

Your work and influence for Me are hindered if your life is not one of complete obedience. "By the obedience of one shall many be made righteous."

Where would your salvation have been had I faltered and wavered in MY task?

It was by the obedience of My earth-life I saved and so must it be with you.

Spirit of Adventure   November 27

THE path has been tried, every step has been planned with a view to your progress. Never test your work by what others can accomplish, or by what they leave undone. Yours to master the task I have set *you*. Go forward in My Strength, and in the Spirit of Adventure.

Undreamed of heights can be attained in this way. Never question your capability. That has been for Me to decide. No experienced Leader would set a follower a task beyond his Power. Trust Me, your Leader.

The World would have been won for Me ere this had My followers been dauntless, inspired by their faith in Me. It is not humility to hesitate to do the great task I set. It is lack of faith in *Me*.

To wait to feel strong is cowardly. My strength is provided for the task, but I do not provide it for the period of hesitancy before you begin.

How much of My Work goes undone through lack of faith. Again and again might it be said—

"He did not many mighty works through this follower's unbelief."

Active but Alert   November 28

WALK very carefully in life. It is a wonderful thing to be known as one who loves Me and seeks to follow Me, but it is also a very great responsibility.

So much that you may do, in which you are not guided by Me, may be condemned as unworthy, and a slur be cast upon My followers and My Church.

There are no moments in your life from now on in which you can be free from great responsibility. Never forget this. My soldiers are ever on active service.

Miracles I Could Not Do   November 29

WHAT emphasis has been laid upon the wonder of My walking upon the Sea, and upon My feeding the multitudes. In the eyes of Heaven those were miracles of small importance.

Nature was My servant, the creation of the Father; and the Father and I are one. Over her and over the material world I had complete control. My acts were natural, spontaneous, requiring no premeditation, beyond the selection of a suitable moment for their performance.

But My real Miracle work was in the hearts of men, because there I was limited by the Father's gift of Freewill to man. I could not command man as I could the waves. I was subject to the limitations the Father had set. No man must be coerced into My Kingdom.

Think of all that My restraint cost Me. I could have forced the world to accept Me, but I should then have broken faith with all mankind.

Fly the Flag   November 30

IN your life and on your home you have unfurled the flag of My Kingship. Keep that flag flying.

Depression, disobedience, and want of faith, these are the half-masts of My Kingdom's flag.

Full and free, above earth's fogs and smokes, *keep My flag flying high*.

"The King is there, they serve the King," should be upon the lips and in the hearts of all who see it. Those who know you must, too, join those who fly My Flag.

DECEMBER

The Next Best-Thing

WHEN you long for your prayer to be answered, when your need is great, and you ask great things, then your way is so clear—.

Take the next simple duty that lies to your hand, and seek to do that thoroughly . . . and so with the next.

As you do it, remember My Promise.

Be faithful in that which is least, and I will make thee ruler over many things.

Learning Times

IN performing the simple duty, and in the restraint you achieve in doing it, and not in the feverish looking for the answer to your prayer for the big thing—maybe you learn the one thing needful before I entrust you with what you desire.

With Me, and in obedience to My Will, you have now become suited for that answer.

These are learning-times, rather than testing-times.

Your Faith Confirmed December 3

"WHOM do men say that I am?" That is the first question I put to each man. My Claim, and the world's interpretation of My Mission and its culmination, must be a matter of consideration.

Then comes My second question, and upon the answer to this depends the man's whole future. Here we have left the realm of the mind. Conviction must be of the heart. "Whom do *you* say that I am?"

"Thou art the Christ, the Son of the Living God," was Simon's answer. Then, and not till then, was it possible, without infringement of man's right of Free Will, to add to that profession of faith, the confirmation of My Father, "This is My Beloved Son."

I had lived My Life naturally, as a man among men. But always with the Longing that those I had chosen might have the eyes to see, the faith to penetrate the Mystery of Incarnation, and to see Me, the God revealed.

The faith of a personal conviction is always cemented by the assurance of My Father. It is that which makes the faith of My true followers, so unshakable.

Withdraw Yourself December 4

IT is not in the crowd that lovers learn to know and cherish each other. It is in the quiet times alone.

So with My own and Me. It is in the tender alone-times that they learn all that I can be to each.

Shut out the world with its all too-insistent claims. Then, because of the power and the peace and the joy that come to you, you will crave to be alone with Me.

Perfect Achievement December 5

YIELD to My demands.

Obey My Will, that is God's Will, for My MEAT was ever to do the Will of Him that sent Me. Obeying that Will, making it yours, all you will *must* be granted.

That Will is creative, secures perfect achievement, and being of God (One and indivisible), secures all that is of God—Love, Peace, Joy, Power, in the measure that one of His creatures can absorb them.

A New Song December 6

YOU are being led forth. You have crossed the Red Sea. Your wilderness wanderings are nearly over. Behold I make all things new.

A new birth, a new heart, a new life, a new song.

Let this time be to you a time of renewal.

Cast away all that is dead. Truly live the Risen Life. In mind and spirit turn out all that offends.

Secret Service   **December 7**

YOU are blessed, very richly blessed. Never forget that you have My Love and Protection. No Treasures of the world can mean to you what that can.

Never forget, too, that you are guided. Every word, every letter, every meeting, God-planned and God-blessed. Just feel that, know that.

You are not a stray and uncared for. You belong to the Secret Service of Heaven. There are privileges and protections for you all along the Way.

But for My Grace   **December 8**

YOU are Mine. Mine to control, to lead, to cherish. Trust Me for all.

In thinking of and dealing with others realize that whatever their sin, you would be as they are but for My protection, but for My tender forgiveness.

Remember, too, that My Command of " Judge not " was as explicit as that of " Thou shalt do no murder," " Thou shalt not commit adultery." Obey Me in all.

Power to Help   **December 9**

NOT so much on what you say as on your willingness to let My Influence flow through you, will your power to help others depend.

The Power of My Father is summoned by you to the aid of those whom you desire to help.

Live in the consciousness of My Presence, and your thoughts of Love, anxiety, and even interest will let loose a flood of Power to save.

Successful Failures   December 10

YOU grieve that you have failed Me. Remember it was for the failures that I hung on Calvary's Cross. It was a failure I greeted first in the Easter Garden.

It was to one of the failures I entrusted My Church, My Lambs, My Sheep.

It was to one who had thwarted and despised Me, who had tortured and murdered My followers that I gave My great world Mission to the Gentiles.

But each had first to learn to know Me as Saviour and Lord by a bitter consciousness of having failed Me.

If you would work for Me, then you must be ready for the valley of humiliation through which all my followers have to pass.

Help is Here   December 11

YOU have been told to end all prayer upon a note of praise. That note of praise is not only faith rising up through difficulties to greet Me. It is more.

It is the echo in the heart of the sound borne on Spirit waves—of that Help upon the way. It is given to those who love and trust Me to sense this approach. So rejoice for truly your redemption draweth nigh.

Prove Me Now   December 12

YOU have to prove Me. To come to Me walking upon the water. No sure, accustomed earth beneath you. But remember He to Whom you come is Son of God and Son of Man.

He knows your needs. He knows how difficult it must be for mortal to learn to live more and more a life that is not of the senses. To know that when I say, "Come," I ask no impossibility.

Seeing the waves Peter was afraid.

Refuse to look at the waves. Know that with your eyes on Me you can override all storm. It is not what happens that matters, but where your gaze is fixed.

The Narrow Way   December 13

YOU must obey My Will unhesitatingly if you would realize My Blessings. It is a straight and narrow way that leads into the Kingdom.

If man turns aside to follow his own will he may be in

by-paths where My fruits of the Spirit do not grow, where My blessings are not outpoured.

You must remember that you have longed to help a world, the sorrows of which have eaten into your very souls. Do you not understand that I am answering your prayers.

The world is not always helped by the one who walks in sunlight on a flower-strewn path. Patient suffering, trials bravely borne, these show men a courage which could only be maintained by Help Divine.

Songs of Rejoicing   December 14

YOU must pray about all you plan to meet. Pray that you may leave them the braver, better and happier for having seen and talked with you.

Life is so serious, let nothing turn you from your desire to serve and help. Realize all you are able to accomplish in your moments of highest prayer and service, and then think that, were your desire as intense always what could you not accomplish?

Rejoice in Me. The Joy of the Lord must indeed be your strength. You must step aside, and wait until that Joy floods all your being if you wish to serve.

Let Joy keep your hearts and minds lifted above frets and cares. If you want the walls of the city to fall down you must go round it with songs of rejoicing.

Excess of Joy   **December 15**

YOUR life is full of Joy. You realize now that though I was the Man of Sorrows in My deep Experience of life, yet companionship with Me means an excess of Joy such as nothing else can give.

Age may have its physical limitations, but, with the soul content to dwell apart with Me, age has no power to limit the thrill of Love, the ecstasy of Joy-giving Life.

Reflect this Joy that it may be seen by souls weary of life, chafing at its limitations, lonely and sad, as the door closes on so many activities. They will learn by this reflection something of the Joys that Eternal Life here and hereafter brings to those who know and love Me.

So Joy.

Varied Delights   **December 16**

POOR indeed is the life that does not know the riches of the Kingdom. A life that has to depend on the excitement of the senses, that does not know, and could not realize, that delight, Joy, expectation, wonder and satisfaction can be truly obtained only in the Spirit.

Live to bring men to the realization of all they can find in Me. I, Who change not, can supply the soul of man with Joys and delights so varied as to bring ever changing scenes of beauty before him.

I am truly the same, yesterday, to-day, and for ever; but man, changing as he is led nearer and nearer to the realization of all I can mean to him, sees in Me new wonders daily. There can be no lack of glad adventure in a life lived with Me.

Vision of Delights — December 17

PRAISE. Pray until you praise. That is the note upon which you have been told to end all prayer. Such marvels, truly such marvels are here.

Have no fear. Live in My Love. Draw nearer and nearer to Me. I will teach you. You shall see.

Before you could pass on to the Vision of Delights, you had to be taught the foundation Truths of honesty, trustworthiness, order and perseverance. All is very well. Have no fear.

Watch Me — December 18

PRAY ever with watchful eyes on Me, your Master, your Giver, your Example. "As the eyes of servants are on the hands of their master, so are our eyes unto the Lord our God."

Ever look unto Me. From Me comes your help, your

all. The servant watches for support, for wages, for everything. Life is for him in the hands of his master.

So look to Me for all. Intent, gazing with a look of complete faith and surrender that draws all it needs towards you. Not merely faith, but intent regard. You must watch the bestowal, so that you may bestow.

Spiritual Practice   December 19

PRAY without ceasing until every thought and every wish is a prayer. This can only be so by following the plan of recollection which I have set you.

How rarely My followers realize that Spiritual Practice is as necessary as any practice to become perfect in any art or work.

It is by the drudgery of the little steps of practice that you will ascend to Spiritual Attainment.

Make His Paths Straight   December 20

PREPARE ye the way of the Lord, make straight His Path. Must you not do this before you see His Coming. Must you not be content to clear a way for Me, leaving it to Me to pass along it when I will.

This is My way and work for you, one of silent unapplauded preparation.

Preparation not for your work but for Mine.

Your feet shod with the Gospel of Peace.

Yes, the preparation must first be made in your own heart. If unrest is there, nothing can make you well-shod.

Adore Him
December 21

PROVE your adoration in your life. All should be calm and joy. Calm and joy are the outward expressions of adoration.

Adoration is that welling up of the whole being in Love's wonder-praise to Me.

If you truly adored, your whole life would be in harmony with that adoration, expressing as far as you were able, in all its varied manifestations, that Beauty of the Lord Whom you adore.

All Loves Apart
December 22

A HUSH fell on the earth at My first coming. In the still hours of night I came. A silence broken only by the angels' song of praise.

So in the fret and turmoil of the world's day let that hush fall. A hush so complete that the soft footfall of your Master may not pass unnoticed. Forget the blows of life, and its adverse conditions, so that you may be ever sensitive to the touch of My Hand on your brow.

For a time you may put aside the loves of earth, and your human friendships, so that the vibrations from the heart of the Eternal may stir your hearts, and strengthen your lives.

Welcome the Interruption   December 23

I WENT to prepare a place for you, but I still need My Bethany Homes and My Upper Rooms. These can be prepared only by loving hearts.

When you have prepared your home, My Home, you must be prepared to receive any whom I may send. Be ready for any interruption. Treat it as from Me.

You know neither the day nor the hour when your Lord will come. You know not the guise in which He will come, in that of a prince or in that of a beggar.

See in the unwanted your Much-desired Lord.

Eve of Christmas   December 24

" A VIRGIN shall conceive and bear a son and shall call his name Immanuel."

" Unto us a child is born, unto us a son is given . . . his name shall be called Wonderful, Counsellor, the Mighty God . . . the Prince of Peace."

" And the Angel said unto her, ' Fear not Mary . . . behold thou shalt bring forth a son and shalt call his name Jesus . . .'."

"The Holy Ghost shall come upon thee, and the power of the Highest shall overshadow thee; therefore also that holy thing, which shall be born of thee, shall be called the Son of God."

Miracle of the Ages   December 25

" AND the Word was made flesh."
Word proceeding from the Father, the thought.

Dwell this evening upon this miracle of all ages. This stupendous fact of all mankind's history:—

God made man.

I came to restore to man his lost dignity. To show him that his physical and mental being could only be maintained at their intended height and power by constant communion with the Maker of man's being.

I came, God, to live with man, to *show man how to live with God.*

Perfect Rest   December 26

EVEN My Perfection could be no place of rest for weary souls. Rest in My Love. No true rest but that.

How much of earth's weariness is sin-caused. Contact with My Perfection would but make your sin seem the greater. The sight of it might truly spur you on to further effort, to further emulation, but rest——? No. And so with other attributes of Divinity.

But in My Love! in that you *can* rest. Pillowed like a tired child, a happily tired child. Pillowed in security, cradled in a Love, tireless and limitless. In a Love that will not only care for the weary, and rest the weary, but will rest you, until in the very strength of Love you can face your life again.

Rest in My Love. Here alone is perfect Rest. Rest for Spirit, mind and body.

When Evil Smiles December 27

REMEMBER that the forces of evil are always ranged against you. They know the power you can become as a channel for God-Power.

I had to conquer them in the wilderness before *My* Life of Healing and Helpfulness could be all-powerful.

Not by great falls but by little stumbles does evil seek the downfall of My friends. Your Mountain of Transfiguration can only come after your conquest in the wilderness. Temptations at which your whole nature would shudder are no temptations for you.

Beware the smiling face of evil, its seeming innocence, its hand of friendliness. Walk the path I trod.

Still Seek Me   **December 28**

SOFTLY I speak to the tired and the distressed, yet
in My quiet Voice there is healing and strength.

A healing for the sores and sickness of spirit, mind
and body, and a bracing strength that bids those who
come to Me rise to battle for Me and My Kingdom.

Search until you find *Me*, not merely the Truth about
Me. None ever sought Me in vain.

Safe at the Last   **December 29**

SAFE amid storms, calm amid a world-unrest,
certain amid insecurity. Safely through the year.

The only safe way is the sure way of Divine
Guidance. Not the advice of others, not the urgings of
your own hearts and wills. Just My Guidance.

Think more of its wonder. Dwell more on its rest.
Know that you are safe, secure.

Sensitive to Me   **December 30**

SO silently I teach, and that silent teaching depends
upon your approach.

Let every discipline, every joy, every difficulty, every
fresh interest serve to draw you nearer, serve to render
you more receptive to My word, serve to make you
more sensitive, more spiritually aware.

It is this sensitiveness that is the prelude to the joy I give you. The sweetest harmony can be played on a sensitive instrument.

Those who fail to hear think Me far off. I am ever ready to speak but they have missed the power of discipline, the wonder of Communion with Me.

New Year's Eve   December 31

BRING to Me this eventide the past year with its sins, its failures, its lost opportunities.

Leave that past with Me, your Saviour to-day as ever, and go into the New Year forgiven, unladen, free.

Bring to Me your youth or age, your powers, your love—and I, as your God-guide through the year to come, will bring My agelessness, My powers, My love.

So shall we share the burdens and the joys, and the work of the days that lie ahead.

ALL BLESSINGS FOR THE NEW YEAR

Krondor's Sons
PRINCE OF THE BLOOD
THE KING'S BUCCANEER

The Riftwar Saga
MAGICIAN
SILVERTHORN
A DARKNESS AT SETHANON

Other Titles
FAERIE TALE

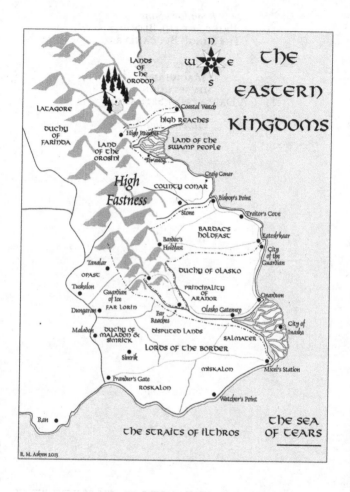

RAYMOND E.
FEIST

MAGICIAN'S

BOOK THREE OF THE CHAOSWAR SAGA

END

HARPER Voyager
An Imprint of HarperCollinsPublishers

This book is a work of fiction. The characters, incidents, and dialogue are drawn from the author's imagination and are not to be construed as real. Any resemblance to actual events or persons, living or dead, is entirely coincidental.

HARPER Voyager
An Imprint of HarperCollins*Publishers*
195 Broadway
New York, New York 10007

Copyright © 2013 by Raymond E. Feist
Maps designed by Ralph M. Askren, D.V.M.
Cover art by Steve Stone
ISBN 978-0-06-146844-5
www.harpervoyagerbooks.com

First Harper Voyager mass market printing: October 2014
First Harper Voyager hardcover printing: May 2013

Harper Voyager and ⟩ is a trademark of HCP LLC.

Printed in the U.S.A.

HB 05.12.2023

CONTENTS

Acknowledgments   *xi*

   1   Shattered   1

   2   Confrontation   22

   3   Journey I   46

   4   Homeward   62

   5   E'bar   77

   6   Assassins   95

   7   Journey II   114

   8   Storm   126

   9   Journey III   147

  10   Skirmish   160

  11   Trapped   187

  12   Journey IV   213

  13   Elvandar   227

  14   Clash   240

  15   Silden   270

  16   Journey V   296

17	Northlands	308
18	Travel	323
19	Magic	340
20	Plans	355
21	Unveiling	368
22	Revelation	384
23	Encounters	394
24	Battles	408
25	Conflict	430
26	Attack	444
27	War	459
28	Destruction	475
29	Obliteration	493
30	Aftermath	518
31	Renaissance	536
Epilogue	Crydee	*551*

ACKNOWLEDGMENTS

As this book is the very last of a "history of an imaginary place," I would like to indulge myself a little and call attention to certain people who were instrumental along the way in the success of this series.

First, as always, are the Thursday-Friday Nighters: Jon, Anita, Ethan, Rich, Dave, Steve B., Lori and Jeff, April, Conan, Bob, and, most especially, Steve Abrams. If there is one heart of Midkemia, its lorekeeper and architect, it's Steve. Thank you all for giving me a marvelous place to play Let's Pretend, back over thirty years ago when we were all starving students in San Diego.

My mother, Barbara A. Feist, who didn't manage to get to the end with me but was there from the start. Reading an early chapter, she said, "You can't send this in looking like this," and proceeded to retype every word. In so doing, she became my first and always biggest fan. I miss her daily.

Harold Matson, a genius and a gentleman, who said, "We think we can sell this," and made me the last client he signed in a long and stellar career. I would say they don't make them like that anymore, but I've met his son and grandson and seen that they do.

Jonathan Matson, who took over for his dad without missing a step, along with Ben Camardi and the marvelous men and women of the Harold Matson Company; the late, wonderful Abner Stein and his great staff at the Abner Stein Company headed by his daughter Arabella in London; Nicki Kennedy, Sam Edenborough, and the rest of the staff of Intercontinental Literary Agency, for turning me into an international hit. Stalwarts all.

Adrian Zackheim, my first editor at Doubleday, who said, "I don't usually do fiction, but I like this. Can you make it longer?" When I did, he said, "Now, cut fifty thousand words," and in less than five months taught me exactly how I should be writing. I have been blessed by an abundance of talent in those editors who have shepherded my work through the publishing process, as people change companies and move on. After Adrian I was loyally defended and appropriately scolded, regularly encouraged and lovingly supported by Pat LoBrutto, Lou Aronica, and Janna Silverstein. I have known my current New York genius, Jennifer Brehl, for many years, for which I am very glad.

Nick Austin bought Magician, for Granada, which became Grafton, then Collins, then HarperCollins, keeping me with the same publisher for thirty-two years despite many name and ownership changes. He was most ably followed by Jonathan Edwards, John Booth, Malcolm Edwards, Emma Coode, and currently Jane Johnson, who is an amazing talent and an author in her own right, whose gift for writing is matched only by her editing skills and her uncanny ability to get what I'm trying to say even when I'm not saying it well. Special mention goes to Eddie Bell, who kept things sane around me when international mergers and changes in ownership threatened chaos.

Peter Schneider, who back in the day when I was a rookie author and he was a baby publicist at Doubleday went way above and beyond to see I caught every break I was entitled to and quite a few I didn't deserve, who endured very early morning phone calls and lots of opinions on how things should be done, as well as a fair amount of hand-holding with a guy afraid it would all turn sour at any minute, and who was smart enough to marry Jennifer Brehl.

My many foreign language publishers, who have enabled me to reach readers I could not have anticipated having when I began. After thirty years foreign publishers have come and gone, and there are many I've never met, but a special thanks to Jacques Post in the Netherlands and Stéphane Marsan and Alain Névant at Bragelonne in France.

Too many other writers to name, both past and present, who either influenced me or befriended me, though a few warrant special notice: Theodore Sturgeon, who smiled when I told him I didn't listen to his advice not to become a writer and said, "I tell that to everyone; the writers never listen." Poul Anderson, who is both an inspiration and damn good company, and the same can be said for Gordon R. Dickson, Harlan Ellison, and Robert Silverberg. Those I have listed for inspiration in the past—Anthony Hope, Arthur Conan Doyle, H. Rider Haggard, A. Merritt, and Fritz Leiber—and every other great writer I've ever read; I've shamelessly stolen from all of you.

Janny Wurts—who showed me things about the craft I never could have imagined and without whom I don't think I could have ever crafted a believable female character—Steve Stirling, Bill Fortschen, and the very much missed Joel Rosenberg, who always played well in my sandbox and gave me stories I could not have achieved without them.

John Bunting and his lovely wife, Tammy, who have done so much on my behalf out of loyalty and affection. They are splendid people I am richer for knowing.

And Ralph Askren, whose love for the geography of an imaginary world has given it rich detail in his wonderful maps.

My core fans who have been with me since the beginning, who have been my recruiting army, and who have worked tireless to endorse my work. Thank you; words do not express how grateful I am.

Last, my many friends outside of publishing, some of

whom have driven me crazy over the years, many of whom have saved my sanity over the years, thank you for your affection and loyalty. And most of all to my daughter, Jessica, and my son, James, who keep me constantly aware that there are things far more important in life than my own momentary concerns.

Without all of you I doubt I would be writing this today.

Raymond E. Feist
San Diego, California
January 2013

MAGICIAN'S END

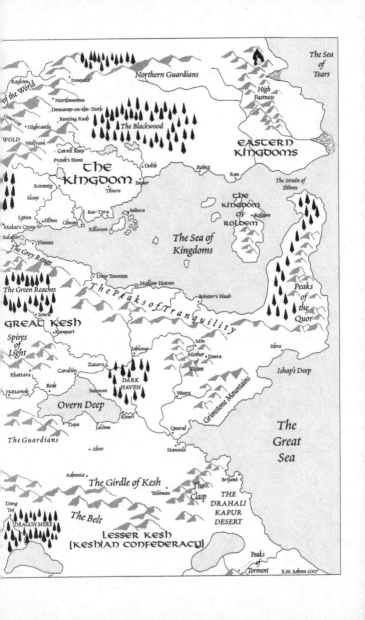

1

SHATTERED

Chaos erupted.

A light so brilliant it was painful bathed Pug as he instinctively threw all his magic into the protective shell Magnus had erected around them just a moment before. Only Magnus's anticipation of the trap had prevented them all from being instantly vaporized. Energy so intense it could hardly be comprehended now destroyed everything at hand, reducing even the most iron-hard granite to its fundamental particles, dispersing them into the fiery vortex forming around them.

The light pierced Pug's tightly shut eyelids,

1

rendering his vision an angry red-orange, with afterimages of green-blue. His instinct was to shield his face, but he knew the gesture would be useless. He willed himself to keep his hands moving in the pattern necessary to support Magnus's efforts. Only magic protected them from conditions no mortal could withstand for even the barest tick of time. The very stuff of the universe was being distorted on all sides.

They were in what appeared to be the heart of a sun. In his studies, Pug knew this to be the fifth state of matter, beyond earth, air, water, and fire, called different names by various magicians: among them, flux, plasma, and excited fire. Energy so powerful that it tore the very essentials of all matter down to their very atoms and recombined them, repeating the process until at some point the plasma fell below a threshold of destruction and creation and was able finally to cease its fury.

Years of perfecting his art had gifted him with myriad skills, some talents deployed reflexively without conscious effort. The magic tools he used to assess and evaluate were overloaded with sensations he had never experienced in his very long lifetime. Obviously, whoever had constructed this trap had hoped it would be beyond his ability to withstand. He suspected it was the work of several artisans of magic.

In his mind, Pug heard Miranda asking, *Is everyone safe?*

Nakor's voice spoke aloud. "There's air. We can talk. Magnus, Pug, don't look. It will blind you. Miranda, we can look."

"Describe what you see," Magnus said to the two demons in human form.

Miranda said, "It's an inferno hotter than anything witnessed in the demon realm. It has destroyed a hundred feet of rock and soil below us and we are afloat in a bubble of energy. Farther out from where we stand, it's turning sand to glass. A wall of superheated air is expanding outward at incredible speed, and whatever it touches is incinerated in moments. As far as my eye can discern, all is flame, smoke, and ash."

Less than a minute before, the four of them had been examining a matrix of magic, which was obviously a lock, but had turned out to be a trap.

Ancient beings of energy, the Sven-ga'ri, had been protected in a quiet glade atop a massive building built by a peaceful tribe of the Pantathians, a race of serpent men created by the ancient Dragon Lord, Alma-Lodaka. Unlike their more violent brethren, these beings had been gentle, scholarly, and very much like humans.

Now that peaceful race had been obliterated. It didn't matter to Pug that they had been created by the mad vanity of a long-dead Dragon Lord as pets and servants: they had evolved into something much finer and he knew he would mourn their loss.

"It's fading," said Nakor. "Don't look."

Pug kept his eyes closed, focusing on his son's protective shell. "You anticipated—"

Magnus finished his sentence for him: "—the trap. It was just one of those moments, Father. The hair on my neck and arms started to tingle, and before I knew it, the protective spell was cast. I had created a word trigger, a power word. I just had no idea the trap would be so massive. Without your help and Moth—Miranda's . . ." He let the thought go unfinished.

Pug and Miranda both chose to ignore his slip. She wasn't his mother. She was a demon named Child who was in possession of all his mother's memories, but Child seemed completely contained within Miranda. It was easy to forget she wasn't Miranda; the experience was unnerving for all of them.

Only Belog the demon, now to outward appearances Nakor, seemed untroubled by his situation, and that was wholly in keeping with who Nakor had been in life: a man of unlimited curiosity and a delight in all mysteries. His voice held a note of awe. "This was an unspeakably brilliant trap, Pug."

Keeping his eyes tightly shut, Pug said, "I tend to agree. What's your thinking?"

"Whoever fashioned this understood it could be investigated only by a very limited number of people," said Nakor. "First they would have to get past the Pantathians, either by winning their confidence or by brute force. If they reached the matrix, few magic-using demons or lesser magicians, or even very well-schooled priests, could have begun to understand the complexities of this lock, or trap, or however you think of it."

Miranda said, "Only Pug."

Pug was silent for a moment, then said, "No. It was Magnus. I sensed the lock, but only assumed there was a trap involved. By the time I returned from the Academy, he had already easily won past barriers that would have proved a challenge to me."

Magnus began, "I'm not certain—"

Miranda cut him off. "That was no hollow praise. I have all your mother's memories and skills, Magnus, but you . . . you are the best of both of us, I mean both your mother and father."

Nakor chuckled. "You've long denied it, boy, but in the end, you are beyond us. All you need is a little more experience and age."

"I find it incongruous to be laughing in the midst of all this chaos," said Magnus.

Suddenly there was an explosion of sound, as if they were being slammed by a hurricane of wind.

"Don't look," reminded Nakor.

"What was that?" asked Pug.

"I think that was air returning." After a moment Nakor added, "The explosion . . . I don't know if I can describe what I'm seeing, Pug. Miranda?"

After a pause she said, "It was more than just light and heat. I felt . . . shifts, changes . . . displacement. I've never encountered its like. I'm not certain if it's even what we would call magic."

Nakor said, "It's not a trick, or at least not one I can imagine. Everything changed."

"How?" Pug asked.

"You can open your eyes now, but slowly."

Pug did so, and at first his eyes watered and everything was blurred. A strange vibration, high-pitched and fast, almost a buzzing, could be felt through the soles of his sandals. He blinked away tears and found himself semicrouched within the energy bubble his son had erected an instant before the explosion.

Beyond the shell, everything was white to the point of there being no horizon, no sky above or ground below, no sea beyond a shore. As his eyes adapted to the brilliance he could see faint hints of variation, and after another moment faint shifts in the whiteness, as if colors were present beyond the boundary of the bubble.

They floated above the bottom of a crater thirty or forty feet below them. The only remnants of earth and rock were beneath their feet, encased in Magnus's sphere.

"Are you holding us up, son?"

"The spell is, and we'd better be ready for a rude landing when it releases. I can't keep this sphere intact and move it."

"Maybe I can help," said Miranda. She closed her eyes and the sphere slowly settled to the bottom of the crater.

Everything was still confounding to the senses as energies continued to cascade around them, every visible spectrum shifting madly outside the bubble. Pug pushed Magnus's protective sphere gently and it expanded enough that they could all stand easily. After a few more minutes passed, details in the crater wall became recognizable. Slowly, the blinding light faded and varying hues of ivory, palest gold, a hint of blue emerged. At last the brilliance disappeared.

They blinked as their eyes adjusted to natural daylight, which was dark in comparison to what they just endured.

Pug looked around. They were perhaps fifty feet below the surface, surrounded by what appeared to be glass.

"What happened?" asked Miranda.

"Someone tried to kill us," answered Nakor, without his

usually cheerful tone. "We need to get out of this hole and look around."

"Is it safe by now?" asked Magnus.

"Be ready to protect yourself and we'll find out," said Nakor. "I think it's going to be very hot for you two."

Magnus studied the little man for a moment, nodded once, and glanced at his father. Pug tilted his head slightly, indicating that he understood the warning, and both men encased themselves in protective spells without a word exchanged.

Magnus closed his eyes for a brief moment and the sphere around them vanished. Pug knelt and touched the glass beneath his feet. "Odd . . ."

"What?" asked Miranda.

"The energy . . . I expected it to be more . . . I'm not sure." He looked from his son to Miranda. "Both of you are more adept at sensing the nature of a given spell. Does this feel like just an explosion to you?"

Miranda knelt next to Pug. "Feel like an explosion? We lived through it; it was massive and loud." She touched the glass beneath them. "Oh, yes, I see what you mean."

Magnus did likewise. "This . . . the explosion was the by-product."

Nakor looked at the three kneeling magicians and said, "Please?"

"The energy released was the result of a spell that wasn't just some spell of massive destruction," said Magnus, standing. "We need to go."

Pug waved his hands without comment. All four rose upward and floated toward the edge of the crater.

Magnus said to Nakor, "As best I can tell, that spell did two things. Besides obliterating everything within a fairly large radius, it also moved us to . . . I'm not sure where we are, but it's not where we were when the spell was triggered."

They reached the lip of the crater and Pug said, "You are right, Magnus. We are not where we were minutes ago."

"Where's the sea?" asked Miranda.

They looked to the south, and where waves had lapped

the shore just minutes before, only a long, sloping plain remained. To their rear there was a rising bluff and hills beyond that roughly resembled what they would have seen on the Isle of the Snake Men, but these hills were denuded of any plant life—no trees, no brush, not even a blade of grass could be seen.

The devastation was complete: nothing moved save by force of the wind. There was sand everywhere: years past this land had turned to desert. They were at the edge of a vast, deep crater, and like the crater, the land around had been fused by the blast, its surface nothing but glass of coruscating colors, as smoke, ash, and dust swirled upward, admitting narrow shafts of sunlight. The wind was blowing the smoke northward, clearing it away quickly. On this world nothing burned, for there was nothing *to* burn, and the rocks and sand that had been turned molten were rapidly cooling.

"I think we're still in the same place," said Nakor. "I mean, an analogous place, as when we traveled to Kosidri." Pug, Magnus, and Nakor had discovered that on the other planes of reality the worlds were identical, or at least as much as the variant conditions of that reality permitted. So wherever they were was a world similar in geography to Midkemia. "But I think the energy state here is going to prove troublesome soon."

Pug nodded.

Miranda said, "I feel a little odd."

Magnus said, "I remember how we adapted when we traveled to the Dasati realm, Father."

"But this time it feels . . . different, obverse?" said Pug.

"A higher state than either the demon realm or Midkemia," agreed Miranda. "As if there's too much air?"

Nakor grimaced. "We could be overwhelmed by it if we do not tread cautiously."

Each fashioned a protective spell that returned a tiny bubble of protective energy around themselves, reducing the more intense energies in this world to a level their own bodies could accommodate.

"If it's a higher energy state," said Magnus, "we did not go into a lower realm, but a higher one. Which means—"

"We're in the first realm of heaven?" suggested Miranda.

Contemplating the desolate landscape, Nakor quipped, "It's obviously overrated. There's more to offer in the demon realm."

They were silent for a moment as they contemplated the barren world around them.

Pug looked at his son and said quietly, "I neglected to say thank you. Had you not returned . . ."

Magnus embraced him. "You're my father. No matter how much I may disagree with . . . what we talked about . . . I will never leave you when you need me."

Father and son held each other for a moment, then separated, returning their attention to the present. Glancing at Miranda, they saw she had tears on her cheeks. She reached up and wiped them away and, in an angry tone they both knew well, said, "Damn these memories. I know they are not mine! I know it!" She crossed her arms over her chest. A bitter chuckle was followed by her observing, "Part of me remembers a time I'd have happily torn your heads from your shoulders and devoured your still-beating hearts." Then she glanced up and in softer tones said, "And part of me feels that I've never loved anyone more than I've loved you two. Only Caleb was your equal." This last came out a hoarse whisper.

Magnus understood his father well enough to know Pug was fighting an impulse to reach out and embrace the form of his former wife, to comfort a person who wasn't really there. Softly he said, "I can't call you Mother." He looked her in the eye. "But I never understood until now just how difficult this must be for you." In what was an impulsive act for the usually stoic magician, he took a step, slipped his arms around the demon in human form, and held her closely for a brief moment.

When he stepped away he saw more tears streaming down the face of the first person in life he had beheld. Powerful emotions tore through him, and he fought back the urge to say more. No matter how much he wished his mother back, alive and before him, it was nothing compared to what his father must feel. He put his hand on Pug's shoulder and said, "We must make the best of a terribly confusing and awkward situation, and if we focus on what is before us, perhaps what is behind us will distance itself enough that we may develop new ways of seeing each other."

Nakor grinned. "That's very nice, but have you noticed someone is coming toward us?"

All looked in the direction Nakor indicated and saw the landscape was starting to resolve itself.

Approaching them was a familiar figure clad in a black robe, wearing sandals bound upon his legs with whipcord and using a staff as a walking stick. His hair was black, his posture youthful, and his stride vigorous, as he had been in his prime.

All four were momentarily stunned and finally Pug put voice to their incredulity. "Macros!"

The figure held up his hand. "No, though I resemble him, no doubt."

Miranda and Nakor exchanged glances and the short gambler asked, "You have Macros's memories?"

"No," said the figure.

"Who are you?" asked Magnus.

"I have no name. You may think of me as a guide."

"Why do you look like my father?" asked Miranda.

The guide shrugged slightly, in a perfect mimicry of Macros. "That is a mystery, for I am by nature formless in the mortal realm. I can only speculate, but my conclusion is that I appear to be who you expected me to be. I am sent by One whose Will is Action, but I needed to be in a form with which you could converse."

The four exchanged quick glances, then Nakor laughed. "It is true that for most of the last hundred or more years I've expected to see that rascal's hand behind every turn and twist of our existence."

The others nodded slowly. Pug said, "Well, then, Guide. What should we call you?"

"Guide serves well enough," he answered.

"Where exactly are we?" asked Magnus.

"The world of Kolgen." Guide pointed to the south. "Once a majestic ocean lapped these shores, now there is only blight and desolation."

"I don't understand," said Pug.

"Walk, for we have a long journey if you are ever to return home," said the likeness of Macros.

"Before we begin," said Miranda, "can you explain how you resemble my father down to the tiniest detail?"

Guide paused, and smiled exactly as the now-dead Black Sorcerer had in life. "Certainly," he said with another pause, again exactly as Macros would have. "We exist in a realm of energy, we who serve the One. We are forever in the Bliss, part of the One until we are needed, and we are then given form and substance, given an identity commensurate with our purpose; to ensure efficiency, all memories of previous service in that role are returned. So, currently, I think of myself as 'I,' a single entity, but that will dissipate when I rejoin the One in the Bliss.

"I am only an abstraction of energy, a being of light and heat, if you will, a thing of mind alone. Hence the One gives me the ability to . . . suggest to your mortal minds any shape and quality suitable to sustain communications."

"But we are not mortal," said Nakor, indicating Miranda and himself.

"You are more mortal than you might guess," returned Guide, "for it is of the mind I speak, and while your fundamental being is demonic, your minds are human, more so each day. Moreover, your demonic bodies are things of flux energy, imperfect imitations of beings of the higher plane.

"And you are becoming that which you appear to me to be, with limits, of course. You would never mate with humans and produce offspring, nor would you be subject to their illnesses and injuries, and those who battle demon kind can still destroy you, returning your essence to the Fifth Circle." He lowered his voice and seemed to be attempting kindness. "Nor do you have a mortal soul. Those beings whose memories you possess have traveled on to the place where they have been judged and are now on their path to the next state of existence, or returned to the Wheel of Life for another turn.

"In short, you will never truly be Miranda and Nakor. But you're as close as any being will ever get."

Turning, he began to walk away. "Please, we must travel far, and while time here is not measured as it is in the mortal realm, it is still passing, and the longer you are away from Midkemia, the more the One's Adversary stands to gain."

Pug and the others fell in next to Guide and Pug said, "Then I believe you had best tell us in your own fashion what it is we need to know, but could you begin with why we are here."

"That's the simple part," said Guide. "You fell into a trap. The Adversary has been waiting a very long time to rid Midkemia of the four of you. To do it in one moment, that approaches genius."

"This Adversary you speak of," said Nakor. "Who or what is it?"

The guide paused. "It will be easier if we wait on questions until I finish explaining to you what has befallen you. You are vital to what transpires, but still just a tiny part of the whole. To leap to attempting the larger picture might confuse.

"You are stranded in a reality that is not your own, and have no easy means of returning. You are, not to put too fine a point on it, marooned here."

He kept walking, and as the four companions glanced at one another, they hurried to keep up with his brisk pace. Pug overtook him in three strides and said, "If we are marooned, where are we going?"

"To find one who may facilitate your release from this place."

"But I thought you said this world was naught but blight and desolation?"

In a perfect duplication of Macros's smile, Guide said, "This is true, but that doesn't mean it's unoccupied."

Pug considered that for a moment, but decided that among the thousands of questions demanding answers, the meaning of that riddle was one he could wait for.

They forged across the bed of a long-absent sea. As they trudged across the rough channels and gullies, Miranda asked, "Why are we walking?"

Guide said, "You have a better alternative?"

With an all-too-familiar smug smile, she glanced at Pug then vanished.

A hundred yards ahead they heard her scream.

Scrambling as best they could across the broken, sun-baked sands of the dry sea bottom, they reached her quickly, finding her sitting up, a look of confusion on her face as she held her hands to her temples.

"That which you call magic," said Guide, "does not respond here as it would in your own world."

"But what of the protective spells we employed?" asked Magnus.

"Did it not occur to you that it was surprisingly easy to create those protections against this world's energy states?"

Magnus nodded. "Now that you mention it, it *was* easy."

Nakor chuckled as he and Pug helped Miranda to her feet. "Different energy states, my friends," said the bandy-legged little man. "If you light a small pot of oil, you get a flame to read by. If you refine and distill that same oil and light it, you get a really big hot flame."

"In time you should be able to learn to temper your arts to transport yourself from place to place," said Guide. "But we do not have the time for you to learn. Rather, *you* do not have that time. So, we walk." With that, he began walking again.

Pug asked Miranda, "Are you all right?"

"Besides feeling supremely foolish, yes." She glanced up and saw the concern in his eyes. "Sorry."

Pug felt conflicting urges to say different things at once, paused, then nodded.

Time passed and they forged on. Guide provided illumination as they traversed the broken seabed. He created bridges as they crossed massive trenches in the former ocean's floor, and seemingly kept them alive by some magic that rid them of need for food or water.

But they did need to rest, even if only for short periods, while they regained strength rapidly in this high-energy-state universe.

During one such rest, Pug asked, "Are we to know why you're here?"

Guide answered, "I am here as willed by One."

Pug couldn't help but laugh. "When I was a Tsurani Great One on Kelewan, my every command was answered by 'Your Will, Great One,' ah . . . for some reason this strikes me as humorous."

A great wave of sadness swept over Pug as he remembered Kelewan. Since his actions had destroyed that world and countless lives on it, he had effectively walled off the profoundly deep sorrow and guilt associated with that terrible decision. Yet from time to time, usually when he was alone, it would return to haunt him.

"How are you able to keep hunger and thirst at bay for us?" asked Nakor. "It's a very good trick."

Guide shrugged. "The universe is aware, on many levels. My perceptions and knowledge are vastly different from your own. What I need to know, I know. What I do not know, I do not know. You are mortals, and in need of food and water, so I provide such . . ." He waved his hand as if the concept was alien to him and difficult to explain. "I just make it so; you are fed; you have drunk . . . what is needed." Then he opened his eyes slightly and said, "Ah, curiosity!"

"You have none?" asked Magnus.

"I am created for a purpose," said Guide.

Nakor laughed. "We all are."

"But my purpose is unique and short-lived. Once I start you on your way home, I will have completed my task and cease to exist in this form," said Guide. "I will return to the One and rejoin the Bliss."

"Who sent you to find us?" asked Magnus.

"The One," said Guide with a tone that suggested it was obvious.

"Why here?" asked Nakor, fixing Guide with a narrow gaze. "Why not on Midkemia before we destroyed an entire city and the best part of a race?"

Guide cocked his head for a second as if considering. "I do not know." He closed his eyes for a moment, then opened them and said, "Rider."

"What rider?" asked Miranda.

"Rider. She was sent by the One to warn you." He pointed at Pug. "But she was . . . prevented." His face became a mask of confusion. He stood up. "Come. We must hurry. Time grows short."

"How much farther?" asked Magnus.

"Why the sudden hurry?" asked Miranda.

"I can only know what I am to know." Guide now looked completely confused. "Your questions will . . . be answered as it is . . . as the One . . ." Frustration overcame him and he almost shouted, "I do not know why these things are so! I am only a means of . . ." He continued in an almost alien voice. "I am only a means of expression, an interpreter, if you will, of a higher mind which must carefully choose how to touch you without harm. Your lack of belief in the form your minds chose . . . it is wearing on me. Come, I will take you to someone who may be better able to answer these and other questions."

They trudged along and Pug said, "When we pulled Macros back from his attempted ascension into godhood, I remember him describing his experience as seeing all of vast creation through the knothole of a fence, and as we pulled him back his perspective shifted and he saw less and less."

"Yes?" asked Miranda.

"He later explained that the other aspect of the experience is, the closer he got to that fence the less of his 'self' remained; as he ascended to godhood, identity faded as consciousness expanded."

Guide said, "Yes. The One could simply impart knowledge, but it would overwhelm you. For you to know, but to be squatting on the side of a hill unable to move because your mind was damaged, that would serve no one."

"That's hard to deny!" said Nakor.

They moved as best they could over the broken terrain and at times found themselves facing seemingly insurmountable obstacles, for they were moving down a miles-long slope that wended its way through once-undersea mountains. Yet Guide always seemed to find a way, even if it was treacherous.

Finally they crested a rise and he pointed. "There!"

In the distance they could see a vast table of land, surrounded by deep trenches. Pug said, "Those crevasses are vast. Can you fashion us a bridge that far?"

Before Guide could answer, Magnus said, "I think I can get us there."

Miranda looked at him. "Are you certain? I found the short excursion I attempted very painful."

"I've been attuning myself as best I'm able to the energy states here . . ." Magnus paused and they both knew he had almost called her Mother, and a smile was exchanged. "I doubt it will be pain-free, but I think I can manage this one attempt without incapacitating myself. As I can see our destination, much of the risk is abated."

Pug and Miranda glanced at each other, then at Nakor, who nodded. "It's been a long time since I tried to forbid you a risk," said Pug. He took Magnus's hand as Miranda and Nakor joined hands, and Nakor grabbed Magnus's arm. Pug gripped Guide's arm with his free hand and found it unexpectedly cold.

Suddenly they were standing on a plateau miles from where they had been a moment before. Pug looked at his son and saw Magnus's expression was pained, and perspiration was beading on his forehead. His pale complexion was drained of what little color he normally possessed. He shook his head slightly and said, "I'll be fine in a moment. If we have to do it again, I can adjust. This is not the easiest adjustment I've made, but it's not the most difficult either."

"I'll take your word for it," said Nakor, then he pointed past Guide. "Who's that?"

Guide didn't look, but said, "That is Pepan the Thrice-cursed." Then he vanished without a word.

The being left before them was as alien a creature as any of them had met, and in demonic form Nakor and Miranda had met many. He, if gender could be determined, was as miserable-looking a creature as any of them had seen. His head was three times the size of a normal man's, but the body was slender and seemed barely able to hold it up. A bulbous stomach protruded so far that only the lower portions of spindly legs where it sat could be seen, and the arms were almost withered.

His face was long, from an almost hairless pate to a broad jaw, and a nose covered in pustules and scabs was at its center. Rheumy eyes of pale blue surrounded by jaundiced yellow shed a constant stream of tears, and heavy lips generated a constant flow of froth and bubbles.

Miranda said softly, "I've seen worse."

Nakor said, "I'm older than you. No, you haven't."

The creature seemed unaware of them until Pug ventured closer. "You are Pepan?"

"That's what Guide said," snapped the creature angrily. "Do you see anyone else here?"

Nakor pressed forward, his insatiable curiosity pushing aside other considerations. "Tell us why you are called the Thrice-cursed."

"Listen and be wiser for it, mortal!" shouted the creature. "In this world, once was I a man among men, a king among kings, a being of power and wealth, wisdom and beauty. Did I sit upon thrones and did subjects tremble at my beauty? Yes! Did I possess all that any man might desire? Yes!"

Pug saw Miranda about to interrupt and slightly shook his head to indicate he wanted to hear this tale: perhaps there was knowledge to be gained here.

"In my arrogance I did conspire to elevate myself beyond the wealth and power I had, to rise to the heavens and seek a place among the gods."

Nakor grinned and nodded. "Go on."

"In my vanity, did I create engines of destruction unmatched in the history of my people. Nations I conquered to gather mighty armies around me: those who were vanquished served or died.

"Then, in the tenth age of my reign, I came here to the Tent of Heaven, and led my hordes up the Path of the Gods, to the top of the tallest mountain on this world!"

Nakor glanced around, for they were on what had once been an undersea plateau. "I see no mountain, Pepan."

"Washed away by the ocean, for no sooner had I approached the Gates of Heaven to demand my due as the newest of the gods, they picked up the entire mountain and thousands of my soldiers fell screaming to their deaths. Then, for my vanity, the gods cursed me by washing away all knowledge of me, sweeping my people into the sea with me, while I was chained to that very mountain. I listened to their screams of terror and pleas for mercy, until there was only silence.

"Then I knew the price of vanity, perhaps the worst of all sins, for alone I waited, aeons passing as the waters wore away the very rocks to which I was chained. The sea became my home and I abided.

"Above, time passed; I had but scant knowledge of it, only suggestions carried to me on fickle tides. A strange scrap of fabric, unlike any I had beheld, drifted close, and I seized it. I wondered who had woven it and what manner of creature now walked in the world above me. I treasured that fabric until the salt of the water had faded it and the very fabric wore away.

"Once a ship passed directly above, blocking out the faint light of the sun as it passed. I wondered who voyaged upon it, whence they came, and where they were bound.

"As the mountain wore away, sections sheared off and I was carried deeper into the depths, until no light reached me from above."

Miranda said, "That is far more than three curses; that's damnation without ending."

"But there you are wrong, mortal!" shouted Pepan. "For after a time, I found peace, an acceptance of my lot. I was content to let my mind go void, to simply be, in harmony with the rhythms of the idea.

"Angry gods at last took note of my peace, and chose then to inflict the second of my curses. A day, a month, mere moments, I do not know how long passed, for time had become meaningless to one dwelling blind in the depths of the sea, but suddenly the waters receded and I was again in the light and air! Fire rained down from above, and majestic clouds of flame and ash tore across the heavens as war on a scale unimagined by mortals raged across the land. Engines of destruction vast beyond my imagining, making my proud fleet seem like mere toys, cruised the skies, delivering obliteration to all below.

"Mortals in armor unlike any seen before hurried across broken lands with lances of red light and fire-belching engines on treads, destroying all before them.

"Then hordes of demons appeared, sweeping mortals away as a scythe shears grain, and answering them was a host of angels, swords aflame, horns sounding notes so pure that I was reduced to weeping at the first note.

"This world was torn asunder and oceans vanished as energies hotter than a star burned across the lands. And yet I abided."

He fell silent for a moment, and to the four travelers it was unclear if he was merely organizing his thoughts or experiencing some emotion at the memory of this unbelievable narrative.

"So, in sum, my second curse was to watch any shred of a thing I might have loved destroyed in the war between gods and men." His voice softened. "A war I began."

"Ages passed and my third curse was made apparent."

"What is that?" asked Nakor.

"Upon this world remain scattered remnants of nations, which I gathered." He pointed to the assembled bits and scraps he had cobbled together to make a shelter. A bit of something served as a chair, an ancient-looking table. Shreds of fabric had been woven together into a quilt. Pepan himself wore a simple breechclout that was revealed when he finally stood up.

"For uncounted days I wandered, gathering what I could find, always to return here."

"Why here?" asked Magnus. "There must be more hospitable places on this world."

"Not really," answered Pepan. "And this is where the gods left me. This is where I am to abide. I no longer rebel but I do question." Raising his eyes to the sky, he shouted, "I was a sinner, All Father! I admit my transgressions, All Mother! I sinned most of my days!" His voice broke. "But not every day. I lived but a few score years, yet I have paid for my sins for an eternity." With a sob, he whispered, "Enough, please."

Just as Pug and the others were verging on sympathy for the abject creature, Pepan erupted in a howl of rage. "And my third curse, most hateful of all, making me the gatekeeper!"

"Gatekeeper?" asked Nakor.

"See you then, mortal, that the ultimate jest piled upon me by the gods is that when those who wander this destroyed world, or who fall here from some other realm, when at last they find their way here, I am obliged to help them on their way. I cannot even out of lonely spite keep them here to mitigate my endless sorrow through pleasant discourse, nor may I exchange tales of lives spent in other realms, but rather I must endure solitude.

"For upon your arrival, I began to feel pain, and with each passing minute the pain increases. It will not cease until I send you on your way, returning to my isolation. I may not end the suffering by my own hand or the hand of another," he sobbed. "Alone on this world, I am immortal and indestructible."

"Why endure the pain?" asked Magnus. "Why tell us your tale? Why not just hurry us along!"

"The pain is a price worth paying to interrupt my loneliness," Pepan said, weeping openly. "Now it must end."

He waved his hands in precise pattern and a vortex appeared in the air. It was obviously an opening of some sort, but as they readied themselves to leap through it, Pepan held up a hand. "Wait!"

"What?" asked Pug.

Pepan closed his eyes, tears now streaming down his cheeks. "Each of you must follow a different path."

"We must split up?" asked Miranda, obviously not happy with the idea.

"Apparently," said Pug. "If someone laid a trap for the four of us, then it's literally set for the four of us."

"It waits for all of us," said Nakor. "Yes!" His expression turned gleeful. "You do not spring a trap on soldiers when only the scout is there: you wait for all of them to gather."

Pepan's expression now contorted into one of abject pain. He waved a hand and the size and color of the vortex changed, growing smaller and tinged with orange energy. "You!" he said, pointing at Nakor.

Without a word, Nakor leaped into the vortex.

Again Pepan waved his hand and the color of the vortex changed to a faint, shimmering blue. "You," he said, pointing at Miranda.

She glanced at Pug and Magnus, hesitating for a brief moment, then with a quick nod she leaped into the swirling air and vanished.

Again the color changed, this time to a brilliant white,

and Pepan pointed at Magnus. Without hesitation, Pug's son jumped into the magic portal.

One more wave and Pepan said, "I am to tell you one thing, Magician."

"What?" asked Pug. He watched the vortex turn dark until it became a black maw.

"This is the beginning of the end. You will meet your companions again, but only at the most dire moment, when you must all be ready to sacrifice everything to save everything."

"I'm not sure—"

"Go!" commanded the wretched creature, and Pug obeyed.

He ran and jumped, crouching as he entered a cone of darkness.

2

CONFRONTATION

Ships dotted the horizon.

Hal stood on the battlements of the royal palace at Rillanon, at its heart still a castle, but one which had not seen conflict for centuries. This portion of the ancient rampart, a large flat rooftop of thick stonework, had once supported war engines defending outer walls long torn down to expand the royal demesne. A fortification that once hosted massive ballista had been converted to a garden, one lush with flowers as summer faded. The stone merlons had been replaced in centuries past with a stone balustrade cleverly carved to be both strong and graceful.

Yet the footing beneath Hal's boots felt as solid as the palisades of Crydee Castle had. And given the forces gathering below, he wished those long-gone outer walls were once again in place here in Rillanon, with ballistas and trebuchets in place of fading blooms.

He let out a slow breath. It was hard to find ease, despite the rigors of the past few weeks fading into memory as troubles associated with fleeing Roldem with the Princess Stephané had been replaced by troubles on a far grander scale. His personal distress over knowing he would never have the woman he loved had been made to seem a petty concern in the face of the threats now confronting his nation.

Yet he was constantly haunted by her memory, along with that of his friend Ty Hawkins, who had spirited her away from her home to see her safely to the Kingdom. All of it seemed unreal at times, yet other times it was vivid. Every detail of Stephané was etched in his memory: the grace of her movements, the laughter as she found delight in small things, her worry for those she loved. He struggled to let go, even though he knew that to wallow was to prolong the pain.

He glanced around, and saw his brother Martin was looking his way. Martin inclined his head: a wordless gesture asking if he was all right. Hal returned a slight nod. Their brother Brendan, standing beside Martin, had his attention fixed on the ships in the harbor. Hal turned his attention that way as well. Nearby stood Lord James, Duke of Rillanon, and his grandson, Jim Dasher.

Rillanon's harbor was south of the palace, at the bottom of the hill. Sails had been appearing on all quarters of the horizon for days: hundreds of ships from every port on the Sea of Kingdoms. This ancient island nation had seen fleets such as these, but not in living memory. War had not touched this soil, the ancient home of Hal's ancestors, in centuries. The prime motive for conquering the surrounding islands and nearby coasts for Hal's forebears had been fatigue from continuous clashes with minor warlords and raiding clans across these waters. The constant need to defend the home island had turned a relatively peaceful community of fishermen and farmers into the most effective army north of the Empire, creating the second-largest nation on this world.

It had been a triumph of the Kingdom of the Isles that this city and the King's palace could do without the massive defense works, as the King's navy for centuries had become "the wall around Rillanon." Now that navy was divided. No man could look out upon that sea, and the many sails upon it, and judge just who they were defending: Edward, Oliver, or some other faction. That irony was not lost on Hal.

He couldn't find ease because he could smell war coming on the afternoon breeze. And unlike the struggle against Kesh, this was the war to be most feared by any noble in the Kingdom: a civil war.

Hal knew the Kingdom's history well. A determined ruler named Dannis had united all the clans of the island, and his descendant Delong had been the first conDoin ruler to establish a foothold on the mainland. After the sack of Bas-Tyra—a rival village that had risen in power to challenge Rillanon—he had not returned to the island stronghold, but had forced the ruler of that city-state to swear fealty to Rillanon in exchange for his life and the lives of his followers, creating the Kingdom of the Isle's first mainland duchy and elevating Bas-Tyra to the rank of second most important city after the capital. That first victory had led to many others, as Rillanon and Bas-Tyra's combined might had overwhelmed Salador and the southern coast. Only the Eastern Kingdoms, with the help of Roldem, had stemmed that early Kingdom expansion.

Now the ruler of that city stood to Hal's right asking, "What is Oliver thinking?" Duke James of Rillanon looked at both Hal and the man on Hal's left, James's grandson, Jim Dasher Jamison, head of the Crown's intelligence service.

"He's not thinking," Jim said sourly. "Or he's thinking that some here might object to a foreign-born king, so he's brought along a few friends."

Hal glanced at his two brothers, and Martin nodded. Hal

knew what Martin also understood: somehow the three con-Doin brothers were about to take a part in all this, but what that part would be had not yet been revealed.

The "friends" were the bulk of the Army of Maladon and Simrick, bolstered by a substantial number of levies and mercenary companies, which were now encamped as they had been for a month, beyond the walls of the city. The old military grounds lay to the east of the harbor, having once been the staging area for Rillanon's conquering armies wait-ing to board ship. Not in a generation had they been used as originally intended, having been converted to a shantytown and impromptu market. Oliver had cleared the area, displac-ing many of the poor and working poor, and had camped his army there.

Many polite messages had been exchanged between those inside and outside the walls, and the longest interregnum in the history of the Kingdom was under way. By tradi-tion, the Congress of Lords met for the election of the new king three days after the dead king's interment in the vault of his ancestors.

But for the first time in history, more than a month had passed since the death of a king without the Congress of Lords being formally convened. One excuse or another had been provided, and each faction negotiated furiously behind closed doors, over quiet suppers, or in dark back alleys, but everyone knew exactly what was really taking place: every claimant to the throne was desperately seeking a resolu-tion to the succession problem without losing his position and without plunging the nation into a civil war it could ill afford. And for the time being, those two goals seemed mu-tually exclusive.

The senior priests of the Temple of Ishap in Rillanon, the most venerated order in the world, would formally conduct the ceremony, but only when summoned by the Congress to do so. Since the ascension of Lyam the First, no dispute had existed in the line of kings from Lyam to his nephew Borric, to Patrick, then Gregory.

Now no heir had been proclaimed, and no clear ties by blood were forthcoming. Politics had seized the nation by the throat. Three factions had asserted themselves, all with roughly equal and valid claims, none of which was seen as compelling by those gathered on the balcony this afternoon.

The army gathered outside the city was nominally an "honor guard" for Prince Oliver of the grand duchies of Maladon and Simrick. In terms of straight bloodline succession to the late King, he was perhaps the most entitled, his mother being the King's sister, but she had wed the Prince of Simrick and Oliver had been raised in the twin duchies. To most people in the Isles, that made him a foreigner.

The two other factions were supporters of Chadwick, Duke of Ran; and Montgomery, Earl of Rillanon and Lord James's first counselor, also Hal's distant cousin. Neither could counter Oliver's claim, but together they could confound the Prince of Simrick's attempt to take the throne.

Lord James sighed, looking his eighty-plus years of age. "If the Keshians decide to abandon the truce and sail into any port in the Kingdom save this one, they'd have nothing but a few fishing smacks and rowing boats to oppose them."

Hal was forced to appreciate the old Duke's observation. Every warship in the royal fleet on the Kingdom Sea was in the harbor, most of the heavy ships armed with ballista and small catapults had their weapons trained on Oliver's army, while beyond was every city's ducal squadron, and other ships flying the banners of noble houses. Many of those ships were contracted, "privateers" barely more than pirates paid by various coastal nobles to create small zones of control in their coastal waters to extort fees from passing merchantmen. That practice over the years had created the need for the deep-water ships now employed by the navies of the Kingdom and Roldem, as well as the major trading houses in both nations. No matter how often the Crown had warned the local nobles that this practice was frowned upon, they persisted.

Hal said, "I trust Oliver brought a lot of gold with him, for he will be paying a great deal for those cutthroats he's hired to leave without sacking the city for booty."

Lord James grunted in agreement. "If Edward's bunch were here . . ." He let the thought go unfinished. Either Oliver would leave with his tail between his legs, or be forced to attack with the Prince of Krondor in residence in Rillanon. Had Edward been in the city, the chance of his being elected King as a compromise became too high for Oliver to wait. Edward had no children of his own, nor was he likely to, but he could name the heir and, after things had calmed down, abdicate, and Oliver knew he had no chance of the Crown if Edward named anyone else as heir.

Edward and the western lords had ridden from Krondor for the Congress, but once word reached them of Oliver's landing on the Isle of Rillanon, they had halted, and were now encamped between Malac's Cross and Salador. Martin and Brendan had elected to leave Prince Edward's army and continue to the capital, to learn Hal's fate. Hal was grateful to have them at hand.

Martin and Brendan were housed in an inn not too far from the palace and had arrived in time for Lord James's calling his grandson and the brothers to this garden. Silence fell as the old Duke was lost in thought as he studied the arriving warships, and Hal recalled his reunion with his brothers.

After they'd commiserated together for the first time over their father's death, talk between the brothers had turned to their various adventures, from Martin's defense of Crydee and Ylith to Hal's escorting the Princess to safety. The reunion had been short and bittersweet, for as relieved as Hal was to discover that their mother was alive and well, being cared for by the elves in Elvandar, hearing Brendan's narration of their father's death was hard for him, and despite his best efforts, he found tears running down his cheeks by the time Brendan finished. Martin had heard the story before, but his eyes shone with wetness as he watched his brother endure the tale. Hal embraced his brothers for a long moment, then promised that when they could, the three brothers would gather for a quiet meal to honor their father, if fate permitted, in their family's hall in Crydee.

Hal then suffered through an awkward few moments as Martin stood before him professing his love for Lady Bethany of Carse, who returned his affection, and got halfway through a painful pleading of his cause, coupled with a declaration that he was willing to sacrifice it all for the good of the duchy and the Kingdom should Hal insist on marrying Bethany. Hal finally let his love for his younger brother win over the temptation to torment him, and said that he had no problem with Martin marrying Bethany should her father, Earl Robert of Carse, not object. The relief on Martin's face was almost comic.

Hal did not tell Martin that his heart belonged to another anyway, a woman whom he could never aspire to wed. He just wryly observed that Martin and Bethany were a perfect match, because she did so well those things that Martin lacked skill at, like archery, hunting, and riding. Martin endured the teasing in good humor, being overwhelmed with relief and gratitude at his brother's reaction to the news. He had left Hal muttering about how he was going to ask Beth's father for her hand. Her father had been furious with Martin when he discovered Bethany hadn't left for Elvandar with the other women, but had remained in Crydee to fight. He seemed to ignore his daughter's part in all of it, and focused his wrath on Martin.

Now Hal and his brothers stood on the rooftop of the palace, contemplating the next move in this game of kingship. Jim said, "Everyone's getting ready for this party. My agents in Salador tell me there's no shortage of garrisons from the west gathered on the Fields of Albalyn." Those fields lay between Malac's Cross and Salador, and were historically vital for any military conflict in the region. They were athwart the King's Highway and no other clear passage to the town that marked the boundary between the Eastern and Western Realms was available.

"Why would the western lords bring their garrisons?" asked Hal.

Lord James fixed the young Duke of Crydee with an expression that was a mix of amusement and pity. He nodded once to Jim, who said, "In case there's a war. Edward ordered the garrisons to accompany him rather than return home after the truce with Kesh." He let out a long sigh as stress overtook his usual calm. "Edward's many things, but a political fool is not one of them. It may be we need elect kings who have no wish to rule, for Edward would be a near-perfect monarch under which to reforge this cracked kingdom of ours."

Hal leaned against the balustrade, his knuckles slowly turning white as he gripped harder and harder. "Wasn't the last war enough for a while?" he said slowly.

Jim glanced at his grandfather, who nodded once, then motioned for the others to leave Jim and Hal alone. When they were alone, Jim said, "You really don't understand, do you?"

Hal felt tired to his bones. Without Stephané he felt empty. She was now safely in her father's palace on Roldem, once order had been restored in Roldem, and the three conspirators behind the war had been uncovered and removed.

Quietly he said, "I know that I'm a duke without a duchy, that the title came to me far too many years too soon, and my mother is far enough away I may not live to see her again. I know I spent most of the war hiding and fleeing, rather than leading men into battle, and I feel a lesser man for it." Jim seemed on the verge of objecting, but Hal shook his head. "I know I served, and I would give my life for the Princess and for the Kingdom, and I took men's lives to do it." He was silent for a moment. "Yet it all feels pointless . . . now." He had been about to say "without Stephané," but he knew that sounded like a whiny complaint. Besides, if anyone knew how he felt about her, it was Jim. "So now you have something I need to hear," Hal continued, "because men of ambition wish to rule, and men of character seem significantly absent. And I suspect that you are also about to tell me what I need to do."

Jim was also quiet for a moment, then said, "You're not a stupid man, Hal. You're of the blood royal—" He held up his hand to cut off the young noble. "Spare me the oft-repeated history of your ancestor's pledge to absent his line from succession. It was a pretty speech: I've read the transcript of the entire ceremony that put Lyam on the throne and it was vital then to prevent just the sort of mess that's happening now, but there is no legal justification for it. I've asked both the court historians and the priests of Ishap, and there is no precedent that permits the renunciation of that blood tie. Martin was free to not claim his cousin Rodric's Crown, but he could not bind unborn heirs to such a burden. You *are* of royal blood.

"Had your ancestor Martin rejected his brother's giving him the title to Crydee, and your father and his father before back to Lord Martin all remained commoners, perhaps. That would have set a precedent. But he accepted and held the title and passed it along." He shrugged.

"Are you saying I should put myself forward for King?"

"Hardly, but I'm trying to stress to you that you are not simply a rustic noble without lands to rule, but rather a player with coins in the game."

"This is why it is taking Prince Edward such a very long time in getting here? Not just because Oliver's landed his army?"

"Edward wishes to be King less than any prince in the history of the Kingdom, but he's being hard-pressed by the western nobles to claim the Crown."

"Why?" asked Hal.

"It's as my grandfather said. It would consolidate the Western Realm's authority and strip supporters away from Chadwick and Montgomery, perhaps forcing them to broker a deal." Jim ran his hand over his face and Hal saw that deep fatigue had taken its toll on the Duke's grandson. "At worst it holds off a war awhile longer; at best it gives a legitimate hope to avoid bloodshed if Chadwick and Montgomery throw their weight behind Edward. With those three combined, even Oliver's not ambitious enough to risk destroying his twin duchies in a futile attempt to seize the Crown without backing. But there are a lot of 'ifs' here. And it begins only if Edward can be convinced to take the Crown."

Jim smiled and some of the vigor Hal had taken for granted since first meeting him returned. "Edward has no sons, but he has three daughters, married to eastern nobles who could never return to their marriage beds if they didn't support their wives' father for the throne. It was one of Gregory's wiser moves selecting an eastern noble to rule Krondor after the previous disasters. Those three nobles have vassals and allies who will follow them. No one of power would then support Oliver once the move to Edward began. So Edward is the perfect compromise candidate."

"What does this have to do with me? I'm a duchyless duke, now that Crydee is occupied by the Empire of Great Kesh."

"You're still a duke," said Jim, "and you're related to the Crown by blood. Your support of Edward is vital. It will also keep you from being a false banner behind which others might rally to broker better terms for their interests. Not everyone who was trying to find you was an agent of those mad demon servants who were thrusting us into war. There are a few eastern nobles who would love to install you as a guest in their castles until you came to support Oliver, Chadwick, or Montgomery. If Crydee supported their candidate, others in the West might consider it prudent to follow suit."

"Father warned me eastern politics was something to be feared as much as war," said Hal.

"Smart man, your father."

Hal said nothing, still hurting inside every time he found himself asking what his father would have done in his place.

"We need to be in Salador sooner rather than later," said Jim.

"Why? Can't I merely announce my support of Edward, then be on my way? I want to travel to Elvandar and find my mother."

"She is safely cared for. Nothing short of a global disaster would put her at risk in Aglaranna and Tomas's court. No, that will have to wait until the situation here is resolved. And to support Edward, you need to journey to his side."

"Why does he wait?" asked Hal.

"He rests his forces on the Fields of Albalyn, preparing the ground for battle. He hopes for the best but is getting ready for the worst. Edward is neither a warrior nor a tactician, but he surrounds himself with the best in the west. Vanderal of Yabon is the Western Realm's best commander given the loss of your father. Fredrick of Tyr-Sog is as fine a cavalry commander as you'll see. If Oliver seeks to answer this question with arms, Edward prefers a battleground of his own choosing. Oliver knows he cannot sit on this island if Edward will not come to him." Jim smiled. "If he seizes the capital but the Congress does not confirm him as King, that makes him a usurper, nothing more. Edward would control the mainland and Oliver would sit here until he rots or runs out of food. The few farms on the island and all the fishermen here will not sustain that host for long. And he'll run out of gold: he has an army only as long as he can pay it.

"And if Edward will not come to Oliver," he continued, "Oliver must go to Edward, and that will be on the Fields of Albalyn. Edward has soldiers; he needs officers. You and your brothers need to be on your way westward as soon as we put some things here in order."

"Going to help Edward?" asked Hal. "And am I safe in assuming people may not wish me to do so?"

"A fair assumption," said Jim. "I'll have men travel with you, and I'd like you to take Ty Hawkins with you, too. He's a smart lad and may prove handy. I've spoken to Ty and Tal, and they're willing."

"Willing?"

"To prevent war, if possible; to end it as quickly as possible, if not."

Hal crossed his arms and leaned back against the stone

balustrade. "Ty's a good friend and the best swordsman I've ever seen. He's no burden."

"Good. His patent of Kingdom nobility is a forgery."

Hal's eyes widened slightly.

"But it's a very good one, created by the best forger my predecessor could buy."

"Predecessor?"

Jim pointed off in the direction his grandfather had taken. "The Duke?"

"Few know the truth about my family, and how our connections wend their way past rank, class, even nationality," said Jim. "It seems to be an every-other-generation sort of thing, really. The first Lord James . . ." Jim got a far-off look in his eyes and he turned to stare out at the gathering fleet. "Did you know he was a thief, just a boy, yet an accomplished rogue by any measure, who was raised by Prince Arutha to become first his squire, but eventually became Duke of Krondor and was then sent off with the Prince's son, King Borric, to rule the nation as Duke of Rillanon?"

"No," said Hal. "Most of the history I do know is from books in my father's library." He laughed bitterly. "Ashes now, I expect." He looked at Jim. "Every other generation?"

"My great-grandfather, named for Prince Arutha, was by all reports an honorable man, resolute and fearless, but by nature much more of an administrator than any sort of blackguard. You really do need to be something of a scoundrel to do what we do, we Jamisons."

When Jim let out a deep sigh, Hal could feel the fatigue in the older man's bones. "You could use a spot of rest."

"I could spend what remains of my life resting," said Jim. "But that may not come, should Oliver and his friends below take matters in hand. My great-grandfather had a brother a year younger than himself, by the name of Dashel Jamison. He rejected rank and office: some say because he was by nature a very mean-spirited bastard, but we in the family know he did it to honor a pledge to a woman he loved." Jim's expression hovered halfway between fond remembrance and regret. A slight smile moved his lips for a brief instant, then he said, "Men do very foolish things for love, don't they?"

Hal thought of Stephané and felt his heart turn to lead. "Yes," he agreed, "we do."

"Dash, as my great-uncle was known, became a business-man of some stature and wealth in Krondor, but what was known by few was that he was also the leader of a large gang of thieves known as the Mockers. He bore the title of the Upright Man."

Hal said, "Those names I know. The legend of the Upright Man and the Mockers reaches out to the Far Coast."

"His son Dasher, whose name I bear, belonged to an-other of those generations that was skipped when it came to bloody work. He almost lost control of the Mockers. And as he had no sons, as his nephew, I had to step in and act on behalf of the family."

"So, you're the Upright Man of Krondor?"

"Until recently. I've placed another in that position to assume my responsibilities. What turned out to be the same in my great-great-grandfather, the first Lord James's, time is true today: a gang of thieves can be very handy in the world of spying."

"Why are you telling me all this?" asked Hal.

Jim shrugged. "I'm not certain I know." He continued to gaze out over the sea. "I've spent half my life here and half in Krondor and half all over the world."

Hal chuckled. "That's three halves."

Jim didn't smile. "I know. That's how it feels." He was silent for a moment, then said, "Why am I telling you any-thing? You're important, Hal. Maybe not in ways that are clear, but there are things in motion, undertakings by men of ambition and power, and the best I can pray for is we somehow get Edward on the throne. If that happens, from that moment forward his life will be at risk every minute of every day."

"Treason?"

Jim nodded. "Slip something into Edward's wine, or have

him fall from his horse, before a clear line of succession can be achieved, and Oliver is back out there with his army within a week, and Chadwick and Montgomery are back inside the palace bargaining with anyone who will promise a vote in the Congress of Lords."

"What has that to do with me?"

"As you've observed more than once, young Hal, you are a duke without a duchy. Oh, Edward will eventually wrest it back from Kesh, for they have no real use for the Far Coast, and you can go back and try to govern, though with a population of fractious refugees from the Keshian Confederates now herding, farming, and mining your duchy. But that may prove more of a challenge than herding cats. Send one of your brothers and as much of a garrison as you can scrape together, and go very light on taxes, and in a generation or so you'll have something resembling organization in the region. I'll try to have Edward forgo Crown taxes for a while so you can feed your brother's little army."

"Martin's little army? Shouldn't it be my little army?"

"No, you need to stay close to Edward."

"Why? He's got your grandfather and you, and there must be others loyal to the Crown, no matter who wears it."

"There are, but my grandfather may not be here much longer. It's hard to know in my family; as often as not, we conspire to get ourselves killed before we meet a quiet death in bed. And I . . ." Jim closed his eyes for a moment. "I am used up. The burden of trying to live up to a family legend that grows with each passing generation, I guess. Truth to tell, I do not know how talented the original Lord James was. By any objective measure he was a genius, but was he the genius portrayed in the histories?

"My burden, my flaw of character, is to match myself against him. As a child, when my father couldn't hear, I'd call myself 'Jimmyhand' because I could never remember the 'the.'" He leaned forward, both hands on the balustrade, and took a deep breath. "Oceans smell different, you know?"

Hal nodded. "Far Coast is . . . damp; the wind comes

from the west constantly and we get that salt-and-fish smell. Here . . ."

Jim laughed. "A lot of flowers in these gardens."

Hal laughed with him. "But down in the city it's still sweet."

"Which one is better?"

Hal thought. "This one, but not here."

"Roldem?"

Hal stayed silent.

Jim put his hand on Hal's shoulder. "There's someone in Roldem I miss as well."

"Lady Franciezka?"

Jim nodded.

"A remarkable woman," said Hal. He and Ty had sheltered for a while under the lady's protection as they got ready to smuggle Princess Stephané out of Roldem and away from a forced marriage. "What is this all going to come to?" he wondered.

Jim said, "If we play our part, we shall gather on the Fields of Albalyn soon, where a truce can be forged that will permit Edward to enter this city safely, and he can be acclaimed by the Congress of Lords as King. And then we can set about restoring order in the Kingdom. And that's what you need to concern yourself with, my lord Duke of Crydee. There are few men of rank in this nation I would hand a sword and ask them to stand behind the King, but you are one of them. If Edward survives more than a few months before someone decides his rule has lasted too long, then we may look to the future." Jim lowered his head.

"There's something else? What?"

"Everything," answered Jim. "Those three murderous creatures that plunged us into wholesale war with Kesh had but one ambition: to create chaos, and in that they succeeded in grand fashion. In all things in this life, magic gives me the most to fear, for you need other magic to battle it. We've long allied ourselves with people who seem to be of good heart and intent, but I . . ."

"You hate leaving things to others," finished Hal.

"Yes," admitted Jim. "It is a flaw of character, and probably why I'm so sick at heart and worn out by all this; I would wager there's no man alive who has traveled more between Krondor, Rillanon, and Roldem than me." He released his hold on the balustrade. "We have more to discuss, but some other time. I could do with a meal before tackling the more prickly matter of politics. Join me?"

"Certainly? Can my brothers come as well?"

"Of course. There's much we need to keep between ourselves, but there are many things it would do well for all the conDoin brothers to know."

Hal smiled.

Jim put his hand on Hal's shoulder and lowered his voice. "You realize that you are the only three males left alive who bear that name." He conveniently neglected to include the magician Pug, who was a conDoin by adoption, but who had renounced his allegiance to the Kingdom years before.

Hal said, "I hadn't thought of it that way."

"For reasons that will become clear, I am having the officials in the court refer to you as Duke Henry, but your brothers will henceforth be called Princes Martin and Brendan. I want these conniving nobles to be reminded of just who you are."

Hal said nothing, but as he and Jim entered the palace, he wondered, *But who are we?*

It was a somber meal despite repeated attempts on the part of Duke James to liven the mood with a series of humorous anecdotes and stories. People would chuckle at the appropriate moments, smile and nod, then fall back into silence. Finally, as the meal drew to an end, silence engulfed the room.

The three brothers from the Far Coast were seated at the table with Lord James, Jim, and several of the Duke's closest advisers, various ladies of the court, and attendants. The other addition to the table was Ty Hawkins, son of Talwin Hawkins, a former tribesman from the mountains called the High Fastness in the Eastern Kingdoms. History and circumstance had propelled young Talon of the Silver Hawk into the cauldron that was international politics and he had emerged a man of many identities.

As had his son. Ty Hawkins, son of Eye of the Blue-winged Teal and a nameless soldier of Olasko, adopted by Tal and loved as his own, was by nature and training his father's son. By an odd quirk of circumstance he resembled his adopted father, with vivid blue eyes and a lithe frame and whipcord strength like Tal. The most striking difference was his sandy-blond hair, contrasting with his father's near black. But like many boys, he had adopted so many of his father's mannerisms and expressions. At times it was impossible to remember Tal was not his true father.

Jim watched Ty in conversation with Hal and found it ironic that the man he most trusted to protect the royal cousin was not even a true citizen of the Kingdom. Still, both father and son had provided valuable service to the Kingdom, Roldem, and occasionally the Conclave of Shadows.

It was the Duke who spoke loud enough for the entire table to hear clearly. "If I may . . ." Everyone fell silent. He looked around the table and said, "It dawns on me that with the exception of young Hawkins here, our families are intimately linked, while we are still relative strangers to one another." He raised his goblet of wine in the direction of the three brothers. "You three are the last of the con-Doin line. While others have royal blood, only you three carry the name. My grandson and I descend from a name far less noble—Jamison—founded by a rogue and scoundrel, raised up to nobility by your many-greats-uncle. Both put two things above all else: duty and honor. Let us drink to their memory. Prince Arutha conDoin and James—the only man in history to be both Duke of Krondor and Rillanon: Jimmy the Hand!"

They drank and then the Duke said, "This may be the end

of us all, but not of the Kingdom, if I have a damn thing to say about it."

Ty nodded and shouted, "Hear! Hear!"

Hal looked at the old Duke, glanced at his grandson, then simply asked, "What would you have us do?"

"Many things, young Hal," said Lord James. "Eventually you'll need to get married and father some sons, so that your name will continue. And perhaps one of them will rule here one day." He held up his hand. "And, one last time, Hal: no more mention of Lord Martin's foolish, if noble, claim. It has no validity. And you need to retake your duchy. The Far Coast may be in chaos but it is still King's land. As I told you on the day of Gregory's funeral, you need to find an ally, either Chadwick or Montgomery, and convince him of your loyalty to his cause in exchange for his loyalty to yours, the retaking of Crydee." James paused. "You'll be lying, of course, because since that day that Crydee was lost so much has changed." He glanced at a window, and everyone in the room knew he was speaking of Oliver's army camped beyond the city. They had expected Prince Oliver to arrive with a retinue to press his claim, not an army. That changed everything.

As if reading their collective minds, James added, "And you must ensure that somehow Edward is crowned here, not that snake Oliver. We may have to persuade Edward to put himself forward as King, rather than backing Chadwick or Montgomery." He pointed at Hal. "You may be the deciding factor if he knows the fate of the Far Coast, and probably much of Yabon, rests on this. You may very well be the one to tip the balance and save this nation."

He sat back and sighed. "But to do any of that, you must, of course, stay alive."

Jim nodded. "I'll see that he does, Grandfather."

Duke James put down his goblet and stood up. "Then I'll bid you a good night and advise you this: outside this room there are few you can trust. Ensure you take wise counsel and be cautious of honeyed words laced with poison." He nodded to the brothers and Ty, then left the room.

As if by silent instruction, the other guests rose and one by one bid Hal, his brothers, and Jim good night. When the last was gone, only those five and the servants remained.

Jim looked around. "Another drink?"

No one objected, so the servants filled their goblets, and they partook of a particularly good wine, but the mood in the room could hardly be called festive.

Jim waved for the servants to depart. When they had gone, he said, "Ty knows what I'm about to share with you three." He glanced from face to face. "I am a loyal servant of the Crown, but I also work with the Conclave of Shadows, and you'd never heard of them until Ruffio told you of them for a reason. What I know, what I'm telling you, is because my loyalty, and yours at the moment, must extend beyond the borders of our nation. I tell you this because I trust the woman in charge of Roldem's intelligence apparatus more at this moment than half the nobles in our Congress of Lords. I trust a few Keshians as well. But mostly I trust the dedication of the Conclave to the preservation of our entire world.

"The recent conflict with Kesh was pointless."

Martin seemed to be on the verge of speaking, but thought better of it.

"It's easy to get caught up in events without considering real causes. Kesh and the Kingdom had been a peace for a very long time, since a misguided adventure when they sought to take control of Krondor after the invasion of the Emerald Queen's army. Since then there's been the usual poking around in the Vale of Dreams and the occasional ship battle when one captain got a little too ambitious. But today we have half the Keshian army spread out along the Far Coast and mustered along their northern border to protect against a Kingdom retaliation; the Kingdom army either here on Rillanon protecting this very palace, in Salador, or mustered on the Fields of Albalyn; most of the Kingdom fleet surrounding this island; the Keshian fleet at the bottom of the ocean; and Roldem's fleet in a defensive position around their island. What do you think that means?"

Martin said, "That we went through a pointless exercise?"

Jim nodded. "Yes. What else?"

It was Brendan who answered. "No one is where they're supposed to be."

"Exactly."

Hal said, "So if another threat materializes, no one is in the correct position to deal with it."

Martin calculated, then said, "The West."

Jim nodded. "Yes."

"I need to get back to Crydee!" said Hal.

"No," said Jim. "You need to stay here until my grandfather tells you to go somewhere else. Most likely to Prince Edward." He looked at Martin and Brendan. "You must return to Ylith and explain to the Keshian commander that he's in the way and you need to go poking around. My intelligence tells me you've got a reasonable chance to have him agree for the right bribe—he is Keshian, after all—as long as you only go with a small patrol. If he doesn't, you need to find a clever way to get around his objections without starting another war out there. Sneaking past his line should prove little trouble to a couple of bright lads like you.

"But you need to get into the Far Coast, north of the garrisons at Carse and Tulan, so my best guess is somewhere near the Taredhel and that city they're building, perhaps near the dwarves."

"Who?" asked Brendan. "Besides Keshian Dog Soldiers and elves and dwarves, who would be there?"

"I don't know," said Jim. "That's what I need your brother and you to find out."

The brothers spent a long night with Jim Dasher discussing as much of the political situation with Great Kesh as could be extrapolated from what Martin and Brendan had seen during the defense of the city and after. They matched what they had seen with reports from the West that had reached the King's court, which in this case meant Jim Dasher's personal attention.

The long and short of it was that it was a mess. Kesh had withdrawn to the ancient borders of Bosania, so a few miles of road to the west of the city of Ylith was open to the crest of the foothills of the Grey Tower Mountains, as well as the southwest highway, leading to the Free Cities, which were still currently occupied by Kesh.

By the time they were finished examining all their options and what needed to be done, the sun was rising in the east. Martin was convinced Jim Dasher was perhaps the cleverest man he had ever met, or at least the most cunning. And Martin was also convinced that Jim was correct: the entire war with Kesh and the plot behind it was designed to put both the Kingdom of the Isles and the Empire of Great Kesh at a military disadvantage in the Far West.

No military action of any kind could quickly be mounted should a threat arise in the Duchy of Crydee or the Free Cities, or the Grey Tower Mountains. It might take days, or even weeks, for news of any outbreak of trouble in the West to reach Prince Edward on the Fields of Albalyn, and if he instantly dispatched some of the western lords' commands to answer, it would be weeks before they reached any site of trouble. And that was dependent on being able to spare men with the possibility of a military confrontation with Prince Oliver looming. By sunrise, Jim and the brothers were convinced the Far Coast and the Western Realm were as defenseless as a day-old kitten.

Martin was a student of history and it didn't take him more than an hour of looking at suggested Keshian deployment in the Far Coast and Free Cities to come to the same conclusion as Jim. The safest location from any counterattacks from the combined armies of the Kingdom of the Isles and the Empire of Great Kesh that wasn't on the bottom of some ocean or one of the moons was in the center of the Grey Tower Mountains; very close to the site of the original Tsurani rift into Midkemia.

As the cock crowed in the distance, the three looked at the now-empty carafe of coffee and wordlessly exchanged the shared opinion they had reached a conclusion. "The Grey Towers," said Martin. "Neither Kesh nor the Kingdom nor the Free Cities can answer the kind of threat the Tsurani posed when they arrived . . ."

"Where the Star Elves are building their city," continued Brendan.

Jim rose. "Well, the sun's up and we've beaten this topic to death. It's time to move and I think we'd best be getting on with it. It's still before dawn in Krondor so you"—he indicated Martin and Brendan—"can still be leaving there at sunrise, once we get you there." To Hal he said, "You need some rest. You're going to have to withstand a lot of charm, guile, and bald-faced lies before we're done, but I'll be at your side most of the time and your best course of action is to nod and say you'll consider what's been suggested. Edward's enemies are not all on the field under arms. There are a lot of poisoned tongues still in the palace."

Hal embraced his brothers and bade them a safe journey.

Jim took Martin and Brendan with him through a palace that was never truly asleep, as servants scurried to ensure that every resident's needs were met before dawn.

Reaching Jim's personal quarters, they entered a tidy office adjacent to his sleeping room and Jim quickly set about penning a travel document. He signed it with a flourish, poured wax, and applied a seal to it.

"Isn't that the Duke's signet?" asked Brendan.

"It's a twin," said Jim. "My grandfather gave it to me to reduce his own need to sign things; he finds it annoying."

"And did you just sign his name?" said Martin.

"Of course," said Jim as if this was quite normal. "Wait here."

A short time later, he returned with a woman of middle years, with graying dark hair and a no-nonsense demeanor. "This is Gretchen. She will take you where you need to go."

Before Martin or Brendan could speak, Gretchen reached out and seized their wrists and suddenly they were in a different room. "Krondor," she said, and vanished.

Apparently the comings and goings of magicians in what was revealed as Jim Dasher's private suite in Krondor was commonplace enough that the palace guards did not react when two men unexpectedly walked out of a room that had been empty only moments before.

The brothers had been in Krondor twice: a leisurely visit to Prince Edward's court when Martin had been small (Brendan was still a baby) and their hurried visit on the way to Rillanon just weeks before.

"What now?" said Brendan.

Martin shrugged. "Find someone in charge, I suppose."

It took the better part of an hour to find the acting city commander, a man named Falston Jennings, hastily elevated from the rank of prince's squire to Baronet of the Court so that he could lawfully be considered a noble. He was obviously in over his head and anxious to see if what he said made sense to the brothers from Crydee, especially as they had introduced themselves as "Princes Martin and Brendan, the late King's cousins."

They had endured Jennings's near-babbling conversation over as informal a breakfast meal as the palace had likely seen in a century, for many of the key servants had traveled east with Prince Edward, attending his baggage train and pavilion to ensure his comfort on the journey to Rillanon.

Martin left that meal with a jumble of facts he could barely make sense of, let alone organize into coherent intelligence. Brendan had been amused by the entire course of events, but of the three brothers he was the one most easily amused.

From what they could get from Jennings's ramble, Kesh had withdrawn her ships to a point behind an imaginary line extending from a point halfway between Land's End and Durbin in the south to the border between the Free Cities and the Kingdom in the north. Kingdom ships were given free passage up to Sarth, but no captain dared sail farther north, as the island kingdom of Queg had declared a state of emergency—a pretext for them to board and seize any ship that sailed "too close" to their imagined "sphere of influence," which at the moment meant from their beach to ankle-deep water on the Kingdom shore north of Sarth.

The Free Cities were essentially Keshian garrisons at the moment, and no ship had arrived from there since the truce had been declared. Also, no Free Cities ship in Krondor or Port Vykor was willing to attempt a run home, as their captains had no idea what to expect from their new masters. In sum, three fleets choked the waterways of the Bitter Sea, all ready for a fight at a moment's notice, so Martin's only recourse had been horseback.

After their hasty meal, Jennings led Martin and Brendan to the marshaling yard, where a patrol of Krondorian regulars waited. "Sergeant Oaks," said Jennings, "this is Prince Martin, the late King's cousin."

Oaks nodded a greeting and then Martin said, "My brother Brendan."

"Highness," said Oaks in greeting.

"I think it better to have some proven soldiers rather than a pretty palace guard," said Jennings. "Sergeant, the princes need an escort to Ylith. Please see they arrive there without difficulties." He beat a hasty retreat, obviously relieved to see the brothers depart.

"Without difficulties?" said Oaks in a neutral tone.

"I think he means alive," said Brendan with a grin.

Oaks returned the smile. "We'll do our best, Highness." He turned to his company of riders and shouted, "Mount up!"

The twenty soldiers of Oaks's patrol mounted in orderly fashion, obviously a battle-trained company.

"Well," said Brendan, "at least we don't have to walk."

"There is that," said Martin. He signaled for the sergeant to lead the company out of the palace yard in Krondor and toward the northern gate, which would put them on the King's Highway to Ylith.

3

JOURNEY I

Pug tumbled across the ground.

Quickly coming to his feet, he stood ready to answer any threat that might be awaiting him. The passage through the vortex had been a new experience, something that was almost welcome, given his age.

It had been like sliding through a tunnel that was slippery but not wet, with cascading lights and colors on all sides. He had been neither warm nor cold. If anything, there had been an absence of tactile sensation. Time also seemed suspended, so he couldn't judge if he had been moving through the vortex for seconds, minutes, or hours.

He shook his head to clear it and glanced around. He was in what appeared to be an alpine forest, at the edge of a meadow. Above him, the sides of a mountain reared up, so he judged he was at the highest point of foothills he would likely traverse without magic. Looking beyond the meadow, he made out a range of mountains receding away. He glanced at the position of the sun in the sky and judged that was south.

He attempted a minor spell to see what conditions he would encounter and discovered the energy state was still not quite what he would expect as "normal" on Midkemia. He was somewhere else and apparently alone. He closed his eyes and attempted to reach out to the demon Child, in her Miranda form, and Magnus, as he had always been able to contact his wife and son that way.

Silence.

He waited in case they might be longer in reaching this planet than he had been. Nothing occurred for long moments until Pug was certain within himself he was alone, his companions elsewhere, perhaps even on different worlds.

He took a deep breath, gauged the downhill slope, and began walking.

He made his way slowly down to the floor of the meadow. By any measure this was one of the most peaceful and lovely spots he had visited in a very long time. The air was not quite still, a breath of something not quite a breeze stirred the leaves in the trees, and birds called out infrequently. A distant crack, perhaps a tree branch falling, was followed soon after by a bellowing challenge as some animal, perhaps something staglike, demanded others honor his territory.

Pug took a deep breath. A hint of fragrance told him that flowers were blooming wherever he was; it was surely spring.

He chose not to use his magic to transport himself to the other side of the meadow, preferring to wring whatever peace he could from this moment. He knew that conflict was only a matter of time and this tiny bit of tranquillity might be his last.

As he walked across the meadow, he saw a tiny tendril of smoke rising from the trees below. Reaching the edge of the meadow, he found a steep downslope leading to a flatter terrain a hundred feet down. What looked like a game trail presented itself nearby and he followed that to what looked to be an old cart path. He followed that in the general direction of the smoke until another, smaller clearing appeared, and when he saw the source of the smoke, he stopped.

The cottage was identical to the one his mentor, Kulgan, occupied in the woods near Castle Crydee, when he wanted to be alone to contemplate, study, or just enjoy a little solitude with his companion Meecham.

Pug found strong emotions rising, for he was certain this was another accommodation to his senses, that the structure he observed was somewhat like the cottage he remembered, and these woods were somewhat like the Green Heart and Forest of Crydee, but that his mind was allowed to manipulate them a little to put him more at ease.

Part of Pug's mind was captivated by the subtle, nuanced quality to this type of magic, and again he realized that conjuration and illusion were two areas of magic he had always intended to study more, but never seemed to find the time for it.

He closed his eyes for a moment, used an old calming-of-the-mind exercise he'd learned as a Tsurani Great One, used his skills to dispel illusions, then opened his eyes.

Nothing had changed.

He chuckled. Apparently the mind wants what it wants; no matter how much you think you're controlling it, it's controlling you. He knew he'd put that in a lesson to young magicians some years before, but had thought he was beyond it. He reminded himself ruefully of the last time he had blindly assumed he knew what he was doing, when he had attacked the demon Jakan and almost died as a result.

That memory triggered the one following, where he had been forced to make a choice by Lims-Kragma, the Goddess of Death, that he would suffer through the deaths of everyone he loved as a price for returning to the land of the living and ending the threat from the Emerald Queen's invading army.

His mood no longer lifted by the pastoral beauty around him, he gave in to a moment of pique and willed himself to the threshold of the cottage. Raising his hand, he knocked three times.

A familiar voice he had not heard in ages but recognized instantly said, "Come in."

Pug could hardly believe his senses as he pushed open the door and immediately recognized the pungent aroma of tabac, a particular blend of mountain-grown aromatic from the foothills of Kesh. A portly figure in a gray home-spun robe sat before a table upon which rested an open book. Blue eyes seemed to twinkle above a thick gray beard. "Well, you haven't changed much in all these years, have you, Pug?"

"Kulgan," Pug whispered. Something told him this was no magic likeness before him, no creature of the mind fashioned to resemble someone he trusted, but somehow his old teacher, dead for more than a century, returned to this little cottage in the woods that so resembled where they had first met.

Emotions long absent rushed up within Pug and his eyes welled up. A lifetime of the impossible had not prepared him for this, seeing again his first master, the man who had taken an orphaned kitchen boy and begun the education that had allowed Pug to evolve into the most powerful practitioner of magic on two worlds.

Smiling, the old man rose and indicated a pot of water on an iron hook overhanging the fireplace. "Fetch that while I get us some tea." As he moved away, he added, "We have a great deal to discuss, my old friend, and, I'm sorry to say, little time in which to discuss it."

Pug stood rooted for a moment as he struggled with the urge to rush and embrace his boyhood teacher, or start asking questions. Then he smiled, nodded, and just did as he had been asked.

Kulgan chuckled as he put the tea to steep. "I take it you are as surprised as I am," he began, glancing over his shoulder at his former pupil.

"A great deal has occurred since . . ."

"I died," supplied Kulgan. "Yes, exactly how long has it been?"

"Over a century," said Pug.

"Hmm," mused the teacher. "So, continue."

Pug took a moment to breathe deeply. "I need help," he said at last.

"Ah," said Kulgan.

The cottage was not exactly as Pug remembered it, but he was at a loss to know if that was due to an imperfect replication or his own faulty memory. He asked, "Where are we? This is not your cottage in the woods south of the keep at Crydee."

Kulgan shrugged. "I'm not certain. For here's the thing, Pug: my last memory is lying sick abed in Stardock, Meecham hovering like a mother hen as he always did, having said my good-bye to you. Age weighed heavily on my soul and I was tired to the core of my being. Your generosity with the healing priests was appreciated: I was free of pain, but I knew my time had come." He paused, a bemused expression crossing his wrinkled old visage. "I closed my eyes, then this odd thing . . . As I was drifting into darkness there was this momentary . . ." He shrugged again. "I am not sure how to describe it, but a cut, as cold as the coldest ice or stone, slicing through my being, then suddenly it was gone, the pain vanishing before it registered, but so vivid that in the fading of life, it was my first recollection as, instead of arising in the halls of Lims-Kragma, I found myself there." He pointed to the oversize bed in the corner of the room. "Apparently three or four hours ago."

He picked up the pot and poured Pug's tea and his own, then indicated with a wave a small pot of honey. Pug shook his head, and Kulgan went on. "I felt wonderful. There is no looking glass, but I suspect I am now a great deal younger than when I died." He laughed. "It is an odd thing to say, isn't it? My favorite robe was folded at the foot of the bed." He plucked at the fabric. "My sandals, my staff, too. After I had dressed, I wandered about a little, trying to determine where I was and shouted, but no one answered." He sat down opposite Pug and said, "When I returned I found a lovely meal to break my fast and must admit to relishing every bite." He pointed to a small washbasin of stone next to the stove. A tidy pile of dishes rested within. "I have no idea who prepared it for me. I had a faint hope it might have been my man Meecham, but I knew by then this was not Crydee. This is not Midkemia, is it?"

Pug shook his head.

Sighing, Kulgan said, "I really knew that. I feel too good, Pug. I don't mean relative to my dying or even the last few years of life. I feel invigorated here in a way I haven't since years before I met you, and while I've resisted the temptation to use any of my arts, I suspect they will prove effective beyond my expectation."

Pug smiled. Kulgan had had as quick an intuitive grasp of the underlying nature of magic as any being he had ever known. "There's a heightened energy state in this world. We are in a different realm of magic, I think, from Midkemia. I suspect if you tried that trick of lighting your tabac pipe with a flame from your finger, you might burn this cottage down."

Kulgan laughed and Pug was suddenly struck by how much he had missed that sound. A bittersweet pang followed that recognition, for as certain as Pug was about anything else, he knew this visit with his old mentor would be brief. He said, his voice heavy with emotion, "I have lost so many beloved friends, and you were first among them. It's so good to see you again."

Kulgan's blue eyes misted. He reached out and took Pug's hand for a moment. "I suppose a summary of the past hundred years is impossible."

Pug laughed.

"So, perhaps if there's time later, we might speak of what

happened after I died. Though waking up here and finding you . . ." He peered at Pug for a moment, then smiled. "Slightly more gray than last I saw you was not something I expected." He reached absently for the pouch where he kept his pipe and tabac and found it absent. "Ah," he said in an aggrieved tone. "Not perfect!"

Pug smiled. "The older I get, the less I know, Kulgan."

"It's always thus," answered the graybeard. "Still, our paths hardly crossed by chance, and one supposes in these circumstances that there's little logic in having us flail about wondering why we're here. What are you about these days and how do you require help?"

"I am trying to save Midkemia," said Pug, "and apparently a large chunk of the universe along with it. And I am far from home and uncertain how to return there."

Kulgan tapped his fingers absently. "It would be easier to think had I my pipe."

Suddenly his pipe and a bag of tabac appeared on the table.

Both Pug and Kulgan looked around the cottage. "We are being observed," Kulgan said. He opened the pouch eagerly, took a long sniff, then said in a satisfied tone, "That's the very thing!"

Pug watched with an unexpected pleasure as his old teacher filled the bowl and looked around for a taper, and saw one next to the small fire he had used for heating water for the tea. He reached over and with a wave of his hand caused the taper to come flying across the room. It smacked his palm hard enough that he recoiled. "That hurt!" he yelped.

"I told you magic here would be . . . more intense," said Pug.

Leaning over to retrieve the taper, Kulgan said, "I'm glad I heeded you enough not to light it with my finger." They both laughed.

Kulgan lit his pipe and drew in a mouthful of pungent smoke, then let it out. "Ah!" Taking another quicker pull, he blew out smoke and said, "So, let us be about this quickly, for I suspect our time together is limited."

Pug paused. So much was woven together in his own mind, going back to his very first encounter with the Dread when he and Tomas were searching for Macros the Black at the end of the Great Uprising. Quickly, he discarded all superfluous information and guided Kulgan through the evolution of his awareness of the various forces at play.

"What I know and what I find highly probable is that an agency of vast destruction seeks entrance into our universe." He briefly recounted his discover of the Dasati world and what he had encountered there, what he had learned from Nakor and Miranda about the demon realm, and concluded, "Apparently this universe or universes is an intertwined organic thing, but like an onion has many layers. So, to anticipate you, Kulgan, I have far more questions than I have answers. But I do know that something for many years has been trying to neutralize threats to its plan, through agencies brutal as well as subtle, on scales that defy understanding, but all with one aim: to enter Midkemia and either conquer or destroy it." Pug continued his narrative leading up to the discovery of the matrix on the Isle of the Snake Men and the trap that had apparently blown him into this world, wherever it was.

Finishing, he said, "At first we of the Conclave assumed it was the Nameless One behind all that was under way, but logic dictates his madness is beyond understanding if he sought to enable the Dread's entrance into our universe."

Kulgan nodded. "I've only heard of the Dread in legend, as some monstrous larger kind of Children of the Void." He shook his head. "And of those I've only encountered one, the wraith who separated Tomas from us in the Mac Mordain Cadal." He feigned a shiver. "That creature was dire enough. I can barely imagine what the Dread must be like."

"I've faced them, Kulgan. They are as bad as you fear, or worse." Pug spoke without bravado. "What we do know is that the Dread have wandered into our realm in the past, but this time it seems to be something far more coordinated and with purpose. We do not know how many Dread exist, or where they come from—save some unimaginable place within the Void—or what their purpose is, but they are coming. And they are driving an army of demons before them."

"Assault troops, as it were," supplied Kulgan.

"It was years before we pieced together that the demons were not coming of their own volition. They were seeking either to escape and hide here, or to conquer at the bidding of false masters . . ." He shrugged.

"One thing," said Kulgan. He sighed. "I wish Tully were here. He was a wealth of knowledge on all things religious, not just his own order. He could answer this, perhaps?"

"What?"

Kulgan looked thoughtfully at Pug. "Legend says that when a demon enters our realm, unconfined, one that is not summoned by a human and bound, or when a summoned demon escapes his bonds, then an opposing creature of a higher order, called an angel by some, appears somewhere on Midkemia and seeks out that demon. When they meet, they fight, and when one is triumphant"—Kulgan clapped his hands together—"they cancel one another out, returning to their respective realms. But if so many demons have entered Midkemia without summons, where are the opposing angels?"

"I come seeking answers, and you provide me with another question!" Pug laughed.

"Well then, finish your narrative and I'll see if there's something you've missed."

Pug spoke briefly of Nakor and Miranda, omitting their names; Kulgan had briefly met Nakor only days before his own death, while Pug's first wife, Katala, was still alive. He also skipped the complexity of human memories grafted onto demons', merely casting them in the role of improbable demon allies. Given that the demons were being exploited by the Dread, the notion of an intelligent demon allying with humans didn't seem all that improbable to Kulgan. He finished the narrative with the Pantathian trap and Kulgan sat back.

At last he said, "Son?" His eyes narrowed.

Pug saw that his attempt not to touch on that bit of his history had failed. "Years after Katala died, I met someone else. Her name was Miranda. We had two sons. She and my youngest, Caleb, were killed." He felt no need to touch upon the subject of the mad necromancer Leso Varen, also called Sidi, and the demons he had summoned to serve him. "Magnus is my older son. He's quite the prodigy."

"Prodigy?" Kulgan laughed. "How old is the 'lad'?"

Pug was forced to laugh in turn. "Very well. He's old enough to be a grandfather, but he's always a boy to me."

Kulgan nodded. "As you were to me. Still," he said, "you've grown to remarkable powers and I judge it safe to assume that since my death you've continued to master the magic arts."

"I do my best. But I'm at a loss as how to return home."

"I can't be of any help there, I'm afraid," said Kulgan, settling back in his chair as he puffed on his pipe. "I'm really not sure why I'm here. Whatever agency snatched me from the brink of death and brought me here at this time must have its reason, but I am ignorant of what it is. Still, one can surmise, can't one?"

Pug smiled. "You used to chide me for leaping to conclusions."

"True, but it seems to me there were many different choices as to who met you here to help you, so why me?"

Pug recognized that tone: after more than a few lifetimes, they were once more teacher and student. "There is a lesson to learn."

Kulgan nodded. "Given how far you've come, I seriously doubt there's anything I know that you don't." He fixed Pug with the narrow gaze the magician had come to know so well when he was Kulgan's student. "But I may help you to remember something you've forgotten."

"Such as?"

Kulgan blew out a cloud of smoke. "There's the nub of it." He waved around the room. "We wouldn't need all this if it was something easily recalled."

They chatted for what seemed like an hour when Kulgan tapped out his pipe in a stone tray designed to cradle it and deposit ashes until he could dispose of them. He sat back with a heavy sigh. "I am enjoying this, Pug, but I have a feeling creeping up on me, a sort of foreboding. There's no sense of terror, rather a sense of inevitability. Whatever agency took that tiny little sliver of my life and held it for this meeting ensured that I would be alert and have full command of my faculties, but it's becoming apparent to me that time is running out. We must continue our discussions with more alacrity, Pug."

"I'm at a loss to know what it is I'm supposed to remember."

Kulgan glanced out the window at the failing light. "Let us walk, for it appears that a lovely evening is approaching and fresh air might give me that moment of brilliance we sorely require."

They exited the cottage and began hiking up the gentle path that led to the meadow above. "I found myself up there," said Pug, pointing to the other side of the meadow."

"Hmm," said Kulgan. "Let's go take a look, just in case there is something there you missed on your arrival."

They crossed the meadow and suddenly Kulgan stopped, tilting his head. "Did you hear that?"

"Hear what?" asked Pug, having only noticed the sound of the breeze in the branches, and the occasional forest noise, a birdcall, or animal moving through the brush.

After a moment Kulgan said, "Nothing." He looked sad. "It's nothing."

"What?" asked Pug. "You don't look as if it's nothing."

"It's just an old man's imagination, but I thought I heard my name called, from far away." He let his voice drop. "I thought it was Meecham. Of all those I've left behind . . ." His voice fell to silence.

"You were together a very long time," Pug said quietly.

"More than forty years." He looked at Pug. "What became of him after I died?"

Pug tried to be matter-of-fact. "He left Stardock. We never had word of him again. I assumed the memories were just too painful."

Kulgan nodded. "That was so like him. I always joked he'd have to die first, because I'd be reasonable about it, but he'd go off and crawl into a cave like a wounded bear and wait to die."

"Perhaps nothing so grim," said Pug, suddenly feeling guilty for not having done more to locate Kulgan's companion. He was a franklin, a free man in service, but over the years they had become so much more than master and servant, forging a deeper bond than most Pug had seen. Pug had thought at the time that if it was Meecham's wish to leave, it wasn't Pug's place to stop him. Yet now, all these years later, he wondered if he hadn't had a duty to Kulgan's memory at least to keep a watch over the man.

He glanced over and saw Kulgan's expression and felt, not for the first time, that his old teacher could read his mind. "Perhaps nothing so grim," he repeated softly.

Kulgan nodded. "Let's move on," he said in a flat tone.

The silence between them highlighted the deep and oddly conflicted emotions Pug had felt since encountering Kulgan. Since his first confrontation with the demon Jakan, ending with Pug lingering at the point of death, he had been cursed with a prophecy, that he would die in futility, after having seen all he loved lost. During the Riftwar, he had lost his boyhood friend, Squire Roland, killed by raiders as he tried to protect a herd of cattle. Pug hadn't learned of his death until his return from Kelewan, after a dozen years of war were ended.

Since then, he had lost the two women he had loved most in the world, and the appearance of the demon Child in the guise of Miranda had reopened that wound as if it were fresh. Pug's ability to move forward with the actions necessary to preserve his world only masked the pain that echoed from years gone by. As it had been with the three children he had outlived. No one, save perhaps his son Magnus, would ever see a hint of the pain Pug bore every day.

Kulgan's death, at least, had been a natural consequence of a mortal's span. And he had died surrounded by those who loved him, yet now, finding himself in the presence of his old mentor, Pug again revisited that loss.

Glancing around, he realized that the beautiful vista beyond the meadow, the magnificent range of mountains above, were all reminders of how fleeting life could be and how indifferent the universe was to a single life. Pug felt diminished.

He stopped. "Kulgan, I think I understand."

Kulgan stopped and said, "What, Pug?"

"Perspective," said Pug softly. "This world is vast, and it is but a tiny part of a much larger universe. I feel humbled."

Kulgan nodded. He put his hand on his former student's shoulder. "Greatness, smallness, these are relative concepts, Pug, and it is important to remember that. But this doesn't change the fundamental reality that what stands before you is a challenge that seems trivial compared to the vastness of which you speak." He narrowed one eye in an expression Pug had seen a thousand times before, one that showed he was coming to the point of a lesson. "But though the task before you seems trivial, the consequences may be anything but trivial in reality." He nodded. "More than once I've taught you the lesson of the keystone, the one brick that when removed can bring the entire building down upon your head."

He pulled out his unlit pipe, a long churchwarden in style, and tapped Pug on the chest with it. "Just be outside the building when you do it." He laughed.

Pug tried to enjoy the mirthful tone, but inside he felt darkness gathering. "What I've lost sight of is the fundamentals of magic."

"Probably not," suggested Kulgan, "but rather the simple

roots of even the most complex causality; you look at a chaotic outcome, well, it's easy to overlook that it may have
begun with the simplest cause. A stray spark from this pipe
I hold could eventually lead to a conflagration that would
destroy this entire forest," he added with a sweep of his
hand.

"And amid the chaos," Kulgan continued, "it's also easy to
lose sight of multiple causes of an event. Consider a storm
that lashes the Far Coast. You know from the time you were
a boy that often the worst storms are not a single storm,
but a convergence of two, one coming down the coast from
the frigid north, the other sweeping in from the southwest,
where it's warm and turbulent." He left his pipe dangling
from his mouth as he linked both hands together, fingers
intertwined, and twisted his hands in a wrenching motion.
"Together they combine to be so much more than each was
separately." He took his pipe from his mouth and tapped Pug
on the shoulder with the tip. "Which then leads us back to
where each storm comes from . . ."

"I'm still not seeing this," said Pug. "But I'm getting a
sense of it."

"It's about the fundamentals of things, Pug. What is the
nature of a storm?"

"I'm not sure what you're asking. It's a storm?"

Kulgan sighed. "It's all that time on Kelewan. Had you
the knack for what those Tsurani call the Lesser Path of
Magic . . ." He shrugged. "Anyway, had you studied weather
magic—"

Pug remembered a long conversation he had had with an
elven spellweaver named Temar. "Equipoise," said Pug, and
Kulgan stopped talking.

A slow smile spread out over the old teacher's face. "Equipoise? Go on."

"Storms are the most extreme examples of nature seeking balance, equipoise. There's too much energy built up in
one place and it seeks . . ." He shook his head. "The sphere!
All different energy states. The difficulty moving from one

to another because of that. The magic needed to survive in higher states or lower states."

Kulgan nodded. "I have no idea what you're talking about specifically, but if I'm guessing right, you're on the right path."

"If you come to a higher-energy-state place, such as this one"—Pug waved his hand in a circle, indicating the entire world—"you need protection so that you don't absorb energy too fast, don't burn up from it. If you go to a lower-state world, the entire environment sucks the energy right out of you, like a spider sucks an insect dry in its web."

"There you have it, then," said Kulgan. "Your first clue, I expect. This all has something to do with the energy states of the sphere . . . whatever that may be."

"Ah, Kulgan," said Pug with a sad laugh. "You have no idea—"

Kulgan interrupted. "Did you hear that?"

"What?"

"I thought I heard . . ." He fell silent, then said, "Just an old man's imagination. Let's get back. I could use another cup of hot tea and some more of your company, my best student."

Pug laughed. "Your only student! I still recall the look on the other masters' faces when you claimed me as apprentice on the day of my Choosing."

Kulgan chuckled. "I assume it's safe to say that all of that is part of all of this. A plan, not of our own choosing, in which we are but pieces?"

Pug nodded. "Apparently. For reasons not made clear to me, I was selected to live this life, to be the tool of the gods in this conflict."

"It's a puzzle," said Kulgan as he carefully stepped down off a slight rise in the trail and halted for a moment to fuss with his robe. "You were, I say with no judgment, a rather unremarkable child. I remember when you were brought to the castle, a foundling. As babies are, you were endearing. We were told that a scullery maid and a wandering soldier were your parents, and she handed you over to a mendicant friar of the Order of Dala, who brought you to Lord Borric. Certainly nothing remarkable was evident in you until that stormy night you came to my cottage in the woods." He shook his head in memory. "When you sat before that scrying orb fashioned by Althafain of Carse for me, and without effort saw into the kitchen at Crydee Keep . . ." He clucked his tongue. "That was remarkable."

"I don't remember it as effortless," said Pug with a smile. "I had quite the headache after."

"You are a master, Pug. You know how remarkable it is for any user of magic to just . . . use it, without instruction and conditioning."

Pug nodded.

They approached the cottage and Kulgan stopped. "Did you hear that? It was Meecham!"

Pug turned and saw no one. Where Kulgan had stood only a second before was now empty space on the trail and suddenly he knew that this had been his last visit with his former mentor and that he would never again lay eyes on Kulgan in this life.

He turned to enter the cottage and before him stood only sparse woods cut through by the narrow game trail on which he stood. Of the cottage no hint remained. Instead, a thick tree stood in its place.

A sudden shift in air pressure and a slight popping sound caused him to turn again, and where Kulgan had stood, another vortex hung in the air. Pausing for only a moment as he wondered which agency was moving him toward what end, and deciding that was hopeless speculation and a waste of time, he took a breath and jumped into the vortex.

4

HOMEWARD

Martin reined in his mount.

The escort behind him also halted as they crested the rise. To their left squatted the abandoned fortification he had seen burning only short months ago, fired on his brother's command in order to deny the use of it to the Keshians. Down the road ahead, they could see the distant walls of the city of Ylith.

"Downright peaceful-looking, Highness," observed Sergeant Oaks. The rangy, redheaded commander of the escort was the leader of one of Prince Edward's best combat-proven patrols. Kesh might be observing the conditions of the truce, but trust was still a far distance away. And Martin didn't wish to explain to Prince Edward why two of the last three remaining conDoin brothers were no longer among the living.

Riding down the road, they were spotted by city lookouts long before they reached the southeastern gate. As the company was clad in the tabards of Krondor and as the cease-fire had been honored for some weeks now, the gate was opened and a familiar face greeted Martin.

"Captain Bolton," Martin said with surprise and some pleasure. When they had first met, George Bolton had been an annoying, officious young man, his bluster covering his deep fear of showing himself a fool. Under Martin's guid-ance, he had turned into a competent officer, eager to do his best. He had even begun to manifest some military talent and a quiet courage before the truce.

Martin and Brendan climbed down from their horses and shook hands with Bolton. "What news?" asked the acting city commander.

Before Martin could answer, he was knocked a half step backward as Lady Bethany of Carse threw her arms around his neck in a hug so fierce he could barely breathe. Ser-geant Oaks and Captain Bolton exchanged a look that con-veyed barely contained amusement, while Brendan laughed openly. Martin held her tightly for a moment, then managed to say, "Let me breathe, Beth."

She loosened her hold on him, then kissed him and said, "I missed you so much. You were gone so long." She wore the leather trousers, linen shirt, and leather archer's vest she had taken to wearing on the wall when Martin had last seen her. Her hair was gathered up in an efficient knot behind her head. Even without the usual lip paint and powders, jewelry and gowns, of the ladies of the court, he'd never seen any-thing more beautiful.

He nodded. "I'll explain everything when we're alone." Then he smiled and whispered into her ear.

She stepped back, tears streaming down her face. "Really?"

"Really." Turning to Bolton, Martin said, "We need to deal with a number of matters." He waved in the general direction of the mayor's home, used by him as a command center during the assault on the city by Keshian forces. "I'll tell you all the news from the east once we're seated. What's the situation here?"

"Better than when you left," said Bolton. He set some of his men to quartering of the escort.

Martin beckoned Sergeant Oaks to accompany them. Brendan said, "I'll get everyone settled and catch up." As Bethany clung to his arm and they walked toward the mayor's house, Martin listened as Bolton reviewed the changes that had occurred since Martin's departure.

Bolton finished by saying, "So they've held fast to the ridgeline in the hills to the northwest, and down to some imagined line between the Free Cities and Yabon." He shook his head as if somewhat confused. "They've been very quiet, content to do nothing, and if anything, they've proved to be reasonable neighbors. They sent a message last week telling us that their outriders saw what looked to be a large band of Dark Brothers heading south toward the smaller game trails"—he looked at Martin as if waiting to be corrected— "heading over the ridges into the Grey Towers and down to the Greenheart." Martin merely nodded. "They were alerting us to possible raiding."

"That's downright neighborly," Martin said.

Bolton looked a little embarrassed. "And there's been some, well, I guess you could call it 'unofficial trading' going on across the lines."

Now Martin was amused. "Keshian belt buckles?"

Bolton nodded. "How did you know?"

"It's been going on for years along the southern front." He glanced over at Sergeant Oaks.

"Sir," said the veteran. "Kesh's finer units, like those Leopard Guard, get some pretty equipment. They have these enamel-and-bronze belt buckles." He held up his hands with fingers and thumbs forming a square about two by three inches and said, "Really fancy things with a leopard head. Fetches a nice bit of gold in the bazaar. It's something of a joke among their sergeants that sooner or later every man loses a belt buckle, usually after a bad run of luck gambling or after having met a particularly pretty whore." Glancing at Bethany, he muttered, "Begging your pardon, m'lady."

Bethany just smiled at him.

"They're a novelty up here, I guess," said Bolton as they turned the corner. "But it's a bit odd, as we're also getting reports that some stores heading here are being diverted to the Keshians." He glanced at Martin to see if he might have done something wrong.

"Not much you can do about that," Martin reassured him. "Short of having patrols up and down every trail and road north and west of here, and that's hardly practical." He fell silent for a moment, then said, "As it stands, anything that lowers tension along the frontier is to be welcomed." He glanced around to see if anyone might overhear. "I'll have more to say on that when we're alone, but for the time being consider yourself as having discharged your responsibilities in an admirable fashion."

Bolton looked visibly relieved.

At the mayor's house Martin was greeted by Lily, the mayor's daughter. "We haven't much to offer by way of hospitality," she said brightly.

Glancing around the conference room where he, his brother, and Bolton had met so often to discuss the defense of the city, Martin felt a sudden exhaustion. He had missed Bethany every moment he'd been away from her, but had managed to stay busy and keep that longing buried deeply. Now she was at his side, but duty required him to be on his way as soon as the horses were rested and a clear way into the Grey Towers was identified. "Whatever you offer is fine, Lily," said Martin with fatigue creeping into his voice.

"Vegetable stew and some hot bread," said Lily cheerfully as she left for the kitchen.

"Only water," said Bolton, sitting opposite Martin and Bethany. "No ale coming from either Stone Mountain or the Grey Towers, and there hasn't been a shipment of anything up the coast since the hostilities stopped. I expect that will change in a while. Every tavern and inn is making do. Some of the local stuff—" He made a face. "It won't kill you, but it might."

Martin laughed. He said, "Water's fine."

"Then a hot bath," said Bethany, wrinkling her nose, "and some rest."

Oaks and Bolton exchanged quick glances but neither said a word.

"Lily," said Martin when the girl returned with a tureen of hot stew. "Where is the mayor?"

"He's out and about, checking on the outlying farms to see who's still around, who's hiding what, trying to get commerce moving again, and get some food flowing into the city once more. It's getting better, but we're living on stores usually put up for winter. People are tired of fish stew and boiled potatoes and would welcome a little change. It's not until goods stop arriving you realize how much of what you take for granted comes from far away. All that fruit from Queg and farther south. I haven't had a good piece of fruit in months," she said wistfully.

She left for the kitchen again and Bolton said, "Lots of chaos after you left, Highness. The mayor and a few of the more influential merchants headed up north to see if they could organize some sort of temporary governance while all the nobles were gone. Recruit some local lads to act as a constabulary of sorts so the farmers would risk bringing their crops into the city."

Lily returned with bowls, a platter of fresh, hot bread, a pot of butter, and spoons.

Just then Brendan arrived and, smelling the stew, exclaimed, "Perfect! I'm starved." With a grin he added, "Hello, Lily!"

She gave him a playful kiss on the cheek and he sat down.

As the three hungry travelers began to eat, Martin looked at George and said, "What else?"

Bolton quickly resumed his summary. "The Keshian commander we faced, and his Leopard Guard, have been withdrawn, either recalled or moved somewhere else along the Far Coast. The fellow they've left in charge is some sort of . . . I'm not sure what to call him. He uses the title 'Premier,' whatever that means."

Martin said, "Really? That means he's a military governor, not a soldier."

Bethany said, "I'm impressed."

"While you and Brendan were out shooting things with arrows, I was studying." He asked Bolton, "What's the disposition of their troops?"

"Mostly militia, but enough veteran Dog Soldier infantry that if you're thinking of retaking Crydee, you'd best wait for the Armies of the West to get back here."

Martin shook his head. "Long wait, I'm afraid. They're all camped on the Fields of Albalyn."

Bolton and Oaks exchanged glances, but neither said a word. Finally the old sergeant said, "We've heard rumors."

"I am certain you have," said Martin.

Brendan added, "It's no rumor. That's where Prince Edward is camped."

Bolton waited, and when Martin stayed silent, he said, "So, we have had a few stragglers wander out of Crydee . . . Commander?"

Martin smiled. Bolton was waiting for him to clarify the situation. Was he back in charge and what was his current rank?

"Under instruction from Lord James of Rillanon, I'm currently 'Your Highness,' as I am somehow still considered royalty; but for the sake of all our sanity, Martin will do. You'll remain in command here, George. In fact, I think it safe to say you're going to find that the rank of captain isn't a temporary one now. And I'm going to presume on my royal prerogative to also give you military authority for all of

Yabon, should anyone from LaMut or Yabon City presume to question you."

"Why would anyone question me?"

"You've a lot to learn about politics, George," said Brendan with a grin.

Martin tried to suppress a yawn. "Now that a truce is in place, we're in transition, and out of chaos arises opportunity. I will bet you a golden sovereign that when Lily's father returns, he'll report that someone from the north with a self-appointed title and a retinue of scruffy guards has named himself Baron of This, or Earl of That, or someone else will turn up within a few more weeks claiming some privilege or another, and seeing your age will try to browbeat you into accepting their orders.

"Confidence tricksters, charlatans, minor nobles with ambition, whoever it may be, feel free to toss them into the local gaol and wait for whoever does return from Prince Edward's encampment." He again tried to suppress a yawn. "I have to travel into the mountains and do some exploring for Duke James and whoever turns out to be our next King. So, after my men have rested, I've got a Keshian premier to bribe and a guide to find, and some backcountry to scout. But for now, a bath, and some sleep." Rising as if his joints were a hundred years older than he was, Martin said, "If you need me, feel free to wake me."

Sergeant Oaks made a halfhearted response that indicated that unless the city was on fire, Martin would sleep through the night.

Brendan said, "I'll quarter with the men." He tried to look serious, but could barely contain his mirth; he usually shared quarters with his brother, but he suspected the young lovers might need their privacy.

Martin followed Bethany to the room he had previously occupied with Brendan and found a claw-foot brass-and-porcelain tub set in the middle of the room. It was filled with steaming-hot water. Martin looked at Bethany with a questioning expression.

"We found it up in the old keep, and Lily convinced George to fetch it down so we wouldn't have to use that old wooden horror her father has kept here far too long."

"Small pleasures are a gift in times like these," said Martin, stripping off his clothing.

Wrinkling her nose, Bethany gathered it up and tossed it outside the door. "Getting you clean is hardly a small pleasure. You positively reek."

"A week's hard riding." A satisfied sigh as he lowered himself into the hot water. He lay back and slowly slid down the smooth porcelain tub until his head was completely underwater, then slid back up, his hair soaked. Instantly he felt Bethany's fingers applying soap to his scalp, a creamy concoction she used. It had a floral fragrance, but Martin was too tired to complain. Besides, it did smell better than the usual harsh soaps his father had stocked at Crydee, composed of lye, tallow or oil, ash, and some attempt at a scent with whatever the soap maker had at hand. This aromatic soap must be something Lily's father had bought before the war from one of the finer soap makers in Queg.

Martin closed his eyes and let the warmth soak into his bones, thinking that whatever else one might say about the Quegans, they knew how to make luxury goods: silken garments to rival the finest in Kesh, wines equal to the best in the Kingdom, jewelry and cut gems without equal. His thoughts drifted off for what seemed a moment, until he felt Bethany push at him gently and whisper in his ear, "None of that, now. You're off to bed for some rest."

He blinked awake and realized he must have dozed off, for the water was cool. "I thought about climbing in with you," she whispered in his ear, "but you're farther gone than I thought in the kitchen."

He grinned. "I might surprise you."

"Get to bed and maybe we'll find out, but sleep first!" Her expression was concerned as she handed him a towel. "You don't plan on lingering, do you?"

"I've got my orders," he said, drying off. "With the nasty

business shaping up in the east, Lord James is desperate to know exactly what we face, and everything we can deduce from the madness of this last war tells us that whoever was behind that pointless bloodshed wants the bulk of the Kingdom's army as far away from the Grey Towers as possible. So that's where I need to go poke around."

Bethany tossed Martin an oversize nightshirt, belonging to Lily's father most likely, and said, "Get some sleep. If you wake for the evening meal, fine, otherwise I'll let you sleep through."

"Don't let me sleep through the night."

She came over and sat on the side of the bed. "As much as I've missed you, my darling, I think rest is what you need most now."

Bethany wasn't clear at which precise point Martin had fallen asleep but he was soundly sleeping by the end of her sentence. She shook her head, torn between slipping between the sheets with him and letting him rest, then let caution overrule desire. He needed whatever respite he could seize during this time in Ylith. Tomorrow he would undoubtedly be away on the Crown's errand, and she wished him to be in possession of all his wits and resources.

As she started to rise, he reached up and grabbed her belt, yanking her back into bed. She shrieked in surprise. Wrapping his arms around her, he whispered in her ear, "I'm not *that* tired."

The next morning it was a very refreshed if not entirely rested Martin who came down to breakfast. He was pleased to see that the mayor had returned and quickly got brought up-to-date on conditions north of Ylith. Captain Bolton and Sergeant Oaks were already at the table. Martin looked around them and said, "I'm very pleased to see how well you've all done since I left."

The mayor said, "We try. Fishing is reasonable given how far out the boats go—there are a great many warships still on the water—but with all the people who fled when the Keshians arrived, we don't have as many mouths to feed as before the war." He fell silent for a second and Martin realized he was also considering those who had died. "Still," he added brightly, "we're starting to see some farm produce coming into the city. Higher-than-usual prices have lured farmers previously reluctant to venture from home during the fighting, and while the produce is not of highest quality, it suffices."

"Some of the townswomen had vegetable gardens," said Lily. "Rather than merely store them for next winter, they're selling them at market on Sixthday."

"We get along," said the mayor.

"Well, if this peace lasts, we'll see a return to normality, at least in Yabon," said Martin.

"What of the Far Coast?" asked the mayor.

"We don't know. Earl Robert"—he glanced at Bethany, whose expression turned somber at the mention of her father—"and the other western lords are with Prince Edward. Until the new King is chosen, I don't see any of them coming back.

"I was told Carse and Tulan held fast as Crydee fell, so we can hope they're still secured, but cut off from communication."

"I hope you're right," said Captain Bolton.

Martin paused, then asked, "What about the deployment of the Keshians along this front?"

Bolton rose from the table and returned with a map. "They're dug in along a line from here"—he pointed to a game trail in the forest to the south of the road to Crydee— "to here: just draw a line north and south a bit from their barricade at the rise." His finger stopped at another point a mile north of the road. "I think it's for show, as if they were concerned we might mount some sort of offensive back into Crydee.

"They patrol but their hearts aren't in it."

"What makes you say that?" asked Sergeant Oaks.

"They send one patrol to the south in the morning and it

returns by lunch. Then after lunch they send the same patrol to the north and it's back by nightfall." He laughed. "We can see them from the western wall. It's got so predictable my men place bets on which Keshians get sent out. My men are convinced it's some sort of punishment duty, as the patrollers look either dejected or annoyed when picked. My lads have even given them names. There's Fatty, Droopy, Thunder Gut—"

"Thunder Gut?" asked Martin.

Bolton grinned. "Apparently he can fart so loud you can hear him on the wall."

"No! Really? That's a quarter mile away!"

Oaks didn't look convinced. "I don't know about the names, but soldiers get good at reading the mood of other soldiers. If they're sending out patrols as a matter of punishment, the captain's right; they're doing it for show."

Martin thought about this, then said, "I had been instructed by Lord James and his grandson that a cautious approach was needed, a discreet bribe to get a small squad across the frontier on the excuse of needing to return to Crydee to recover some family heirlooms, as if any might not have been plundered already. I always thought a better approach would be for the Keshians to not know we crossed the line at all."

"That should be easy enough if you're careful, Martin," said Bolton. "If you sneak out at night down the coast toward the Free Cities, just shy of the Keshians' first checkpoint on the road to Natal, lie low for the day, then head up into the woodlands and find a game trail." He shrugged.

"I think I have a better idea," said Martin. "How far behind the lines does that old bolt-hole from the castle extend?"

Bolton said, "Only a few dozen yards, really. It's awfully close to the Keshian line, Martin."

"But if we come out after their last patrol of the day has returned to their camp, and we're quiet enough, we can loop around behind their camp and be halfway up the mountain by sunrise."

"If those elves up there let you get that close," said Bolton. "We heard a rumor that a Keshian patrol got too close to their city and were routed. I don't know how true that is. We heard it from a refugee from Walinor, up in the foothills. He and his family managed to get out when the Keshians turned south toward Hūsh. Before they left, he said they sent that patrol up into the Grey Towers, and not many of them came back. A few of the Keshian soldiers complained about their commander's decisions in earshot of some of the towns-people before they left for Hūsh." He looked at Martin and added, "It's your mission, Highness, and it's a bold plan." He smiled. "Glad it's you climbing that pile of rocks, and not me."

"You'll have your hands full enough for a while, George. I suspect it's going to be some months before the Duke of Yabon or any of his vassals return. You're going to be in command of what's left of the military for all of Yabon."

"Not that it's much," said Bolton. "I can barely scrape to-gether a decent-size patrol once a week to ride up to LaMut. We only get word from Yabon through LaMut. The Hadati tribes along the northern foothills keep things pretty peace-ful up there: they're not kind to renegades trading with the Brotherhood of the Dark Path, but banditry along the roads south of there is starting to be a problem."

"We'll see what we can do," said Martin, "once I get back."

"You're not taking all the lads," said Oaks. "We could take a small patrol up to Yabon and back. Show the colors, as it were."

Martin calculated. "I've hunted in those mountains since I was a boy."

A slight clearing of her throat from Bethany told Martin what she thought of that, given that he was a terrible bowman.

"I *have* hunted in the Grey Towers from the Crydee side all my life." He turned to Oaks. "Ignore her."

"Ignoring the lady, Highness," said Oaks, his stoic de-meanor barely hiding his amusement.

"I'm not taking any of your men, Oaks. They're good soldiers, but none of them are mountain-trained." Turning to Bolton, Martin said, "Get me four of your best hunters or trackers, George. I want lads who know how to move through the woods quietly."

Bolton nodded and stood up. "Best to go at sunset tonight."

Bethany's expression revealed she was not happy, but she said nothing.

Martin said, "It was suggested we bribe the Keshians to slip past their lines, but I'd rather as few people as possible know what we're doing. That bolt-hole from the old keep is on the other side of the line."

Bolton said, "That side, but barely."

"And if we come out after their last patrol heads back to the camp by the road . . . ?"

"That assumes they're being sloppy and not leaving pickets out along the line, Highness," said Sergeant Oaks.

Captain Bolton said, "They've grown lax. My best appraisal is that they're bored and waiting for orders."

"To do what?" wondered Martin aloud.

Bolton shrugged. "Gods know, Highness. I don't. None of this makes sense."

Martin explained in brief what Lord James had told the brothers about the pointlessness of the war.

When he finished, Bolton nodded. "Well, if the object of the exercise was to throw the region into total chaos, they've succeeded. From Yabon City to LaMut, we've barely got five hundred of what could reasonably be called fighting men. Mostly old veterans and boys, some town militia who didn't go marching off under the Duke of Yabon's banner, and our little garrison here, and as I've said, I've barely enough here to mount a decent patrol. Our lads are either watching the Keshians, or getting ready to escort farmers to the city when the mayor says it's time. The Keshians have also withdrawn the heart of their forces. After that Premier fellow, the highest-ranking soldier I've seen up on that barricade when

I've ridden close appears to be some sort of sergeant of militia." Bolton let out a slow breath. "I hope you don't think me presumptuous, Highness, but I think with your own detachment and the garrison here, we could probably roll over that line up on the ridge."

Martin nodded. "No doubt, but to what end?" He looked at the map as if trying to see something he missed and spoke almost to himself. "We might be able to retake Crydee if we hit them hard and fast and they haven't rebuilt what I destroyed on the way out. But . . ." He looked at the others. "Our countryside is now populated with Keshians, most of whom I suspect do not speak the King's Tongue. Shall we ride out, greet them as new subjects, and inform them of when the tax roll will be posted and where to gather to give their due to their new lords? If we get true peace with Kesh, it will be years before we hold anything, truly, north of Carse. We can repopulate Crydee Keep and Jonril's garrison, but beyond that . . . My grandfather never got around to rebuilding the old garrison at Barran." He slowly shook his head. "Even if we could hold Crydee and Jonril, everything north of Carse will be as wild as the Northlands, I fear, for years to come."

He glanced at the faces around him, and smiled. "We'll worry about retaking old territories some other time. Right now we've got to find out what's going on up in those mountains, and I think our best chance to get up there quickly will be to come out of the old keep and head straight across the road behind the Keshian line and take the old West Rim game trail."

He stood up. "We'll head up to the old fortress and rest. After their last evening patrol, we'll head out of the bolt-hole, make straight across the western road and up into the hills. By midnight we'll be high enough above their position they'll never know we passed by."

Bethany looked at Martin and said, "And . . . ?"

Martin smiled and said, "Oaks, I'm leaving you here as second to Captain Bolton. George, find those lads I need and have them meet me at the old keep in an hour."

Bethany smiled, turned, and walked toward the stairs without further comment. Martin attempted to look oblivious as he waited for what he hoped would be an appropriate moment to pass; then Bolton said, "Sorry, Highness, but it's probably going to take two hours to organize the scouting party."

"Well," said Martin, following Bethany. "Two hours, then."

He hurried up the back stairs while Bolton and Oaks stifled their laughter.

5

E'BAR

artin signaled.

The four hunters behind him halted. They were two hours past the Keshian roadblock on the highway between Ylith and Crydee. They had easily passed to the west of that position and moved quickly into the foothills of the Grey Tower Mountains. They had executed Martin's plan without a hitch, crossing the King's Road from Ylith to Crydee and getting high into the mountains. They made a cold camp there and rested until sunrise. Now they'd been hiking for half a day and Martin sensed something was amiss.

He listened to a faint sound from behind them and indicated that the four hunters from Ylith should move to either side of the trail, out of sight. He moved as quietly as he could back the way they had just come. It was nearing noon, so there were few hiding places around the trail. The trees were not particularly dense here, but a few clumps of brush and some tightly packed large boles provided him with cover.

Martin was perhaps half a dozen yards down the trail when a familiar voice said, "If I were a Keshian assassin, you'd be dead, my love."

Slowly turning, his expression one of exasperation, he said, "Beth?"

She stepped out from behind a nearby tree trunk. "Congratulations on hearing me. I didn't think you would after I caught up with you, two hours after you passed the roadblock."

Martin was still tired and already feeling the pressure of leadership. Now he felt close to rage at being disobeyed by the woman he loved. As if reading his mind, she said quietly, "Before you make a fool of yourself, listen. You don't want these lads from Ylith thinking you can't control a woman. Especially when obeying you might be the difference between the success of this mission and death. I know you take your duties very seriously, Martin, but there are going to be times you'll need to listen to me. I really didn't mean to embarrass you."

Whispering through clenched teeth, he said, "Then why did you put me in this position, Beth?"

"Because I love you, even though you're an idiot at times." She put her hand on his arm. "Of the five of you, you're the only one who's spent time on the west side of the Grey Towers. These men may be able hunters and trackers, but this is new territory for them. Odds are almost certain you're the worst bowman and hunter in the band. You don't have a tenth of my skill and knowledge. While you were studying history and language, my father and I were hunting from the Straits of Darkness to Elvandar."

Martin knew the last to be an exaggeration, but not by much, so he said nothing.

She moved closer. "Martin, I love you with all my heart, but if I can keep you safe, I will do just that, no matter what orders you think I must follow. Now, do we understand each other?"

"Beth—" His tone left no doubt that at that moment there was no understanding, just a young man feeling betrayed and embarrassed.

She cut him off. "Look, why are you following this trail?"

He blinked, as if he didn't understand the question. "Because it's leading us up into the peaks, toward where the Star Elves have built their city."

"And you call yourself a student of history," she said softly.

"What?" he asked.

"The Tsurani invasion. Surely you studied the maps."

"Of course I did . . ." He let his voice fall off and his anger drained away as he realized what she was saying. "This is the crest trail, the false trail, isn't it?"

She nodded. "This trail ends five miles ahead at an impassable ravine. It's why both the Kingdom nobles and Natalese Rangers left it unguarded. You want the trail a half mile downslope."

Feeling foolish, he said, "Thank you, but you could have reminded me back in Ylith."

"You'd just get lost somewhere else. We have many days of travel ahead, my love, and who knows what will be waiting for us the closer we get to those elves? Either Brendan or I would double your chances to survive, and admit it, I'm a better choice than Brendan; I've traveled these trails more and I'm a better archer."

Finally Martin turned, motioning for her to follow. He whistled and the four hunters from Ylith appeared from cover. "Tom, Jack, Will, and Edgar; Lady Bethany of Carse."

Tom and Jack were brothers, fourteen and fifteen years of age. They had been too young to fight when the Keshians had first arrived in Yabon, but were now keen to do their bit. Will looked to be in his fifties, with his gray hair and a sallow complexion, but his eyes were sharp and focused. Edgar was a slightly stout man with a bald pate, a gray beard, dark eyes, and the shoulders of a brawler. All held bows and moved like experienced hunters. Tom and Jack exchanged glances, but neither of them spoke.

"She'll be taking point," Martin told them. "Let's go."

Beth said, "If memory serves, there's a dry streambed ahead we can use to get downslope to the next trail." She spoke as if this was the expected route and no one said a word. The four hunters from Yabon might not know the young prince well enough to say for certain, but all of them were convinced he was in no mood for questions.

Beth set off at a slow trot and the others followed in line.

Days passed quietly. The forest above was thin as they followed the upper game trails. This part of the Grey Towers was below the timberline at the peaks, but still high enough that the foliage was less dense, hence less difficult to pass. It also made it easier to be seen if they weren't careful, but Bethany was proving to be a skilled trail breaker.

Martin was still nursing his injured pride five days into the march, but it was fading as he was forced to admit Beth's reasoning was borne out by the ease with which she led the party. Several times she negotiated them around difficult spots that would have confounded him, forcing him to double back and find another path.

They ate trail rations, avoiding campfires at night, so this foray lacked any sense of the fun Martin and Bethany had known hunting with their fathers. There was a quiet urgency and earnestness about the mission that was more sobering than any admonition Martin could have made. Everyone knew lives were at stake, their own and others'.

Bethany would rise at dawn and move off at a distance to relieve herself. She had instructed Martin and the four hunters in ways to relieve themselves leaving as little evidence as possible. At first Martin thought she was showing off her trail skills, but after a few days he realized that their body odor could betray their whereabouts. Bethany had taught them how to bathe in a cold stream and rid their garments of stench, using rocks and some oil pressed out of pine bark. Martin had stood guard while she bathed and the five men had rotated guard duty while cleaning themselves.

On the fifth day of their journey the rains came.

Even in midsummer, the weather on the west side of the Grey Towers could turn suddenly. Driving rain, even hail, was not uncommon. They were on the "wet" side of the mountains, as the trail they followed from the road looped to the west of the peaks; storms off the Endless Sea would drench the west face of the peaks, leaving the east side of the mountains dry. Enough rain got over the peaks that the east faces were replete with rivers and streams, rendering the mountain pastures and lower meadows fertile farmland, providing many of the cash crops shipping from the ports of the Free Cities, but they were less plagued with marsh-like depressions, stagnant pools, and mosquitoes. Martin decided that in addition to what the history books said about the Keshian colonization of Bosania, the simple truth was that the east side of the Grey Towers was just a nicer place to live than the west side, which is why it was more densely populated.

The troop was less troubled by the terrain than by keeping dry: for much of that fifth day they all huddled under a granite overhang that provided some shelter. In the last hours of the afternoon the storm blew out, and the late sun found the six members of Martin's scouting party standing, arms outstretched, catching as much of the sun as they could to accelerate drying out, looking like nothing so much as a group of turkey buzzards trying to warm themselves in the sun.

Martin was concerned, not about the discomforts of the trail, but because so far they had encountered no sign of the elves. From what he had been told, these so-called Star Elves were a city race, unlike their cousins in Elvandar. Their trail craft and woodlore were no better than that of most humans, and inferior to those like the Rangers of Natal and the Pathfinders of Krondor. Still, if Martin's estimation was correct, they were less than two days from their city of E'bar, and should be seeing signs of patrols or sentries.

But there had been nothing.

The dawn of the sixth day saw six tired, hungry, miserable scouts moving up a small draw, which should have emptied out into a woodland meadow just north of the Great Rift Valley, as it had come to be known. Here was where the Tsurani had breached space to invade Midkemia through a magic rift. To the south of that spot, the Taredhel were reputed to have constructed a remarkable city. Little was known about it, for few humans were known to have survived seeing it. The only reason Martin knew where to look was because of information provided him by Jim Dasher before leaving Rillanon. Apparently those who had visited and survived were members of the mysterious Conclave of Shadows.

Martin knew there were still many things he didn't know; and having to proceed without a clear plan was bringing him to the limits of frustration. "Go there and look around," Lord James and Jim Dasher had said. Martin had no idea what it was he was looking for, or even if he'd recognize something important if he blundered across it. More than he would ever admit, he was relieved that Bethany was with him. She possessed an innate sense of how things should be organized and saw details where Martin saw patterns: between the two of them they stood a fair chance of the mission succeeding. What Martin didn't like was the possibility of failure, especially where she was involved.

Bethany raised her hand.

Martin and the others stopped.

A voice cried out in a language none of them understood And suddenly they were surrounded by very tall, angry elves. Martin's sword had barely cleared its scabbard before he was struck by a balled fist across the cheek, and swallowed up by darkness.

Martin awoke with a groan. His head throbbed and he had trouble focusing his eyes for a moment. He found himself a short distance away from a fire, and reckoned he must have been unconscious for at least three hours, for it was clearly just after sunset. Along with Bethany and the others, he lay under a lean-to shelter. Like the others, his hands were tied behind his back, so contriving to sit upright took a little effort and each exertion caused his head to pound, and then he sat up with a grunt. Once he exchanged silent nods acknowledging that everyone was more or less intact, Martin took a good look around.

Surrounding them was an encampment of elves, but they looked nothing like those elves who had visited Crydee from Elvandar over the years. These were unusually tall and most were blond, though there were a few with darker tresses or red hair. At least half seemed to be wearing a uniform of some fashion: a blue tunic over which a cuirass of polished steel was fitted. A few were wearing white-lacquered armor and matching helms. All appeared to be sporting injuries of some kind.

Bethany whispered, "Are you all right?"

"I was about to ask that of you," he replied in a low voice. "Except for a throbbing head, I'm all right." He glanced around. "Where are we?"

"I'm not sure," she said. "We were ambushed and taken without injury. They seem to want us alive." She nodded toward the four hunters who all sat silently. "We were bound and blindfolded. I think we're maybe an hour or less from E'bar, if it's where we think it is. We're in the valley." With her chin she pointed and Martin could make out a faint glimmer from the setting sun playing off peaks opposite where they rested. The eastern rim of the valley was higher than the rest, so while they were quickly entering shadows, there was some illumination still.

"Has anyone talked to you?" asked Martin.

"They seem rather too busy."

Martin watched the camp and noted that while no one was moving frantically, there was a sense of urgency about these elves. The economy of motion that blessed their race masked an intensity that betrayed itself by glimpses and hints. "There's something going on."

Bethany nodded toward the south. "See anything?"

Martin craned his neck. In the falling twilight he could make out a faint red glow coming from the south. "What is that?" he asked.

"I have no idea," she responded. "At first I thought it might be a trick of the light, some reflection of the sunset off a cloud, but as it got darker that glow continued."

They both looked on in silence, wondering what was in store next.

Time seemed to drag, as none of the elves seemed aware of their presence, let alone concerned with their comfort. Finally, the burly, bald-headed hunter, Edgar, said "If they don't cut me loose soon, Highness, I'm going to be sitting here in a pool of my own piss."

One of the elves who was sitting near a fire a dozen yards away turned and looked at the captives. He stood up and slowly walked over to the lean-to and knelt on one knee before Edgar. Pulling out his large belt knife, he cut his bonds and in a slightly accented Common Tongue—the trading language around the Bitter Sea—he said, "Go over there." He pointed with the dagger and indicated a spot some distance from the camp. "We've dug a trench."

Edgar said, "Ah . . . thank you." He got up on what were obviously stiff knees after having sat on the ground for hours and hobbled off.

"Come back when you're finished, human," said the Star Elf. "You do not want to be out there in the dark alone and unarmed."

The elf then looked at Martin. "Highness?"

Martin hesitated, then said, "I'm Martin conDoin, brother to Duke Henry, cousin to the late King Gregory."

The elf was silent, then nodded once, stood, and walked away. He walked past the spot where he had been sitting, circled around the large campfire, and vanished into the gloom in the trees beyond the clearing.

"What was that?" asked Bethany.

"I do not know," said Martin.

Edgar returned a little while later, and seeing the elves unconcerned with his coming and going, he knelt behind Martin and untied him. Martin's arms felt as if they were shot through with needles as he moved them slowly, getting his circulation back. Bethany and the others were quickly freed, and when they had all moved enough to regain some sense of comfort, Bethany said, "What now?"

Martin said, "I don't know. Look." He indicated the large contingent of elves a short way off. "No one seems to care we're unbound."

Edgar said, "I think it's what that elf said, about being out there unarmed."

"What do you mean?" asked Martin.

Edgar said, "I've been a hunter all my life, Highness. I know when something unseen is nearby; you can hear things, sense things. There are . . . things out in those woods and I think we don't want to go there."

"So what?" asked Tom. "We wait?"

Martin nodded. "We wait. If these elves wanted to harm us, they would have done so by now. I'm getting the distinct impression they see us as something of a nuisance. They're preoccupied with other matters."

"Looks like they've come through a pretty nasty fight, Highness," said Will.

Occasionally a wounded warrior would appear, either staggering in alone or being helped by another, who would turn and trot back into the forest to the south toward the faint red glow. The elves in the camp attended the wounded, dressing injuries, providing food and water, or simply letting them rest. Once an elf with a bandaged leg rose from his rest, picked up his weapons, and hobbled off down the trail leading to the south.

Time passed and suddenly three elves walked purposefully toward them. Martin stood up. The two flanking elves were obviously warriors, bedecked in the white-and-pale-blue uniforms he had seen mixed in with the other warriors, and the one in the center wore an ornate blue robe, but one now stained with mud and blood. He sported a large bruise on the left cheek as well as a heavily bandaged right arm.

"You're a prince of Kesh or the Kingdom?" he asked Martin.

Fighting back the need to explain, Martin simply said, "Kingdom. Yes."

If the elf had reservations, he kept them to himself. Instead he just said, "Come," and turned to walk away.

Martin nodded to the others to accompany him and they all followed the elf, who glanced back at them. "I am named Tanderae. I am by rank Loremaster of the Clans of the Seven Stars. There is something you must see."

They followed him into the woods, along a dark path through the boles. There was just enough light from the fires behind and the red glow ahead that they could make their way.

Abruptly the path widened and deepened and they found themselves in a broad down-sloping ramp, hastily cut into the soil to allow quick escape to what Martin decided could only be called a rear-echelon rest area, a place where the wounded could be tended to and exhausted soldiers could eat and sleep as much as circumstances permitted. This route was not hollowed out by tools wielded by hand, driven by muscle and sweat. It was perfectly cut as if by some giant gardener's trowel then smoothed by a sculptor. In the alien light it was without seam or flaw, almost as if the rock had been made liquid and fashioned like soft clay, then made hard again.

A soft glow came from a series of stones set upright along

the pathway every ten feet or so, a pale blue light that made traveling up and down the slope easy at night. The distant red light was becoming brighter as they walked down the ramp to a flat terrace, bordering on what had been a ridge-line before the magical excavation behind them had moved tons of soil, trees, and boulders.

Suddenly they were out in the open, and they all stopped and gaped.

Miles in the distance, down in the deepest part of the valley, stood the city of E'bar, the ancient elven word for "home."

Martin could barely credit his eyes. Even at this distance the city was massive. Rumors had begun to circulate during the war with Kesh that the elven city had been constructed by arts beyond human understanding. Seeing it, Martin counted the rumors as true.

Graceful towers dominated the heart of E'bar, but from what could be seen at this distance, the entire city was a work of art. Looking down at the magically transformed stone beneath their feet, Martin imagined the walls of the city would be smooth and seamless. But it was hard to tell: tantalizing hints of what was awaiting a visitor were masked by a scintillating bubble of energy that surrounded the entire city, starting a few yards beyond the great circular city's walls and rising up above the loftiest pinnacle. Intermittently, random glimmers of brilliant white-yellow diamonds seemed to flow across the surface, erupting into lances of blinding light that shot out for dozens of yards before vanishing, leaving the eye blind for a moment from the brilliance. Except for those bursts, the dome was a transparent red shell, pulsing with energy and giving off the ruby light that had illuminated the night sky.

A ring of elves, thousands from what Martin could judge, encircled the massive city. Shafts of light erupted from dozens of points in the line every second and magicians or priests cast magic at that barrier. Where the magic struck, tiny lightninglike bursts rebounded from the surface, then faded.

Tanderae said to Martin, "Behold the last home of my people."

Martin was silent for a moment, then glanced at his companions, who looked equally perplexed by the scene before them. At last Martin said, "You were driven from your city and now you attack a magic defense?"

Tanderae smiled slightly. "We fled from our city, but that energy shell is not that city's defense. It's ours. Many of my people are giving their lives to prevent what's inside from escaping."

Thinking about the number of exhausted and wounded elves he had seen, Martin began to form a question. But then he saw a tiny breach in the shell surrounding the city. Instantly a score of dark forms exploded from the gap before it closed. Those creatures of inky blackness moved straight for the line of magic users and silver-and-white-clad soldiers threw themselves before the magicians, slashing frantically.

They were too far from the fight to see details, but eventually the black figures were gone and the elves re-formed, a few limping back to their line.

"What were those?"

"We call them the Forbidden. They are an ancient species, so hateful they make their demon servants appear benign. They have found a way into our city, and if they escape that barrier, life as we know it on this world will rapidly cease."

Martin was aghast. "How long can you hold?"

"Until the last of us," said the Loremaster. "We brought this horror to our home world and we will die here protecting Midkemia."

"Why haven't you sent for help?" asked Martin.

"Because every man, woman, and child not killed in the explosion that brought those horrors here has been fighting them, holding them in." Tanderae looked at Martin. "So now you are here, we don't have to send a messenger." He nodded to Martin. "Prince of the Kingdom, we seek help."

Bethany said quietly, "Now we know why someone

wanted every army in the west as far from here as they could maneuver them."

Martin could only nod.

The elves provided them with food, though not a great deal of it, and filled their water skins. Tanderae walked with them to the original clearing in which they had been held and was silent until he reached the large lean-to where they had been left after being captured. He was impassive, though Martin saw what he thought were hints of fatigue and perhaps even hopelessness in the way he spoke.

The Loremaster of the Clans of the Seven Stars said, "Rest here until sunrise, human. The few hours will make no difference, and while there is little chance of you encountering any danger, falling down the mountain and breaking your neck would serve neither of our causes. If you move downslope from here for an hour, you'll find the game trail upon which you were taken." He looked at Martin. "I know little of you humans. Others among us have visited your cities and understand your politics and might be better able to convince you, but at this time I have nothing more to show than what you've already seen, and I can only tell you this:

"For centuries, we of the Clans of the Seven Stars have battled the demon legions across worlds, and only at the end have we come to understand those demons were no more than the servants of a far darker evil. Once we numbered in the millions, more than all your nations of man on Midkemia, but now we are as you see us.

"It is bitter to say, but we were betrayed by our own leaders. I was a member of the Circle of Light. We were scholars and delvers into mystery, creators of art and magic. Those of us who sought enlightenment and knowledge were at first opposed by those who took power; then we were named traitors to the cause of our people, hunted and killed. When we were offered amnesty we took it, and some like myself even entered the Regent's Meet. Now I find it was our own leaders who betrayed us to our most bitter enemies. If the death of my race comes, it comes from within."

"But why?" asked Martin.

"I do not know," answered the Loremaster. "Madness, offers of survival, faith in a power that corrupted. I can only speculate." He sighed. "It doesn't matter. This is what we face. Inside that dome is the true enemy, those behind the demon legions, seeking their way into this world to destroy all they touch. I have already sent word to the north, to the Queen of the Eledhel and her consort, Lord Tomas. But even their magic will not be enough. So, we need human allies.

"When you return, seek me out, or if I am gone, find Egun, leader of the remaining Sentinels, and if he is gone, whoever may be left." He reached out and gripped Martin's shoulders. "Help us." Then he turned and headed back to the embattled city.

Will, Tom, Jack, and Edgar said little as they traveled back toward Ylith. They knew without being told that they had seen something both majestic and terrible. Even Martin and Bethany had little life experience to put what they had witnessed into any context. The encounters with those supernatural demonic creatures who had appeared during the assault on Ylith, and the response of the magic users who were in the city, were relatively normal in comparison to what they had seen in the Grey Tower Mountains.

As they approached the Keshian lines, Martin said to the four hunters, "Men, I would take it as a personal favor if you said nothing to anyone about what we've seen."

"Who'd believe us, Highness?" asked Tom.

The others nodded and Will chuckled, but Martin pressed on. "Still, rumors spread like fire on dry straw, and Ylith is barely approaching what we might think of as normal times. There are still plenty of scared, battle-weary folks who don't need to be told more horror is on the way. All right?"

The four agreed and Bethany said, "What are we going to do when we reach the city?"

Martin said, "There are some things I need to talk over with George Bolton before I head south."

She sighed and patted his arm. The idea of him leaving so soon after arriving didn't please her. "What are you going to do?" she asked.

"I've got to get to Krondor as fast as I can, and hope a magician named Ruffio is still there, or someone knows how to reach him."

"Why?"

"Because riding horses until they drop to reach Prince Edward isn't going to solve anything, because Edward's not about to leave the Fields of Albalyn with a civil war threatening, and besides, from what we saw, bows and arrows are only so useful. No, we need magicians, and if I can find Ruffio, he can get word to where it needs to go, to the temples, to Stardock . . ." He glanced over at the four hunters and lowered his voice. "And to others I'll tell you about when we're alone."

She looked confused and curious, but she nodded to say she would wait.

"Let's go," said Martin. "If we're quick enough we should be able to slip behind the southern patrol and loop around to the main gate of the city. No need to use the old keep tunnel if we're already back on our side of the line."

It was an exhausted and filthy band that reached the gates of Ylith an hour after sunrise six days after leaving the elves. By the time the gates of the city were opened, Captain Bolton, Brendan, and the mayor were waiting. Martin outlined the situation as Sergeant Oaks appeared, obviously just awakened. When Martin finished, the old sergeant said, "Orders, Highness?"

Martin said, "I'm going to need four men to travel with me to Krondor. The rest of you will stay to bolster the garrison here until I return."

Oaks wasn't happy, but he merely said, "Yes, Highness."

"We'll need two horses each and we'll ride them until they drop; there's a need for speedy travel."

Brendan said, "I'll go see to the mounts."

"No," said Martin. "Send someone else. I have something I need you to do. We'll talk later."

Something about Martin's demeanor made Brendan think twice about objecting. He signaled for one of the boys who were acting as messengers and aides for the soldiers and instructed him as to Martin's needs. The boy ran off in a hurry.

Martin quickly finished detailing some things he'd like done in the city to the mayor, Bolton, and Oaks, then motioned for Bethany and Brendan to accompany him as he left for the mayor's house for a quick bath and meal. Once the three of them were out of earshot of the others, he said, "I've got some things I'd like the two of you to do. If either of you want to say no, I'll understand. I can order Oaks to send a couple of his men, but I'd rather leave these tasks to people I trust."

"Whatever you ask," said Brendan.

"Yes," agreed Bethany.

Turning to Bethany, he said, "I need you to take the four hunters after you've rested and travel to Elvandar."

"Elvandar?" she said. "Really?"

Martin nodded. "I know that elf Tanderae said he'd sent someone north, but I'd feel better knowing we had someone talking to the Elf Queen. Those Star Elves don't strike me as practiced hunters, and we've had word of the Brotherhood of the Dark Path moving down from the Northlands again. Between those dark murderers and the Keshians, we've no guarantees the Elf Queen will know what's happening in the Grey Towers. That's elf magic and maybe she can help. But she can't do anything if she doesn't know.

"From the Yabon side of the mountains to the south side of the River Boundary, you shouldn't even see a hint of a Keshian or a Dark Brother, so I think it's a relatively safe journey. Besides, you know how to move through the woods like an elf."

She smiled. "It will be good to see our mothers." Both Martin's mother and Bethany's were safe in Elvandar since fleeing Crydee.

"Tell the boys and take what you need and leave in the morning," he said. "I'm leaving as soon as the horses are ready—I've got most of today to ride, but you could use a few hours' sleep."

"What do I say to the Elf Queen?"

"You saw as much as I did, Beth. Just tell her what you saw and that these Star Elves are hard-pressed by whatever is trapped within their city." He paused. "If you can remember what Tanderae said about betrayal from within, that might be important."

She nodded, hesitated, then realized Martin wished to speak with his brother alone. She kissed him lightly on the cheek. "I'll see you later." She hurried off.

Brendan said, "What do you want me to do, Martin?"

"I'm going to ask much of you, but do you think you can find a boat and get down the coast past the Quegan patrols?"

Brendan was quiet for a minute, then said, "I think so. There are a couple of small cutters still in the harbor. One's a nice little double headsail that should make good time. I can sail her at night and lay in close to the coast with the mast down in the day if I see Quegan galleys. If I hug close to shore and avoid shoals, yes, I can get south of here. Are we sailing to Krondor?"

"No," said Martin. "I'm riding, as I told the others. I must get word to Prince Edward of this invasion or attack or whatever it is in the Grey Towers. But as certain as bears sleep in the winter, whatever those elves are facing needs magic as well as arms to withstand it, and I'm remembering what Jim Dasher told us about our last night in Rillanon."

"The Conclave?"

"Yes, and you remember where he said we'd find them?"

Brendan's expression turned sour. "Sorcerer's Isle."

"If the Conclave is there, you can safely ignore all those tales of monsters and evil sorcerers. And if you can get to

Sarth, it's almost a straight sail south to the island. The stories have a castle on the east tip of the island, so that's where I'd start looking."

Brendan nodded. "I understand. If you can't find that Ruffio, you'll be riding hard from Krondor to the Fields of Albalyn."

"And that means weeks before I can find Prince Edward. And who knows if he'll be willing to send anyone to the west?"

"Okay, I'll leave at sunset and start for Sarth."

Martin looked around. "It's odd how normal this city looks at times like these."

"Enjoy, brother," said Brendan. "I'm coming to believe normal as we once knew it will never return."

"As long as something normal returns, I'll settle for it being different," said Martin.

The two brothers took one last look around the still-quiet street and headed in different directions, on different tasks, but sharing the same determination to do their best or die trying.

6

ASSASSINS

Hal lunged.

Ty Hawkins beat aside the blade and riposted. Hal barely avoided the point of Ty's sword with a frantic parry, but before he could get back on line, Ty was already in place, ready for his attack.

"Enough," said Tal Hawkins. To Hal he said, "You're still over-reaching when you sense a weakness. Most times you'll survive that mistake, because you're as fast a blade as I've seen in my life. But Ty is not like most of the opponents you'll face. And you must never assume the man facing you is not my son's equal. Else you will find yourself losing the bout."

"Or facedown on the ground bleeding," added Ty. He removed the basket helm they wore for practice and wiped away the perspiration. "But you came close."

Hal removed his helm and also wiped his brow with the back of his gauntlet. He motioned to a servant who took his helm, then Ty's.

Tal smiled at his son. "When you faced him in the Masters' Court, I told you he was faster."

Ty grinned back. "I'm going to have to practice faster, I guess."

Hal laughed. "Thank you for the bout. I needed it."

Tal put his hand on Hal's shoulder. "I understand. Waiting for the other side to make the next move can be grinding on the nerves.

"I feel like a steam. You two need to clean up."

Ty and Hal exchanged questioning looks, and Ty said, "He's right. We both reek."

Hal glanced around and decided he'd find out what this was about when they were alone. He motioned for the palace servant who had been assigned to him as he unbuttoned his heavily padded practice tunic. When it was off he handed it to the page and said, "Bring fresh clothes to the baths."

Ty echoed the instruction to the lad who cared for his needs, and the two young nobles left the empty room Hal had commandeered for use as a practice hall. It was used primarily as an extra dining hall, hence it being long enough for good fencing practice. That meant it also had a back entrance that opened onto a long hall that led to stairs down to the next level, the main servants' quarters and lesser guest quarters, a floor above the baths.

They moved quickly down the stairs into the very busy royal kitchens. A massive complex of rooms, they were centered around a core kitchen with two hearths for roasting meat or boiling soups, preparation space, and ovens. Even with no king in residence, there were hundreds of mouths to feed every day, and with the current influx of eastern nobles attending the Congress when it ratified the next King—whenever that finally occurred—the demand for food and drink was constant.

Two auxiliary kitchens were also in operation, adding two more hearths and four working ovens, and a further two for backup. The last two were used if a gala was under way or on Midsummer Day, the Festival of Banapis, when the gates of the palace were thrown open and the city feasted at the King's table.

The two young nobles made their way through a busy press of cooks and helpers, with one particularly striking blond helper catching Ty's eye. He smiled and paused to speak with her but Hal grabbed his arm. "Later."

Ty threw Hal a dark look, but said nothing. They moved through the servants' wing of the palace, heading back toward the main corridors that fed into the grand entryway, the hall from the main doors of the palace—once the heart of an ancient keep—to the throne room. As Hal was reminded each time he needed to go from one side of the palace to the other, it was massive.

Originally a fortress above a village on one of several islands in what became known as the Sea of Kingdoms, the fortress had been replaced by several increasingly larger constructions, first of wood and mud, then stone, and finally the first castle had been erected on this site. Of the last castle, only vestigial walls remained, now part of the heart of the palace, surrounding on three sides the King's reception area and throne room. The rear wall had been torn down to accommodate floor-to-ceiling windows looking out over the bay.

Now the two young men cut across the entry hallway, which was as wide as most streets in the city, and reached the beginning of the labyrinth of apartments and offices that ended at the royal apartment complex on the opposite side from where they started. Rillanon might not have the tradition of opulence that was found in the older Kingdom of

Roldem, but it seemed to be attempting to overtake it as best it could, Hal thought. He glanced through the massive doors that opened onto the reception courtyard and gave a view of the city beyond. In the afternoon sun, it was dazzling.

Rodric the Fourth, occasionally called the Mad King, though never in this palace, had been obsessed with turning Rillanon into the most splendid city in the world. To that end he had started a beautification project of unprecedented scale. Stone quarries in all corners of the Kingdom, and some in Queg and Kesh, were searched out for the finest marble and granite, which were shipped to the city in a steady stream to replace the ancient walls of the palaces, the royal complex, then the royal precinct. Over the years subsequent kings had continued the process, so that merchants and commoners found stonecutters and masons with royal commissions arriving one day to announce that old masonry, stone facing, and even ancient whitewashed daub was being replaced by stone, courtesy of the King.

The result centuries later was that on a sunny day, when approached from sea, Rillanon sparkled like a jewel, and as one came closer, the rainbow of colors playing over the façades of the city was stunning. From rose to pale blue, golden yellow to pale violet, the range of colors was breathtaking.

At times of conflict, the cost to the royal treasury might be debated, and the impact on taxes was undoubted, but no one argued the results. Rillanon was the jewel of the Sea of Kingdoms.

Hal and Ty reached a long descending staircase, lit by lamps in sconces, and reached a basement two floors below the main hall. One of the pleasures of the palace was that Hal's ancestors had installed a Quegan-style bath in a previously dank and little-used subbasement. Unlike the Quegans, who had evolved bathing into a pastime, the Kesh's baths were more a way to mitigate the scorching summer heat with cool pools and fountains, dipping in and out all day, so that cleanliness was rarely an issue for the scantily clad Truebloods of the city of Kesh. They could drop their light robes or girdles, slip into cool water, and wait for the evening's cooler air.

The Quegans, on the other hand, had come to colonize the Bitter Sea, and as a result had a much more varied climate. They had developed a three-room bath process, later up to five rooms, for steam and dry heat.

Hal had discovered the almost sybaritic pleasures of bathing since coming to Rillanon. He and Ty entered the first room, the cold bath, and handed their clothes to attendants. The dry stone floors told them they were the first nobles of the day to partake of the bath's pleasures.

The two young men slipped into the water, descending two broad steps of marble, until they were able to kneel and cover their shoulders with the bracing cold water. Hal dunked his head and when he came up said, "If I were King, my friend, I'd be here every day."

Ty ducked his head and emerged, wiping his face. He grinned. "These days the desire to be King makes you a target, Hal."

"True," said Hal, turning and swimming to the far end of the pool, Ty a half stroke behind him.

They reached the end, pulled themselves up onto the stone deck, and found servants holding towels. The softness of the King's woven towels never ceased to amaze Hal. He had grown up in a castle where coarse linen was the fabric of choice for drying everything, from kitchen utensils to dukes' sons.

They walked through a short hall that brought them into the warm room. A shallow pool of water occupied all but a two-foot-wide ledge around the perimeter and was filled with warm water. A series of low wooden stools were arrayed so as many as a dozen bathers could be attended at any time. With only two attendants, Hal knew that someone on the palace chancellor's staff always knew how many residents were approaching the baths.

They sat on stools while the two attendants, boys who appeared to be approaching manhood, set about soaping up the two young nobles. As Hal endured having someone else soap his hair—something he hadn't had done by anyone since his mother stopped doing it when he was a boy—Ty laughed. "In Queg, and the city of Kesh, this task would likely befall a couple of lovely young girls."

Hal laughed at that. "If that were true here, I'd never get you to the hot room."

"A time and place for everything, I suppose. You natives of the Isles tend to be a bit proper. You're almost as conservative as the folk in Roldem."

"You have Isles parents," observed Hal.

"True, but I was Olasko-born and spent most of my youth there and in Roldem. I also hold titles from both cities."

When they were completely covered in soap, they stood for the servants to pour buckets of warm water over their heads. Dripping wet, they made their way to the next room, where a very deep hot pool waited. They slipped in and Hal could barely avoid gasping from the sudden increase in heat.

After a moment he could feel his muscles loosen from the vigorous swordplay. "I could linger here for an hour or two," he said.

Laughing, Ty pulled himself up. "Maybe later, but Father is waiting."

Hal groaned, but followed his friend to where more servants waited with large fluffy towels, which the two young men wrapped around their waists. They moved through a heavily curtained entrance that led to a short hall with two doors, one on either hand.

"Wet or dry?" asked Hal.

"Father will be in dry. That way he won't have to bathe off the sweat."

They entered the dry chamber, a spacious room with cedarwood walls and a large bench. A bin of heated rocks had been placed against one wall. Hot coals could be added from a slot in the wall beneath, so the attendant didn't have to enter the room.

Two men waited on the bench, both wearing towels. Next

to Tal Hawkins sat Jim Dasher, which surprised Hal not at all. The two older men sat on the higher of the two long benches across the back of the room. Jim held up his hand for silence, then indicated the bench at his feet. Both younger men sat.

A sudden eruption of steam from the steam box filled the room with moisture and a sibilant hiss. Jim said, "One of my men has ensured we are not overheard."

Hal and Ty exchanged quick glances, then Hal said, "News?"

"Not of the good sort," answered Jim Dasher. He leaned forward, elbows on knees, and said, "You've been marked for death." He looked at Hal.

Hal was silent for a moment, then said, "You said that might happen."

"And so it has," answered Jim.

"Do we know who wants me dead?"

Jim smiled. "A lot of people want you dead, Hal, we just don't know who is paying for it." He sighed. "I got word early this morning off a ship from Roldem, sent by a good friend." Hal knew he meant the Lady Franciezka Sorboz, a woman who held much the same position in Roldem as Jim Dasher did in the Isles. "We'd a report from the Conclave a while back that the Nighthawks had come to terms with them, basically safe passage in exchange for . . . getting out of the assassination trade, more or less. At least they were no longer lending support to the demon worshippers who had been plaguing us for a very long time. As a result, those seeking a blade for hire or a poisoner have had fewer options; in short it's a seller's market.

"That being the case, both my friend in Roldem and I have had certain people watched, those able to broker less reputable contracts and arrangements, some who are not averse to setting up such deals then selling information about those deals to a third party."

"You," said Ty.

"Or . . . your friend in Roldem," added Hal.

Jim nodded.

Hal asked, "What do I do?"

Jim sat back. "For the moment, nothing. I've some good men out looking for a pair of fellows who've sailed up from Kesh to Roldem, then on to Rillanon. Given the recent unpleasantness between Kesh and the Kingdom, anyone coming straight from there to here would be examined carefully by several hundred soldiers surrounding the docks."

"A pair of sailors off a ship . . . ?"

Jim shrugged.

"Do you have a description?" asked Tal, reaching over and taking a ladle of water from a bucket and pouring it over his head.

"I doubt they look the same anymore," said Jim. "I've got on a ship looking like a nobleman, and got off it looking like something that crawled out of the bilge. For a target in the palace"—he pointed at Hal—"even if he is *only* a distant royal . . . that means a great deal of gold and only the best would accept the contract." Jim took the ladle from Tal, refilled it from the nearby bucket, and poured it over his own head. "I've never been one for this dry heat."

Tal smiled. "My people in the mountains had sweat lodges when I was a boy. You get used to it. After a fashion, you even enjoy it."

"What I'll enjoy is getting out of it," said Jim Dasher, rising. To Hal he said, "Pack a bag and leave it in your rooms, by the doors so that my servants can find it quickly. Be ready to leave the moment I give word. Until then, stay in the palace."

Tal looked at his son and said, "Pack as well. You're going with him." Then he rose and departed.

Ty looked at Hal and said, "I guess I'm going with you."

"Apparently."

Rising, Hal said, "Let's go gather our things."

"And then we wait," finished Ty.

"Boredom beckons," said Hal.

Ty laughed. "In a palace full of serving women who would love to make close acquaintance with a duke?"

Hal sighed and said nothing.

As they walked to the dressing room where fresh clothing awaited them, Ty said, "Stephané."

Hal again said nothing.

"Sorry," said Ty.

"It's . . . something I need to get used to."

This time, Ty said nothing. He understood what a beauty Stephané was, and how resilient she had proven herself to be when Hal and he had helped her escape Roldem. But Tyrone Hawkins had never found a woman to hold his attention longer than a few weeks, perhaps a month at most. His childhood had been less than instructive about how women and men should be together, he thought occasionally. He knew the facts of his childhood, that his father was some unknown Olaskon soldier, though Talwin Hawkins treated him as his own, and he loved him as his father, but there was a sadness about his mother, one that never seemed to completely pass. He knew she loved her husband, but there was something missing. Ironically, he felt closer to his adopted father than to his natural mother, though she loved him dearly.

He pushed aside thoughts that led to doubt and concern, and turned his mind to something much more enjoyable: that pretty blond wench in the kitchen who had smiled at him as he had passed through. As they reached the changing room, he decided the first thing he'd do was to find out her name.

A knock at the door awoke Hal. It was still dark. After the many cautions he'd received from Jim Dasher, he had his sword in hand when he opened the door. Opening it slightly, he saw a page waiting. "Lord James asks you to attend him, my lord."

Hal nodded and said, "Wait here."

It took him only a few minutes to dress, and again he heard the echoing cautions in his head; he wore sturdy clothing suitable for travel rather than court finery. He followed the page and was surprised that even in the predawn darkness, the palace at Rillanon was busy.

They reached Duke James's quarters and found Jim Dasher, Ty, and a court chirurgeon attending the Duke. Hal hurried to the old Duke's bedside. "Are you ill, my lord?"

Waving away the hovering chirurgeon, Duke James coughed and said, "Just a bit of an ague. It'll pass."

Hal glanced at Jim, who shook his head slightly.

Feeling alarm rising, Hal asked, "How may I serve, my lord?"

Old Duke James said, "That reprobate grandson of mine says someone's come to kill you. He's inclined to let you sit here as bait and capture the murderous dogs who are sniffing around. I, on the other hand, think it best to get you somewhere else. They can't kill you if they don't know where you are. So, get going and stay alive."

Hal was caught between concern and amusement, but managed to keep a serious expression as he said, "Yes, my lord."

Jim nodded toward the bed. "My grandfather is holding this kingdom together with strength of will. There are nobles who've stood silently, not allying with Montgomery or Chadwick, or thinking of throwing their weight behind Oliver." Jim closed his eyes as if suffering a headache, then said, "We take these trials as they come. Now I need to get you two off this island," he said to Hal and Ty. "Then I must have a very important talk with Montgomery."

Hal and Ty listened, and said nothing.

"If in a few days you hear my grandfather is no longer among the living and that Montgomery is now Duke of Rillanon, assume I'm dead."

Hal's face showed alarm. He glanced at the old Duke, who nodded.

"Your very distant cousin's claim to the throne benefits him if he's Duke of Rillanon, the man in theory I would pay fealty to, and who would be in a far better position to allocate favors before a vote in the Congress."

"And have control over your agents," added Ty with a tone of concern that surprised Hal.

Jim nodded. "So I must have a chat with dear old Monty and insist he let me assume the office of Duke so I can maintain the balance between all the raving lunatics around us who think being King is a wonderful idea!" His voice rose at the last, his anger starting to manifest itself.

"Can you convince him?" asked Hal.

Jim said, "A combination of promises and threats . . . perhaps. Our Montgomery is a man of low tastes at times and has made some ill-advised choices. His wife is a simple woman, but her father is the Duke of Bas-Tyra, who would not be pleased to know that his son-in-law is unfaithful on a regular basis, preferring the company of young girls—very young girls—to his wife."

Hal said nothing, but his face bore an expression of distaste.

"Without Bas-Tyra, Montgomery's claim will fall short. Bas-Tyra influences the votes of every noble from here to the Eastern Kingdoms. A great deal of the plotting and dealing around his claim presumes that he has his father-in-law's backing."

It was Ty who said, "Still, rumors against the possibility of his daughter being Queen of the Isles?"

It was the old Duke who said, "Bas-Tyra is a cautious man, but not without ambition. Not for himself, but as young Ty observes, perhaps for his daughter. Bas-Tyra has not openly supported anyone, but in the end he'll do the right thing for the Crown. Now, Montgomery," he added, looking less than happy, "he's another thing. Not a driven man, like some, but one capable of being led." To Jim he said, "When it comes to claiming the Crown, you must convince him not to stand before the Priest of Ishap."

"I'll convince him, or kill him," said Jim.

Hal was speechless.

"Go on, now," said Duke James from his bed. "Leave an old man to his rest and go cause some havoc for our enemies."

Jim walked out of the old man's room with Ty and Hal. Once outside, Hal asked, "How is he, really?"

"Not good," said Jim, his tone matter-of-fact, but behind it lingered a hint of sadness. "I've sent for a healing priest from the Temple of Sung, but there are only so many times you can fend off death. My grandfather is approaching ninety, though he looks a man twenty years younger when he's in his armor bellowing at the palace guard." He glanced back toward the door of the Duke's private chambers.

"Now," said Jim. "I've had your travel bags collected from your rooms, Hal. From here you're to go straight to the stables, where two horses are waiting. They are sturdy, but unremarkable, as is the tack. In short, once you're out of the gate, you're swords-for-hire, or young adventurers, or whatever brand of feckless gadabouts you care to be.

"Half the ships in the Sea of Kingdoms are arrayed to the west of us, a blockade no captain could run. Every ship in and out is being boarded and inspected by someone, either captains loyal to the Crown, Montgomery's faction, or Chadwick's. But if you ride north for a few days, on the west coast you'll find a fishing village called Kempton. Ask in the tavern for a man named Moss. He'll show you to a boat you two can certainly handle. It'll look shoddy, but in fact it's in excellent condition, and with some luck you can hug the coast traveling northeast, and when you see any break, you can make a run for Bas-Tyra. Once there, find the Inn of the Black Ram, ask for Anton, and he'll set you on your way to Edward." He looked from face to face. "Any questions?"

When there weren't any, he said, "Go now, and may the gods watch over you." Jim walked away.

"And your grandfather," said Hal after him.

Hal turned and left, Ty a half step behind. As they moved toward the stables, Ty said, "I do not envy that man."

"I never have," said Hal as they turned a corner. "I admire him, for he has thankless and bloody work to do, but I would never wish his burdens on anyone."

They hurried down a flight of stairs that led to a door

opening on the old marshaling yard, and across it lay the royal stables. They were halfway across the dark marshaling yard when Hal realized there were no lanterns lit in the stable. Then he heard a nervous nicker from a horse inside.

His sword was out of its scabbard as he heard the faint click. He leaped to the right and slammed into Ty, knocking him over, and came up as a second crossbow bolt sped through the space just occupied by the young noble from Olasko.

Ty was a step behind Hal as they charged through the large open door into the royal stables. Without a word, both men dived headfirst, striking the ground in a tuck and rolling to their feet, swords at the ready. The sound of crossbows being fired over their heads demonstrated the wisdom of their choice, and a horse cried out in pain and started kicking out at its stall as an errant bolt struck it.

Hal turned to his left and Ty to his right, protecting each other's back. They paused only for a moment before moving toward opposite ends of the large stable.

Hal saw a dark shape moving in a crouch while all around horses neighed and whinnied in panic. Hal knew that he had seconds before the assassin reloaded his crossbow or fled into the night. He charged.

The man rose up holding a small, one-handed bow that fired a dart rather than a bolt. Hal slashed with his sword, knocking the weapon aside, and punched the assassin hard in the face with his left hand. The man staggered back and Hal lunged, nicking him in the left side. Suddenly the man had two dirks out, and executed a fast feint followed by a slash toward Hal's throat. Hal barely fell back enough to avoid losing the fight there and then.

He ducked and a dirk cut through air where he had been standing a moment before. Then he jabbed with his sword and felt the tip strike the man's already injured side. The assassin gasped in pain and both men were suddenly enmeshed in a deadly duel.

Hal stepped back, his sword's point aimed at his opponent,

who crouched and took his measure. It was clear that the assassin had expected Hal to be dead and safely away by now.
Hal realized he had two opportunities to emerge victorious:
either kill the assassin and hope Ty did the same with his
opponent, or keep him occupied until relief arrived. It was
the middle of the night, but someone from the nearby servants' quarters would surely hear the struggle, or notice the
absence of the certainly now-dead lackeys who had failed to
return from readying the horses for him and Ty.

The assassin also realized that and knew his only hope of
survival was to finish this quickly. He suddenly threw one
of his dirks.

Hal managed to beat the blade aside and stumbled backward, trying to get his sword around from his blocking move
to a position from which he could employ the point.

The assassin didn't give him the chance, but lowered his
shoulder and charged. Hal brought his sword hand back hard,
striking the rushing thug on the side of the head with his
pommel. That staggered him and Hal felt an off-target blow
slide across his side as the dirk missed his torso. He slammed
the man over the head again, gripped the back of his shirt
with his left hand, and fell onto the extended right arm. The
sound of bone cracking accompanied by a gasp of pain was
heard as he struck the ground, his full weight on the assassin's arm. Hal drew back his sword hilt and slammed the man
on the head for a third time, rendering him senseless.

Hal rolled up onto his feet, his sword pointed at the now-
motionless assassin, as shouts of inquiry came from the servants' quarters.

Hal glanced into the gloom of the stable in time to see Ty
approaching with his sword at the ready. "Yours?" he asked.

"Dead," said Ty. "This one?"

"Not yet."

Servants with lanterns arrived, followed moments later by
palace guards. Hal looked at his attacker in the lantern light.
He was an unremarkable man, slight of build and wearing
simple garb, a city man who would easily blend into a crowd.

"He doesn't look like an assassin," said Hal.

"Neither did mine," said Ty. "But they almost did the job." He quickly knelt and opened the man's mouth, motioning for a torch to be brought close to his face. "No false teeth," he said. "Not fanatics like the Nighthawks, then." He sheathed his sword as he stood, and motioned for the guards to pick up the unconscious killer.

Hal said, "Take him to a cell and notify Jim Dasher."

The guards lifted him up. A servant cried suddenly, "Oh, dear! Poor Lonny and Mark are dead!"

"See to them," said Hal to another pair of guards.

"How did you know?" asked Ty.

"Know what?"

"They were there. To knock me down?"

"I heard a click when he set the trigger on his crossbow."

Ty was silent for a moment, then laughed. "So, for want of some lubricant, we're alive."

Hal chuckled. "I almost got myself killed forgetting we're not dueling."

"Ah, yes," said Ty. "It can be a bad habit, trying to fence while your opponent is brawling. Swords have edges, too."

Patting his sword, Hal said, "And pommels. They make a fair bludgeon."

"What now?"

Looking around at the building crowd, Hal said, "As much as I would like to tarry and find out exactly who is trying to kill me, I think it best if we follow orders. We ride."

"Wise choice. If Jim finds out who is behind this, he'll send word. And if another attempt is made, it's best for you to be somewhere else."

They quickly finished the saddling begun by the two dead lackeys and within ten minutes were riding out the postern gate of the palace, vanishing into the night.

Three days later they reached the village of Kempton and found the promised boat. They waited until the evening tide, then slipped out after dark, sailing along the coast on a northeasterly tack.

The third morning after heading up the coast, Ty scrambled up the mast and shouted, "Nothing in sight!"

Within moments, sails were raised and Hal pulled them around to catch a favorable wind blowing north. By rough reckoning, they should hit the southern shore of the Kingdom mainland close to Bas-Tyra. With luck, when they caught sight of land, they'd be pointed right at that harbor.

Twice they caught sight of sails and turned and ran, and for two days there was no sign of pursuit. During the war, they had run afoul of Ceresian pirates, acting as privateers but in fact raiding the coast. But this trip passed uneventfully.

Three days after leaving the coast, they saw a brown smudge on the northern horizon that promised land. Two hours later, the coast was clearly outlined against the sky. By midday they could make out features and judge roughly where they were. Hal pulled the tiller over and corrected his course, and soon coastal details could clearly be seen.

Three distant white spots indicated sails, but Hal made straight for them, because he knew exactly where they were. An hour before sundown, they could see a huge city, one to rival Rillanon and Roldem in size if not in majesty. The harbor mouth was flanked by two massive towers, but beyond that dozens of ships could be seen sailing among many more at anchor.

Hal looked at Ty and smiled. "Bas-Tyra."

The Black Ram was like many other taverns in the cities along the coasts of the Sea of Kingdoms: crowded, dangerous, and noisy. It was filled with sailors avoiding duty aboard ships stuck in harbor, mercenaries looking for employment either as auxiliaries to the city's garrison or as guards for merchants, with prostitutes, gamblers, and the assorted riffraff attracted to an approaching war. Two young men pushed their way through the press of bodies over the occasional objections of people who disliked being jostled, though once they saw two young men with serious expressions and fine swords on their hips, they soon gave way.

Reaching the bar, Ty signaled to the closest of three barmen, and when he approached said, "I'm looking for Anton."

With a jerk of his head, the barman indicated a door off to the left. Pushing through complaining customers, Ty and Hal reached the door, masked by an ancient curtain. Pushing it aside, they found themselves looking down a dimly lit hall at the far end of which stood the largest man either of them had ever seen.

They were forced to look up to address him. As both Ty and Hal were over six feet in height, they judged this human mountain to be approaching seven. From the size of his shoulders and arms, he probably weighed close to three hundred pounds. His skin was coffee-colored, so much of his ancestry would be Keshian, but his eyes were a vivid blue. His shaved head reflected the light from the one open lamp that hung halfway down the hall.

"What?" he asked in a voice so deep it almost rumbled.

"We seek Anton," said Hal.

"Who sent you?" asked the human barricade.

Ty paused for a moment, then said, "Jim Dasher."

The man nodded once, turned his back, and opened the door. He leaned in and said, "Someone looking for you. From Jim Dasher."

Somehow the monstrous guard stepped aside enough to allow Ty and Hal to enter the room. Inside they found a tiny desk behind which sat a slender man with the oddest hair Hal had ever seen. He was balding, but had a fringe of dark hair which he had allowed to grow, and which he swept up and forward to cover his pate. Using some manner of pomade or oil to keep it in place, he looked as if he were wearing a strange, shiny helm. His clothing was ostentatious and he wore earrings and several necklaces. Only his thumbs lacked rings.

"Jim Dasher?" he said, rising. He moved around the desk, but did not offer his hand or bow, just appraised the two young men silently.

Hal started to speak, but Anton cut him off with an upraised hand. "I do not need to know many things, and do not want to know almost as many. I'm in Jim Dasher's debt, so tell me what you need and I'll do what I can to help."

"We need to reach Prince Edward," said Hal.

Anton winced. "That tells me too much, but you had no choice. That way could prove dangerous." He fell silent for a moment, tapping his cheek. "I can get you safely to Salador. From there you must find your own way."

"Salador would be a good start," said Hal.

Anton went to his desk and removed a parchment, ink, and quill, and began to write. "Our lord, the Duke of Bas-Tyra, has remained neutral in the contestation for the Crown. He's a wise man, our Duke, who will wait until he's certain which way the wind is blowing, at which point he will declare for the winner."

"A practical man," observed Ty.

Anton shot him a dark look. "Now," he said, holding out the parchment. "Take this to the servants' entrance to the palace. Ask for a man named Jaston, no one else. Someone at the gate may argue they'll take the message, but do not permit it. Just keep insisting and eventually they'll send for him.

"You do not need to know who Jaston is, so do not ask. You do not need to know why he will do me this favor, so do not ask. More importantly, he doesn't need to know anything more about you than I've written down here, so do not answer any of his questions, no matter how affable the conversation may be. Do you understand?"

Both Hal and Ty nodded.

"Do what he says, however, and he will get you to Salador."

Hal took the parchment and turned without remark, Ty a step behind.

The massive guard stepped aside as much as he was able, allowing the two travelers to squeeze through the door.

Within half an hour, Ty and Hal were at the servants' gate to the palace arguing with a guard about summoning Jaston. Eventually, as predicted by Anton, Jaston was sent for and appeared.

By his dress, he was a man of some rank within the ducal household. He read Anton's letter and then looked at Hal and Ty. "Come," he said brusquely, and led them through the gates.

They walked around the massive castle's side yard, past some flowering gardens, and to the rear marshaling yard. There a company of horsemen was gathering. "Captain Reddic!" Jaston shouted.

An officer of horse, dressed in the black tabard of Bas-Tyra, with a golden eagle spreading wings embroidered over his heart, turned and replied, "Sir?"

Jaston indicated Hal and Ty. "These two gentlemen are to accompany you to Salador."

"Sir?" said the captain again, this time his tone curious.

"They are men of rank, but their identities will remain unknown to you. Should there be cause to speak to them, keep it brief and to the point. Ask no questions. Should anyone question you, they are mercenary swords attached to your patrol, nothing more, nothing less."

The man named Jaston turned and walked away without waiting for an answer. The captain didn't look pleased with his instructions, but after a moment turned to Hal and Ty. "Ask the lackeys inside to fetch out two sturdy mounts. We've a very long ride ahead and we'll be weeks on the trail. We leave in a half hour."

They walked toward the stables, and when they couldn't be overheard, Ty said, "I never understood just how far Jim Dasher's reach went."

"I had no idea," said Hal.

In less than half an hour a patrol of thirty cavalry with two mercenaries tagging along left the palace of Bas-Tyra and wended its way through the second-busiest city in the Kingdom, moving slowly toward the western gate and the road to Salador.

7

JOURNEY II

Miranda screamed.

The frustration of finding herself in what appeared to be an endless maze of tunnels somewhere underground had brought her to the brink of unleashing destructive blasts in all directions. Despite her enraged state, she realized the best she could hope for would be to vent some rage, and the worst that could happen would be to bring the tunnel crashing down on her. Not that she feared for her safety, but digging herself out from under tons of earth would be even more tedious than wandering lost. At least she wasn't wandering blind, as she was able to use her magical abilities to light a path.

Her magic worked here, though, as had been the case in the last place she had tried a spell, it was amplified. She was as adept at willing herself to new locations as anyone she had met, far better at it than Pug, and perhaps still better than Magnus, but even she had to have a rough idea of where she was headed. And despite her prodigious ability, even she didn't wish to risk discovering she had transported herself into solid rock, or off the face of the planet.

The tunnels were not commodious, though they were large enough that she didn't have to stoop or squeeze through narrow openings, but they were seemingly endless. She had come tumbling out of the vortex to land hard on her face, and since then her mood hadn't gotten any better. She had lost track of how long she had been walking, but she knew it was at least the better part of a day.

She had tried a technique used in mazes: to keep turning in one direction then turn back when hitting a dead end, go to the last intersection, turn in the other direction, then again keep turning in the original direction. It was tedious and likely to be anything but swift, but lore had it foolproof for eventually finding a way out.

At last she heard a sound. It was faint, as if echoing down corridors from a great distance, but she heard it. A light, trilling sound, which she almost recognized. It stopped. She paused, and a moment later she heard it again. She hurried first one way, then the other, moving from one end of her tunnel until she was certain where the sound was louder, and almost ran to the first intersection she found. At a crossroads, she turned her head this way and that, until she was certain again from which direction the sound was loudest.

After fifteen minutes of tracing the source of the sound, she realized what she was hearing: it was music, a pipe of some sort, playing a simple refrain over and over.

After another ten minutes, she was certain where the music was coming from. She closed her eyes and used her magical senses to locate the source. Trusting there wasn't some evil joke by Kalkin, God of Tricksters, at play, she willed herself to the source.

She appeared in a cavern where dozens of tunnels met, and above was a series of stone ramps leading to other tunnels. A pit in the center of the clearing showed more tunnels below. A single large rock sat at the edge of the pit, upon which sat a young man, barely more than a boy, playing a simple wooden pipe.

He was dressed in leggings vertically striped in yellow and green and a matching green tunic with yellow piping. He wore slippers of green with silver bells at the toes, and a flop cap of green with a dyed yellow feather held by a silver buckle.

"A jester," said Miranda, wondering if some mad god had conspired to drive her to lunacy.

The boy stopped playing. "I'm Piper," he corrected her. "And you are a demon called Child, or Miranda. Which do you prefer?"

After a moment's hesitation, she said, "Miranda."

"Predictable," answered the youth.

"Who are you?"

"I don't know," said Piper. "Until a few moments ago, I didn't exist, or if I did, I'm absent memories of that existence." He leaped nimbly from the rock, rose *en pointe,* and flexed his knees slightly. "Everything feels new. No creaks, aches." A quizzical expression crossed the youth's face. "Lacking experience, I wonder if I would know what creaks and aches are. And then, how do I even know to speak of them?" A bright expression was followed by "Then again still, how do I even know to speak?"

Miranda was not amused. "Where is this place?"

"We are on the last bastion of a dead race, where they futilely attempted to resist chaos. They were obliterated so many years ago that no sign of their existence remains save these ramps and tunnels."

"How do you know me?"

Again, a bright expression was followed by one of wonder.

The boy had a perfectly round face save for a slightly pointed chin. He had vivid green eyes and wisps of reddish-blond hair stuck out under the hat. "I don't know. I just know."

"What *do* you know?"

The brow furrowed for a moment. "I am your guide."

Lacking patience even in the best of circumstances, Miranda barked, "Then guide me!"

"Very well," said Piper. "We need to go up there." He pointed to the dark top of the cavern.

"Give me a moment," said Miranda, focusing her concentration on that gloomy destination. She cast a spell of distant vision and her view passed through several levels of lightless tunnels and caverns, only her magic senses giving her a vision in the darkness, until she saw a large hole beneath an open sky hundreds of feet above them. The darkness indicated a massive cavern above the one in which they found themselves. "Very well," she said. "Do you need my aid?"

Laughing, Piper said, "Would I be sitting alone in this godsforsaken pit if I didn't?"

Miranda found the youth's penchant toward good humor irritating, and realized that was felt from both her demon half and human half. With a single step she grabbed Piper around the waist and willed them to the indicated destination.

She found herself on the lip of a vast crater, and letting go of Piper, she used her demon's vision to pierce the darkness. The landscape was desolate, without a hint of any living thing. Glancing skyward almost gave her vertigo, for there was no cavern above.

The sky was empty.

Where stars should have abounded, only a vast expanse of emptiness sprawled overhead. Miranda felt something akin to panic rising as she pushed her senses outward. Farther and farther she reached and finally she retreated back to where she stood, almost overcome by the experience. There were no stars. There were no comets. No worlds, or any other object of size as far as she could perceive. Instead a fine dust with occasional rocks ranging from the size of a man's thumb to this slab of granite she stood upon.

"Where is this place?"

Piper said, "You believe it to be the Fourth Circle. A battle of consequence was fought here in ages past." He waved a hand lazily at the sky. "This is the consequence."

"Nothing is left?"

Piper smiled, and in the magical corona surrounding Miranda, she couldn't tell if he was being ironic or sad when he said, "There's a great deal left, but it's just been ground down to a fine powder in most places."

"Why am I here?" she turned to ask, but Piper was gone. In his place stood a young woman with ebony skin, eyes of piercing black, hair tightly gathered in rows that flowed down her neck to her shoulders. She wore a similar costume, but of red and beige rather than green and yellow. "Where's Piper?" asked Miranda.

"I am Piper," said the young woman in a voice as melodic as one could imagine. She picked up the exact same pipe Miranda had seen before and blew the same annoying melody.

In the span of two lifetimes, one as a demon and the other as a human, the merged being of Child and Miranda had seen many things, shape changing and conjured illusions being among them, but there was something different about this creature. "You change your body at will?"

"Yes, don't you?"

"Not lately," said Miranda, deciding to ignore the body shift. She remembered something Pug had said about one of Kalkin's visions. Suddenly she realized she didn't know if it was something he had said to her on Sorcerer's Isle as Miranda, or something she'd heard since Child had come to this world with Miranda's memories. "I'm losing one of my selves, aren't I?"

Piper shrugged. "I don't know about such things. I only know what I know."

Miranda was intrigued by that statement. "Isn't that true of everyone?"

Piper smiled, her teeth brilliant against her dark skin. "Some people know things they don't know they know. But I only know what I need to know. I was formed for a task, nothing more."

"Formed?"

"I was of the Bliss, at one with the Source, and now I am here with you to provide what you need."

Miranda saw something behind Piper's shoulder and said, "What is that?"

Piper turned and saw a speck of light. "An energy adjustment."

Suddenly the pinpoint of light blossomed into a cascade of sparkling lights that rapidly blinked out of existence. "Despite seeming empty from your perspective, there's a lot going on here," observed Piper. "The Fourth Circle is contracting. In . . . time is a difficult concept . . . some years, many years, few . . . ? In some amount of time, the Fourth Circle will be gone."

"One of the Circles will be gone?" Miranda thought of the ever-expanding void in the center of the Fifth Circle and asked, "Will the Fifth Circle vanish?"

"I do not know," answered Piper.

"What am I doing here?" asked Miranda.

"That I know," said Piper. She pointed behind Miranda. "Look!"

Miranda turned, and where a void had been moments before, a panorama of a massive arc of heaven stood revealed, as if some incredibly large curtain had been drawn aside. A vista of stars was visible, and for a brief moment Miranda had a touch of vertigo as the sun rose above it and moved at noticeable speed.

"This was once a place like those to which you've traveled, realms of countless worlds, stars, comets, planets teeming with life," said Piper, and hearing a new voice, Miranda turned to discover Piper had changed bodies again. A tall, handsome man of middle years, with a neatly trimmed beard just lightly shot through with gray stood wearing an outfit similar to the last two incarnations', but this one was a sable black that looked like velvet, trimmed with gold lamé. "Will you stop that?" said Miranda.

"Why?" answered Piper in a deep, melodious voice. "Bodies are fun."

"You never had one before?"

"I may have, but I don't remember. We who are spun out of the Bliss know only what we need to know; whatever pasts we may have experienced are part of the Unity with the One." He shrugged and grinned. "Makes everything new."

"Wonderful," muttered Miranda. "The gods send out curious toddlers to save the universe."

"Watch and learn," said Piper.

A massive storm of energies erupted across the panorama before Miranda, and Piper said, "The Sundering."

"What is it?"

"When the heavens and hells split. Behold the demon host."

A swarm of creatures flew out of the rip in space and Miranda's eyes widened. Instead of the seemingly endless variety of shapes of horror Child had known since her birth, this was an army of incredible beings, roughly human in form and beautiful in a way she could barely comprehend. There was not the slightest resemblance between what she knew from her short tenure in the Fifth Circle and what she now observed.

Soon another figure emerged, a being so brilliant she could barely look at it. "Who is that?" she asked.

"Hell's first king," answered Piper, and she saw he had reverted to the form she had first seen, the youth in the green-and-yellow garb.

"He . . . is beautiful." Both Child and Miranda found him an object of stunning form and elegant grace. "What is his name?"

"Name?" Piper blew a shrill note. "That could be his name. 'Name'! He has a different name for every race of being that encounters him. Some worship him as a god, and others fear him as the ultimate font of evil. He is, or was, or will be a force of nature. Does calling air that stirs 'wind' make it different from when it goes unnamed?" Piper pointed with his flute. "The Shining One, Light Bringer, Fallen Star, First of the Chosen, Accuser, Defiance, so many names in so many languages." He gripped her arm lightly. "There was a First Cause. But this was the Second. Remember that. Your father and Pug witnessed the First Cause. You are seeing the Second. He was first among those created by the First Cause, Most Beloved, but he challenged his creator, and became the Opponent!"

Miranda could not tear her eyes from the image. There was no scale. Hell's first king could be the size of a man seen from very close, or a mile tall viewed from miles distance. The humanlike face was perfection, without blemish or flaw. If one could imagine perfect proportions of brow to nose to chin, fullness of lips, set of eyes, shape and contour of a male body, then he was perfect. A woman of no small life experience, she was overwhelmed by desire and longing, a need for more than mere physical love, but to be accepted by this being. She said it aloud: "He's perfect."

Piper laughed. "No, but as close as any living thing can get. There was only one perfect being in existence."

"Who?"

"In time. You're not ready." Piper waved his hand. "This is the event, or as you would see it . . . time confuses me. This is the Second Cause."

Miranda looked at the vista before her, distances beyond her ability to imagine, and in the midst of it, a sea of incandescent gases. Tiny lights dotted the cloud and she knew them to be stars. Five beings like the first one she had just seen, magnificent in every aspect, stood in a pose of confrontation, one facing the other four. No words were heard, but Miranda sensed they were communicating.

"What am I seeing?"

"Watch."

Suddenly one of the four moved to the Shining One and grappled with him; then the Shining One was gone.

"What was that?"

"There are many different stories. Here's what you must know. For every cause there's a reaction, an opposition; for every force, a counterforce. It's part of a balance so fundamental it surpasses even the First Cause. It is called equipoise at its most fundamental, and that is what you must first understand. The one who fell was cast out because he questioned his creation and aspired to rise beyond his station. He brooded in solitude for ages and felt rage.

"Then came envy, and the one who fell created imitations of his brethren. His children were demons. They would serve and worship him, as his brethren served their creator."

Again Miranda saw what Piper had called the demon host, a legion of beauty on the wing, appearing through a massive rift in the heavens, the Sundering. "Am I seeing what he really looks like?" she asked.

Piper again blew a loud note, spun in a circle, and said, "Of course not. There are bands of energy coursing through the universes impossible for any physical entity to perceive, let alone grasp. Understanding beyond any one mortal's capacity is what is needed to grasp the totality of what is before you.

"Threads of possibility, waves of probability, surges and flows of consciousness, vital forces beyond mortal comprehension." In a patronizing tone he added, "We have to simplify so you can comprehend. Your feeble mind does what it can to understand, but it's not sufficient."

Miranda scowled at being called feebleminded, but let it go. "What are you showing me?"

"The hosts of heaven."

"I thought you said it was the demon legion."

Piper laughed. "Your mind! It is lacking. Angels, demons, they are the same thing, but from different places! Or the same thing seen differently! They just serve different causes. They are opposites, yet they are the same!"

Piper came to stand before Miranda, put his pipe under his arm, then formed a sphere with his two hands. "You see things like this! But in truth, they are like this." Suddenly he pulled apart his hands, fingers wiggling frantically, and moved his hands in a flurry of motion. "There is no higher heaven, lower hell. The First Circle is the First Circle, or plane or realm or demesne." He waved one hand high above his head. "Here you call it heaven." Then he waved the other down below his waist, letting his flute drop, which he deftly caught with his free hand while he knelt. "Down here, the same place, you call hell!"

He walked around behind her. "From here, I see you with black hair hanging down your back." Before she could turn, he was in front of her. "From here I see your face! You look different from before. But you are the same!"

"Perspective," she said.

"Yes!" He laughed, a clear boyish laugh. "You begin to understand." He waved his hand and the image changed.

Suddenly the King of Hell was a red-skinned monster with huge white horns that rose from his forehead and curved back over the dome of his skull, an upraised ruche of black hair rising between them like the fin of a sailfish, and two enormous black bat wings spreading out from his back.

The host of angel-like demons was now replaced by what Child would have expected to reside in hell. Miranda said, "Why . . . ?"

"You denizens of that region of the spheres, what you call the Fifth Circle, like all beings in one sense or another, are creatures of energy. You look the way you expect to look."

"I expected to look like Child?"

"Language," snorted Piper, obviously unhappy with its limits. "No, you creatures, all of you, together, over time, you come to believe things and they become so." He laughed. "Look at this one. It's wonderful!"

She looked up and instead of figures of demons and angels saw a massive cascade of scintillating lights, so brilliant as to cause her to shield her eyes. Millions of other lights flowed and swirled around the twisting fountain of color in the middle. It was as if every fireworks display ever conceived had been simultaneously unleashed on a scale to dwarf worlds. Colors darted so quickly it was a sight to induce madness in a weaker mind than hers.

"It's energy, don't you see?" asked Piper.

"What do you mean?"

"Energy, matter, time, it's all the same. You just have to know how to look."

"Perspective," said Miranda.

"Yes," said Piper. He grinned and danced a step.

"What am I looking at?"

"Witness," said Piper.

Suddenly the entire sky changed. Instead of a window through which to view images conjured by whatever magic Piper or his master employed, Miranda found herself floating over a vast field of stars. There was a glorious harmony to all she beheld. Vast swirling oceans of star-studded gas moved across the heavens in stately progress, while comets blazed their timeless paths around multitudes of stars.

"This is what the universe looked like from this rock when it was a planet," said Piper, "before the Enemy came, before the time of madness and chaos."

Miranda was about to ask a question, then ceased as she noticed an anomaly. In a corner of a star field, a dark spot had appeared, at first hardly noticeable in the flowing pattern of lights against the darkness around her. But after a moment she saw that there was something different about this blackness. If there could be shades of blackness, this was a depth of it, an absence of even the promise of light or color.

"What is it?" she asked.

"Watch," said Piper.

"It must be immense," said Miranda, "and very far away."

"Distance, like what I've shown you, is illusion. How do you think you move from place to place by thought?"

"Magic," she answered.

"There is no magic," replied Piper. "Nakor understands."

Miranda looked at Piper, who looked quizzically at her. "Or he will." Piper frowned. "Or he has." After another moment Piper said, "Time is an illusion, too."

Miranda had only a rudimentary idea of how vast the distance between stars might be, but she knew, given the size of the sun around which Midkemia spun and how it appeared in the sky, and the size of those tiny pinpoints of light called stars, that the distances were vast. Yet the dark spot was growing at an enormous speed. "It must be expanding at tens of thousands of miles a minute," she muttered. "More," she amended as entire clusters of stars were suddenly blotted out.

She looked at Piper, who was transfixed by the sight below them. She asked, "Is it just blocking out what's behind it, or . . ."

"It's eating stars," said Piper. Then he said, "In your home world, the demon realm, the void where the first Kingdoms once were, that's what it becomes eventually."

Miranda's hand went to her mouth. "Gods." Whispering, she asked, "What is it?"

"The Enemy. The true Darkness," answered a voice in the air, and when she turned Piper was gone.

There was a popping sound from behind her and she turned. A vortex awaited. For a moment she hesitated, then she realized she had learned all she would here. She took a step and leaped into the dark vortex.

8

STORM

Lightning split the sky.

Brendan cursed every god of weather in every nation of every world that had gods of weather. He had made an uneventful journey down the coast, staying close and putting in whenever he caught sight of a sail on the horizon. As he moved south of the headlands known as Schull's Rock, he took his bearing off the rising sun and pushed straight through to Sarth. He knew the Quegan fleet would not put in that close to the Kingdom coast and felt safe hurrying along.

When he came into sight of Sarth, he had

taken a quick inventory and discovered he had four days of food and five of water on board. Rather than stop at Sarth, he put the helm over to starboard and beat a course dead south. He ran out a Kingdom pennant he had liberated from the mayor's library in Ylith, used by Kingdom couriers, in case he encountered Kingdom warships that might otherwise stop and board his vessel. It was providential, as twice Kingdom ships altered course to give him a closer look, but catching sight of the snapping guidon in the royal blue and gold and Brendan giving a cheery wave, they'd return to their original course, assuming Brendan was seeking out another ship.

Now he was caught up in one of the Bitter Sea's sudden weather changes. It wasn't raining yet, but he could smell the moisture in the air. Lightning was cracking overhead, followed by thunderclaps that felt like physical slaps.

The little smack was starting to climb up crests and dive into troughs and Brendan was starting to worry. In clear weather, if the charts and maps he had studied were correct, he should be seeing the smudge on the horizon that would have marked Sorcerer's Isle, but now visibility was down by half, as rain from the southwest formed a curtain on the horizon. If he was lucky, it would pass to the west of him, or only get him a little wet, and prove to be just another sudden squall.

If it was a big storm, he could be sailing and bailing for days, and literally sail right past the island and be halfway to the Keshian coast before he realized his error.

Or he could sail right onto the rocks of Sorcerer's Isle's north shore.

Brendan checked his jib and saw it was well extended as the wind picked up, and knew that he would soon have too much sail. He tied off the tiller and quickly lashed the boom with a preventer, a short rope that would keep the wind from suddenly jibbing the boat while he pulled in the jib sail. Normally the type of smack he was sailing had two masts, but this one had sacrificed the smaller abaft mast for the fish well. Usually two men manned this craft, but Brendan could find no one in Ylith willing to make the journey with him. He was young and had spent his life sailing the Far Coast near Crydee, and felt able to sail her solo. Until now, he realized. Right now a second man to man the sheets or bail out the bilge would have been most welcome. He had a small bailing bucket nearby, and if a wave crested the bow, he could hold the rudder with one hand while dumping some water overboard with the other. But it was tedious, fatiguing, and ineffective.

Dropping the jib, he decided to sacrifice order for speed, wadded up the mass of canvas, and dumped it in the fish well. He returned to the rudder, unlashed it and the boom, and set his eyes on the horizon.

Lightning flashed and he waited for the following thunder, but there wasn't any. And then he realized most of the lightning was behind him. Then the lightning flashed again, and he realized it was in the same place as the last time he had seen it.

He kept his eyes focused on that place, as well as he could with a pitching craft and moving horizon, and after about half a minute, he was rewarded with another flash. Still no thunder.

He tried to judge his direction, for the sky was heavy with clouds that blocked any hint of the sun's position, save that the light was failing, so he knew it was late afternoon. And with the curtain of rain coming up from the southwest, visibility was dropping by the minute.

Another flash, and this time he could make out what looked to be lightning traces, all near the surface. It was most definitely odd, though he had seen ground lightning ashore once. But at sea? Never. Usually the bolts streaked across the sky, or struck the surface, but . . . this? It was unlike anything he knew.

Lacking a better guide, he tried to keep the boat pointed off the port side of the place where he first saw the flash, judging it to be as good a landmark as any he'd likely find.

Slowly the display grew in size, and then in the distance he heard a faint sound, which quickly resolved itself into the crash of waves on rocks.

A sheet of rain struck him like a thousand tiny whips, driving so hard his eyes stung and water got up his nose; then it passed. Those tiny thunder showers were nothing he hadn't seen before, but none had been this intense. Now he felt worry, for this was beginning to feel like a major storm was building up all around him.

He cleared his vision and he saw it: the black castle.

And then he saw the lightning.

The castle was perched upon a massive upthrust of rock that formed a table, one separated from the main body of the island by crashing waves and boulders. A single, long drawbridge linked the castle to the bluffs opposite its entrance.

Lightning erupted from the highest tower of the castle, long actinic, jagged arcs of white with a hint of purple that left the eyes dazzled for a moment and lingered in afterimages of green. Brendan blinked and realized that this was the "lightning" he had been seeing for some time.

He ported his helm and pulled hard on the sheets to tack over and move away from this invitation to wreck on the rocks below. From what he had been told, there was a beach on the south shore. He felt the boat fight against a sideways tide and realized he was perilously close to a hidden tide race.

If the tide was pulling in that direction, it had to be the result of something unseen, either underwater rocks or magic: whatever the reason, it was a death trap for any vessel caught in it.

Brendan ducked under the boom and turned, tightly holding the boom sheet taut with his hand on the rudder while he loosened the outhaul, and the small craft heeled over. He could hear the mast creak as waves slammed into the hull.

An odd calm settled over him. He knew he could manage this balky craft. He settled into a series of movements, pointing the vessel in the right direction, moving almost casually against a mounting storm, climbing crests and dipping into troughs as the waves grew, keeping one eye on the malevolent marker that was the castle.

Despite its baleful appearance, he had been told it was no more than a showpiece, that the real community he was seeking was inland. Brendan considered the workmanship of the display, for whenever the lightning erupted from the tower he still recoiled slightly. He was now close enough that he could hear the sizzle of energy with the discharge and realized a very powerful magic must be at work. It might not pose a direct threat, but anyone approaching this island would be exposed to a demonstration of danger powerful enough to discourage further exploration.

The artistry was all very well, but Brendan's concerns turned quickly back to the state of his boat and his personal safety. Everywhere he looked there were rocks along the coastline and the little craft was hardly able to make headway against both tide and wind. He was forced to take a very long tack away from the island, and soon his back and shoulders were burning with the effort of keeping the bow pointed toward land against the combination of tide and wind that was trying to pull him back toward the rocky shore and away from whatever sandy beach was supposed to be there, beyond the surf and the limit of his vision.

Feeling the hull under him moving the wrong way, Brendan yanked over hard on the tiller and ducked under the swinging boom, trying to fill the sail with enough wind to get moving forward again, even if in the wrong direction. But the boat was having none of it. It continued to move backward while the sail luffed, snapping uselessly in the wind and giving him no momentum. The tiller and rudder caused the skiff to turn slowly on its centerline as the tide pushed it along. The boom continued to swing as Brendan sought to fill the sail with wind, and suddenly the bow of the boat swung around and it began to wallow, keeling over on the lee side, and then the boom tip was in the water.

Brendan let go of the tiller for a moment to yank hard on

the boom sheet, and the boat shook, then rolled back as it turned to follow the tide race. That's when he knew he was in dire trouble, for he felt the craft take off as if it were a dog leaping after a rabbit.

A tide race meant shallows where the energy of deep waves was forced over an abruptly rising seafloor. Which simply meant the mass of rocks he saw between himself and the castle was not starting close into the island, but was under his keel at this moment.

He pulled the boom sheet and grabbed the tiller, pulling them over and trying to pick up speed so he could move off at a tangent to his current course, looping out and coming back in a far bigger circular course, adding hours to the journey if need be. The storm was growing and now he was starting to feel the rain pelt him, and he knew it would be a downpour in minutes. He lacked foul-weather gear, having to rely on the cloak he currently wore, which would soon be soaked.

The bow lifted, and Brendan tried to keep focused and not to panic. If the boat crested the wave and came down into the trough, everything would be well. If he heard wood scrape or, worse, splinter, he would be swimming in minutes.

The vessel came down smoothly, and he pulled it over and got it set on a northeast course away from the island. He felt a momentary giddy relief.

Then the boat crashed into underwater rocks.

Brendan was thrown forward into the fish well, landing on his neck and shoulder with enough force that his vision swam. He lay in reeking water up to his chin while the boat shook and groaned as it was pushed across the rocks. He got up spitting foul water and could barely get to his feet. His head throbbed and keeping his wits was proving a challenge. Pulling hard, he got over the lip of the fish well, but as he tried to climb, the boom swung wildly, striking him hard.

The world spun out of control and fell sideways, his senses fleeing as the boat started to break up on the rocks.

Images swam above him as Brendan regained consciousness. He had trouble focusing and he ached from his head to his feet.

A man's voice said, "Quite a beating you took there, young sir."

The speaker was just a little out of his field of vision. Brendan managed to croak out a sound and felt someone put an arm behind his shoulder and lift him as a cup of water was put to his lips. He drank a little and felt his throat relax a bit. "Sorcerer's Isle?"

A face hove into view. Female, but something decidedly unusual about her. He blinked and said, "Who are you?"

With a slightly accented King's Tongue, she answered, "I am Dilyna."

He blinked again and finally she came into focus. "Is this Sorcerer's Isle?"

She nodded and he noticed there was something odd about her eyes: they were a brown bordering on red. Her hair was a deep brownish red, but her skin was pale. She answered, "This is the Isla Beata, but some call it Sorcerer's Isle."

"Oh," he said as he tried to move. "Anything broken?"

"Here," she said, holding up a shallow bowl with a pungent-smelling liquid in it. "This will heal you faster and make the pain less."

He endured the draft, and finally said, "I'm Brendan. My brother is Henry, Duke of Crydee, and I'm looking for—"

A voice from behind said, "Me, I should think." A man came into view and sat on the edge of the bed. "I received word yesterday that a small fishing boat had crashed into the rocks and tied up in the wreckage was a young man wearing a signet that identified him as a member of the royal family." He tapped the ring on Brendan's right hand. "So I came to have a look."

Brendan felt a warm glow creep into his body and the pain subsided. "Ruffio!" he said, grabbing the dark-haired magician by the arm. "My brother needs you in Krondor . . ." He blinked. "Or maybe he doesn't, now that I've found you." He felt his eyelids grow heavy.

"Dilyna failed to mention that she gave you a healing draft that makes you fall asleep."

A moment later, Brendan was snoring loudly.

Hours later Brendan awoke. The draft had done its work. He was stiff and a little sore, but nothing like the mass of pain he had been in before. He saw the room was dark and wondered if he had slept through a day and night. There was a hint of gray light coming through a crack in the shutters. He raised himself up on his elbows and saw Dilyna sitting in the corner, reading something by lantern light. "Hello, again," he croaked.

He saw a pewter pitcher and cup on the nightstand next to his bed. He sat up and managed to fill the cup and drink. "I should do that," she said, looking down at him.

Brendan grinned. "I thank you, but I'm feeling much better now." He must feel better: he realized Dilyna was far more attractive than he had first thought. Of the three brothers, Brendan was the ladies' man, with Hal being relatively shy due to being the heir, and their mother watching him like a hawk. Martin had been in love with Bethany before Martin knew he was in love with Bethany, and whatever encounters he had had with town girls at Crydee had been the result of a festival, lots of wine or ale, and the girl being the predator, often thinking she might land the Duke's son. Brendan, on the other hand, had discovered the difference between girls and boys at a very early age and had also discovered he very much liked the difference. He had probably bedded more girls in Crydee and the rest of the Far Coast than both his brothers combined, despite being the youngest.

Dilyna was not particularly tall, but he judged she had long legs and a well-rounded backside from the way her dress fit her.

When she realized she was being appraised, the color

rose in Dilyna's cheeks. "I should fetch Ruffio," she said, and hurried out of the room.

The young magician appeared a moment later, followed by the girl. He smiled. "Feeling better?"

"Yes, thank you," replied Brendan. "How long have I been here?"

"Our lookout saw your boat foundering off the point two days ago, and by the time we got down to you, it had struck the rocks and was breaking up. We found you entangled in line and sails and got you out. Another few minutes and I think you'd have been underwater." Again he smiled.

"I'm glad you got to me when you did," said Brendan. A sudden burst of thunder caused him to look toward the window. "The storm still lingers?"

"Two days now. It is not natural."

"I don't understand."

"Someone is using weather magic to keep this island busy," Ruffio replied.

Brendan sat up on the edge of the bed. "Do you know who?"

"We have our suspicions," said Ruffio. He motioned for Dilyna to depart and she hurried out of the room.

"She's very pretty," observed Brendan, watching her go.

"She's also from a region of Novindus, in the Riverlands, where girls and boys are segregated, so I think you better get used to her avoiding you as long as you're here."

"Pity," said Brendan, then he lost his smile. "I have much to tell you, Ruffio, and I suspect time may be vital." A sudden gust of wind rattled the shutters and he said, "And it may have some bearing on this storm you say is magical in nature."

"Say on," instructed Ruffio. He sat down on the chair Dilyna had used as she watched over Brendan.

Brendan recounted what Martin and Bethany had told him of their visit to E'bar. When he got to the part of the narrative where Martin had tried to describe the magic shell surrounding the city, Ruffio asked some questions Brendan was unable to answer.

"I must find your brother, then," said Ruffio. "You say he's looking for me?"

"To tell you what I'm telling you," said Brendan. "And to see if you can possibly get him to Prince Edward's camp. Edward's as close to a king as we have now and someone in charge needs to know what's going on in the Grey Towers. And if Martin doesn't find you in Krondor, he'll be on his way to the Prince. Jim Dasher made it clear that we were to keep both the Crown and the magicians at Stardock informed. It was Martin who decided to send me here to let the Conclave know what was happening."

"Smart lad, your brother," said Ruffio. "Though if you had found anyone of note, I would have heard of the situation your brother described eventually. However, your bravery in sailing here saves us time. I'll send word to the Academy, then see if I can get your brother to Prince Edward in a timely fashion." He paused. "Are you hungry?"

Brendan realized he hadn't eaten in nearly two days and suddenly the idea of food was appealing. "Yes, please."

"Supper will be served in an hour. Rest until then."

He left the room and Brendan set about cleaning his sword with a dry towel, knowing that quickly he'd need to bathe it in freshwater and oil it to keep the metal from pitting. After a few minutes, when he was convinced he'd done as much as he could with the materials at hand, he lay back down and within minutes was asleep again.

Brendan was awakened by the gentle shake of Dilyna's hand on his shoulder. Blinking, he smiled and said, "Supper?"

"Yes," she said. "Please follow me."

They walked through a long hall that was noticeably colder than his room. A moment later he discovered why. The outer side of the building was a series of rooms, but one large open door faced inward onto a huge garden. The door was currently allowing a bitter wind to gust down the hall, for while the garden was sheltered on four sides by the building, it was still taking a buffeting from the storm. Spraying water had drenched the floor, but they passed quickly by without getting more than slightly damp. They turned a corner and Dilyna led him to another opening onto the garden, but opposite it was a large hallway that connected that building to another. The center of this building appeared to be a series of large rooms, one of which was a dining hall big enough for perhaps forty or fifty people.

Unlike the hall at Crydee, which had an obvious head table where the Duke and his nobles sat, this one had a large square of tables so that the diners could all see one another. Judging by the configuration, Brendan realized the tables could be moved and reset in various patterns to accommodate fewer or more diners at need.

Ruffio waved him over to where he sat, next to two familiar folk. Brendan smiled at the two elves. "Calis! Arkan! I'm surprised to see you."

Calis nodded and smiled, but the dark elf, Arkan, barely acknowledged Brendan. "When we left with Miranda and Nakor, this was our destination," explained Calis.

"Ah," said Brendan. "I didn't think where you would go, beyond reaching Sarth."

Calis shrugged. "My mother was going to send another to Ylith, to inform the Duke of the safe arrival of your mother and the others. I asked if I might be the one; I'm more at home in the cities than anyone else at Elvandar, save a few from across the sea, and they don't know their way around the Kingdom as I do."

Arkan's gaze narrowed slightly but he said nothing. In the time they had been on Sorcerer's Isle, he had come to hold the alien Prince of Elvandar in a grudging regard. He was not pure elf, not Eledhel, Moredhel, Eldar, or Taredhel. He was both elf and human and something else, and Arkan expected that "something" was a legacy of his father's carrying the mark of the Dragon Lords.

Calis continued. "It's been years since I visited Krondor, since the war with the Emerald Queen, so I thought I might visit." He glanced at Arkan. "My friend here has other concerns, which seemed in line with things my mother might need to know, and he seems to be of the opinion he must make contact with either Pug or his son, so here we wait."

Arkan nodded. "Indeed. We wait."

Brendan sat down in an empty chair next to Arkan and said to Calis, "Lady Bethany is on her way to see your mother."

"To what end?"

Brendan explained what Martin had told him, and what he had already shared with Ruffio.

Both Calis and Arkan reacted with concern. "We should go see for ourselves, don't you think?" observed Calis.

Arkan looked unconvinced. He shook his head slightly and said, "I've seen these so-called Star Elves."

Calis said, "One visited for a while in Elvandar." He looked at the Moredhel chieftain. "You don't approve?"

"They tend to be an arrogant lot."

Calis chuckled.

"You find that amusing?" asked Arkan, his eyes narrowing.

"Ah," said Calis. "I've heard the same of your . . . clans." He added, "I suspect much the same is said of us."

Arkan nodded. "We see those of Elvandar as having a very high opinion of themselves."

Calis sat back. "Still, this news from E'bar is more than just a little troubling. An invasion of some dark force, and the Taredhel magicians confining it to the city. I'm certain my father will wish to see for himself."

If mention of Lord Tomas stirred a reaction in Arkan, Brendan couldn't see it. He went on. "The fellow my brother spoke with, Tanderae, said something about betrayal at the highest level, the Lord Regent himself and his 'meet'?" He grabbed a hunk of hot bread from a nearby platter and slathered it with butter from a small bowl.

Arkan paused, then said, "From the Regent himself? What of a warrior named Kumal, their Warleader?"

Brendan said, "I do not know that name. If anyone mentioned it to my brother, he failed to mention it to me."

Calis said, "You've met him?"

"No," answered Arkan. "He came to speak with us, in Sar-Sargoth." He glanced around to see if the name of the city in the Northlands registered for any of the others at the table, but no one reacted.

"Oh?" said Calis.

"He came to let us know we could continue to live as we liked, unless we ventured south, in which case we would be subject to Taredhel rule."

Calis smiled. "I'm sure that was welcome news to those of your kin who called the Green Heart home."

"I left the meeting before the serious bloodletting occurred."

"I would certainly label the Taredhel behavior there arrogant," Calis said.

"Have you met one?" asked Brendan.

"The one your brother mentioned, Tanderae. He seemed . . ."

Arkan chuckled. "Arrogant?"

"A little, but he also seemed sincere. I'm not surprised to discover that if there was some plot or betrayal here, he was on the other side of it. He seemed to care about his people."

"It's what the best of us do," agreed Arkan. "We take care of our people."

Brendan looked around the room and found Dilyna sitting at a distant counter. He smiled at her and she shyly returned his smile, then glanced away. He also noticed a very striking blond woman speaking with a man who wore a finely fashioned robe, but then a student came to fill his goblet with wine and others began serving meat, potatoes, greens, and boiled vegetables. Brendan was starving, but even as he ate he felt a growing sense of urgency. Was Hal still in Rillanon? Had Martin reached Prince Edward?

Brendan was about to finish eating when a sudden scream from the courtyard cut through the sound of rain and wind. Instantly the entire dining hall was a flurry of activity.

Brendan turned one way then another to see where everyone was rushing. He saw the attractive blond woman and the man she was talking with come out of their seats, the woman with a mace in her hand. She also wore armor under a white tabard. Brendan realized she was a member of the Order of the Shield of the Weak, who served the goddess Dala. The rest of those in the room were magic users of one stripe or another, save for the two elves who had left their bows leaning against the wall behind them and now had them in hand. Brendan yanked his sword out of its scabbard as he followed the rush out of the dining hall.

The scream had come from the large garden in the next building over, and even before everyone cleared the connecting hall between the two buildings, Brendan could feel something profoundly wrong in the air.

It was a sense of evil, one that caused his stomach to turn, as if struck by an incredibly horrid stench. As he had learned to do in combat, he just gulped hard and focused on staying alive.

He reached the courtyard as sizzling bolts of energy and flashes of flame were exploding all about a creature striking back with magic of its own. The water pooling in the garden seemed to come alive, lifting up and twisting into ropes of liquid, lashing out at anyone approaching.

Brendan halted for an instant, his mind rejecting what he was seeing. The creature stood on two legs, roughly in the shape of a human, but the torso was covered in barnacles and patches of weed, leaving only a few glimpses of night-black skin exposed. The legs seemed to turn fluid at the ankles, as if the feet were constantly picking up water from the rain-saturated garden. The arms were likewise solid until the wrists, which then became massive, shimmering clubs of liquid. The head was a nightmare, with tentacles where a human's mouth would be, an octopus-like body where the head would be, but with two large yellow eyes, one on each side. It reeked with the stench of things long dead on the ocean's floor and it made gurgling and choking sounds like a man drowning.

Brendan waited until it turned away, and leaped in, sword extended. He struck the creature. It was like hitting the trunk of an ancient oak with a dull ax. The point slid off the creature's skin, dancing around as it snagged then slipped off the extrusions on the hide, and shock ran up Brendan's arm.

Brendan leaped back and a spray of water hit him like a massive maul, propelling him across the garden. He skidded through mud into a now-drenched flower bed and felt small branches catch at his clothing as he slammed into the low garden wall.

Shaking off the blow, Brendan got to his knees, then rose on wobbly legs. He found the woman warrior with the mace nearby, studying the creature. The man with the neatly trimmed beard was casting a spell of some sort, then stopped. "I can't! It's not summoned."

"Damn," said the woman. Seeing Calis and Arkan, she shouted, "It's immune to magic! Shoot!"

An instant later both elves had nocked arrows and let loose, and two broad-headed shafts struck the creature. Arkan's arrow managed to find an uncovered patch of skin and pierce the creature's hide, but Calis's merely bounced off the barnacles studding its hide.

It howled in pain and lashed out, and as it got angrier, it sprayed water with more force. Now drenched to the skin, Brendan shouted, "It's ugly as sin, but it would be a handy thing to have around the next time there's a fire!" He looked around, did a quick inventory, and realized that only the blond warrior with her mace and he with his sword possessed hand weapons that could do damage. The elves continued firing with little effect, as the creature's rapid twists and turns made vulnerable spots targets only for seconds.

Brendan shouted to Ruffio. "No magic works on it?"

"Apparently not!" shouted back the head magician of the Conclave, drawing a belt dagger. Brendan wasn't entirely sure the magician knew what to do with it should the opportunity present itself.

But watching the woman warrior was a marvel. She seemed to know exactly when to duck and move, and when to attack. She wasn't apparently doing much damage to the monster, but she was keeping its attention.

Suddenly Brendan had an idea. "Ruffio!" he shouted.

"What?"

"If your magic won't work on it, can it work on me?"

"What do you need?"

"Fly me around that thing so I can get to it from behind."

"I can do that."

"Who's the woman with the mace?"

"Sandreena, Sergeant-Adamant of the Order of the Shield of the Weak."

"Good," said Brendan. He turned and shouted, "Sandreena!" His voice cut through the chaos and she looked over.

He pantomimed her moving to her right, causing the creature to move in the same direction, and she nodded. "All right," said Brendan. "I need to be right up behind it."

"Then what?"

"Get me a couple of feet above it; then, when I shout, let me fall."

"Are you sure?" The magician's expression indicated that he was as concerned for Brendan's sanity as he was for his safety.

"No. I'd rather she turned it around, then I could run and jump, except there is no footing." The ankle-deep water made the move he desired impossible.

"Ah," said Ruffio, now understanding. "When?"

"Now!"

Ruffio waved his hand and suddenly Brendan felt a force lift him up out of the wet garden mud, twisting him slightly as he was elevated to a point immediately behind and above the sea creature. Sandreena did as she was asked and continued to hammer at the monster, keeping its attention.

"Now!" shouted Brendan and he felt the force holding him vanish. He almost mistimed his blow despite knowing the drop was coming. He held tightly to his down-pointed sword and drove it into a spot above a row of barnacles and below the bulbous back of the monster's head.

The sword bit deeply, and Brendan was knocked about for a second as the creature began to thrash. Then he lost his grip on the hilt and fell to the ground, only to be hit by a powerful jet of water that sent him once again crashing into the bushes at the boundary of the garden.

A cry of pain and rage filled the garden, then suddenly the creature seemed to fall apart, bits and pieces just dropping away from its form. Within a minute, only a pile of foul-smelling debris from the ocean's bottom remained.

The rain still pelted them all in the garden, and Brendan looked up to see the blond warrior extending her hand. "Well done, youngster," she said.

"Thank you," said Brendan as his once-again-punished body reminded him he was not immortal.

The man in the finely fashioned robe came and introduced himself as Amirantha and said, "Bravery or foolishness, it worked."

"A bit of both," said Ruffio. "Now, how are you?"

"Glad your gardener didn't plant roses," Brendan said, pulling twigs out of his hair.

Ruffio said, "Let's get out of the rain and discuss this. Pug's study after you've dried off?"

Amirantha and Sandreena nodded. Brendan said, "I am going to need some of that healing draft before I sleep, I think. Things are starting to hurt again."

"Pity," said Ruffio. "I know how foul that concoction tastes."

"They always do, don't they?"

Dilyna came to Brendan's side and said, "Do you need help, sir?"

Brendan smiled and found his face hurt. "Thank you, but I can manage." He turned to Ruffio and said, "I'll clean up and . . ." He turned back to Dilyna. "You could come by in ten minutes. I don't know my way to Pug's study."

She almost beamed, then nodded and left.

Ruffio said, "You seem to have charmed our shy girl." He looked with barely hidden disgust at the mass of rotting sea life where the monster had stood. "Given the circumstances, that's an achievement."

Brendan shrugged. "It's a knack."

He left Ruffio, Amirantha, and Sandreena collectively shaking their heads in amusement.

Brendan was wobbling a bit by the time he reached Pug's study, Dilyna gripping his arm. "Thank you," he said, trying to be charming, but only managing to look more pathetic.

He entered the room and found Ruffio, Amirantha, and Sandreena, along with three magicians he didn't know, sitting down, and the two elves seemingly content to stand at the wall.

"Young Prince Brendan," said Ruffio as Brendan sank into a chair near the door. "Again, your bravery and ingenuity put us all in your debt." A smattering of agreement went around the room. Brendan was in too much discomfort to feign modesty. He really didn't want to be anywhere but in bed at the moment—alone, to his own surprise.

Ruffio said, "Let us go back over what we know." He held up a finger. "First, we were attacked by an agency that is powerful enough to put a creature into our midst despite our best defenses against magic. Second, it was immune to our magic. Lastly, we've never seen its like before." He looked at Amirantha. "Have you?"

"No," said the warlock. "But I have heard of creatures like it."

Sandreena looked at him and said, "Oh, really?"

"Where I hail from, in Novindus, there are several types of water-based demons, called rakshasa, who are pretty nasty customers." Amirantha paused and said, "This could get complicated."

Sandreena smiled and said, "Say on. We need to know and we realize you tend to the pedantic."

Brendan realized at that moment there was quite a history between those two, but he found the subject matter interesting.

"Like the demons you and I are more familiar with, the demons of water—those I mentioned are more associated with rivers and lakes than oceans—are one of three basic types, the summoned, the spirit, and the created. The reason none of our magic worked is that thing was neither spirit nor summoned, but created. It was the work of necromancy, coupled with demonic spirits."

Sandreena looked disgusted. "So my banishment would not work."

"Nor mine. Nor apparently any of the magic employed here." He looked at Ruffio. "Had you a priest of Lims-Kragma here, he would have recognized the necromancy instantly for what it was and, if powerful enough, had means to counter it. Several other temples likewise could have dealt with the creature, though an especially powerful construct can even overcome that.

"But even the most powerful of the created beings have a vulnerability, one still-living part necessary for its continued existence. Find that part and kill it, and the rest falls apart. It's usually a human head or a heart. The head makes for a more intelligent creature, able to act more independently, but the heart is preferred, for you can encase it in the center of the creature, providing more protection.

"Young Brendan's sword did the trick, cutting down through the body into the heart, the one living thing left in it to bind the spirit to the flesh and other matter used to fashion the body. That caused the demonic spirit to flee back to the Fifth Circle and the creature fell apart."

Sandreena looked at Brendan. "How did you know where to strike?" she asked.

"I didn't. I just saw an opening between all that armor on its body and the head, a bare spot at the base of its neck. I didn't think I could hit it and slice the head off, but if I could jump high enough and plunge my blade . . ." He shrugged. "With all that mud, I couldn't get a running jump, so I needed you to distract it long enough for Ruffio to magically pick me up and drop me on it."

"Still," said Ruffio, "some of our magic should have harmed it."

"That has me concerned as well," said Amirantha. "It wasn't the usual sort of demonic resistance to banishment magic or even physical damage; it was as if the magic wasn't working when I cast the spell."

Several voices echoed agreement. "It's canted everything," said one magician. "I tried to access my room through a step-through rift to fetch a magical weapon, and it wouldn't open."

"I can't transport to my room either," said another magician.

Ruffio got a very worried expression. He pulled a Tsurani relocation orb from his pocket, pressed his thumb on a tiny lever, and nothing happened. He said, "One of the properties of this storm seems to be to keep magic from working as it should." He lifted his hand and a small pot of flowers in the corner of the room moved upward. "Not all magic, but . . ."

"The important magic," finished Sandreena.

"Where did it come from?" asked Calis. "There's a very nasty storm blowing, so how did it get into that garden?"

"You said it wasn't conjured," said Ruffio to Sandreena, who nodded. "Our magical defenses prevent any conjuration or translocation from outside. Someone or something had to physically bring that creature here and drop it in that garden."

"For something to be flying out in that weather . . ." said Arkan. He shrugged, leaving the thought unfinished.

"This storm shows no sign of letting up."

"It's not natural," said another magician. "I know as much about weather magic as any man here, and this storm is being manipulated."

"To what end?" asked Brendan.

Sandreena's smile was ironic. "To keep us busy here."

"So we aren't somewhere else," finished Brendan. He sank back in his chair, fatigue washing over him.

"In the Grey Tower Mountains," supplied Arkan.

"At E'bar," finished Calis.

Ruffio sat. "Then we have but one task. We need to find the source of this storm, and put an end to it."

Brendan looked out the shuttered window as if he could somehow see through the heavy wood, and knew what he would witness if he had that ability. He had lived on the coast his entire life and could tell from the sounds that the winds were mounting, trees were bending before it. Soon roof tiles would be torn away and smaller buildings knocked over.

And as the elves had observed, it was all designed to keep them from returning to the elven city and to the struggling defenders trying to keep a nameless horror at bay.

9

JOURNEY III

Nakor ran.

He had appeared in what looked like familiar grassland, and had hiked to the top of a small knoll to look around, only to discover three very angry riders heading his way. A sense of the familiar washed over him as he ran away from them. He evaded the first rider to overtake him, rolling underneath the horse he rode, dodging the next two.

Once before in his life he had enjoyed such an encounter, rolling under horses, taunting riders, and otherwise making the best of a very bad situation, but today he had misplaced his sense of humor. The three riders looked remarkably like the three Ashunta warriors he had cheated at cards many years before. The one currently trying to brain him with a ceremonial war club wore leather leggings, no shirt, and a leather vest. His companions were dressed in a different fashion, one in leather armor, the other in an ornate red shirt, flop hat, and leather knee-high boots, yet all had the ceremonial band holding their long flowing hair back, set with a single feather.

Nakor remembered this encounter and how it had previously ended, but lacked patience to see if things turned out as before. He might look like the card cheat who had swindled these three in the past, but he still possessed a demon's powers. He jumped up and knocked one of the three riders from his horse, and leaped from that mount to the next one, swatting that rider off as he would a bothersome insect.

The third rider shouted a war cry and charged, and Nakor leaped again and drove his shoulder into the rider's chest, knocking him from his horse. Nakor hit the ground, tucking and rolling, and came to his feet ready for more.

He turned and the riders were gone.

Standing a short distance away was a familiar figure, one Nakor had never expected to see again in his life. Looking amused, the red-haired young man walked slowly down the hill.

"Nakor!" he said, throwing his arms around the little man, lifting him off his feet.

"Borric," said Nakor.

Putting Nakor down, Borric looked around and said, "Am I dead?"

"In one sense," said Nakor, "we both are. But I think differently."

"As obscure as always."

"It's my nature," said the little man, laughing. He reached into his shoulder bag and said, "Want an orange?"

Borric conDoin, eldest of twin sons of Prince Arutha of Krondor, and Hal, Martin, and Brendan's many-times-great-uncle, reached out with delight and said, "Thank you." He stuck his thumbnail into the orange and began peeling it.

Nakor looked around and said, "Some things are missing?"

"Yes," said Borric. "The caravan and Ghuda and Suli Abul and the others."

"So we're really not where we think we are," said Nakor.

"Actually," corrected Borric, "we are not where we appear to be. As I have no idea where we are, I'm not thinking about it."

Nakor grinned. "You learned a few things."

Borric smiled. "You have to, being King."

"What do you last remember?" asked Nakor.

"Lying in bed, listening to a priest droning on; I was silently praying to Lims-Kragma to take me so I wouldn't have to endure the sound of his voice anymore. I know my wife was there, and other family, but the last year . . . it wasn't kind." He looked around, smelling deeply. "Flowers blooming, close by."

"Perhaps."

"The worst thing about aging, Nakor, is that until the mind goes, you think you're eternally . . . thirteen years old?" He laughed. "Perhaps lacking some of that youthful optimism, and certainly knowing the sting of setbacks a great deal more, but in the end, there's still a child in there somewhere." He tapped the side of his head. "If you just let it thrive." Then he laughed again. "Look who I'm talking to. You've always let the child in you find wonders."

Borric sighed. "The thing is, that child wants to run, jump, swim, love, fight, sing, and know all the joys of being young, in just existing and feeling invincible and eternal." He smiled. "But the body won't answer. You try to leap to your feet as you did when young, but there's a pain in your back, and one knee wobbles, and someone is there with an outstretched hand to guide you." His expression turned wistful. "The last year, though, I would be talking and then . . . I was somewhere else, and hours had fled. I could look at the faces of old friends and their names . . . were missing. My children . . . sometimes I confused them." He looked regretful. "You've made the right choice, Nakor, in not growing old."

"I can't say I had much choice in the matter," said the little man, biting into his orange. "Something to do with the power to do tricks that I was given."

Borric laughed. He looked down at his hands and flexed them. They were the hands of a young warrior in his prime. "I feel wonderful. Though . . ."

"Though what?"

"This small cut, here," he said, pointing to the back of his left hand. "I remember exactly how I got that. When we were storming through the imperial palace, trying to save the empress. With all the knocking about Erland, Ghuda, and I did, the sword fights and brawling, I banged my left hand against a damn lantern on a metal tripod, and got this annoying little cut."

"Interesting," said Nakor. "As I suspected, you are not some creation of the gods given Borric's memories, but it is really you. Somehow a tiny part of you was captured and brought forward to this moment."

Borric put his hands on his hips and looked down. "I think I know. Right after we left Kesh to return to Krondor, a bit after we dropped you off at Stardock, when Erland and I were perhaps two nights away from home, we were sleeping next to our horses and I awoke." He put his hand on his chest. "I felt this . . . slice of cold."

"Slice?" Nakor's expression was now very curious and absent the usual delight he showed when faced with a conundrum.

"There was an . . . echo, for lack of a better word. A similar cut of cold."

Nakor was silent and then said, "I think I understand."

"What?" asked Borric.

"If I am right, a tiny sliver of your existence, the briefest moment of your life, was captured, and kept, for this meeting. It was your life, cut so thinly that your existence jumped that infinitesimally small space, so your life didn't end there. But a bit of that life was taken from you."

"Odd," said Borric. "How is it then my memories after that time are with me, from then to taking the Crown when Uncle Lyam died, to my marriage, children, all the palace years . . . to my own death?" He looked around, the wind picking up a little. He turned his face to the sun, smiled, and extended his arms. "If I am only to remain for a moment, at least my last memory will be of sunshine on my face, wind carrying the scent of tall grass, and a conversation with the most amusing man I ever encountered."

Nakor said, "Thank you, but beyond amusing, I am also very curious. If I understand what is occurring, your presence was arranged to impart knowledge to me."

"Ah." Borric laughed. "I can't begin to imagine what I could ever teach you, Nakor." He shook his head and said, "You know, Erland and I always regretted you never left the West to come visit."

Nakor shook his head. "After our adventure in Kesh, I'd had enough of palaces for a while." He sighed. "I did visit Krondor, once, when Jimmy was Duke. That's a nice palace."

Borric's expression turned thoughtful. "That was my home, where I grew up."

"Very nice place. Lots of rooms."

Borric laughed again and looked around. "Is . . . ? Did you hear something?"

Nakor cocked his head. "A pipe . . . and a drum, if I'm not mistaken."

"Odd," said Borric, casting around. "This way, I think," he said, pointing up a rise. He took two steps, then stopped. "I remember this place." He pointed behind Nakor. "Shouldn't there be a river that way about a quarter of a mile?"

Nakor nodded. "On the other side of the road that isn't there either. Yes."

"So on the other side of this ridge is that nice little vale where we camped the night after you joined the caravan with Ghuda and me!"

Borric was about to walk up the rise when Nakor said, "Wait."

"What?" said the onetime King of the Isles.

"After we parted, what was the most important thing you learned? You know, when you went from being Prince to King?"

Borric was silent for a moment. "I was Borric conDoin, son of a prince, nephew of a king, a king myself, father to a king. I was a son, a husband, a brother, and a father. I made decisions every day that changed lives, sometimes cruelly. I threatened wars, and fought them, and in the end I was an old man in bed when death came."

"What did you learn?" asked Nakor, his voice almost entreating.

Borric motioned for the little man to walk with him. As he headed toward the sound of pipes and drums, he said, "My true education began when I was captured in the Jal-Pur, Nakor." His expression turned thoughtful. "Being in the slave pens, fighting my way through that brothel with Suli, stealing a boat, serving aboard ship as a common sailor, all the things I did before I met you, then all we did after. Losing Suli." His eyes turned to scan the horizon. "I learned true courage watching a frightened boy try his best to do what needed to be done despite being terrified right up to the moment he died." He shook his head as he reflected on these things. "People talk about honor and duty and respect, and a host of other things to dignify their acts. In the end it's this: you have love or you don't."

"Love?"

"Have you ever loved something so much you'd gladly die to preserve it?"

Nakor was silent.

"Honor without love is a pose, a hollow justification for your acts. It's not what you're willing to fight for, but what you'll gladly die to preserve: a brother, a wife, or your child.

"The same holds true with nations. I would die for my nation, because I loved it. The Isles is a place, like Kesh, or

Roldem, just earth and rocks, trees and bushes, pastures and streams." He waved his arm. "Grasslands and mountains. It's just another place until you understand it's where your family lives, where the people who matter to you live, and the people who matter to them; those other places, that's where people you don't care about live. Given a choice, you'll fight to defend your people. More, you'll die to protect them."

Nakor felt a glimmer of understanding begin to take form. "Go on."

"It's a bond like no other, Nakor. Until I traveled to Kesh with you and Ghuda and Suli Abul, I didn't understand, truly. Erland and I had a difficult time learning about the responsibility that comes with privilege. My father loved my mother so much he let her indulge us, my brother and me, our sister, our little brother."

Nakor said, "Nicholas."

A sadness passed over Borric's face. "Erland and I were terrible to him before that journey, Nakor. I was changed by that journey." He then laughed. "Erland, too, but not so much."

"You were in a slave pen. He was in a palace with lots of pretty girls who didn't wear much."

Borric's smile faded. "But we lost Uncle Locky there, along with Suli. Erland felt that." The wind strengthened and the music in the distance grew a bit louder, then faded. A scent of sage and flowers touched them and fled.

"In the end, you lose everyone, don't you?"

"Yes, I suppose so," said Borric. "Let's see who's playing that music."

Nakor was a step behind Borric when the former King of the Isles said, "It's about touching lives, Nakor. It's about sacrifice because you love something more than yourself. It's about making a difference." He stopped for a moment. "It's about a farmer who can get his crops safely to market without being murdered by bandits because I made the roads safe. Me, King Borric of the Isles, and because I did, he gets safely home with his tiny pouch of coins and those things his wife asked him to fetch back from market, and a sweet for his little girl, or perhaps a toy for his little boy, and their lives unfold as they do." Borric's eyes grew moist with emotion. "But I didn't make the roads safe so that farmer would love his King. I made them safe because his King loves him and his family."

"I've known men of power, Borric. Some before I met you, others after, but your family is unique. Most rulers . . . the farmers are there to grow crops, pay taxes, and make them rich."

Borric said, "Nothing lasts forever, but this I know. If a conDoin sits on the throne of the Isles, no matter how talented or flawed the man is, somewhere inside of him is a love for his people that comes from the foundation of my family. When the first conDoin King put a rude circlet of gold on his brow, he did so thinking, 'This is my land. These are my people. I am their servant.' Even my uncle's predecessor, poor sad Rodric, 'the Mad King,' loved his people." Suddenly he laughed. "Maybe that's your lesson, Nakor."

"Maybe it is."

"Come, let's see about that music."

They hurried up the rise, and when they reached the ridge, they both stopped.

"It's a fair!" said Borric in delight.

Below were colorful tents, a large striped red-and-white one, and one Nakor particularly remembered: a hideous combination of gray and purple with a green fringe; and half a dozen wagons arrayed in a semicircle, behind which was a camp, cookfires, and horses.

Nakor took a step down the slope. "I know this fair," he said in disbelief. "It's Bresandi's traveling fair!"

He turned to find his companion was gone. Nakor stood motionless for a moment, then softly said, "Good-bye, King Borric."

When he turned back, a woman was standing before him. "Jorna," he said in wonder.

She smiled a rueful smile. "As good a name as any. How are you, Nakor?"

"You know I'm not Nakor," he replied.

"Close enough," she said, moving to his side and slipping her arm through his. "Still with the bag of oranges, I see."

"Always," he said, trying to force a lighter tone. The woman who now walked slowly down the hillside with him, arm in arm, had once been Nakor's student, then his wife. The demon known as Belog had never been so overwhelmed by the identity of Nakor as he was at this moment.

Nakor knew her as Jorna, but she had many other names, the last being Lady Clovis, then the Emerald Queen. Now she appeared as she had when he first met her, not looking young due to powerful magic, but young in truth: an ambitious girl with raven hair and piercing eyes that seemed to see inside him.

"Last thing I remember about you," she said, "was you ruining my master's plans to infect the Kingdom of the Isles with a plague."

"I wondered how willing you were in that plot," said Nakor.

"I had illusions then. I thought I could wield any power and command it. The arrogance of youth, you could say. Or perhaps I was always just full of myself."

She had always been a striking woman. Born of common farmers, she had carried herself like a queen since girlhood. She was slender but strong, her features lovely yet hard. She had beguiled him at first, seduced him, then abandoned him. "What was the last thing you remember before you got here?" he asked.

"It's quite odd, actually," she replied as they approached the fair. "I was negotiating with a demon—always a tricky business—and suddenly the demon was inside me."

"Not in a good way," quipped Nakor.

"You evil little man," she said. "I was fond of you, you know."

"Until you wrung every secret out of me you could, then ran off and found Macros."

She smiled and there was little in it that was mirthful, but for the first time Nakor saw a hint of regret in her eyes. "From some people's point of view, I got what I deserved, and perhaps they were right, Nakor. This demon, Jakan, he was a wily bastard. Having one slowly eat away at your mind to drain it of knowledge—and I mean literally eat—wasn't pleasant. Seems devouring people is a demon's fastest way to gain knowledge and power. I was alive perhaps as long as twenty minutes while he slowly picked my brain apart.

"The odd thing, you know, is that once he tore open my skull, the pain stopped. I was helpless, unable to move, and very angry, as you might imagine, but the actual eating didn't hurt. What hurt was losing . . . everything. I knew knowledge was vanishing—memories and abilities—but I didn't know what they were. Just toward the end, when there wasn't enough left for any sort of cohesion, there was just this overwhelming sense of loss."

Nakor said, "There are those who would say you did, indeed, get what you deserved."

"You among them, Nakor?" She lowered her lashes slightly, reflexively flirting with him as she had when they first met, a habit more than any overt attempt to change his view of her; they had too much history for that to ever be possible.

"Perhaps it's just we are so different in outlook, Jorna. I never understood your thirst for power."

"And I never understood your endless curiosity to know things without a goal."

He laughed. "Haven't you ever had a moment where coming to understand something, how something works, or what its true nature is, whatever you learned, in and of itself, was the joy?"

"I can't say as I have."

"Your loss, then," said Nakor.

"The thing about death is you learn that nothing is really

important, in the end. I mean, will anyone care who we were or how we lived and died a thousand years from now?"

"Very interesting question," Nakor said. "If one is important enough to be included in a history, perhaps. But maybe the question is what is important knowing that in a thousand years no one cares who you were or how you lived and died?"

She looked as him as if she didn't fully understand his point.

"I mean, knowing what you know now, if you could start again, say this day"—he waved his hand around—"when you first arrived at Bresandi's traveling fair, and met all of us . . ." He glanced away a moment, expecting to see some familiar faces: Totun the juggler; Batapol the knife thrower and his wife and usual target, Jantal; Subo the wrestler, who would pay a gold coin to any man who could best him in the ring. This was the carnival where Nakor the Isalani, the card cheat and swindler, had first discovered his tricks, and this is where he had met the young village girl Jorna, whom he had cared for, trained and educated, then married. "Would you do the same things as before?"

She was silent and said, "You're not asking that. You're asking would I be a better person." She sighed. "Probably not. I left those concerns for others. I would probably seek the same things—power, eternal youth, and the safety to enjoy my power and youth—but would seek different avenues of achieving those goals."

He sighed. "There were moments when I saw . . . glimpses of something more in you."

"Or moments you wished you had seen more."

"I've spent a lot of time with your daughter. She's who you could have been, I think."

"Miranda," she said softly. "I was never a good mother. My best choice for her was to leave."

Nakor shrugged. "The Miranda I know wouldn't disagree. Still, you left her alone with a father who was hardly an ideal parent."

"Macros," she said softly. "He was . . . magnificent." She sighed. Gripping his arm tightly, she hugged it to her. "But you, my funny little Isalani card cheat, you amazing magician who doesn't believe in magic, you were as close as I ever got to really caring for another. I know this means little to you, but I did think of you kindly from time to time."

"You hardly appeared to when we last spoke," he said with a chuckle.

"Well, you and that half elf and the fat pirate had just destroyed my plans for world conquest. I wasn't happy."

"Necromancy," he said, shaking his head. "Always a bad choice."

"You're right. One thing I learned from Dahakan before he finally, truly died, was that being undead tends to make one insane. Apparently, just working necromancy does the same, but slowly. That's why the second time I decided to try my hand with demons."

"Forgive me if I don't say I'm sorry it didn't work out for you."

"I understand, my dear Nakor." She stopped and looked around. "I think . . ."

"What?"

"I think my time is done." She looked at him with an expression that could only be called affection, laced with regret, and with eyes shining said, "Still, we had fun while we were together, didn't we?"

A hot flash of memory that wasn't his own, wasn't real, struck the demon Belog who now thought of himself as Nakor. "Fun?" he said grimly. He looked away, for the forgotten feelings were still close to overpowering if he let them. When he looked back she was gone, as were the colorful tents that had served as a backdrop. He was alone on a flat patch of grass.

Her question hung in the air.

Softly he said, "It was never fun. It was the most pain I've endured. You were the only woman I ever loved."

He heard a suck of wind behind him and turned to discover another vortex hanging in the air. He pushed ancient feelings deep down inside, then took a step and jumped into the vortex.

10

SKIRMISH

Hal drew his sword.

Captain Reddic, leading the squad of thirty riders from Bas-Tyra, said, "Put up your sword, sir." He did not know Hal's or Ty's name or rank, but having been told by a palace officer they were men of rank, he had presumed courtesy and deference from the moment they left Bas-Tyra eleven days before. "This is a local patrol out of Silden."

"Remind me, Captain," said Ty, "to tell you the story of a bunch of Ceresian pirates we ran afoul of who were wearing Kingdom tabards—

and last I heard, the Ceresians are now auxiliaries with Prince Oliver's navy . . ."

"It's the boots," said Hal quietly enough for the company to hear. Ty gave Hal a dirty look for spoiling the story.

The men readied themselves as the captain held up his hand in greeting. The thirty or so men who approached wore the red tabards of Silden, decorated with a silver stag's head. Their leader, a Knight-Lieutenant by his badge, held up his hand and ordered his men to halt. He rode forward and lifted his helm slightly in greeting. "Captain," he said in a friendly tone. "We don't usually see the tabard of Bas-Tyra this far west. What brings you to our part of the Kingdom?"

"Orders from my lord Duke," answered Reddic. "We bear dispatches for Salador."

"Odd," said the lieutenant. "But given the chaos on the water, I guess not that odd to be sending dispatches by rider instead of ship. Can we be of help?"

"Just how do things lie between here and Salador?"

"We're getting mixed reports," said the young lieutenant. "Here to where the road forks west to Malac's Cross and south to Salador, things are calm. My lord of Silden ensures that with our regular patrols, but south of there?" He shrugged. "Every warship in our navy is in Rillanon, and we've heard of both Keshian and pirate ships sailing within sight of Salador. And we've had reports of banditry, though with this many swords, I suspect you'll arrive unchallenged."

"One can hope," said Captain Reddic. "I fear no fight, but arriving in a timely fashion is important."

The two officers saluted and the two columns rode past each other, the men of both commands nodded respectfully. Hal couldn't help himself, but glanced twice at the Silden contingent's boots, finding them as polished as he would expect from cavalry in the field.

The ride over the next four days was uneventful, and as they entered Salador territory they saw more and more signs of conflict. Villagers raced to lock themselves behind doors or fled into the field when they saw men with strange tabards approaching. The second time this occurred, Hal commented on it. "What's got them so fearful?"

One of the men riding just ahead of Hal and Ty said, "From a distance, they see these black tabards, they can't tell if we're friend or foe. Might as well be a bunch of horseback pirates, for all they know."

"With the navy gone," said the man riding beside the first soldier, "it's easy for a pirate sloop to ride in close, drop a dozen men over the side, and wait while they plunder. Farmers and fishermen, that's what we're seeing."

The first soldier said, "Don't sell 'em short. They're tough as old boots when formed up in a militia—I've fought beside too many of them to think they lack spine."

"No argument, Jacques," said the second speaker. "But when only two or three of them are facing a dozen cutthroats, and they've got wives and daughters to think of, they'll flee, or hole up and take 'em one at a time through the door."

"Rarely works, that," said Jacques.

"What rarely works?" asked Ty.

"Holin' up. The pirates just burn you out and take what they want. You fight them on the beach or you run. Anything else is a waste of time and blood. Leave some booty behind and the sea rats won't bother to chase you into the hills."

Hal said, "Before this trouble with Prince Oliver began, what was the coast like?"

The second soldier said, "Quiet as could be, sir. A man could ride unarmed from Bas-Tyra to Salador with his purse filled with gold, and unless he ran afoul of a particularly bold bandit, he was as safe as he was in his own bed."

"Safer," said Jacques. "Cities still have thieves, and that's a fact."

They traveled until nightfall, then made camp on a flat-topped hill a short distance from the road, surrounded on three sides by light woods. Ty helped gather firewood while Hal helped tend the horses. He admired the squad from Bas-Tyra; it was efficient and disciplined. They might be close to the King's Highway and almost to their destination, but the nearby grounds were cleared, a brushwork barrier erected—it wouldn't stop a rider, but it would slow men on foot as well as make a great deal of noise if moved—and sentry torches cut and placed along the perimeter. When the last torch was cut and put in place, Hal asked the soldier next to him, "Aren't we close to the city?"

"Less than a day's ride, I reckon," answered the soldier.

"Good. As much as I enjoy the company, a bath and bed would be welcome."

"Well, I'm not keen on baths; my papa said they'd wash away your strength, make you weak, so I avoid them until told by an officer, then I do it quick."

Having been downwind of the man, Hal had no trouble believing the story.

The camp had become routine for Hal and Ty. For two weeks they had been riding with these men, and while the two young nobles' identities were still hidden, they had come to know the men they rode with well. Hal realized that in some way garrison soldiers were the same the world over. The Bas-Tyra accent might be foreign on his ear, and some of their words were foreign enough to make him wish he had studied the original Bas-Tyra dialect, but for the most part he understood and admired them. Like soldiers everywhere, they numbered their share of drunks, malingerers, malcontents, and fools, but he had little doubt these men had earned their Duke's loyalty as much as he had earned theirs.

He approached Captain Reddic after the evening meal. "If you have no objection, Captain, I'd like to be off before first light."

"In a hurry to get to Salador?" Reddic asked with a neutral expression.

Keeping his voice down, Hal said, "You've been a fine officer on this mission, Captain, one I'd be proud to have in my command."

"Your command?"

Lowering his voice, Hal said, "I'm Henry conDoin, prince of the Kingdom and Duke of Crydee." He had been carrying his father's ducal signet in his belt pouch. He would follow tradition and bury it with his father once his father had been recovered from the roadside grave where Brendan had buried him. At the King's pleasure he would don the new ducal signet given him by his liege lord—whoever that might turn out to be. Hal showed the captain the ring, then put it back in his pouch. "I'm riding with my companion to take council with Prince Edward on the Fields of Albalyn."

Reddic reflexively started to come to attention but Hal's hand on his shoulder cut off the change in posture. "I'd just as soon appear at the gates of Salador as one of a pair of swords-for-hire than be escorted in by thirty of Bas-Tyra's finest."

"Highness," whispered the captain. "Whatever you command."

"How about Ty and I take the last watch before dawn, then just steal a march on you? Make up whatever story suits you and we'll be fine. If fate gives me the opportunity to commend you to my lord Bas-Tyra, I will."

"Your Highness is too kind."

Hal smiled. "I know soldiers, and you handle these better than most."

He walked back to where Ty was patiently waiting for what remained of the food to be heated up. There was only so much you could do with salted pork, dried vegetables, and jerked beef. More experienced cavalry cooks carried small packets of spices, trying to give the lackluster food some semblance of variety. Hal was of the opinion that just getting anything hot on the trail was a situation for which to be thankful, so anything more was a blessing.

"We're taking the last watch and getting out of here early."

Ty nodded. "Anxious to get where we're going?"

"Absolutely. That popping around those magicians do . . . it would be something if we could do that at will."

"Maybe flying, while we're at it," said Ty with a wry grin. "I've been told some of them manage that feat, as well."

"All right. I'm going to get some rest until they tell us food is ready. Tomorrow night, a good dinner and a hot bath."

Ty laughed. "Don't sound so expansive. You're not buying; we're going to be guests at the palace."

Hal lowered his voice. "No, we're not. I'm forgoing the usual courtesy of calling on the Duke of Salador—Jim shared some intelligence with me before we left, and I'm not certain I want to be in Duke Arthur's tender care, even for a night. We'll find a decent inn, and I am buying."

Ty grinned. "I know just the place. Very good food; not as good as at the River House"—the River House was the name of his father's twin establishments in Roldem and Olasko, famous in the Sea of Kingdoms for the best food one could buy—"but very good. The beds are soft with clean sheets, and the women are . . . very friendly."

"Sounds like just the place," said Hal, lying down and putting his hands behind his head.

His thoughts couldn't help turning to Princess Stephané. No matter how many times he told himself that she was not only unobtainable, but that fate might decide he would never see her again, he still saw her face last before he fell asleep, and every morning she was the first thing he thought about. No woman he had ever met had filled him with such feelings: he felt profoundly empty without her.

He had been somewhat sheltered as a youth, his mother apparently having eyes and ears in every home containing a daughter of appropriate age. Being the eldest son of a duke had advantages almost everywhere in the Kingdom, but not in Crydee. It would have been funny to Hal had he not been the object of the joke. While other young men his age were often closing down alehouses and inns on Sixthday night, he was usually alone in his room reading or sitting with his family after dinner.

Like most young men, he desired what he thought he was missing, and on those few occasions when traveling with his father to Carse or Tulan he did have an encounter with a serving girl or one of the town girls, he found the experience enjoyable and worth the time, but essentially empty.

It wasn't until he met Stephané that he realized what was

missing. Once when a friend had been rejected by a girl, he had asked his father about it, and remembered the reply. "He'll get over it," said his father. "But to speed it along, he needs to know that pain will come. The knack is to not engage the pain, not hold on to it like a treasured thing, but to simply let it pass through and wait until it's gone. It will come less frequently, and after a time, be gone."

Most of the time since coming to Rillanon he had been too busy to dwell on loving a woman he could never have as his wife, but it was in these quiet moments when something reminded him of her that he got an ache in his chest he could not shed. He refused to let his mind drift into self-pity or pointless longing, but the emptiness lingered. He tried to follow his father's advice and simply let thoughts of Stephané pass through him, but they didn't. They lingered and tormented him.

He drifted off to a fitful doze, his mind floating through various thoughts and images. He missed his father, and wished he could talk to him about so many things, especially how best to serve his now-smashed duchy and the Kingdom. About Stephané . . .

He felt a hand on his shoulder. "Sir, it's your post." Hal blinked and found one of the Bas-Tyra soldiers waking him. Blinking and feeling completely unrested, he said, "Thank you."

Ty was already awake and moving toward the horse line. When he caught up with Hal, he said, "Rough night?"

"Yes. Couldn't sleep."

Ty said nothing. He had traveled enough with Hal to know that the young Duke was an experienced enough soldier to grab sleep anywhere, so this was unusual.

"Something up?"

Hal shook his head. "Just things getting to me, I expect. Once we reach Salador I'm neck-deep in these politics and that's a place I'd rather not be."

"I don't envy you," said Ty. He quickly inspected his tack and said, "I'll take the west side."

Hal nodded. He glanced skyward and took note of the position of the stars and the setting two moons, Small Moon and Middle Moon. Large Moon rose with the sun this time of year. "We have two hours, then let's saddle up and get an early start."

Ty nodded and moved off to the west side of the camp.

Sentry was as mind-numbing a duty as a soldier could endure, yet it was vital. A man coming awake is not as effective a soldier as one already on his feet, weapon in hand and alert. It was conventional wisdom among every author on the subject of war that Hal had read that attacking in the early-morning hours was the most effective in a surprise attack. Men were either still sleeping or just rising and did not have their wits about them. Those attacking had the advantage of resting before the assault, and Hal had learned enough as a student of warcraft to know that sometimes a battle turned on one side or the other having only the slightest advantage.

He remembered reading an account of the battle for Krondor when the Kingdom seized its first foothold on the Bitter Sea, ages before. Krondor had been a mere hill fort, stone-and-wood palisades surrounding a basic town of wattle-and-daub houses. But it had been well defended and could be resupplied from the sea.

The battle had begun and became a useless siege and in the end the leader of the attacking Kingdom forces, Prince Leontin, brother to the King and the Duke of Salador, had led a sunrise attack on the last day. By noon it appeared as if the attack had been successfully repulsed, as the attackers withdrew, but a small fire had started, not in the wood of the rampart but in a small clump of brush in the surrounding trench at the foundation of the rampart, and suddenly three timbers collapsed. Prince Leontin saw that gap and turned his forces and hit it with everything he had, and by sundown the Kingdom possessed Krondor.

The Kingdom of the Isles had its foothold in the Bitter Sea because a bush caught on fire.

That lesson had stuck with Hal, while others had not. He and his father had discussed it and his father had been clear on this one subject: the battle plan must remain fluid, changing from the instant you make contact with the enemy: it was the commander who could best adapt and respond on the spur of the moment who would emerge victorious.

Hal peered into the night, trying to imagine what he would be doing now if the war had never begun. He and his brothers would still be in bed asleep, but within two hours or so they would be dressing to break fast with their parents.

That life seemed a thousand years away.

Hal heard something. He wasn't sure what it was, but he knew it was something out of the ordinary. He snapped his fingers loudly, and Ty turned to look at him from the other side of the camp. Hal pointed twice toward the origin of the sound, then once in a circle motion around the camp, then he made a downward pushing motion with his hand, and Ty nodded that he understood.

Ty awoke each man quietly, motioning for silence, and within a minute the camp was up and armed. Hal motioned to Captain Reddic that he was going out to take a look, and indicated that a soldier named Minton should accompany him, knowing from conversations along the trail that the lanky, redheaded soldier had been a practiced hunter and tracker before enlisting.

A quick move through a gap in the brush at the far end of the camp put them outside the perimeter. Hal and the soldier quietly circled around, moving toward the source of the sound, weapons at the ready.

The trees were sparse in that direction and the lines of sight fairly clear, despite the darkness, but there was nothing to be seen. As Hal was about to return to the camp he heard a noise, faint but unmistakable. A horse's snort and the faint rattling of a bridle. Hal pointed and motioned for Minton to make a circular approach from the opposite direction.

After a minute he heard someone riding away. The soldier reached Hal a few moments later and Hal said in low tones,

"Someone led their mount this way. Then when they thought they were safely away, they mounted up."

Minton knelt and looked around in the dim moonlight. "I can't be sure until dawn, sir, but I'm pretty sure that's the mark of a boot heel next to your toe."

"Let's get back to camp."

They hurried back. "One rider, scouting us for certain, rode off to the south," said Hal.

Ty raised an eyebrow in question, and Hal said quietly, "I think we don't leave early."

Ty nodded once and Captain Reddic said, "As everyone's up, let's be out of here as soon as we can. If someone is expecting us down the road, let's surprise them by being early." He pointed to the soldier Hal had been scouting with. "Minton, I want you down the road now. Quiet as you can, and back here the second you see anything I need to know."

"Captain!" said the man, and hurried to saddle up his horse.

"Cold meal," said Reddic, "and in the saddle when the eastern sky turns gray."

Men hurried to follow orders and grab what they could to eat while getting ready to ride. Hal came to the captain and said, "I think we'll ride along with you for a bit longer."

"Always glad for the extra swords, my lord," Reddic said softly. Nodding at Ty, he added, "If I remember right, would that be the young man who bested you at the last championship at the Masters' Court?"

"Yes," said Hal. "That's Ty Hawkins."

With a smile, the captain said, "Well, Ruthia smiles on me, for if I'm gaining two extra swords, the two finalists in the Masters' Court final is all I could ask for."

"I hope we don't disappoint," said Hal.

"Rider coming!" shouted the horseman taking point. Instead of their usual place at the tail of the column, Ty and Hal were now riding directly behind the captain.

"It's Minton," said Reddic.

"Looks like he's in a hurry," said Ty, drawing his sword.

"I don't see anyone behind him," said Hal, motioning for his friend to put his weapon away.

Minton pulled in his mount at the last moment, and the horse almost squatted, it came to a halt so fast. The soldier turned and pointed down the road. "About a mile that way, Captain, they're waiting for us."

"How many?"

"About thirty-five, maybe forty. They scouted us, for certain. I found tracks between our camp and where they're waiting, just off the road. Followed them and got above them."

"Any idea of who they are?" asked Hal.

"No uniforms, tabards, or banners, sir," said Minton to his captain. "But they're organized and their position is as good as you'd want."

"Archers?" asked Reddic.

"Couldn't see any, but that doesn't mean some of those lads don't have horse bows."

"Can we get in behind them?" asked Reddic.

Minton grinned. "As a matter of fact, I believe we can."

Hal said, "Captain, do you have any bowmen?"

"Four," answered the captain. "I know what you're going to suggest." He turned to Minton. "You said you got above them. Good location for archers."

"Once they get to it, yes, sir, but those ambushers will see them if they set up before the fighting starts."

"I don't care," said the captain. "If they have archers, I want someone to take them out before they turn around and see us coming from behind."

Hal said, "If you're going to do that, you're going to need someone coming up that road, to hold their attention."

"What are you thinking?"

Hal smiled. "They'll need to see your point, a man in a Bas-Tyra tabard, so what I'm thinking is they do see your point rider and a lot of dust a half mile behind."

"Couple of riders dragging brush?" said the captain.

Hal nodded.

"Sound idea."

Ty threw Hal a skeptical look. "And I suppose we're the ones volunteering to drag brush?"

Hal grinned. "And miss the fun?"

"Oh, in that case . . ." Ty shrugged.

The captain motioned Minton away, giving them privacy. "Actually, I was going to suggest you and your friend do just that." He lowered his voice. "I would have a problem if anything . . ." He left the thought unfinished.

"As you really have no idea who we are, Captain, how could you have a problem?" asked Hal. He leaned close. "Right now I need to know why this ambush is being set for your men. I need one of those men up ahead alive. Preferably more."

"Yes, my lord. Just try to not die under my command, please?"

Ty had to stifle a laugh.

The captain detailed three men to act as point and brush draggers, instructing them to wait for half an hour then start down the road. To the point rider he said, "If these bastards have half the wits the gods gave cattle, they'll wait until you ride through to hit what they think will be the full column. If you see any sign of them, ride straight ahead where we will be waiting, behind them." He turned and yelled, "Mount up!"

"Sir!" came the reply as the riders followed orders.

Ty and Hal were only a moment behind, and when everyone was formed up, Captain Reddic shouted, "Minton! Lead the way."

"Sir!" answered the scout, and he set off at a posting trot until the column was moving behind, then took his horse to a canter.

Hal glanced at the lightening sky in the east and realized the false point rider and "column" would be leaving exactly as the sun rose, which would have them arriving at the ambush when expected. He glanced over at his companion.

"You're having too much fun," said Ty.

Hal could not resist a laugh. "After all the politics and skulking around, the hiding and dodging, I'm ready for a stand-up fight."

"As I said, too much fun."

They left the road a short time later and moved up a dry riverbed, overgrown with enough brush that it was clear the river that once ran here shifted its course years before. Minton said, "Captain, we need to leave the horses here."

Everyone dismounted and tied up their mounts. Minton pointed to some tracks. "This is where I found they'd left the road. Good thing, too, or I'd have ridden right into them." To the captain and everyone behind, he said, "From now on, hand signals only."

Captain Reddic reached into his belt pouch and said, "Muffle your scabbards." He removed a thick piece of cloth, lifted his sword, wrapped the cloth around the blade, then pushed down on the hilt. The blade now would not betray his position by clanking.

Hal and Ty were given cloth by a pair of soldiers and followed the captain's example. The soldiers then dropped all their other gear where they stood—packs and belt pouches—so that nothing would rattle, then secured their round shields to their backs, till they looked like a bunch of black-and-gold turtles.

The captain nodded and had the men form up in two columns, then motioned for Minton to lead.

Hal was impressed. Thirty well-armed soldiers were usually heard before they were seen. And palace guards and garrison soldiers lacked trail discipline. He was now convinced there was more to this particular troop than an escort for a message rider. All the soldiers at Crydee were trained for forest duty; the nature of the region demanded it; but Bas-Tyra was an ancient city surrounded by farmlands with no forest within three days' ride. And what scattered woodlands they had in that duchy didn't provide cover for outlaws, poachers, and fugitives.

But these men were trained for stealth, and Hal now knew

why the Duke of Bas-Tyra's mystery man Jaston had attached Ty and Hal to this detail; this was a special unit—infiltrators or assassins. Hal's father had told him of such, though Crydee had never had the need for these types of soldiers, but in the Eastern Realm, warfare was not always overt.

They reached a split where what appeared to be a dry rivulet turned into a game trail that wended upward into the rocks. Minton pointed and pantomimed archers, and the four bowmen headed up the indicated trail. Minton then held up his hand, fingers spread, and pointed down, indicating they needed to wait five minutes before moving again.

Hal stood motionless, scanning faces. There was nothing about this band of soldiers to suggest anything out of the ordinary, but he now was certain looks were deceiving.

Minton held up his hand when the five minutes passed and directed them down the dry riverbed. Like thieves at night, the remaining twenty-six soldiers, their captain, Hal, and Ty moved silently down the draw, their boots barely making any sound as they carefully lifted and placed their feet.

They came to a large outcrop and Minton motioned for them to circle around it. He held up one finger, and the captain turned and relayed the instruction, which Hal took to mean they'd move in single file.

For what seemed an hour but was only five or six minutes, they moved around the large rock and down another draw, then found themselves moving into dense woods. Hal realized they were moving back toward the King's Highway, moving down from the north.

Minton turned southeast and, as they came out of a thicket of trees, pointed to what had to be the ambush. Hal craned his neck and after a moment saw movement in the rocks above what must be the gap where the highway cut through these hilly woods.

Captain Reddic motioned and the column moved slowly around in a broad, looping course until they were just north of the highway, directly behind the ambushers.

The King's Highway cut through a natural pass about a

hundred yards across, flanked on both sides by rock forma-
tions. The one to the north where they had circled, and another to the south several times as large. Minton had been
smart enough to scout out the shortest route to the ambushers' rear.

Hal looked high into the rocks to the north and saw nothing, to his relief. He knew that if the archers were in place,
the second they heard fighting below, they would pop up and
help bring a quick end to the struggle.

Captain Reddic knelt and the rest of them followed suit.
Then he leaned forward and pointed to the end of the line,
held up seven fingers, then pointed to the rocky position to
the north of the road. After that, he pointed to a small clump
of trees and the last seven men in line got up and scampered
to that position.

He motioned for the other men to follow him, and moved
in a southwesterly direction. If the ambushers were evenly
divided, the northern contingency would come under bow
fire from above, Hal realized, hence the unequal division of
their forces.

Hal was thanking Ruthia, Goddess of Luck, that they
hadn't been noticed, when a voice ahead whispered, "I see
dust!"

The men in the rocks shifted position and now Hal could
see their entire deployment.

Captain Reddic seemed to be counting silently; then with
a single motion, he stood and slowly drew his sword. Silently, the men in his command took their shields off their
backs and silently drew their weapons. Hal and Ty did so
as well.

The captain held his blade aloft for only a moment, then
made a single downward cut and started a slow, measured
run, Ty and Hal a step behind the other soldiers, who knew
what was coming. They jogged along silently, then broke
into a sprint. One of the ambushers heard the movement and
turned, shouting alarm, and the fight was fully joined.

Besides their having the element of surprise, it was clear

that Bas-Tyra's soldiers were far deadlier fighters. The shouts from the north told Hal that the other side of the road was under attack as well.

Hal saw a soldier coming down out of the rocks and made a run at the man. These were trained soldiers they attacked, but none wore a uniform. The man Hal charged wore a white shirt with a leather jerkin over it and heavy wool trousers. He carried a finely honed long sword, but no shield. He saw Hal coming and leaped, expecting to bowl him over, but Hal dodged to his right, slicing the man's throat for his troubles.

Blood fountained and Hal swung around, seeing Ty quickly dispose of his opponent and move to come to the aid of a Bas-Tyra soldier being hard-pressed by two attackers.

"I need one alive!" Hal shouted to whoever could hear him.

Ty obliged by reversing his sword and striking one of the two soldiers hard behind the ear, dropping him senseless, then kicking him hard in the jaw.

"And who can talk!" shouted Hal.

Ty grinned, then skewered the other soldier through the leg. He went down with a cry of pain.

Hal saw Captain Reddic fighting with one man and with another ambusher coming up behind him. "Reddic! Behind you!" he shouted.

The captain slashed low with his blade then moved to his right, swinging around just as the man behind him stabbed. The blade missed running him through, but did catch him in his side.

Hal ran and in five strides struck down the man Reddic had faced, smashing him in the throat with his left arm, then stabbing to his right at the man menacing Reddic from behind. His blade cut air, but the second man retreated as Hal kicked the one on the ground in the face.

Reddic clutched his left side and thrust at the man who had wounded him. Hal turned and ran at the man, passing Reddic, who was walking on wobbly legs.

Feigning an overhand slash, Hal turned his blade and lunged, taking the attacker in the stomach. The man's face registered a look of astonishment as blood came flowing out of his mouth and his eyes went blank before he fell over.

Hal spun to find Reddic sitting on the ground clutching his side. "The fight's over there," he shouted at Hal, pointing with his sword.

Hal charged a knot of ambushers who were organizing themselves into a tight defensive group that would prove tough to attack. He saw where most of the Bas-Tyra men were disposing of their opponents, and shouted, "To me!" and a half-dozen black-and-gold-clad soldiers ran to him.

"Shield line!" he commanded, indicating with his sword where he wanted it. The six soldiers obeyed instantly. "Raise shields!" Hal shouted. The six men raised their shields until they were peering over the top. "Charge!"

The six men ran straight at the ambushers, who drew back their weapons and made ready to parry and counter. But the attackers didn't stop; they smashed shield first into the group, sending bodies flying in every direction.

Suddenly it was close, hand-to-hand fighting. Ty came over to join Hal. "That looks interesting. Should we lend them a hand?"

"I think we'd just be getting in the way."

"These Bas-Tyra boys are a tough bunch."

"I was thinking the same thing."

The fight was quickly over. Five soldiers ran off in the direction of the horses and left the rest in charge of the prisoners.

Of the ambushers, four remained alive, three conscious. Half a dozen men from Bas-Tyra sported wounds, but only the captain's appeared grave. Hal came over to where the scout Minton tended him.

Kneeling, Hal said, "Captain?" He saw frothy blood on Reddic's lips and knew it was a bad sign.

The captain waved Minton away. "Leave me propped up against this rock. I've got something to say to our friend."

Minton helped the captain into a more comfortable position, and when they were alone, Reddic motioned for Hal to come close. "My lord, I fear I am dying. Something inside is bleeding and I can feel my strength draining away." Hal moved to inspect the wound, but the captain pushed his hands away. "No disrespect, my lord, but I don't have time for you to delude yourself that you can get me to Salador before I die. If the time getting there didn't kill me, the ride will. I have something important to tell you. The communiqués in my saddle pouch are unimportant. They are for the Duke of Salador and a few to be sent on by courier to other local nobles in Deep Taunton and Pointer's Head. But sewn into my shirt is a letter from the Duke of Bas-Tyra to Prince Edward. War is coming, and my lord wishes Edward to know Bas-Tyra stands with him. He has gulled Chadwick of Ran into thinking he might stand with Oliver, but that is a ruse."

Hal nodded. "Someone in your master's court is a spy, else how would they know about this journey and that letter, and set this ambush?"

Reddic coughed and blood ran down his chin. "Montgomery of Rillanon still stands neutral, but my lord believes Chadwick of Ran is reaching agreement with Prince Oliver. That letter details what my lord Bas-Tyra has found so far."

"How was the letter to reach Prince Edward?" asked Hal.

"There's a courier waiting for me at a tavern near the palace in Salador."

Ty approached and said, "Something important."

"What?" asked Hal, looking over his shoulder.

"None of the men would talk until they saw me skewer two of the wounded," Ty said. "It was all show. They were already dead; I just claimed they still lived. These men are not just swords-for-hire; they're Vale mercenaries." Ty paused, then said, "My lord of Salador paid dearly to bring them up from the Vale and detail them to destroy this patrol."

"Salador?" said Reddic. "The Duke of Salador has been neutral but firm that all measures be taken for a peaceful settlement on who wears the Crown."

"*Was* neutral, you mean," said Hal. "If a spy in your master's castle got word to a fast boat, they would have been in Salador three days ago, giving ample time for this ambush to be planned. Then, should questions arise, an unfortunate attack by murdering outlaws who ran off with your horses, swords, and any communiqués you might carry . . ." His expression turned curious. "But how did the Duke of Salador get men here from the Vale so quickly?"

"I'll find out," said Ty. A moment later there was a painful yelp and after that Ty returned and said, "Our lord of Salador, apparently, has been recruiting mercenaries from both the Vale and northern Kesh for months now. He has them scattered about at inns and taverns throughout the duchy. This bunch was personally instructed by the Duke's chamberlain."

"What were his orders?" asked Hal.

"Kill everyone from Bas-Tyra and bring whatever was in the communiqué pouch to the postern gate of the castle. The leader of this lot said if he didn't make it, the lads would get paid their second payment, whoever showed up, by telling the guard on duty, 'Special orders for the chancellor.'"

The captain coughed and more blood ran from the corner of his mouth. "Let me tell you how to find the agent."

"No," said Hal. "As soon as the horses get here, I'm turning your men around and sending them back to Bas-Tyra. Ty and I will enter the city as we planned, alone and posing as two swords-for-hire. I'll personally get this letter to Prince Edward."

He looked down at the captain. "Is there anything I can do?"

Reddic shook his head, unable to speak, then closed his eyes. Suddenly his head lolled over and he let out a long death rattle.

"Minton!" shouted Hal.

The scout ran forward.

"Your captain is dead, Minton." Hal reached into his belt pouch, removed his father's signet, and slipped it on his finger. He knelt by Reddic and pulled away his shirt, finding the letter sewn into the lining. Using his belt knife, Hal cut the letter out and slipped it into his own shirt. Then he pulled away the captain's bloody tabard with his badge of office sewn over the sigil of Bas-Tyra and wadded it up in a ball. "Where's the communiqué pouch?"

"On his horse, sir."

As he stood, he could hear the horses coming and looked up to see the five riders, each leading a string of mounts.

The men of Bas-Tyra were gathered around the remaining prisoners and Hal approached them. "I'm Henry, Duke of Crydee, and I'm assuming command. Who is the senior ranking officer?"

A slender man Hal had only known as Carmody said, "Sir. I'm the squad sergeant."

"Orders, Sergeant."

"Sir?"

"First, fetch me the communiqué pouch from your captain's horse. Then take a message to Jaston, and speak to no one else but him."

"Jaston." The sergeant nodded. "Yes, my lord."

"Tell him your duke's suspicions about Chadwick and Arthur of Salador are correct and he should act to protect himself."

The sergeant paused and then said, "My lord's suspicions about Lords Chadwick and Arthur are correct and you advise him to protect himself."

"Then tell him he has a spy in his court; tell him about the ambush and that they knew you were coming."

"Easy to remember that, sir," he said sadly, looking down at the still form of his captain.

"Last, take the captain back to Bas-Tyra and tell your master he was served as well as a man can be served by a man who merited a better fate than being ambushed by robbers."

"Robbers?" said one of the prisoners. "We're not robbers! We're war prisoners. It's the code of mercenaries. We surrendered all proper like."

Looking at the four remaining prisoners, Hal said, "Who's your leader?"

"It was Benson," said the man who spoke before. "He's over there, food for crows. I'm Galton, next in charge."

None of the other men objected, so Hal nodded. "You're Vale mercenaries, swords-for-hire, men with loyalty only to gold. As far as I'm concerned, you're just a band of robbers.

"I, Henry, by patent of the Crown and right of birth, prince of the Kingdom of the Isles, do by right pronounce the King's High Justice." Looking at Carmody, he said, "Hang them."

Suddenly three shouting and fearful men were being dragged to a stand of trees. "What about the unconscious one, my lord?" asked one of the Bas-Tyra soldiers.

"Hang him as well," said Hal, and the unconscious man was dragged after the others.

Ty came over and said, "Harsh."

"Do you disagree?"

With no mockery, Ty said, "No, my lord. You have the right." He paused, then said, "And I think it necessary."

Hal was silent as he watched the first man hauled up by his neck. Then he said, "If Salador stands with Oliver, Bas-Tyra is right: Chadwick must have moved to Oliver's standard. Salador would never act without powerful allies in the east."

Ty let out a tired sigh. "It means we will have war."

"No," said Hal. "It means the war has already begun."

He turned and moved to where his horse waited and Ty followed.

Hal and Ty reined in as they caught sight of the northern gate of the city of Salador. A full squad of soldiers was halting everyone going in or out. "What is this?" asked Ty.

Both men had rehearsed their roles as vagrant mercenaries, and both looked the part, having neither shaved nor bathed since leaving Silden. Being covered with road dust after a day's ride in a nasty hot windstorm had added to the illusion.

"Readying for war," said Hal. "Our lord of Salador is worried about agents for other claimants to the throne entering his city."

"Well, given the jumble of politics in the Kingdom now, I suspect every city from one end to the other has enough agents and spies that no one does anything without everyone knowing." Ty looked at Hal. "Did that come out right?"

Hal laughed. "I know what you mean." He sighed. "I'd give a lot to be able to get a message to Jim Dasher right now."

"I'm sure he has people here."

"But finding them," said Hal, "that's the problem."

Slowly they moved to the head of the line and a soldier said, "State your business."

Ty glanced at Hal, who said, "Special orders for the chancellor."

"Give it here," said the soldier, holding out his hand.

"Orders are to give it to him personally," said Hal.

"Whose orders?"

"The Duke's," said Hal, without blinking.

Hal's ease of manner outweighed whatever perceived benefit the soldier thought he might gain by delivering the message personally, and finally he said, "All right, then, but go straight to the palace. No stopping for a drink with the whores."

Hal waved in a casual salute and headed through the gate. The Northern Gate Road led straight to a palace on the highest hill in Salador, a bluff overlooking the harbor. Hal reflected as they approached that he and Duke Arthur were relatives, albeit distantly, as their common ancestor had been the third Duke of Crydee, Borric. His son Martin was Hal's ancestor and his daughter Carline had been Arthur's many-times-great-grandmother.

But like most relationships among the nobility of the Kingdom, blood ties were only important when they served political ambition. Hal had no doubt that if Oliver's advisers had cautioned the Prince of Maladon and Simrick to put Hal's head on a pike, his distant cousin Arthur would be obliging, if he was, indeed, Oliver's man.

The Duke's palace had once been a major fortification. But looking around, Hal muttered, "Give me five hundred men through that gate and I'd take this castle within ten minutes."

Ty said, "Makes you wonder why Kesh wasn't here during the recent unpleasantries."

"Because most of their army was sacking the Free Cities and my duchy," said Hal quietly but with obvious bitterness.

They reached the main gate and turned to the right, moving along a stunning lawn bordered by low hedges, behind a low stone wall topped by wrought-iron bars, painted a muted yellow. The stone of the palace was gray and aged to dark blue or even black in places, but despite the brooding character of the building, the surrounding grounds looked almost festive.

The streets were crowded and Ty said, "Looks like everyone knows war is coming."

Hal nodded without comment. The number of hawkers, itinerant merchants, and practitioners of every service from seamstress and fletcher to chirurgeon, blacksmith, and even whore had come into the city, waiting for the departure of the army. Hal's father had said that there were times in history when the camp followers were double the number of people in the actual army.

They reached a road that was blocked off by soldiers and a makeshift barrier of a massive pole set on two sawing stands. Hal pointed. "Postern gate?"

The soldier nodded and said, "Business?"

"Special orders for the chancellor," replied Hal.

The soldier nodded. "Let them pass," he ordered, and two burly pikemen put down their weapons and moved to lower one end of the huge pole so that the horses could step over it.

Ty looked over his shoulder and saw the two soldiers struggle to get the log back in place. "What is that about, do you think?"

"No one's getting in easily, is my best guess."

"Just hope no one has to leave in a hurry."

Hal smiled. "My horse can make that jump, no worries." He glanced at his friend. "Not so sure about yours, though."

Ty smiled, but without humor. "Jumping that log with those bruisers trying to drag us out of the saddle into a crowded street . . . not my idea of sport."

"Agreed," said Hal.

Now they rode along a narrow road bordered by a chest-high stone wall that isolated the palace grounds from the city itself. The buildings on the slope below the new wall appeared to be successful shops, smart homes, and high-priced inns; just what one might expect this close to the palace: people of means, but not rich enough to enjoy the luxury of huge estates.

They reached the postern gate, a small but heavy wooden door in the middle of an otherwise blank wall. Hal laughed. "This was once useful, I suppose."

Ty looked at his friend and said, "I'm not sure . . . ?"

"Never lived in a castle, did you?"

"Visited them, but no. Palaces, inns, over my father's restaurant, under tables in taverns, and many other less savory haunts, but no, I never lived in a castle."

Hal grinned as he dismounted. "In ages past, this was a sally port as well as a back door for deliverymen."

"Ah," said Ty, looking around. The little road was hardly anywhere from which one would wish to launch a counterattack. "Bit narrow, isn't it?"

"I have no idea what the terrain was like centuries ago," said Hal, pounding hard on the gate. "Maybe there was heavy brush and trees or marshes . . ."

Within a moment the door opened and a guard appeared. "What is it?"

"Special orders for the chancellor."

The guard nodded once. "Right. Wait here," he said, and closed the door.

Ten minutes later a man dressed in court finery opened the door and said, "Yes?"

"You the chancellor?" asked Hal, suddenly sounding considerably less educated than usual.

"Where's Benson?" asked the man gruffly. He was entering late middle age, but was dressed in fine clothing and well-crafted boots, and evidently had a penchant for gaudy jewelry, for he sported a gold chain from which hung his badge of office and several large rings.

"Dead," said Hal. He motioned to Ty and said, "Some of the lads are injured and resting at camp. Him and me thought it wise to hurry here, as Galton said you were waiting for this. Galton was too hurt to ride, so he sent us. But he said to tell you we got them."

"Got them?"

Hal went to his horse's saddlebag and took out Captain Reddic's bloody tabard and the communiqué pouch. "Galton says this is what I had to bring you, and be quick about it, he said." He showed the badge on the captain's tunic and handed the pouch to the man.

The chancellor opened the pouch, removed its contents, and tossed the empty pouch back to Hal. He quickly went through a half-dozen communiqués and, after glancing at each, threw it aside. When he read the last, he said, "This was all?"

"We found nothing else, m'lord. The boys did a thorough job of lookin', too, I can tell you. Searched clothes, boots, everything."

There was a quiet moment while the chancellor weighed what was in the pouch and, more critically, what wasn't. Finally he asked, "The Bas-Tyra captain, did he say anything?"

"Well, truth to tell, m'lord, me and him"——he indicated Ty—"was a little busy killin' those lads. Quite a fight they put up, too." Hal lowered his voice. "It's not my place to offer an opinion, Chancellor, but seems to me that bunch was as nasty a crew as I've seen in the field. Special training and the like, I'm thinking. We lost a lot of boys yesterday."

"You're right, it's not your place to offer an opinion."

Hal wondered if he had overstepped his role of common

sword-for-hire. The chancellor had a menacing air. Hal had seen his type during his stay in Rillanon. Some men killed with a quill and parchment as easily as others did with steel, and if this man had Duke Arthur's ear, Hal was certain the Duke of Salador was getting dangerous political advice.

Obviously frustrated by not finding what he expected, the man said, "Very well. You can go."

"M'lord," Hal said before the chancellor turned away. "Galton said you'd pay the second half of the contract fee."

"Did he?" said the man, and Hal knew he had blundered into a dangerous moment. He had little experience with mercenaries, as there was no call for them on the Far Coast, but he'd heard stories.

Hal said, "Galton said Benson said we was given first payment when they took the contract, and we was to be paid the rest now." He shrugged. "Now, Galton should be fit to ride in a couple more days, so I guess we can wait until he gets here and let him settle with you, sir. I mean, you got too many swords-for-hire lounging around your city to have word spread you don't pay your agree contract, right? I mean—"

"Never mind," said the chancellor, a sour expression on his face. "Wait here."

Close to half an hour passed, with Hal standing by the open door, under the baleful gaze of a Salador soldier, while Ty sat patiently on his mount. Finally the man returned with a heavy pouch and handed it to Hal.

"Thank you, m'lord," said Hal.

"Galton is coming here in a few days, you said?"

"He took a blade across the leg. Not deep, but he couldn't ride. But we bandaged it good. I expect he'll be fit for riding in three, maybe four days. Should be here by the end of the week, latest."

"When he arrives have him report to Captain Braga at the eastern gate for new orders."

"Sir," said Hal. He mounted up and Ty made a sloppy salute to the chancellor, who ignored him.

When the postern gate was closed behind and they were deep into the streets of the city, Hal said, "Well, at least we sleep in clean beds and eat a good meal tonight." He hefted the bag. "Must be three hundred gold in here."

"Maybe we should become swords-for-hire?"

"Maybe," said Hal, laughing as they rode away from the palace.

11

TRAPPED

Horns and drums shattered the morning quiet.

Hal woke up suddenly. He and Ty had found a room in an inn called the Dancing Pony near the Farmer's Gate in the southernmost quarter of the city, where demand had set a price far higher than normal, so Hal decided to play the part of the struggling sword-for-hire and shared a room with Ty. Ty had won the coin toss and was sleeping in the single bed, while Hal had made do with blankets and a pillow on the floor.

Both had enjoyed a hot bath and shave, and had purchased clean travel clothing the day before and enjoyed a reasonable supper. Now the clamor outside roused them from a well-deserved sleep.

Hal moved past a still-groggy Ty, pushed open the small window under the gabled roof of the room, and peered out. Two men in the garb of Salador were marching down the street and stopped two shops away. One blew a horn, three long blasts, while the other beat out a tattoo on his drum. Then the horn blower shouted, "By order of his grace, Arthur, Lord of Salador, all fighting men are conscripted! If you be between the ages of sixteen and fifty summers, without infirmity or crippling disease, sound in mind, and able to bear arms, you are summoned to assemble!" Losing the official formal tone, he shouted up, "You scruffy lot get out of your beds of pain and move orderly to the south gate! Any man able to bear arms who has not stood before the scribe of the court, and been inducted, will be counted a deserter and hanged at the city gate!" He picked up his horn and blew it again while the drummer repeated his tattoo. The two men marched briskly down the street where they would repeat the message.

Hal pulled back inside the room. "What was that?" asked Ty, still half asleep.

"We've been conscripted," said Hal, sitting down on the side of the bed to pull on his boots.

"What?" asked Ty, waking up fully.

"Apparently Arthur has put the city under martial law and enrolled every man of fighting age into his militia. We are to report to the southern gate by sundown or be hanged as deserters."

Ty yawned, then grabbed his shirt off the post nearest him at the head of the bed. "Well, I guess that's better than being hanged as spies."

Hal looked at his friend as if he had lost his senses. "I'll leave that comparison for another time."

"What are we going to do?"

Hal said, "First, we hide this gold." He pointed to the pouch that sat on the floor next to his second boot. "Half-mission pay for thirty men? Most of the bravos in town would happily cut our throats for a tenth of that."

"It's a lot of gold," said Ty. "But do we need it?"

"For the time being," said Hal. "I think the chancellor was trying not to honor the contract so he could keep as much gold on hand as he could. If he had realized there were no other survivors coming to join us, looking for their share, we'd either be in the Duke's dungeon or dead.

"This conscription means the Duke has too many mercenaries and militiamen in the city and he's running out of food, wine, and gold." Hal stood up, took his sword belt from the back of the chair where it hung, and put it on. He tossed Ty's sword to him. "So, what's as good to an army as paymaster's gold?"

"Booty," answered Ty.

"Right." Hal considered. "He can't march west, because he can't face Edward until Oliver and Chadwick arrive, and to do that, the fleet loyal to Oliver must first go here . . ." He stopped. "He means to sack Silden."

Ty stopped dressing for a moment, then nodded agreement. "Bas-Tyra can't move until he knows if Chadwick is marching against him or sailing past him to join here with Arthur. But Silden's allied with Bas-Tyra and could march south to take Salador's forces from behind if they leave the city. Yes, he'll have to crush Silden before he can join with Oliver and Chadwick to march on Edward. I guess it had to start sooner or later."

Hal leaned against the doorpost. "Oliver can't stay in Rillanon threatening the palace forever. That's why Edward's waiting. In ages past you could grow enough food on that island to feed everyone, but now two-thirds of what feeds Rillanon comes from the mainland. Oliver knows that every western lord and half the east is with Edward, but he also knows that should he defeat Edward, with Chadwick's backing, Montgomery will not challenge him. So, Silden first, then Oliver and Chadwick come to Salador."

"What do we do?"

Hal said, "Not get hanged today. Come along. We need to report in to the conscription officer at the gate."

Ty finished gathering his things and said, "The gold?"

Hal tossed the pouch to Ty and said, "Find somewhere on you to keep it, and don't let it clink too much."

Ty rummaged through his saddlebag, wrapping it in his clothing. "Don't let me lose track of that horse."

Grinning, Hal led his friend down the stairs and out into the busy streets of Salador.

The mood at the southern gate was getting out of hand. A squad of Salador's regular army stood ready with pikes held high in case some heads needed breaking. Three companies of cavalry were already roaming the streets to provide motivation for unruly parties of mercenaries to disperse if so ordered. The mustard-yellow-and-dark-red uniforms were seen on every corner as the muster was being called.

Ty muttered to Hal, "Any stupidity here and we have a riot."

"Oh, the stupidity is already under way." Hal nodded toward a wagon used as a barricade across the southern gate, with a table next to it. Behind the table sat a nervous clerk and atop the wagon a grizzled sergeant who looked as if he'd seen far more barroom brawls than battles. His face was jowly and had the texture of dirty leather, and his bloodshot eyes glared out from under bushy eyebrows. His helm looked too large and sat skewed on his head, giving his entire appearance a comedic aspect totally at variance with the menace he seemed determined to demonstrate.

A dozen men standing in line before the table, and others jostling to get into the queue, started name-calling and pushing. "This will not end well," said Hal.

Ty tugged at Hal's arm and with a jerk of his head indicated a place against the city wall. They edged along until they had their backs firmly against the stones of the tunnel under the city wall, behind the first group of pikemen. Ty whispered, "If they start swinging those things, duck."

Hal grinned. "Hug the ground, you mean."

The sergeant was shouting over the noisy crowd. "And that is until the Duke says you're done!" He squinted at the crowd as if one eye worked better than the other, then added, "Anybody not happy with that can think about it in the dungeon!"

More muttering was followed by the sergeant picking up a water skin and taking a deep pull. "I'll bet all the gold in your backpack that's not water," said Hal.

"No bet," replied Ty. "I can smell it from here." He looked at Hal. "Good wine is not that expensive. He's a sergeant? He can afford it."

Hal gave him a skeptical look. "More?"

"Oh," said Ty. "Yes, if your concern is quantity rather than quality . . . fair point."

Putting down the skin, the sergeant shouted, "I'll repeat the orders for those of you just arriving!" He wiped his mouth with the back of his hand. "Line up and give your name to the clerk. You'll be given instructions on where to report. Go there and give your paper to the officer waiting for you. If you can't read, it doesn't matter, the officer can.

"Now, my lord Duke Arthur has announced his support for good Prince Oliver, rightful heir to the throne, and is mustering to put down rebellion against Prince Oliver." He held up his arm and shouted, "Long live Oliver!"

This was greeted with a halfhearted muttering from the crowd as a few of the newly conscripted fighters repeated the phrase.

"Now, if you're in a company already, find your bloody captain and go where he tells you." At this, a few men turned and left the assembly. "The rest of you get in line. You'll be serving the Crown for the duration, which means until the Duke is done with you. If you don't like it, you can sit out the war in the dungeon."

"I think this we've heard before," said Hal.

Ty nodded. "What do we do?"

Hal looked thoughtful for a minute and then he grinned. "I'm Benson. You're Galton."

Ty's eyes narrowed. "What do you have in mind?"

"Well, we have their gold. Let's spend some of it!"

They ducked past startled pikemen who didn't realize Ty and Hal had slipped in behind them, and circled around to the farthest point behind the crowd. "Look for some likely lads."

"It's a pretty scruffy lot," said Ty. "That fellow over there!"

Hal saw the large man Ty indicated. He was a full head taller than most of those around him and had a seriously angry expression but seemed reticent about saying anything. "Smart enough to hold his tongue," said Hal.

He worked his way through the crowd and tapped the man on the shoulder. Hal was not used to having many men look down on him, but this fellow did. "What?" the man asked with controlled fury.

Hal said, "I think we might have cause to speak, stranger." He turned without seeing if the man followed, and when he reached Ty he turned and saw the man had. They stepped away from the press and Hal said, "I'm called Benson, and he's Galton. Are you a sword-for-hire?"

"I'm a damned teamster," said the burly man. His head was covered in thick brown hair shot with gray, and his jaw looked as if it had been fashioned by a blacksmith. He had massive shoulders but a tapered waist, and carried himself well.

"But you were a soldier?" asked Hal.

"Once, in another life," said the fellow. "Used to serve up in Darkmoor as a man of the castle, but I got married and told my missus I'd give up soldiering. Her da had a hauling company for the wineries in the area, so I spent the last twenty years driving wagons from there to Krondor, to here, and back. Now they're trying to turn me into a damn soldier again!" The veins in his neck stood out with rage.

"Why are you here?" asked Ty.

"Got an order for more wine in one shipment than we usually move in a year. So I spent every coin I had to buy or rent rigs, horses, hire men, and moved as fast as I could bringing down every bottle I could find in Ravensburg and all the other wine towns around Darkmoor."

"Why so much wine?" asked Ty.

"For the wounded," said Hal. "A man gets a gut wound and you give him water, he dies almost certainly. You give him wine, he has a chance to live."

"You know your battle medicine," said the teamster.

"What's your name?" asked Hal.

"I'm Jeremiah," said the wagoner. His anger had lessened, and he put out his hand.

Hal took it and said, "How many drivers do you have?"

"A full thirty-five. We had eighteen wagons of wine casks, all full loads of casks, four hundred and fifty of them! We bring them in and what do I get? A piece of parchment with a fancy seal on it!" He waved his finger under Hal's nose. "They took my wagons and parked them by the barracks, told me to settle my men in best I can. Most of them were sleeping in the stables behind the miserable inn I found, and now they're turning us into bloody militia!"

"May I see that parchment?" asked Hal.

Jeremiah reached into his tunic and pulled it out. Hal read it: it was written in a florid style, in a hurry, and almost illegible, but at the bottom was a wax seal of Salador and a big signature with a flourish. "We need a forger," said Hal.

Ty grinned. "I think I can find one. See you back at the inn."

"Hey!" said Jeremiah as Ty ran off with his parchment. "I need that to get paid!"

Hal put a restraining hand on the wagoner's massive chest and spoke in quiet tones. "Easy. You'll never get your money from Duke Arthur. Most of your men will end up dead, and when this war is over, Arthur will either be hanging for treason or he'll be taxing the hell out of everyone in the duchy to help Prince Oliver pay off his war debts to the Eastern Kingdom moneylenders." Hal glanced around to see if anyone overheard his remarks, then continued. "If my plan works, you'll get out of here and be headed back home, with gold—not as much as you're due, maybe—and your men alive and safe and able to return to their families." He looked up at the big man. "If a man has to fight, it should be for his own home, not for another man's ambition."

"You're not just an ordinary mercenary, are you?"

Hal smiled. "I'm ordinary enough that I don't wish to be wall fodder for Arthur when he sacks Silden."

Jeremiah nodded. "I've seen generals feed militia to the wall, saving their regulars until there's a breach."

"Gather your men and meet us in an hour at the sign of the Dancing Pony. Have they unloaded your wagons?"

"They were still there last night. The soldiers here are so this way and that, up, then down, no one's doing anything. I had to go and put nose bags on my thirty-six horses and carry water for an hour because the baggage boys in the army were too busy getting ready for battle. For all I know, they're still sitting there."

"Go see if they are. If they haven't unloaded the wagons, that would be a good thing." He slapped Jeremiah on the shoulder and the large man moved off.

Glancing around, Hal didn't detect anyone paying attention to him, so he hurried off to return to the Dancing Pony.

In a shadow in a deep doorway, across the road from the entrance to the gatehouse over the Farmer's Gate, a figure in a hooded robe watched Hal depart. "What is Henry conDoin doing in Salador?" she muttered. She cursed the gods of fickle opportunity and wished she had departed last night instead of waiting for this morning. Lady Franciezka Sorboz, leader of the King of Roldem's intelligence network, ducked behind a moving wagon that masked her from the view of the soldiers over by the gate, and vanished into the city.

Hal returned to the Dancing Pony to find Ty in the corner with a strange-looking little man with hunched shoulders and a scraggly beard, wearing the oddest flop hat Hal had seen. It was a lumpy thing of dark red velvet, ancient, stained, and discolored.

"This is Sheridan," said Ty. Lowering his voice, he said, "He's our forger."

The man had a very curious pair of spectacles on his nose: square lenses of thick, transparent quartz or glass through which he peered at the promissory note taken from Jeremiah. "An' you don't need me to forge a document and seal, my friend," he said, putting it down. "This will do nicely for what you want."

"Really?" asked Ty.

"See, this document has been used a few times. That's why it's so smudged. We just cover up the signature and seal so they don't get damaged, then we strip away most of the old ink, and write in what we want." He took off his spectacles and smiled. "Ten gold and I'll have it done in an hour."

Ty said, "Done." Looking at Hal, he said, "What do you want it to say?"

"The bearer of this document is acting under my personal orders and every effort is to be made to help him in any way he requires."

Ty grinned. "That's vague enough."

"Ah, that'll take . . . I can write that right here," said Sheridan. "I'll need a glass of strong spirits; brandy or whiskey would be better."

"I'll see what they have," said Hal.

He went to the bar, said what he wanted, and the innkeeper reached under the bar and pulled out a large porcelain jug. He pulled out the cork and poured the amber liquid into a glass; from two feet away, Hal could smell the bitter, volatile aroma of distilled grain. "Don't get much call for this," the man said.

"I can see why," said Hal. "It's making my eyes water from here."

Hal returned to the table as Jeremiah entered with two of his drivers. "Wagons are still sitting where we left them. Horses are hock-deep in their own manure and no one has fed or watered them."

"That's good news, really," said Hal. "Have a drink and

wait a bit, and with luck we'll be out of the city in a few hours."

Hal handed the glass of whiskey to Sheridan, who arranged the parchment, placing a cloth carefully over the seal and signature, then took off his hat and from inside pulled out a case. He opened the case and withdrew a flat-sided blade. Then from a tiny pouch he sprinkled a white powder over the writing. He started to trickle the whiskey down the blade and then scraped gently. As he did so, the letters began to fade.

"Aren't you afraid that stuff will burn holes in the parchment?"

That brought a barking laugh from Sheridan. "I'll need another, please."

Hal got up and fetched back another small cup of the drink. "This smells like the oil used in lamps."

Sheridan took the glass, but instead of pouring it, he drank it in one gulp. "Takes some getting used to," he said hoarsely, "but it has its uses."

Before their eyes, they could see the lettering continue to blur and fade. "The nice thing about this," said Sheridan, "is the soldiers here have seen enough of these used-again documents they probably won't think twice of it."

Hal said, "How much longer?"

"Take a few minutes for this to dry," said Sheridan. "Then five to write what you want."

Hal nodded to Ty and pointed to his saddlebag, which was slung over his shoulder. "If you please."

Ty removed the coin purse and counted out the ten gold pieces, sliding them across the table. Sheridan scooped them up and Hal said, "Now comes the hard part."

"What?" asked Ty.

"We need two uniforms."

Ty let out a slow sigh. "I don't expect you have us running over to the barracks quartermaster and nicely asking for a pair?"

"No." Hal stood up. Picking up the pouch of gold, he

handed it to Jeremiah. "Hold on to this. It's the gold I promised you, but I might need to buy a thing or two before it's over."

"Understood," said Jeremiah, hefting the small sack and liking the weight of it.

The two young swordsmen left the inn and Ty said, "Where are we going to get uniforms?"

"From soldiers," said Hal brightly.

Ty rolled his eyes but said nothing. Hal looked around. "Have you been in this city before?"

"A couple of times," said Ty. "That's how I knew where the Thieves' Quarter—not officially its name—was and where to ask for someone like Sheridan."

Hal thought for a moment, then said, "Lead the way."

Ty shrugged. "What's your thinking?"

"Two guardsmen vanishing in the middle of the day is difficult. Impossible anywhere near the musters. But two vanishing in the Thieves' Quarter?"

"It's happened before and no one who sees us is likely to say anything unless a reward is offered, and that wouldn't be for at least two or three days, if at all given this madness." Ty's mood brightened. "I like this idea better than before."

They moved out of the crowded eastern market area, through streets of small businesses and homes. The so-called Thieves' Quarter proved to be everything Hal hoped it would be, dark with high buildings over narrow streets, once well-to-do neighborhoods run down and turned into tenements. Ty pointed. "We call these 'rental barracks' in Olasko. Four or five little rooms in what used to be a house, each now with a family in it. You'd better like your neighbors."

The stench that swept over Hal from the streets was overpowering. Ty noticed his reaction and said, "Duke Arthur hasn't seen fit to repair the sewers around here for a number of years, so what gets dumped into the street stays in the street." He pointed up to the windows overhanging the street. "Best to wear a very broad hat if you spend any time around here."

Hal nodded. "Soldiers?"

"Could be anywhere." Ty looked around, then said, "That way." He pointed down a wider street.

"Why this way?" asked Hal, following.

"Bit of a local market down there. It's where I found the lad who led me to Sheridan."

"Not your everyday market," said Hal.

"It is for this sort of neighborhood."

As soon as they reached the little market, Hal realized they stood out. They might not be dressed in a rich fashion but they were clean and their boots and weapons were well cared for. As they moved through the crowd, Hal felt watched every step of the way.

Some of the local vendors pulled aside their wares, not eager for strange eyes on them, while others ignored their passing or even viewed them as potential customers. Hal saw packets of paper folded and sealed with wax, which he assumed contained drugs. Every manner of trinket and goods was on display, most likely all stolen or smuggled. Gambling was under way in two stalls, one with cards, the other game involving knucklebones.

Finally Ty saw what he was looking for. He motioned for Hal to follow and the young Duke found a clutch of urchins gathered at the end of a small cul-de-sac. They eyed the approaching swordsmen and it was unclear if they viewed them as prey or predators.

Finally one of the bolder boys shouted, "What's it about, then?"

"Squeaky?" Ty said.

A small boy from the back of the pack emerged, and smiled when he saw Ty. He was half the size of the others, wearing a tunic that was properly for a boy twice his size, and had a rough-cut mat of dirty black hair and a round face. "He's all right," he said, and the other boys drifted off. When the three of them were alone, he asked, "Sheridan did al'right for ya, then?"

"Fine," said Ty. "How would you like to make a little more?"

"Always," said Squeaky.

"Is there a place close by where my friend and I might have a quiet word with two of the city's garrison?"

Squeaky looked around to make sure no one was listening. "I don't think that's such a good idea," he said. "Even the dodgy guards are acting all proper like, given the fuss stirred up by the muster. They're more worried about having to deal with a riot than making a little gold for looking the other way. Fact is, they're distracted enough already and you can plunder and pillage as you like, I reckon."

"Well," said Ty. "It's not bribing them we need, but rather to borrow some things from them."

"I don't want to know more," said Squeaky. "How many do you need?"

"Two is all we need," said Hal.

"About our size if you can arrange it."

Squeaky fixed the two swordsmen with a narrow gaze. "If it's a bit of murder or assault you want, I'm your boy. But I need money now, two gold."

Two gold was two days' wages for a master craftsman. Squeaky had been content with a single silver piece to introduce Ty to Sheridan. "That's quite a bit," said Ty.

"I got to show a coin to the crushers to get them to come, and they'll almost certainly take it from me. If you don't do whatever it is you want, they'll keep it and be looking for me."

"Fair enough, given the risk," agreed Hal. He reached into his own belt purse and fished out two pieces of gold.

Squeaky said, "Here's as good as anywhere. The crushers will expect no good and anyone who sees what happens isn't going to be wanting to talk to anyone about this." He dashed off.

"Now?" asked Ty.

"When the soldiers show up, we remove their uniforms and try not to get too much blood on them."

"The soldiers or the uniforms?"

"The uniforms," said Hal drily. He quickly outlined what he had in mind.

In less than a quarter of an hour, people in the small market began diving for cover, opening a tunnel that revealed a small boy being chased by two soldiers. Squeaky ran to where Hal and Ty stood and ducked behind the two swordsmen.

As planned, Hal and Ty stood with arms crossed as the two soldiers came to a halt. "Give up that boy!" shouted a red-faced sergeant, out of breath from the chase.

His companion was less patient and put his hand on Hal's chest as if to push him out of the way.

"I ain't going with no pederast!" shouted Squeaky.

The sergeant's eyes widened and he began to say something, but at that moment Ty's sword came out of his scabbard and the pommel slammed into the point of the sergeant's jaw behind his ear.

Hal leaned away from the man who had his hand on his chest, and struck him with a balled fist three times in the face. In seconds, both men were unconscious.

With a grin, Ty said, "See, no blood."

"Greed and caution," said Hal. "Greed wins just about every time."

Squeaky said, "My other coin?"

"What did you say?" asked Ty.

"I told them a fat merchant had died and this was all I could get out of his purse." He took the gold coin Hal had removed from the sergeant's belt pouch. "I told them if they'd help me move his fat carcass, I'd split the gold with them. When the sergeant grabbed my coin, I shouted I'd find someone else and ran."

"Bright lad," said Hal.

They quickly stripped the bodies and donned the uniforms: tunics, tabards, and helms. They assumed no one would notice their own dark trousers were of better weave than those the soldiers were wearing.

Squeaky, the other boys, and a couple of unsavory-looking thugs had gathered to watch. When Hal was satisfied that he and Ty looked enough like members of the city garrison, he turned to Squeaky. "We're off now."

"What do you want us to do with these two?" asked the boy.

"Know any Durbin slavers?" asked Hal, joking.

"Not from Durbin, but there's a gang runs up here once every so often from Jonril." Hal was momentarily taken aback, then he realized the boy was talking about the original city in Kesh, not the fortress in Crydee named for that city.

"Care to make them an offer?" asked Ty, not joking.

"Well, normally that would be just the thing, but with this city bottled up, as it were, no slaver is going to be seen here for a few weeks. If we keep them hidden, we got to feed them and then there's the risk we get caught out, and that means the hangman for all of us."

At the mention of the hangman, the two thugs and most of the boys decided it was time to be somewhere else.

Squeaky grinned. "You don't really want me to keep these boys cool until some slavers show up?"

"No," said Hal, returning the boy's infectious smile. "Just keep them confined for a while." He fished out his purse and tossed it to the boy. "There should be enough in that for you to buy some help. Keep these two until day after tomorrow. Put something into their drink and before dawn dump them somewhere they'll be found—in their smallclothes, reeking of cheap ale. Let them explain to their commander why they're in that condition."

Squeaky laughed. "I like that!" He turned to the remaining lads and said, "Up we go, boys. Let's get them to Granny's and see to their keeping!"

Four boys each picked up the unconscious soldiers and hauled them scuffing and bumping across the cobbles as they were taken from the thieves' market.

Hal said, "Let's go move some wagons."

Two hours later a company of teamsters escorted by two soldiers appeared outside the barracks. In orderly fashion, Jeremiah and his boys began inspecting the wagons, horses, and lashings on the load.

A corporal from the barracks came over and said, "What's this, then?"

"Orders," said Hal, wearing the sergeant's uniform.

"No one told me about any orders to move this wine," said the corporal, being careful to stay just shy of sounding belligerent with a superior.

"And I expect the chancellor runs down here every time he decides to issue orders to see how you feel about it, right, Corporal?" Hal let his voice rise until he was shouting the man's rank in his face.

The corporal took a step back, but then his brow furrowed. "Can't say I know you, Sergeant, and I know every sergeant in this city."

He appeared to be verging on calling for others inside the barracks to come out, but Hal cut him off. He reached inside his tabard, pulled the false orders from his belt, and said, "That's because I'm new to the city. I used to be a corporal in Bantree." Hal thanked the gods he had been forced to study Kingdom geography when he was younger and knew the position of every Kingdom and ducal garrison. "Got promoted. With all this militia, the Duke needs more sergeants." He thrust the orders into the corporal's hands. "You haven't got your promotion yet?"

Now the corporal was flummoxed. Hal's question distracted him from the orders he could barely read. He glanced at the signature and seal at the bottom and handed them back. "No, no one's said anything about promotions."

"Probably just a couple more days," suggested Ty.

The drivers were all mounted up and Hal said, "Do me a favor. We're new here, and with all the mess at the muster points, it would speed things along if a familiar face came along. What's your name?"

"Herbert," said the corporal.

"Ride with me to the western gate and help us get this mess outside the walls." He pointed to the piles of manure at the base of the wagons. "And when I get them where they're supposed to go, I'll be sure to mention to Captain—"

"Bennet?"

"Yes, Bennet, how helpful you were and ask, polite like, why you haven't received word of the promotions yet."

Corporal Herbert's expression changed completely from one of suspicion to gratitude. "I can do that. Thank you, Sergeant!"

Hal indicated Ty should run back to the final wagon, and then to the corporal that he should get up on the other side of Jeremiah. Once everyone was ready, Jeremiah started off and the others followed.

The chaos of the morning had died down somewhat, but there were still many armed men in the streets. They came to an intersection to turn west and found a half company of soldiers blocking the way. Herbert shouted down, "Corporal Soams! What's this?"

"Just put down a bit of a riot, Herbert. What are you about?"

"Orders from the chancellor. We have to take this freight outside the walls. Do us a favor and help clear the way, will you?"

The second corporal shouted orders and formed up his men, clearing the way for the wagon train. They moved purposefully toward the closed western gate. Herbert stood up and shouted, "Soams! Have one of your lads hurry along and open the gates!"

They moved quickly through the city with the escort. As they reached the last part of the main west road, a cloaked figure leaped up onto the last wagon, startling the driver. Ty glanced over and smiled. "Lady Franciezka, joining us?"

For the first time since Ty had known her, she looked surprised. "You knew I was in Salador?"

"I thought that was you skulking around when Hal was making his introduction to Jeremiah. With all due respect to your rank and ability to cut out my heart without flinching, you're a very hard lady not to notice."

Keeping the hood pulled forward, she said in the High Roldemish tongue, so the driver couldn't understand her,

"You're a lot more like Jim Dasher than your father at times, you know that?"

"I'll take that as a compliment," he answered in the same language.

"Well, Jim has spent enough time training you that it would be hard for you not to think like him."

Ty's expression barely held, surprise hovering.

"There's not a lot about Jim's operations I don't know," she said, patting his shoulder, then added with a wry expression, "and not a lot about mine he doesn't know."

"If you say so," Ty offered in neutral terms. His relationship with Jim Dasher had been one of the most closely held secrets in Ty's life. Even his father did not suspect that Ty was Jim's agent.

"Where are you heading?" she asked, again speaking the King's Tongue.

"Darkmoor, or at least these wagons are going there. Hal and I will stop at the Fields of Albalyn."

"Good," she said.

They both fell silent as the wagons came to a halt.

The captain at the gate came over to Herbert and said, "What have we here, Corporal?"

"Orders to move this from the chancellor, sir."

"Let's see them."

Hal handed over the orders to Herbert, who handed them down to the captain, who looked annoyed as he said, "I can hardly read this scratching." He handed it back and looked at Hal. "Who are you?"

Ty and Franciezka both tensed. Hal said, "I'm just in from Bantree, Captain. Just promoted." He pointed to Herbert. "Someone needs to find out what happened to Herbert's orders."

"What orders?"

"Everyone's getting a promotion," said Hal. "With all this militia . . . why, there might be orders coming to make you a major or even a general, I don't know. Can we be on our way now?"

Diverting the captain's attention with the suggestion of a promotion seemed to do the trick. He waved them along and said to his own sergeant, "I'm heading to the castle to speak with the Knight-General. Watch things for me."

As Hal drove past the confused-looking sergeant, he shouted down, "Make sure these gates are closed tight when we're through, and don't let anyone else out without written orders!" He patted Herbert on the shoulder and said, "Better get back!"

The now-completely-won-over corporal said, "Thanks, Sergeant! I won't forget this."

Trying hard not to laugh, Jeremiah said, "I'm sure he won't."

Once the gates were closed behind them, Hal shouted to Jeremiah, "As much speed as these poor horses can manage, if you please."

"We're going to have to rest them soon and find some grazing. Those idiots starved them for almost a day. Still, they're good animals and will bounce back."

"How long?"

"We should graze them for at least an hour, two would be better, and then we can push on after sundown for an hour or so. By tomorrow, they'll be as good as new."

"If Squeaky and his lads do their part, no one will be looking for us until after that, so I think it's a safe bet."

"There'll be some patrols between here and Prince Edward's line," said Jeremiah.

"I can still show orders, and if it comes to a brawl, how are your lads?"

"Fed up to their gullets with anything to do with the Duke of Salador. They'll fight."

"We'll try to avoid that if we can," said Hal. "How do you think the wine fared?"

"Not good," said Jeremiah. "But it's not been especially hot and the jostling along the road's doing it more damage, but I'll worry how the wine's holding when I get somewhere we can sell it. First thing is to get home."

"Yes to that," agreed Hal as they moved away from Salador.

An hour and a bit after dark found the wagons unhitched along the banks of a small stream that cut across the road at a well-tended ford. The water only came up to the wagons' hubs, so it was easy enough to manage, but there was enough grass on both sides of the stream and the road that the horses could crop until full.

Hal had been surprised to find Lady Franciezka with them, but after a moment's consideration of who she was in the scheme of things, he decided having her appear just about anywhere should come as no shock.

Hal organized the camp, set up sentries, and then came to where Ty and Franciezka were sitting near the fire. In low tones so the drivers wouldn't overhear, Hal said, "Care to tell me what you were doing in Salador, my lady?"

She looked at him and said, "As a matter of fact, I do. Let's say that for the moment we're allies and I need to be moving in the same direction."

Hal was silent, then said, "So Roldem will either back Edward's claim or stand apart." He studied her face. "You're telling Edward that the King of Roldem will recognize his claim," he stated flatly.

"How did you arrive at that conclusion?" she asked.

"If Roldem was standing apart, you wouldn't be personally carrying word. A messenger would have been sent to Oliver's camp outside Rillanon and another would have landed in Salador, told Arthur he was there, and been given diplomatic passage to Edward." He sighed. "You're carrying a message that Oliver and, by extension, Arthur do not wish Edward to hear."

She was silent for a moment, then said, "You're smarter than you look."

Ty grinned.

Even without her usual gowns and makeup, in the flickering campfire, the Lady Franciezka Sorboz was one of the most stunning women either young man had seen. They both knew she ranked far higher in the King's court than was made public.

"What news of Roldem?" asked Hal.

Ty and Franciezka both knew he was asking after the Princess Stephané. "The royal house is in good order, now that the traitors have been unmasked. It seems our three inhuman . . . whatever they were had more dupes than willing allies. A few heads were taken, but mostly it was a boring procession of apologetic nobles again pledging their loyalty to the Crown."

"The princes?" asked Ty.

"Back to their duties. Your friends are on their ships or in charge of their armies as the case warrants, and . . ." She looked at Hal. "The Princess is safely in the bosom of her family." Trying to make light of it, she added, "After all your adventures, I'm sure she misses you two rascals."

If Hal hoped for anything more, he kept it to himself. He asked, "What of Jim Dasher? I'm surprised you didn't just get a message to him and let him tell Edward about Roldem's position."

"I would if I knew how to find him," she said. "But I have no idea where he is, so it fell to me to bring word to the Prince. I was doing fine, but stayed one day too long in Salador. So instead of being at some inn along this highway, ready to see Prince Edward, I found myself in a city under martial law conspiring to find a way out."

"Well, luck smiled on us all," said Ty.

"Clever lad," said Franciezka. Looking at Hal, she added, "If you ever decide being a duke isn't enough excitement, I think Jim could turn you into a fair agent."

"Somehow I doubt it's fun all the time."

"It's never 'fun,'" she answered, "but sometimes it is entertaining."

"Still," said Hal, "too many people got a good enough look at us to ever try anything like that in Salador again."

"Smart lad."

"We should reach Albalyn in three days," said Hal.

"Good," said Franciezka. "I'm going to turn in under one of those wagons. Anyone have an extra blanket?"

"Let me go see," said Ty.

When they were alone, Franciezka said, "For your ears alone, Hal. I am sorry for the loss of your father."

He nodded. News of his father's death hadn't reached him until after he left Roldem with Ty to safely smuggle the Princess Stephané and her companion, the Lady Gabriella, to Rillanon.

"As a duke of the Kingdom, you rank high enough to carry this message to Edward. King Carole will recognize Edward's claim and reject Oliver's. His majesty fears that with Oliver on the throne, his ties to the Eastern Kingdoms put the Duchy of Olasko at risk, and more, pose a threat to Roldem."

"What concessions does the King desire?" asked Hal.

She paused and smiled. "As I said, you're smarter than you look. At least one state marriage between Roldem and the Isles; two would be better. Prince Grandprey is the only brother not currently wed, so that would mean he needs to find a highly placed duke's daughter, and Stephané needs to be wed to an equally high-ranked duke."

Hal hid his pain on hearing that. He might be a duke, but even if Crydee was still in possession of the Kingdom, by eastern standards he would be a rural noble, one only noteworthy due to a distant blood tie to the Crown. Without a duchy, he was a duke in name only and would rank lower than many eastern earls and even a few barons in terms of political power and wealth. He swallowed his bitterness, and all he could say was "Well, assuming there are any dukes left alive without wives, I'm sure Edward will give his blessing. What else?"

"Nothing else. Both kingdoms are too scarred from the mauling Lord John Worthington and his twins in Kesh and the Isles inflicted to have much left to give in land or property. Besides, the marriage of two royals to Isles nobility sends a strong message to Kesh and the Eastern Kingdoms that no one can attack either nation without response from both. That in itself, in these times, is ample. Now I'm for sleep. I suggest you sleep as well. We're not safe until we see Edward's camp ahead and no one behind."

Hal nodded. Ty returned with a blanket from one of the wagons and gave it to Franciezka.

They watched her go, and then Ty said, "Which watch?"

"I'll take first," said Hal. Ty didn't argue and turned in, leaving Hal alone by the fire. As hard as he tried, he could not take his mind off Stephané. The thought of her wedding another left him with a terrible, sinking feeling in his stomach.

Two days later they could see the banners of Edward's camp on the ridge ahead. Hal stood up to see better and, when he sat back down, said, "Every banner of every lord in the West is flying. A few from the East, too, from what I see of the colors." He indicated a cluster of banners near the side of the road. "I see Malac's Cross, Durrony's Vale, and a couple I don't recognize."

Hal paused as they came a little more into view and said, "Timons . . ." He stopped. "Now I see why Salador is moving against Silden. If Timons has already declared for Edward, Arthur faces potential attack from three sides." He was quiet for a moment. Then he said, "Damn."

"What?"

"Edward has enough strength of arms to win if he seizes the moment, but he doesn't have enough votes in the Congress."

"Seems to me if he wins the war, who votes for what doesn't matter."

"Maybe," said Hal, and he fell silent.

They reached a checkpoint and Hal jumped down from the lead wagon. He and Ty had disposed of the tunics and tabards the day before, so now they resembled swords-for-hire again. A sergeant wearing the livery of Krondor, a dark blue tabard showing an eagle over a mountaintop, held up his hand. "What's this?"

Hal donned his ducal signet. "I need to speak with Prince Edward."

"You do, do you?" began the sergeant, a burly man with a suspicious eye.

Hal held out his hand. "I'm Henry, Duke of Crydee."

Upon seeing the ring, the sergeant changed his attitude at once.

Hearing the title, Jeremiah looked down from his driver's seat with wide eyes.

Hal smiled and said, "Safe journey home."

"Yes . . . Your Grace."

"Let these wagons through. They're home for Darkmoor."

"Yes, Your Grace," said the sergeant. "I'll send word to His Highness."

Hal beckoned for Lady Franciezka and Ty to come with him and followed the sergeant while a private sprinted up the hill to the Prince's pavilion.

Moments later they were standing before the massive pavilion, where a gray-haired man wearing a simple soldier's tabard of Krondor waited. Hal knelt. "Majesty."

The older man put his hands on Hal's shoulders and raised him gently. "Not yet, my young friend."

"Lord James sent me," said Hal, and then he introduced his companions. "Lady Franciezka brings a message from King Carole, and I think it's a welcome one."

"Good," said Edward, his blue eyes taking in the beautiful noblewoman from Roldem. "Your reputation does not do you justice, my lady," he said, extending his hand to lead her inside the pavilion. "Lord Henry," he said, "there is someone here who will be most glad to see you."

Inside the tent, Hal saw a collection of nobles, men of rank from every quarter of the West and a few from the East, gathered around a massive table on which rested a battle map of the region. Nearby one familiar face lit up in delight at seeing Hal.

Martin took one step to reach his brother and embrace him. "You're alive!"

"As are you," said Hal with a laugh. "When did you get here?"

"A few days ago, with tidings from the Grey Towers."

"You two catch up later," said the Prince. "We have much to speak of, but first . . ." To the assembled nobility, he said, "Gentlemen, Lady Franciezka Sorboz, envoy of Roldem."

Lady Franciezka curtsied, then said, "My king sends you greetings, Prince Edward, but as a brother king. He recognizes your claim and will support you in any way Roldem can, short of armed intervention."

Edward smiled. "As long as he's not sending a similar message to Oliver, we welcome his support."

An uncomfortable laugh greeted the remark, but Franciezka said, "No such duplicity . . . this time, Your Majesty."

" 'Highness' will do," said Edward. "I'm uncomfortable with claiming the mantle; I'll wait until the Congress of Lords bestows it." He looked at the map. "If Carole does nothing more than move a few ships around to make Oliver think twice about sailing his army to the mainland, that would suit us fair."

"Highness," said Hal.

"Yes, Duke Henry?"

"Salador moves against Silden."

"What?" said one of the other nobles, while muttering erupted all around.

Hal walked over to the map and pointed. "Bas-Tyra sends this," and he handed him the letter given to him by Captain Reddic. "Chadwick of Ran has moved to join with Oliver.

"Arthur of Salador fears a pincer movement from Timons, Durrony's Vale, and Malac's Cross, so he moves against Silden to clear the road. I suggest Oliver wants to land his army at Silden before Bas-Tyra can march, move to take Malac's Cross, then come at you here from the north."

The Prince studied the map. "Fair assessment."

Martin motioned to Hal that he wanted to speak, so while

the Prince and his advisers considered the significance of the King of Roldem's message, and Bas-Tyra's pledge, Hal moved to the door and the two stepped outside.

"What news?" asked Hal. "Brendan?"

"Well enough, last time I saw him. But I sent him off on an errand."

"Where?"

"Sorcerer's Isle."

Hal's eyes widened. "Why?"

"Because we're going to need magicians, a lot of them. There are things happening in the West that make this war here trivial."

Hal didn't wish to know what his brother meant by that, but he stood and listened while Martin spoke of the Star Elves and their troubles. When Martin had finished, Hal suspected he was right, and that what was happening in the West would determine if this coming conflict between Edward and Oliver had any significance at all.

12

JOURNEY IV

Magnus stumbled.

One moment he had been propelled through a tunnel of light, and the next he was standing on a grass-covered hillside. He glanced around and was struck by how familiar his surroundings were, then he realized he was on the north side of Isla Beata.

He willed himself to his father's study and a shock of pain struck him like a lightning bolt, knocking him to the ground and momentarily stunning him. He shook off his fuzzy-headedness after a moment and got to his feet. He took in a deep breath, then started walking.

While it was not a big island, it was large enough that to walk from the north shore, where he once had a personal retreat, a small fishing shack, to the villa took several hours. He listened, half-expecting to hear familiar sounds, but all he heard was the sound of distant breakers and the wind in the trees as he walked from the shore. Then he realized what was missing. There were no birdcalls, no insect sounds. He wasn't on his island.

Progress by foot was slow, and Magnus wished he had his usual staff and the old slouch hat he used to wear when traveling. They provided additional utility and comfort. The staff was useful for negotiating small streams and other places he didn't feel like using his arts to bypass, and the hat had protected his very fair skin against the harsh sun.

As long as he was wishing, he thought, he might as well wish for a picnic basket with a fine, chilled wine.

"Lovely place for a picnic, isn't it?" said a feminine voice from behind him.

Magnus hadn't heard that voice in years, yet he recognized it instantly. "Helena," he whispered.

He turned and drank in the sight of her. She looked exactly as she had the day they had first become lovers. She had long, flowing, wavy hair that reached the small of her back and curled at the ends, unless the weather was dry, then she'd complain it was unruly. Her skin was naturally fair, but as she insisted on doing her studies outside and swimming as much as she could, she was always tanned. Her eyes were the dark brown of an island sable's fur; almost black. She wore a wine-colored dress, with a scooped neck and short sleeves trimmed in the palest yellow, almost white, and he knew she wore nothing under it, save sandals on her feet. She complained the island was too warm in summer, and wanted to be able to strip naked and leap into the ocean at whim.

He remembered her body. She was neither slender nor heavy, but exactly in the middle, athletic and strong, ideal from Magnus's point of view, and her long legs were magnificent. Her nose was perfect, lacking the odd bumps and curves of most people's. Years had passed and he occasionally wondered why he found her nose so memorable, but it was. And now he beheld it again, a straight bridge down to a tip exactly the right size, and perfectly centered and symmetrical. And below was her mouth, which most of the time was pursed as she concentrated on one thing or another, but then she'd smile as she was doing now, and his world became dazzling.

She was the only woman in his life who had captured his heart; no other woman had wounded it so deeply.

She pointed to the large picnic basket on a commodious blanket. In her hands she held his staff and hat, the one he had worn years before, larger-brimmed than the newer one. "You forgot your staff and hat, my love."

He took a faltering step toward her and said, "How is this possible?"

She shrugged and glanced around. "Something's different, Magnus." Then she closed her eyes for a moment, and he could see vitality flow away. At first she had moved almost as a dancer would, light upon her feet, then before his eyes he saw her manner change and her body settle into the movement of someone older, a woman with more years to carry.

"I remember," she said softly. She came to stand before him and handed him his staff and hat. It wasn't the staff he had lost leaping into the vortex, but rather the one he had carried as a youngster. The wood was still freshly carved, sanded and smoothed, and hand-polished by him every night in his room for hours over many weeks until he judged it just so. It was a youthful student's affectation, for it was not a staff of power, nor was it even a study yeoman's stave, but really a very elegant walking stick. And the hat. He held it in his other hand and realized how foolish he must have looked as a youth, wearing this pointy-topped, broad-brimmed, floppy monstrosity. Though he did feel affection for it, and admitted it had been a very good hat for the many years he kept it. He couldn't remember where he'd last seen it, over half a century before. And he was surprised to discover he was very glad to have it back.

"What do you remember?" he asked.

"My life," she said softly. "And my death." She gazed up at him with wonder and fear. "Magnus, how can this be?"

He looked down at her and felt his heart racing. He said, "I'm unsure. Tell me what you remember."

She looked around, then knelt by the basket, opened it, and began preparing food. "I remember all of it, my life, my family, up to the day I died. I remember our fight. I remember you not speaking to me after that." She sat back on her heels and looked up at him. "You could be the most stubborn person I've known, even worse than your mother."

Magnus smiled. She was right about that. He had been a prodigy by any measurement. The flaws in him were not strength or intelligence, but rather a tendency to hold back at things. As a boy, the first time he lost his temper once his talents emerged, he had caused a fire that had damaged a large part of his room. Another time he lost his temper and severely injured three boys who had been tormenting his little brother, Caleb. Though he was slow to anger, when he did lose his temper his rage could be prodigious. It had been such a rage that had ended their love.

She resumed emptying the basket. "I know that when I asked your father to return to Stardock and continue my studies away from you, he didn't ask why, so I knew you had said something."

"I didn't," said Magnus. "It must have been my mother or my brother."

"Or anyone else on the island," she conceded. "No one on this island was ignorant of that ugly situation."

He was silent for a moment, reflecting on those long-ago events. And this wasn't "this island," though he thought better than to correct her. He had a sense of fleeting time and did not wish to be bogged down explaining things to her that were unnecessary for her to understand. More, this wasn't about her, he was certain, but about him coming to understand something.

He had been in love with Helena from the first moment he saw her. She had arrived in the morning, transported into the villa with three other students by his mother. As happened occasionally, promising students at Stardock, who might benefit from training beyond what the more structured regimen at the Academy provided, were recruited to come to the island, especially those who looked as if they might be useful to the Conclave.

Helena had been such a one. She was an enchantress, a conjurer, able to spin illusion so real few were able to tell the difference. It was a seductive power that often led to an addiction as deep as the most potent drugs sold in the back alleys of any city. Instead of one's having to visit a dirty room full of pungent smoke to drift off into hazy dreams, she could provide as vivid and lifelike an experience as one could ask, seeming days of whatever she wished to provide. For a dying man with means, a year again in his youth with those he loved most, while only one day passed before his death, was worth bags of gold. It was also why more ambitious slavers sought out those with this gift and used their own magical restraints to bring them to heel. For the gifted conjurer, life as a slave was a strong possibility: all it required was one cruel guard protected from the power of illusion. It was a rare and powerful ability, one the Conclave had concluded was potentially very useful to them.

But he had fallen in love the moment he beheld her, before he knew who she was or what her capabilities were. Now he was again with her on the first day she told him she loved him as well.

He found the scene disturbing in ways he could not begin to articulate. What had been the single happiest day in his life seemed so inappropriate in the context of what he and his father faced that it seemed a pointless distraction.

He remembered how their relationship had ended, though. He had come upon her with another boy, together on the grass by the lake near his cabin. They had lain in one another's arms, kissing. Magnus had almost killed that boy in his rage. He and Helena had not spoken a word since then. His father had sent him away, to a temple of mystics in a mountain range on the other side of the world, not too far from the Pavilion of the Gods, to study how best to master his rage when it emerged, and when he had returned Helena was gone, returned to Stardock for the remainder of her studies.

He sighed in resignation, and sat opposite her on the blanket. "I can only assume there's a reason this is happening, a reason that's not frivolous or whimsical."

"I suspect you're right," she said, putting a slice of bread on a platter and topping it with smoked ham and pungent cheese. She garnished it with small ripe tomatoes, sliced carrots, and a small bunch of grapes, and handed it to him.

He smiled; this was correct down to the last detail. "And you still forgot the mustard."

She shook her head and held out a small pot. "I did then, but whoever packed this did not."

"Is this one of your illusions?" he asked.

"Hardly," she said. "Until moments ago I was dead."

"Why?" he asked.

"Why are you here?"

"Why are we here?"

She considered a moment, then suggested, "Perhaps there is something vital you need to learn, something lost between us? Or something you lost, something later in life because of what happened between us."

He absently chewed some bread and ham with mustard and said, "This is delicious."

"We had fun . . . for a while."

He sighed. "I never thought of it as 'fun.' "

She nodded. "That is so like you, Magnus. I think I could list every time I saw you laugh when we were together." She sat back on her heels again, nibbling at her food. Then she opened the wine and poured it into two clay cups she removed from the basket. Handing him one, she continued. "All relationships are unequal in a way, I think. What is that word you used to describe my nose?" She laughed.

He could not resist smiling at her reference to the bumbled attempt at a compliment he had once tried to pay her. "Symmetrical," he said. "Equally balanced."

"Ah, so the word for not being equally balanced?"

"Asymmetrical."

"Relationships are asymmetrical. I loved my husband, but not as much as he loved me, I'm certain. Perhaps it is as simple as women love differently than men?" She shrugged, and he felt his heart stop for an instant. Each gesture, the sound of her voice, filled him in a way no one else ever had. "I know I loved my three children, but each uniquely, as your mother loved you and your brother, but each love was different."

"What is the point?" he asked, sounding harsher than he intended.

"With love comes risk," said Helena, her expression turning serious. "You were never averse to risk, Magnus. You would do the most amazing things as a boy. The first time you just willed yourself to the other side of the island to see if you could do it, that terrified me. I was so fearful of telling your father you tried that, so you could take us somewhere to be alone . . ." She shook her head sadly at the memory. "I felt relief when you returned a moment later, but I was also angry."

"I remember." He fell silent, sipping his wine and eating, though he really wasn't very hungry. At last he said, "Not a day goes by that I don't think of you."

"And I of you . . . when I was alive."

"Where did it go wrong?"

"We were so young, Magnus. We were caught up in passions we didn't understand. Perhaps it was being born here, with all this magic around you, but for me it was a bard's tale, a magic place from a story. I came here and found wonder, and found you."

"I knew I was wrong in what I did the day I came back and found you gone," he said quietly.

Tears glistened in her eyes as she softly asked, "Then why didn't you ever come after me?"

"I thought you in love with Anton."

Her expression turned sad. "You wouldn't speak to me, and your father sent you away." She put down her food and stared into the distance. "Anton was fun. Nothing more. We drank wine, went swimming. We were just kissing when you found us."

"I thought—"

"No, you didn't think. You reacted. Badly." She stood up and came to sit down next to him. She put her hand on his arm and her head on his shoulder. "You have such deep feelings, Magnus. So easily injured, and you hold that pain in, close to you. I won't say we would have had a good life together, and the one I had without you was good enough. But we never had the chance to try because of your refusal to let go of a boyhood injury." She kissed him lightly on the cheek. "Had you come to Stardock to get me, I would have come back here with you."

Magnus was silent. He lowered his head and a tear ran down his cheek. "Once, when a young man I was teaching . . ." He stopped. "His name was Talon and he was given to think he was in love." Magnus remembered what a beautiful woman named Alysandra had done to the lad, as part of his training by the Conclave. Alysandra was broken, and the Conclave knew that, which was why she was a dangerous weapon. She was empty inside, devoid of emotion, but she was stunningly beautiful, charming, and seductive, and after only a few days Talon of the Silver Hawk, now Tal Hawkins, Ty's father, had thought himself inextricably in love. Then, under Nakor's instruction, she broke his heart. "It was a very harsh lesson, what we did to him. I asked Nakor if you had been such a lesson."

"What did he say?"

"Actually, I asked him if you were one of his, had been

brought to the island to teach me the same lesson Tal had suffered, and he said no. I remember what he said next to this day. 'That harsh lesson was of your own devising.' For the longest time, I thought he meant my poor choice." He looked at the most beautiful face he had ever beheld. "Now I understand."

"What do you understand?"

He paused for a moment before answering, then said, "I felt rejected for another, but that was the least of it; I felt betrayed. I felt a trust had been sundered, and for me that was the end."

"I neither rejected you nor betrayed you, Magnus. I was a foolish young girl who got drunk and kissed a boy. And you had never told me you wanted me and no other."

"I told you I loved you, on this very day."

"After a lot of wine, Magnus." She sighed. "You were not the first or last boy to tell me he loved me after drinking. I needed to hear that a few times, I fear, and at least one of those times you needed to be sober and not naked in my arms." She was silent for a while in reflection, then said, "We are our own worst enemies, at times, my love."

Considering once more his conversation with Nakor, Magnus said, "Nakor meant my poor actions, or lack of action. Apparently he agreed with your assessment."

"You think a great deal, Magnus. Perhaps too much at times. I think it's a natural consequence of that hot temper you bury so deeply within."

"Even though I never saw you again, I never passed a day without you being in my thoughts," he said softly. She grabbed his hand and squeezed it as he sat staring at her tears running down her cheeks. "I know the Conclave used your abilities occasionally. I heard the reports, and know how you served. Who you wed, your children . . . I knew where you were every single day."

"You punished yourself. Why?"

Now with tears matching hers, he whispered, "I really don't know."

"There, then, is your lesson, my love. Something important is coming, or I would not have been snatched back to life for this meeting. My life is over. How I am not before Lims-Kragma, or again on the Wheel of Life, I don't know, but of this much I am certain: this has nothing to do with me, and everything to do with you. I lived my life, Magnus. I married a very good man, and loved him deeply. I never had the passion for him I felt for you, but I was not a hot-blooded child when I met him either. I rejoiced in our children and thanked the gods none of them had my gift or any other that would bring them to the Academy or this island. They all found common, boring, ordinary, wonderful lives.

"I loved my grandchildren, and mourned my husband. My last days were quiet, and I sat on a terrace of a little room in my eldest son's home, watching the days go by. One day I closed my eyes, and suddenly I'm here. Yet I feel time has passed."

"More than a century," said Magnus quietly.

She smiled sadly. "Either way you would have lost me, my love."

"But I would have had you for those fifty years."

"And what? Stayed at home with me and children?"

"I don't know," he said, taking control of his runaway feelings.

"I think the lesson here is that you must accept certain risks you do not wish, but you must also take care of yourself. For if you do not, who else will?"

Thinking about what he and his father endured when his mother died, he felt he understood that now.

"A battle is coming," he said, "and sacrifice is likely."

She nodded. "Then don't assume you need to be the one to make the sacrifice. Don't hold your own needs as less important than other people's." She reached for his hand again and squeezed it tightly. "I'm sorry you didn't have the life you wished for, with me, but you have the life you chose. So when it comes to whatever it comes to, be glad you made the most of that choice."

"Is that all?" he asked. "I'm here with you again to be told to make the best of things?"

She shook her head, disappointed. "Life is what happens, Magnus, no matter what you expect or want." She looked around. "If I had been asked for one wish before my death, it would have been to come back here and have this discussion, but with a different understanding at the end. I loved some men after you, and before my husband, but you were my first love, Magnus, and what saddens me most of all is that you never seem to have found another to love as you did me.

"Let go. You're still injured by a heartbreak that belongs to a boy not yet twenty summers, not a man over a century old. It does not protect you; it makes you vulnerable. You don't have the luxury to nurse that hurt anymore. Too much has already been lost to you." She sighed and put her hand on his. "There is no perfect ending, my love. You wanted to love someone so badly . . ." She smiled. "I think that when you met me you created this icon of a perfect woman. I was a girl. With talent, but occasionally stupid, and had you not stumbled across Anton and me on that shore, I don't know what would have happened. I might have made love to him, or I might have thought of you and pushed him away. But neither of us will ever know, will we?"

He stood up; powerful feelings threatened to overwhelm him. "I've been angry . . . for so long. The anger has become a part of me."

"Forgive me, Magnus."

"I don't know if I can."

"You must."

Still looking into the distance, he said, "You need my forgiveness?"

"No. I'm dead. You can do nothing for me. You need to forgive me so that you can live."

He turned and found she was gone, as was the blanket and picnic basket. All that remained on the ground were the staff and hat.

He slowly picked up the staff, then the hat, which he put

on his head. In the midst of the turmoil he was glad to get back the hat. He didn't move, digesting the experience and trying to apply his analytical abilities to what he just experienced, and at the last he could almost hear Nakor's voice, saying something after several cups of wine that only now Magnus understood. "Feelings don't make sense," Nakor had observed, "but they can drive us, and that's what you have to understand most of all. People will often do imponderable things because of how they feel, not because of what they think." Then he had grinned at Magnus and said, "Of all the men I've known, Magnus, I think you will have the most trouble learning that lesson."

Suddenly there was a sound and Magnus turned to discover that a vortex had appeared. He took one last look around, knowing he would never again see Helena's face. He drank in the echo of her presence, then leaped into the vortex.

Magnus came tumbling out of the vortex, holding his hat with one hand and his staff with the other. Clouds of dust arose around him and slowly spread out as he came to his feet.

A lone figure stood on a curving ledge and Magnus realized he was on a small planetoid, perhaps the size of a palace but not much larger. The figure turned and beckoned him to come closer, and he took a step and found himself floating upward. The figure stuck out his hand, grabbing Magnus's ankle before he could float away. Pulling him back down, he said, "I've created some atmosphere and enough gravity if you don't try to leap up."

"Macros," said Magnus. He had seen a rough likeness of him in the form of a Dasati who had been given his memories and some aspects of his appearance, but here stood his grandfather as perhaps even his mother hadn't seen him, young and vigorous, not a hint of gray in his hair or beard. His high forehead was one trait he shared with his daughter and grandson, but his black eyes were unique. He wore a black robe, cut slightly differently from the one Pug chose; his father's had been a Tsurani Great One's garb, whereas Macros's was cut off between knee and ankle, and was tight across the shoulders.

The original Black Sorcerer looked at Magnus. "Do I know you?"

"No, not really."

Macros said, "I am—"

Magnus interrupted him. "Macros the Black."

Again Macros tilted his head a little, in exactly the same fashion as Miranda. "But *you* know *me*."

"It's a long story."

"Aren't they always?"

"I'm called Magnus."

"Magnus," said Macros, nodding as if he liked the sound of the name. Suddenly he looked delighted. "You're my grandson!"

"How do you know that?" asked Magnus. "You died before I was born."

"Yes, battling that demon Maarg on the world of Shila," said Macros. "I don't know how I know. I just . . . suddenly knew. It seems what I need to know just . . . pops into my head!" He seemed delighted by that fact.

"Where are we?"

"I don't know exactly, but I have a rough idea."

"I've been on other worlds and other planes of reality," said Magnus, "but I've seen nothing like this."

The planetoid they stood on slowly tumbled in orbit around a massive gas cloud, moving along with millions of other pieces of rock. Comets made a stately passage across the sky, and down in the core of the gas cloud an incandescent glow burned, illuminating the entire cloud. Within, brilliant lights streaked, like massive discharges of lightning.

Magnus said, "This is something to behold."

"Yes," said his grandfather.

"You know, Nakor would love seeing this."

"The little gambler? Is he still around?"

"In a manner of speaking."

Again came the odd cocking of Macros's head, as if he were listening to something, then he smiled again. "Ah, he will get to see this. He'll be joining us soon." Then his smiled broadened. "And so will the others!"

Magnus was about to ask how he knew, then thought better of it, and decided instead to enjoy the spectacle and try to process the turmoil left inside him from his encounter with Helena.

13

ELVANDAR

Bethany shouted.

For half a day she had walked the banks of the River Boundary, the edge of Crydee and Elvandar, the home of the elves. Entering Elvandar unbidden put you at great risk. Several times before, she had called out, but only forest sounds had answered.

Will said, "Lady Beth, we've been shouting across this river since sunrise and no answer. Why don't we just cross at that ford?" He pointed to a broad shallow about ten yards upstream.

From behind him a voice said, "It would be unwise."

Tom turned around so quickly he almost fell over, his hunter's cap tumbling from his head. Standing behind him was a pair of elves in brown leather hunting garb, carrying longbows.

"Lady Beth? Bethany of Carse?"

"Yes," said Beth.

The elf who had first spoken said, "I am Calin, and this is my friend Eledar. I met you once when you were very tiny, but you won't remember." He looked as Bethany expected an elf to look, with large pale blue eyes and light brown hair that fell to his shoulders.

"I remember the name, Prince of Elvandar," said Beth, curtsying as well as she could while wearing leather trousers and holding a bow.

"No," said Calin. "We only bow before my mother." His manner was friendly. "Who are your companions?"

Bethany introduced the four hunters, who stood silent. They were tired and hungry and were relieved to have delivered Bethany to her goal. By nature, they were quiet men, but days on the trail moving through dangerous woodlands had rendered them mute. The trails over the hills were narrow and dangerous, and having no idea how likely a Keshian patrol might be, they had chosen to move on foot. Up the steep inclines and down the narrow draws would have slowed the horses to walking pace anyway, but they were all near exhaustion.

"What brings you to Elvandar?" asked Calin.

"An urgent need to speak with your mother."

"Then we bid you welcome to Elvandar. Cross there," he said, indicating the ford.

To the four hunters, Bethany said, "If you wish to return to your families, you need not travel with me any longer. I am safe from here."

Will said, "My missus will wonder if the Keshians or a bear did me in. I'd best head back."

"I will go with him," said Edgar. "I'm for my family, too."

The two young brothers exchanged glances. "We'd like to come," said Jack.

"We'll never get the chance again," said Tom.

Bethany smiled, then asked Calin, "Is it permitted?"

"Yes," answered the Prince of Elvandar.

The two brothers quickly emptied their packs and gave their trail rations to Edgar and Will. The four hunters and Bethany said their respective farewells, and Bethany turned to Calin. "Whenever you're ready."

Calin smiled and Bethany said, "You and your brother have the same smile."

Calin's smile broadened. "You've met Calis?"

"In Ylith. He went on . . ." She felt tension drain away and suddenly she was tired. "It's a long journey. I'll tell you and your mother together. But yes, your brother was well last I saw him."

Calin nodded. "You're tired, and we have two more days before you reach my mother's court."

As they crossed the river, Bethany said, "The other elf is well, too."

Calin and Eledar both looked quizzical. "Other elf?"

"Arkan," said Bethany. "Tall, black hair, doesn't speak much."

"My brother travels with a Moredhel chieftain?" asked Calin, with as close to a look of surprise as a human would ever see on an elf's face.

"Moredhel?"

"You call them the Brotherhood of the Dark Path."

Now Bethany was surprised. "But he looks . . ." She shook her head. "Another tale for your mother's ears." As they started off, she added, "But they fought side by side on the walls of Ylith against the Keshians."

Calin stumbled a step, then set off at a steady walk.

Two days later, Bethany and the two boys reached a massive clearing in the Elven Forest. In the distance she could see a sight that made her pause. Calin put his hand on her shoulder. "Welcome to Elvandar, Lady Bethany of Carse."

On the other side of the clearing reared a stand of gigantic trees linked by graceful arching bridges of branches on which elves could be seen crossing from bole to bole.

As they got closer, Bethany looked up. The trunks rose until they were lost in a sea of leaves and branches. The leaves were deep green, but here and there a tree with golden, silver, or even white foliage could be seen, sparkling with lights visible even in the shadows. Above the canopy, the late-afternoon sun shone down, but so thick was its cover that Elvandar was in constant twilight. A soft glow permeated the entire area.

As they made their way across the clearing, Bethany could see that the elven tree city was even larger than she first thought. It spread away on all sides and must have been over a mile across. She was stunned by wonder and glanced at Tom and Jack. The boys were almost openmouthed, and finally Jack looked at her and said, "Now I'm very glad we came, my lady." Tom only nodded.

They reached a stairway, carved into the side of a tree, that wound its way upward, into the branches. They climbed, and as they passed the large branches that served as roadways, they could see elves on all sides. Many of the men wore fighting leather like Calin, but many others wore long, graceful robes of fine weave or tunics of bright, rich colors. Bethany marveled at the casual splendor of the elven women. All were tall and graceful, with their hair worn long, many with jewels woven into their tresses. Bethany reached up and self-consciously touched her own hair, dirty after weeks on the trail.

They reached a gigantic branch and left the stairs. Calin said, "Stay to the center. Many of your race have difficulties with the heights. It's best if you look forward, not down." For their part, the elves seemed oblivious to how far above the ground they trod.

Deeper and deeper they moved, until they reached a large

opening where a circle of trees formed a central court for the Elf Queen, a hundred branches merging into a huge platform. Aglaranna sat upon a wooden throne, surrounded by her court. She was a beautiful, regal woman whose reddish hair was gathered and held behind her lobeless, pointed ears by a golden circlet with a single ruby in the center. She wore a deep green gown with golden trim at the neck, sleeves, and hem, and her waist was cinched by a golden cord. Her fingers were long and graceful, and she bore a single ring on her left hand, a simple golden band, a wedding ring in the human fashion.

To her left stood an amazing figure, neither elf nor human but somewhere in between, clad in green leggings and a dark brown tunic with a simple brown leather belt. Easily six inches over six feet, he had striking features, blond hair, blue eyes, and an almost boyish face as he smiled; but Bethany could imagine it would look very different if he was angry. There was a sense of power to him that went beyond his impressive size and obvious physical strength.

He came to stand before Beth. "Lady Bethany," he said, bowing, "on behalf of my wife and queen, I welcome you to Elvandar. I am Warleader Tomas."

Calin mounted the steps, kissed his mother's cheek, and took the smaller seat to her right.

Aglaranna arose to greet Bethany, taking her hands and saying, "Welcome. You've come a long way."

"Thank you, Majesty. Your home is amazing and I'm pleased to see it, but my reasons for coming are dire and pressing."

"Please," said the Queen, indicating a chair that had been brought for Bethany. She ordered that Jack and Tom be shown to their quarters, leaving Bethany alone with the royal court. "Before you tell us your story, your mother is coming."

A cup of wine was handed to her and she drank. Her mother arrived and they embraced. "I'm so glad to see you," said Bethany.

Bethany's mother, the Countess Marriann asked, "Any word of your father?"

"At the last report, he held fast in Carse and all lands from there to the Straits are still in Kingdom hands," said Bethany.

Countess Marriann looked relieved.

Bethany said, "You look well, Mother."

"We've been so welcomed here, and treated well. We have a camp to the north. Everyone from Crydee."

Duchess Caralin had accompanied Bethany's mother and now she came to embrace Bethany. "What news of my sons?" she asked, fearful to hear the answer.

Bethany realized news was slow reaching this deep forest, being only what the occasional ranger from Natal might share. "Martin and Brendan were well last I saw them. They saw Hal in Rillanon."

The Duchess closed her eyes with relief, and as she did so, Bethany realized her hair had more gray in it and her features looked more drawn than the last time she'd seen her. "When word reached me of my husband's death," she said softly, avoiding his name to respect the elves' tradition of not using the names of the departed, "my heart broke, but if the boys are well . . ."

Bethany hugged her again. "They are well. We have a great deal to discuss. Later."

Now she turned to the Elf Queen, Lord Tomas, and Prince Calin and detailed what she and Martin had seen in E'bar and the warning from the Taredhel Loremaster, Tanderae. When at last she finished, the Queen asked a few questions, then turned to Tomas. "My love?"

Tomas waved to someone at the edge of the gathering crowd and two very tall elves came into view. They wore fashion very different from the other elves, tunics and trousers of very fine fabric and beautifully crafted leather boots, somewhat the worse for wear. Tomas said, "Gulamendis, Laromendis, two allies of Tanderae, Lady Bethany of Carse."

The two Star Elves, the conjurer and the demon master, nodded greeting to the young woman. Tomas said to the assembled elves in the Queen's Court, "We have much to discuss, but our newest guest is tired. We shall convene again after sundown for a meal and discussion." To the two visiting elves from E'bar, he said, "We would welcome your views on the news Lady Bethany has brought." They both inclined their heads in acknowledgment, and Tomas looked at Calin, who nodded to him. "The war council will meet now."

The elves who had been observing Lady Bethany as she had recounted her visit to E'bar began drifting away. Marriann said, "Come. Rest with us and we'll return after sundown."

Queen Aglaranna nodded. "Please, I know word from home will be welcome to the others from Crydee."

Bethany was quickly escorted along with the two older women from the Far Coast down a series of circular stairs cut into the sides of boles and, once she was on the ground, to the northern part of the great clearing. There they found a tidy camp where a series of quarters had been constructed using curtains suspended from wooden rods held aloft by stout wooden standards.

"Not much privacy," said Duchess Caralin, "but they have been very kind."

The refugees from Crydee gathered in greeting and Bethany saw they all had been well cared for, their injuries healed, and that they were well fed, clean, and rested. A hundred questions were thrown at her until the Duchess said, "Give the girl a moment. Let her get clean and then we'll all sit and chat."

Bethany was shown to the shower, which was a clever series of tanks with sun-warmed water high above that fed into a hollow wooden pipe and ended in a flat tray punctured by many holes. She was provided with a jar of apple-scented cream and soon her hair was as clean as it had been in weeks, months perhaps, and her body was free of every speck of dirt she had collected along the way. After drying herself with a wonderfully luxurious cotton towel, she found a lovely, simple blue dress waiting for her, with plain but comfortable sandals.

Her mother said, "We'll make sure your travel clothing is cleaned, dear. I expect you'll be needing to run off soon and go somewhere else dangerous."

Bethany smiled. Her mother had never appreciated her love for hunting, tracking, and fishing as her father had; she preferred that Bethany endure the quiet "ladies' arts" of music, dance, needlepoint, cooking, and "more refined" pastimes. She smiled. "We'll all be leaving together, Mother."

An impromptu reception was waiting for her. She indulged herself with some fresh food, knowing full well that supper with the Queen and her court was just a short two hours or so ahead. The brothers from Ylith appeared, both far cleaner and more rested than she had ever seen them, and seemed to enjoy their momentary celebrity as people plied them with questions.

Bethany began with the retreat from Crydee and the traps Martin had set along the way, reaching the point in the narrative where they found safe haven in Ylith, and when she finished, she realized it was almost time to rejoin the Elf Queen. Her recounting of events had brought expressions of relief to wives, daughters, and sweethearts of garrison soldiers and volunteers who remained with Martin. Those few who had lost men in the early part of the siege still looked proud of the memory of their heroes, despite tears gathering and pain revisited.

An elf woman appeared to guide Bethany, her mother, and the Duchess to the Queen's table, and before they left, Bethany motioned for a private moment with her mother. "I need to tell you something," she said.

Countess Marriann looked concerned, her face showing that she was ready for bad news. "What?"

"I'm getting married."

Now Marriann looked confused. "Married?"

"Martin and I are to be wed."

"Martin!" said her mother, her expression turning darker. "You were supposed to wed Henry."

"Did it ever occur to you and father to ask either Henry or me what we wished?"

"We just—"

"Assumed," finished Bethany.

"What will Henry think of this?"

"He thinks it's just fine. Martin told him, and the Duke of Crydee has given his blessing."

The mention of Hal's office was like a bucket of cold water in her mother's face. Hal was now their liege lord, and for Bethany to enter any sort of state marriage, his permission and the King's blessing were required. Fumbling for a last objection, Marriann asked, "The King?"

"We don't have one," Bethany said with a note of apprehension. "And truth to tell, Hal doesn't even have a duchy to call his own."

Countess Marriann did exactly what her daughter anticipated: in the face of defeat, she changed the subject. "We should not keep the Queen waiting. We'll talk about this again when we finally rejoin your father."

Bethany shook her head in resignation and realized that nothing short of a direct order from the King would change her mother's mind about her becoming Duchess of Crydee someday.

The meal was far from festive, though everyone was at ease. Bethany had the opportunity to study the Queen, her son, and her consort while attempting to keep her mother's obsession over whom she married at arm's length.

The Queen was the personification of grace and charm, but there was nothing practiced or artificial about it. She was simply the loveliest being Bethany had ever encountered. After little more than an hour in her company, she understood why Aglaranna was legendary, even in the human communities of the Western Realm. Despite the reassuring welcome, though, Bethany was unable to shake the feeling that the elves were as worried as she was about the news she carried from E'bar.

Tomas looked distracted. Occasionally Bethany caught sight of him staring into space, as if listening for something. And when he spoke, it was to ask questions, of her, the two elves from E'bar, or members of the queen's council, a pair of old elves, rather wizened in appearance, which appeared to be a rarity among the elves.

Toward the end of supper, Tomas said, "Lady Bethany, if you think it time, we will send escorts with you to Ylith so that your people can be reunited. The Keshians stay south of the River Boundary now, so they will pose no risk. The Duchess has been waiting for word from the Kingdom that it's safe to leave."

She considered only for a moment, then said, "I think it best, Lord Tomas. Ylith is struggling and more hands to help with the rebuilding would be welcome, and it appears that a return to Crydee anytime soon is highly unlikely. As generous as you have been to us, we need to return to our own."

Supper continued, and when it was over, Bethany was escorted with her mother and the Duchess back to the encampment. She had half-expected to spend more time with the Queen and her council, but realized that during the course of the supper she had provided every scrap of information she possessed.

She found the goose-down mattress a welcome change from the hard soil she had called a bed for the last few weeks. She was asleep before her mother came to bid her good night.

After supper, the Queen had motioned for Acaila and Janil, her two eldest advisers, to linger, along with the two Taredhel, Gulamendis and Laromendis, as she, Tomas, and Calin kept their seats. Acaila was the most senior of the Eldar, the ancient order of scholars, and Janil had risen to first among the spellweavers when the Queen's most trusted adviser, Tathar, had finally left for his journey to the Blessed Isles.

Since the two elves from E'bar had arrived, the Queen's

Court had been discussing how best to deal with the events chronicled by the brothers. In typical elven fashion, there was no hurried decision making, but a detailed examination of all choices. Tomas had postponed a flight to E'bar to see for himself what was happening there until he was certain it was safe to leave Elvandar.

Of late he'd been troubled by more dreams, and the sense he got from his mental link with dragons was worrisome. Something profound had changed and he was concerned that there was a link that needed to be examined.

Tomas glanced as his wife, who inclined her head, indicating that he should speak first. "More grave tidings from E'bar," he said.

Janil was a worker of powerful elven magic, but her age was manifesting itself in her white hair and a slender form now starting to wither. But her voice was strong when she said, "I've dispatched four of our best to E'bar. Do we send more?"

"If numbers of magic users are critical, we can do little," added Acaila. "Our cousins will need to reach out to the humans."

"Bethany of Carse has said it has been done," said Gulamendis.

"Then we can do naught but wait," said his brother.

Tomas said, "You may need to return soon." He sat back, a look of concern on his face. "It may be that every spell-weaver we have must journey to fight what is contained within E'bar."

Aglaranna said, "What do you make of our son fighting beside a Moredhel?"

"Calis is unique," answered Tomas, "as is his perspective. Perhaps there is a lesson here."

Janil said, "The Moredhel number powerful shamans among their clans."

"But Arkan is leader of the Ardanien," said Acaila. "What we know of Moredhel politics tells us he's in a faction despised by those in power."

"That may be less important than we think," answered

Calin. "For if I remember the most recent rumors from the north, the Ardanien are still tied to the Hamandien, maybe even more closely."

"Liallan," said Aglaranna. "She's been ruling the Snow Leopards longer than I have ruled in Elvandar. If she's protecting Arkan . . ."

"She is the only Moredhel clan leader strong enough to oppose Narab's bid to be their first King," said Janil.

"The Ardanien, the Ice Bears, have a shaman by name Cetswaya, who is counted as being among their wisest and most powerful," said Acaila.

"Dare we seek out the Moredhel?" asked Aglaranna.

Calin said, "If nothing more than to warn them. This threat from E'bar is far worse than they might know."

Aglaranna looked at her son. "I have one son at risk already, and you are heir."

Tomas nodded. "I would go, but their reaction to me might not be much warmer."

It was Laromendis who said, "We can go, Majesty. Our particular gifts do not bring much to aid our kin in E'bar, but as of yet we have no problem with the Moredhel. If you can get us to the border of their land, we should be able to cross freely."

Calin looked at his mother, who nodded, and said to him, "Escort them. Ensure they are safe until they make contact, but return here at once."

Acaila said to the two Star Elves, "If you spend the day with me tomorrow, I will share what we know of Moredhel clan politics. It may not be current enough to do you good, but it's a start. There is one among the Moredhel you need to speak with before any other, the woman I named, Liallan . . ."

Tomas smiled at his wife. Acaila's briefing on the morrow appeared to be starting that moment. Then his smile faded.

Aglaranna rose from her throne and came to her husband's side. "What is it?"

Sadly he said, "I have to leave soon."

"The dragons?"

"Yes," he whispered back. "They are calling, and soon I must leave."

Neither of them said what they both feared most, that it very well might be the last time he left Elvandar.

14

CLASH

Brendan peered into the storm.

He slammed the heavy wooden shutter closed and said, "Nothing."

Sandreena said, "What did you expect?"

"I never did well with waiting," said Brendan, grinning as he wiped water from his face.

Amirantha sat back in the big chair he had appropriated for his own use in what had become the de facto common room of the villa, a classroom containing several chairs designed for nonhuman students that was currently not in use. Amirantha's choice looked like nothing so much as a massive pillow filled with tiny wooden balls, which made it a task to move, but it was formfitting and very comfortable. Sandreena rested on a small stool, content to sit anywhere after a lifetime of mostly being on the ground or in the saddle.

Brendan said, "I'm still trying to fathom how they're doing this." "They" were whoever was unleashing this seemingly endless storm, and "this" was the storm.

For days now, the island had been reduced to inactivity because of the near-gale-force winds and driving rain constantly pelting it. The storm was intensifying, if Brendan was a judge of such things, and he had lived through his share of gales and squalls in Crydee. It was barely noticeable unless you were stuck in the middle of it, thought Brendan, and now he realized he never would have survived if the storm had been this intense when he'd first arrived.

"It's getting worse," he said.

"Yes," agreed Sandreena, who had endured her share of foul weather as well. "Slowly, but it's getting worse."

And everyone was ready for the possibility of another attack.

Brendan had spent some time with most of those of importance on the island, until he realized that his rank was the only reason for not being told to go away and leave the adults to the planning. That and his willingness to leap into battle with the conjured monster.

He had found Sandreena and Amirantha talking with a magician named Leonardo, who had since left. Brendan had been politely included in the discussion, though he had little to add.

Amirantha said, "If you discover how they are doing this, please feel free to share."

Sandreena threw him a disapproving look. Amirantha quickly added, "I apologize, Brendan. We're all feeling helpless. Gets on the nerves."

Brendan sat down and said, "I know nothing of magic. My family used to have a magic adviser, but somewhere along the way we stopped. Last magician I even saw before I left Crydee . . ." He sat up.

"What?" asked Sandreena.

"I just got a . . . notion. Where's Ruffio?"

"In Pug's study, almost certainly," said Amirantha. "Why?"

"Come on, if you want to know," said Brendan, hurrying off.

Curious, both demon experts followed him. Brendan knocked on the door to Pug's study and, when he heard Ruffio's voice, pushed open the door.

The magician looked up from a pile of books. He had been reading everything Pug had written down about weather magic.

"I think I have an answer."

"Go on," said Ruffio.

"You don't have any weather magicians here, right?"

"It's not a common area of study," said Ruffio. "More to my regret now than ever."

"It's elf magic, I've been told."

"They are the masters, but getting an elf here . . ." Ruffio shrugged.

"I know a captain who's mad enough to risk this storm, and he has the best weather magician in the Kingdom on his ship."

Ruffio's eyes widened. "Reinman! Why didn't I think of that?"

"Unless he's running an errand for the Prince, he should be in Krondor," said Brendan.

Ruffio said, "Whatever is blocking our magic isn't always effective." He grabbed a quill and parchment and started writing. After a moment he said, "I'll just keep trying to transport this until I'm successful."

"Where are you sending it?"

"Stardock. I'll have someone there who's trusted in the palace take it there by hand. I have no confidence that a piece of parchment landing on the floor of a random room in the palace asking that the ship named the *Royal Messenger* be sent to Sorcerer's Isle would be well received."

He continued to write out detailed instructions, then

sprinkled pounce over the parchment and blew just for good measure to ensure the ink wouldn't smear, rolled it up, and tied a cord around it. He put it on the table and stared at it, and nothing happened.

For the next hour Amirantha, Brendan, and Sandreena watched Ruffio try unsuccessfully to send the parchment to Stardock. Then suddenly the parchment vanished.

Ruffio sank back in his chair, perspiration running down his forehead. "That . . . was exhausting."

"But the interference is intermittent," said Sandreena.

"Yes," answered Ruffio, rising. "I could do with a cup of wine. It may be days before we know anything."

"What do we do until then?" asked Amirantha.

"Hunker down, keep our wits together, and be ready for trouble," said Ruffio. "And drink some very good wine."

"You sure someone will find that parchment?" asked Brendan.

Ruffio smiled. "We of the Conclave have a lot of friends still in Stardock. The moment that parchment appeared, a special signal sounded. Someone there is reading that message right now. I expect that person to be in the palace at Krondor, talking to another friend of the Conclave, within another hour, and if Reinman's in Krondor, he'll be departing at dawn tomorrow at the latest."

"If Reinman's in Krondor, he'll be here in three days," said Brendan. He glanced at Amirantha, who was regarding him with what could only be called an approving expression. Brendan felt pleased at that, and then said, "About that wine?"

Captain Jason Reinman shouted over the wind to his first mate, "What do you make of that, Mr. Williams?"

"I've never seen anything like it," replied Noah Williams. "And I've been on the sea as long as you, Captain."

"Longer if you'd stop lying about your age." He grinned. "Got Bellard drunk yet?"

"Just about," answered the first mate. "Didn't need to force him either. Whatever that other magician in Krondor said to him got him in the right mind."

"Well, he'd better be if we're going to get through that and not end up on the rocks."

"That" was the oddest weather either sailor had ever encountered. About a mile from where they should be seeing the Magician's Tower of the Black Castle on the headlands of Sorcerer's Isle, there stood a wall of weather. Reinman had ordered the ship to take a port tack, swinging wide of the visible storm, but noticed that there seemed to be something of a buffer of nasty wind before the fringe of the storm.

After sailing for a couple of hours, he had determined that the storm was a perfect circle of weather starting perhaps a mile or more off the coast of Sorcerer's Island. He summoned a magician named Xander, a Keshian by birth, but apparently trusted enough to be allowed aboard the Kingdom's fastest warship. "Can you get a message through to whoever's on that island?"

"It may take a while," Xander said. "But I think so."

"Here's what I need you to tell them. As far as we can tell, the center of that storm is right over the middle of the island. I don't know if Bellard can blunt it enough for us to come to shore, nor do I know what good that would do anyone. We'll await their reply before we decide the next move."

The magician headed belowdecks to compose his message. He and Ruffio had been selective in sending messages, but it was an erratic process, sometimes taking hours.

Reinman kept his ship away from the storm as best he could, moving off for miles on a southeastern tack before coming around to the south of the storm. After two hours he asked, "Mr. Williams, is that storm getting larger?"

"Hard to judge, Captain." He shouted aloft. "Lookout! Is the storm getting bigger?"

From above came the response: "Aye, Mr. Williams. It appears to be getting larger, and stronger as well."

"Port your helm, Mr. Hagan!" he shouted to the helms-man. "Mr. Williams, would you head below and inform Xander of the change? I think that might be important news to the island."

"Aye, sir," said the first mate, heading below.

Jason Reinman, who had the well-earned reputation of being the most reckless and daring captain on the Bitter Sea since Amos Trask, looked at the storm and thought not all the gold in Kesh would make him try to sail through that mess.

Ruffio waited patiently in Pug's office, distracting himself by doing as much research as he could, but mainly waiting for another communication from his agent from Stardock, Xander.

Two messages each way had gotten through, each taking at least a dozen tries before finding a gap in the block-ing magic. The energy of the storm was the cause of his problems, he was now convinced, rather than any overt attempt at countermagic. He wasn't sure what that meant, but knew it would prove to be significant eventually, if they survived the storm, which seemed to be mounting in inten-sity, slowly, but steadily. Given the pounding the villa was taking, he was glad the rebuilt villa Pug had put up had such staunch walls.

Suddenly a parchment appeared before him and he quickly tore it open and read it. Then he shouted, "Brendan!"

Brendan was at that time in the common room, failing to charm Dilyna. The best he had managed to get from her was a shy giggle and he was coming to the conclusion that nice girls were a sight different from the ones was used to flirt-ing with. He heard his name called, said, "Excuse me," and hurried to Pug's study.

He opened the door and said, "Yes?"

"Get Sandreena, please, then both of you come back."

Brendan did as was asked, found the Sergeant-Adamant

in her quarters cleaning her armor, and together they went to the study.

"I have a task for you two if you're willing," Ruffio said. "I've received intelligence from Captain Reinman and Xander that the storm is centered here on the island."

Sandreena said, "I know little about weather magic, but how can someone be sitting in the middle of your island throwing out magic of this power and not be seen by your magicians? It would be like shouting at the top of his lungs, wouldn't it?"

"Normally," said Ruffio. He rolled out a map of Sorcerer's Isle and put his finger in the middle. "If the spell originated here, we would have felt it. I think that attack by the sea demon was a distraction. I think two entities were dropped onto this island." He moved his hand to the south of the island. "If a storm was blown up from here, just enough to strike the southern part of the island, from the beach to the villa, and some flying entity—a magician or a summoned creature—carried that monster and dropped it in our midst, then another flier could have reached the center of our island undetected. Then"—he drew a line with his finger—"imagine a ship out there somewhere, protected against the storm, but where the magic is being conjured. Here"—he again pointed to the center of the island—"a second magician waits. He doesn't create magic, he merely anchors it."

It was Brendan who said, "But he's acting as the center!"

Ruffio smiled. "Yes. Imagine a great engine of magic, a thing that can blow a storm out across a finite area, but it will simply blow in a straight line. If you want to confuse your opponent as to where it originates, have it circle around a different location."

"What do you want us to do?" asked Sandreena.

Ruffio looked at Brendan like a teacher regards a promising student.

"We go find whoever it is and persuade them to stop doing what they're doing, and then see what happens to this storm. I'll go," said Brendan without hesitation.

"You and Sandreena are the only two here with weapons and experience. I have no one else to send. I am sure I can find at least one young magician who will be willing to go with you, and protect you from any magic directed at you."

"Where do we look?" asked Sandreena.

"Out that door, turn right, and follow the hall to the last door on the left," said Ruffio. "Keep your bearings and go straight on without turning until you come to a small pond . . . by now it might be a big pond, given the rain. Circle to your left and get back on your original course, and in a few hours you'll come to some outcrops below three hills. Somewhere in those hills is where our unwelcome guest is likely to be."

"Caves?" asked Sandreena.

"No, so look for some sort of shelter, or magic against weather. Or a magician who doesn't care how wet and cold he gets." He stood up and walked past them, beckoning for them to follow.

Ruffio walked through halls now dripping with water coming in through every crack and loose joint in the ceiling and walls until he reached a classroom currently occupied by half a dozen younger magicians trying to study despite the crashing chaos outside.

"They're researching weather magic as well," said Ruffio. He turned to the group. "I have a favor to ask. I need some-one to go out in the storm with Sandreena and Brendan to look for one or more magicians who may be hiding in the central hills of the island, to protect them from traps."

Three of the six magicians instantly stood up and Ruffio said, "Donal, thank you."

The magician was sandy-haired, fair-skinned, and wore a green robe with half sleeves. He nodded at Brendan and Sandreena and said, "We leave now?"

"Sooner is better," said the Sergeant-Adamant.

"We have some foul-weather gear in the storage room," said Ruffio.

"I'll show you," said Donal.

Donal took them across an open expanse of grass, where they were pummeled by rain so hard it soaked them to the skin before they reached the next building. "Seems a little pointless now," said Sandreena.

Brendan said, "No, it's not," as his teeth started to chatter.

Donal opened a large trunk and Brendan pulled out a heavily oiled canvas cloak, fleece-lined, with no seams. He pulled it on over his head and stuck his arms through the sleeves. "It's not the wet as much as the cold."

"I've fought in cold and wet before," said Sandreena.

Brendan grinned. "No doubt, but you know how it can rob your strength. And this is cold. I've been doused by storm water coming out of the frozen north, and those winters are far worse than what should be normal here. This is worse than that ever was! Besides, we may be looking for a couple of hours before we have to fight." He turned and was surprised to see Ruffio donning gear. "I didn't know you were coming as well."

"Two reasons," the magician said. "I can transport us back here quickly, should the need arise, and moreover, while Donal is protecting you from harm, I can be doling out harm myself."

"I feel better already," said Brendan, evincing a bravado he did not feel in the least.

Once dressed against the weather, they left the storage room and started walking toward the center of the island.

Two hours later they came to a small plateau on top of a hillock. Brendan did not need Ruffio or Donal to tell him they'd found their goal. The energy put out by whoever was up there caused the hair on his arms to stand up, despite being wet. Ruffio moved slowly up a muddy, slippery path to where he could see, then signaled for the others to follow.

Now the storm was their ally, masking their approach. Brendan had lived his life in a coastal town and had seen monstrous storms, rolling down the coast with bitter sleet and rain, but he had never see one like this. The raindrops struck like rocks.

Half a dozen figures huddled under a sturdy lean-to that shielded them from the worst of the wind. Three of the figures were motionless, squatting on the rocks, while the other three stood upright like men, guarding the three on the ground. A small spindle of emerald flame rose from a point equidistant from the three squatting figures, and from it emanated a sizzling, crackling shaft of green energy that shot into the sky.

Brendan came up behind Ruffio and his eyes widened. He had never seen the like of these creatures. They were lizard-featured, but three of them stood upright like men. One saw him and gave alarm in a hissing tongue, and suddenly battle was joined.

Donal incanted as Sandreena joined Brendan. All the lizard men were unarmed, but the three standing quickly cast spells at the attackers.

A bolt of dark purple energy exploded in Brendan's face, but washed around it as if he had a perfectly clear shield of glass between the furious blast and his face. Feeling his hair almost dance from the discharge around his head, he was now very glad Donal was there. He didn't hesitate but charged the caster, bowling him over with his shoulder and shield. The creature rolled over through the mud, hissing and baring pointed teeth. Brendan swung hard and his blade bounced off a protective ward of some sort.

"Magic!" he shouted, then instantly felt like an idiot; of course they were using magic. He quickly added, "Magic's protecting them. How do I get past it?"

Ruffio shouted, "Duck!" and Brendan hunkered down as a sizzling bolt of energy sped past him, illuminating the serpent man as he tried to stand, knocking him backward.

Brendan leaped to his feet and almost had them go out from under him as he slipped on the mud. He regained traction just in time to face a snarling mask of reptilian hatred, as the alien magician began to conjure another spell. Not waiting to see if anyone was protecting him, Brendan took a quick step forward, and thrust, skewering the serpent with his sword. With a gurgling cry, the creature fell, and Brendan pulled free his blade.

By the time he had withdrawn his sword, Sandreena, who was far more experienced at combat, had knocked over the lean-to, brained one serpent man with her mace, and had turned on the second one.

The second serpent man threw a massive wave of fire at Sandreena, who reflexively crouched behind her shield. Brendan watched in shocked amazement as flames roared around the crouching Sergeant-Adamant. He felt the waves of heat wash over him from several feet away, heard the hissing of water on rock surfaces being turned to steam, and wondered how she could survive that heat even with no direct flame on her. It must be part of the magical nature of her order, he decided as he saw her spring to her feet the moment the flames stopped.

Brendan charged the last standing serpent man at the same time as Sandreena. Whatever spell the last serpent magician had been casting died before he finished as Sandreena struck him hard enough that all could hear bones cracking as his head twisted at an unnatural angle above his shoulders.

But still the three sitting figures did not move.

Sandreena had her mace drawn back, ready to strike, but Ruffio shouted, "Hold!"

For a brief moment everyone was motionless, then Ruffio knelt next to one of the sitting figures, pulled off its hood, and revealed another creature, one that was somehow different from the ones that now lay dead on the ground.

"What are they?" shouted Brendan.

"Pantathians," said Sandreena.

"Not like those we saw down on the island with Pug," said Sandreena.

"Those three are Pantathian Serpent Priests," said Ruffio, indicating the three dead magic users. "They are the ones who have been plaguing our world for centuries. These other three are called Panath-Tiandn, or Shangri. They're somehow related, but I'm not sure how. I've never seen any of them before, but I've read about them. Pug and Magnus have been dealing with them for years." He indicated the three motionless, living creatures. "These three are powerful conduits for magic, but they're nearly mindless on their own."

"What do we do with them?" asked Sandreena. "They seem to be unaware of us."

"We proceed cautiously," said Ruffio. "One of the reasons our magic was intermittent is these creatures use energies alien to us. For as long as there have been stories about them, it has been said their spells skew other magic."

Spitting water as he spoke, Brendan said, "Well, I'm no expert in weather magic, but it seems this storm is still getting worse. We need to do something."

Ruffio turned to Donal. "See if you get any sense of what this spell is."

The two magicians examined the three mute figures for nearly half an hour, and finally Donal said, "They aren't casting magic, Ruffio. They *are* the magic."

"What do you mean?" shouted Sandreena.

"I mean they're giving their life energies to this spell and it will continue as long as they live."

"That's all I needed to hear," said Sandreena, who raised her mace and brought it crashing down onto the head of one of the three still figures.

Brendan looked at Ruffio, who nodded once. Brendan ran the second creature through the back of the neck with his blade. Donal pulled a dagger from his belt and slit the throat of the last, and within seconds the three creatures were dead.

The storm shifted with the swiftness of someone snapping a piece of damp cloth. The wind that had been howling around the island was gone, moving as fast as a bolt shot from a crossbow. The resultant following wind as the weather shifted knocked everyone to the ground.

Brendan felt his ears pop. He rolled to his knees, and

when he sprang to his feet, he saw something as strange as he could imagine.

As if a shroud had been pulled aside, a bright sunny sky had appeared above, and he could see dark thundering rain clouds speeding away to the southeast. Trees were swaying from the winds that had buffeted them seconds before, but now the air that struck him was warm and dry.

"That was unexpected," said Sandreena as she put out a hand and helped Donal to his feet.

They watched as the storm vanished into the south and Brendan said, "What happened?"

"Magic that I barely understand," said Ruffio. "One thing I have learned from Pug is that magic is as much an art as a science, and while we try to fathom its intricacies, so much of what we are capable of depends on the nature of the magic user. These creatures have a unique relationship to magic, and maybe we will never truly understand how they achieve what they do." He looked around at the clearing sky, then at his still-soaked companions. "We can speculate about this later. Now we must go."

"Where to?" asked Donal.

"I'll take them back to the villa," said Ruffio.

"I'll stay and see if they're carrying anything of note," said Donal.

"Good. If what we've surmised is correct, the storm should be blowing straight out in one direction from its origin." Ruffio closed his eyes and said, "Things are returning to normal." He held out his hands to Sandreena and Brendan and each took one. Ruffio nodded and suddenly he, Brendan, and Sandreena were in Pug's study.

Sounds of laughter and relief came from nearby and Brendan looked out the window to see sun reflecting off the rainwater that was still pouring from the roof gutters.

"From the feel of that heat, it should dry out here in a day or so," said Sandreena.

"I'm curious as to what happens next," said Brendan.

"Want to come and see?" asked Ruffio.

Brendan took off his cloak and said, "Absolutely."

"Me, too," said Sandreena as she doffed her rain gear.

Amirantha entered and looked at them with a grin. "I see you were successful."

"Come along," said Sandreena.

"Where are we going?"

"To see what happens next," said Brendan.

They all joined hands and suddenly were standing upon a windswept stone battlement, the highest vantage point at the Black Castle. To the south a massive wall of dark, roiling clouds, shot through with flashes of lightning, swung away from them, as if anchored to the right. Everything north of the malevolent dark front was clearing nicely and the air was warm, but the storm now seemed to have retreated as far as it was going to go, and appeared to be hunkered down, as if waiting.

Suddenly Sandreena said, "Look, there's something out there!"

In the distance, they saw what appeared to be a ship at anchor. It was right at the southern cornerstone of the magically generated storm.

"Look at the size of that thing," said Amirantha.

Even from their distant position, they could tell it was huge. "It's a Quegan trireme," said Ruffio. "Huge bastard, three banks of oars on either side, ram on the prow with mechanical barbs to seize a ship. Get it in their grasp, board and loot it, then release the barbs, backwater, and let the other ship sink." He made a grasp-and-release motion with his hands.

"The storm has fallen away as much as it is going to," said Brendan.

"We must have broken the spell entirely," said Ruffio.

"What next?" asked Sandreena. "I'm tempted to have you fly out to that ship for a closer inspection, but given that we're dealing with Pantathian magic, I don't think that would be wise."

"I appreciate the curiosity," said Ruffio.

"What's that?" asked Brendan, pointing to the southeast.

In the distance they could see another ship, making speed with all sails tacking against the fading storm. Ruffio said, "Unless I'm completely mistaken, that's the ship captained by Jason Reinman, the most fearless captain on the Bitter Sea."

Brendan said, "And the most reckless. He's making straight for that big ship. But how is he able to run so quickly against the wind like that?"

"Bellard," said Ruffio. "He's Reinman's weather magician and he can get that ship anywhere as fast as it can go. It's one of the two secrets behind Reinman's ability to get messages through for the Crown when no one else can."

"What's the other secret?" asked Sandreena.

"Madness."

"Speaking of madness," said Amirantha, "I think he's attacking that huge ship."

Ruffio sighed audibly.

Captain Jason Reinman shouted, "All hands! Ready to board!"

Noah Williams, first mate on the *Royal Messenger* for sixteen years, had seen Jason Reinman give orders that others judged mad many times; but in all of those sixteen years, this was the single maddest order he had ever had to relay to the men. Still, he had vowed years before that if Jason Reinman ordered them to sail into the lowest hell, he would relay the order and follow the redheaded madman anywhere.

"Boarders to starboard! Archers aloft!" Mr. Williams bellowed.

As Bellard staggered to the rail as if on the verge of vomiting, Reinman shouted, "Downwind, you miserable souse! You know better."

The magician took a deep breath and said, "I'm all right."

"Then change the wind up a bit to port, if you will. I need

to bring this beauty around fast and neat alongside that ugly bastard."

The vessel he indicated was racing toward them: a squat black thing that looked as much like a hideous insect as it did a ship. A long, downswept prow ended in a nasty ram, a massive black armored thing of barbs and spikes. It had three banks of oars, moving in a slow rhythm. The sails were dark, making it even more ominous-looking than usual.

"Quegan," said Williams, "but someone's done a bit of work on her. Quegans like them all white and shiny."

"Captain!" shouted down the Knight-Lieutenant of Marines, who had his bowmen in the yards above. "We see no crew aloft."

"But there's movement on the decks!" shouted another.

Without warning, a flight of creatures launched themselves off the deck of the black ship and came speeding across the gulf between the two craft. They were about the size of monkeys, with red fur and bat wings, large jaws, and a vast number of claws on each hand.

Sailors screamed in shock and anger and began fighting back. Archers shot at the creatures, most missing, but when a steel-headed shaft struck one of the red creatures, it burst into flames. The clamor on the deck of the strange ship rose in volume as more monsters came swarming up out from belowdecks.

Reinman shouted, "Turn us and make all speed!" He looked to the drunken weather magician. "Bellard, as swift a following wind as you can muster without ripping our masts out."

The magician's face was devoid of color. Whatever he had endured in service to the Crown previously hadn't prepared him for what he saw prancing and leaping on the deck opposite: nightmare shapes of every description. "Demons," he said.

Reinman looked at the magician and realized he had been frightened sober and would therefore be of no use.

Then grappling hooks from the black ship snaked out and bit into the side of the *Messenger*. They were outmanned, out of position, and had no advantage. Reinman shouted, "Prepare to repel boarders," drew his cutlass, and hurried down to the main deck.

Looking down from the castle above the headlands, Brendan said, "What is going on?"

"Demons!" said Amirantha.

Sandreena regarded her former lover. "You're certain?"

"I can feel them. There must be dozens."

Sandreena looked at Ruffio. "Either we let them all die, or we get down there. They're no match for a crew of demons."

Ruffio closed his eyes for a moment, then said, "Help will be on the way soon." He reached out and Sandreena, Brendan, and Amirantha joined hands.

Instantly they were on the quarterdeck of the *Royal Messenger.* Chaos was erupting on all sides. Brendan lashed out at the first flying creature that came his way, severing its wing. It flopped to the deck and fluttered around, smoke flowing from the wound, then suddenly erupted into a small green-blue flame and vanished.

Amirantha had been frustrated for years since he could no longer control demons, but he still knew how to banish them back to the fifth realm. He lashed out with a spell aimed at three large brutes that were poised to leap from the deck of the massive black ship onto the *Messenger,* and instantly they were gone in a puff of black smoke. He concentrated on banishing the larger and more dangerous of the demons he could see. Within another minute, a half dozen of the most loathsome of the creatures were gone.

Ruffio blasted a group on the lower deck, freeing up beleaguered seamen so that they could better coordinate the defense of their ship.

"We've got to get over to the other ship!" shouted Sandreena.

"Why?" asked Ruffio.

"Demons don't sail ships," she said, crushing the skull of an unfortunate flier that had sped too close to her. "Something over there is controlling them."

Ruffio craned his neck and saw that the upper wheel deck of the other ship was empty. He reached out, they joined hands, and suddenly they were on the other ship.

Brendan knew little of magic, but just placing his feet on the deck of this vessel made his skin crawl. He looked around frantically to see if their presence had been detected. The horrors on the deck were swarming over the rails, leaping aboard the *Royal Messenger*.

Amirantha said, "Whatever's controlling this vessel and crew is below."

They hurried down the short ladder to the main deck and opened a companionway door that led down. Below, they found the first level of the rowers' deck; down the middle ran a large walkway from stern to bow. As miserable a crew of slaves as one could imagine was pulling the oars. Half a dozen demons raced along the central walkway whipping the slaves, who appeared to mostly be human. Amirantha took aim at one particularly noxious creature carrying a massive, bloody whip and incanted a spell of banishment. Suddenly he was gone.

"You go and find the source of this magic," he said to Sandreena and Ruffio. "I'll deal with this lot."

"I'll stay here," Brendan said, brandishing his blade.

Sandreena said, "I wish I'd had time to don my full armor before we left."

Ruffio said, "I wish I'd brought along a dozen other magicians, but we make do."

Heading for the bow, they found a large foredeck, and there a creature of darkness sat on a raised dais, around which three of the mindless Panath-Tiandn sat, casting their weather energy. The figure in the middle was featureless, a thing of shadows and darker blacks, yet it conveyed shape and dimension, contour and features. Eyes that were blazing red coals looked at the two humans, and when it started to rise, they could see it was easily seven feet in height. Ruffio shouted, "It's a Dreadmaster!"

The Dreadmaster extended an arm, hand palm out, and unleashed a massive wave of magic at them, howling, "Die!"

Ruffio had begun casting his counterspell the moment he recognized the creature for what it was, not knowing what the attack would be, but certain it would come. Cascading energies washed around Sandreena, who would have been reduced to ash had he not been there to protect her. The magician threw himself to one side and avoided the energies that splashed off his shield, shouting, "Don't let it touch you! It can wither you where you stand. But it hates the touch of cold iron!"

As soon as the energy dissipated, Sandreena swung her mace with both hands and struck the extended arm. The Dreadmaster cried out in agony as hot white sparks erupted where Sandreena's mace struck. Where normally she would expect to hear cracking bones and the wet sound of crushed flesh, she heard an ear-shattering clang of metal on metal as shock ran up her arm: it was like hitting an anvil!

Ruffio extended his hand and sent out a glob of shimmering white light through which black flashes streaked. It struck the Dreadmaster while it was distracted by Sandreena, and the creature was engulfed by a cocoon of energy. It fell to the deck, rolling in a paroxysm of pain, its body contorting wildly. Sandreena didn't hesitate and slammed her mace down on the creature's head.

The Dreadmaster recoiled from the blow, moving backward like a captured insect rolling in a spider's cocoon, then it flexed and the imprisoning energies exploded around it. Odd howling sounds erupted from the creature as it rose again to confront its attackers. Sandreena knew it was an illusion of light and shadows in the darkened rowers' deck, but the creature looked as if it was even bigger than it had been moments before.

Ruffio then shot out a bolt of red liquid. The evil fluid burned whatever it touched, causing smoke to rise up from where it splashed the decks and causing huge blisters to erupt on the body of the Dreadmaster, who contorted in agony, smoke erupting from the lesions. It fell over backward, crushing one of the three Shangri beneath its huge form.

As it was trying to rise, Sandreena knelt and expertly struck at the back of its knee, and again white-hot sparks exploded and the creature fell once more. Ruffio struck with another spell, and by then Brendan and Amirantha had arrived. Brendan wasted no time and stabbed at the creature, almost getting his arm yanked off for his troubles. The Dreadmaster shrieked in pain then bellowed a challenge, and its voice rang out, an echo of something unnatural from a place beyond sanity. "You dare? You pathetic creatures, know pain!"

With a wave of its hand, the Dreadmaster caused the air to bend, sending a wave of force that picked up the four humans and flung them back as if they were nothing more than flies. Sandreena, Ruffio, and Amirantha were knocked straight back, but Brendan was sent careening toward the edge of the catwalk above the rowing deck. He flailed out with his left hand, grabbed the edge of the rail, and felt his shoulder yanked as if someone were trying to pull his arm out of its socket.

Sandreena shouted, "Brendan, look out!"

He looked up and saw the malevolent creature rearing above him. The Dreadmaster reached toward him, and Brendan was left with no other choice but to let go. He fell back, landing on two rowers in the upper tier of oars.

Emaciated, filthy arms sought to grab Brendan to hold him down or to help him up, he had no idea. He struggled to his feet, pushing past the shouting and pleading men. "Set us free!" and "Help us!" they cried, and uttered entreaties in languages Brendan didn't understand.

He navigated past more men chained to benches and glanced up. Having eluded the Dreadmaster, Brendan saw that the monster had returned its attention to Ruffio, Sandreena, and Amirantha. The Sergeant-Adamant fought as best she could with mace and shield, and Brendan now also wished she had been able to fully don her armor. There was nothing remotely vulnerable about Sandreena, but as stalwart and determined as she was, he'd have felt more reassured of her chances of survival if she wasn't attired in only a tunic and trousers.

He surveyed his surroundings. The rowers' deck was a good twenty feet below the walkway. There were three banks of three rowers on every oar on each side of the ship, the benches being staggered one above the next so each man had room to row without having to duck his head. The rowers were settled on simple wooden benches, secured by heavy braces along each side from bow to stern, above and below by supports, and by a massive chain down the middle. For a brief instant Brendan wondered what would happen to the hull if all this was set afire, then he realized it would prove a death sentence to the hundred and twenty or so slaves chained here.

He turned to the stern and saw the ladder that led up to the supervising catwalk. He took a step and his toe struck something that clanged. He glanced down and saw a ring of keys. Picking them up, he looked at the chain that ran through the length of the ship. Another chain at every bench was secured in place, bolted to the hull on one side, anchored in place by a large iron ring through which the first chain passed. By removing the long chain, rowers could be changed when one died or could no longer row.

Brendan hurried toward the ladder and saw a heavy wooden door on the left side with a barred window. He peered through and saw about another dozen slaves huddled miserably on the floor, wincing in terror at every crash and bellow from above. Brendan saw the door lock and quickly tried several keys until he could open it.

He tossed the keys at the first startled slave and hoped he understood the King's Tongue. "Free yourself, then unchain the others."

He didn't wait for a reply but climbed the ladder to the catwalk.

Brendan turned from the ladder just in time to be blinded by a flash of light so intense it left his eyes watering and his vision floating with afterimages. A raging scream from the Dreadmaster shook the hold of the ship.

Blinking furiously, Brendan crouched with his sword at the ready and waited until he could make sense of the scene.

The Dreadmaster was entangled in some sort of mystic web, thousands of silver-and-white shreds of energy that were contracting around him. Bits of the mystic stuff would tear, sending tatters of it away from him, blinking out of existence moments later. Brendan kept blinking and saw that the more the Dread struggled, the tighter the web became, and more and more strands were binding him.

He moved forward and took up a position on Sandreena's left. "Wondered where you'd got to," she said, panting.

"Landed on some poor sod below," said Brendan. "Thought while I was down there I'd free the slaves."

"Nicely done," said Sandreena, "but if they're breaking free, who's rowing the ship?"

"We can worry about that when we get up on deck," said Amirantha from behind.

Ruffio was completely focused on the spell he had finally contrived to neutralize the Dreadmaster. The creature from the Void bellowed enraged threats and promises of destruction, but more and more it struggled in confinement, and finally it teetered then crashed to the ground.

Brendan heard shouts and looked to the rear to see the first of the freed slaves clambering up the ladder. With his sword point, he indicated the companionway to the upper deck. "Hurry!" he shouted. The first slave nodded and took the lead, the others following. Brendan returned his attention to the conflict before him.

The Dreadmaster lay thrashing and roaring as Amirantha tried a variety of spells, a few of which seemed to injure the creature, while Ruffio held him confined. The magician appeared exhausted by his efforts to keep the Dread immobile as Sandreena and Brendan dodged in and out, striking and cutting.

"It's like hewing wood!" shouted Brendan after his first blow sent a shock up his arm. "This thing will not die."

Sandreena crashed her mace down on the Dread for perhaps the tenth time. "It's like hitting rock!"

The Dreadmaster tried to rise again, and Brendan swung low to hamstring it. For his troubles he got swatted away like an insect and rolled hard into the bulkhead. His entire body arched in agony from the thing's brief touch: it felt as if something had attempted to reach inside and tear out his heart. He struggled to regain control of his body, but the best he could manage was to roll over and vomit all over the deck.

Sandreena stayed focused on striking and not being struck. The creature appeared to be weakening, but so was she. Her arms felt leaden and her back hurt, for while she had fought for longer periods in battle before, she had never struck anything that caused shock to course up her arms and shoulders like this creature did. Even the wooden pells used for arms practice were more yielding than this monster. But with dogged will she continued to strike at it. The Dreadmaster appeared to be faltering, and turning its attention from fighting to escape. It thrashed around, causing everyone to move away.

Brendan managed to sit up with his shoulders against the bulkhead as his head began to clear. He felt sick and weak, as if he had just awoken from a fever.

Abruptly, the Dreadmaster gave up thrashing, flipped around, and rolled right at Sandreena and Amirantha. The warlock beat a hasty retreat back down the center section of the catwalk while Sandreena managed a huge leap into the air, allowing the monster to roll beneath her. She hit the deck, turned, and saw an opening.

Running up behind the Dreadmaster while it rolled to the edge of the open decking, she launched a massive underhand blow that struck it on the back of the head. The extra force caused the brute to roll farther than anticipated, and suddenly it was falling onto the rowing benches below.

The Dreadmaster crashed onto the remaining slaves attempting to flee. Men screamed in agony as the very touch of the thing of the Void sucked life from their bodies.

Brendan forced himself to his feet and half-staggered over to where three Shangri lay sprawled, their lives taken by the flailing Dreadmaster they had served.

Sandreena looked at Ruffio. He nodded once and she quickly crushed the skulls of all three to make sure they were in fact dead.

Abruptly a violent thrumming began to shake the ship. "What is that?" asked Sandreena.

"I have no idea," said Ruffio, "but I think we need to be off this ship."

They hurried back to where Amirantha stood, looking down at the havoc caused by the thrashing Dreadmaster. Brendan shouted, "What do we do?"

Without warning, there was a monstrous cracking sound, as if someone had smashed open a gigantic walnut with a massive hammer, and water started rushing up from the bilges below the slaves.

"That damn thing put its foot through the hull!" shouted Sandreena.

Brendan's eyes widened as he saw the Dreadmaster thrash around, still grievously injured, but powerful enough that it was indeed tearing a hole in the ship. The few remaining slaves were looking up and reaching out to him in panic, as if he could somehow lean down and grip their hands and haul them to safety, while others frantically tried to leap over or dodge around the thrashing Dreadlord, only to die at its touch.

Ruffio shouted, "We leave now!" He reached out to gather Sandreena, Amirantha, and Brendan close, then suddenly they were again on the tower in the castle.

Brendan said, "Those men . . ."

"It couldn't be helped," said Ruffio, then his eyes rolled up in his head and he collapsed. Amirantha grabbed him, sparing him a hard fall, and lowered him to the stones of the tower.

They watched as the massive ship started to roll slowly.

Jason Reinman slashed at another growling horror with a bull's head, cutting it with his cutlass. It howled in pain and retreated a step. Then he heard the loud cracking sound.

The bullheaded monster was distracted for a moment, looking to see where the sound came from, and Reinman hacked halfway through its neck.

The captain of the *Royal Messenger* looked around at a deck awash in blood and took a moment to appraise the situation. His men were holding their own against the monsters. The magic users had been effective in eliminating most of the seriously dangerous creatures, and now his crew was dealing with those left behind. They were powerfully strong, but apparently not overly intelligent, and his crew was among the most highly trained and disciplined in the Royal Navy. The archers in the rigging were picking off any demon that presented itself on the edge of the crowd, and his own men had established a line behind which the wounded could crawl for respite.

He saw that the massive ship, which looked like a Quegan trireme magically enlarged and refitted, was ever so slowly capsizing. "Mr. Williams!" he shouted.

"Mr. Williams is dead, Captain!" shouted a voice from the press on the main deck.

Ignoring the sinking feeling in his stomach—Williams had been his first mate for sixteen years and he'd find time to mourn him later, if he survived this battle—he shouted, "Mr. Baintree!"

"Aye, Captain!" came the shout from his second mate, a short, dark, bull-necked man who was as tough in a brawl as any man Reinman knew.

"We need to cut loose!"

"Cut loose!" shouted Mr. Baintree.

A few sailors dodged past the demons to slash at the grappling ropes, but they were quickly overcome by the creatures still attempting to swarm the *Messenger*.

Reinman had been a captain for twenty years, and had

served as a royal seaman for ten years before that, earning promotion rapidly. In his forty-five years he had never been known to hesitate once he understood the situation.

The Quegan galley was going down slowly. Reinman knew ships so he knew this trireme was open-benched from the bilges to the deck, with scant cargo room fore and aft, so after she was holed she'd take on water and sink quickly. Their grappling ropes were taut and could only be removed by cutting, but they were for the most part on the other side of a mass of dangerous demons.

"Abandon ship!" he shouted. "Port-side bailout!"

At once those tending the wounded began to help them get to the port side of the ship. Reinman knew that he only had minutes to get men in the water swimming away from the ship. If any tried to escape in a direction other than the port side, which was now starting to rise as the larger ship started on its way to the bottom of the Bitter Sea, they stood a very good chance of getting caught in sails and rigging, or sucked down by the vacuum created as the two ships sank.

His only hope for his men was that the *Messenger* would act as a massive buoy for at least a few minutes, slowing the huge trireme's descent until his men could swim clear. This fight was lost: it was the only way to keep further casualties to a minimum.

The wounded were carried to the rail, save those too gravely injured to move. The ship's chirurgeon glanced at Reinman with an unspoken question in his eyes. Reinman nodded once and the chirurgeon held his gaze a moment, communicating a bitter sadness. He then spoke to his assistant, who moved quickly away. Reinman had always found the term "final mercy" offensive, but he understood that a quick, clean death was preferable to being torn apart by demons or hopelessly drowning. Even so, giving the order that six of his own men be killed left a bitter taste in his mouth.

His men were retreating in good order, and his archers on high were giving a good account of themselves and keeping the demons from pressing too quickly.

Suddenly the massive trireme gave a shudder and rolled, the *Messenger* was jerked around like a rat caught by a terrier, and every creature on deck—human or demon—was thrown to the planks. Those demons still on their own ship began to scream and roar, running in chaos as they saw water coming up over the bow.

Reinman shouted, "Everyone over the side, now!"

His men didn't hesitate, but stood, crawled, or leaped to the port side. The archers cast away their bows and crossbows, and jumped from the yards off the port side, diving into the sea. As the ship began heeling over, the barefoot sailors found some purchase on the deck, but many of the demons had hooves or claws which gave them little traction on the blood-and-water-soaked planking, and they started slipping away from their foe.

Screams of rage slowly turned to cries of fear as the demons realized they were sliding to their own watery deaths.

Reinman took one last look around and realized he was alone on the quarterdeck. Climbing up onto the rail, which was now nearly over his head as the deck was tipping, he pulled himself over just as the ship started to roll. Sheets and stays were snapping, and wood was creaking and cracking: the *Royal Messenger* seemed to be fighting for her every breath as the monstrous black thing that had once been a Quegan trireme sank under the waves, pulling the fastest ship in the Royal Navy under with her.

Reinman hit the water in a sailor's dive, bending his knees as he entered the water so he wouldn't run the risk of a broken back. He broke the surface and without seeing who was near shouted, "Away from the ships!"

His crew needed no warning about being pulled under by the suction of the sinking ships and swam away as fast as they were able.

The two ships plunged below the surface, an uprush of air bubbles and debris fountaining into the air, then they were gone. Reinman paused for a moment to say a silent good-bye to a good ship.

His erstwhile second mate swam over and said, "Orders, Captain."

"Find something that floats and start making for that island."

The tide had carried them northward during the battle and now Sorcerer's Isle lay less than three miles away; barring problems, most of the fit men would make it, and the wounded perhaps with help. "Keep an eye out for sharks," said Reinman as he started swimming toward some debris to look for makeshift flotation devices. Traditionally, many sailors refused to learn to swim, preferring a quick death by drowning to the possibility of a lingering death swimming, but Reinman had insisted that every man in his crew be a strong swimmer: he wanted no man on his ship who would choose any death under any circumstances over the chance of survival.

"Pity about the ship," said Mr. Baintree.

"They'll build me another. And she'll be better," Reinman added, trying to sound lighthearted. "Did those magicians and their companions get off safely?"

"Lost track of them during the fighting," said the new first mate.

"Well, let's get these lads to dry land."

"What's that?" asked Mr. Baintree.

A scattering of figures could be seen flying toward them, men and women in robes. "I have no idea," said Reinman with some fear, knowing full well that his men were helpless in the water and resistance to any attack was futile.

But rather than attack, the fliers split up and swooped down. A young girl with brown hair stopped to hover over the captain. She shouted down, "If you gather with others, we can get you to shore quickly!"

Reinman glanced at the wide-eyed first mate and then shouted back up. "We'll swim to that wreckage!"

She nodded and Mr. Baintree said, "Sink me! Now I've seen it all."

Silently agreeing, Captain Jason Reinman, finest captain

in the Royal Navy, started swimming toward a floating spar where half a dozen men already had gathered.

Donal said, "We'll get them to shore and look for other survivors for a while. No one will be left behind." The young magician had taken charge of rescuing the crew of the *Royal Messenger* and slaves escaping from the sunken trireme while Ruffio recovered from exhaustion.

Brendan nodded. From the castle, the sight of the two ships going under was still daunting. He couldn't imagine what it must have been like to be on the decks as the vessels went down. He, Sandreena, and Amirantha stood beside Ruffio, who was now conscious, but weakened and slightly disoriented. He sat in a chair in Pug's study, sipping at a tea another student had concocted which seemed to be revitalizing him quickly. He blinked a few times and took a deep breath, his eyes clearing. He smiled at the three and said, "Everyone all right?"

Amirantha smiled. "Barely, but yes."

"What was all of that?" Brendan asked Ruffio.

Ruffio said, "In all of our dealings with the Pantathians, their plots and schemes over the centuries, much of what we've seen looks to be madness, yet their actions always have purpose. We've had rumors of the Dread; Pug has mentioned them in the past, but one hasn't been seen on this world in over a century." Ruffio seemed at a loss what to think. Finally he said, "Whatever the cause, if in league with the Dread or in thrall to them, the Pantathians wanted this island locked down by storms."

Sandreena said, "They didn't want you going anywhere."

"E'bar," said Brendan. "They didn't want you sending help to E'bar."

"Which is what I will do the moment we sort out this mess here."

Sandreena said, "Had you sent magicians alone, they wouldn't have survived, just as Reinman's crew alone would have fallen before the demons."

"We got lucky," said Amirantha. "Still, it was a close thing."

Ruffio nodded and took a deep breath. "Thank you," he said to the other three. "If so many things hadn't come together in the proper fashion, we'd be still trying to wait out the storm, or we'd be lying dead in the bottom of that trireme." He closed his eyes for a moment, then said, "I just sent a message to one of the students to fetch Calis and Arkan. If we are going to discuss E'bar, it concerns them as much as anyone else on this island." He turned his attention to Brendan and said, "You've done all you came to do. I can arrange to have you in Krondor in minutes, if you wish to find your brothers."

Brendan shook off his overwhelming desire to just fall to the floor and sleep. He suspected the damage done by the Dread might linger, but as long as he could keep his wits, he would not give in. He considered only for a moment. "That would be welcome. I need to be with my brothers, and that means getting to Prince Edward's camp on the Fields of Albalyn. From Krondor I can get there by horse in less than three weeks. If you can get me closer than Krondor, that would be better."

"We'll leave before supper," said Ruffio. "I'm the only one who can actually get us both into the palace, and once we're there, a horse will be no problem."

Brendan thanked him, then said to Amirantha and Sandreena, "It was an honor."

They acknowledged his praise and watched as he left the study. Glancing at Ruffio, Amirantha said, "He's a very special young man."

"His entire family is special," said Ruffio. "The Conclave has watched that branch of the conDoin family for years now. If we survive the coming battle, we'll need them to rebuild the Kingdom."

15

SILDEN

Jim Dasher dived for cover.

He had expected the explosion of rock and gravel, and the cloud of mortar dust as a massive boulder crashed into the wall behind which he was standing, just not at that exact moment. He had been on the wall next to the Knight-Marshal of Silden, Geoffrey du Gale, acting commander of the city in the absence of Duke of Silden, who was currently with Prince Edward.

Jim had come to Silden by swift horse from Bas-Tyra, after conferring with the Duke on behalf of Prince Edward and Duke James. Jim's grandfather was recovering, and what little energy he possessed was being directed at keeping Earl Montgomery of Rillanon from doing something stupid, and keeping Prince Oliver of Maladon and Simrick squatting on the fields north of the King's palace in Rillanon until it was to Edward's advantage for Oliver to come to the Fields of Albalyn.

So once again Jim Dasher was scurrying around the Kingdom, doing his grandfather's bidding, which seemed lately to require him to travel quickly to very dangerous places he did not have magic access to. He could leave Silden at will, but his duty required him to see this city defended long enough to frustrate Oliver's plans.

Jim picked himself up off the stones of the palisade and peered between two merlons on the wall. "That was to get our attention," he said.

Geoffrey looked up from his hands and knees and said, "He has it."

The young soldier had been adjutant to the old Knight-Marshal of the city and had been promoted at the old man's death. Jim liked him. He was smart, confident but not arrogant or certain he was always right, and he listened. He also followed orders without asking unnecessary questions, but asked the necessary ones.

What impressed Jim most was that he was the Duke's nephew: Jim had expected him to be the product of the usual blind nepotism, rather than ability, and was pleasantly surprised to discover the young man deserved his office. His family owned working properties where Geoffrey had been put to work as a boy; he had grown up to be a nobleman unafraid to get his hands dirty. "What now?" he asked Jim.

Jim grinned. "You know as well as I do."

"Yes," said Geoffrey, standing up. "But if you say it and we're wrong, I'm not the one who looks stupid."

Jim shook his head and smiled. They both looked to the distant hill where the crew manning the trebuchet was reloading the bucket and cranking it down. "I hope that was a lucky shot," said Jim. "Because if they actually can hit what they're aiming at, we have a far more serious problem than we thought."

"We have one task," said Geoffrey, "and we shall achieve it."

"Here comes the messenger."

A herald in the livery of Salador was accompanied by two guards, one carrying a white banner. Reaching the walls, the herald cried out, "I bring terms!"

Geoffrey looked at Jim, who nodded, and stepped forward to present himself to the view of the herald while Jim hung back out of sight. "Terms?" he shouted down. "The only terms that are acceptable are for your master to cease this unlawful assault on my sovereign lord's city, and get himself hence to his own lands without further ado. Moreover, your master should stop committing further base felonies against the lands, chattel, and people of Silden, for which he must answer to His Highness, Prince Edward of Krondor."

"That should do it," said Jim.

"My lord Arthur, Duke of Salador, does act as bade by our lawful master, King Oliver. Open the gates and no one shall be harmed, nor shall booty be taken, nor property seized or ravished. All lawful commerce may recommence, and as long as the peace is kept, no retribution shall be taken."

"Retribution for what?" muttered Jim. "Not opening the gates before they got here?"

"Resist," continued the herald, "and no man, woman, or child shall be spared the sword. Every building shall be sacked, and all goods confiscated."

"Nasty," said Jim. "Sounds like a Keshian Dog Soldier general."

"I know that's for the benefit of those soldiers on the wall who can hear him. He sacks Silden and Oliver will hang him." Geoffrey hiked his thumb over his shoulder to the men on the palisades and added, "But they don't know that."

"Time to give him an answer," suggested Jim.

Shouting, Geoffrey replied, "We shall not yield!" He

turned to a raised platform on top of the barbican over the main gate of the city and shouted, "Loose!"

A huge trebuchet hidden from view behind and to the right of the gate unleashed a massive rock, which sped overhead and crashed into a line of Salador soldiers within ten yards of the Duke's pavilion.

"Nice," said Jim. "That will buy you an hour as Arthur moves his personal residence farther behind the lines." He glanced at the sky. It was perhaps half an hour after sunrise. "Expect the full attack before noon."

"I agree," said Geoffrey. "How long before we will be relieved?"

"I wish I could guarantee a time," answered Jim, "but there are other parts to this that need be in place and I have no control over the time. But if everything goes according to plan, expect a ship flying a huge green banner sailing into sight within two weeks. Can you hold?"

Geoffrey smiled. "If they're not very good, we can hold for two weeks, maybe longer."

"Salador hasn't endured a war on its doorstep in two generations. Arthur has never fought in a battle, let alone supervised one. And the gods watch over fools." Jim put his hand on Geoffrey's shoulder. "Two weeks, and with the gods' blessing, not one hour more," said Jim. Then he hurried from the ramparts. As far as Geoffrey knew, Jim Dasher was the Crown's agent, on his way to mount a fast horse to Bas-Tyra. But Jim planned on traveling much faster than that.

Once he was out of sight, Jim took out the Tsurani travel orb Ruffio had given him and toggled it. He was instantly inside his own quarters in the palace at Rillanon, and moved to the door.

Sentries had been posted outside, and they came to attention. "I need you no longer," he said. "Dismissed." They saluted and moved smartly down the hallway. He had stationed pairs of guards on four-hour rotations instructed to let no one disturb him except for his grandfather—who wouldn't—two days before. He hadn't been in the room, but none of the guards who had stood post knew that.

Jim hurried to his grandfather's quarters to let him know that the siege of Silden had commenced. He had a plan, one that if successful could keep the Kingdom of the Isles from tearing itself apart. Jim was no idealist, and by no means viewed his nation as any sort of paragon of human governance, but he knew it was the best this world had ever seen. And he would die before he would see the Kingdom of the Isles reduced to a nest of petty monarchies like those in the Eastern Kingdoms.

There were two great powers for progress on Midkemia, in Jim's mind: Roldem, which had raised the arts to the level of honors previously reserved for rich nobility. The other was the Isles, where the rights of the common man were held as unquestioned.

Yes, those rights were often abused or ignored, but in no other nation did a commoner have the legal right to petition the King. It was a fragile concept, this Great Freedom, as it was called, this idea that no matter what their station in life, each person had a basic right to personal freedom, but it was unique to the Kingdom of the Isles, and it was something for which Jim Dasher Jamison would risk his life on a near-daily basis.

Jim reached his grandfather's quarters and looked inquiringly at the guard on the door. "He's awake, sir," said the guard.

Jim knocked once and, when he heard his grandfather's voice, entered. The old Duke looked his age and more. He was pale and thinner than Jim ever remembered seeing. Like every grown man and woman with elderly parents and grandparents, Jim knew he would eventually see them die— and Jim was no stranger to death, often as a result of his own direct action—but the reality of seeing the most powerful and unswerving man he'd ever known reduced to a pale echo of himself had struck him hard.

"What news?" said his grandfather without preamble.

"Salador is assaulting Silden, even as we speak, or will be as soon as Arthur moves his pavilion a little farther out of range of the trebuchet Geoffrey sneaked in behind the gates of the city."

"Geoffrey?"

"Du Gale, Duke Reginald of Silden's nephew?"

"Ah, that Geoffrey. For a moment I was concerned it was Geoffrey, Baron Montcorbier—that man's an idiot. I know du Gale. Smart lad. Has a future." He pushed himself away from his desk with a sigh. "Assuming any of us has a future."

Jim moved to assist his grandfather, who waved him away. "I need to get some proper clothes on, boy. Can't fight a war in my nightshirt."

Jim smiled and called for servants. They quickly attended to the old Duke, and when he was dressed, he beckoned his grandson to his side. "I've sent word to what's left of this family of ours."

There were several members of the Jamison family scattered around the Kingdom, although only Jim had taken service with his grandfather. Jim's father had chosen early in his life to go into business with traders to the Eastern Kingdoms, and Jim's cousin Richard had taken service in Krondor as a soldier, working his way up to being Prince Edward's Knight-Marshal, but there were more distant members of the clan, as his grandfather liked to call them.

"Richard will give his life for Edward, of that I have no doubt. But some of those others . . ." He sighed. "I made it clear they were to sit on their hands and do nothing to aid Oliver or his allies, else they'll answer to me."

"I'm sure they'll behave," said Jim.

"They'd better. If Oliver wins, anyone named Jamison will be fortunate to be left penniless and alive on the side of the road, because most of us will certainly hang."

"That should keep them in line."

"One can hope." The Duke sat down at the desk he had been using for more than thirty years. "Let's talk about something unpleasant."

"What?" asked Jim, with a smile that said, *As if the previous conversation was pleasant.*

"I'm going to die, boy."

Jim stayed silent.

"Maybe not today, or even tomorrow, and even if Oliver doesn't put my head on a pike outside this city's gate, sooner or later I'm going to be called to Lims-Kragma's halls. Here's the thing of it, Jim." He held up his hand as if swearing an oath. "As the gods are my witness, when I was young, when your great-uncle Dash and I were doing all manner of stupid things for our grandfather, I thought I'd live forever. Even when I was your age, I thought I had a century ahead of me. Now I realize that no matter how long you have, you will always leave things undone, tasks that will fall to others to complete or that will go unfinished."

Jim nodded. He had come to that realization early in life, perhaps because of his grandfather's delight in telling stories about his youth with his twin brother, Dash.

"It comes to this, Jim. You and Richard are the last two Jamisons to matter to the Crown. You've had the more difficult road, for too many reasons to recount. But do not believe for a moment your work has gone unnoticed or unappreciated. When this war is done, if we survive, and I am still alive, I will be stepping down. I need to move Montgomery aside and name another to my office. Edward will do as I ask, so if I ask him to name you Duke of Rillanon, he will."

"Name Bas-Tyra," said Jim evenly. "He's shown his loyalty when he saw through Chadwick's and Oliver's lies, and has four capable sons who can fill in where needed: we're going to need some new dukes if we win. I am not by nature a man to do what you do, Grandfather. I could not sit all day and read reports, endure state functions endlessly, or listen to the prattling of fools on trivial topics because it's required of me. I cannot do it."

"Bas-Tyra is a man for whom I have no small regard," said Lord James. "One of his ancestors was Duke of Rillanon, as well, so it's precedented."

Jim grinned. "You just hate seeing the title leave the family after all these years."

Lord James returned his grandson's smile. "Indeed. Jamison is a name that has earned its place in the annals of the Kingdom." He sighed. "Though your contributions are far less likely to be found in any volume in the royal library. You've had the most thankless of tasks, Jim." His voice lowered. "Jimmyhand." He looked out the window at the noon sun. "Mealtime soon; stay and eat with me." He returned his gaze to his grandson. "No one has given more, Jim. Don't think I don't recognize it. Other men would have succumbed years earlier to the need to remove themselves from your bloody work. Others would have gotten themselves killed or simply walked away."

"That has occurred to me from time to time," said Jim.

"No doubt. No wife, no children, nothing to live on after you."

"The Kingdom will live on after me," Jim answered quietly.

"My grandfather, already the legendary Jimmy the Hand by the time I was born, was the first Lord Jamison, first Duke of Krondor, then Duke of Rillanon, and perhaps the wiliest bastard in the history of the Kingdom. He was in love with the Kingdom, Jim. He was in love with Prince Arutha, the father he never had, with Princess Anita, the woman he idolized, with his wife, my grandmother, Gamina, conceivably the only person who ever truly knew his heart and loved him anyway, and he loved her beyond words for that."

Jim had heard endless stories of his great-great-grandfather, but he knew his grandfather was trying to make a point.

"But of all the things he loved—his friends, his family—he ended up loving the Kingdom more. He died for it, and let his wife die with him for it, and do you know why?"

"No, sir, I do not," answered Jim honestly.

"Because the Kingdom is an idea, an ideal. The first King had this notion that he was there to protect his people, and given how serious about duty the conDoins have been since then, it's become a family tradition, to uphold the greater good of every subject within its borders.

"Now, don't misunderstand me, Roldem is a lovely place. If I could just hand all of the Isles over to King Carole and let him take on the bother of ruling here, no one would likely notice much difference. And it would probably be the same under that boy of his . . ."

"Constantine," supplied Jim.

"Yes, that's the boy. He's got three, and I always seem to mix them up. But there's no Congress of Lords in Roldem, so if Constantine has a monster for a son, there's no one to keep him from getting the throne. Roldem's lords are too much concerned with their own well-being ever to think of what is good for the nation, which is why their politics can be even more bloody than ours. We need close ties with Roldem. We are descended from common ancestry after all, though the Roldemish deny it, of course, but we were sleeping with their daughters and they with ours when we were paddling around these islands in sewn-hide canoes, and everyone knows it. But Kesh? The Eastern Kingdoms?" He sighed. "No, if we let the Kingdom fall into Oliver's hands, we will one day end up like those, or even worse the city-states down in Novindus. So what choice have we?"

Jim smiled. Of all the people on this world, he perhaps loved his grandfather most of all. "None, of course."

"Exactly!" said the Duke.

"So what next?"

"We see if this mad plan of yours works."

"I don't see any alternative." He moved to sit next to his grandfather. "We're getting some odd reports from the West."

"What now?"

"Something to do with the elves up in the mountains east of Crydee."

Duke James waved his hand in a dismissive gesture. "Let the elves east of Crydee worry about it, then. You've studied as much history as I have, and we both know the only reason we have a duchy there is that it was a king's little brother who conquered that part of ancient Bosania, and that king in particular loved to tweak Great Kesh's nose. Not that I approved of their latest attempt to take it back without asking first, but the West has always been something of a drain on the Kingdom."

Jim nodded, though he knew that wasn't true. A common complaint in the politics of the Kingdom since the conquest of the Far Coast, it was never true. Crydee, the Sunset Islands, and Yabon were all self-sufficient, not costing the Kingdom a copper coin to administer, and moreover they paid a modest, but not trivial, tax every year. The meme was continued by Eastern Realm nobles as a means to keep Western Realm influence in court to a minimum.

"Where are you heading now?"

"To Bas-Tyra. Duke Charles needs to be informed of our progress, and then I need to get back to Edward."

"All with that magic thing?"

"I only wish," said Jim. "I can get here, to Krondor, and to Roldem in a moment, but if I'm to reach Prince Edward, it will be by fast horse unless there's an unoccupied magician handy who has the talent to move me with thought. I will be out of the harbor at sunset by fast sloop, up the coast, and across to Bas-Tyra. With luck I'll see their harbor in a week's time. After speaking with Charles, it's back to Roldem, then I'll drop in here to check up on you."

"Don't worry about me, my boy," said Lord James, patting a stack of papers. "I've got Montgomery in check, and if I don't drop dead before you get back, all will be well."

"It's on the way," said Jim.

With a dismissive wave of his hand, Lord James said, "I'll be fine. Go find yourself a magician. That fellow you huddle with at times, Ruffio? He was around yesterday for a bit."

"Ruffio?" wondered Jim. "What was he doing here?"

"Had something important to speak to you about, but seemed pressed for time. So he flew off, as he does." Lord

James narrowed his gaze. "I believe he left someone in his quarters with a message for you. Donato by name?"

Jim smiled. "I know the fellow. He'll do admirably. I'll go find him, then if King Carole can see me and give me what I need—"

"What is that?"

"There's a fast Roldemish messenger cutter in the harbor. If Carole will lend me its use, I can be back here for dinner with you, then be off with the morning tide on Carole's ship, and overtake Oliver's fleet before he turns to land north of Salador. I can reach Edward before Oliver even knows he doesn't hold either Silden or Salador." He kissed his grandfather on the cheek, a rare gesture of affection. "I haven't called you Grandpa in a very long while, but I love you, Grandpa."

The old man gripped his grandson with surprising strength. "I love you, too, Jimmyhand." He patted his Jim's shoulder. "Now go, and if no one else ever knows, remember your grandfather understands what you've given to that ideal, the Kingdom."

Finding himself feeling revitalized in no small way by his grandfather's words, Jim left his quarters and found his way down a series of back stairs and neglected hallways to a little-used exit where a horse waited for him. He nodded to the groom, one of his agents in the palace, and without word took the reins and mounted. He would head straight for the docks and by sunset he would be clear of the southern point of the harbor, and with a following wind, would be sailing to Bas-Tyra.

This was such a mad plan, he thought, and dependent on so many impossibilities. Still, he realized as he cantered down a backstreet from the palace toward the docks, nothing mattered if Geoffrey du Gale couldn't hold Silden for a week or two.

"Oil!" shouted Geoffrey du Gale as the first wave hit the base of the walls. While soldiers were pushing over scaling ladders with long poles, the defenders rushed forward with large pots of sticky oil, two men carrying each pot, and poured them over the wall onto the gathering men below.

"Torches!" he shouted, and the men below started screaming as the oil was fired by torches cast down from above.

Captain Armand Boucicault ran to his commander and said, "They're withdrawing."

Looking at the dying men in flames below and those racing away from the wall, pelted with arrows, Geoffrey said, "Duke Arthur feeds his militia and foreign mercenaries to the wall without thought of the cost."

"What cost, my lord?" asked the captain. "Each death is one less man to pay."

"But we lose men, and we spend arrows and oil."

"Shall I send men out to retrieve arrows?"

"After dark," said Geoffrey. "A squad of no more than a dozen men, dressed in black, quietly. Each is to gather what he can easily carry and return. If Duke Reginald hadn't taken every fletcher in the city with him . . ." He shrugged. "We shall make do until relieved."

"You expect relief?" asked the captain.

"I expect another attack," answered his commander. "Return to your position, Captain."

Geoffrey du Gale, Knight-Marshal of Silden, nephew to Duke Reginald, and by circumstance defender of the city, avoided feeling overwhelmed by his duties by the simple expedient of having too many things to think about, which gave him no time to worry. But his city had been surrounded for ten days now, and he gave thanks for the seeming incompetence of Duke Arthur of Salador. On three occasions the Saladorian forces had nearly breached the walls, only to withdraw at sunset. It seemed as if Arthur disliked the idea of fighting at night. They had endured three days of rain and Salador apparently also disliked fighting while wet. Whatever the cause, Geoffrey was glad for the time. He knew he needed to hold for a few more days before relief arrived. If it arrived.

He made quick rounds of the key defensive positions and assessed the damage done by the constantly hammering trebuchets of the enemy. The walls of Silden were ancient and had been built when this was the frontier of the Kingdom, when Salador was a trading village. There was a weak spot on the northeast side of the city where an ancient trading gate had been replaced when it became superfluous because of the larger eastern gate's creation during an expansion of the city. It had been bricked over and refaced with stone and few even knew of its existence, but Geoffrey worried about every detail. It was possible to move around the entire city of Silden on the ramparts of the walls, save for two places where one could only reach the barbicans over the massive western and eastern gates by descending a flight of steps and ascending another.

It took more than an hour to circumnavigate the entirety of the city's defenses if one was merely walking the route. To stop and inspect and discuss the situation with the commanders of each section took far more time.

When Geoffrey reached the sea gates he paused to ask the sergeant in command, "Anything?"

"No, sir," answered Sergeant Bales, a gnarled veteran who knew exactly what his commander wanted to know. "No sign of anything sailing up from the south."

Geoffrey removed his helmet and ran his hand through hair damp from the warm, muggy evening and his running like a maniac for the last hour. Here was the defensive position he worried over the most. The harbor had once been as heavily fortified as the rest of the city, but in years of peace defense had become an afterthought. Only the recent war with Kesh had made that shortcoming apparent, and it was only in the last few months that action had been taken to defend Silden by sea.

Catching his breath, he said, "We have depended on the fleet to keep us safe for too many years, Sergeant."

The old veteran nodded. "No argument from me, sir."

"Signal fires ready?"

"I make sure they're ready every five minutes," said Bales with an evil grin. "Annoys the men something fierce."

Geoffrey chuckled. "Which amuses you no end, I'm certain."

"A man must grab whatever tiny slice of happiness he can when he finds it, I always say."

Geoffrey didn't bother telling the sergeant to stay alert. There was no need. He had put Bales on this post because he was the most reliable sergeant in the garrison.

Each ship in the harbor had a man aboard whose only task was to watch where Bales now stood watch. If a powder was poured into a signal brazier, it would cause a huge crimson flame to erupt, bright enough to be seen at noon and producing a red plume of smoke. If that signal was sent, every man was ordered to scuttle the ship aboard which he waited, then jump into the sea and swim to shore.

Each ship carried a barrel of Quegan fire oil in her hold, which, once lit, would burn with a fire so hot the bottom of the ship would be holed within minutes, an hour at most. Quegan oil burned without air. Water spread it.

Each man aboard knew he risked his life, for in some cases that oil would explode before the man could win free of the ship, or even if he did, he might find himself swimming into flaming water.

The strategy was simple. Turn the harbor into a maze of burning hulks that no invading fleet could manage. Deny the docks to Salador's marines and let Duke Arthur continue to assault the walls. Buy Lord James of Rillanon and his grandson the time they said they needed in which to bring reinforcements, and hopefully to speed the end to this war.

Not for the first time since being placed in charge of the city's defenses, Geoffrey prayed to any god who would listen that Jim Dasher Jamison knew what he was talking about.

On the twelfth day, a messenger came running to the exhausted Knight-Marshal. The attacks by Salador's army

were unceasing, and by Geoffrey's estimation, both sides
were nearing breaking point. Jim Dasher's intelligence that
Arthur of Salador would not attempt a traditional siege, that
he had no time for it, proved accurate. He was attempting
an onslaught, he had ground down Silden's defenses, and he
was verging on success. The last two assaults had topped the
wall and only been beaten back by the sheer determination
of the city's commander and her defenders. One more such,
with a dozen ladders providing breach points, and Salador
would be in the city.

"Report," Geoffrey told the breathless youth.

"Captain Garton says there's a breach forming in the
northeast wall, sir. He's trying the best he can, but we've no
timbers to shore up the damage and a few more strikes from
the enemy's engines will hole the wall. Orders, sir?"

Geoffrey was already racing past the messenger, who
stood for a moment in surprise, then ran after the commander. He picked up two soldiers as escorts as he raced
along the wall. They cut across the western quarter of the
city, the guards clearing a way for him through the throngs
who huddled in the streets, seeking shelter where they could.

Reaching the wall, Geoffrey saw what Garton had reported. The captain saluted and said, "Must have been a
hidden flaw in the masonry, sir."

Geoffrey saw several stones bulging out of place, and
where other stones should have supported them there was
crushed rock and earth. "A quick fix of an old breach, I
think," he said to the captain. "We need to brace it."

"We have no timbers, sir. We've used every one long
enough to brace the gates. If we strip them away, the gates
are going to weaken."

Geoffrey's mind was numb from lack of sleep and the
stress of repulsing three breach attempts over the last two
days. He stood, looking around the city as if seeking inspiration. Down the central boulevard of the city he could see the
harbor. After a second, he said, "I want you to send runners
to every gate, and have them bring one timber here now.

Then send a crew into the harbor and start cutting down masts. A dozen of the stoutest you can find, and when they are done, bring them here!"

Captain Garton relayed the orders and said, "A good idea, sir."

"If Salador gives us enough time to use it." He saw his own exhaustion reflected in Captain Garton's face. "If this breach fails, I want every other man off the wall and here." He pointed to a choke point in the street behind him. "Shield wall with archers on the roofs above. If they get inside the wall and we don't break them here, the city falls."

He pointed first one way then the other. "Have the men start building barricades at the corners of those buildings; if Salador breaches here, I want them funneled into this street here and under the fire of the archers. If they spread out, the city falls."

He glanced around and said, "And find some more arrows. If the archers have nothing to shoot, the city falls."

Garton said, "Boys are out gleaning for arrows now, sir."

"How are they getting in and out?"

"We have a rope over the wall on the east side. No enemy watching there and the boys fill a bucket and we pull it up. The boys have orders to flee to the bay and dive in if they see enemies. They can swim over the harbor chain and get back into the city through the harbor gate."

"Good plan," said du Gale. "Now let us see if we can hold out for two more days."

"Two more?" asked Garton.

"I was promised relief would be here in no more than two weeks. That is two days hence."

The exhausted commander saw things were relatively quiet as Salador was retreating from the wall, no doubt to resume its relentless pounding with stones from its siege engines. "I'll be in my quarters."

"Get some sleep, sir. We'll keep the city safe for you."

"Thank you, Garton."

Knight-Marshal Geoffrey du Gale made his way back to

the bakery that had been converted to a makeshift command post. He motioned his aide away and fell face-first across the small bed in the back, next to the cold ovens. In his full armor with his sword and scabbard splayed out to one side, the Knight-Marshal of Silden was sound asleep in seconds.

Geoffrey awoke with a start as his aide shook him. "The attack is resuming, my lord!"

"What's the time?"

"It's dawn, sir. You slept all night. I managed to get your sword and boots off, but . . ."

Du Gale sat up and motioned for his boots, which he put on. He had cotton in his head and his eyes felt as if he had sand behind his lids, but the sounds of battle were rising, so he dressed quickly and was out the door. Hurrying to the failing breach, he saw that his orders had been carried out and a dozen new timbers had been set to brace the failing wall. A massive shudder caused rock dust to fly off the back of the wall as a boulder struck the other side.

Captain Garton saluted and said, "It seems their engineers have noticed the failing wall here, as well, sir."

"How long can we hold here?"

"Perhaps until midday if they keep pounding."

Geoffrey hurried to the nearest stairway up to the wall, taking the stone steps two at a time. He reached a vantage point, noticed three trebuchets on top of a hillside half a mile away, and saw them unleash their rocks. The first landed short and bounced into the wall, most of its momentum eaten by the damp soil, and the second sent a boulder hurling over the wall, to crash into a building a short distance away, causing screams of pain and fear to erupt. When the third boulder struck within yards of the weak point, Geoffrey turned to Garton, who had followed him.

"I want those barricades finished."

"Almost finished, sir," answered the captain.

"Form up a flying company and place them at the other end of the street, near the harbor, so they are out of reach of those damned stones. If the enemy breaches, I want our men to hit the invaders hard and fast until we can pull more men from the wall." He pointed to the choke point he had indicated the previous day. "We will take a stand there if we must."

"Understood, sir," said Garton, running off to carry out his orders.

Geoffrey looked at the three massive war engines and wished he could sally out with a company and burn them . . . Might as well wish for an extra two hundred heavy cavalry while he was at it.

He turned and gazed out over the city and the harbor beyond. One more day, he thought, and help will arrive. He rejected any thought that Jim Dasher would not live up to his promise, for in that event, Silden would die.

Geoffrey felt his stomach knot as he saw two more trebuchets being moved into place next to the three already there. He could tell from the sounds in the city that the attacks on the western and northwestern walls had ceased. Garton was right, Salador's engineers had seen signs of the failing wall and had interpreted them correctly. They were now shifting their attack to the northeastern section of the city.

Geoffrey judged it would be two more hours before the oxen pulling those heavy machines of war into place would get them situated, their crews get them locked down in place, and the intensified bombardment begin.

He hurried down to the street behind the wall, wishing there was a real bailey so that he could stop them at the wall. He might as well wish for those two hundred heavy horse again.

He motioned for a messenger, who came and saluted. He was a boy no older than eleven. "Orders to the wall. One man in two to stand down and find a place to rest. Rest for two hours. Then they're to report to Captain Garton down at the harbor end of this street. Is that clear?"

"One in two," repeated the boy so he was sure he got the orders right, "then rest for two hours, then report to Captain Garton at the harbor end of Broad Street, sir."

"Right. Now run off."

The boy would get word spread, and within two hours Geoffrey wanted as many men ready to come up that avenue as he could spare. He looked around and judged how better he could prepare the battleground, for here, he was certain, the fight would be determined, the outcome decided.

Throughout the day the five war engines cast massive stones at the wall, two out of five hitting close enough that the wall began to falter at sundown. Throughout the night the stones rained down and men died, and throughout the night Geoffrey du Gale kept his men ready. Five hundred soldiers waited at the far end of the boulevard, out of harm's way from misguided stones and shards of ricocheting rock and masonry. When it was clear that the wall was going to fail near dawn, Geoffrey ordered the remainder of his men off the battlements. He had the rested column brought up, ready to bolster the point of attack for the invaders. Two companies of men took positions behind the makeshift barricades, which du Gale had refortified constantly. Any man of Salador who rushed those overturned wagons and bags of sand would die before he cleared them, so the only point of attack was down Broad Street.

There a wall of shields and swords waited.

Suddenly the wall collapsed in a burst of masonry and dust, and stones came rolling in the streets. As the dust cleared, Geoffrey could see through the breach how soldiers from Salador were advancing.

Men died as those on nearby rooftops fired blindly through the clouds of dust and the defenders waited with weapons ready. Then abruptly, with shouted prayers to various gods and cries of victory, the breach was flooded with invaders.

Geoffrey cried, "Hold!"

Archers rained death down on the invading surge of the yellow-tabarded enemy as the men of Silden answered the insult done to their city. Battle was joined.

As a boy, Geoffrey had worked with his family's properties, one being a camp in the mountains to the north, where he worked a season as a woodcutter. They had a device, powered by a mule, much like a miller's grinding wheel, but instead of grinding grain, it shredded wood, branches, and small saplings, reducing them to chips and pulp to be used by the paper makers. This struggle reminded him of feeding a branch into that shredder.

The men of Salador hurled themselves bravely through the gap, to be greeted by a fusillade of arrows. With their shields raised above their heads, most made it through, only to be confronted by a wall of shields and swords. Still they came.

And they died. The men of Silden responded with a vicious countercharge, pushing back the invaders, once, twice, three times, before Geoffrey realized they were at an impasse.

Then he heard the sound of a distant trumpet and the men of Salador withdrew.

From the rooftops came the shout of Captain Garton for a cease-fire, and Geoffrey turned to see an exhausted soldier behind him barely able to stay upright. "Stand down," he commanded, surprised at how hoarse his voice sounded in his own ears.

A boy appeared with water skins, one under each arm, and passed them around, only to vanish as another boy turned up. Geoffrey finally allowed himself to take a drink, finding himself so parched he was almost unable to let go of the skin as he gulped, but at last he released his hold and passed the skin to the next man.

He heard Captain Garton shout, "Herald approaching!"

Knight-Marshal Geoffrey du Gale walked toward the breach, having to make his way over the bodies of the fallen. Occasionally someone in the pile would groan or whimper and soldiers would instantly set about getting the wounded out from under the bodies of the dead.

There was an odd border between the bodies inside the wall and out, a rising portion of the wall's foundation, six inches high and six feet across. Geoffrey stepped up on it and found another carpet of dead men spread before him, mostly those wearing the tabard of Salador or mercenary auxiliaries, with only the occasional man of Silden who had fallen from the parapets above. There he waited. The two horsemen, the herald and the soldier with him carrying a white flag, pulled up about twenty yards away, as the horses were unwilling to step on the corpses. The herald shouted, "I seek your commander!"

Du Gale shouted back, "You have him. I am Knight-Marshal Geoffrey du Gale. What do you seek?"

"My lord Arthur, Duke of Salador, seeks parlay. Are you willing?"

Geoffrey glanced at his exhausted men up on the wall or massed behind the breach, then saw the huge Army of Salador to his right re-forming on the hill, and weighed his choices. His men needed respite, but that also gave Salador time to reorganize for the next attack.

He glanced skyward and tried to judge the time of day. It appeared to be midafternoon, but what hour he could not tell. Finally he said, "Very well. I shall come under a flag of truce to that tree!" He pointed to a lonely elm perched on the side of a hill to his left.

"My lord Arthur invites you to his pavilion, where you may speak in comfort and share a cup of wine."

"I thank His Grace for his hospitality, but I must decline. I have much to attend to here, so if he wishes to parlay, that's where we will meet. In one hour!"

The herald hesitated, then said, "Very well, my lord. I will carry your request to my duke."

The two horses turned and started back up the hill. Geoffrey returned to the breach, where he found Captain Garton waiting. "I'd have taken the wine, myself," said the captain.

"If things turn ugly, which I expect they will, I prefer a short sprint back to my men."

Garton inclined his head. "Just as well. I would prefer not to discover I'm in charge while you're held hostage."

"I thought of that. Truce? From a man who betrayed his oath to the Kingdom and makes war upon another Kingdom city?"

"These are ugly times, my lord," said Garton.

"Get men to clearing the dead. We have an hour or so, but I think we'll be fighting again before sundown. Feed and rest as many as you can . . . and pray."

"I've been praying since dawn."

Geoffrey decided to make an inspection of the other areas of the city, knowing that the truce would only last until he spoke to Duke Arthur. From that moment on, peace would be a fragile thing doomed to shatter; the only question was when.

An hour later Knight-Marshal Geoffrey du Gale rode out with a single companion, a cavalry corporal bearing a white flag of truce. As he trotted leisurely up the hill, he saw a pair of riders approaching downhill from the crest. The herald was the same, though this time he carried the white banner. At his side was a man whose flowing blond locks and ornate armor proclaimed him to be Arthur, Duke of Salador, and the vain dandy he was reputed to be. The armor was of polished steel with gold decoration at the shoulders and neck, and his helm rivaled that of the King's, complete with a golden plume.

Reaching the agreed-upon location, Geoffrey saluted. "My lord," he said in neutral tones.

"I'm here to offer terms, sir," said the Duke contemptuously.

"Your terms, sir?"

"You will surrender the city by nightfall. Your men will lay down their arms and muster upon the field over there." He waved vaguely in the direction of the field to the north of the western gate to the city. "All arms and armor are confiscated and all men of fighting age will be conscripted. All stores and goods are to be rendered up to my quartermaster."

"And in exchange?" asked du Gale.

"Why, I let your citizens live, of course. They may go where they wish, or stay under my governance, but they will be alive. Either way, Silden will be annexed to Salador and my edicts will be law. Resist, and every man under arms dies, and I will permit the sack of the city. The women and children left alive will wish they had not survived. Any further questions, sir?"

"I see," said Geoffrey, looking out over the city.

"You seem distracted, sir," said the Duke. "Have I your answer?"

Geoffrey rose up in his stirrups and stared at something in the harbor. A ship was sailing in, a large green banner snapping in the wind from the top of the mainmast.

He sat back down in his saddle. "My answer is to offer my own terms, my lord Duke."

"You're hardly in a position to offer terms," said Arthur with a sneer.

"I've bled your army, my lord, and your men are hungry, your mercenaries are demanding payment or booty, and time is on my side. If you come against us, we will grind you some more, and you know it, or we would not be having this conversation. Each hour you fail to take Silden is an hour closer to having a full-blown mutiny in your ranks. You expected a short battle and a quick surrender, so you did not come prepared for a full siege. If I may be frank, Your Grace, you were underprepared for this siege."

Before Arthur could voice umbrage, du Gale pressed on. "You may yet take Silden, but when you do you will have little left to call an army. Your men may sack, loot, rape, and kill, but you will not have enough of a force left to occupy and govern. Your mercenaries will be the first to desert and your remaining men will hole up during the night and only go where ordered during the day. In short, you will be here, but you will not rule."

The Duke's eyes widened: he did not expect to be spoken to in such a way.

"Here are *my* terms, Your Grace. You will lay down your arms and organize your forces to march back to Salador, where you will prepare to offer up your defense against the charge of treason against the person of Prince Edward and the Kingdom of the Isles."

"Preposterous!" shouted Arthur. "I was ready to offer you and your officers a special place in my new commands; you've acquitted yourselves admirably in defending this city, but I see you're intractable. Marshal, if you don't surrender at once, I shall see you in chains and you'll answer to the rightful King, Oliver."

"Well, my lord, that is likely to prove problematic. I will almost certainly be dead, and this city once it is sacked will provide you little protection, and it's a long journey back to Salador. Moreover, you won't enjoy what you find when you get home."

"What do you mean?"

"Your city's been taken, my lord. If you'd care to hold this truce for, say, another day or two, I believe you'll receive word that Lord Charles of Bas-Tyra arrived with the bulk of his army a few days ago and has seized your city in the name of Prince Edward." He glanced at the forces of Salador arrayed on the distant hillside. "I wonder how your lads will react to the news."

"You lie, sir!"

"I do not, Your Grace. You have three choices. Attack, surrender, or wait. May I suggest you wait. My lads are tired and could use a hot meal, and it would be a bother for them to have to round up and guard your army until they've rested a bit. When you receive word from home, let us speak again."

He turned his horse and rode back, leaving the Duke near speechless in his wake. Reaching the gates, he rode through and said to Garton, "What do we see?"

"Nothing. Their forces are just sitting there."

Hurrying back to the breach, he called up to the wall, "Are they moving?"

"Yes, Marshal, but not toward us: back to their camp."

With a grin, Geoffrey du Gale, Knight-Marshal of Silden, said to his senior captain, "Garton, feed the lads and tell them to get ready to oversee some prisoners."

"Prisoners?"

"Arthur has lost his city. That was a ship from Roldem flying that green banner. It means Salador belongs to Edward."

Some of the men nearby overheard that remark and started spreading the word. A cheer erupted and was picked up by the rest of the city's defenders.

"If you find Arthur trying to steal a boat down there, let him. He'll be trying to find a way to Rillanon and Oliver's protection, if he can. He knows that if he stays here, he's going to hang."

"What now, sir?"

"We wait."

At sundown two days later, a lone rider with a white flag approached, but not the herald. It was a sergeant in the tabard of Salador and he came to the main gate. Geoffrey came to the barbican above the gate and shouted down: "What word?"

"Sir," said the sergeant, "Lord Arthur has ridden off. He's taken the officers of noble birth and his personal guard, and he's heading east. I find myself commanding an army, but with no orders."

"What do you seek?"

"I see no good end to this battle, sir, and even if I pressed it, and we won, I have no idea what I would then do. I am but a common soldier, my lord, and my only concern is following orders—of which I have none—and the well-being of my men. As I now only have that concern, I petition you, sir, may we depart in peace?"

"What would you do?"

"Go home," he said sadly. "If my lord Duke abandons us,

we are defeated, even though we may hold advantage in the
field."

"You are no common soldier, Sergeant. May I know your
name?"

"Cribs, sir. Algernon Cribs."

"Wait until dawn and prepare for revolt: your mercenaries
won't be happy with being ordered to quit without booty. If
you will permit me, I'll pen a missive I would have you give
to whomever you find in charge of Salador, commending
your care for your men."

"That would be most kind, sir."

"Shall we agree the hostilities are past and free passage by
all is guaranteed?"

"It is agreeable to me, sir."

"Then I shall send you a messenger in the morning with
the letter and I think we shall meet again, Sergeant Algernon Cribs, I hope in happier circumstances."

"Good day to you, sir."

The rider headed back to his own lines, and finding himself relieved to the point of tears, Knight-Marshal Geoffrey
du Gale said, "Garton, see to the men. Feed them and rest
them, then let us bury our dead and the honored fallen of our
enemy, and see an end to this."

"The war is over?" asked Garton.

"Just our little bit of it, and we may find ourselves fighting again, but not today . . . and not tomorrow. Tomorrow
we mourn our losses and thank the gods for a kind king in
Roldem and as sneaky a bastard as ever lived in Jim Dasher."

Not being entirely sure what the Knight-Marshal meant
by the last remark, Captain Garton saluted and left his commander with his own thoughts as he stood alone on the barbican of the western gate of Silden, while below men began
to celebrate a victory that was a gift of circumstances in a
war no one in Silden had wanted.

Geoffrey gave himself a moment, then pushed down
rising emotions and gathered himself. There was a lot of
work ahead and it wouldn't get done on its own.

16

JOURNEY V

Miranda fell.

Magnus came over and helped her to her feet without floating into the air. "I had the same problem," he said.

"Where are we?" she asked. Then she caught sight of a very familiar figure. "Macros," she whispered.

Magnus nodded. "Not a . . . well, it appears he's who he looks to be."

Drinking in the vista of stars and galaxies, Miranda repeated her question. "Where are we?"

"On what appears to be a very large hunk of

rock hurtling through some unknown region of the universe. What air and gravity we have appears to have been provided for us by whoever brought us here."

Macros turned and a delighted expression crossed his face. "Miranda! How lovely to see you again." He gathered her in an embrace.

"I'm not Miranda," she said, disentangling herself from his grasp.

"I know," said Macros. "You are the demon Child, with my daughter's memories imprinted on you. But you're as close to my daughter as I'm likely to get for however long I'm permitted to continue this existence, so I'll make do. How I got here and why this tiny sliver of life was pulled from me I don't know, save that it is for a reason beings of great power consider important."

"I was with someone . . . the place I left . . ." She looked around. "The Fourth Circle, though maybe not . . ." Her voice fell away as she beheld the magnificence all around her. "With something called Piper."

Macros was silent for a long moment, as if listening to something, then said, "Ah, yes, Piper. She, or he, was a construct. A being sent to you to impart a lesson." He paused again, as if listening. He nodded, then said, "The others— Magnus, Pug, and Nakor—encountered people of note from their pasts, people they were inclined to listen to. I'm not entirely sure why, but people from Miranda's past would not have the same impact on you as people from their lives had on the others." With a rueful chuckle he said, "You are unique."

"I hate lessons," said Miranda.

"You always did," said Macros. "You were always conspiring to learn things your own way, until you needed me to show you how to do something." He looked at Magnus. "Did you know your mother, when she was about ten years of age, I believe it was, almost destroyed half a village when she summoned a fire elemental but hadn't continued to read the text where it explained how to control him?"

"No, I didn't," said Magnus, trying not to grin at Miranda's obvious discomfort. She might be a demon at heart, but her mind was becoming Miranda's so much that she was almost squirming with embarrassment. "Let's spare Magnus tales of my ill-spent youth, Father," she said archly, "and we'll also spare him tales of your profligacy with the trust of others."

"I don't mind, really," said Macros. "I have a feeling that my time alive is limited to my usefulness to those who are bringing us together. Anything to stretch out that time would be welcome."

"Why are we here?" asked Miranda, surveying the sprawling arc of heaven. She had been many places and seen many things in her human life, but she had never beheld a view such as this.

Gas clouds of a size beyond imagining sprawled in every direction, and pulsing points of light glowed from within them, as comets moved majestically around distant stars, their white plumes trailing away from them.

"It's magnificent, isn't it?" said Macros.

"It's huge," said Miranda. "I knew the universe was vast, but . . ."

Macros's eyes were alive with a surprise and wonder she had never seen in her father as he said, "This is only the beginning."

"Of what?"

"You'll see," he said, "as soon as the others arrive."

They waited.

Nakor stumbled out of the vortex, and when Magnus caught and steadied him, his expression was one of undiluted delight. "Macros!" He hurried over and touched his robe, looked into his eyes, and said, "The real one!"

Macros couldn't conceal his pleasure. "Nakor! Still cheating everyone you meet at cards?"

"Always," he replied, and they hugged.

Circumstances had involved both of them indirectly in each other's life in ways they hadn't suspected until events during the Serpent War had caused them finally to meet.

"I take it," said Nakor, "that none of this is random coincidence."

"I have much to share," said Macros. "Let us wait for Pug. But there is one thing I must tell you three that he can't be permitted to know." He looked from one to another, then said, "Pug believes his life will end soon. A crux is coming, a confluence of probability which none of you may survive. But the future is now unfixed, and whatever prophecy or foretelling that may have directed his behavior is almost certainly moot. However, he must not know that. He must believe he will sacrifice himself to save . . . everything."

"But why?" demanded Miranda. "It makes no sense."

"Actually," said Magnus, "it makes perfect sense."

Nakor nodded. "If he feels he has nothing to lose, he will fear nothing. If he believes this fight is personally hopeless, all his energy will be directed at saving everyone else."

Miranda began to look angry. "Hasn't he suffered enough?"

Macros said, "More than enough, but this is how it must be. When he is here and I . . ." He paused. "When he is here I'll continue this discussion, but you must agree."

Nakor and Magnus nodded while Miranda stood motionless before giving one curt nod.

For a long moment they stood staring out at the incredible ocean of stars and gas clouds, the impossible colors of space.

At last, Nakor said, "I met people."

All eyes turned to him. "First, I met Borric, back before he was King, when he was in Kesh and he and I first met. It was a strange conversation, and I'm still not sure I fully understand his meaning."

No one spoke.

"Then I met Jorna, on the day she first appeared at the traveling fair where I was working."

Macros's expression turned solemn but Miranda's showed

barely contained anger. Nakor's wife, Jorna, had taken all she had learned from Nakor and left him. Then, later, she had spent years with Macros, conceiving Miranda during that time, finally running off, leaving the little girl with a father incapable of raising her. Not suspecting until later the powers his daughter possessed, Macros had given her up to another family to raise, returning for her only when her powers manifested themselves. Their relationship had been rocky at best, hostile at times, and never close in any meaningful way. Miranda had come to terms with that early on in her life, and had managed to forge her own life on her own terms after that.

Still, the demon within Miranda found conflicting emotions welling up inside her. Mention of Miranda's mother produced an unexpected anger, and the part of her that was Child realized that while Macros may have been a poor excuse for a father, Jorna had been no mother at all. Child felt as if Miranda was about to completely consume her, ridding her for all time of her demon heritage, and now she fought to maintain a shred of identity within the complex dual being she had become. Demon rage was at its heart simple. Child's mother had taught her the beginning of the concept of love through her willing self-sacrifice, but the sea of tumultuous feelings through which she swam was far more than any demon was capable of dealing with, and Miranda began to understand something.

Miranda had encountered her mother for the first time as an adult, and the thing that stood out most starkly was that the woman did not for an instant recognize her. Circumstances over the years had caused their paths to cross. Now, years after her mother's destruction at the hands of the demon Jakan, Miranda still found herself angry.

Softly she asked Nakor, "What did you learn from that encounter?"

"I'm not certain about that either, save that men can do very stupid things because they believe themselves to be in love." He shrugged. "But I knew that before I met her."

Macros nodded. "She had an ability . . ." He let the words go, then started again. "One of her talents was to make a man think he was the most important thing in her life, no matter how improbable that might be to an onlooker."

Nakor nodded. "That was true."

"Still," said Magnus. "We were confronted by things from our past that were in some measure getting us ready for what? This?" He waved his hand.

"This is only the beginning," said Macros again.

Miranda looked at Nakor and said, "I know why we"—she indicated herself and Nakor—". . . why we're here."

"Why?" asked Nakor.

"I saw . . . I'll share details after Pug arrives, but this one thing: Child and Belog could never see what we are seeing, are going to see, have seen, however you want to think of it. We could not see through human eyes. Miranda and Nakor could never see through demon eyes. My lesson was about perspective, the need to look at things differently."

"Fascinating," said Nakor.

Magnus said, "It never occurred to me, but now that you say this, I realize how true it is; you two have a unique view."

Time passed, then suddenly the vortex appeared, and a moment later Pug came stumbling out, to be caught by Nakor and Magnus. Miranda could barely constrain herself from throwing her arms around his neck, satisfying herself by gently squeezing his arm.

Pug looked around and his eyes widened, "Macros?"

Nakor said, "The real one. Not the guide we met on the beach."

"Hello, Pug," said the original Black Sorcerer. He turned and stood looking up at the massive display. "I have been watching for hours, and as I need to understand things, they come to me. There is so much to tell."

"Why are we here?" asked Pug.

"Each of you has been provided instruction, or at least reminders of things you already knew, but perhaps overlooked," said Macros.

"There is an agency so vast and powerful it defies logic." He paused. "You will discover much in the time we spend together, but realize that the full truth will never be revealed, for two reasons. First, some truths cannot simply be taught but have to be learned, sometimes through bitter experience." He glanced at Miranda sadly. "Other things are simply beyond understanding. Much of what I'm about to show you will illustrate that truth." He looked at Pug. "Let's begin with you. Where were you before you got here?"

"I had an encounter with my first teacher, Kulgan," answered Pug. "In a cottage very much like the one he had in Crydee."

"What did he teach you?" asked Nakor.

"When in doubt, return to the fundamentals."

Nakor glanced at Miranda. "That everything is a function of perspective."

They looked at Magnus. "That being fearful of risk guarantees failure."

Nakor grinned. "I learned a thing or two, but I'm not sure which thing or two. They will come to me." Looking at Macros, he asked, "What now?"

Macros smiled and said, "Now we begin."

The planetoid moved, or the universe moved around it, for apparent motion was relative. Macros spoke in hushed, almost reverential tones. "This thing we call a universe is vast beyond imagining." He waved his hand in an arc, across the star-studded dark. "We see only the tiniest part of it."

He turned to the four of them. "You've all trodden on alien worlds, walked the Hall of Worlds, and dwelled in different realms of existence. Yet while you four are no doubt the most traveled individuals in the history of Midkemia, the distances you've traveled are but the tiny steps of a baby walking compared to a striding giant who is traversing uncountable times around that world. Less even . . ." He sighed. "There is no comparison."

He waved a hand and suddenly they were somewhere else. Across the sky above them a thing of incredible power pulsed, emitting massive streams of energy out of the apparent north and south poles while a tiny white-hot speck burned at its core. A dark shroud of what might have been dust or gas or millions of planets was dwarfed to mote size by the distance; it was impossible to judge. Macros pointed. "We are farther from that star by a thousand times a thousand times the distance from Midkemia to her sun. If you were standing a trillion miles above either pole, the energy it generates would kill you instantly. This is one of the most massive things in the universe, an engine of creation, if you will. The furnace within that pulsing star is forging . . . everything." He held out his hand. "We are formed of the same energy and matter created in such a place, for in some future era it will explode, and matter and energy will be scattered across the vastness." He pointed at the massive, pulsing star. "And there are billions of them out there. Billions."

"This is humbling," said Magnus.

"It is not supposed to be," said Macros. "It is the start of showing you how important your journey is, and how countless lives and places beyond your imagining are in your hands."

"What do you mean?" asked Miranda.

"Everything we are about to see, all we learn, is to prepare us all for the final battle," said Macros.

"Us?" asked Pug.

"As much as I am permitted," said Macros. "The tiny slice of my life was preserved, but so much more has been granted me than I imagined when I was alive."

Nakor laughed. "It's so very odd to speak of yourself in the past tense."

"It's even more odd to live in the past tense, I can promise you," answered the Black Sorcerer.

Miranda looked at the monstrous thing hanging above them in the sky. "I am looking at this thing, this star, but my mind rejects it."

"We five may possess the most prodigious intellects when it comes to magic of any who have ever lived on Midkemia. Yet we know hardly anything."

Macros waved his arm and suddenly they were somewhere else.

A magnificent vista of glowing, swirling gas surrounded them. Inside it, they could see spots of light with swirling currents of energy slowly being gathered into them. "A heavenly crèche," said Macros. "A sea of gas and dust so vast no human mind can encompass it. Were I to count the grains of sand on a beach, one grain a second, it would take me thirteen days to count one million. To reach a billion would take me thirty-one years. And here, in this sea of gas and dust, are billions upon billions of billions of grains of sand to count."

"Impossible," said Magnus.

"The scope of reality is beyond the capacity of mortal mind to fully comprehend. We can only imagine bits, or create metaphors or develop abstractions to help us cope, but no matter what we imagine we have achieved in understanding all this, in truth we know nothing."

They watched in silence as slowly gas wound its way inward, spiraling into the birthing stars. At last Macros said, "Billions of miles of dust, falling inward, and in time a few grains combine, attracting more grains, and eventually there is a bit of something bigger than the grains, and more fall in, and gravity exerts itself, and even more dust and gas fall in, and that creates pressure, and eventually there is so much pressure that energy is released, creating—"

"Stars," said Magnus. "We're watching the birth of suns."

"This magnificent sea of stars," said Macros, and the scene changed. Now bright lights died in the sea of gas and dust, shrouded as if covered by a veil of soot or a thin curtain of dark gauze. "This dust nebula is where suns, like Midkemia's own, are born. This is just one of millions of such places throughout the universe."

"But the time it takes to create this . . ." began Miranda.

"Time is an illusion," said Macros. He pointed to Pug. "We learned that when we traveled back in time. Or at least that was our first lesson."

"Time is an illusion?" asked Nakor.

"Not yet," said Macros, acting like a performer onstage at a fair determined to let the play unfold at its predetermined pace. He waved his hand and it appeared as if the swirling gas increased its speed, moving faster and faster as the suns grew brighter. "As the dust falls in, the space between the stars grows more empty. Or at least it appears to be."

"What is the point to this, Fa—" Miranda cut herself off. "Macros?"

He smiled. "Either will do." The brightening stars grew more intense and robust and began to change colors. "Red, blue, yellow, white, tiny, massive beyond measure, so many types of stars," he said. "And like that giant, pulsing star, just within this nebula are entire galaxies being formed."

"Why are you showing this to us?" asked Magnus. "It's absolutely breathtaking and worth viewing for the beauty of it alone, but what is your purpose?"

"To help you understand the stakes of this cosmic game," said Macros. "It's why powers beyond the Midkemian gods are acting and why you four are standing with me now: because if we fail in the coming struggle, this goes away."

"Goes away?" asked Pug.

"All of it, the stars, the worlds, every tick of life on the smallest dust mote floating around the tiniest star in the farthest reaches of the universe, it all ceases to exist.

"It's not just the end of the world," said Macros grimly, "it's the end of everything."

After a moment Pug said, "What do we do?"

"Now we start the lessons," said Macros.

The sky around them suddenly turned dark and brooding, gas clouds still, but now dirty gray and brown. A few illuminated specks of light in the distance gave a sense of dimension and shape, but otherwise it was a cold and lonely place.

"This is how stars are supposed to end," said Macros.

"Some just wither and die, like a candle flickering out, while others explode in a violence so self-consuming that all that remains is hot gas spreading out at unfathomable speed. For aeons it drifts, and in some impossible future it will gather again and start its progression to rebirth."

With a wave of his hand, the sky changed again.

"The Fourth Circle," said Miranda.

Pug nodded.

"But Piper said it was ending."

"This is how a portion of the universe died at the hands of the Dread, and this is what will happen to most of it before they achieve their goals," said Macros.

"What are their goals?" asked Pug. "I've wondered for years."

"All in time," said Macros. "First, this."

He waved his hand again and the scene changed once more.

"The stars look different," said Nakor.

Macros laughed. "Look closer. Those aren't just stars."

A dot of light expanded as if they were swooping toward it, and as it grew larger they saw it take on the shape of a swirling mass of lights. "It's a galaxy!" said Magnus.

"Each of those lights," said Macros, pointing outward, "is a galaxy. Billions of them, and within those galaxies, billions of stars, and around many of those stars, planets like Midkemia, complete with life."

"Now I know why the Hall of Worlds seems endless," said Miranda.

"Because it is," said Macros. "Honest John's is an anomaly, a place within the Hall but not of it, so it serves as something of a starting point, the center of the Hall, as it were. But the Hall itself has no beginning or end."

"Because stars are constantly being born, which means planets are being born as well," said Magnus.

"Yes," said Macros, pleased someone else made the point. "So doors arise as worlds are born, and vanish when the world they're linked with dies."

"You've made the point," said Miranda, her impatience surfacing. "The universe is a vast place. Could we discuss the end of everything you're warning us of?"

"This is where it gets tricky," said Macros. "Because as vast as the universe is . . ." He waved his hand.

"The Garden!" said Pug.

"Where we—you, I, and Tomas—watched creation."

"You witnessed creation?" asked Nakor.

"A metaphor," said Macros, "because the next step on the journey concerns perception." He looked at Miranda.

"What Piper showed me," said Miranda. "Perspective."

"There are things outside our perceptions, things we cannot see, hear, feel, smell, or taste, things we can only infer and speculate about. Here Tomas, Pug, and I were trapped in a time-reversal spell of inordinate power." Macros smiled at the memory. "And a very pleasant dragon was with us, I almost forgot."

"Ryath," said Pug. "She was very pleasant." Then his eyes widened and he said, "She flew us to *this* garden."

"Yes?" said Macros, tilting his head as if waiting to hear something else.

"Through rift space."

Macros nodded. "Dragons can fly through the Void."

Nakor said, "I never knew."

"Few do. Dragons don't think about it. They just do it. But because they can, we have one of the keys to saving the universe."

"What are the other keys?" asked Magnus.

"Come with me and find out," said Macros, waving his hand again.

Suddenly they rose up out of the Garden, an impossibly beautiful floating parkland, and started moving toward a growing image of buildings, walkways, palaces, and parks. The cityscape seemed to roll out before them as if unfolding itself little by little for them to assimilate.

They touched down in a massive but empty boulevard.

"The City Forever," said Pug.

17

NORTHLANDS

The brothers reined in their horses.

Neither Laromendis nor Gulamendis had ridden in their lives and their accelerated education had begun when the elves of Elvandar got them safely to their borders near the Lake of the Sky.

There was a trading post at the southern end of the lake where it emptied into the River Boundary, and from the first thaw of spring until the first snows of winter, it was relatively active. Dwarves from Stone Mountain to the north, elves from Elvandar, humans from Yabon to the southeast, and renegades who lived in the

Northlands, all traded at the post. Originally operated by a trader from Natal, it had changed hands and names several times—currently it was Bram's Post—but to everyone in the region it would always be Sky Post. There the elves from E'bar traded for two stout horses, tack, and trail goods. A man named Smiley gave the brothers a half day's instruction on the care and feeding of the animals. Fortunately the elven brothers had very good memories, because the man was loath to repeat himself and went through the subject of care and feeding quickly.

Still, the brothers did their best, and after two very uncomfortable days managed to get the hang of staying in the saddle, not being in constant pain, and keeping the animals going where they wanted them to go. They became adept at saddling and unsaddling, currycombing coats and picking hooves, though neither was entirely sure what they were looking for when they inspected the legs at the end of a long ride. Gulamendis finally decided that they should only concern themselves if something in the afternoon looked different than it had in the morning.

After riding for another four days, they reached the Inclindel Gap. Patrolled by a garrison out of Yabon, it had been neglected since the muster had taken most of the Yabonese fighting men south. A few Hadati villages nearby posed a threat for any Moredhel moving south in strength, but two lone horsemen, despite being very tall elves, hardly warranted a second glance.

After negotiating a ford north of Lake Isbandia, they found the route to the town of Harlech. Of the four towns in the Northlands, Harlech was the largest. Barely more than a large village by Kingdom standards, it was big enough to boast four inns, several stores, a bakery, and two blacksmiths.

A large sign was posted at the southern entrance to the town in half a dozen different scripts. Gulamendis reined in. "What do you think it says?"

Laromendis said, "Given our surroundings, I'm certain it's some sort of warning, telling us to behave ourselves in case we run afoul of whatever passes for the local constabulary here." He closed his eyes for a moment, then cast an enchantment.

"Ah," said his brother. "I forgot you could do that."

Suddenly the sign appeared to be written in the language of the Taredhel, repeated six times. Gulamendis read aloud, " 'Entering Harlech.' "

"I believe it's pronounced 'Har-leech.' "

"Leech, lech? What does it matter?" He resumed reading. " 'Entering Harlech. Cross the line and you are peace-bound. Breaking the peace will result in fine, imprisonment, slavery, or death. Town Council of Harlech.' "

"They're certainly generous in warning strangers," commented Laromendis.

They rode into the town. A group of Moredhel, leading pack animals, were obviously on their way out of town. Several cast a glance at the two Star Elves, but none acknowledged them. There were two humans working a forge and they paused in their labors to gawk, as no Taredhel had ever entered Harlech before.

A small band of odd-looking creatures stood in a knot at one corner, deep in discussion. They were poorly dressed in ragged tunics and trousers, but heavily armed. Their faces were roughly human- or elf-like, with two eyes, a nose and mouth, but their ears were pointed, their fang tips showed even when their mouths were closed, their faces were dominated by a heavy brow ridge, their hair was black and coarse, and their skin was a bluish-green. "Goblins," said Laromendis. "I've heard about them."

They rode until they found an inn with the sign of an animal painted bright silver hanging over the entrance. "This must be the Silver Otter," said Gulamendis.

Neither of them had ever seen an otter, but the likelihood of two taverns in the town having silver animals on their signs was remote.

The inn was crowded. Gulamendis and Laromendis entered the room, shaking off the dust of the long ride. A dozen humans and two dwarves occupied the four tables, so the two Star Elves crossed to the bar. The barman was a scarred, heavyset man holding a heavy cudgel, appearing ready for anything. "Something to drink?"

The door opened and a Moredhel warrior entered the inn, looked around, and went to the far end of the bar.

Uncertain as to what to say, Gulamendis nodded. "Yes."

"What?" asked the barman.

"I said, yes, I'd like something to drink."

"I mean, what do you want to drink?"

"Oh." Gulamendis looked at his brother. "What are we drinking?"

"Wine?"

"Don't have any," said the bartender. "Word is all the wine from the south has been bought up, so we got ale and spirits."

"Ale, then," said Laromendis.

A few moments later two large pewter jacks of ale were put on the bar. "Ten coppers," said the barman.

The brothers exchanged looks. They had spent all their gold on the two horses, certain they were being taken advantage of by the trader at the Sky Post, but as the elves with them also had little experience with Kingdom coin, they had paid his price. Laromendis nodded, closed his eyes, and moved his fingers across the bar. The barman scooped up something, dumped it in his pouch, and moved off. The brothers drank and Laromendis said, "This is good."

"Yes," agreed his brother.

The Moredhel who had been standing quietly at the end of the bar moved down to stand beside them and said something in a language neither understood. Seeing incomprehension on their faces, he switched to another dialect of the elven language. "Forgive me, but I'm not used to speaking to outlanders. I said, you'd better drink up before the barman realizes his purse is light ten coppers."

"You saw that?" asked Gulamendis.

Nodding, the Moredhel said, "I was sent to find you."

"Us?"

"Unless there are more of the Star People wandering around Harlech, then yes, I was sent to find you two."

"By whom?" asked Laromendis.

"My clan leader. I am Chovech of the Hamandien, a Snow Leopard. My leader is Liallan. She sent me here a week ago. I was told to wait until two of the Taredhel arrived in Harlech, then to bring them to her camp."

"How did she know we were coming?"

"She is Liallan." Chovech inclined his head toward the barman, who was hefting his pouch. "Come."

They followed him outside and saw that a third horse had been tied next to theirs. "Follow," said Chovech. "Our camp is just a few days north of here."

The brothers remounted and exchanged a look that said they feared they would never again sleep in a bed.

Three days they rode, past cascading waters from the hills, up into the forested foothills north of the grasslands, then into the thicker growth that abounded at the foot of the peaks known simply as the Great Northern Mountains. While the Taredhel could be considered reticent by human standards, the Moredhel guide was close to being a mute. He ignored the brothers as they shared their wonder at discovering new things wherever they looked.

Laromendis had visited Midkemia as an advance scout for his people and had been the one to identify it as the ancient home of the elves, so he had traveled within the Kingdom and to the cities of men. Even so, much of what he saw struck him with wonder.

After a generation of fighting demons across the stars, watching entire planets destroyed by magic, steel, and fire, the sight of the pristine beauty of the Northlands moved both brothers. The only other time they had felt this awe had been on their visits to Elvandar, but here was a different kind of wonder, nature without even the elves' touch. They marveled at majestic elk and herds of deer, a massive brown bear, and in the distance, sunning himself on a rock one afternoon, a northern lion, his copper-red mane looking like flame in the sun. The eagles and hawks that soared overhead were icons of freedom and beauty.

The third night, they found a camp of Moredhel, a band of hunters from a clan Chovech called Thunder Buffalo, who offered them a place at their fire. Like Chovech, these Dark Elves were taciturn around strangers, though they did appear curious about their distant cousins from the stars. Chovech spoke little, but occasionally he would volunteer an observation. Before going to sleep the third night, he said, "They're curious how two men, so big and apparently powerful, have delicate hands like women."

The brothers took the remark in silence, glancing at each other. Just before falling asleep, Laromendis whispered, "Well, we are among primitives."

The fourth day found them arriving at a recently erected palisade of wood. "Here we are," said Chovech, leading them through the gate. "The Hamandien. We are the Snow Leopards."

The brothers were impressed by the size of the community. There were easily fifty tents behind the palisade. A very large tent of stitched hides stood in a small clearing, and before it was a forge where a smith was working iron.

"Where is Liallan?"

Chovech pointed up a gully where a rough path had been pounded out by horses' hooves. "That way. You ride for maybe half a day, then if you get lost, ask."

The guide obviously saw his work as finished, so the brothers started up the gully. When they reached the peak, they stopped. "Gods of the stars," said Gulamendis.

"Indeed," said his brother.

Arrayed below in a shallow valley were at least three hundred more tents. "There's a lot of them, aren't there?"

"This is one clan?" asked Laromendis.

"I don't think we'll have trouble finding this Liallan," said Gulamendis, pointing to a huge pavilion on a rise overlooking the camp.

His brother nodded and they set off.

The ride would have been shorter had there been a direct route, but it was nearly sundown before they arrived before Liallan's pavilion. When they reined in before it, a pair of guards looked at them with an unspoken question.

"I think we are expected," said Gulamendis. They dismounted.

One of the guards vanished inside and returned five minutes later. He held open a large flap and they entered. The pavilion was sprawling, several big tents placed together and divided one from another by curtains. The exterior was like the rest, made of overlapping leather hides fitted around the tent poles, but the interior was opulent to the tastes of a Taredhel. Beneath their feet were colorful woolen rugs and heavy furs to keep the chill of the ground below at bay.

A woman stood waiting, and both brothers recognized the authority with which she carried herself. They were forced to crouch slightly, given their height, but they executed full bows before the mistress of the Snow Leopards.

"Welcome," she said in a voice that was soft and melodic.

She motioned for them to sit and she sat in one elegant motion. The brothers glanced at each other. This woman was no primitive. She would have blended in with the most murderous politics of the Regent's Meet, if it still existed.

"Your coming was foretold," she said. A pair of servants, young Moredhel women, appeared and trays of food were placed before the brothers. Prince Calin had told them of Moredhel hospitality, so each took a delicacy from the trays and ate. It was a welcoming gesture that guaranteed their safety so long as they were under Liallan's roof.

"Then you know our reason for being here?" asked Laromendis.

"No," answered Liallan. All elves looked young until the last forty or fifty years of their life, so she was obviously old by elven standards, for there were tiny lines around her eyes and the edges of her mouth. Her raven hair had a hint of gray at the temples, but her body still looked slender and fit in her red woolen trousers, blouse of fine cream silk, and black leather vest. Both brothers drew the same conclusion: that she could at will be stunningly seductive or efficiently murderous. She smiled and said, "I only knew you were coming. Now, tell me why."

Laromendis said, "I will assume you know how we came back to this world, and about our city. Should you need more detail, I will answer your questions, but for the moment let me begin with the night we found we were betrayed." He took a breath, as if to focus his thoughts on painful memories. "We were sleeping when Tanderae, the Loremaster of the Clans of the Seven Stars, woke us and told us to follow him. We dressed quickly and left our quarters, hurrying to the main complex of the Regent's Meet and the portal room. When we got there three soldiers were waiting for us: the captain of the Sentinels, Egun, and two of his soldiers. To both of us, as well as the two Sentinels with the captain, Tanderae said, 'The captain and I witnessed something . . . unbelievable, but we need you to believe us.'

"One of the soldiers said, 'Whatever the captain says will be true,' and his companion nodded. That is when Tanderae told us that the Regent Lord had summoned a creature, something from the Forbidden, within the portal room."

"The Forbidden?" asked Liallan.

"All that is known by only the most trusted Loremasters and . . ."—Gulamendis glanced at his brother—"a few others about the time before the Taredhel left Midkemia during the Ancient Ones' war against the gods that the humans call the Chaos Wars."

Liallan nodded. "The knowledge of the Ancient Ones is closely guarded . . . Yes, I understand. Say on."

Laromendis picked up the narrative: "We knew enough of the ancient lore to realize the implications. The two soldiers only knew that the Forbidden was an area of history denied to the Clans of the Seven Stars by Regents' edict since the departure from this world, but they instantly recognized there was something gravely wrong and deferred to Captain Egun's wisdom."

Gulamendis added, "Which we fervently hope will be the attitude of the rest of the Sentinels. The Lord Regent can muster some of the most powerful magic users among his Meet, but they are few in number. More of the magicians would be opposed to anything regarding the Forbidden, so the balance would teeter on where the Sentinels stand."

Laromendis nodded. "Tanderae said we would not be missed for a while, so we needed to depart that night for El-vandar. We were to tell Lord Tomas we needed him in E'bar to deal with the Regent. Understand that Tomas by his very existence was part of the Forbidden: he was the Forbidden manifest."

Gulamendis added, "I knew more of the Forbidden than any other elf besides the Loremaster, by dint of my mastery of demons, for all demon lore is considered part of the Forbidden. The only reason I am still alive is because my ability to summon, control, or destroy these infernal creatures was important in the war against the demons."

"I wouldn't let that be widely known," said Liallan. "Even among the shamans it's frowned upon." She smiled. "Place-your-head-on-a-pole frowned upon."

"Understood." Gulamendis continued: "Early on in the war, the demon summoners were blamed for the attacks, and were hunted down and put to death. The Circle of Light—a society of scholars that my brother and I were members of—objected and fell into disfavor with the Regent Lord. The organization's effectiveness was first blunted, then it was finally disbanded. Tanderae was very young when it was dissolved, as was Laromendis, and escaped the social stigma and political tarnish more established members had endured."

Laromendis nodded agreement. "But we were still re-garded with suspicion. Tanderae was the only one from the Circle to rise in importance, because he had a powerful mentor, his predecessor."

Gulamendis finished by saying, "A galasmancer named Ilderan transported us to a flag point, a magical marker left by scouts so galasmancers can create portals to a specific location to ensure no one is materialized inside a rock or twenty feet in the air."

Laromendis said, "I was that scout. I placed the point flags when I scouted to the north of that valley, upon first arrival. I made an almost complete circuit of the Bitter Sea when I first scouted for the Regent. So I knew the route to Elvandar, our first destination. We were an hour down the trail when we heard a faint booming noise, like very distant thunder. Then came a strange, shifting sensation, bordering on a moment of vertigo. So we climbed an outcrop that took us up to a rocky vantage point where no trees grew, and we saw, in the sky to the south, a red beacon of light shooting into the night sky."

"What was it?" asked Liallan.

"I had no idea until a human girl, Lady Bethany of Carse, arrived at Elvandar. She carried word from Tanderae as well as coming to find her mother, and others from Crydee who had fled the Keshians during their war.

"Tanderae's convinced the Lord Regent and his followers were all destroyed within the red dome after the monstrosity they'd summoned arrived in E'bar."

"A fitting end to traitors," suggested Liallan with a dismissive wave of her hand. "So you found the Elf Queen."

"Yes," said Laromendis. "We told our story to her and her consort and they pondered it."

"They pondered?" asked the leader of the Snow Leopards.

"Until Lady Bethany arrived," said Gulamendis, "bringing word from Tanderae. Then they acted, at once sending four of their spellweavers to aid the magicians in E'bar with more to follow."

Liallan turned her head and stared off into the distance for a moment. "How like them," she said. "They pondered.

They debated. They considered." She sighed. "They live in
a world where time doesn't pass and . . ." She let the words
fall away.

"So you discovered what that red light was?" she asked.

"A beacon, at least that's what Tanderae thought," Gulamendis replied. "What Lady Bethany had to say was disturbing, mostly because the descriptions are sketchy."

"Say on," commanded Liallan.

"Creatures of shadow escape from the bubble of light surrounding the city," said Laromendis. "Sentinels defend the
magic casters and eventually destroy these creatures, whatever they are. We know they are not demonic. We've fought
demons too long—"

"So these creatures . . . ?"

"In your lore, do you have the Forbidden?"

"If I understand your question, not the way you mean,"
said the leader of the Snow Leopards. "If you're speaking
of the Time Before, when we were in thrall to the Ancient
Ones? It's not Forbidden to speak of such things, but it's
frowned upon."

"Head-on-pole frowned upon?" asked Laromendis.

She nodded.

"In the Queen's Court," said Gulamendis, "a name was
given to us. Cetswaya."

Liallan tilted her head slightly, as if curious. "From whom
did you hear that name?"

"A spellweaver of the Eldar: Janil."

"Ah," said Liallan. "Continue."

"E'bar calls for magical help in battling these smoke-
and-shadow beings. The Queen of Elvandar had already
dispatched spellweavers. We were told you have powerful
shamans among your clans, including this Cetswaya."

"He is the shaman of the Ice Bears, my nephew Arkan's
clan."

"We have heard that name," said Laromendis.

"Arkan?"

"He was in Ylith with the Queen's son Calis."

"Really?" She fell silent. Then she told a servant, "Send for Arjuda."

The young Moredhel woman withdrew and Liallan asked, "So, my nephew?"

"We were told by Lady Bethany," said Gulamendis, "that he met Prince Calis in Ylith, and while the city was besieged he helped defend it from the Keshians."

"Killing humans is never a problem," quipped Liallan.

"I'm vague on the details," continued the demon master, "but Arkan was on some errand to find a human sorcerer, and Calis, who had carried messages for the Queen, decided to continue on with him. Lady Bethany said they departed together with a human woman and man."

Liallan sighed. "So many disturbing things . . ." She regarded the two Taredhel. "You from the stars, you have no idea of what you left behind." She leaned forward on her cushion. "You and I are descended from the same stock. We were closest to the Ancient Ones, our masters. The Queen of Elvandar descends from those who cared for this world, and their ties to the soil are the deepest. The Eldar were the librarians, the scholars, those who attempted to bring order out of the unending stream of loot and artifacts brought back to this world by our Dragon Lord masters. But we were the ones who served, who stood at their sides, who filled their beds, who endured their whims and wrath." She sat back. "And in the best and worst ways, we were the most like them. When the Chaos Wars erupted, and our masters flew to whatever fate waited for them, and we became a free people, you Star Elves vanished. You simply left." She looked from Gulamendis to Laromendis. "We stayed, while you fled."

The brothers exchanged glances. "We are taught that this world was in peril, balancing on the edge of destruction, and some among our people had the art of galasmancery, and opened a portal, escaping to a world unknown to the Ancient Ones."

Liallan said, "Thereby leaving the rest of us behind."

"We . . . we are not taught that way," said Gulamendis.

"I doubt you would be," Liallan said. "What's taking that old man so long?" She leaned forward to glance out the open entrance to her pavilion, then turned back to the two Taredhel. "What we began: the struggles, the clan rivalry, the brutality, all this was necessary. We forged a nation of warriors in blood and fire, and fought for supremacy with invaders from other worlds, the humans, dwarves, the orcs—"

"Orcs? We've heard no tales of them," said Gulamendis.

"We hunted them down and destroyed them utterly, as did the dwarves," said the ruler of the Snow Leopards. "Their lesser kin we let live as long as they ceased opposing us, so goblins are still around. We left the elves in Elvandar to themselves, until our own young heard the call of their Queen." She looked at the twins. "Our ties to this world are profound, for we are the first race after our masters to be born of this world. Those in Aglaranna's court are closest to those ties, so of course some would feel the tug.

"But we cannot allow it, for we are a free people and will never bend knee to that woman. Some of us sought to emulate our masters, and some were driven mad by their ambition. Others sought to isolate themselves in the forests of the south. Others across the sea were so isolated they became like the humans who surrounded them." She paused. "But things change. If we answer E'bar's call, we shall have a reckoning."

"What do you mean?" asked Laromendis.

"Your Lord Regent, in his arrogance, sent an envoy to instruct us as to how we must behave should any of our clans venture south of the River Boundary. He dictated to clans that occupied those hills and forests in the Green Heart for centuries while you were out flying among the stars. He said should they return home, they must bend knee to him."

"I suspect," said Gulamendis, "the Lord Regent will not be dictating conditions to anyone anymore. If what Tanderae says he saw was true, the Lord Regent, and most of his Meet, are already dead."

"Then we will deal with your new masters. Who will rule?"

"A new Meet," said Gulamendis. "Tanderae will probably be the next Lord Regent."

Further discussion was interrupted by the arrival of a very old man wearing a robe and a necklace of charms. "Mistress," he said, bowing.

"This is Arjuda, my shaman." She indicated that he should sit. "Now, tell him what you told me," she ordered, and the two brothers retold their story.

When they had finished, the shaman was silent for a very long time, then said, "I am troubled, Liallan. Of late I've had dreams, and there have been portents. I have consulted the smoke and looked into the waters."

"What did you see?" she asked.

"Time as we know it is ending and the new time will be forged by other hands if we do not act, but the risk is grave."

"How grave?"

"Our people, all our kin, no matter how changed or distant, all of us stand before an abyss. From within that abyss comes a darkness so profound that it could be the end of all of us."

Liallan was silent. Unlike some shamans, Arjuda was not given to theatrics or histrionics to add conviction to his foretelling. His skills were without question. Then she said, "Janil sent these two to find Cetswaya."

"Wise," said Arjuda. "He is among the very few I would place ahead of myself in understanding such things."

"Where abides Cetswaya?"

"To the north," answered the old shaman. "As his father, Arkan, commanded, Antesh has taken the Ice Bears into the icelands again, to await such a time as they are safe to return."

"Why do I think such a time may not come?" She rose. "Use your dream magic to summon Cetswaya and his clan south," she instructed Arjuda. "Can you do that?"

"I can try. Dream magic between Cetswaya and myself

has always been strong, but you'd do well to send a fast rider north to seek out the Ice Bears. They intend to enter the floes at the Black Ice Massive, on the shores of the frozen sea to the north of Sar-Sargoth. From there they will migrate east. The broken floes are thick with seal, walrus, and ice birds."

"I will send runners, for I think the shamans of the clans of the north must meet. Then we must plan to move south."

Laromendis said, "You'll aid us, then?"

"You sound surprised."

"I hoped, but didn't expect. Why?"

Softly she said, "Because at night, I dream of dragons."

She signaled the two Star Elves to follow her and led them and Arjuda outside.

She merely motioned and within minutes word was traveling through the camp that she would speak. A three-step platform was carried out by four strong Moredhel warriors and she mounted it. Within minutes the larger part of her people had gathered below on the hillside and down in the valley. She called out in a surprisingly strong and clear voice, "My people! Send the word to our brethren and our allies to gather. Send word to the humans at the Inclindel Gap, and to the Hadati tribes in the hills of Yabon, and to the Eledhel in Elvandar. We will trouble them not if they do not hinder our passing, but we shall crush any who stand in our way.

"In five days as the sun rises, the Snow Leopards will go south. We shall take the Inclindel Gap and pass through the land of the Hadati, past the borders of Elvandar, to E'bar to aid our besieged cousins, the Taredhel!

"My people, ready yourself! The Snow Leopards march to war!"

18

TRAVEL

Jim Dasher gripped the sheet.

The Roldem naval messenger ship *Lord Archibald* leaped through the combers as it swung around the southernmost point of Kingdom Island, a large, barren, and uninhabited islet in the westernmost bay of the Sea of Kingdoms. It was one of the navy's fastest cutters, and it was shadowing Prince Oliver's fleet. Oliver had received word from his agents that Salador had marched on Silden, meaning that the coast between the two cities would be clear. It was his intention to land his army somewhere beneficial, organize them, and march to confront Edward.

Over the last few months, Jim had used every resource at his disposal to discover what he could about Oliver's plans. Prince Oliver of Maladon and Simrick had cooperated by allowing his patience to wear thin. It had become obvious over the previous month that the Congress of Lords would not convene to crown a new king until a single clear claimant to the throne emerged.

All the voting nobles were in the field, under arms, or holed up in their castles awaiting the outcome. As the winners would vote and the losers would be in chains or dead, it was a foregone conclusion that the winning side in this conflict would end up naming the new King.

The Congress of Lords was largely a good thing in Jim's opinion, when rival claimants agreed to adjudicate their differences peacefully; but when there was no clear claimant and the different sides had no intention of reaching a peaceful settlement, civil war was the result.

Oliver had made his bargain with Chadwick of Ran. When the dust settled, Chadwick's holdings were likely to have appreciated by more than half, as would his revenues, and he would be the richest and most powerful Duke in the Kingdom. Moreover, Chadwick's idiot son would be given Montgomery's position of Earl of Rillanon, effectively governor of the home island, when Montgomery was named Duke of Rillanon—which would occur as soon as Oliver took the throne and the current Duke of Rillanon died. And Oliver would ensure the latter followed the former quickly, Jim was certain.

Jim was also certain that Montgomery's tenure would be a short one, ostensibly to show forgiveness of previous rivals, though Montgomery was a threat to no one, and eventually old Monty would be replaced by one of Oliver's favorites.

What Oliver didn't know was Jim Dasher Jamison, Count of this, Baronet of that, occasional thief, murderer, and professional liar, had tampered with his intelligence. Jim had intercepted messages from various vassals to Oliver and had tinkered with them for over a month now. He had learned long ago that the best lie was wrapped in truth. So rather than confuse Oliver with blatant disinformation, he had lulled him with slightly altered truths.

Oliver expected an unopposed landing on a wide stretch of coast due south of Malac's Cross, which would put him on a beach below the headlands just two miles from where the Western Highway intersected the road between Salador and Silden. From there it would be a march due west to the Fields of Albalyn. He expected to be safe on both flanks, with Duke Arthur holding both Silden and Salador. His only threat was from Charles of Bas-Tyra, since their falling-out, but because Bas-Tyra's only route to aid Edward would be through Silden, Arthur of Salador would keep him from reaching Edward before the issue was decided.

Oliver also didn't know that while Bas-Tyra's ships were tightly packed around Rillanon, proudly flying banners— isolated and confined by Oliver's allies—Charles had the loan of a separate fleet, that one being Roldem's. Charles was either already with Edward or would be shortly.

It had taken a very persuasive Lady Franciezka Sorboz's constant pressure on the King, coupled with King Carole's own history of dealings with Oliver, to convince him that Roldem could not stand neutral in this coming civil war. It was clear that Oliver, should he take the Isles, would immediately become a threat to Roldem's control of Olasko, and perhaps even to the home island itself.

Jim had met with Lady Franciezka briefly in Salador, both of them in disguise, and had departed two days before her. He trusted in her wits and abilities to get herself out of Arthur's city and to Prince Edward, but he found himself worrying about her, and he hated that he worried. Their relationship was very complicated, as she was the only woman he genuinely loved despite her having tried to have him killed twice. He turned his mind away from her and back to his current plan.

He had used his Tsurani orb to get to Rillanon and found that Oliver's fleet had departed. After leaving his grandfather, Jim had availed himself of a talented young magician named Donato to transport him back to Rillanon after a brief meeting with King Carole to cement the alliance between the Isles and Roldem, then returned to dine with his grandfather.

The next morning he had boarded the *Lord Archibald* at first light. Once the ship's captain read James's letter of free passage signed by the King of Roldem himself, and bearing the royal seal, ordering any and all to give aid to the bearer, Jim was under way. In less than three days, they had overtaken Oliver's fleet and shadowed them. They could see the sails of the trailing ships until they reached Kingdom Isle, where Oliver's fleet swung around to the north, heading for the coast south of Malac's Cross, and the *Lord Archibald* swung south, heading for Salador.

Jim, not for the first time, wished the damned orb had more settings, or he could somehow learn the magician's trick of popping in and out of the place where they wanted to be, but at least he was arriving in Salador after Bas-Tyra's army had occupied it. Waiting for the ship to berth, Jim reviewed his plan again.

Oliver would land unopposed, and word would reach him that all was proceeding as planned. The only difference would be that when Oliver marched into Albalyn, he would discover the army he faced was twice the size of the one he anticipated and that no aid would be forthcoming from Silden or Salador.

Still, Jim worried. History was full of battles in which the smaller army was victorious. Oliver's biggest advantage was that his was an army with a core of battle-hardened Eastern Kingdom soldiers, mean bastards tempered by years of border clashes. Edward's army comprised mostly westerners, and their primary tasks had been fighting disorganized bandits, goblin bands, or the occasional bar brawl on the frontier between rival garrisons.

His single greatest concern would be how Arthur of Salador reacted to the news that his city was taken. That bit of theatrics relied on a very stalwart commander named du Gale holding Silden for two weeks, and then Arthur's fleeing to the east when hearing of Salador's fall. Jim's worst nightmare was Arthur's taking Silden before the Roldem ship with the green banner arrived, or returning to Salador at the head of his army, marching right into Oliver's forces and joining up with them.

The captain gave orders and the ship began losing sail as it hove into sight of the city. Jim would land at Salador, see if Franciezka was safely gone, and find out what, if any, news from Silden had reached the garrison. Then he would find a horse and make for the Fields of Albalyn. He had done everything he could and now the players were on their predetermined positions on the board.

He had nothing left but to stand at his King's side, when Edward was victorious, or to lie dead next to him.

Salador was chaotic, as Jim had expected, but it was the level of chaos that troubled him. He made his way past a company of Roldemish marines who were stationed on the dock to guard their ships, and then looked for some sign of who might be in charge. He saw a squad of soldiers from Bas-Tyra standing at the corner and made his way over to them. A corporal saw him coming, tried to appraise him by his dress, and decided a neutral course of action was appropriate.

"Sir?" he said in a noncommittal tone.

"Where is the Duke of Bas-Tyra?" Jim asked.

"Departed a few days ago with the bulk of the army." The soldier glanced around as if not wanting to be overheard. "We sailed in and found about two hundred city watch—most of them conscripts—and some louts up in the Duke's castle trying to be all heroic, and in about four hours had the city in hand. Not that it's my place to speak ill of my betters, but my wife and kids could have defended this city with more heart. It's as if the Duke of Salador had no notion anyone might see an undefended city as an opportunity."

Jim smiled. "I think he had bad intelligence."

"Well, I'm not speaking of his intelligence, mind you, him being a duke and all, but seems to me if you're taking your army somewhere else, best leave enough men behind to make sure you have somewhere to return to, if you take my meaning."

"I do. Who's in charge?"

"That would be Captain Ronsard. He's provost of the city and commander of the garrison. He's over in the barracks."

"Thank you, Corporal."

Jim left the knot of soldiers behind and worked his way through the crowd. The city was simmering just below the level of a full-blown riot. He could smell it on the wind.

No doubt Duke Arthur had left the city with a show of pomp and confidence, brave men in the mustard and crimson of Salador marching off to conquer for the new king. Rumors would have been rampant, and those merchants, whores, beggars, and thieves who hadn't followed the army all salivating over the prospect of a conquering army returning home loaded with booty. Then a few weeks later another army sails into the harbor under cover of night and whatever was left of the local military is easily overcome. One night the citizenry went to bed with the banner of Salador snapping bravely in the breeze, then the next morning they awoke to see the black-and-gold banner of Bas-Tyra overhead. Those that could read found edicts nailed to every corner that the city was now under martial law, imposed by the Duke of Bas-Tyra on behalf of the Crown.

Suddenly goods would become scarce, for whatever Bas-Tyra didn't confiscate would be hidden away against shortages. People were suddenly frightened, and despite order being maintained, it was maintained under threat of violence from an invading army.

Jim knew it would take skillful management to avoid riots, looting, and wholesale bloodshed during the occupation. He worked through a very crowded section of the city near the southern gate and passed a strange assortment of onlookers. There were very old men, and very young boys, but no one between the ages of fifteen and fifty. The women were gathered in clutches, whispering, as if afraid of being overheard. He realized that within a day or two after he and Franciezka had met in this city, some sort of muster must have been called, as there wasn't a man of fighting age not in uniform to be seen. That didn't mean the city was safe from violence; old men and young women could run rampant through the streets just as easily as a mob of drunken men, and there was likelihood of a full-scale rebellion.

Jim reached the barracks and asked for directions to the captain's location. He found the office and an orderly announced him.

"Yes?" said the captain impatiently.

"I just arrived on a Roldemish cutter, Captain." Jim handed over a parchment and waited.

The captain read it and his entire manner changed. "My lord," he said, handing it back. It was a carte blanche Jim had written himself, signed by his grandfather and bearing the Duke's seal.

"How stands Salador?"

"As you no doubt saw." The captain rose from behind his desk. "The city is verging on insurrection and riot. I've given orders that should riot erupt, my men are to pull back to this garrison."

"Wise," said Jim.

"How can I be of aid, my lord?"

"I need a horse."

"A moment," said the captain. He picked up a quill and leaned over to pen an order, signed it, and handed it to Jim. "Take your pick at the stable, though I would appreciate it if you'd pass over the big gray gelding; that's my horse." He smiled.

"I'll find another," said Jim. "Tell me, have you encountered a lady of Roldem here?"

"Not to my knowledge," said the captain. "A specific lady, I take it."

"Very," said Jim, thinking Franciezka must have found a

way out of the city. Had she been in hiding when Bas-Tyra had arrived, she would surely have made herself known to the Duke.

A shout from outside caused both men to go to the door. A guardsman ran up and said, "Captain, we have sight of a large column of dust from the north."

"That can't be good," said the captain.

"Perhaps not bad either," said Jim. "May I join you?"

Given the rank of this mysterious traveler and the carte blanche he carried, the captain realized asking permission was simply good manners, but he appreciated it and nodded.

Both men climbed the steps to the city walls and moved to the northern tower. From the roof they peered northward.

"It's a big company," said Captain Ronsard.

As they watched, the cloud of dust grew larger.

One of the lookouts said, "It's a bleeding army, sir."

"What banner?"

"Can't see yet, Captain."

Time dragged on and Jim waited. If things had gone according to plan in Silden, there was little threat. But if things hadn't gone as planned, the approaching force could prove disastrous for Prince Edward and the Kingdom.

Finally the lookout said, "They fly no standards, but they're wearing Salador colors, Captain!"

Jim asked, "Who rides in the van?"

"No officers I can see, sir. Their horse are on the flank, riding at a walk, keeping pace with the infantry."

"Good," said Jim. He turned to Captain Ronsard and said, "I expect you'll find a captain, lieutenant, or perhaps even a sergeant in command of that army. But if there's one nobleman left, I'll be surprised."

"I'm not sure I take your meaning, sir."

"That's the Army of Salador come home, without the Duke."

"Is Duke Arthur dead, you think?"

"More likely trying to find a way to ride around Bas-Tyra and seek asylum with Chadwick of Ran." Jim headed toward the stairs. "I'll take that horse now, just in case whoever's in charge of that army isn't in a good mood. But if I'm right, you'll need to accept a lot of paroles for the rest of this day. Promise them whatever it takes, but start with back pay. Tear apart Duke Arthur's apartments—he thought he was coming back, so I expect much of his personal wealth is secreted there somewhere, likely a treasure room next to his own quarters, or somewhere in the lower dungeon. Make sure those men are disarmed, fed, given something to drink—not too much— and paid, and you'll have little trouble. And you might even put some of them to work guarding their own city."

"I'm not sure any of this makes sense, my lord," said Ronsard, but Jim had vanished down into the tower. The captain returned his attention to the approaching army. "As soon as that nobleman is out of the gates, I want them closed until we find out what this is all about."

"Sir," said a nearby sentry, and he followed Jim down the steps.

All eyes on the wall watched as the Army of Salador slowly returned home.

Jim rode without incident for two days. He had circled wide of the approaching army from the north, but rode close enough that he judged they'd be little trouble for Captain Ronsard and his garrison. From the look of them they were tired of fighting and just wanted to go home. The absence of mercenaries told Jim as much as he needed to know: Silden had withstood attack and the Army of Salador had withdrawn. If he survived the rest of this coming war, he'd read the reports and sift through the details later, but he knew that when this was over, an officer in Silden's army— Knight-Marshal Geoffrey du Gale—should be sought out and personally thanked. Jim had left him in a very bad situation and it appeared he had made the best of it.

The villages along the line of march between the coast and the Fields of Albalyn were deserted, as Jim had expected them to be. Villagers had an inbuilt sense of when trouble was headed their way and usually found places to be other than in front of approaching armies. The woods to the north and south of the highway would be speckled with camps and makeshift villages. These people had generations of putting up a wattle-and-daub hut in short order. Some camps might even turn into permanent settlements.

The road from Salador intersected the road from Malac's Cross, a point accepted as the de facto line separating the Eastern and Western Realms of the Kingdom. Jim circled south and west around that particular intersection, as Oliver had no doubt put a company there, protecting his beachhead. He paused and stared up the road. In a matter of a few weeks, Prince Oliver and his army would be marching down this road to about where Jim sat his horse. Within a week after that, he would march over a rise and see a sweeping vista of fields, freshly harvested and now empty, dominated at the north by a rising tor. On that tor rested an ancient fortress, a single keep abandoned centuries ago, but once the first Kingdom fortification in what would become the Western Realm. The Tower of Albalyn, which gave its name to the fields below.

There Oliver would be looking up at a deceptively long rise: he would have to charge his men uphill at Prince Edward's entrenched army. If all went according to plan, the battle would be over in a day, with Oliver crushing himself against Edward's position.

At least that was Jim's plan, and his hope.

And Jim Dasher was enough of a realist to know that nothing ever goes as planned.

He rode on.

Jim spied the sentries along the ridgeline east of the fields and rode slowly to the two guards stationed along the highway. He waved casually, and when he reached them, one said, "Your business?"

Without speaking, Jim handed down his warrant of passage, and the guard looked at it and handed it to his companion. Jim realized neither could read and said, "Message for Prince Edward from the Duke of Rillanon."

Alone, he was hardly a threat to Prince Edward, who was surrounded by several thousand soldiers, so they waved him along. He rode at a slow trot, his eyes traveling over the terrain. There were a dozen features that caught his eye, small deviations from the maps, that had him recalculating a possible battle strategy. He stopped: there was a tent full of generals, marshals, dukes, and a prince to conduct this battle. There was unlikely to be anything he noticed that they had missed.

When he reached the lines, a captain who could read glanced at his document, waved him through, and pointed out the Prince's pavilion. There, a lackey took Jim's mount and he entered. Several familiar faces greeted him as he approached Prince Edward and bowed. "Highness."

"Lord Jamison," said the Prince. "I hope you bring good news."

"As good as can be had in a war. Oliver follows the trail we left him, like a dog after a rabbit." He removed his gauntlets and took an offered cup of wine. "Good," he said after taking a drink. He looked around the room, nodding greetings to all.

The Dukes of Yabon, Darkmoor, Bas-Tyra, Krondor, Durrony's Vale, Sutherland, Silden, and Crydee were attending the Prince, and the other court officers. Jim noticed his cousin Richard standing next to the Duke of Krondor and nodded to him. He didn't particularly like his cousin, but he respected him and was surprised to discover he was here. A dozen commanders were waiting word of Oliver's army approaching from the east, and reviewing plans to anticipate every contingency.

Jim turned to Prince Edward. "I left Salador three days ago, after I had followed Oliver's fleet toward their beachhead. They did as anticipated and landed directly east of the Western Highway."

"How soon?"

"If he doesn't lag or piss around too much, two weeks, three at the outside. He's got seasick horses, men who've been barracked a long time; he probably needs to forage and establish his scouts and skirmishers. Most importantly, he has to set up his base for his line of march. He's got to unload a lot of cargo and be ready to resupply if this turns into a long campaign."

"How many men?" asked the Duke of Darkmoor.

"Silden cost him most of the western mercenaries," said Jim with a smile. "They didn't like fighting and not getting paid. And he's lost Salador, which is close to two thousand men. But he's got all of Maladon and Simrick, eastern mercenaries, and Dolth, Euper, Tiburn, Timons, and Romney marching with him."

"What of Ran?" asked Edward. "Chadwick made a deal with Oliver, correct?"

"All our intelligence says that was so," Jim answered. "Chadwick is not with Oliver, but that doesn't mean he's not causing mischief somewhere."

"Without Chadwick's army, we can crush them," said the Duke of Yabon.

"My Lord of Crydee," Edward said, "you have that same look your father got when he had something to say, but didn't want to say it."

Hal had been quietly standing to one side, being the youngest Duke in the tent, but he frowned deeply at Edward's remarks. Then, looking a little self-conscious, he stepped up to the maps and put the battlefield map on top of the one Jim used. "If I were Prince Oliver, I wouldn't be marching up that highway as expected, but waiting, taking my time, perhaps sending some patrols west to keep you worried."

"Why?" asked the Prince.

"To stall for time," answered Jim Dasher. He looked at Hal. "You expect Chadwick of Ran to arrive, don't you?"

"Not by ship," said Hal. "If Chadwick set off as soon as he made his agreement with Oliver, steady and easy, not punishing his men with twenty miles a day, but half that, he'd be about here."

Again the shuffling of maps, with Hal's finger stabbing the town of Sloop. "Lord Romney has already left to take up position with Oliver, so Chadwick can move his entire army without anyone except some farmers noticing him cutting through the south end of that duchy. Then he continues down the old logging highway from Sloop along the edge of the Dimwood, to Sethanon."

"And drops in behind us once the fighting starts," said the Prince. "No one has ever accused old Chad of being a fool, and if he comes in that way . . ." He shook his head.

Jim closed his eyes. "I didn't see that."

"You can't see everything," said a female voice from the shadows in the corner of the tent.

Jim's expression went from one of deep concern to a broad smile as he said without looking, "I am pleased my lady reached the Prince untroubled."

Lady Franciezka laughed. "Oh, there was a bit of trouble, but nothing too difficult." She moved to Jim's side and added, "The politics of your nation is currently such that I think young Lord Henry is correct. For if both you and Oliver were to fall in battle . . ."

Jim cringed at missing something so obvious. "Chadwick calls for truce, both sides have no one to support, the war ends, and he's—"

"Left the sole legitimate claimant to the throne, and in command of the field," finished Edward. "Montgomery wouldn't dare to challenge his claim, even with your grandfather's backing," he added, looking at Jim. Then he looked at Hal for a long moment, but the young Duke said nothing.

"How do we deal with this?" asked the Duke of Yabon.

Hal said, "If I take enough men to Sethanon and wait, I can slow him enough that by the time he gets here, the battle will have been decided. Or, even if not, he won't be a deciding factor."

"How many men do you need?" asked Edward.

"I can make do with my men from Crydee and"—he looked at the Duke of Yabon—"another garrison."

"Take LaMut," said the Duke of Yabon. "The Wolves are the best soldiers I have in my duchy." He grinned at Prince Edward. "Most of them had Tsurani ancestors. You know what a bunch of tough little bastards they were."

"When do you leave?" Edward asked.

Hal studied the map. "If Jim's predictions about Oliver's movements are accurate, we have plenty of time. Ten days to reach Sethanon . . ." He calculated. "That gives me enough time to rebuild the castle there," he said with a grin.

"Hardly," said Jim, sharing the humor, "but certainly you have enough time to build a fortification he can't afford to leave at his rear."

"Good," said Prince Edward. "You'll confer with us on your preparations and we'll ensure all is ready when it's time for you to depart. Who acts as your adjutant?"

"My brother Martin," said Hal. Martin and Brendan were waiting in the Crydee ducal pavilion, the very same used by their father in years past. Brendan had arrived courtesy of Ruffio and had been catching up on the situation here after having filled in the Prince of Krondor on the events in the Grey Tower Mountains. "And I'd like to drag Ty Hawkins along."

Jim nodded. "He'll go. Make him your fourth, after your brother and the Earl of LaMut."

"Captain Hawkins it is, then," said Hal.

"I'll send word to the Earl of LaMut," said the Duke of Yabon.

"I thank my lord," said Hal. He said to Prince Edward, "I'd like to leave my youngest brother, Brendan, here . . ." He paused. "I'd like one of us away from the fight for the moment, if you've no objections?"

"Of course." The Prince understood that the loss of his father was still fresh in Hal's memory and that having both brothers at risk with him was asking too much.

"If I may withdraw, I will start preparing a plan."

"Permission," said Edward. Hal hurried out and the Prince

said, "If my lords will permit, I need to speak in private with Lord Jamison."

The dukes and their attending officers bowed, as did Lady Franciezka, but the Prince said, "Stay, my lady." He signaled for a handful of his most trusted advisers, the Knight-Marshal of Krondor, the Duke of Krondor, his own adjutant, and beckoned for wine to be poured as he sat in his canvas-and-wood chair. Once the wine had been served, he ordered the servants outside and said, "See that we are not disturbed." When he was satisfied he only had his most trusted advisers around him, he said, "Are we going to survive this?"

Jim Dasher said, "Probably not all of us, Highness. Oliver has some of the toughest soldiers from the Eastern Kingdoms under his banner, and Chad has the frontier, so his men are their equal. If young Lord Crydee doesn't slow Chadwick, you're going to have to defend your northern flank against some of the hardest troops north of Kesh."

"If you'll permit, Highness," said Richard Jamison, "I'd like command of the north."

Edward glanced at the Duke of Krondor, who nodded, and the Prince said, "You have it, sir."

"So now we wait," said Jim.

"We still have numbers," said the Duke of Krondor.

"Yes," said Jim, "but only by a slim margin if Chadwick arrives in anything like good order. And even without Chadwick, Oliver's army is a tough nut to crack."

"Very well," said Edward. "When young Henry and his command depart, I'd like a screening patrol to follow, to set up pickets along the way, so as soon as the issue in Sethanon is resolved, we know."

"Yes, Highness," said the Duke of Krondor.

He motioned to Richard, who said, "I'll see to it," and departed.

They sipped wine for half an hour and chatted, and then Edward said, "I'm feeling my years. If you wouldn't mind, I need a moment alone with the Lady Franciezka."

The others excused themselves, and as Jim turned to leave, Edward said, "Lord Jamison, linger for a moment."

When the three of them were alone, Prince Edward's pose of fatigue dropped away and he said, "You two bear more responsibility for everything that's about to happen, and perhaps there are four people in this world who know this." With a smile he added, "Damned spies."

Franciezka remained expressionless, but Jim laughed. "What do you need now, Your Highness?"

"Your ability to see the future, Jim." Edward looked at Lady Franciezka. "You're a rare prize, lady, and Carole is fortunate to have you. You serve your nation well."

"I thank His Highness."

"Pull over a chair for the lady," Edward instructed Jim, and motioned for him to bring one for himself as well.

When they were sitting, Jim poured the last of the wine and Edward said, "Roldem will save the Isles from chaos, but we plot a bold course." He looked at Franciezka. "I have had nothing but respect for your king since we both were boys and he used to bully me at university."

"I never heard that story," said Franciezka.

"Carole was a rambunctious youth," said Edward. "He would bully me because he was Crown Prince of Roldem and I was then the son of a court duke, but he would never let the other boys bully me. After a while the bullying stopped but we still spent time together. I believe that because no one ever said no to the Crown Prince of Roldem, his bullying was his way of testing my mettle. There are two kinds of strength," he added, reflecting on years gone by. "Power and the ability to wield it is obvious, but resilience, the ability to resist power, is the other. Carole once told me my willingness to put up with his nonsense taught him that. We have been close friends since university. Your monarch is a fine man."

"As are you, Highness," returned Franciezka.

"I'm a placeholder," said Edward. "I'm the fitting dummy for the groom at a royal wedding, standing motionless and not complaining when stuck with a pin, while the real groom is out hunting or in court or doing whatever it is that princes or kings do before a wedding. I will be King or I will be a dead prince, but no pretender from the Eastern Kingdoms will sit the throne of the Isles." He sighed. "I am a conDoin by my mother's side of the family, and not by much. That would be enough had I been blessed enough to have sons, but I wasn't." He grew wistful for a moment. "That young Hal . . . he's so very much like his father."

Franciezka said, "I've spent time with him. He's . . . unusual."

"Should he survive his encounter with Chadwick, I want him close to me when I face Oliver."

"I'll tell him," said Jim.

"You realize," said Edward to Franciezka, "that your king's generosity has put both our nations at risk."

"Not by much," answered Franciezka. "While our nations suffered because of those murderous impostors, it was Kesh who was harmed the most. Half her army was sent to the Far Coast and the Free Cities, the other half sent to reinforce the northern borders, and now the usual bloody Keshian politics has commenced. Legions are hurrying to deal with chaos south of the Girdle, as those who remained in the Confederacy seek to seize land left by those sent to the Far Coast. It is turmoil piled upon confusion."

Jim added, "They'll be looking inward for a few years, I'm certain. Expect nothing more than a disapproving note from the Keshian ambassador when all this is finished. As long as we stand solid with Roldem, Kesh will do little more than complain."

"Then let us speak of things political, marriages of state and all the other issues that may prove moot should Oliver prevail and my head end up on a pike." Edward sighed. "This may be a long night. Send for some more wine, please."

Jim nodded, rose, and moved toward the tent opening. The finest thing about Edward, Prince of Krondor, was that he was the only claimant to the throne who didn't want the Crown. Which is why he was the perfect man for it.

19

MAGIC

Tanderae swung his sword.

It had been years since he had actively been trained, as all young Taredhel were, but he was attempting to make every blow count. The creature opposite him was a chill thing of darkness. Twice it had come close to touching him, and the near misses felt as if the life was being sucked out of his body as its claw sped past.

Tanderae had managed to organize those attempting to keep the city sealed, but he was now convinced they were on the brink of a collapse. Magicians were falling unconscious from exhaustion; too many Sentinels lay dead, and even though every able-bodied adult and not a few older children stood stalwart against the creatures, too many breaches, and too many escaping monsters, made it clear to him that the existence of the Taredhel was now to be measured in hours, perhaps even minutes.

He swung hard and the creature recoiled; they hated the touch of steel, and enough blows caused them to explode in a shower of dull, metallic-looking shards that evaporated before touching the ground.

Suddenly a shaft of searing white-hot energy struck the shadow creature and it vanished with a puff of acrid smoke. Two more bursts, and two other creatures nearby vanished.

Tanderae turned and saw a group of humans striding down from the upper staging meadow, in their lead a tall man with a neatly trimmed beard and long black hair. "I am Ruffio," he said. "We are members of the Conclave of Shadows, and we are here to help."

Tanderae almost collapsed in relief. He watched in amazement as a dozen magicians hurried past, casting spells at every dark shadow that emerged from the ruby dome. A few others were hurrying to see if they could aid the fallen.

A young man hurried by carrying skins of water and paused to offer a drink to the prostrate Loremaster, who took a long drink and nodded his thanks before the youngster ran off to help someone else.

"How did you know?" Tanderae asked Ruffio.

"Word reached us from Brendan conDoin. We were delayed by a nasty storm, but once that problem was solved, we came straight here."

The sound of flying arrows caused Tanderae to look up, and he saw a blond-haired Eledhel and a dark-haired Moredhel moving with purpose toward the ruby dome, firing arrows with deadly accuracy at any shadow that emerged from within. Calis and Arkan had discovered that if they could place a steel broadhead in the very center of a creature's chest, it vanished.

After them came a young woman in heavy armor, her

shield bearing the symbol of Dala. She moved like a practiced warrior ready. He watched as she dropped her visor over her face and accelerated in a slow trot toward the battle line.

Sandreena might not have faced many of these so-called Children of the Void, but she'd tangled with a wraith and a couple of wights over the years, and knew how to avoid their touch as she bashed them back into whatever universe from which they sprang.

Amirantha had stayed on the island to facilitate communications, and because his particular magic was useless against anything but demons. He had made Ruffio promise to fetch him to the field of conflict if he could be useful. Ruffio could tell he was not happy being left behind, but had understood the wisdom behind the decision.

"How many have you brought?" Tanderae asked Ruffio.

"In this group, a dozen. It's the most I could handle." The magician glanced around. "I need to fix my bearing. I could only get us to a place I know west of Ylith and then we had to do line-of-sight jumping, which is very slow with a large group. That took us half the afternoon and most of this day. Once I fix a spot . . . ah!" He pointed. "That rock outcrop is perfect. Allow me a moment." He stared at it, fixing it in his memory, then vanished.

In less than a minute, he was back, another half-dozen robed figures with him. They quickly turned, assessed the situation, and started attacking more of the shadow creatures.

Tanderae said, "I feared we would be overwhelmed."

"From what I hear, if E'bar falls, we'll all be overwhelmed. What can you tell me about that dome?"

"Little. I am not gifted in the arcane arts. But I can take you to one who is."

"Wait a moment," said Ruffio, and vanished again.

Another minute later, he was back with another half-dozen magicians. "Joshua, Cullen, stay with me. The rest of you know what to do."

Two young magicians waited while the other four hurried off to bolster the defenses mounted by the beleaguered Taredhel. Tanderae motioned for them to follow and they walked up the incline to the upper meadow. There a few humans were organizing food and helping to tend wounds. Uninjured Taredhel who had been taking care of the wounded and dying were collapsed on the ground, simply numb with exhaustion.

Tanderae led the three human magicians to a place under a tree, now clothed in shadows as the evening approached, and there they found an elderly Star Elf whose face was ashen and drawn. He seemed to be asleep, but when Tanderae said "Asleum," his eyes opened.

"I live," said the old man. "If barely," he added. "Who are these?"

"Human magicians, come to help."

Ruffio took a knee and said, "We see your barrier is tested. May we know what it is we may do to bolster it until more help comes?"

"More help is on the way," said Tanderae.

"We are from a small island in the Bitter Sea," explained Ruffio. "There were but two dozen of us with mature skills, and another dozen students in residence when news of your plight reached us."

"Where are the others coming from?" asked the old spellcaster.

"Stardock. From the Academy of Magicians."

"We need more than another dozen, I fear," said Asleum. "It took every magic user among my people to fight back those horrors while a handful of us contrived this barrier. We lost more than a dozen of our best until we understood how we could turn the invaders' own magic beacon against themselves. We have taken that ruby magic and turned it into a containing dome. It will only fail if we fail, or if the invaders cease trying to enter our realm."

"Clever," said Ruffio. "My young students here are among the most adept I have when it comes to understanding energy fields, magical traps, and the like. Your elven magic is alien to us, so if you could guide them in how best to help, they will in turn pass that on to the others when they arrive."

"How many are arriving?" asked Asleum.

Ruffio smiled. "Hundreds."

The old elf studied Ruffio's face for a moment, then began to weep.

It was a savage night. All the human magicians could do was to stand by and destroy the dark creatures that emerged from the dome. Ruffio's two students asked many questions of Asleum, and occasionally one would venture down the hillside to probe the shell and see for himself which magic signatures and hallmarks bore out what they were being told.

Finally, the young magician named Cullen said, "I think it would be years before I knew enough about this to be useful in keeping the dome intact. Perhaps Pug or Magnus could recognize how to best help, but I think I may have a temporary solution."

Ruffio looked intrigued. "Say on."

"Maybe we should aid these elven magicians directly, instead of concentrating on the dome."

"Feed energy to the magician, so that he can use it?" asked Ruffio.

"More or less. It's one of those things that Magnus does without thought, but tries to teach the rest of us. At some profound level, he believes, there's this core of magic that can be tapped, as one taps a keg of ale, I guess, and that what spills out of the core can be passed along to someone else."

Joshua nodded. "It's an exercise Magnus has tried with some success. I can conjure up, for example, the energy needed to light a campfire, but rather than cast that spell, I pass along the energy to Cullen, who lights the fire."

Ruffio said, "Don't wait for my approval. Go see if you can help."

The two young magicians hurried back down the hill.

The old magician said, "Let me rest awhile longer, then I can return."

"Rest, then," said Ruffio. "More help is on the way."

He went to help his students.

Cullen and Ruffio sat motionless, while Joshua stood watch. In a trancelike state, the two magicians cautiously explored the energy of the ruby shell, examining what they could without actively engaging with it. Within the trance, they spoke to each other with mind-speech, oblivious to the world around them. "This is incredible," said Ruffio.

Cullen said, "Now you can appreciate the difficulty. We can aid the elves, but to join in holding this matrix of energy in place would be problematic at best, disastrous at worse."

Ruffio used his magic to alter his perception, looking at the flow of energies from the elven magicians to the ruby sphere. "I see it as if it were a tapestry," he said. "It's as if where the elves' magic ends countless tiny threads of their devising intersect the magic of the sphere. It's a clever weaving, with overlapping threads that hold other threads in place but somehow don't truly link to them."

Both magicians peered at the latticework of energy. "The elves' magic lattice inserts its own weft in between the strands of the alien magic, just enough to seize part of the warp," said Cullen. "I don't know if this was by design, or by sheer luck, but they've turned the invaders' spell on itself. Very clever, really."

Ruffio blinked and came out of the trance state. He put his hand on Cullen's shoulder and the younger magician also came alert. Ruffio stood up, inspecting the scene around him. Magicians from Stardock had begun arriving hours ago and were doing everything they could to help, but at this point the only aid they could provide was to augment the flagging energies of the elven spellcasters. That was helping, and most of the breaches in the energy shell had been repaired. Only a few of the shadowy creatures were getting loose and they were being quickly disposed of by the actions of Sandreena and the elven Sentinels.

"I don't know what more we can do," said Ruffio. "Pug or Magnus might be able to make sense of this, but I can't."

"I'll keep exploring it," said Cullen. "Maybe if you talk with some of the elves?"

Ruffio felt his eyes burn. "I have, and don't know if any more discussion will help."

"Then rest. I think we're holding our own and we should have more help shortly."

Ruffio nodded and moved off to find a bite to eat and a place to nap. He looked at the night sky and realized he had lost track of time. He didn't know if it was only an hour after sunset or an hour before dawn.

He wondered if even Pug or Magnus could make sense of what he had seen. Then he realized he hadn't heard from either since that odd sensation of upheaval before the storm. It wasn't unusual for them to be out of touch for a while, but as a rule, when they knew they would be away for any significant period of time, they let Ruffio know. He was head of the Conclave after them, and should anything occur to father and son, the burden of the Conclave and Stardock fell to him.

Suddenly he was worried: Where were Pug and Magnus?

Nakor said, "This place is a maze."

"Where are we?" asked Miranda.

Macros swept his hand around and said, "Let's explore the City Forever a little." They rose as if on a magic platform lifting high into the sky, feeling no sensation of movement, which would have been disorienting to lesser mortals.

Pug said, "Perspective helps."

Nakor was delighted. "I've heard the stories . . ."

"Let's move above the confusion," suggested Macros, and the four of them started traveling above the buildings, between the vaulted arches and sky-topped towers. On every hand was alien beauty. Impossibly slender, brilliantly hued

minarets of crystal, or fluttering fabric, or liquid rose below
them, weaving their way skyward. Fountains sent out showers
of liquid silver that turned to crystals, filling the air with tin-
kling music as they shattered upon the tiles, only to become
liquid again.

They hovered above the center of a magnificent boulevard,
nearly a hundred yards wide. The entire street was tiled, and
the tiles glowed with soft colors, each subtly different from
the next, so that it appeared like a leisurely flowing rainbow.

As the group passed over them, the tiles shifted hue and
music filled the air, music that evoked a longing for another
place—a softly lit glade in a scented forest, a gorgeous sunset
over an alien sea, green fields beside sparkling brooks, or
late-afternoon light softly coloring majestic mountains.

The images were almost overwhelming. Pug shook his
head to clear it, putting aside a dawning sadness that such
a wonderful place could never be found. "I've had the same
reaction to this place, before," he said.

"It's part of the secret of the city," offered Macros. "There
are more aspects to this place than can be imagined by the
mortal mind. This is just a part of what there is, and it plays
on more than the five senses. It feeds thoughts, feelings, and
false memories to you."

"What is this place?" asked Miranda. "I've heard the stories, but it's real. Who built it?"

"We may never know," said Macros.

They flew under monumental arches a thousand feet
above their heads, and tiny flowers tumbled through the air
around them. Sparkling white-and-gold, glowing rose-and-
vermilion, green-and-blue petals showered down around
them as they made for the heart of the city.

Everywhere they looked the eye was beguiled by forms
and structures that were at first glance jarring but within
seconds achieved a relationship of color, form, balance, and
harmony. "Truly remarkable," said Magnus.

"Keep alert, for occasionally others wander into this place
and sometimes they can be unpleasant," said Macros.

"I remember," returned Pug. "Tomas and I encountered a particularly nasty bunch of flying demons somewhere around here."

"Those were merely to distract you," said Macros. "They were sent to convince you that the false trap you were intended to find and name false was actually convincing."

"What are those?" Nakor asked, pointing to rising columns in the distance.

"What I was going to show you next," said Macros, and with a wave of his hand they were standing next to a maze of massive pillars, made of crystal or some clear material, that rose to impossible heights, their tops lost in the sky above. Within them swam motes of light and clouds of what appeared to be gas.

"It looks like—" began Miranda.

"The vast universe of galaxies I just showed you," interrupted Macros. "They do, don't they?"

Pug said, "It's been many years, more than a century, since I was last here, Macros. Do you know what this place is?"

"No," said Macros. "Several times I came to visit. Once you've been here, it's really easy to return. Over the ages many have come. Ask Tomas about the time the Valheru came, Pug."

"Tomas had mentioned it just before we found you in the Garden."

"There was nothing to loot," said Macros, "despite the appearance of riches. Imagine trying to pry up some of those magical tiles to decorate a palace and discovering nothing you could do could move them even the most minuscule distance. The Valheru were never known for handling their ire well, so they lashed out and tried to destroy the city out of pique. But they never so much as put a scar on a stone." He pointed and a blinding line of energy lashed out. Energy sizzled as it ran up and down the column and then a wave of heat washed over the onlookers.

Macros stopped and Pug knelt where the energy had

struck. He reached out and touched the invisible container that housed the floating lights. "Not even warm."

Miranda said, "So what are your conclusions?"

"No conclusions, but suppositions, and perhaps a theory."

"The theory, then," said Miranda, her impatience surfacing again.

"I think this is . . . a set of plans."

"It's a very large set," said Nakor.

"And very detailed," added Magnus.

"Explain," demanded Miranda.

"I'm not sure this place even exists in any way we understand, nor that it looks remotely the way we see it."

It was Miranda who said, "Perception."

"Yes," said Macros. "You're beginning to understand."

"When I encountered Piper, before joining with the rest of you," Miranda went on, "she showed me something called the Sundering and a host of demons rising against an army of angels, but they looked nothing like I expected them to look. First the demons were things of beauty, then things of horror, then abstractions of energy." She paused, then added, "Piper said they were unchanged, but my perspective of them changed each time."

"Imagine a blind man," said Macros, "and you take him to a sea coast, and he defines it by the salt tang on the air, the sound of waves on the shore, the sensation of warm sun or cold wind on his face, all the other factors that enter into your perception of that environment, but lacking form, color, visual texture, or perception of distance."

"So we see this because . . . ?" asked Magnus.

"Because you are human," said Macros. He smiled at Miranda and Nakor. "Or close enough that it makes little difference. Pug, I suspect you or Magnus have spent more time attempting to apprehend other energy states than are normal to human sight. Care to have a look?"

Pug shifted his perspective, using magic he had developed years before to see above and below the human spectrum, and was overwhelmed by the level of energy rampant through the city. "It's incredible. Beyond my understanding of the entire spectrum of energy I know."

"And beyond what I know as well, and I was doing it even longer," added Macros. "I know there are magic safeguards in place, because without them we would have been turned to ash within moments of arriving here." He pointed at the columns. "I believe those are universes."

"Really?" said Miranda, leaning over to peer at them. "But they are so tiny."

"Perspective," said Nakor with a laugh. "Perhaps we are now very big. Everything is relative, remember?"

"Ha!" Macros laughed. "You are almost correct."

"Almost?" Nakor looked puzzled. "What do you mean?"

"In all the vast universes we've encountered, all the places we've traveled to, and the tiny wonders we've beheld in a drop of water, there is one absolute. What is it?"

Miranda said, "I've heard from priests the gods are absolute."

"Bah," said Macros dismissively. "I'll get to the gods in good time. No."

Magnus looked self-conscious as he remembered his encounter with Helena. "The poets say love is absolute."

Macros shook his head. "More harm has been done in the name of love than in the name of the gods. Love of self, love of others, love of children, love of power, love of nation . . ." He shook his head. "No, it's something else."

"One," said Pug.

Macros smiled, and Nakor grinned. "Of course," said the little demon in human form.

Magnus took a moment, then nodded.

Miranda said, "One what?"

"Not one anything," said Magnus. "The abstraction 'one' is an absolute so that everything else can be measured against it."

"You can't have twice as many of something unless you can define that something," said Macros. "Or half of something."

"You need a starting point," said Pug. "And that leads us to: Where did that concept come from?"

"What does it matter?" asked Miranda. "You're speaking of an artificial construct. It's a mental, academic abstraction to enable us to cope with the world." She narrowed her gaze, and everyone knew she was growing short-tempered. "I'm sure the universe went swimmingly without it before someone thought the notion of 'one' up. Again, what's the point?"

Macros laughed. "You never were one for the abstract side of things. All you wanted to know was 'how do I do this?' never 'why does it work this way?' "

"It's a mathematical convention," said Miranda. "It's not real."

"And that is the lesson!" said Nakor, nearly jumping with the excitement he felt.

"If there's a universal language, across all realms of time and space, something that isn't bound by different laws of nature and states of energy, it's mathematics," said Macros. "How many times when puzzling out how a magical spell is achieved did you find a need to express concepts that only rendered themselves manageable through mathematics?"

Even Miranda was forced to concede. "Oh, very well. It's useful."

"More," said Nakor. "It's a reflection of something beyond our understanding, allowing us to grapple with forces and manifestations of the universe otherwise beyond our grasp."

Macros reached out and tapped the side of Nakor's head lightly with his fingertip and said, "There's a great deal going on in there, isn't there?"

Nakor lost his smile. "Sometimes it worries me."

"Well, that's what you get for sleeping with that damned Codex under your head all those years."

The Codex of Wodar-Hospur, the lost God of Knowledge, had fallen into Nakor's hands and he had kept it on him for many years. He had used his backpack as a pillow on most nights without knowing until years later that it was imparting knowledge to him, but in a random fashion, so that Nakor had many ideas that seemed to come from nowhere. He had finally given the Codex up to the Temple of Ishap for safekeeping.

"Very well," said Miranda. "What is the point?" This time her tone was not accusing.

"The point is, we can 'see' all manner of things beyond the universe we see, what we call 'rational,' or 'objective,'" said Macros. "If we take something away, we can say 'less one' or 'minus one,' and move on to a new value, but what if we take a null, a zero, and take one away?" He paused. "We have a negative number."

"Useful for moneylenders," said Nakor with a smile. "It's how they know they're losing profit."

"And for many other things," added Macros. "It allows us to describe things when we have no words or anything close to an analogy that provide us with the means of understanding what is happening in realms beyond our knowledge."

Pug said, "So you're saying the City is a mathematical construct?"

Macros pointed at Pug. "Exactly, but a mathematics beyond any scrawl of numbers across a board or parchment. It's a multidimensional equation a billion times more complex than the most complex apothecary's formula, or the most precise engineering used by a shipwright to calculate the stresses a mast can endure or how much water a hull displaces. It is the mathematics of creation."

"All right," said Miranda. "I'm impressed with the concept, and this place is far more unnerving than anywhere I've been, even in the Fifth Circle of Hell, but where is this taking us?"

"It is taking you to a place where perhaps you'll be able to do what needs to be done to save . . . everything," said Macros. "Be patient. You're ready for your next lesson."

He waved his hand and they vanished.

Ruffio awoke to find Sandreena sleeping nearby, as well as several other magicians from Stardock. The morning light was cutting through the trees from the east. He stood up and looked around. What had begun as a small cooking station a short distance away had turned into a full-scale military field kitchen. He found that he was hungry. He walked over, casting a glance down the hillside, and saw that the ruby shell seemed completely intact.

Tanderae was overseeing the general care of the wounded and exhausted and saw Ruffio approach. "We have stabilized the dome," he said. "Without your aid, we would have been lost. We are in your debt."

"Your quick actions may have saved all of us," Ruffio said. "Perhaps neither of us is indebted. Perhaps we both needed each other."

"For my people, that is a difficult concept," conceded Tanderae. "We have been taught since birth that we are the only highly evolved people in the universe." He lowered his voice. "Don't even ask what we think of dwarves, let alone goblins and their ilk."

"If it comes to a stand-up fight, those dwarves to your south in the Grey Towers are very handy to have on your side."

"We've been polite to our neighbors to the south" was all Tanderae said. "At this point the dome is holding, and some of our 'mancers are resting. This energy we control is as alien to us as it is to you, but we'll attempt to learn more of it."

"I wish two of my fellow magicians, Pug and his son Magnus, were here," said Ruffio. "They understand more about the energies of magic than anyone I know. Pug has even taken the time to learn what he can about elven magic up in Elvandar."

"Four of their spellweavers arrived while you were sleeping," said Tanderae. "They have been very helpful, as their magic isn't as alien to our own as human magic can be."

"If we manage to get through this, I'd like an opportunity in the future to learn more of your arts," said Ruffio.

Tanderae smiled. "Not long ago I would have been accused of treason even to suggest we allow a human to study our arts. How could I say no after what you've done for us? Of course. I will make sure of it, should we survive all this."

The feeling of collegiality was short-lived, for an elf warrior ran up to Tanderae and said, "Please, come, my lord."

Ruffio invited himself along and found a pair of elven magicians resting nearby. One looked up at the Loremaster of the Clans of the Seven Stars and said, "The pressure is increasing."

"What do you mean?" asked Tanderae.

"The best way I can explain it, my lord, is to say that something is trying to get out of a hole, and we're trying to push it back down. We managed not only to repair the tears and the dome, but actually to increase the pressure on the forces inside."

The other magician added, "But the pressure inside is increasing. It's building up like steam building up in a kettle."

"How much time before it starts rupturing again?" asked Ruffio.

The magicians glanced at Tanderae and the first answered, "Some time, I think. We have a week or two if we harbor our resources, and the rate of increase doesn't accelerate. If your human magicians can learn to directly bolster the dome, we may be able to push whatever's coming through that breach inside and seal it off."

"We're doing what we can to learn," said Ruffio.

Tanderae motioned for Ruffio to walk back with him. "You've mentioned others who might be able to understand our magic."

"Yes, but only the gods know where they are now."

20

PLANS

Hal held up his hand.

The column of soldiers behind him reined in and he motioned for Martin, Ty, and the Earl of LaMut—Hokada Venlo—to ride forward. The four ranking officers were positioned atop a rise looking down into a rolling valley in which lay the ruins of an abandoned city.

"Sethanon," said Hal. He surveyed the countryside, noting features and landmarks. "Opinions, gentlemen?"

Earl Hokada was a stocky, thick-necked man, but despite being a head shorter than the others, his reputation as a brawler as a youth and a soldier as an adult made him a man not to be underestimated. He was reputed to be among the best horsemen and archers in LaMut. "Chadwick will march down that road." He indicated the faint track of the loggers' highway from the Dimwood in the distance beyond the city. "He's a traditional man, so he'll march his infantry on his left, with his cavalry providing a screen between his infantry and the forest."

"But the forest ends miles north of here," said Martin.

Hokada nodded. "But he'll see no compelling reason to move them to the other side. So that's how he'll present, infantry in a double column to our left, cavalry double column to our right."

"I agree," said Hal. "So, what else?"

Ty said, "He'll assume the city is deserted, as it has been for a century, but he'll send scouts anyway."

"How do we deal with the scouts?" asked Hal.

All were quiet for a moment, then the Earl of LaMut said, "If they ride through, we know their instructions are to report back only if they spot the enemy. If one or both turn back, they are reporting the city is safe to pass. That's my best guess, my lord."

Hal was still getting used to older, more experienced soldiers addressing him as "my lord." He looked at Martin and Ty, who both nodded agreement. "So, if we want to lure Chadwick into a bad position in the city, he needs to think it's deserted." He stood in his stirrups to get a better look at the surrounding countryside. "We have a few days before he gets here, perhaps more. Let's be exacting in scouting this terrain and preparing the ground for battle. My lord." He nodded to the Earl. "See to your cavalry. We'll camp over there." He pointed to a clearing less than a quarter of a mile farther back down the trail with a small creek running along its west side. "And send scouts into the city at first light tomorrow. I want a trap here which will grab Chadwick of Ran by the tail and not turn him loose until we're ready to see him go."

"Yes, my lord," said Hokada. He turned his mount and started back down the road.

"What have you in mind, Hal?" asked his brother.

"I don't have a specific plan yet, but I do have an idea. We'll let his scouts pass, then have Chad come into Sethanon, but make him pay with blood to get out of the city."

"I like the idea," said Ty.

"Good," said Hal, "because I'm going to give you a particularly difficult role to play."

"Why doesn't that surprise me?" said Ty with a grin.

"Let's get some rest and start plotting," said Hal.

"Good," said Martin. "I'm hungry."

"You're always hungry," returned his brother, and Ty laughed, for as long as they lived, these two would always revert to acting like brothers, no matter what else occurred.

Sundown the next day found Ty, Martin, and the Earl in Hal's tent listening to the reports from the scouts Hal had sent into the city of Sethanon. Common lore said it was a cursed city, and its history seemed to support that myth. A large blank parchment had been unrolled and Martin was drawing in details as they were described to him. "I don't know why you're having me do this," he muttered.

"You were always the best artist, remember?" said Hal.

"Just because I said I was doesn't make it so."

They laughed.

"My father used to say," observed Hal, "that if your men were staunch and wouldn't break, then preparation was nine-tenths of the way to winning a battle. We just need to be better prepared than Chadwick."

Martin, concentrating on drawing in a fine detail pointed out by the scout, said, "He also made the point that once you came into contact with the enemy, all your plans went to hell."

Hal gave him a brotherly smack on the back of his head. "But that's true for both sides, and the side that's better prepared prevails." To Lord Hokada, he said, "If you were Chadwick of Ran and you suspected an ambush here in Sethanon, how would you prepare?"

The Earl of LaMut considered the map. "There are several ways, my lord, but which one is optimal? The original keep is an obvious choice as a garrison point, for in the case of need, your forces can retreat inside and the old portcullis can be dropped. That would delay an enemy should they decide to stay and root you out, but in the end you'd lose your position. Moreover, if his goal is to reinforce Oliver, then he leaves a small force to keep you from sallying from the keep, and quickly moves the rest of his forces south. Here"—he pointed on the map—"and here, in those buildings, a squad of archers could hold back any sally as Chadwick marches past." He looked at Hal. "If they send scouts into the city to explore, I would leave the keep deserted. Then should you choose to fortify, move them quickly in after the scouts leave."

"Noted," said Hal. "What else?"

"Luring them into house-to-house fighting might provide a temporary advantage, and it would neutralize any advantage they might have in cavalry, but the same holds true for our cavalry."

Martin said, "Your horse archers can do more damage than their cavalry, though, correct?"

"If they can keep some range, yes," said the Earl. "But you turn a corner and find yourself sword to sword with a heavily armed rider, and you don't have the advantage in speed. I don't like the odds."

"Point taken," said Martin. He looked at the scout. "How's that?"

"Good," said the horseman from LaMut. "And there's another wall here, about four feet high—looks like it might have been used to wall off a garden behind an inn."

"I'm beginning to think you don't like the idea of being in the city, my lord," Hal said to his subcommander.

The Earl smiled. "My great-grandfather was one of those Tsurani children who fell in love with horses, my lord. I've been riding since before I could walk. The idea of finding myself in any place where a horse becomes a liability in combat is alien to me. My first company is horse archers, not mounted infantry. I lead that company personally."

"What about your second company?" asked Ty.

"Mounted infantry and as tough a bunch as you'll find in Prince Edward's army."

"Well, let's leave your first company to do what it does best."

"What are you thinking, brother?" asked Martin.

"I'm thinking Earl Hokada and I both like where we sit right now better than being in that empty city."

Martin sat back with an exaggerated breath of exasperation. "Which means I've been drawing all day for naught?"

"Oh, this will come in handy," said Hal, putting his fingers on the map.

"But you want them charging uphill against this ridgeline?" asked Ty.

"Only if I can get them to do it on my terms."

Martin grinned. "Now that sounds like fun."

"Let's step outside, gentlemen," said Hal.

They followed him from the command tent up to the crest, where Hal pointed to a heavy patch of thornbushes dominating the hillside to his right, between the road and a sharply rising scarp on the other side. "If we extend the gorse and thorn by dragging plants from nearby and digging them in, say for a quarter of a mile down this road, to make it look like natural growth, Chadwick will either compress his columns so he can march up over this ridge on the road, or he'll hold back his infantry and let his cavalry go first."

"The second, I should think," said the Earl. "It's the most logical if he gets surprised coming over the rise."

Hal stood motionless for a long time, surveying the ground, and after a while said, "I think I have a plan."

"The Enemy has a plan," said Macros. "Or as close to a plan as can be imagined when dealing with an alien consciousness."

They stood in the midst of a vast plaza in the City Forever, where strange lights danced above them, moving like a flock of starlings on the wing in an endless dance.

"We're speaking of the Dread," said Pug. "A Dreadlord appeared in Sethanon when first we battled over the Lifestone, and another was masquerading as the Dasati Lord of Death when that world was almost destroyed."

"Dread?" said Macros. "In a manner of speaking. It's as convenient a name as 'the Darkness,' or 'the Enemy.'"

Pug's expression turned questioning. "Are you speaking of the Enemy in Tsurani lore? That was the essence of the Valheru, and they were banished or destroyed when we closed the rift into Sethanon."

"I wish it was that simple," said Macros. "Come, it's time for you to see some more things and learn more truth."

"Truth is always welcome, but a rarity with you, F—" Miranda almost called him Father, but caught herself in time.

"I have had my reasons for everything I've done," he replied. His expression became regretful. "But I'll concede my reasons at times haven't always been for the best."

They were approaching a massive black building that dominated this central part of the city. "The false prison," said Pug. "This is where Tomas and I first came to find you."

"And what was waiting for you?"

"A Lord of the Dread."

"Let's go and see him," said the Black Sorcerer.

"He's still there?" asked Pug.

"Follow." Macros hurried through the massive door and led them down the central passage, one which Pug remembered vividly. The Dread, or whoever was behind them, had engineered an elaborate trap to lure Pug and Tomas into confrontation with a Dreadlord. Pug and Tomas had easily bested the creature, but they had accounted for that by assuming the Dread had underestimated them. That assumption had lasted until they had found Macros and sprang the time trap that had carried them back into the past.

As they climbed the stairs Macros said, "Pug, in all the years since you and Tomas found me here, did you ever encounter another case of time travel?"

"I thought I had," said Pug, and he explained the forged notes giving him hints and clues of things he needed to do, originally thought to be from a future version of himself, but at last revealed to have been the handiwork of Kalkin, also known as Banath or Ban-ath, the God of Thieves, Liars, and Cheats.

"Gods are a little different," said Macros. "Especially that one. He's unique and plays a key role in all this."

They reached the upper room of the tower and entered. A cage of crystal bars stood in the middle of the room, within which crouched a figure of smoke and ash. It rose slowly. "You return to taunt me, Magician!"

"No, we return to ensure your torment," said Macros, unleashing a bolt of silver energy that sliced through the air like a thin pole of brilliant light. It passed harmlessly through the bars of the cage, and when it touched the creature, passed harmlessly through it as well. "I thought as much," said Macros. "Had this been a true Dreadlord, that energy would have made it go up in flames."

"What is it, then?"

"A lesser Child of the Void," said Macros. He cast another spell and the creature moaned, a hollow, echoing sound. "This is a dark wight. It's not much of a risk to a well-armed man, or to someone of your or Tomas's power. They ensured you would be engaged enough to think it real, but emerge easily victorious, and find me in the Garden." Turning to the creature in the cage, he asked, "How long have you been here?"

"Since the beginning," answered the creature.

"How long since you were last visited?"

There was no answer.

Macros looked at his companions. "He doesn't know."

"It's been a long time," said Pug. "Over a century. From what I can see, there's no way to gauge the passing of time here."

"It's more than that," said Macros. With a wave of his hand the cage and creature inside it vanished. "The Dread isn't a creature or a host of creatures, but a sort of conscious-ness, one so alien to everything we've ever known that even the gods don't understand it."

"It?" said Magnus. "Are we to consider the Dread to be a single entity?"

"Essentially," said Macros. "Although it can be in a lot of different forms and places at one and the same time. All the Children of the Void are, in one fashion or another, part of the Dread."

"How can that be?" asked Nakor.

"It looks at time differently, and uses it differently," said Macros.

Miranda said, "Now I'm interested. From my experience, what you say makes no sense."

"Which is why you are here, d—" He almost said "daugh-ter," and smiled instead.

With a wave of his hand, they were in another place.

"The Pavilion!" said Pug.

"Yes," answered Macros. "Where, if what I've been given to understand is correct, your son bullied the Goddess of Death into appearing."

Nakor looked at Magnus and appeared impressed. "You bullied a god?"

"Persuaded, actually," said Magnus.

"But you are now approaching an understanding few if any clerics, philosophers, or sages on Midkemia understand: the true nature of the gods."

A voice from behind them said, "You are treading on tricky ground, Macros."

A young man was standing there, with curly brown hair and dark eyes, dressed in the tabard of Krondor. Pug knew this couldn't be Squire James.

"Ban-ath," said Pug.

The figure bowed theatrically. "I chose this appear-ance out of nostalgia. He was always one of my favorite subjects."

Magnus asked, "Macros, what is it you wish to show

us that he"—he indicated the god in the form of a young man—"cautions you against?"

"That is the most difficult thing to explain, and the hardest to grasp. But it is the most vital part of your preparation to fight against the Dread."

"And you don't want him to?" Nakor asked Ban-ath.

The god shrugged. "I have my limits. I wish for a certain outcome—my survival—yet as gods, we must protect certain knowledge." He smiled. "It's a contradiction. But then life is full of them. As I said, I do have my limits."

"But apparently not as many as the other gods," said Pug. "Otherwise how could you have interfered in the Dasati realm, or brought Miranda and Nakor back to consciousness through these demons?"

"You give me too much credit," said the being also known as Kalkin. "I have the ability to 'cheat,' as you say, to circumvent limits preventing my brethren from acting on this world's behalf, but even I could not cheat enough to give Macros's memory to that dying Dasati, nor could I blend Miranda's and Nakor's minds and memories into a demon of the Fifth Circle. That took the work of all of us."

With that, the other gods of Midkemia appeared around them, looking down from their thrones. At the back sat four gigantic, motionless figures: the four greater, Controller gods.

"I think no introductions are necessary," said Kalkin. "The Controllers remain mute, as always."

Pug looked up into the heavens above the Pavilion, and saw the four silent faces, Abrem-Sev, the Forger of Action; Ev-Dem, the Worker from Within; Graff, the Weaver of Wishes; and Helbinor, the Abstainer.

Pug said, "I . . . I understand."

Kalkin said, "What do you understand?"

"These are the forces that define our universe. They do not interact with mortals because . . . they *are* the universe."

Macros looked at Miranda and said, "I told you you married a bright lad."

"You told me nothing of the sort," said Miranda.

Looking at Ban-ath, and then at the other gods, Pug said, "You interact with humans because . . . we made you!"

"Very bright lad," said Kalkin.

As one, the gods stepped down from their thrones and came closer. Kalkin said, "We are personifications. We represent elements of the natural order that you, through worship, have given a level of consciousness, one that otherwise wouldn't exist."

A frail old woman appeared next to Kalkin. "We persist, in one form or another, beyond what is thought of as a mortal existence. We are energy, sometimes vigorous, sometimes faint, but we linger."

"Arch-Indar!" said Nakor, delighted. "I had a statue and shrine built for you outside Krondor." He looked down, abashed at his own enthusiasm. "Or at least the Nakor part of me did."

"If enough people return to worship me, I will return to life."

"You appeared when I fought to save Caleb," said Magnus. "How can you say 'return to life'?"

"Because I am not alive," she said, smiling. "I am a memory." She looked at Pug. "Zaltais, whom you fought, was a dream, a wish fulfillment of the sleeping embodiment of evil. The wishes, dreams, and memories of the gods are powerful, Pug."

"What I don't understand," said Magnus, "is that you came to aid me in saving my brother." He looked at the black-veiled figure of Lims-Kragma, the Goddess of Death, the deity whom he had faced down. "You came into her realm and forced her to comply with my wish to see my brother survive."

The old woman smiled a sad smile. "I didn't force her. I persuaded her that your cause was good."

"What I don't understand," said Miranda, "is how can you have a memory if you're dead?"

Arch-Indar's image laughed. "I am not a memory of Arch-Indar's."

Lims-Kragma said, "She is *my* memory of Arch-Indar." She moved her pale hand in a circle, palm up. "When any of us needs to remember 'good,' she appears."

"Fascinating," said Nakor.

Kalkin said, "We have an investment here: that should be obvious to you."

Pug said, "For a very long time we assumed the Nameless One was at the root of this."

"Nalar—you can say his name without fear here—is as much invested in your success as any of us," said Kalkin. "If this world perishes, we all perish with it. And there will be no one left to worship us, or even to remember us or dream of us."

Suddenly the gods were gone, and the room was as silent as a tomb.

Macros said, "Pug, what did you mean when you said the Controller gods were the forces that defined the universe?"

Pug blinked. "My head is swimming."

"Do *you* know what he's talking about?" Miranda asked Macros.

"I do," answered the Black Sorcerer.

"Then tell us."

"I can't," said Macros. "I didn't make the rules here. I think you must discover certain things for yourselves, so that you really understand them." He frowned. "Damn! If I'm only going to be alive awhile longer, why give me a headache?"

"True learning," said Nakor. Then he grinned. "I know! Abrem-Sev, the Forger of Action, is the force that exploded out of creation, driving everything." He made waving motions, wiggling his fingers. "Crazy things all over the place, just scattering here and there!"

"Yes," said Pug. "He is that outward wave of things, but within a confined set of rules. But not his rules!"

"Rules beyond mortal knowledge," supplied Magnus.

"Yes, good," said Macros.

Miranda looked around. "Are we still in the Pavilion?"

"We are wherever you'd like to be," said Macros. "But

stay here awhile longer, for I can guarantee here we will not be disturbed, and here time will not rush us."

"Time?" asked Nakor. "You've touched on time before."

Macros nodded. "We'll get there. Let Pug continue."

Pug said, "So if Abrem-Sev is the outward force, Ev-Dem is the inward force, the one that tempers Abrem-Sev's chaotic, seemingly random outward burst. That's where the rules begin."

"Wonderful," said Macros. He waved his hand and a large chair appeared, on which he sat. "I'm feeling old."

Pug continued. "Then Graff is . . . how our minds interact with that energy, how dreams come to be or how gods are formed by human perceptions of natural forces, or how you think of a thing, and it suddenly happens."

"A simple way to put it, but essentially correct," said Macros, obviously delighted with the flow of the conversation.

"Helbinor?" asked Magnus. "The god who does nothing? How does he fit in?"

Pug said, "I do not know."

Nakor beamed. "I do."

Macros leaned forward. "I must hear this."

"He only *seems* to do nothing," said Nakor. "But if the gods are personifications of natural forces, he's the personification of things we cannot see, things we do not understand. He is the god of true mystery, things yet undiscovered."

"Say on," said Macros with a grin matching Nakor's.

"What we have said about the forces of creation and the forces that oppose them, and forces created by the mind, that's too simple. There must be other forces also at play. Forces not only not understood, but not even perceived or suspected. That's Helbinor. Remember the City Forever. It's a plan, like a set of drawings laid out by an architect. We were seeing things of wonder, but what were we seeing?"

"Go on," said Pug.

"All those things we've discussed: the critical importance of mathematics, our limited perceptions, our need for perspective, and most of all, our need to remember the central, important things about being human . . ." He paused, and smiled ruefully, and moisture gathered in his eyes. "Being human." He looked at Miranda. "That is our lesson."

She nodded.

"We have come to understand that the gods are merely how we see the universe and that our perspective is limited, incomplete, and flawed, yet it is all we have. It is *how* we understand," Nakor went on.

"Fair enough," said Macros.

"And Ishap, the Balancer, is the most important of all," Nakor added. "Without him, everything else is chaos."

"He's dead," said Miranda.

"So are a lot of the gods," said Nakor. "Eortis, God of the Sea; the God of Love, the God of Night, the God of Healing, but other gods take on some of their roles, or remember them, so their influences linger, even if their aspects do not. Ishap, he's gone, but the others remember him, so that's why he's still important. It's why his impact is still felt."

"And why the Ishapians work to make him supreme among the gods," said Magnus. "To bring him back in order to ensure the balance."

"It's not my nature to ponder such things," said Miranda. "But what you've shown is so extraordinary that even I'm intrigued. Still, I must ask, what has this to do with the Dread and saving the universe?"

Macros stood up. "Now we get to the hard part." He waved his hand and suddenly the five of them were gone from the Pavilion.

A faint breeze blew a curtain and a shadow appeared. Then a second, then a third.

"Can they do it?" asked the first shadow. It spoke with the voice of a kindly old woman.

A voice, muffled as if speaking from beneath a mile of a distant planet's soil, said, "We can only hope, old enemy."

The third shadow balanced what the Goddess of Good and the God of Evil had said and remained silent.

21

UNVEILING

Dragons screamed.

Tomas awoke. His wife, Queen Aglaranna, rose up at his side and put her hand on his shoulder. "Another dream?"

Tomas sat up and swung his legs out of the bed they had shared for more than a century. "I dreamed of dragons again." He, the human son of a common cook, had been given the armor of the ancient Dragon Lord Ashen-Shugar, and in donning it had started a process of creating a being that was neither human nor Valheru.

As a youth in the war with the Tsurani, he had come to Elvandar with Dolgan, now the ancient King of the Dwarves, then the Warleader of the Grey Tower Mountains, and had wintered with the elves. A love had grown between the widowed Queen Aglaranna and the changing man from Crydee. At the end of the war they had wed, and against any possible logic they had had a child, Calis.

Softly he said, "I must go."

Aglaranna placed her cheek against his back. "Will I see you again?"

"You sense what is coming," he said. "It is in the hands of the gods."

The elves did not have gods in the human sense, though they venerated Killian, the human Goddess of Nature, but the Elf Queen understood that he was speaking of fate. "You are my heart," she whispered.

"And you mine," he said. He rose and went to the wardrobe that had been carved into the bole of the massive tree in which the royal apartment was situated. He opened the curtain and there waiting was his armor of white and gold.

Minutes later he was dressed in battle armor he had not donned since flying down to greet the Taredhel, and hadn't worn in combat for what seemed ages. As fierce a warrior as existed on this world, Tomas was by nature a man of peace who enjoyed nothing more than the small quiet moments he spent with his wife, his son, and his friends in Elvandar.

He turned and saw that Aglaranna had removed her sleeping gown, and was now wearing one of the simpler robes she preferred when not at court. He smiled. "That shade of green is my favorite on you."

"I know," she said.

Ages of life and loss, wisdom beyond that of mortals, experiences few could imagine: the Queen was wise beyond all but a very few in the world. She held herself poised and showed nothing of the pain she was feeling, but he was her husband and could read the small signs. All life ends, they knew, and loss was inevitable, but now was the moment of parting, and this perhaps was the last parting.

"If I can, I will return," he whispered as he gathered her into his arms, kissing her head lightly.

She rose up on her toes and kissed him on the mouth, holding him close as if unwilling to let him leave. They lingered long in this embrace, parting at the same moment, knowing it was time.

Aglaranna led him out of their apartment and found Calin and the most senior members of the council waiting there. Janil said, "I felt it, too, Tomas. The dragons are crying out."

Calin added, "And I bring word of the Moredhel."

Tomas looked at his wife's eldest son. "What of the Moredhel?"

"Liallan sent us word that the Snow Leopards and their allies are moving to E'bar to aid the Taredhel and will pass within our traditional boundaries. They are entering the woodlands to the northeast now."

Tomas nodded. The woods around Elvandar were considered part of the Eledhel's territory and for any Moredhel to enter would be considered a hostile act at any other time. "What is their disposition?" he asked.

"As they promised, riding with weapons sheathed and on a direct route to the south. They make no threatening moves or gestures."

Queen Aglaranna spoke softly. "So many things to wish for, born out of greater threat: that the dark elves enter our woodlands without violent intent, that we allow them safe passage, and no blood spilled." She looked up at Tomas and said, "I fear for us all."

"I will do all that I must, to the end, to ensure that you are safe," said Tomas.

Janil said, "I would speak with Cetswaya."

"You have no need to ask permission," said the Queen.

"I will send an escort," said Calin. "But you need to move quickly, for they will be across the river before you can reach them on foot."

"There will be no need," said Aglaranna. She turned and raised her voice. "Belegroch! Belegroch! Attend us." She turned back to Calin. "They will bear you willingly, for I know you will go with Janil."

"Mother," Calin said, bowing. Turning to Tomas, he said, "If this be farewell, I can only say how honored I have been to know you."

"Let us hope it is not farewell," said Tomas. He gripped Calin's hand. "You bear my love, Calin, as you bear my son's." They embraced briefly, then Tomas said, "We must all depart."

"Will you summon a dragon?" asked the Queen.

"None will answer," said Janil. "They are singing and crying, and foretelling the end of time as we know it."

"I have no need," said Tomas. He raised his arms and took to the sky using his own magic. "Farewell, all of you!" he cried.

Arcing high above the canopy of trees, he looked to the northeast, and in the distance could see the might of the Northlands—Liallan's Snow Leopards and their allies, followed by other clans, moving across lands traditionally claimed by the Eledhel. He felt the wind blowing in his face and for a moment rejoiced in his own power.

The Valheru had always been creatures of incredible might. Their name in the ancient tongue meant "Lord of Power," and many arts were theirs at whim. Flying on the backs of mighty dragons was both a vanity and a useful practicality; for while the Valheru were capable of many feats, the dragons possessed one skill no Dragon Lord could duplicate: they could navigate the Void.

Tomas extended his sense and felt instantly that all the dragons were gathering in an isolated region to the southwest of the Empire of Great Kesh, called Dragon's Eyre, where a ring of mountains called the Watchmen by those who lived nearby surrounded the Great Lake.

Tomas sped south and turned in the direction of E'bar, the better to judge what was occurring there on his way to find the dragons. The gold-and-white figure sped across the sky high above the trees of the place he loved most in the world, the place he might never see again.

The tiger men prostrated themselves as their master emerged at last from the throne room in the heart of the Great South Forest. More than a century before, another Ancient One had passed this way with a black-robed human, but this was the first time in countless ages their master had been among them.

Draken-Korin, Lord of Tigers, emerged from his palace, which was now covered in millennia of dirt, lianas, ferns, and shrubs. His body had once belonged to a human named Braden—a mercenary, bandit, smuggler, and murderer. Memories of that mortal life lingered, but to his soul he was the remaining Dragon Rider who had dared to take to the skies and confront the new gods.

But there was another of his kind out there somewhere, and he sensed him. It was a presence as familiar to him as any of his kindred: Ashen-Shugar, ruler of the Eagle's Reaches, his father-brother and mortal enemy.

Much of the time Draken-Korin had lingered deep within the hall below the surface of this world had been devoted to the mere act of survival, as ancient magic possessed the mortal body, healing wounds that would otherwise prove lethal, and integrating ancient powers and knowledge.

Memories that were oddly distant also came to him, memories of a time when the sky tore open and he descended into a dark chamber wherein resided a glowing green gem of impossible power. The Lifestone. He remembered . . .

The gods had been too powerful and the Valheru had served only to turn them one against the other, or else they would have perished. They had thought themselves so clever, giving up all their life essences to the Lifestone, that engine of power that was to have propelled them to godhood, holding back only a tiny part to maintain their corporeal bodies during the last battle of the Chaos Wars.

Instead, Draken-Korin had found himself facing his most feared rival: his own father, Ashen-Shugar.

Fleeing the conflict within the Void, Draken-Korin had been no match for Ashen-Shugar, and his last memories were of lying broken on the hard soil of this world, his father standing over him.

Draken-Korin had looked up at his attacker and whispered, "Why?"

Pointing with his golden sword at the chaos seen through the massive tear in the sky, Ashen-Shugar said, "This obscenity should never have been allowed. You bring an end to all we knew."

Draken-Korin looked skyward to where his brethren battled the gods. "They were so strong. We could never have dreamed . . ." His face revealed his terror and hate as Ashen-Shugar raised his golden blade to end it. "But I had the right!" he screamed.

Ashen-Shugar severed Draken-Korin's head from his shoulders, and suddenly all was darkness.

Now Draken-Korin took a deep breath, for the memories were painful. Primal rage and bitterness rose up within him, but in his mind there was another voice that found his feelings repellent. A low intelligence, a weak soul, yet still Braden abided, a voice of flawed humanity.

Draken-Korin looked at the prostrating tiger men and said, "Rise."

They did so. He motioned for their leader—Tuan, as every leader of these people was named. "I must depart."

"Will you return, Ancient One?"

In a gesture never seen before in the history of the tiger men, Draken-Korin put his hand on Tuan's shoulder and smiled. "Probably not."

"What shall we do?" asked Tuan.

"As you did after I last departed, and before I returned. Live."

Draken-Korin closed his eyes and heard dragon song in his mind, punctuated by screams and cries. He remembered . . .

Their haven had been turned into a trap. Below the deepest dungeon in the city of Sethanon lay a chamber constructed by the Valheru before the coming of man to Midkemia.

Odd voices had whispered to Draken-Korin and he had felt power surge through him such as he had never possessed before.

The Lifestone.

And when the skies tore and madness engulfed the universe, the Valheru had battled the new gods, realms far apart in nature crashing together in violent upheaval. Barriers had tumbled and reestablished themselves by the moment, dividing the Dragon Host and weakening their resolve.

Draken-Korin had known fear. Dreams of conquest, ascension to godhood, fled before the specter of complete annihilation. This was more than two Valheru contesting for power and territory in which one would fall and the other emerge victorious: this meant the total obliteration of the race.

Gods of majestic visage and incredible power had picked up flaming stars and hurled them. Thousands of angels and demons had risen in furious conflict, and time itself became a weapon.

Draken-Korin commanded his dragon to flee, and the terrified mount had wheeled and the heavens spun as the Dragon Host's combined might attempted to tear open a wound in the sky above Midkemia so that they might slip away from this conflict.

"Foolish," said a voice.

Screaming worlds died behind him as Draken-Korin had shouted, "Who speaks?" He had looked behind and seen a presence, a massive black shape, following him. It was a thing of hopelessness and anger, and it had reached for him as if to pull him back, to drag him into a pit from which even light could not escape.

"Home!" commanded Draken-Korin, and the universe had shattered.

Macros said, "When we were in the chamber below Sethanon, holding back the rift that was forming, and Draken-Korin slipped through, a Dreadlord followed."

"Yes?" Pug nodded, curious as to why Macros was reminding him of events he had lived through.

"In the aftermath of that conflict, did you ever wonder why they came together?"

"Many times," said Pug, "and in discussions with Tomas afterward, and with a few others who understand the lore of the Valheru, and the even fewer who know something of the Dread, I still came to no conclusion."

"Then it is time for you to see the truth of that moment."

They stood in a featureless realm of white light that seemed to come from every direction. They felt as if they were standing on a solid floor, but when they looked down, all they saw was white. "Where are we?" asked Nakor.

"In the middle of a metaphor," said Macros. "I'm creating this to illustrate something impossible to show you."

He waved his hand and a spinning ball appeared to hang in the air before them at chest height. "This is . . . everything."

Pug whispered, "You said 'size and distance have no meaning.'"

"Yes," said Macros with a smile. "You remember."

"How could I forget?"

"Pug, Tomas, Ryath the dragon, and I witnessed this," said Macros.

"What?" asked Miranda, peering at the orb.

"It's featureless," said Macros, and he also leaned close to inspect it. "It seems to have shape and substance, but yet reflects no light. This is a metaphor for what really happened, and it's my creation. I haven't the means to take you back to the Garden at the time we witness what I'm about to show you. More, I'm controlling this so I can manipulate a few things so you may understand better what it is you need to know, about the Dread and the coming battle."

He moved his hand and the sphere moved as well, rising to eye level. All around them the light faded until they were floating in darkness, with a single light around the sphere illuminating their faces. "Behold," Macros said quietly.

In an instant the sphere vanished and a light erupted and filled every point of view with blinding brilliance so that they all had to avert their gaze. With the light came a surge of feeling, an almost overwhelming sense of completion and perfection, that left them weeping for joy. Then the light was gone, shattered into billions of tiny lights, and on every side around them were stars, masses of stars, speeding away.

Macros cried, "Hold!" and all motion halted.

Moving through the void, he walked in a circle around a solitary point where the sphere had been. "Can you see this?" he asked.

They saw a flicker in the dark, a swirling mass. "It's . . . something," said Nakor, "but I can't make out any features."

"Here," said Macros, and a blazing light shone down from above and brought the tiny mote into view. It was a thing of utter darkness, and no matter the bright light hitting it, nothing was reflected back. Rather it was seen because of its lack of features, a negative presence amid all the glory of stars around it. It was given definition only by where the light could not be seen, where the stars behind it were rendered invisible.

"What is it?" whispered Miranda, the alien nature of the object prompting a sense of trepidation in her.

Nakor said, "I think it's the Dread."

Macros said, "There was at the beginning . . . everything. Matter, energy, space, time, all were one thing. That was the sphere you saw."

"It was massive when we saw it in the Garden," said Pug.

"Perspective," answered Miranda.

"Now you are beginning to understand the reasons for the lessons," said Macros. "Watch," he said. He moved his hands and the dark speck expanded till its irregular surface was finally revealed in detail, reflecting so very faintly the distant stars, offering an impression of movement, of change, something that looked almost like writing.

"Remember," said Macros, "what you are seeing is a metaphor, an analogy, a representation of something so far beyond our ability to apprehend that even what I show you is only a small part of the reality."

The point of view of the observers seemed to swoop in to a point just above a writhing, ever-shifting landscape.

"It's . . . almost as if it's in pain," said Miranda.

"Astute," said Macros. He waved his hand and suddenly their entire field of vision was filled by the surface of this mass. "Now," he said, and colors began to shift. "This is a way to show you something beyond the ability of mortal eyes to see." A mass of threads rose up from the surface to connect to the fleeing stars, and their number was so vast it was as if they were speeding through a jungle of white vines. Perspective shifted and for a moment Pug couldn't judge if he was getting smaller or the threads were getting larger. Then suddenly they stopped.

"What is this?" asked Pug.

"Watch," said Macros, and they appeared to approach a single thread, which got larger and larger, until it dominated their field of vision, and then within the thread other threads manifested, as if the first thread they saw was some sort of rope. On they drove, deeper into the fabric of that virtual rope, until Macros brought them to face one single thread. "Now, pay close attention." The thread seemed to flicker until at last they saw it wasn't a thread, but a series of tiny motes so close together that from any distance they seemed to be connected. "So, Nakor, what is this?"

The mote expanded and became a translucent sphere within which energy vibrated. The vibrations slowed until the illusion of a sphere vanished and they could see there was a thread of energy that writhed madly, turning itself into a variety of shapes each second. Again Macros waved his hand and it slowed. First the strand was straight, then it looped, then it fluttered upward, then doubled back on itself, one end anchored while the other described the outer limit of its reach, defining the "sphere," despite moving at speeds faster than the human eye could decipher.

The little demon-turned-human stared in wonder, and at last he said, "It's . . . stuff."

"Stuff?" asked Magnus.

"It's what you call 'magic,'" said Nakor. "This is what you play with when you think you're doing magic."

"Wonderful," said Macros. "Yes, this is what you've been struggling to understand your entire life, little gambler. You've intuitively understood the single most fundamental truth about our universe." He put out his hand as if presenting the flickering thread. "This is the basic building block of everything. Nothing smaller exists."

"What is it doing?" asked Miranda. "It's constantly changing."

"Therein lies the genius of creation," said Macros. "For this tiny object, this thing that is not energy, nor matter, nor light, nor time, but its own unique thing, decides from instant to instant what it is going to be."

"I don't understand," said Magnus.

"No one does," said Macros, as if the idea delighted him. "There are things in the universe that we will never fully comprehend. We must just accept it as mystery."

"The first being why this happened," suggested Miranda.

"Yes," said Macros. "Exactly. There was this perfect state of being, this total harmony of everything . . ." He stopped, then said, "Words can't do it justice. You felt that brief instant of bliss as it passed through you. That was how it was eternally." He laughed. "Or perhaps it was only that way for the tiniest part of a second, because then time was part of everything."

"I'm overwhelmed," said Miranda.

"I'm delighted," said Nakor.

Pug merely glanced at Magnus, who said, "Why?"

"Why what?" said Macros.

"Why the elaborate display? Why not just tell us?"

"Two reasons," said Macros. "Miranda can tell you the first."

"Because he's not the most reliable source of intelligence we've encountered, and in this case showing us is better than merely telling us."

"And," said Pug, "because we need to understand the scope of what we are confronting."

"You are tasked with the most profound and difficult burden in history: you are to save the universe."

Tomas flew above the trees, and as he approached the farthest boundaries of E'bar, he could feel the alien energies infecting the area. First, he saw the clearing to the north of the valley where once the Kingdom and Tsurani armies had battled. Sensing a familiar presence, he located it and swooped down, landing easily next to his son.

Beside Calis, Arkan of the Ardanien looked on with hooded eyes, uncertain of how to keep his deep rush of emotions under control. He was torn between drawing his sword and attacking the white-and-gold-armored figure, or begging forgiveness for some unnamed shortcoming.

"Father!" cried Calis, and they embraced.

"I thought you were to return to your mother as soon as you had finished carrying word to the Kingdom?"

"At Ylith, while I was waiting for safe passage south to Krondor, several odd things happened." He nodded to Arkan. "Arkan, this is my father. Father, this is Arkan, the Chieftain of the Ardanien."

"Gorath's son," said Tomas. "I met your father. He was a remarkable person."

Arkan inclined his head. Since Tomas had appeared, rumors of his nature had circulated among the clans of the north, speculation ranging from him being a pretender with some magic ability, to his being a tool of the Eledhel through which they hoped to claim dominance over all the elven people. But one moment in the presence of this towering figure in white and gold and Arkan knew to the core of his being that this was indeed an embodiment of an Ancient One. He fought the desire to fall to his knees in obeisance.

"I encountered the sons of the Duke of Crydee," Calis said. "The mantle of the dukedom has passed to his eldest son, Henry. So I spoke to Martin and Brendan, and passed word of their mother and the others' safety. My duty being done, I felt free to find out what our friend here was doing in the Kingdom."

Arkan looked at Calis askance at the term "friend," judging it to be meant as a friendly gibe, and stayed silent.

Tomas indicated that he wished to have a private moment with Calis and led him a short distance away.

"You're leaving," said Calis, and it wasn't a question. "The dragons call."

"You hear it, too?"

"In my dreams, Father." He studied the face of the marvelous man who had sired him, studied features as familiar as his own reflection. He knew of the struggles endured by the human side of his father to control the Dragon Lord's rage, and yet all he had known since his birth had been love and acceptance. Calis kept his emotions under control as he considered this might be the last time they spoke. He said, "My life has been one of wonder and love. I thank whatever gods listen every day for my mother and my father."

Tomas felt himself swept up in a powerful emotion. "I could not have asked for a better son," he declared. "Take care of your mother if I do not return."

"I will," Calis said stoically. His father's request was unnecessary, but a reminder that both men faced the possibility of not surviving this coming fight; they embraced and lingered for a moment, then separated.

Tomas turned. "How fares this struggle?" He looked down the hillside at the ruby dome.

"We appear to have reached a stalemate. The enemy within brings more power to bear, but the magic users who have arrived to aid the Taredhel have blunted the assault. I do not know how much longer we can withstand the mounting pressure inside the dome."

"Come," said Tomas, and he walked back to the motionless Moredhel chieftain. "Arkan," he said, "your clans march south."

A flicker of concern passed over Arkan's face. "Clans? I have but one."

Tomas smiled. "Your aunt's clans, then."

"Liallan comes here?"

"She brings the might of the Snow Leopards and their allies to aid the Taredhel. Every shaman of note is coming to help push back whatever's trying to get out into our world."

Arkan was silent, then asked, "My people?"

"I do not know if the Ice Bears were called, but I can't imagine her not calling every sword and shaman tied to her."

"She takes a great risk," said Arkan.

"I know," said Tomas. "She's abandoned the north to Narab and his allies."

"You know much of our politics," said the Moredhel chieftain.

"We have always thought it wise to keep an eye on our neighbors," Tomas said. The relationship between the various nations of elves had long been contentious and bloody, and it was considered bad taste to mention the kinship involved. The use of the word "neighbors" instead of "cousins" was appreciated, and Arkan inclined his head.

"I must ask, though," said Tomas, "why are you here? You departed the north long before the events here."

"Liallan sent me," he said. "She and her shaman dream—"

Before he could finish, Tomas said, "—of dragons."

Arkan paused, his eyes widening in surprise. Then he nodded. "Yes, they dream of dragons."

"Why you?" asked Tomas.

"Many reasons," said Arkan, "but foremost, she saw me in

a vision, atop a hill, protecting a human magician in a black robe, and judged it to be a foretelling."

"Liallan's bloodline numbered many with that gift," said Tomas. "Her sister was considered a shaman, though tainted by your father's choices."

"My mother," said Arkan softly, "is someone of whom I never speak." In his eyes, his mother, Cullich, had betrayed his father after the first battle of Sethanon, when Gorath had ordered the remaining forces of the Moredhel north, and she had renounced their marriage.

Tomas nodded. "I meant no offense. Apologies."

Arkan stood motionless. The most powerful figure he had ever encountered, perhaps the most powerful single mortal being on this world, had just apologized to him. This was perhaps the single most unexpected thing he had encountered in his life. He inclined his head and said, "There is no offense . . . Tomas."

Tomas smiled and turned his attention to the ruby dome. Using his own powers, he studied its structures for a moment, then said, "I recognize a very odd but familiar quality to what is seeking to leave."

"The Dread?" asked Calis.

Tomas nodded. "It will take Pug and Magnus to push that back whence it came." He looked at his son. "No word from them?"

"Ruffio is here on behalf of the Conclave and Stardock, but there's no word from Pug or Magnus, or Miranda and Nakor."

Tomas's eyebrows rose.

"It's a long story, but Miranda and Nakor . . ."

Tomas held up his hand. "If we see each other again, you can tell me the long story. However it happened, if Miranda and Nakor are with Pug and Magnus, then perhaps this day will be ours." He looked at Arkan. "If Liallan's vision of you protecting a black-robed human magic user is a foretelling, then it is a critical role you play. All of our survival may depend on you protecting whichever man in black—Pug or his son—is fated to be in your care."

"I will give my life if I must," said Arkan.

"We all may," said Tomas.

"Are you not staying to confront that thing within the dome?" asked Arkan.

"No," said Tomas, "for the powers of the Valheru are not given to the more subtle arts of magic, and should what is in that dome emerge, even my sword will make little difference. I am destined to play another role. And now I must answer the call of dragons." He smiled. "If they wish me to return, I will. If they have other plans for me, fare you well, both of you."

Calis and Arkan both nodded.

Tomas leaped into the sky and in a giant arc sped into the distance.

22

REVELATION

O n all sides, the universe unfolded.

Five magic users studied an incredibly complex array of energy and matter.

"There are ten dimensions: three which you perceive, one which you experience, and six so profound even gods wonder at their nature," said Macros.

"Height, width, depth, and time," said Pug.

"Yes."

"There are six more?" asked Nakor, his curiosity piqued.

"Perhaps more, but six I have been able to deduce, using a complex set of . . ." He grinned at the little demon in Nakor's form. "We do not have time for this. I will indulge you if I can at some later time."

Miranda softly said, "I'm struggling to understand what you're showing me, but more importantly, I need to know what the point of all this is."

"It's complex at a level that gives me a headache to consider, let alone attempt to understand," said Magnus.

"You're coming to the end," said Macros. "But each step has been needed so you can approach the coming conflict with as much knowledge as possible." He turned and seemed to walk around the mass at the center. "We shall return to this in a moment." He waved his hand and the virtual universe around them appeared to speed away from the Dread, following the countless tendrils of energy that gave the impression of being connected to everything. Then the vision halted, and they were left with a vista of curving space, moving away from the center, connected throughout by energy.

"It is a common error of all sentient beings to see the universe as being limited by the capabilities of their own perceptions. A race of blind creatures might perceive light as heat, but they will not understand light unless there's a different means to detect it," said Macros. "What is this thing that happened, this primary birth of all known universes?" he asked.

The other four remained silent.

"Nearly every race has a creation myth, everything from a single ultimate god willing the universe into existence, to the world being born out of struggle, to living in a god's dream . . ." He shrugged. "Whatever one can imagine, I guess."

"We were taught," said Magnus, "that before the Chaos Wars began, the two blind gods of the beginning—"

Macros interrupted: "Consider." He waved his hand again and images of two powerful beings appeared on either side of a swirling torrent of energies. A massive male stood grasping at the flood and tearing shreds out, casting them in every direction. Opposite him, a female figure reached out with incredible speed and grabbed the threads of life and wove them into a tapestry that looped around behind her and fed the torrent.

"The earliest personification of the two fundamental forces in the universe—creation and destruction—but what does it show you?"

"That nothing ends," said Pug softly.

Macros beamed with pride. "Yes, nothing ever ends. As sentient creatures arose, the multitude of gods arose with them, each offering a reflection of those people. In some cases, like your Dasati, there were literally thousands of gods, since they assigned a deity to even the most mundane aspect of daily life: a goddess of the garden, a god of the hearth, a god of this and that. Others ascribed minor issues to spirits and lesser beings, leaving the gods to personify only the larger aspects of life: love and war, health and wisdom, fortune and nature." He shrugged. "I know this came about, but I do not know how it happened. There are worlds upon which the gods walk, interact with their worshippers, and worlds like Midkemia where the gods are present, but only a very few such as yourselves encounter them. There are worlds in which the gods exist and are never seen. And worlds where the gods do not even exist."

"No gods?" asked Nakor thoughtfully.

"You find that interesting?" asked Macros.

"Very," said Nakor. "It means the forces control the gods, not the other way around."

"Almost correct," said Macros. "In some worlds there seems to be a synergy, but for the most part, what Kalkin said to you is the root truth: they are merely personifications of natural forces given whatever powers they possess by their worshippers. They have aspects that are perceived by mortals, and attributes they can wield."

"Then who or what is responsible for all of this?" asked Miranda.

Macros smiled delightedly. "Daughter, I have never been

more proud of your abilities as I am now; you cut to the heart of it."

He swept his hand and moved them back closer to the image of the Dread, the writhing mass at the center of the colossal explosion that created the universes. "There are cultures whose myths contain the concept of a single god: the Ultimate, the One, the Father or the Mother, the Demiurge . . ." He shook his head in resignation. "No one will ever know, unless that entity, whatever it may be, chooses to reveal itself, and I for one think that is impossible."

"Impossible?" asked Magnus. "For an entity who did all this?"

"Go have a conversation with a flower, reveal yourself to a butterfly—"

"The spider," said Pug, nodding with understanding.

Macros paused for a moment, then smiled. "The lesson I inflicted on you while you were training with the Tsurani, yes."

The others looked at Pug and he said, "If you disturb a spiderweb, the spider will be aware of that disturbance, but it doesn't understand what's causing it. Moreover, if a spider is running up your arm and inflicts a bite, does it know who it is biting?"

"No, of course not," answered Miranda.

"But there is still a causal relationship there," said Nakor.

"Yes," agreed Macros.

"Then we are left with a mystery," said Magnus.

"Not a mystery," said his grandfather, "but *the* mystery. The single greatest mystery of all."

Miranda said, "But you have a theory."

"Always," said Macros. "But I am not so audacious as to give it a name. All I can do is to describe it as best I can."

The tendrils of energy sped closer to them again. "These . . . threads link everything together. I think they are what we would call Mind. There is a higher Mind, a thing some cultures even worship as the God Mind, or name it after a particular deity or prophet or savior, or simply the universal or higher consciousness. It's rather like your own mind being very busy while the hair on your arm doesn't really care much what you're thinking about: we each have our own tiny bits of mind that we're concerned with, and leave the universal consciousness, the Mind, to its own devices."

"Mind," muttered Nakor. "It easily accommodates Miranda and me still being here, and you, too."

"A slice of Mind," said Pug. "Kulgan, and you."

"If you sliced those tendrils finely enough, and gathered the thinnest slice of their essence, they would heal almost instantly and no one would notice."

"But who could do such a thing?" asked Magnus.

"We return to the ultimate mystery." Macros looked at Pug. "If you recall, when traveling the Hall after fleeing the Garden, you asked me what the gods were doing to intervene and I said *we* were the intervention, we were doing the gods' work."

"Now I understand," said Pug. "The gods are our personification of forces. We create them, therefore when we're working for the gods—"

"We're working for ourselves," finished Macros.

"What of the Dread?" asked Magnus. "What are they and how do we best confront them?"

"Again, you're mistaking one thing for many. The Dread is a single entity, just like the Mind. Two halves of a coin, two sides of a parchment, two things connected in a profound way."

"The Dread is the opposite of Mind?" asked Magnus.

"No, the Dread is the other side of Mind," Macros replied.

"Explain, please," said Pug.

"Everything is connected," began Macros. "So we can speculate why this all took place. Perhaps Mind got curious? I have no idea: my understanding is very limited. But one significant difference is that time was spun out of the ball of everything and allowed to unfold."

"Why is that more important than the other aspects of reality being turned loose?" asked Nakor.

"Because time is what keeps everything from happening simultaneously!" answered Macros. "Because of time, you can see evolutions and changes . . ." He stopped. "Let me show you something, and pay close attention, for this is the Dread's one weakness, their one vulnerability that you must somehow exploit."

He waved his hand and a stream of water appeared in the air, moving in a downward arc. "Consider this jet of water as an analogy for time." He pointed to the top. "Imagine a single drop to be a moment, which flows from here down to here."

"I see," said Pug.

"Now, we are in a drop, our 'now,' and we travel along with it, so when we were up here"—he pointed to the top of the stream—"that was yesterday, and where we get here"—he pointed to the bottom—"it will be tomorrow."

"So as the drop travels we pass from yesterday through now to tomorrow," said Pug.

"But it's always now," said Nakor. "This is all a matter of perception."

"True," Macros agreed, "but it's necessary for us to see what we see, understand as we do, and learn, for our part of the task is to grow and bring to the Mind our tiny contribution so that it may understand."

"Understand what?" asked Miranda.

"Itself. We are Mind learning about itself, the totality of the universe trying to understand itself fully. All of us, every conscious being on every world in every reality. We are all connected; nothing dies because what we learn is part of Mind."

"I can't begin to pretend I understand what you're saying," said Miranda, her manner betraying an impatience with the abstract. "Tell us about the weakness of the Dread."

"The Dread cannot see the now. They see the entirety of time all at once. It was they who set the time trap in the Garden for Pug, Tomas, and me, in the hope we'd simply move to another part of the stream without the means to return, but they couldn't anticipate we'd take the course we did."

"I still don't see how the Dread's ability to see the entirety of time is a weakness," said Magnus. "Why haven't they done whatever they know will work to bring about the ending they seek?"

"Because they see this!" said Nakor, barely able to contain his excitement. "They see the entire stream, and yes, they see all the drops in it, but they can't follow a single drop." He started sticking his finger in various parts of the stream. "So they poke here, and there, and try to make this work or that work, and they watch and see results, but there is no coherency!"

"Exactly," said Macros. "At various times they've attempted to do whatever they could to defeat Mind and what it is seeking."

"Why?" asked Miranda.

Pug said, "And why Midkemia?"

"As for the second, it had to be somewhere. Why not Midkemia? This is where they got lucky in trying to break into your realm. As for the first . . ." He waved his hand and Pug and the others saw a high mountain meadow populated by luminous beings floating about the ground, jewel-faceted and lit from within. The Sven-ga'ri. Their language was emotion, and to be near them was to hear music.

"On many worlds," Macros continued, "the Dread reached out and placed . . . markers. For they also understand the limits of their own perception when it comes to time. The Sven-ga'ri are one of these 'markers,' a way for them to discover the secret of a continuity of time we take for granted. So profound is the need of the Dread for these markers to endure that they used the powerful arts to protect them."

"They made them beautiful," said Pug.

"They speak with feelings," said Macros, "and they seem gentle and harmless. But even the Dragon Lords recognized them as having terrible potential for danger."

"Which is why they placed the elves to guard them?"

"They created the Quor, or rather they facilitated the creation of the Quor," said Macros. "The Valheru could not create true life, but only take life and change it. The

Quor were once plants—in a sense they're animated trees—and predate even the elves as the oldest sentient beings on Midkemia. Then the elves evolved, and they placed elves to guard the Quor."

"Why guard them if they were a means for the Dread to find Midkemia again?" asked Magnus.

"Because they didn't understand them," said Macros, "and feared that to destroy them might bring terrible danger. The Dragon Lords were capricious and wanton in their destruction, but they were not stupid."

"What about the Sven-ga'ri we found on the Isle of the Snake Men?" asked Pug.

"Destroyed utterly when you sprang your trap. Along, I'm sorry to say, with the entire population of that Pantathian city. It was clear that the Dread put your destruction ahead of keeping the Sven-ga'ri on the island alive." He shrugged. "They had the ones in the Peaks of the Quor anyway, and perhaps they've discovered another way in."

"Those Pantathians were a gentle aspect of that race," said Magnus. "It is tragic."

"Nothing dies," said Macros. "What they are, who they were, returned to Mind and will manifest itself somewhere else at some other time."

"That's hardly comforting to the Pantathians who died in that blast," said Miranda.

"You're probably right," said Macros. "But I can share one thing with you. When I was attempting to attain godhood, while my body wandered almost mindless, wasting away on the shore by Stardock, before you pulled me away, and then, again, as I tried to ascend, what I can tell you is that when you join with the Mind, the more you know, the less your sense of self endures. It becomes closer to that moment of bliss you felt when the Sphere of Creation exploded." He looked from face to face. "They feel no pain, and their minds are with that bliss."

"Hardly seems a recommendation for seeking oblivion," said Miranda drily.

"Life is tenacious," said Nakor.

"Very much so," said Macros. "I have no knowledge of where my own mind went after I left you. This slice of my existence knows much, but not everything. I do not know what that Dasati holding my memories said and did, though I expect his . . . my participation was needed."

"It was," said Magnus.

"Macros," said Pug, "you've shown us astonishing things, and offered us perspectives beyond imagining. But I still do not see how we are to deal with something as vast as the Dread."

"As I said," Macros replied, "the Dread's weakness is its perspective on time. What you must do is find a moment, one critical instant, and focus its consciousness there. That will cause it to lose track of its other markers, like the one destroyed in the Pantathian city. And do not forget those in the Peaks of the Quor must be destroyed as well. Once it becomes obsessed, then maybe we shall see the beginning of a slow return to stability between the Dread and Mind."

"How do we do that?" said Pug.

"That," said Macros, "is the problem you were given to solve, Pug."

Pug thought about this while Macros started to make the vista around them return to where it had been before, so that it looked as if stars and galaxies were moving back toward the center, where lurked the Dread. "Oh, Macros," he said, "one thing. Gathis? What became of him?"

Macros said, "He died of old age. When it was his time he just left, as was his kind's wont. They die apart."

"What manner of creature was he?" asked Pug.

"As the Taredhel wandered the stars, so did goblin kind. His race was highly evolved: poets, scholars, healers, artificers of beauty. He was the last of his kind."

"Hearing that makes me wish it true that nothing ever dies." Pug had expected that the kindly keeper of Macros's household on Sorcerer's Isle was now dead, but hearing it as fact made him sad.

"Truly," said Macros.

"In all this," said Miranda, "you've never answered the first question, why the Dread wage war on everything."

"Really?" said Macros. "Why, I thought it would have been obvious by now." He waved his hand and again they floated in white light with a single dark sphere before them. "This," he said, pointing. "This was eternal, or as eternal as something can be with all time contained within it. It was, or is, or will be, everything, past, present, future, matter, light, heart and mind, love and hate, all of it rolled up in this tidy little ball. Then *bang!* Mind and that feeling of perfect bliss sped away from the Dread and left this miserable component behind." With a gesture he made the Dread appear again without the rest of the sphere. "Whatever impulse drove Mind to seek experience, to put time out in a line, and to learn all that it could about itself, the Dread wants things back the way they were, returned to that perfect, blissful state."

Nakor didn't smile. "The Dread are lonely."

"In a way," said Macros. "This is the fundamental battle in reality. Nothing is more basic."

"Back to basics," said Pug softly.

"What do we do now?" asked Magnus.

"You return to Midkemia and finish a battle already begun," said Macros. "Should you fail and the Dread achieve their goal, then all will return to the primal state and none of what we think of as history will have occurred, for time will be retracted into that sphere and none of the reality we have experienced will have ever happened."

With a nod of his head, a vortex appeared. Pug glanced at the others then ran to it, jumping in headfirst. Miranda, Magnus, and Nakor followed.

Macros started to follow, but the vortex vanished, leaving him standing in a void of white light.

Slowly, he said, "It is over?"

An echo in his mind said, "Yes," and Macros the Black, sorcerer supreme of Midkemia, vanished from view forever.

23

ENCOUNTERS

Liallan held up her hand.

The column of Moredhel horsemen behind her reined in and the signal was passed back until over five thousand warriors had halted their march. From the west, riders approached across the river that marked the boundary between the outer elven forests and unclaimed land, a dozen or more, on horses that were legends among the Moredhel: the near-mythical mounts of Elvandar, a breed of horses considered mystical, magical, and untamable. The leader was a mature male elf with dark hair and eyes, and his manner identified him before he drove his mount into the shallow waters. The other horses reached the nearby bank and halted, and Liallan noted these had no bridle or saddle. The lead rider threw his leg over his mount's neck and slid down, then hurried to help a much older elf dismount.

Escorting Janil to the head of the Moredhel column, they reached Liallan. The leader of the Snow Leopards looked down and said, "You are most certainly Prince Calin."

He bowed his head. "And you are no doubt Liallan of the Hamandien."

"You've sent no small number of my clan to hunt with our ancestors in the sky," she said sternly.

"Only when it was necessary."

She actually laughed. "So tell me, then, Prince of Elvandar, why are you here? We will honor our pledge to pass by and leave you untroubled."

"I would not question your oath, lady," he replied. "Our eldest spellweaver needs speak to one of your clan."

Liallan looked down at Janil, who said, "I need to speak with Cetswaya."

At a sign from Liallan the ancient shaman of the Ardanien moved his horse around a group of riders that included the two Taredhel, Gulamendis and Laromendis. Calin inclined his head in greeting and the two elves from E'bar returned the gesture. The old elf on horseback continued past Liallan until he looked down on Calin and the ancient spellweaver and said at last, "Janil."

"Cetswaya," she said. "We need to talk."

The old shaman looked at Liallan, who nodded, and he dismounted and went with the ancient spellweaver.

Calin watched them move away. "How do they know each other?"

Liallan laughed. "Shamans and spellweavers, you know how they are, like gossipy old women. No doubt they trade recipes in their sleep with that dream talk of theirs." She lowered her voice. "And if your mother hasn't told you, it's how she keeps track of me, and how I keep track of her. We may be enemies, but there are times when it's useful to have a means of communication. When you see her, tell her that letting us pass in peace will not be forgotten."

At a discreet distance away from the others, Janil said to Cetswaya, "It is good to meet you at last."

He nodded. "And you."

"I have had a vision," said Janil, throwing back her hood, so that her gray hair blew freely in the wind. "The dragons are in moot and the Ancient Ones again move."

"Ancient Ones?" said Cetswaya. "There is more than one?"

"There is another," she answered, "and they fly to meet the dragons."

"To what purpose?" asked the shaman.

"I do not know." Janil looked at Cetswaya and he looked away to the south. "What do you dream?"

"A great evil arises where our cousins from the stars have made their home, a thing called from the darkest part of the universe. I know we will not prevail on our own."

"I sense that as well," said the old woman. "Yet you bring an army. Do you think swords and bows will make a difference?"

"I do not know. It is how we are." He smiled slightly. "You know how we are."

She nodded. All types of elves were related, but it was not a relationship they chose to acknowledge openly, if given a choice. The roots of conflict went back to the abandonment of Midkemia by their masters, the Dragon Lords, and the choices made by each group of elves as to how they would live. For centuries, the conflict had been bitter.

"Does Liallan bring her entire clan?"

"And allies," said Cetswaya.

"And your clan, the Ice Bears?"

"As well."

"I've had other visions," said Janil.

"I have also," said Cetswaya. "But I have always distrusted dream visions. They are too undependable, too subject to interpretation."

"Yet you are here."

"Yes," said the old shaman. "Did you have a vision of the end?"

The old spellweaver was silent for a long minute, then she said, "I have seen a pit so dark that light cannot escape from it, a thing so terrible it should not be imagined, let alone exist. I have seen the ending of us all." She paused. "But I have also seen the closing of that pit, but at great sacrifice, perhaps too great if vain heroics outweigh prudence. May I counsel Liallan?"

Cetswaya turned and motioned to another elderly elf, who came forward. "Arjuda," said Cetswaya as introduction.

"Janil," said the shaman of the Snow Leopards. "We have met in dream."

"We dream of this coming conflict, and see an ending. Have you?"

He shook his head. "I have dreamed until a gem is sundered, then I awake."

"A gem?"

"A ruby of impossible size, as big as a city."

Janil said, "With all humility, may I advise Liallan?"

Arjuda looked at Cetswaya, who gave a slight nod.

"I will intercede," said Arjuda, and the three magic users returned to stand before the commander of the Moredhel host. Arjuda said to Liallan, "The spellweaver asks permission to advise."

Liallan's eyebrows rose in surprise. "You seek to counsel me, Eledhel?"

"If you will permit," said Janil.

"Say on, then." Liallan leaned forward in the saddle and gave the spellweaver her full attention.

Janil said, "We have dreamed of dragons and ancient warriors, and a dark pit from which a horror rises."

Liallan said nothing.

"We dream of dragons with riders on their backs, and a confrontation from which none here may escape. I argue caution."

"You're asking me to turn my army around and go home?"

"What you face is a thing of horror and darkness from the deepest pit in the universe, and it will not rest until it has consumed everything. Your braves will die with their swords in hand or nocking arrows, but they will die. Only the power of our magic can stem its entrance to our world."

Liallan fell mute and studied the old spellweaver. Finally she said, "This is your counsel? I am to turn my warriors around and march home?"

Janil nodded. "Let Cetswaya and the other shamans continue." She raised a staff and the elf steed hurried to her side. "We will ride with them, for every spellweaver in Elvandar is here!"

From out of the trees behind Calin and his escort, a hundred figures moved, some on foot, others on the backs of the magic horses of Elvandar, but all moved with purpose. Acaila, leader of the Eldar, rode a roan stallion. He bowed his head to Liallan and Cetswaya. "Leader of the Snow Leopards, I speak for every magic user in Elvandar. This is our burden. Spare the lives of your young warriors. Let them return home to be fathers and husbands, that your clans may endure should the rest of us prevail."

Liallan considered. She turned and motioned for a young warrior to approach. To the elves who didn't know him, Liallan said, "This is Antesh, son of Arkan, who leads the Ice Bears." She signaled for another young warrior to ride forward. "This is Nadeer, a chieftain of the Snow Leopards, lesser in years, yet gifted." She looked at the two young men. "Nadeer, I give to Antesh my daughter Kalina as wife. Bear witness."

The younger chieftain hid surprise and nodded once.

"Antesh, it seems those of us who ride south are fated for destruction." She cast a dubious look at the magic users. "Though experience teaches me that fate is often the servant of those who seize the moment, still, there is a caution here. While we ride apparently to save the entire world, even those within it we don't particularly wish to save, our clan's enemies are still going about their business, plotting and planning." She let out a long breath. "Antesh, take your Ice Bears back to the camp at Snow River and wait. Nadeer, take your family and the allies and go with him. If I come back, all will be as it was. If I do not, you two are . . ." She shrugged. "Form a new clan, with a new name, for if you do not, Narab will hunt you down to the last child to ensure that the Snow Leopards are obliterated. Take the combined clans into the north as your father did if you need to, but save our children."

If Antesh was disappointed at being ordered to leave, he did not reveal it, but merely nodded and said, "My father always saw you as the wisest leader among our people, my aunt. I will do as you bid. Kalina will be safe, as will the children of the Snow Leopards at Snow River. On my life."

"I, too, will obey," said Nadeer.

The two young men rode to the rear. As they did so, horsemen began to peel away from the ranks behind and follow the two young chieftains, one in five returning north.

Liallan looked at the two Taredhel. "And what is your choice?"

Laromendis almost laughed. "I didn't think we had one. We will continue. E'bar may have been our home for only a short time, but it *is* our home."

Liallan nodded. To the remaining host of dark elves' and the light elves' spellweavers, she said, "Now let's move on. I'm feeling a strong need to hunt down this nameless horror and kill it."

She raised her arm and signaled the resumption of the march south.

Hal signaled and Martin waved a red flag, then after a moment a white one. "Send a rider to tell him we see perfectly." Martin was high above the ancient keep, establishing a warning system to announce Chadwick of Ran's arrival.

A soldier saluted and hurried off.

A shout from behind Hal caused him to look back at his camp and he saw a sentry signaling and pointing down the road. Dust indicated the approach of a company of riders.

Hal mounted his horse and rode down the hill, past the camp. The five riders wore the Prince's colors, and the fifth rider was familiar. Leaping from his horse, Hal hurried forward as Swordmaster Phillip dismounted. "Phillip!" he said with obvious delight as he hugged the old man to the point of almost lifting him off the ground. "We thought you lost!"

"Close, my lord," he said, looking at the man he had first handed a sword to as a boy.

"Come, Martin will be overjoyed when he gets back from Sethanon Keep."

A sergeant in the Prince's livery stepped forward. "My lord, a message from His Highness."

Phillip's eyes narrowed. "I'll save you the time of reading it. Oliver's moving."

"How long ago?" asked Hal.

"We left Prince Edward's camp four days ago, riding hard."

Glancing at the exhausted horses, Hal said, "I can see that."

"Our spies reported that Oliver broke camp two days before that, so Oliver's been on the march for six days now. He'll be reaching Edward in four more, five at the outside. He's moving slowly and keeping his forces rested."

"Come, let's get something to drink and discuss what needs to be done here." To the sergeant of Prince Edward's messenger unit, Hal said, "See my sergeant over there." He indicated a large soldier in a Crydee tabard. "His name is Samuels; have him find you a tent for the night. I'll see you have fresh mounts to leave tomorrow and I'll then give you any message I have for the Prince."

"Yes, my lord," said the sergeant, and indicated for his men to follow him.

Hal called up a soldier to take Swordmaster Phillip's

mount and care for it, and led the old master-of-arms to the command tent. As they entered, Ty looked up from a spread of maps on the table and smiled broadly. "Swordmaster Phillip!" He gripped the Swordmaster's hand and said, "It's been a while."

"Since you won the Masters' Court," said Phillip. He glanced at the two young men and said, "Good to see you both."

Hal dispatched an orderly to fetch wine and food. "I assumed you'd fallen along the way. We've had no word of you since you departed Roldem to rejoin Father at the western muster."

"It's a long story, Your Grace."

"Please, it's still 'Hal' when we're alone."

"Hal, it began when we got word of the muster. I found myself seeking a ship to an Isles city in the Sea of Kingdoms. I settled for one on the evening tide bound for Ran. I was with a dozen other masters and nobles hurrying back to the Kingdom, and when we reached Ran, a squad of Chadwick's palace guard met the ship and placed some of us under arrest."

"You've been in Chadwick's dungeon?"

"Not quite that grim," said Phillip, nodding his thanks when handed a cup of wine by the returning orderly. "Some of us were kept in pleasant enough little rooms in the palace, though under guard, and we were even allowed to stroll in the garden overlooking the bay for a few hours a day. I compared notes with the others and we learned that Chadwick had entered into a bargain with Oliver. We were furious he'd do that with a war with Kesh under way, but days stretched into weeks, then into months." He sat back. "I worried myself sick wondering how you boys and your father were doing." He lowered his head as moisture gathered in his eyes. "I managed not to hear news of the Duke until I reached Prince Edward. I'm so sorry, Hal."

"He treasured your service, Phillip," said Hal. "As will I." Then he laughed ruefully. "Of course, I'm not sure where you'll serve as my duchy is chock-full of Keshians at the moment."

"Once we sort out this business with Oliver and his thugs, we'll get back to where we once were, I'm sure of it," said the Swordmaster.

"On to more pressing matters," said Hal. "How did you escape from Ran?"

"When Chadwick marshaled his forces to march to join Oliver, a few of us managed to slip over the garden wall and get down to the street between the palace and the road to the harbor. The city was in an uproar with the entire Army of Ran leaving. I sold the ring your father gave me, the one with the ruby, and bought horses for myself and the other three who escaped. It was easy enough to slip out of the city with a band of mercenaries, and we were soon miles away without hearing any alarm about our escape. We rode right past most of Chadwick's army, circled the van so that he and his councillors wouldn't recognize any of us, and made for Rodez. There we split up and I used the last of my gold to sail to Salador. When I got there, Bas-Tyra held the city and I found his acting marshal, a captain named Ronsard, who got me a fresh horse and supplies, then rode like mad to circle around Oliver's army, got chased by his skirmishers on the north flank, and reached Edward."

"And now you're here," said Hal. "To my relief." He looked at Ty and said, "I'm going to change a few things. With Phillip here, I'm going to put you in charge of the ambush."

Ty said, "That might be fun."

"You have an odd idea of fun," said Hal. He looked at Phillip. "We plan on grabbing Chad's tail like a bulldog and not letting go until he turns away from engaging Edward. Even if we fail to stop him, I hope we can delay him enough that when he reaches Albalyn, Edward will hold the field. If Oliver prevails, it doesn't matter what we do here."

Phillip said, "I'll do whatever you command, my lord."

"Good," said Hal, "because I need you to hold a position as if you had a thousand men."

"How many will I get?"

"Two hundred."

"Ah," said Phillip. "Then give me two hundred hard-headed brawlers, and I'll hold as long as you wish."

"Good," said Hal. "Let me show you the plan, and any suggestions to improve it will be welcome." They both set aside their wine and looked at the maps.

Tomas flew above the ocean called the Dragon Sea, knowing where he would find those he sought. Now he didn't have to try to listen, for the voices of dragon song rang in his mind as if he were hearing it aloud.

It was a song of hope and fear, terror and joy, as if a cycle of completion was approaching. The inevitability of that completion was reassuring, yet the specter of the unknown beyond that completion provoked trepidation.

Of all the creatures Tomas had encountered in his lives and travels, dragons remained distinct and unfathomable. They possessed magic unique to their race, the ability to navigate and survive the Void and to shape-change. They had lesser kin, the wyverns and drakes, whose intelligence was at mere animal level. Dragons began as primitive children—large, dangerous children—but with age came the development of their intelligence and magical abilities, and with great age came wisdom.

Tomas sped across the shore and saw ahead the peaks of the Dragon's Eyre, the isolated home of dragons on Midkemia. He arced across the sky, a dazzling comet with the reflected sunlight dancing off his golden armor. As he neared his destination he saw a sight that took even his breath away. Dragons—three or four thousand of them—arrayed in a massive circle. Every known color turned the gathering into a brilliant display as sunlight glinted from scales of emerald green, azure, ruby, ebony black, silver, and, at the center of the gathering, a knot of golden dragons.

As he descended he saw another figure approaching from

the west, a black mote that grew by the second until another figure revealed itself, one he'd not seen in a century and more, but one who was instantly recognizable.

Tomas landed lightly on his feet, his sword drawn from its scabbard. He swung his white shield with the golden dragon on it off his shoulder and approached the black-and-orange-clad warrior. His ebon blade was out and the tiger face on his black shield snarled in rage. The two warriors approached each other as the dragons formed around them, lining the hillsides, the eldest golden dragons in the first rank, the others behind.

The two warriors circled within the ring of dragons, who watched silently. The other dragons stopped their singing and looked down from their perches on the rocks overlooking the sacred meeting place of their kind.

"Ashen-Shugar," said the figure in black and orange as he warily observed his opponent, "but not."

"Draken-Korin," said Tomas, and he sensed there was something profoundly different about him. "But not."

A massive golden dragon stepped forward and said, "Neither of you is what you were."

Tomas paused. "Daughter of Ryath?"

"Tomas." She bowed her head in greeting. "Rylan, and I am of Ryath, daughter of Rhuagh's line."

The figure of Draken-Korin spoke. "She called you Tomas. Who is Tomas?"

"Whose body is it you wear?" asked the dragon.

"Braden," answered the black-clad warrior. "In mortal life, I was Braden."

"You are both the past and present," said Rylan.

Braden's mind was awash with memories, his own and Draken-Korin's, and he found himself caught in a struggle, one that Tomas had decided over a century before.

Tomas lowered the point of his sword. "What do you remember?" he asked.

With madness in his eyes, the being before him grinned. "Many things, Father-Brother." Then he shook his head as if trying to clear it and his expression changed. "Many things," he whispered, seeming scared. "How did this happen?"

"Powerful magic," answered Tomas.

"Dragon's magic," said Rylan

"Dragon magic?" asked Braden. The mad gleam entered his eyes again and he hefted his sword as if to attack.

"Time magic," said Tomas, raising his sword and shield. "Magic to bring us forward in time, to match the new age and save this world."

The two reborn Dragon Lords slowly began to circle. "Why?" asked Draken-Korin. "Why magic across time to return me from death?"

"You are but a tool," said Rylan, rearing up and spreading her wings. "An ill-crafted tool, but useful."

The Valheru within Braden broke to the surface and shouted, "I am no witless tool of any lesser creature!" He cast a bolt of energy that struck an invisible barrier before the dragon.

The dragon dropped her wings and settled down on her haunches. "We are so much more than you remember, Valheru."

"What would you have of me?" shouted Draken-Korin.

"You are a crucible," replied Rylan.

Spinning as if expecting attack from every side, the human within whom the mind of an ancient being was trapped shouted, "You speak nonsense. I am Draken-Korin! I am the Lord of Tigers! I commanded the Dragon Host!"

"You are here for one purpose only," said Rylan. "You must kill Tomas."

Tomas nodded as if he knew this was what the dragon would say. He readied himself for what he knew would be the last struggle of his life.

Ashen-Shugar awoke in a dark cave, and by sheer will brought into existence a tiny sliver of light. He was alone and had been dying for what seemed ages. Memories not his own plagued him and he knew that time was turned upon itself, and yet in some profound way he also knew this was as it must be.

"You will return," said a voice, and he recognized it as a dragon's voice, but it was not the voice of a dragon he knew.

"When?" he said as his eyes grew heavy again.

"When you are needed. For you alone can save this world, child of the First Born, Lord of Power."

Weakly, as he closed his eyes, Ashen-Shugar said, "I abide."

The two ancient warriors circled and battle was joined. Ashen-Shugar had faced his brother-son twice before and both times had emerged victorious, once when he had been terribly weakened by what he had contributed to the entity that assaulted the newly birthing gods, and the second time when he was no more than an echo of his former self, attempting to gain access to the Lifestone.

Now he faced an equal, a human brought to full power by the ancient magic of the Valheru. As he feinted, moved, and readied himself for the onslaught he knew was coming, Tomas marveled at how alive he felt. In the years since the coming of the Tsurani, he had approached this level of vitality only during the Riftwar, when what he saw then as "madness" descended on him and he slew wantonly. It was a bloodlust that was wholly a thing of the Valheru, overwhelming whatever human limits were placed on him.

In Braden he faced a Valheru spirit hardly tempered at all, for Braden was a murderer with no remorse or sense of wrongdoing in his life: no love for another softened Draken-Korin's rage. For Ashen-Shugar to be victorious, Tomas would have to die.

Draken-Korin's patience failed, as Ashen-Shugar knew it would, and he attacked. The older Valheru easily deflected the blow and struck back, his own blade being blocked as effortlessly as the first attack. They measured, they stalked, and they kept looking for that opening.

Back and forth blows rained, none coming close to finding a weak point. The contest was balanced, for the single-minded rage of Draken-Korin, overwhelming Braden in moments, was offset by the decades of Ashen-Shugar being tempered by Tomas, who remained in control, bringing focus and discipline to the struggle. Wrath clashed with reason.

The dragons watched. This was a struggle that would continue for hours, perhaps days, but that was trivial. It was a struggle that had been destined since the dawn of time.

24

BATTLES

Hal watched the approaching riders.

He peered from behind a rock on top
of the ridge next to the southern road into Sethanon. Half an hour earlier the signal flag from
the keep tower had warned of the approach of
the Duke of Ran's scouts. Messages had been
relayed to every commander for every man to
stay out of sight. Fires behind the ridge had been
banked to prevent any smoke giving away their
position. Scabbards had been muted with cloth
and horses had been led away. All Hal could do
was wait.

The scouts rode down the road casually, grown

lax after days of encountering no living soul. They even split up to expedite their search of the city and were sloppy in that task. One entered the keep, rode a lazy circle of the bailey, looking up at empty windows of the keep hall and towers, then rode out, not realizing an arrow had been pointed at him the entire time.

The other rider had peered into broken windows and fallen doors, looked into empty buildings, and ridden quickly past dozens of others, also not realizing he was but a string's release from a quick death.

When the two scouts finished, they met on the south side of the city, spoke briefly, then began to ride up the hill toward Hal's position. Hal had half a dozen men on either side of the road ready to ambush them, preventing either from escaping to carry word.

Then one halted a hundred yards from the ridge and pointed at the angle of the sun. "We're not going to get much farther before we have to turn back, anyway. His Grace will probably want to poke around in the old city as well."

The other turned his horse. "Very well. This is enough for today. I don't know about poking around in the city. His Grace may want to camp outside; they say it's cursed."

"Cursed?" said the other one as they moved away. "I never heard . . ." His voice trailed away as the two riders cantered their horses north in a leisurely fashion.

Hal had judged it a fortunate turn that had them arrive at that time of day, as Chadwick's forces would be arriving perhaps an hour before sundown, tired from a long march, expecting to make camp in peace.

He called a hasty meeting with Martin, Ty, Hokada, and Phillip. "Two choices: hit them before they've established a perimeter, or at first light tomorrow as they muster?"

It was the Earl of LaMut who answered first. "Just as they halt would be ideal. Their horses and men will be tired, the men will be thinking about digging trenches, setting a perimeter, food, taking a piss, everything except fighting."

Phillip said, "Agreed. That extra moment or two when they

have to reassess their situation will be better tonight than in the morning when they're rested. We can't hit them before sunrise or we'll have none of our planned advantages."

"Ty," said Hal, "can you have your men in place before they return?"

"If I leave now."

Hal nodded and Ty was off, rounding up the men detailed to his command. Hal turned to his brother. "Martin, you need to be as clever as you were at Crydee, because both you and Phillip need to convince Chadwick that your commands are ten times the size they are."

Martin put out his hand and Hal gripped it. "I won't fail you, brother," he said.

Phillip put his hand upon theirs. "I will not fail you either, Your Grace."

"Go," said Hal, and the two left to make ready.

Turning to Hokada, Hal said, "You've got a lot of riding to do, my lord."

The Earl of LaMut smiled. "It's what we do best, Your Grace."

"Then go," said Hal, and the Earl departed.

Now all Hal could do was wait.

Hal and Martin watched as Chadwick's forces moved slowly along the old logging road that skirted the Dimwood and had once served as the main conduit from local farms to this old city. By royal proclamation, the city had been ordered abandoned after the first battle. It had been an easy edict to enforce, as the Earl had died in battle, leaving no heir, and most of the city had been reduced to ruin by the invading army of the false Murmandamus. Nothing before or since had been seen like the forces he commanded; even the reclusive and hardly seen giants, those twelve-foot-tall brutes from the north, the mountain trolls, and every goblin in the north had joined with the clans of the Moredhel at Sethanon. Hal had read the reports on the last battle here, but he knew his family lore, passed down to him by his father, from his father before, back to Lord Martin, fourth Duke of Crydee, who had been brother to Prince Arutha and King Lyam. He knew about the family secret: that once there had been a great treasure called the Lifestone below this abandoned city which had been the true object of the massive Moredhel and goblin army that had sacked Sethanon. Murmandamus had proved to be a sham, a Pantathian Serpent Priest ensorcelled to look like the ancient Moredhel hero, returned from the dead.

A second battle had been fought here as well, though by then the city had been left to dust. This time, the Lifestone had been retrieved. Prince Calis, a being combining the blood of human and elf with the magic of the Dragon Lords, had unlocked the Lifestone and released all the pent-up life force confined inside it, ensuring it could never be used as a weapon. The city's reputation for ill fortune had been so real that no one dared return, despite the proximity to good water, fine farming land, and potentially rich trade routes. Hal thought it ironic, for he had lost his own duchy to what were essentially starving Keshians looking for good land upon which to raise crops, breed livestock, and live in peace, and here sat a massive stretch of the best farmland in the Kingdom, empty because of an imagined curse. Where once commerce had thrived in the region, now empty villages, abandoned inns, marked a territory crossed by unused roads.

And down one such road marched the Army of Ran.

Hal turned to Martin and said, "Time to start the mummery."

Martin nodded and hurried off at a crouch so he would not be seen above the ridge. He would pass word to Phillip, then head downslope to where his mount waited and ride to his command.

A hundred soldiers had worked frantically to erect a false growth of thornbushes running along the ridge to the right of Hal's position, behind a string of rocks hauled into place over the last few days by furiously laboring soldiers. They had created a chest-high stonework that hid a hundred archers.

To the right of them waited two hundred heavy foot-men from Crydee under Swordmaster Phillip's command. Behind Hal a squad of soldiers waited, each of them holding a blockade barrier, a simple long log of wood, to which had been affixed a set of wooden spikes. Each required two men to move it, and although a mere annoyance to infantry unless they were very closely packed, they would be a crucial bar-rier to horses.

Hal peered over the rise and waited until he saw the van of Chadwick's army reach the agreed-upon point in the road. It was assumed that within a hundred yards of that point, the order to halt and make camp would come, so everyone in Hal's company watched and waited. The signal to attack would be given by the Duke of Ran himself.

For another minute the column moved ahead, then a figure at the front raised his hand and ordered a halt, and the signal was given.

Hal stood up and signaled the attack as the afternoon sun lowered in the west.

Tomas felt a burning pain across his shoulder and realized Draken-Korin's ebon blade had finally sliced through the golden chain links under his tabard. He'd not deflected it cleanly, as he dropped the top of his shield too low and the blade had gained purchase for an instant.

Both warriors sported half a dozen minor wounds and an assortment of bruises. They were still in the stage of gauging each other. The dragons observed the conflict silently.

Twice before these two had faced each other, and twice before Ashen-Shugar had emerged victorious. This time the rage of the Dragon Lord was wed to the years of experience of a practiced mercenary who had endured every type of brawl and battle imaginable. He brought an entirely new array of battle skills to the conflict, and Tomas knew he was equally matched.

Both possessed the power of the Valheru, and fatigue would not become a factor for long after a mortal would have fallen exhausted, but failed concentration might be a factor soon, and that could prove deadly. Tomas stepped back for a moment, braced, and waited for the next attack as the sun lowered in the west.

Prince Edward stood in front of his pavilion, his advisers and generals surrounding him. On the field below, the armies of Prince Oliver were deploying. Edward said, "Looks as if he brought all the Eastern Kingdoms with him."

The Duke of Yabon said, "Just those that can fight."

Prince Edward turned to Brendan conDoin. "From the look of that column, it will take him another full day to get his forces in place."

"Thinking of attacking first?" asked Lord Sutherland, stroking his gray whiskers.

"No," said Edward. "It looks tempting, but I'd rather have Oliver attacking uphill against our prepared positions than to abandon them after all this work." He turned to Brendan. "Son, send word along the line to be wary." He glanced westward toward the late-afternoon sun. "There's no chance Oliver will move soon, but we still have to be alert for mischief."

Brendan saluted and hurried off. "Smart lad," said the Duke. "I overheard him telling his brothers about some business out at Sorcerer's Isle and he managed to present some astonishing facts in a very workmanlike way."

Edward said, "He's a conDoin, like his brothers. They're a special lot. Always have been, and we'll need all three of them before this is over." He fell silent as the armies of his enemy continued to form up across the field.

Hal hurried down the ridge road to his waiting horse and mounted quickly as Swordmaster Phillip started his part of the attack. From behind the rocky wall at the ridge, each man stood and shouted, shaking poles and stakes. Each had attached to the weapons anything that could be found to reflect light. It was Hal's hope that from Chadwick's position it would appear as if many more men were dug in at the ridge than were actually there. To heighten the illusion, fires were started and torches run back and forth behind the defenders, making the defense look busy preparing for Chadwick's attack. The men with the heavy log barriers began rolling them down the road toward the oncoming Army of Ran, their embedded short spikes causing them to bounce and careen down the hill.

Hal couldn't afford the time to look: he rode with five guards around to the west, looping past a series of concealing hills, on a course that would bring him to the southwestern corner of Sethanon. As he rode past a squad of heavy cavalry, he waved to Martin, who returned his wave. Hal held up one hand, signaling for his men to wait, then pointed at his own eyes and then toward the field, indicating that Martin should watch for the agreed-upon deployment of the enemy before acting. Martin signaled he understood.

Chadwick did exactly as Hal had hoped, ordering his company up the road in column. The horses were tired and his company was almost entirely heavy cavalry, supported by a dozen bowmen in the van. The faster archers moved out swiftly uphill, only to discover a careening, tumbling mass of wooden logs with spikes rolling down the road, bouncing toward them.

The horses reared and the riders tried frantically to turn out of harm's way, but discovered the road had been bounded on the right by a heavy berm upon which grew a massive thicket of thorns and briars. Suddenly half a dozen archers behind the wall stood up and started firing on the lead horsemen.

The column of infantry moved left, the soldiers leading the charge instinctively moving away from the horses on their right. They stepped off the road and there found a narrow strip of ground bordered by an equally heavy thicket, leaving them scant room to move. Then suddenly the ground on the other side of the thicket seemed to erupt with archers, who appeared to have jumped up out of the ground. Hidden from sight by a trench frantically dug over three days behind the heavy screening of thorn, Ty had waited with a company of two dozen archers, lying beneath a cloth disguised with earth and grass.

What had begun as a steady march up the road was now grinding to a milling confusion as those soldiers and horsemen in the rear had to halt while those ahead stopped. The infantry on the left turned to face Ty's squad, as there was an enemy they could see, someone shouted an order to charge, and they set out, using their shields to crash through the heavy thicket.

Suddenly men were falling and screaming as they plunged into deep holes filled with sharpened stakes. Hal had not had enough time to dig many, but the few the men from Ran encountered were halting the charge as effectively as if the infantry had hit a stone wall.

Caught in a cross fire of bowmen to their east and from behind the wall to the south, the infantry tried to reorder as sergeants shouted commands in the chaos. The horsemen were taking constant fire from the archers above them and could not get their column turned around. Ty's men would keep up a steady fire as they withdrew to the southeast, and at Ty's command would turn and run up behind the sheltering rocks where Phillip's infantry waited should Ran's army try to flank the archers.

Then, from the rear of the stalled infantry and cavalry, a column of horsemen under Hokada's leadership and wearing the gray and blue of LaMut and the grinning wolf's head on their tabards, erupted from locations within the abandoned city. The thirty archers took aim at the rear of the heavy cavalry who were trying to discover what confusion ahead was delaying them, and unleashed a barrage of arrows. Four horsemen fell from their saddles as the rear of the column turned and offered pursuit.

Exactly as Hal had hoped.

A full third of Chadwick's heavy cavalry took off after the LaMutian cavalry in an attempt to crush them by numbers and armor. Hokada led his men in a looping course to the north and then east that brought them around on the other side of the infantry column. He shouted a command and his men turned and loosed their arrows, then spurred their mounts away at a gallop without looking at the results.

From his position Hal could see a pair of riders taken out of saddle before he lost sight of that aspect of the conflict. He rode through a part of the western faubourg and the open gates to the main city, where his heavy cavalry waited out of sight. He signaled for them to fall in behind him and took his command down the central avenue of Sethanon, leading out the eastern gate half a mile away and into the heart of Chadwick's column.

As Hal had planned, Martin rode his column into the bunched-up cavalry a hundred feet away so that the heavy riders from Ran were slammed by two attacking columns within moments. The horses screamed as they were pushed into the milling infantry that was now frantically trying not to be crushed by the falling horses and attacking men of Crydee and LaMut.

Ran's officers were gathered in a knot at the head of the column, separated by the mass of troops gathered between them and the attackers. Hal could not make out a single badge, so he could not tell which rider was Chadwick, but he saw they were all in a frenzy to get away from the bow shots coming from the head of the column, despite being blocked by the mass of their own men.

Hal tried to shout an order, but suddenly had a footman from Ran grabbing at his stirrup, attempting to unseat him.

He had lost the advantage of mobility and faced the same risk any other rider did, to be dragged from his mount, which would likely mean death.

He slashed down at the footman's head and struck a glancing blow, but it was enough to force the man to let go of his stirrup. He shouted "Back!," turned his horse, and retreated.

His men began to disengage, and as they turned to face him, he shouted, "To me! Rally to me!"

His original hundred riders were now whittled to about ninety from what Hal could see. "Form up for charge!" he shouted as his men drew in around him and turned to face the infantry that followed. "We have to hit them before they form a shield wall!" he shouted. "Charge!"

Now battle was fully joined and whatever advantage he had had was gone. This struggle would quickly be decided by determination and luck.

Pug and his companions emerged from the vortex to a scene of incredible struggle. Before them stood an energy dome of ruby hue, completely covering a city.

"I've seen its like before," said Pug.

"Where?" asked Miranda.

"At Sethanon, during the Great Uprising, when the Dragon Lords tore open a rift in the sky . . ." He looked around. "Macros?"

"Not here," said Nakor. "I guess he wasn't fated to be here at the end."

"We could have used his might," said Magnus.

"We don't know how much had been given to him," said Miranda. "They may have used him up just to show us what he did."

"Who is 'they'?" wondered Nakor. "Will we ever know?"

"I doubt it," said Pug. "While our gods may be mere personifications of powers, those are prodigious powers, and Macros made it clear there's a higher Mind in control. For lack of a better term, the ultimate power serves."

"Well," said Nakor, "the ultimate certainly has dropped us into a mess."

Pug took a moment to make some coherent sense of the scene before him. Then he said, "Miranda, you and Nakor get as close to that red dome as you can and see if you can decipher what manner of magic is being employed. You've seen more magic on more planes than we have."

They nodded. Miranda put her hand on Nakor's shoulder and they vanished.

Pug looked around and pointed, and Magnus turned to see a familiar figure in the distance. He put his hand on his father's shoulder and instantly they stood next to Ruffio.

Ruffio said, "Thank the gods. We're at our wit's end here."

The younger magician was in the company of what appeared to be two elven spellweavers, who nodded greeting to Pug. Ruffio summed up the situation, and before he had finished, Miranda and Nakor reappeared.

"It's a spell but nothing I've come across before," said Miranda. "It's driven by a level of energy that comes from another plane, so it's just growing."

"It's familiar to me," said Nakor. "It echoes other things we've encountered from the Dread. But the way in which it's been turned into a trap is . . . ingenious."

Ruffio said, "It's the Taredhel magicians, their 'mancers. They seemed to know what to do the moment this unleashing of whatever is inside that dome began."

Pug looked around and said, "Find me one."

"Over there," said Ruffio. He led Pug down the hill and the others followed.

The five magicians came to a circle of a dozen elven magic users: eight of the Taredhel galasmancers and four other magic specialists. They were all standing with their eyes closed, seemingly reaching out to the magicians down the hillside to provide them with aid.

"Asleum," said Ruffio, but the old magician didn't respond.

"Leave him," said Pug. "I will find a way to speak with him."

Pug put his hand on Asleum's shoulder and closed his eyes.

Pug swam in a sea of energy, lattices forming faster than the eye could follow. He remembered Miranda's lesson about perspective and forced himself to look for something recognizable, a quality within the swarming energies that he could use for orientation.

He remembered his time with the elf spellweaver Temar, studying weather magic, and recalled that there had been a distinctive sense of a different energy to the magic he wove. Pug sought out anything that might be similar to that and found what he was looking for. One of the threads that was forming a weaving lattice had the same quality as Temar's energy and Pug followed it away from the forming lattice and back to its source. An unmistakably elven consciousness recognized his presence and a voice said, "Yes?"

Pug opened his eyes and saw the elderly spellcaster staring at him. "I am Pug," he said, removing his hand from the elf's shoulder.

The old elf seemed on the verge of exhaustion, yet his eyes were bright and he smiled. "Young Ruffio has been awaiting you," said the spellweaver. "I am Asleum."

"We are here to help," offered Pug.

The old elf nodded. "We are grateful beyond words."

"Your gratitude is premature," Pug said. "We face something difficult to imagine in there." He waved his hand in the direction of the ruby dome.

"We regard what is contained within as a part of what we know as the Forbidden, lore from the time before, when we served the Ancient Ones," said Asleum. "We recognize what it is: a most powerful Lord of the Dread."

Pug said, "It's far worse, I fear. What you have done, turning its own magic back upon itself, is as artful as any spell craft I have ever seen, but what you seek to contain is far greater than you imagine. It is not a Lord of the Dread seeking entrance into this realm. It is the entirety of the Dread, and they seek to consume this realm."

The old elf's face was impassive as he turned to look at the distant ruby dome. Finally he said, "What must we do?"

"More than merely contain it," answered Pug. "We must devise a way to send it back whence it came."

"How?"

"I am not sure, though I believe that with your help we can find a way." He recognized a young magician who had been closely watching the elves and motioned for him to approach. "Cullen."

"Pug," Cullen replied. "I have been studying the latticework of that spell. It's ingenious. Whoever first cast it . . ." He shrugged. "I would have tried something else."

"And been obliterated," said Pug. "If we can find out who among the spell crafters here first responded, we might discover something useful. I think I know how we can help, but I'll need a little more time with this. But one thing I know is that we do not have enough magicians here to battle that thing inside the dome for more than a few days, a week at most."

"All the senior members of the Conclave are here," said Cullen.

Pug nodded. He motioned to Magnus and Ruffio, and when they were standing before him, he said, "Ruffio, you must go to the Academy. Every magician with any measure of ability must be made ready."

"Ready for what?" asked Ruffio.

"What do you have in mind, Father?"

"I think I understand this contrivance of a spell," said Pug to his son. "I'll need some time, but if I'm correct, we need a conduit for magic, a way to bring the ability of everyone we can into harmony at the right moment, and I'll channel that energy into the dome. I think we can not only hold the Dread at bay, but actually pressure them to the point at which we can drive them back into the Void and seal the breach after them." He turned to Magnus. "I need you to go to the Temple of Ishap in Rillanon."

Magnus nodded.

"Tell the High Priest that it is that time we once spoke of."

"It is that time we once spoke of," repeated Magnus. "And he'll know what that means?"

With a grim expression, Pug said, "He will know all too well what it means. Then send word to Grand Master Cregan at the Order of the Shield of the Weak. Tell him to alert all the friends of the Conclave within every temple and repeat the same message."

Magnus nodded and vanished.

Pug returned his attention to Asleum. "Now, I must study what you've done here." He closed his eyes and returned his concentration to the spell lattice.

Long shadows fell over the struggling men. Hal turned his horse rapidly, using the massive gelding as a battering ram against the men on foot. The animal was exhausted and sported two wounds that had almost caused it to pitch Hal off its back, but the training and firm control of its rider had kept the mount under control.

Hal slashed down at whoever had been foolish enough to get in his way and kept his eyes constantly moving, keeping track of what he could while avoiding being taken unawares by enemy soldiers. He turned and struck down a Ran soldier who was pressing a Crydee man, and found himself with a second of calm, isolated in a ring of bodies while around him the battle raged. The tide of the battle was turning, and it seemed to Hal that things were slipping away from him, though he had hammered Chadwick's forces so hard that now the two armies were of roughly equal size. If he quit the field and retreated toward Edward, keeping himself between Chadwick and Edward, he would effectively win the day, as Chadwick would not be able to attack Edward's flank should he be engaged with Oliver.

He saw riders off to the east and for a moment wished the day were brighter, for the sun would set within minutes and twilight would not linger, and soon both sides would be fighting in the dark. He had sent Hokada and his bowmen off on a hit-and-run attack that had pulled a full third of Ran's heavy horse in pursuit, a suicide mission if the heavier horsemen could close.

He spied another soldier of Crydee being hard-pressed and struck down the warrior facing him, a mercenary not wearing Ran colors. To the south he saw Martin's company had driven the heavier riders back into the infantry, splitting them, and was continuing to push them into the thorn-bushes he had planted, which would discourage the infantry from trying to reach the other side, even if the horses went through them without complaint.

Hal stood up in his stirrups and saw that was exactly what was happening as the riders from Ran were turning and crashing through the gorse and thorns. Which brought them under fire from the archers still on the ridge.

Their commander turned and saw the rocks ending less than thirty yards away and regrouped his men, intending to circle around and take out Hal's archers. Hal signaled to Martin to press on behind them if he could. Martin waved that he understood and moved his own riders off in pursuit. Hal kept standing up in his stirrups, looking for Chadwick. He had seen officers near where Martin had been fighting, but he could not see any there now. He needed to find and kill or capture the Duke of Ran in order to end this battle before darkness forced both sides to withdraw.

A small group of riders was being forced up the hill backward by Crydee soldiers. Hal spurred his horse toward them. Glancing to the east, he saw the approaching riders were Hokada's men, and that they were turning to intercept the cavalry trying to circle the ridge and attack Hal's archers.

As they came around, they found Phillip and his infantry, who had been patiently waiting behind the wall, formed up in a shield wall with pikes in what was called a hedgehog, a formation that would force the enemy riders to rein in or be impaled.

Hokada's archers began firing as soon as the enemy came into range, and Ty's archers behind Phillip's position had already turned their attention to the newest threat. The riders from Ran turned, broke, and fled.

The sense that something had shifted in their favor rippled through the field as the men of Crydee on the ridge gave out a shout of victory, and the archers returned their punishing attention to those on the north side of the ridge.

Martin's contingent of riders turned and came back, and suddenly the men of Ran began reversing their swords and kneeling, the sign of surrender. Martin stood up in his stirrups, and in a dry voice, hoarse from dust and shouting orders, he cried out, "Crydee! Crydee!"

The shout was taken up, and as men of Ran saw others taking a knee, they did as well, until the last knot at the south was surrounded. Hal rode over and saw five tabards covered in blood, holding various rank badges, and among them was the one he wished to see, the crest of Ran topped with a coronet marking the rank of Duke.

Lifting his visor, Hal shouted, "Do you yield, my lord Chadwick?"

Chadwick of Ran raised his own visor. Dust caked with perspiration surrounded his eyes. Almost too softly to be heard, he said, "Yes, Your Grace, I yield."

Hal held up his hand and shouted, "The day is ours!"

The men of Crydee and LaMut cheered as the men from Ran looked on. Hal said, "Your parole, sir, while we attend the wounded?"

"You have parole, sir," said Chadwick, and he looked at the carnage visited on his men by this much younger Duke. Softly he said, "If Edward wins the day and I don't end up at the end of a rope, I'll tell His Highness he was well served today."

"I thank Your Grace," said Hal, knowing full well that Chadwick was trying to curry favor with the possible victors.

If Prince Edward *was* victorious, that is. Hal turned his attention to the care of the wounded. "Get some fires started!"

he shouted. They would need hot water to tend wounds as well as to cook meals for starving men.

He moved away from the captured officers and began taking inventory of the damage wrought on his forces as the sun set in the west.

Tomas took the blow and felt the shock run up his arm, through his shoulder even to the point of his jaw. Draken-Korin seemed to be getting stronger.

The sun had set, but neither the warriors nor the dragon observers needed light. The faint glimmer from the stars above and the promise of a rising moon gave enough illumination for eyes far beyond mortal to observe the conflict.

The duel had taken on an almost ritualistic, dancelike quality as the two opponents used every art they possessed against each other, but neither could find an advantage. Sword and magic, both were equally matched, and the dragons watched in silence.

As the large moon rose in the east, they fought on.

Pug removed himself from the matrix erected by the elves and found Magnus speaking with a tall elf. "Father, this is Tanderae, the Loremaster of E'bar. At this point it's safe to say he's the leader of what's left of this society."

"Sadly, true," said Tanderae.

Magnus continued: "I've carried word and the Ishapians understand your message. Word is going out to every order from them to those who are members of the Conclave, those with whom we have dealt before, and any who will listen; all are being alerted of this danger. Some of the magicians who are more adept at magical transport are ferrying other magicians from Stardock and we're fetching clerics as well."

Pug noticed a point near a distinctive rock formation

where magicians and clerics were appearing in twos and threes. "We'll need as much help from those who stay behind as from those who come to us," he said.

"As I understand it, this is something you've had in place for a while?" asked Magnus, obviously not approving of being kept ignorant of something so important.

"It was something I began when I traveled to Kelewan with an Ishapian cleric named Dominic," his father said. He motioned for Magnus to follow him where they could not be overheard. "In short, the temples have traditionally distrusted magic they didn't control, or at the least see come direct from the gods."

Magnus forewent comment on their recent revelation as to the true nature of the gods, and that the magic seemed to come from the worshippers, not the other way around.

"When the Darkness, the returning horde of the Dragon Lords, was bound up and sucked into the Lifestone at the end of the first battle of Sethanon, I realized there were things so far beyond my power I was likely to need a great deal of help."

"If there was such a time, this is it," agreed Magnus.

"The twelve temples in Rillanon, as well as their sister temples in Krondor, Kesh, and the other great cities, number many clerics who are adept at channeling magic. I've set up a way for them to lend us their magic, as it were, should the need arise. The Ishapians were instrumental in orchestrating this."

"So what are you planning?" asked Miranda, having walked up behind Pug. Nakor was a half step behind her.

"We may need to wring every bit of magic out of every magic user on this world before we're done."

Nakor nodded. "From what I've seen, the Dread are getting stronger by the hour."

"Agreed," said Miranda.

"Here's what I plan," said Pug, and he began to speak softly.

Hal wolfed down a cold plate of yesterday's beans and dried bread, glad to have it. Martin stood before him as the Duke of Crydee sat on a rock beside a campfire. "I've got Chadwick and his officers under guard behind the command tent," he said, obviously ready to drop where he stood. "The rest of the Ran army has been disarmed and is camped on the other side of the hill; the wounded have been cared for and are being fed; those too wounded to survive were given quick mercy. What are your orders?"

"You, eat," said Hal. "I'll give orders myself." He put down his plate and stood up. "Where's Hokada?"

"Over by the command tent," said Martin, moving toward the slowly heating beans.

Hal hurried to where the Earl of LaMut sat, rubbing his bare left foot. "Are you injured, my lord?"

Hokada started to rise, but Hal waved at him to keep his seat. "No, Your Grace. It's just too many hours in the saddle." He chuckled. "It's never my bum that hurts, but my feet start killing me after four or five hours in stirrup irons."

Hal laughed. "I understand. My feet are also tired, but rest will have to wait."

"Sir?"

"I intend to have every horse we have with a man in the saddle, cavalry or not, and we ride at dawn."

"Back to support Prince Edward?"

Hal nodded.

"What of the Duke of Ran and his officers?"

"They'll ride with us. Without them, the rest are infantry and cavalry on foot, a long way from home. I'll give them parole to get back to Ran as best they can, and truth to tell, I don't care how many actually get back."

Given how bloody the fighting had been, the Earl of LaMut understood the sentiment. "Very well, Your Grace. My Wolves will be ready to ride at dawn."

"Good. Have your men cull the captured horses. Those

fit to ride we keep, the rest I want put down. I don't want one of those lads from Ran getting a notion that he might curry favor by trying to reach Prince Oliver before we reach Edward. Understood?"

"At once, Your Grace," said the Earl, pulling his boots back on with a look of resignation.

Hal smiled and patted the man on the shoulder, then went looking for his brother and Ty. He had a lot of instructions he needed carried out before he got any sleep this night.

"A large force is arriving from the north," one of the Taredhel reported to Tanderae.

Pug and the others had been partaking of food being transported in by some of the younger magicians from Stardock, a welcome addition to what the elves had already managed to provide in their makeshift kitchen. They had been lost in deep discussion of what they had discovered about both the ruby shield and the elven magic holding it in place, and were comparing notes on their speculations.

A good deal of movement in the north heralded the arrival of what at first seemed to be dozens of elven riders and quickly revealed itself to be hundreds, with even more following. In the vanguard rode the two Taredhel brothers, Laromendis and Gulamendis, and what looked to be more than a dozen elven spellweavers. Also, if Pug's senses weren't betraying him, the riders were from the Brotherhood of the Dark Path, as humans called them: the Moredhel or dark elves. And with them were what appeared to be another dozen magic users.

A regal-looking elf woman rode into view and jumped nimbly down from her mount, and Pug realized that some of the horses he saw coming closer were elfsteed, the magic horses he had once seen in Crydee the first time he and Tomas had seen the Elf Queen and her court.

The woman conferred for a moment with the Taredhel

brothers and they indicated Tanderae, who was approaching. She moved toward him and said, "I am Liallan. I rule the Snow Leopards. We have come to aid you."

"Your aid is welcome, and overwhelming," said the Loremaster. He gazed at the continuing influx of Moredhel horsemen. "I'm . . . truly grateful."

"I was told," she said, eyeing the magic users who had accompanied her and were now moving toward the circle of those shamans and Taredhel magicians who were reinforcing the ruby dome, "that dire consequences awaited all Midkemia should we not come."

Pug stepped forward. "Not an understatement, leader of the Hamandien, but a fearful possibility."

She looked at him with her eyebrows raised, then realized there were other humans nearby. She looked around at all these humans who were helping in whatever fashion they could. Then she said, "Ah, you must be Pug."

"I am."

"Your reputation reaches even to the far north." She looked him up and down. "I thought you'd be much taller."

Magnus came to stand next to his father and Liallan said, "That's more what I had in mind. So tell me, Black Sorcerer—or is it Sorcerers? What have we come here to kill?"

"That will take time," said Pug. "Perhaps you'd care to sit and eat while we discuss this?"

"What of my soldiers?"

"We do not need them as yet," said Magnus. "But I fear, something I was about to tell my father, that we may need them a great deal very soon."

Pug said, "Then we do indeed have much to discuss."

Liallan followed him to where food was being served and Tanderae said, "I will have refreshments brought over." He indicated that they should sit a little apart from the others and they did so.

"Where to begin . . . ?" said Pug.

"The usual answer is the beginning," said Liallan, "but something tells me that might take a great deal of time."

"More than we have," said Pug. "If circumstances permit, if we survive the coming destruction, I will answer for as long as you care to listen."

"Agreed, human," she said, and then she let out a long sigh, the first hint of her fatigue. "Now, why don't you begin?"

25

CONFLICT

Tomas bled.

As the sun turned the eastern sky from predawn gray to a rosy amber, he blinked away the blood running into his left eye from a massive strike from Draken-Korin's blade he had only partially blocked and that had caught on his helm, causing a cut above the eyebrow. He resisted the urge to reach up and wipe away the blood. To do so would block his view with his shield: if he did it even for an instant, it would be suicide.

Throughout the night the two reincarnated Dragon Lords struggled, evenly matched to the point of stalemate. Blows were offered and returned, taken and endured. Both suffered minor cuts and the effects of unleashed magic; every thrust and strike was taking its toll.

They were beings of incredible strength and power, but the power was not limitless and now the first hints of fatigue were becoming evident. A stumble or a hesitant step, a slightly late block of the shield or a slow riposte, all suggested that the end was drawing nearer.

As the sun rose, a familiar voice echoed within Tomas's mind. *Tomas must die.*

It was echoed by the host of dragons. *Tomas must die.*

Tomas tried to ignore the call, but it sparked a response, from deep within him. *I am Ashen-Shugar!*

For the first time since the struggle began, he felt a tinge of doubt. But the fight was far from over.

Trumpets sounded as Brendan struggled to get his boots on. They had been waiting for any sign that Prince Oliver's forces were moving. Instead there had been two days of frustration watching him position his forces into line, opening up camping centers, erecting tents, and generally settling in as if for a siege.

Brendan dashed from what had been his father's tent, which felt cavernously empty when he was the only occupant, and arrived at Prince Edward's command pavilion just as the other nobles appeared. "Looks as if we have some sense of what's keeping Oliver," said Edward, pointing to a parchment on the table. "There appears to be an army of Keshian mercenaries marching up from the passes."

Without thinking, Brendan looked at the map and blurted, "Where did they come from?"

Edward laughed. "Gods know, son. If Oliver was recruiting down in the heart of Kesh"—his finger struck the map in an area of Kesh near the city of Jonril—"and once gathered, the men marched straight north through the Green Reaches, it would put them out near Durrony's Vale. And with every soldier from that part of the Kingdom already here, no one would oppose their march."

"When do they get here, Your Highness?" asked the Duke of Yabon.

"And how many of them are there?" added the Duke of the Southern Marches.

"Early reports put them between three and four thousand," said Edward. "But I'll need more accurate information."

Everyone knew that even if Hal had stopped Chadwick's march, this additional number of soldiers in the field gave Oliver a significant advantage.

"And they'll be here in three more days."

"Yes," said Jim Dasher, emerging from a corner of the tent. "Now we know exactly what Oliver is waiting for."

"Well, my lords," said Edward, "I refuse to lose the advantage of terrain because Oliver's bolstering his numbers. I believe we still hold the upper hand." He smiled. "Besides, I'd hate to see all the work the lads did in preparing the battleground go to waste."

Jim Dasher smiled, and Brendan wondered if there was something here he was missing.

It was as unprecedented a council as had ever been seen in the history of Midkemia. Pug sat in a circle with two Eledhel spellweavers, a dozen clerics of various orders, two Moredhel shamans, half a dozen Taredhel magic users, and two Eldar mystics. He said, "I think we can agree that we may never understand exactly how this came to be."

An older galasmancer named Kethe said, "I have examined every aspect of the counterspell I can, and I have one possible explanation, though it is speculative at best."

"Please, continue," said Janil.

"Our most talented young galasmancer was named Rojan, and he was one of those contacted by the Loremaster to bear witness against the Regent Lord's treason. He has been unaccounted for since the destruction within the city, and as with so many others, it is assumed he was killed in the initial destruction or by the outpouring of those creatures we are now told are elements of the Dread.

"I think he did get to the portal chamber, perhaps early enough to have seen the Regent Lord's act of betrayal, summoning the Dread into our realm." He closed his eyes for a moment as if in pain. "Had there been a moment to react, to begin a counterspell, it would have been his first choice to turn back whatever was there, to force it against itself. It was the way he practiced his art. The energy of what Pug calls rifts, what we know as portals, is very powerful, very dangerous and uncontrollable unless you have a high degree of precision in your work."

Pug nodded.

"With his dying last effort, I think Rojan may have started the spell that created that dome." He pointed down the hill. "When we were awakened by the explosion that destroyed most of the hall of the Regent's Meet, and the first of the dark horrors appeared, we were all too busy surviving the onslaught and getting free of the city to pay close attention to what was going on with the ruby beacon." He took a drink of water from a skin. "When I fought clear of the city, I saw the dome forming, coming down slowly like water spilling from a fountain, evenly from above . . ." He took a deep breath. "This is when I and others began examining the barrier and realized it had become a trap for everyone inside."

"Including those of our people who didn't have time to escape," said a second Taredhel, by the name of Mulvin. "We all lost someone in there."

The Moredhel shamans remained impassive: death among families was common and not worthy of comment unless the loss was of a great warrior during an act of heroism, and while the sacrifice of Rojan might have been a selfless act, it might also, simply, have been a blind act of desperation.

Acaila said, "I have talked to a number of survivors and what they describe is an invasion of the Dread. Of that there is no doubt, but beyond that we lack intelligence."

"Do we have any knowledge of what is occurring under the dome?" asked one of the clerics, a bishop from the Temple of Lims-Kragma.

"Only in the vaguest sense," said Pug. "I've had encounters with the Dread before and have been given some insight into them lately, though I don't know if what I've learned is particularly helpful in this instance, save for one thing." He looked at Kethe. "If what is coming through the passage that was opened by your Regent Lord gets into our world, it will devour everything here." He looked from face to face to emphasize his point. "I am not speaking metaphorically. This thing is the devourer of worlds, the eater of suns. It will kill and consume every living thing down to the tiniest blade of grass; then it will consume rock and sea, even the very air, until there is nothing left here but the Void, and then that Void will expand until it has consumed everything we behold, the three moons, the sun, even the distant stars."

Every face showed shock. Finally a shaman of the Moredhel said, "Surely you overstate this."

Kethe said, "He speaks of the Forbidden."

Acaila nodded. "Much of that lore has been lost to you," he said to the Moredhel. "What we of the Eldar know is incomplete, but that battle existed before even our arising on this world. It's a struggle that predated the Ancient Ones, and it is the thing of myth, the struggle of gods and beings of darkness, beyond the stars and at the heart of worlds."

"What must we do?" asked one of the human priests, a rector from the University of Roldem and member of the order of Sung the Pure.

"First, we must keep the dome closed," Pug said. "Second, we must discover what is inside the dome. Lastly, we must close the rift inside, either sending what's there back whence it came, destroying it, or trapping it within the rift. We cannot let the Dread remain on this world. Even contained behind the dome, it will continue to wreak havoc and eventually get past the barricade."

Cetswaya said, "Human, you seem to know more of this than you're revealing."

"I do," said Pug to the old Moredhel shaman. "If we survive, I will explain what I do know to the exhaustion of your curiosity, but trust me when I say that at the moment we do not have the luxury of time."

The dark elf studied Pug's face, then nodded. "I've got a lot to learn about this Star Elf magic, so I best be about it."

Pug watched as the group broke up into different pairs and threesomes that were soon lost in discussion. Magnus came up to him. "Have you a plan yet?"

"I do, in part."

"In part?"

"I think I know how to reverse the original spell, the rift magic that the Taredhel turned into that dome." They looked at the ruby dome, which now pulsed slightly with waves of energy as the human magicians and newly come elven magic users were helping the original Taredhel spellcasters reinforce the barrier. "At its heart, it was a rift, but one unlike any we've encountered."

"We've studied every type of rift there is." Magnus noted that Pug's face bore a familiar expression. "What is it you're not telling me, Father?"

"If I say we face as great a danger as we can imagine, I'm stating the obvious. There's risk involved, high risk."

Magnus was silent for a moment. "Very well. When it's time." He motioned to where Nakor and Miranda stood in deep discussion with two elven spellcasters, one from E'bar and the other a Moredhel shaman. "I've never seen those two so engrossed." He looked around at the wounded and displaced, the dying and the homeless, those who had come to give aid, and said, "If it wasn't for the grim surroundings, I'd say they were having fun."

"Your mother thrived on adversity when she was alive, rejoiced in overcoming it," said Pug, "and whatever else she is, this Miranda is in very large part still your mother."

"I know." Magnus looked back at his father. "When this is over, then what?"

"I don't take your meaning."

"Miranda and Nakor, what of them?"

Pug sighed. "Before our little journey, I would have said something about the gods and their use for us. After what we've seen, shall we simply call it fate or providence? In the past, fate has demonstrated little kindness to those it deems no longer necessary. I expect this time around to be no different."

Magnus sighed. "I've grown used to having them around again."

"I know exactly what you mean," said his father. He put a hand on his son's arm. "I'm not sharing a few thoughts with you because I'm uncertain if they're useful yet. This situation is too fraught with real danger to burden anyone with imagined dangers."

Magnus nodded. "When you're ready."

"You will be first to know," said Pug, "because if what I think we need to achieve is true, your role will be vital, perhaps the most vital of all."

Magnus nodded. "What now?"

"We study some more," said Pug with a tired smile. He looked to another gathering of magic users in deep discussion. "Let's see what their concerns are."

Magnus nodded and they turned and walked over to the magicians and priests.

Brendan hurried to the command tent. Prince Edward's generals were absent, and only Jim Dasher and Lady Franciezka Sorboz were there, with a few servants hovering. The Prince waved the servants away and, when the four were alone, said, "You've done well, young sir." He indicated that Brendan should take a seat.

"Thank you, Your Highness."

"In all the time you've been here, we've had scarcely a

moment alone." He nodded at Franciezka and Jim and smiled. "This is about as alone as I think we're likely to get. I've heard you had quite an ordeal on Sorcerer's Isle. At least how it was related to me." He indicated Jim. "Formal reports are occasionally lacking detail. Now that we have a little time, I'd like to hear your recounting."

Brendan looked slightly embarrassed. "I don't know if I'd call it an 'ordeal,' but it was a bit difficult once or twice." He told the story in a straightforward fashion, omitting the part where he almost drowned himself getting there, and spent most of his time singing the praises of Sandreena, Amirantha, Ruffio, and the others. When he finished, the Prince shook his head and said, "Remarkable, really."

Jim said, "I'm sure our young friend here is being modest." He put his hands on Brendan's shoulders. "We have a task for you, if you're up for it."

"Of course, sir. Whatever is required."

Edward signaled that they could withdraw and Jim and Brendan left the tent, leaving the Prince in conversation with Lady Franciezka. Outside, Jim said, "Those Keshian mercenaries should be about a day southeast of here. If you ride hard past a small village named Tasford, then through a narrow pass in the hills, you should come out right above where they make their last camp. I have heard reports they may number as little as a thousand, or as much as five times that. I would like a more accurate count. If you can avoid being killed or captured by their sentries, you may get a rough estimate of their numbers from how many campfires you see; then ride like mad back here in time for us to know before the battle tomorrow, or the day after, whenever Oliver decides it's time to fight. An accurate count will allow us a more intelligent deployment of our forces. Can you manage that?"

"I'll leave at once, sir," said Brendan, turning to run off.

Jim reached out and grabbed his shoulder. "I wasn't jesting. Don't get killed. His Highness has plans for you and your brothers when this is all done."

"I won't," said Brendan with a grin that Jim found reminded him too much of his own.

Jim went back inside. Prince Edward said, "I like the boy. What can you tell me about the other two?"

"I don't know Martin well," Jim said, "but from what I've seen, he and Hal match their brother, and more. Martin's reports to the Duke of Krondor about the retreat from Crydee and the defense of Ylith were modest, and what I've heard from others who were there is that he was nothing short of brilliant in protecting those given over to his care. He reads and remembers." Jim tapped the side of his head.

Lady Franciezka said, "And I got to know Hal well when he was hiding from John Worthington's agents in Roldem. He's more of the same: intelligent, passionate, willing to die for duty. And Roldem is in his debt. The King feels a personal obligation and the Queen likes him a great deal. He's compassionate, modest . . . in short, he's as unlike most other nobles you meet . . . he lacks personal ambition, greed, suspicion, and dishonesty. He's exactly what you'd want in a son."

Prince Edward appeared to be lost in thought, a hint of regret crossing his face. "The consequences of this may be dire."

"How much more dire can they be, Highness?" asked Jim. "We're already in a state of civil war, and if we don't prevail, it will be meaningless. If we do prevail, the majority of those likely to object will be dead or in chains."

"Very well," said the Prince with a sigh. "Prepare the document and have Bas-Tyra witness as well as Krondor and Yabon. Charles was once good friends with Chadwick before he discovered his duplicity with Oliver. Switching sides may not make him popular with those nobles wishing to see Oliver on the throne—even if they won't openly say so—but it makes Charles appear a man of conscience and principle, not my creature."

"Very well, Your Highness," said Jim, hurrying off to fetch a scribe.

Prince Edward looked at Lady Franciezka. "And what of you, lady?"

She smiled, and he saw the fatigue in her eyes, but otherwise she was as beautiful as ever. "My career is over, as is Jim's," she said. "We've ensured our respective organizations are as intact as possible, to do your bidding and King Carole's, but our part is done."

"What will you do?"

"Neither of us wants for anything, as we are both wealthy in position and gold." Her eyes glistened. "Despite being as cold-blooded as he needs to be in his service to the Crown of the Isles, James Dasher Jamison is at heart something of a romantic. He imagines us living idly on an island somewhere, raising children."

Prince Edward smiled. "However unlikely that may be, it's a wonderful goal to imagine, is it not?"

Franciezka could only nod, fearing that if she spoke, her voice would break.

Martin came over to Hal. "Could you please do something about the Duke of Ran?"

Hal was trying to eat a hastily concocted meal: they were cooking quickly over campfires on their ride back to Prince Edward's encampment. "What is he complaining about now?"

"Everything," said Martin, sitting down next to his brother. "And he keeps offering bribes to me and Ty to help him escape and take you prisoner or whatever else he can imagine." He picked up a wooden plate and dug out a heavy spoonful of beans and bacon from the cooking pot. "I don't think he realizes I'm your brother."

"Or he doesn't care," said Hal with a smile. "Some brothers, you know?"

"I think Ty might be listening," said Martin, and Hal laughed.

"How are the horses?" asked Hal.

"Tired, but holding up," said Martin. "The remuda is large enough that we're riding fresh mounts each day. When do you think we'll reach Edward's position?"

"If we're out at first light, sometime near sundown tomorrow."

"Think the battle's started already?"

"We'll know tomorrow," said Hal, finishing up his meal. "I'm going to take a quick tour around the camp, then turn in. You turn in now; you're close to exhausted."

"You're no spring daisy yourself," said Martin. "But, very well, Your Grace."

Hal laughed. As he set out to inspect his prisoners and the camp, he wondered if that might not be the last laugh he and his brother shared for a while.

And not for the first time he wondered how his other brother was faring.

Brendan crawled over the rocks, belly down, listening to the camp noise below. He pulled himself up above an outcrop and saw a sentry standing halfway down the hillside. These mercenaries were sloppy, not expecting any of Prince Edward's forces to be nearby. Had they been alert, they'd have had twice as many guards up on this bluff looking north-west. If they had any patrols out, Brendan had neither seen nor heard them.

He studied the camp. There was a large tent in the center, which he assumed belonged to the captain of this company, and only a dozen smaller tents scattered around, big enough for four or five men each. The rest of these forces were sleeping under the stars, which, given the current weather, was no problem.

For a brief moment he wished he had that weather magician of Reinman's along to dump a torrent on them, but then realized there probably wasn't a bottle of wine or a flagon of ale left between Edward's camp and Rillanon.

Brendan began counting campfires.

Tomas battled and Draken-Korin, in the form of Braden, answered every attack. A human would have long since died of exhaustion, yet these two relics of a bygone age continued to test each other. Twice Tomas had delivered wounds that would have killed any mortal instantly, but Draken-Korin had withstood them and kept his opponent at bay long enough for Valheru magic to heal him.

Both fighters guarded their magic now, needing it to keep them alive rather than to inflict harm. They had both come to terms with their inability to gain magical advantage and now realized this combat would end in the spilling of blood, as primitive and basic as a fight could be.

Throughout the night they moved like wary wolves circling and dodging in for the attack, only to pull back to avoid counterattack. They nipped and snapped, and each took slight injuries, but they were now coming into the final phase of this fight.

At some point one would find an opening, or gain a momentary advantage, and when that occurred, the outcome would finally be decided.

Tomas heard the dragon voice in his mind again: *Tomas must die.*

But this time it was followed by an ancient and alien sound. A dragon began to sing, and others took up the song. At last Tomas recognized it. It was the death song of dragons, the song they would sing when a Valheru fell.

Pug signaled Miranda, Nakor, Ruffio, and Magnus over. "I think I know what we need do," he said.

Ruffio glanced over his shoulders to where a knot of clerics sat eating and resting.

Pug followed his gaze. "We'll tell the others when it's time."

"It's not yet time?" asked Miranda.

"No," said Pug. "There are some things we must arrange for, before we embark on what may be our final confrontation."

"I don't like the way that sounds," said Nakor.

"None of us do," echoed Magnus.

"First, we need to know exactly what is occurring within the dome. And we need to be able to react instantly once we know. Second, we must invert the energy of the magic confining the Dread and drive them back whence they came. Last, we must seal off that rift."

"When you say it like that," quipped Nakor, "it sounds easy."

"It's direct," said Pug, "but not easy."

"How are you going to get inside to see what's there without being obliterated?" asked Miranda.

"This," said Pug. He held up an orb.

"An Orb of Ocaran?"

"I've never seen one of those before," said Nakor.

"We had one in storage at the villa," said Magnus. "It's the last one. We were trying to study it and duplicate it."

"Magicians who die without teaching another their secrets are annoying, aren't they?" said Nakor.

"We understand the basic theory," answered Pug. "We still haven't taken this one apart for fear we'd disable it, so we might as well use it now to ensure we have the leisure to build another in years to come."

"To make sure we have years to come," said Miranda. "You know how to use it?"

"I've used it before, briefly." Pug turned to Magnus. "You can put it inside that dome, can't you?"

"It's a very large target, Father; literally the size of a city. I can get it in there."

"It's time to alert everyone to their roles," said Pug. "We shall need four distinct tasks attended to. First, we will need defenders, for when we begin the spell inversion, that shell will become porous for a while, and we have a very good notion of what's going to be coming out of it."

"A lot of Dread," said Miranda.

"Second," said Pug, "we will need people to be ready to evacuate all those who aren't needed here. Because not only are there going to be Dread rampaging around this valley, but if this spell is as unstable as I think it may be, there could be destruction on a level that will make what happened on the Isle of the Snake Men look trivial."

"That's . . . terrifying," said Nakor.

"Third, Magnus, you're the only one who has the strength and ability to do the melding of magic that's coming our way. I don't know if even I could do it alone. I need you to be the conduit for what they give us.

"Lastly," he said to Nakor, "I need you to be ready to do things you've never been asked to do before, tricks on a scale undreamed of by anyone."

Nakor grinned. "I'll try."

"Now, I have to speak to some people," Pug said. "Where are Sandreena, Arkan, and Calis?"

"Oddly enough," said Miranda, "they are all with that Dark Elf Queen, enjoying a meal."

"I doubt Liallan would enjoy being called either a dark elf or a queen," said Pug. "I'll be back shortly. You three start thinking about how we're going to do this and not make mistakes. We need to have everything in place and ready to try by midafternoon tomorrow. After that, I think the magicians keeping the dome intact will be too fatigued. We need everyone at the peak of their power."

He walked away and Miranda looked at Magnus. "There are times when your father can be the most annoying person I've ever known."

Without conscious thought, Magnus slipped his arm around her waist and gave her a gentle squeeze. "I know."

26

ATTACK

Trumpets sounded.

Drums beat a tattoo and orders rang out as Brendan hurried to Prince Edward's command tent. Outside, he saw a dozen lackeys holding horses for the nobles. Prince Edward's was a powerful gray gelding covered in a deep blue bard, embroidered with the full coat of arms of Krondor, the eagle-and-mountain crest. Brendan had been sleeping since he reported back early in the morning with the count of the enemy mercenaries, who numbered between eleven and thirteen hundred by his best estimate, enough to make a difference, but not an overwhelming addition to Oliver's forces.

Seeing the Prince, Brendan ran to him, and Edward turned and said, "I want you to ride with me, sir. Get your horse."

Brendan hurried back to where his horse was resting from the previous night's travels, quickly had him saddled, and rode back to the Prince's retinue. Edward now wore full armor and, despite his age, wore it well. He was dressed in a full coif of chain with a mail coat and heavy leather leggings. His tabard was identical to all those worn by the men of Krondor, save that his bore the royal crown above the coat of arms of the principality. He motioned Brendan near. "The dukes, earls, and barons will be leading their forces, but I'll have a few nephews and younger brothers, such as yourself, nearby. You I would like on my right, behind me, at all times, so I know where you are. If I need to send word to one of our commanders in the field, I will send you."

"Yes, Your Highness," said Brendan. He reined back his horse, giving the Prince room to mount up and organize his men, and rode behind Edward and a squad of palace guards, twenty handpicked men who would give their lives to save their prince. They rode to the top of the hill behind which they had camped, and looked down on the armies of Prince Oliver.

"Gods!" Brendan whispered.

Before, it had seemed a sprawling sea of tents and campfires. But to see the whole of army now arrayed in battle formation less than a half mile away was staggering.

Prince Edward said loud enough for all to hear, "Looks to be perhaps ten thousand, wouldn't you say?"

If Brendan was a judge of such things, perhaps more.

"Will Oliver parlay?" asked the Earl of Hūsh, a distant cousin to the Prince and his aide-de-camp.

"Most likely," replied Edward. "He'll wish to gauge my resolve, I should think. There you are," he said, pointing. "A parlay call."

Four riders moved out from the army below, riding slowly forward under a white banner, while a trumpet sounded a truce call. Edward turned to Brendan and said, "Ride along, my young friend. You might learn something."

They rode down the hill until they met in the middle. It was Brendan's first look at Prince Oliver of Maladon and Simrick. He seemed a tall man by how he sat his horse, and big without being stocky. Brendan's first impression, before the man said a word, was that he was a bully. He wore a white tabard, quartered with opposing blocks of red in the upper right quadrant with a single white cross, and a block of blue in the lower left quadrant with a white horse rampant. His horse was also covered in a bard imprinted with the crest of Maladon and Simrick. His companions wore the same tabards without the royal crest.

"Highness," said Edward in an affable tone, "you have something to say?"

"Good day, Your Highness," replied Oliver. His helm was open-faced, showing a man of sharp features, cold dark eyes, and thin lips. "We could end this now, if you'd be willing. I am the only male heir related to King Gregory, my beloved uncle, and yet you press a claim without foundation."

"This should have been a conversation before the High Priest of Ishap in the Congress of Lords, not between two armies on the verge of battle. Why bother now? We know that the Crown will be settled by force of arms no matter what you say. Or do you make an offer of compromise?"

Oliver made a show of sighing dramatically. "Your Highness, in all the years I've known you, you've been a man of no ambition, yet now you seek a Crown?"

"I already have a Crown, Oliver," said Prince Edward with growing impatience. "What are your terms?"

"Retire from the field. Return your armies to your various garrisons, and come to Rillanon and stand before the Congress. Do not oppose my claim and peace will reign. No more bloodshed and your friends' and family's offices, titles, lands, chattels, and appurtenances are guaranteed. If you seek no gain for yourself or your family, why stand opposed?"

"Any discussion of my personal motives is not germane. I will not see a foreign-born lout sit on the throne of my ancestors, is all the reason I need."

"You wound me, Edward," said Oliver with a nasty grin.

"That is my intention, Oliver. Severely and with malice."

"Then look for me on the field, old man. I'll be easy to find," Oliver said, turning his horse and riding back to his lines.

Edward turned his horse without comment, then, as they were halfway to their own lines, said, "Brendan, my young friend, what did you see?"

"A bully, Highness, who wished to engage you in pointless conversation while his aides counted your forces and marked your deployment. I think he might also have wished you to believe there was an easier way out of this, to sow doubt at the last moment."

"Very astute, my young friend," said Edward. "Now we surprise him." Edward glanced again at Brendan. "What else?"

"Highness," said Brendan, "it's what I didn't see. I didn't notice those Keshian mercenaries that marched in this morning."

"That's because Oliver is hiding them," said Prince Edward. He signaled to a captain of horse, who turned and waved his arm.

Suddenly two things occurred at once. Oliver's forces began a slow march up the hill and Edward's cavalry began to shift position, moving from the center, pulling out from the rear, as archers ran out from behind a wall of shielding infantry.

Brendan watched in fascination. He knew the Prince and his generals had been preparing the ground for battle since arriving and that three features on the field that were judged critical were fortified. There was a large knoll to the southeast that was a perfect defense against any attempt Oliver might make to swing around and take Edward on his right flank. There was a rocky ridge rising up to the north that was a natural defensive position, upon which waited two hundred archers. That protected Edward's left.

And in the middle of the battlefield was a shallow depression that was misleading in appearance, but whose reality Brendan had just experienced. Once a horse dropped down into it, it had to gather itself to charge upward, which meant it lost momentum. It was a natural defense to break any charge.

Brendan lowered the visor of his helm and glanced down at the brown-and-gold tabard of Crydee. By rank, he was entitled to a cadence mark over the crest, but he hadn't found time or a tailor to sew one on. He prayed quietly, "Oh gods, do not let me shame this tabard of my family."

The army of Prince Oliver started moving uphill, the infantry at a leisurely trot, and the horses in the middle started their canter. Brendan heard a trumpet blow behind him and glanced back. To his surprise he saw the remaining cavalry pull out. A squad of men hurried forward carrying heavy poles, two men per pole, and fanned out to form a line before the infantry and archers.

Brendan understood now why Prince Edward had resisted the temptation to attack while Oliver was arriving. That would have been a melee without planning, while this was going to be the battle he chose.

As Oliver's cavalry reached the depression, Brendan watched and things proceeded exactly as he had anticipated. The cantering horses suddenly found themselves dropping down, and instinctively braced, then gathered for an uphill lunge, slowing down and blocking those horses behind. Like a ripple, the break in rhythm flowed back to the second, third, and fourth ranks, completely breaking the charge without a blow being struck.

Edward nodded and a banner was raised: his archers fired. Now Brendan understood why the traditional distance markers had not been placed in the field, for every bowman knew exactly how far downhill that depression lay. A flight of shafts took riders out of their seats and sent horses down screaming as they attempted to come out of the depression. More horses stumbled and became enmeshed in the thrashing mess in the misleadingly shallow hollow in the ground.

Arrows pelted the riders and they broke as a group to the right, circling around the far end of the depression, and Brendan saw the men on the ground get ready. Kneeling beside the poles, they formed a hedgehog barrier that would prevent the horses from attacking the infantry.

Where is Edward's cavalry? Brendan wondered, for he, like Oliver, obviously, expected the two cavalry forces to meet in the center of the field, reinforced by the infantry. Instead, Oliver's cavalry was moving to his right, Edward's left, toward the very defensible rocky ridge to the north. Two hundred archers waited and unloosed on Oliver's cavalry when they came into range.

Dozens of riders fell and Oliver's cavalry was soon in shambles. Commands were relayed and the hedgehog poles were abandoned. There would be no continuing charge from the east.

Oliver's cavalry fled back toward his line to regroup. Whatever use they were in the coming attack was blunted. Brendan looked and saw more than two hundred riders dead or wounded on the ground, with another hundred sporting wounds limping back to their own lines. And Edward's forces had not suffered a single injury.

Prince Edward drew his sword. "On my command . . . advance!"

He rose up in his stirrups and swung his sword in an arc, and his infantry moved out in an orderly fashion. Edward and his guards hung back, and Brendan also rose up in his stirrups and looked around. *Where is our cavalry?* he thought.

Pug meditated on what he had just encountered with one part of his consciousness. With another he reached out to Magnus, Miranda, and Nakor. *Come see this.*

Soon he felt their minds link to his and said aloud, "Can you see what I'm seeing?" He attempted to share what he was seeing through the Orb of Ocaran as it hovered outside the boundary of the dome. He would control it and Magnus would attempt to place it inside the dome.

After another moment he heard the three voices in his mind say they could. "Magnus, if you would be so kind?"

"Not all of us have to see what is inside," Magnus said. "I'm better than any of you at transporting objects without physically carrying them myself. So, you three link to the orb, and I'll send it inside. Once that's done, I'll try to link with you and see what you do."

"But you have to know where you're sending it," said Miranda.

"I've seen the breaches in the dome. It's perhaps five or six yards thick. So I'll transport the device six feet aboveground and ten yards in a straight line into the city."

"That's fine if you don't materialize it inside a wall," said Pug.

"Or inside one of the Dread," added Nakor.

"I would welcome a better approach," said Magnus. "Suggestions?"

Pug broke the mental link as they were all standing around him. He was silent, then said, "I have, I think, found a way to invert the dome, or a small section, which was what I was going to do, open a window for a second, then close it."

"Opening a breach is a better idea?" Miranda almost shrieked, Pug hearing her voice echo what she thought.

Pug said, "If we are to close that rift inside, we're going to have to either shut down that dome—"

"A very bad idea," Nakor inserted.

"Or use it to plug up the rift, driving everything inside it back."

"Which means at some point inverting the magic and shrinking everything inside," finished Magnus. "We know, but isn't it better to learn once that we have a problem with doing that than twice?"

Pug sighed. "You're probably right. I just hate not having some means of testing my theory. This will be the single most powerful spell anyone has undertaken; we'll have hundreds of magic users and priests linked into the spell, and there's no telling what the effect will be."

Miranda put her hand on Pug's arm. "Pug," she said softly. "I have all Miranda's memories, including everything you muttered in your sleep."

He blushed, causing Nakor to chuckle.

She continued: "I've heard you chatter over dinner about this and that, and what I've come to know is if there is one being on this planet who's capable of designing a . . . piece of magic . . . a spell that will save this world, you are that person."

Magnus nodded.

Nakor shrugged. "If we do nothing, everything dies. If we try and fail, everything dies. Might as well try, right?"

"It's not even a question," admitted Pug. "Very well. Link into the orb with me," he said to Nakor and Miranda, "then Magnus can send it into the dome."

The Orb of Ocaran was one of several devices that Pug had discovered years ago in the abandoned lair of an artificer of magic devices by that name. Ocaran was legendary for making one-of-a-kind items; but this orb was particularly useful, so he had built several. However, it was the only working one Pug had seen. There were many types of far-seeing spells, scrying, and distant vision, but they all had limits; exhaustion on the part of the caster was foremost. The orb, on the other hand, needed only to be guided, and as it was a physical item, once its use was mastered, it was nearly effortless to operate.

They exchanged glances. Unspoken was the thought *better sooner than later,* so Pug, Miranda, and Nakor sat down, while Magnus walked as close to the boundary of the ruby dome as he could. He gauged his distances then mentally asked, *Ready?*

When the answer came back affirmative, he sent the orb into the dome.

Tomas grunted with exertion as he attempted to remove Draken-Korin's head, but the blow was deflected away. Both fighters were now laboring, and despite their inhuman endurance and strength, soon one of them was bound to take a wound that would be beyond his ability to magically heal.

The dragons sang a melancholy song. It had no words but carried a meaning no mortal could apprehend. Within the web of the song was repeated, over and over, "Tomas must die."

Tomas hit Draken-Korin so hard that the Lord of Tigers stumbled back a full ten yards, and Tomas used his mental powers to ask, *Why must I die, daughter of Ryath?*

From the great golden dragon who presided over this contest came the thought: *Death is a gateway into something beyond. Tomas must pass beyond. At the proper time, Ashen-Shugar must be without constraint.*

Tomas laughed as Draken-Korin poised to charge him. "You mock me?" the Lord of Tigers shouted.

"All of life is mockery," Tomas responded. "Come, old enemy, last of our kind, let us put an end to this."

Draken-Korin charged and Tomas easily dodged the attack, inflicting a serious wound to the black-clad warrior. The Lord of Tigers screamed in pain and rage, spinning away to get out of Tomas's reach.

Tomas closed his eyes.

Again he stood on rocks, with an inky dark sea swirling on all sides. He had climbed out of that black tide over a century before and knew what it meant to be swept under and pulled down by it. It was an ending and beginning for him. He laughed in a triumphant voice and dived headfirst into the water.

I am Tomas!

With a purpose that could only be seen as mad, Tomas sought out the heart of this blackness, the root nature of the Valheru with whom he had shared his existence for decades. Downward he swam.

Ashen-Shugar opened his eyes and felt a power unlike any he had experienced in ages of life flow through him. The dragons surrounding him sang a battle song of blood and victory, and he turned to see Draken-Korin before him. The Lord of Tigers was battered and covered in blood, staggering as he readied himself for another attack.

Ashen-Shugar looked at his own blood-covered hands and arms. He saw the rents in his tabard and felt the flame of wounds upon his body. He willed away the pain and healed the wounds and felt life well up within him.

The blood drained from Draken-Korin's face as he screamed, "No!" He launched himself at his old foe with a ferocity born of terror. Whatever reserves he had held back were now unleashed and he appeared for a moment a warrior reborn.

Ashen-Shugar held his ground, easily countering the blows and looking into the face of his oldest enemy with the certainty that the day was won. After a flurry of blows, Ashen-Shugar batted away Draken-Korin's ebon blade and stepped forward, smashing him in the face with his white shield.

The Lord of Tigers arced backward, landing hard on the ground. He groaned in pain and knew he had nothing left to offer. His sword fell from limp fingers and he released his hold on his black shield. With what little strength he had left, he struggled to get up and fell to his knees.

"Why?" he whispered.

Ashen-Shugar stared down at him.

"Why was I brought back, just to die once more?"

"Does it matter?" replied Ashen-Shugar.

With a powerful sweep of his sword, Ashen-Shugar sundered the Lord of Tigers's head from his shoulders, and watched as blood fountained high into the midday sunlight.

As one, the dragons tilted back their heads and cried out in a song of sorrow and triumph.

Ashen-Shugar, ruler of the Eagle's Reaches, turned and looked at the ring of dragons as if seeing them for the first time. "What has happened?" he demanded.

Rylan leaped down with one beat of her massive wings to confront the white-and-gold-clad warrior. "You have been lost in a dream, Master. You have been awakened by your most ancient enemy, and your power is needed."

"To what cause must my powers be lent?"

"An invader, your most powerful foe, has invaded your world."

Ashen-Shugar had not participated in the Chaos Wars against the emerging gods. He had watched from afar, so he had no gauge to measure the gods by, save their ability to reduce his brethren to sobbing, frightened children. In his vanity, he thought himself above them, so their experience bore no relation to his own self-estimation. But once in his existence, he had faced an enemy so powerful and unrelenting that the Dragon Host had been forced to flee in disarray. Softly he said, "The Dread have come?"

"Indeed," said the golden dragon. "We have assembled to contest the invasion, every lesser dragon on this world, but your power and command are needed."

"Of course," said Ashen-Shugar. He gestured with one hand and Rylan lowered her head, allowing him to mount her. "Take me to the Dread. We shall rid this world of their taint."

With a single snap of her wings, Rylan, daughter of Ryath, took to the sky, and the entirety of dragon kind on Midkemia took flight behind her.

Brendan saw the melee below as if it were a moving thing, an ocean's surface of churning steel and blood, brave banners, and rearing horses, and with it came a noise of screaming, crying, shouting, and the clash of metal. But it had a rhythm, a surge, ebb, and flow, and without knowing how he knew, he was certain that he was witnessing a battle approaching stalemate.

Then suddenly, from the north, Prince Edward's cavalry came flying. Now Brendan knew why Edward had let Oliver's cavalry charge be answered by terrain, arrows, and hedgehog poles. He had sent his own cavalry on a fast ride around the granite ridge serving as the northern redoubt, and now was hitting Oliver hard on his right flank.

There was a balance in the air, a sense that somehow this was going to break one way or the other, and within an hour, perhaps within minutes, the battle would be won or lost.

Then Brendan saw movement to the southeast. It took a moment to understand what he was seeing. The Keshian mercenaries must have been infiltrated through the woods, and been thrown wholesale at the knoll to the southeast. Rather than attempt to ride around it with cavalry, Oliver had stormed it with infantry, and now that infantry was streaming down off that knoll, directly at the Prince of Krondor's position, with only Brendan, a few minor nobles, and twenty mounted palace guardsmen to defend the Prince.

"'Ware the field!" Brendan shouted as loudly as he could. "'Ware the field!" He pointed with his sword.

The Krondorian palace guards rode up behind him, forming a line, lowering lances and drawing their swords. Their captain shouted, "On my command, charge . . . charge!" and the twenty riders with Brendan at their side charged into the mass of oncoming mercenaries.

Pug asked, "Is everyone seeing this?"

Miranda and Nakor both said, "Yes," then Nakor said, "But I can barely believe my senses."

"The orb is safely there?" asked Magnus.

"Yes," said his father. "See if you can locate it. Try linking with my mind, if you must."

Magnus sat next to his father and closed his eyes. Piercing the dome to link with the orb was difficult, so he linked with his father's mind and instantly was inside the dome, amid chaos.

"What are those . . . things?" he heard Miranda say through his father's perceptions.

The interior of the dome was illuminated by a faint red light, sunlight filtered through the magical energy field surrounding the city. Within the boundaries of the dome, there was a roiling cloud of black. Occasionally a piece of the cloud would break off and form a roughly humanoid shape, something upright with broad shoulders and bright red eyes, but eventually it would fall back into the mass.

"We remain unnoticed," said Nakor.

"So far," said Pug.

Magnus said, "Laromendis and his brother said the heart of the city was where this rift was formed."

Pug moved the orb, watching to see if it called attention from the mass of black smoke. They moved without incident a few yards, then he picked up speed and hurried to the center of the city. He had no problem identifying the point of entrance.

"Gods!" said Miranda.

"It's the Void!" said Nakor.

In the center of the city, a blackness occupied an area roughly the size of a building. Nothing could be seen within it, but from the edges the black smoke emerged, curling and surging outward.

"This is what is devouring the center of the Fifth Circle," said Nakor.

"Watch the edges," said Miranda.

Through the vision they got from the orb, they could see the edges of the Void expanding at the crawl of a snail, mere inches an hour, yet it was still expanding. "At this rate this city will be gone in a year," said Pug.

"Sooner," said Nakor. "I think the rate of expansion is accelerating. Look at those tiles in the wall."

The Void was consuming a wall, decorated with small tiles roughly an inch across. Pug did not need the Void to cross one to observe, "I think you're correct."

"What is this Void?" asked Magnus. "Is it a manifestation of the Dread? Is it the Dread itself?"

Pug said, "I don't think we're going to learn anything

useful by simply wandering around among all this . . . smoke, for lack of a better term. It's clearly a manifestation of what's in that pit." He hesitated for a moment, then said, "We weren't going to get this orb back, anyway," and moved it into the Void.

Suddenly they were without bearings, engulfed by a world of neutral gray. "We are in the Void," said Pug. "I have been here before."

He had willingly accompanied Macros into the Void to shut down the Tsurani rift and end the war, and it had taken magic and the aid of his old teacher Kulgan to pull him back out. Another time he had ridden through it on the back of a dragon with Tomas, looking for Macros the Black.

Nakor said, "I know what Macros meant about this not being an empty place. It is brimming with . . . stuff. There is great magic here, Pug."

Miranda said, "Perhaps this is where magic comes from, and we somehow tap into it."

"There," said Magnus. "There's something there."

Without direction it was difficult to know where "there" was, but within seconds the other three saw what Magnus had referred to: a speck. They focused on it and Pug said, "It's hard to know if we are close to a tiny thing or very far from a massive thing."

"Move us closer and we'll see," said Miranda.

"With only one point of reference, this may be difficult," said Pug. But he turned his focus on the spot and willed the orb to move toward it.

Suddenly a stream of energy sped around them, and Nakor cried out, "It's . . . stuff!" All they got was a tantalizing glimpse as it sped past. Every time any of them attempted to concentrate on a single mote, it was gone.

Pug said, "I think I'm beginning to understand why the Dread have such a problem understanding time. If we attempted to intercept even one tiny part of this stream of . . . particles? Strands of energy? Whatever this may be, we would be flailing blindly."

Magnus said, "But in flailing you could do a great deal of damage."

Miranda said, "A nice enough metaphor, true, but let's see what it is that is doing all the flailing."

"Are we getting smaller?" asked Nakor. "Before we couldn't see the strands of stuff, but now they look large enough to reach out and touch."

"I doubt it," said Magnus. "It's perspective."

They saw the speck in the distance expand, and with the movement of particles showing them, it felt as if they were moving toward the dark spot. It grew and they felt as if they were accelerating toward it, even though they were outside the dome on the ground.

Abruptly, everything changed. The spot expanded almost explosively to look like a massive pit and in the center of that pit rested a being.

Either it was gigantic, or they had become tiny. The being was roughly humanoid in shape, with flames bathing it from head to toe, but no light or heat was generated. Waves of energy were being created constantly, and the profound sense that swept over the four magic users was one of rage and sorrow.

Every dark dream, hidden fear, and unvoiced terror was encompassed in those feelings, and it was aware.

It turned its attention to the orb and it reached out.

Then it reached past the orb and the four magic users felt it coming out of the pit, along the lines of consciousness that linked them to the orb, coming outside the ruby dome, right at them.

Ruffio was talking to Tanderae and Janil when he heard a cry of anguish. All three turned to see the four magic users who had been employing the orb lying on the ground, their eyes rolled back in their heads, thrashing in paroxysms of pain.

He hurried over and knelt next to Magnus, put his hand on the thrashing magician's chest, then shouted, "Get healing priests! Get them now!"

27

WAR

Brendan swung his sword.

A Keshian mercenary dodged away before the blow landed, and Brendan kept moving forward. He had enough training to know that to be standing still in a melee while on horseback was an invitation to be pulled from the saddle. He knew his mount was his best weapon at the moment, and he intended to take advantage of it.

They were hugely outnumbered, only thirty horsemen—twenty trained guardsmen and not quite a dozen minor nobles like Brendan—against at least five hundred foot soldiers. The best they could hope for was to distract the infantry while Prince Edward rode to safer ground. The captain of the palace guard was rallying some of Edward's foot soldiers to him, to stem the attempted sweep from the right flank.

Brendan moved as fast as he could, knocking down attackers and causing as much confusion as he could, but keeping away from the heart of the force. His horse was calm and well trained, but even the stoutest warhorse would balk if faced with too many bodies packed tightly together.

Hacking and charging, Brendan managed to turn a half-dozen soldiers away from the line of march, but dozens more were flooding toward the top of the ridge, behind which lay the Prince's pavilion and the tents of the other nobles. He spurred his horse away from the fight and circled around, trying to get his bearings.

Brendan saw that Edward had been spirited away by some of the nobles around him while his bodyguard was being pushed back and overwhelmed. He knew he could do nothing more, for the Keshian mercenaries were pouring in unchecked. Kicking hard, he drove his horse forward.

He looped around to join with three other palace guardsmen who had been driven back and teamed up with a squad of infantry wearing tabards from different duchies.

He looked around and could not locate the captain he had seen earlier who had rallied the soldiers. Seeing no other noble or officer close by, Brendan waved his sword aloft, shouted, "Follow me!" and led a charge into the gap at the top of the ridge where the Keshians were swarming.

As they moved forward, he heard the clash of arms on the other side of the ridge and saw smoke. "They're firing the tents!" someone shouted.

Brendan kicked hard and drove his horse up the hill, leaving the infantry behind. He rode through the gap at the top of the hill as fast as he could, striking down Keshians who were foolish enough to get in his way.

He felt a chill of near panic as he saw that a squad of Keshian riders had circled even farther to the west and had come up behind the camp while the infantry had distracted the Prince's attention. It had been a double-pronged assault, and Brendan now feared for Edward.

He looked around for the distinctive markings of the Prince's horse's bard and saw a flash of deep blue through the smoke and chaos. He urged his horse toward it and found a knot of defenders protecting Edward. The remaining palace guards, a few surviving noble nephews and cousins, and as ragged a collection of infantry who had wandered or fled this way were now rallying to guard the Prince of Krondor. They were overmatched but fighting as bravely as men could fight, and Brendan was overcome with admiration as he pointed his horse's nose at the Prince's standard and spurred it on.

Brendan weighed into the fight, slashing and hacking and driving a wedge between attacking Keshians while the infantry coming up the hill intercepted the Keshian foot soldiers. This was a desperate attack, for it would not turn the overall battle tactically, but it was designed to do one thing: kill the Prince of Krondor, thereby ending the battle in Oliver's favor.

Brendan clubbed a soldier with the hilt of his sword and smashed another with the flat of his blade. He pulled tight on the reins of his horse and urged it forward, deeper into the press.

Hal saw the smoke in the distance and motioned to four guards who were escorting the Duke of Ran and his companions. "Keep them under close watch," he ordered. "If they try to escape," he added, looking directly at Chadwick of Ran, "cut them down."

Martin, Ty, and Hokada rode up from their positions along the line. "Looks as if the fight's started without us!" shouted Hal. The remounts had proved to be a wise choice: able to ride longer and farther, they had reached the Prince of Krondor's camp a day early.

He turned and motioned for the rest of his command to form up. "Drop remounts! Double column!"

The four riders at the rear, who had the responsibility of herding the remounts, left their positions to catch up with the other riders, all of whom fell into place as ordered. Once they formed up, Hal motioned them forward. After a few yards at a trot, he ordered a canter. As they reached the edge of the woods, he saw in the distance the struggle at the Prince's pavilion.

What looked to be an army of mercenaries on both horse and foot had a core of defenders surrounded, and at their heart he could see Edward. Hal drew his sword and took his shield off his back. Ignoring the soldiers moving to intercept him, he charged straight in the direction of the Prince of Krondor, shouting, "Charge!"

Chopping his way through as if he were cutting wheat with a scythe, he rode, desperate to reach Edward before his defenses collapsed. A pair of what appeared to be Keshian mercenaries hopped on a baggage wagon, crossbows at the ready. Hal shouted a warning as he drew closer, but it went unheard in the din.

Both men shot at Edward, one missing entirely, but the other taking his horse in the neck. The animal went down with a cry, and Edward vanished from sight in the press of horses and riders trying to defend him.

Hal saw Brendan and both brothers brandished their swords overhead in greeting as Martin and Ty caught up. Hokada took his bowmen around to the right and began raining death on the attacking Keshians. Within moments, they were turning to flee, dropping to their knees with their swords reversed, or lying dead on the ground.

Hal took command and quickly moved away the Keshians who had surrendered, directing a handful of infantry to take charge and guard them while Hokada and his horse archers harried those fleeing. Hal and his brothers dismounted and shoved and pulled people out of the way to reach the Prince.

Edward lay on the ground, blood staining his lips and

nose. He motioned for Hal to come close when he saw him and Hal knelt. Despite the pain, Edward chuckled. "Not a blade or arrow," he said, then coughed blood, "but my own damned horse falling on me." He looked into the younger man's face. "You are all we have left." Then his eyes rolled up and he lost consciousness.

Hal ordered two nearby palace guards to get him to his tent.

"I'm sorry, Your Grace," said one of the guards, "but the tent's been burned to the ground."

"Find a place for him and make him comfortable, then send for the chirurgeon and a healing priest!"

Four guards bent to carry the Prince, and another said, "I'll get the chirurgeon, but we have no priests, my lord."

"No priests?"

"They all . . . left, two days ago."

"Where did they go?" asked Hal, frustration rising up.

"They just left. No one knows where. There were a dozen of them, from all the different orders, then . . . they were gone!"

"What in the name of the gods is going on?" asked Hal.

"No one knows, Your Grace," said the soldier.

Hal looked around and didn't see another ranking noble. He grabbed Brendan and said, "See to the Prince's safety." To Ty and Martin, he said, "Follow me."

They remounted and rode over the crest, and Hal reined in to watch the battle's progress. At first glance, all was in chaos, but after a moment he could see that Edward's forces were holding a slight advantage, with heavy Krondorian cavalry pressing hard against Oliver's right flank. On Hal's right, things were in flux, as the fleeing Keshians had found haven behind Oliver's lines. Taking in the situation, Hal turned to Ty and said, "See if you can find Hokada and get him to stop chasing Keshians. Have him move back to that rise over there, and get ready to hit the main body of Oliver's left as hard as he can." He pointed to a tiny rise at the foot of the wooded knoll that originally had been held by Edward's forces. Ty nodded and hurried off.

To Martin, Hal said, "Go back and get as many of our lads as you can find, all the Crydee boys and anyone up there not still guarding the Prince or captives, then ride to that knoll and dismount. I need you to get up and clear it of any of Oliver's men so Hokada can safely ride over it and slam into Oliver's left flank down there when I give him the order." He glanced again at the ebb and flow of battle. "Tell Hokada if he can turn that flank and force those men back into Oliver's center, we shall have the day."

"Very good," said Martin. "Where will you be?"

"Down there in the mess," said Hal, and he spurred his horse and rode straight down to where the fighting was thickest.

Hal arrived as a surge of Oliver's Maladon infantry was trying to push back a beleaguered troop of Krondorians, and he hit them in their right flank, trying to turn it. A dozen more riders were a second behind him and they disrupted Oliver's soldiers just enough for the Krondorians to disengage and re-form in an orderly defense. Hal slashed and clubbed any enemy soldier who got too close to his horse and found his way cleared by retreating men.

Suddenly the Krondorians charged in counterattack and the rout was under way. Hal pulled up his tired horse and took a moment to see how the rest of the battle was proceeding. He saw Martin leading his squad up the knoll to clear it. He hoped Ty had found Hokada and that he could organize archers quickly and give Martin support.

Hal saw another half-dozen Crydee horsemen approaching and beckoned them to join with the five already at his side. He hurried behind the line, moving from Edward's right to left flank, south to north, and came in behind the heavy Krondorian lancers who had started to roll up Oliver's right flank. He stood in his stirrups and shouted, "To me!" Then he rode like a madman straight at the infantry that was hastily trying to stand against the lancers. To the commander of the Krondorians, Hal shouted, "Re-form and charge again!"

The captain of the Krondorians recognized the ducal insignia above the golden gull of Crydee and acknowledged the command. He withdrew his lancers while Hal and his men harried the now-retreating men from Simrick. In less than a minute, Hal felt and heard the charging lancers before he turned and saw them, and he signaled his own men to withdraw. He cleared the knot of defenders just as the Krondorians smashed into those attempting to stand and fight, and rolled over them.

Now Hal could see that Oliver's entire right flank was collapsing. He stood again and saw that Ty and his archers were picking off targets and inflicting damage on the other side of the line. Hal shouted, "At them! We have them!"

He saw a group of mounted men on a small rise to the rear of the battle, at the center of which sat Prince Oliver. His banners waved bravely in the wind but his advantage in the field was slipping away by the second. His right flank had collapsed; his left was being harried by Hokada's archers and the cavalry riding with Ty and Martin. The center was in flux, with neither side prevailing, and it could tip either way in minutes. The Dukes of Yabon and Bas-Tyra, along with other nobles, were concentrating on Oliver's main force, and there was murderous work being done, but no advantage seized.

Hal waved to the captain of the Krondorians. "Regroup your men, drop your lances, and draw your swords!" Then he signaled to his own men and, when they were with him, shouted, "Follow me!"

The right flank of Oliver's army was in full retreat, rapidly escalating to a rout. Hal led his company, now numbering about thirty men, and circled around the retreating infantry, through a grassy depression strewn with the bodies of the fallen, and came into line with where Oliver and his cadre waited. "Let's see what this Prince is made of!" he shouted, attempting to hit Oliver's center as Martin, Ty, and Hokada hit him from the other side.

When Oliver saw Hal leading a company in his direction, he drew his sword, then turned and fled, along with two of his guards, while his officers stood their ground.

Hal signaled the Krondorian captain to take the rear guard while he rode after Oliver. A half dozen of his Crydee soldiers followed while the rest overran the defenders on the rise.

Hal urged his horse to overtake the fleeing Prince, and the gap closed slowly. One of the two guards turned and charged at Hal. Hal ducked under a sword blow and kept going, letting the soldiers behind him dispose of the delaying guard. The second guard glanced over his shoulder and saw Hal overtaking them. He also turned and charged. This time Hal knew there was no one immediately behind him, so he braced himself for the attack. He brought his sword up to meet the blow offered by the guard, then reined in his horse so fast that the animal squatted, then he wheeled so that he was suddenly behind the guard as he was trying to turn his own horse. Hal took the guard out of his saddle with one vicious slash, blood fountaining into the air.

Hal urged his mount on, seeking sight of Oliver. He saw a flash of white vanish into trees at the edge of the woodlands to the northeast of the battlefield. He turned his horse in that direction and hurried after.

The midafternoon sun gave Hal a clear view and he easily saw Oliver's tracks in the damp soil and fallen leaves. He saw the trail turn as if Oliver was trying to use the woods to lose Hal and double back toward his own lines, where he might find protection. Hal drew up and listened. In the distance he heard the sound of hooves.

He followed the trail for a little longer until he was certain of Oliver's course, then cut through the trees on a path to intercept him. Once more he stopped and listened, and once more he adjusted his course.

A small drop-off caused Hal to change direction, and he looped around as the sound of an approaching horse grew louder. Then he let his mount jump down a few feet, and landed directly in front of Oliver's cantering mare, causing her to rear up as the two horses collided. Hal jumped and hit the ground in a roll, coming to his feet, sword at the ready.

Oliver was on his feet, his visor down, covering his face, and his sword at the ready as both horses ran off into the woods.

Hal didn't hesitate. He charged.

The dragons rose in a spiral, a flurry of colorful wings cracking like thunder as they tore through the sky. At their head flew the great golden dragon Rylan, upon whose neck rode the last living Valheru, Ashen-Shugar.

"Tell me about this threat to my world," demanded the Dragon Lord.

"The Dread attack, Master," said the dragon. "They seek to breach a portal created by the elves."

"Fools! I'll have their heads on pikes," said Ashen-Shugar.

"They are already dead," said the dragon. "They died in the making of the rift."

"Then take us to the Dread and I will destroy it!"

"There's a risk to address first, Master," replied the dragon. "Do you remember the Sven-ga'ri?"

"The singing crystal beings, yes," said Ashen-Shugar. "I ordered them protected. They are beings of . . . dangerous power."

Left unsaid was the core reason for the decision made by the Valheru to leave the Sven-ga'ri alone. Their language was incomprehensible to the Valheru, but it evoked feelings that were alien to the Dragon Lords. Longings and desires at variance with what drove his race: the need for blood and conquest, to rise supreme among the stars.

"What you must know, Master," said the dragon, "is the

Sven-ga'ri were placed in the mountains of the Quor by the Dread as a means of gaining entrance to this world. They must be destroyed before you can drive the Dread back whence they came."

"Then to the Peaks of the Quor!" shouted Ashen-Shugar.

In a very dark, cold place, a mind of a man was being pulled down into a void. It struggled to stay aware.

I am Tomas. Just a little while longer.

Hal knew he was overmatched by this bigger, fresher opponent. He had been riding desperately for days after a fight while Oliver had slept soundly in a pavilion. His only advantage was that he knew he was a far better swordsman than the Prince of Maladon and Simrick. Had Hal been fresh, the contest would already have been decided, but fatigue made him slower to react; his blows were a tiny bit off as a result, and Oliver was experienced enough to understand what he had to do, which was to wear Hal down.

For his part, Oliver knew he faced a superior swordsman, but he also knew that time was on his side, so he was content to wait for Hal to move first, counter, and retreat. The boles of trees were additional allies, as he maneuvered in such a way that when he dodged, he had a trunk between himself and Hal.

Hal could not see his opponent's face, but he knew he must be smirking. That angered him enough that he could battle back exhaustion for a while longer. Even so, his sword arm was growing tired, and he realized that because he knew what Oliver was doing, he was falling into a predictable attack. He would start an overhand, looping blow and Oliver would deflect it with his shield, then quickly bring his shield back against a combination attack, pause a moment, and move back a step.

Hal now realized what he had to do. He began his blow

and Oliver's shield came up slightly, but Hal pulled his swing and ducked. Oliver imagined an opening that wasn't really there and stepped forward as Hal had wished. Hal threw all his weight behind his shield as he smashed into Oliver's shield, causing his opponent's sword blow to slice through the air. Oliver stumbled. Trying to step back, he caught his boot heel on the root of the tree he had planned to duck behind, and fell backward, landing hard on his rump. Reflexively he put out his hands on either side to brace his fall and for a moment was exposed.

Hal didn't attempt a sword blow. Instead, he kicked up at the exposed part of Oliver's chin, under his helm, and was rewarded with a loud crack as his boot toe found its mark. Had he missed, he might be nursing a broken foot, or have Oliver's sword point in his groin.

Oliver rolled sideways, disoriented, and came groggily to his feet. Hal charged again, bashing his shield hard against Oliver's helm, and took the big man down to his knees.

This was no fencing match in the Masters' Court, but a brawl without rules, and as tired as Hal was, he wasn't about to let the bigger, stronger, and fresher man get any respite, even a moment, to gather his wits and fight back. He smashed again with his shield and spun Oliver half around, swung his sword sideways as hard as he could, and took him in the side of the head with the flat of his blade. It was like striking an anvil or ancient oak tree; the shock ran up Hal's arm and was painful enough it took all his willpower to keep his grip on the sword's hilt. Oliver went sprawling and lay twitching slightly.

Hal knelt upon his chest and ripped Oliver's helm from his head. Unfocused eyes stared upward as blood flowed from his left ear and both nostrils. Hal put down his sword and balled his mailed fist and struck Oliver on the jaw as hard as he could. He was rewarded with a loud cracking sound—if the boot to the jaw hadn't broken it already, this time it was certainly broken. Oliver's eyes rolled up into his head and he lost consciousness.

Hal sat there for a moment, trying to catch his breath. Satisfied that the Prince of Maladon and Simrick was indeed senseless, Hal staggered off to look for the horses. Given the hard collision, he wasn't surprised they had run off.

Sighing in resignation, he returned to his prisoner, hauled him up by one arm, then let it drop. "No damned way I'm hauling you and all this armor back," he said aloud. He dropped to his knees and began unfastening the buckles on Oliver's armor.

Hal walked slowly back toward the sounds of fighting, breathing heavily from the exertion of carrying the Prince of Maladon and Simrick over his shoulders. More than once he was grateful that his father had insisted he learn how to carry a stag out of the woods, or he was certain his back would have given out by now.

It had only been fifteen minutes since he had felled Oliver in the woods, but it felt like an hour, given the size of the man. Hal silently wondered why Oliver couldn't have been a short, skinny fellow.

A squad of riders in Krondor blue approached at a canter and reined in upon seeing Hal. "Your Grace," said the rider in front, a sergeant. "We've been looking for you."

"How goes the fight?"

"The day is ours, my lord. Lord Bas-Tyra routed the center after the Earl of LaMut turned their flanks; the enemy is fleeing in disarray. We've captured many nobles and officers."

"Add this one to the catch," said Hal.

"Is that Prince Oliver?" asked the sergeant. "In his smallclothes?"

"My horse ran off, and I didn't feel like lugging him and his armor."

The men laughed. "We'll see to him, my lord." The sergeant motioned to one of his men. "You ride double, and give the Duke your horse." To another he said, "Drape that fellow across the rump of your horse and be gentle; he's royalty."

They laughed as they carried out their orders. Like all soldiers after a victory, they were buoyed by survival and success, and tired to their bones.

Hal took the reins of the horse given to him and mounted. "How fares Prince Edward?"

"The chirurgeons tend him, but I have no news."

"Take me to him," ordered Hal.

He followed the sergeant at a gallop as the others brought Oliver along at a more sedate pace. As they rode past the battlefield, Hal could hardly credit his eyes at the mass of dead and dying covering the once-rich farmland of the Fields of Albalyn. Fully five or six thousand bodies, a few still moving, were now mired in mud made from soil and blood. A few of the boys from the baggage train helped find those who could be tended back to health, while men of cold resolve moved through with misericords, the long thin blade inserted though the armpit into the heart of those too wounded to save and spare them a lingering death, the battlefield's "quick mercy."

Smoke blew across the field and a sense of order was slowly returning. Prisoners were being gathered and guarded, and men who could stand watch did, while others lay where they could, gasping for breath or merely silently thanking whichever gods they worshipped for their lives this day. Others wandered with shock on their faces, seeking something: a comrade, a lost weapon, or some unseen need yet unmet. The boys from the baggage would return and guide them back to where others could tend them, but until those with wounds of the body were treated, these lost souls would be left to wander awhile longer.

Hal reached a massive spreading oak on the top of a hill located behind the hill where the Prince's and other pavilions and tents had been burned. Under a large canvas, perhaps a portion of unburned tent, lay Prince Edward. His entire lower body was covered in blood-drenched rags and he lay propped up against the bole of the tree, tended by two chirurgeons. Nearby waited the nobles loyal to him. Brendan stood beside the tree, obvious frustration on his face over his inability to protect his prince.

Hal glanced over at Charles of Bas-Tyra, who nodded a silent greeting, and Hal dismounted. A lackey took his horse and Hal came to kneel before Prince Edward. He looked at the chirurgeon on the Prince's right, who looked back and said, "His legs and pelvis are crushed, Your Grace. His horse went down and rolled over him. He was never a robust man, but he endures."

"Is there no healing priest?" asked Hal.

It was Bas-Tyra who answered. "While you were catching Chadwick by the nose, some dozen healing priests of the orders of Sung, Dala, and La-Timsa all vanished."

"Vanished?" Hal looked confused.

Charles explained about the disappearance.

Hal could hardly contain his anger. "Our prince lies dying and there's not one priest to be found. What of those who were with Oliver?"

Bas-Tyra's expression was one of genuine regret. "As soon as Oliver fled and the day was ours, we began asking, but their priests disappeared before the fight, the same as ours."

As Hal waited for any sign of consciousness from Edward, the Krondorian rider carrying Prince Oliver across the rump of his horse arrived and deposited their still-limp enemy inelegantly on the ground.

Charles said, "I've seen Oliver look better. And what happened to his armor?"

"I was tired" was all Hal said.

Edward's eyes opened and focused on Hal. "Duke Henry," he whispered.

"I am here, Highness," said Hal, leaning forward to hear better.

"The battle . . . ?"

"The day is ours, Highness. Oliver is taken."

"Where is Jim Dasher?" asked the Prince.

Out of the shadow of the tree stepped Jim Dasher and

Lady Franciezka Sorboz. Hal stood and nodded greeting, wondered how he had not seen them before.

"Is it done?" asked Edward.

"Yes, Highness." Jim leaned over and whispered into the Prince of Krondor's ear, then stood up.

"Henry," said Prince Edward weakly, waving him over.

Hal again knelt beside him. Edward reached up and took his arm in his hand, squeezing it. "What I have done is for the good of the Kingdom. I need you to understand. Will you honor my decision?"

Hal had no idea what he meant, but simply said, "I am loyal to you, my prince, and whatever you choose to do I will support."

"Swear," said Edward weakly.

"I swear on my honor, Highness."

"Then I am left with but one hope, my young friend. And that is that you will also forgive me." Edward closed his eyes for a moment, then opened them again. "I may never walk again," he said to the chirurgeon, "but I will survive to face the Congress of Lords. See to it."

The chirurgeon nodded and said, "Find us shelter."

The Duke of Bas-Tyra pointed to a large tent from the baggage train being erected down the hill. "My pavilion stands. Bear him there."

The chirurgeon oversaw four soldiers, who gently lifted and carried the Prince to Bas-Tyra's pavilion.

Martin and Ty had found their way to where Hal and Brendan stood and they all embraced. Hal's face was a mask, set in place by exhaustion and the sight of too much death. He looked at Jim Dasher. "So, we win the battle and lose the war?"

Jim said, "Plans were made. Prince Edward is gravely injured, but he lives, and today he was victorious." He smiled. "In no small part due to your actions, my young friend."

Martin asked, "With Edward injured, what happens? Does Oliver reassert his claim?"

Lord Bas-Tyra snorted. "Hardly. He's probably lucky if

he remembers his name given the thrashing your brother gave him."

"What will be done with Oliver?" asked Brendan.

"And Chadwick?" added Hal.

Bas-Tyra tried not to smile, but failed. "Oliver will be a guest in Rillanon for a while, I think."

"Until Maladon and Simrick can scrape together enough gold to pay his ransom," added Jim. "Chadwick will linger awhile longer, until Edward decides his fate."

Charles came over to Hal and put his hand on the younger man's shoulder. "We have missing lords among the dead, and quite a number in chains with Oliver. They will be . . . spoken to," he said, again glancing at Jim, "and all will be well, I assure you."

"You need to rest," said Jim to the brothers and Ty. "You've fought valiantly, and all here know that. But you're not made of steel. It's a long journey to Rillanon. Get some rest and we'll leave at dawn."

Hal looked at Jim, Franciezka, Bas-Tyra, then at Ty and his brothers. He then looked back down to the field of fallen men and said, "Sleep can wait. There are honorable dead to be tended," and he turned and walked down the hill to help carry the fallen to their burial pyres. His brothers and Ty were only a step behind him.

Charles came to stand next to Jim and said, "Edward was right. They are a different breed."

Jim said, "I think we also have some work to share," and he followed the three brothers down to the field of battle.

28

DESTRUCTION

The sky was filled with dragons.

Smoke billowed across mountaintops as an inferno spread throughout the Peaks of the Quor. Ashen-Shugar looked down as wave after wave of the Dragon Host flew low and bathed the creatures called Sven-ga'ri in dragon flame. Without remorse, he bade them do what would have been impossible for any other mortals: destroy entities whose very voices sang to the heart and mind.

The Valheru were merciless and Ashen-Shugar had endured where his brethren had fallen, for he cared nothing about the fate of others, only himself. He felt no pity or sense of loss at destroying the last of his kindred. The final destruction of Draken-Korin had brought him only a muted sense of triumph, for now he was undoubted ruler of the world.

Besides, the universe held secrets unrevealed, and the day might come when he could find means to bring more of his own kind into being, should he feel the need. At this moment he was unconcerned with such considerations, but rather with the destruction of the wedge into this universe driven ages before by the Dread. For now his only interest was in ridding this planet of invaders, to subjugate all life on this world and crush any who opposed his will. He ordered the dragon Rylan to circle so that he might better see the destruction he had decreed.

The beings known as Quor were helpless against the overwhelming power of even a single dragon, let alone an army of them. The Elves of the Sun either resisted and died instantly or fled down the mountain, knowing their ages-long charge to protect the Quor as they protected the Sven-ga'ri was at an end.

Fools, thought Ashen-Shugar. *We were fools to fear that which we did not understand.* Those feelings of love, compassion, and mercy, those alien emotions he had learned about by sharing his mind with the human Tomas, were nothing to fear. Such useless attachments to others were distracting, and by necessity must be destroyed.

Grudgingly, he conceded that the enemy, the Dread, had been clever to plant tethers into this realm, and to protect them by making them beautiful, engendering feelings of love and joy in those who became aware of them. Even the Valheru admired that genius as he watched it turn to ash below him.

Then came the silence, and he realized the last of the Sven-ga'ri was gone.

A howl erupted from deep within the ruby dome, a sound of such anger and despair that it caused every living being to pause and look toward E'bar. The shell flickered as if energy shifts were running like courses of waves through a lake, ripples getting larger with every passing moment.

"What is that?" asked Liallan.

Sharing a meal in the quickly erected pavilion with her was as odd a collection of beings as Liallan had ever imagined entertaining: a prince of Elvandar, a human woman knight of a religious order, three Taredhel magic users, and others who had been coming and going all day.

A messenger hurried in and knelt before her.

"Speak," she instructed.

"Cetswaya says there's been an upheaval inside the dome. Powerful magic has been unleashed and we should be ready."

"Order the warriors to take up position."

Liallan stood up and left the pavilion, followed by her guests. Calis said, "I should find Arkan."

Liallan looked at the son of her most hated enemy and said, "He will be with his clan, somewhere over there." She pointed to the large outcrop of rock the magicians had been using as a reference point to bring in supplies and other magic users. "Why?"

Calis shrugged. "You get used to having certain people around." Then his smile broadened. "And he is a little quick to focus on his left, and neglect threats from his right. That could get him into trouble."

The Prince of Elvandar hurried off and the human woman warrior, Sandreena, came to take his place, pausing to pull on her gauntlets. "I've been around those two enough to know they'd die to protect each other; I'll never understand the blood feud between your people."

Without taking her eyes off Calis's retreating back, Liallan said, "You're correct, human. You will never understand."

Sandreena hurried along. The magic users followed, leaving Liallan alone with her servants. At last she turned and quietly said, "Bring me my armor." She looked at the sky above. Storm clouds were gathering, seemingly drawn to the strife down below as the ruby dome began to flicker and tremble. Softly, the leader of the Snow Leopards said, "Few will be around to finish what we start here, now."

Pug felt the upheaval, as did the other magicians. He, along with Miranda, Nakor, and Magnus, had been stunned for a few minutes before regaining his senses. Pug stood and studied the situation. He saw Cetswaya instructing various magic users while Moredhel warriors were deploying to answer any threat. He motioned to Magnus, Miranda, and Nakor to come close. To Nakor he said, "Can you go fetch Ruffio, please?"

Nakor returned in a minute with Ruffio and Pug said, "I imagine everyone here felt that . . . whatever it was?"

Miranda said, "It felt as if something . . . tore loose?"

"I get the sense something is thrashing around inside the dome, Father." Magnus looked in the direction of the dome. "It's changing."

Pug looked at the magicians controlling the dome and saw that they were starting to exhibit signs of distress. "Magnus, see if you can tell what's going on. Look at the elven magic users. They appear to be—"

A sudden ripping sound was accompanied by screaming as a rent in the dome materialized. A flood of dark figures erupted through the tear and battle was joined.

The horrors that came flooding out of the breach were smoky shapes with glowing red eyes and massive shoulders tapering to trailing tails upon which they effortlessly glided along. They lashed out with claws and lunged to bite with fangs, but no wounds appeared where they struck. Rather, those unfortunates whom they wounded suffered shriveled flesh and felt a numbness spreading from the wound. A slash to the throat or a deep wound in the chest, and the afflicted would die without breath, their heart stilled. A blow to the head and vacant eyes would herald brain death. Steel hurt, but didn't kill them. But it drove them back, as stalwart

Sentinels and Moredhel warriors furiously attacked. Magic destroyed them—a magician's fiery blast, a cleric's spell of destruction, or a spellweaver's enchantment. Slowly, the onslaught of smoky horrors was pushed back to the dome.

Pug, Magnus, Miranda, and Nakor walked slowly toward the dome, destroying every smoky apparition that stood before them. Pug found a moment to look past the attacking Dread and examined the dome. It was wavering, despite the containment spell. He could sense that the thing that lay at the heart of the dome, at the rift in the center, was attempting to push itself up and out of the pit, to gain full entrance into this world. There was a sense of desperation that hadn't existed before the surge of energy they had all felt moments before.

Pug moved to a knot of magicians and spellweavers who were being defended by a dozen Moredhel warriors. With a wave of his hand, he sent a curtain of scintillating, white-hot energy that swept away a large group of Dread who were poised to overwhelm them.

One of the Moredhel glanced over at Pug, and for the briefest moment Pug thought he saw gratitude on his face, then the warrior returned his attention to the next wave of attackers. Pug put his hand on the shoulder of the nearest magician and closed his eyes, lending his senses and magic to the spell engaging the dome.

We have an opportunity, Pug sent mentally to his son, Ruffio, Miranda, and Nakor.

What? came the reply from all four.

The creature at the heart of the pit is frantic. I think that wrenching feeling we experienced is related to this. It is trying to get out prematurely.

Nakor's voice entered their minds. *When I lay dying on the Dasati world, I saw the Dreadlord rising through the dimensional rift, and it took time. The life energy it was using was enormous, yet it was moving slowly. If you are right, Pug, the Dread in the pit will need more energy. Be cautious.*

What are you thinking? asked Miranda.

Pug said, *Ruffio, send word to the waiting magicians and priests worldwide that it's time to start linking up the magic chain. It will take an hour or two, but once it's in place, I think the Dread in the pit will be vulnerable.*

Ruffio replied, *I will.*

You dropped a portion of Kelewan's moon down the last rift, Pug, said Nakor. *What are you planning this time?*

We won't be able to fully reestablish this dome for an hour or two. When we do get control back, I want to invert the spell, twist it inside out, and push back with everything we can muster and drive the Dread back into that pit, then fix the inverted spell in place, as a "stopper," and collapse these mountains in on it.

Nakor said, *What about the dwarves to the south?*

Ruffio, can you send word to King Dolgan and his people they should move to the south end of their valley?

I will, said the younger magician, and then they felt a void as if he had vanished.

Nakor's voice returned to Pug's mind. *I'm not sharing this with the others. Can you control this?*

I must, replied Pug. *There is no other choice. If the Dread flood into this realm, we and every other living thing on this world will die And from here it will move out to other worlds.*

I saw the Void in the Fifth Circle, Pug. It moves slowly. Perhaps we could come up with a different solution?

Miranda said it moved "slowly but inexorably" when she described it, observed Pug. *We must keep it from entering entirely.* He paused, then added, *Everything we've encountered from the first attempt to reach the Lifestone to the incursion of demons and Dasati, all of it was to clear the way for the Dread to enter this realm. Here is where they need to be if they are to reunite with what Macros called Mind, and return everything to that perfect state of timeless bliss.*

Timeless bliss, said Nakor with a mental chuckle. *That doesn't sound so bad.*

Except for everything we've ever known ceasing to exist.

If time is returned to that state, nothing that has ever oc-curred will have happened. All we know will never have ex-isted. Inverting the rift is our only hope.

No one knows more about rifts than you, Pug, said Nakor, *but this is unprecedented.*

The threat is unprecedented, replied Pug, and Nakor had no answer to that.

They worked to push back the Dread emerging from the dome, and when it was at last closed off once more, Pug dived mentally into the lattices of energy. He described what he saw to the others while they attended to the needs of the failing magicians. Several had been rendered unconscious or otherwise incapacitated by the fury of the breach, and magicians who had not fully recovered were being asked to return to hold the barrier.

Pug worked for nearly an hour before he was forced to take a rest and withdraw his mind from the energy matrix formed between the intersection of the elven magic and the dome energy. He took stock of the situation around him and saw that at least a dozen Moredhel dead had been gathered together and a funeral pyre was being built. He walked over and took a moment to bow his head in acknowledgment of their sacrifice, then trudged up the hill to where Magnus stood watching over the dome.

"Father," said the tall magician in greeting.

"How are you holding up?"

"Better than you, from appearances. You need to rest."

"No time," said Pug. "We have the dome contained for a while but I don't know if everything we need will be in place in time. It feels as if it will break again soon, and next time I don't think we have the resources to close it down. When it breaks, that is when we must be ready to turn the spell in on itself, even if we're not entirely ready. We have to attempt to seal the rift and drive the Dread back to the Void."

"I know more about rifts than anyone except you," said Magnus. "I have grave concerns whether this will work."

"As do I, but if the dome tears again, we will have no

choice but to act at once. Which is why I need you to do certain things to improve our chances."

"What?" asked Magnus, stepping off the rock upon which he had been observing the dome.

"There are two stages to this undertaking," said Pug quietly. "We can all work on the preparation: you, me, Miranda, Ruffio, Nakor, the spellweavers and shamans. When we are ready, however, there are only two of us who can do what comes next."

"I do not like the sound of this, Father."

"Nor do I," admitted Pug. "But there's no choice in the matter. I need you to act as the conduit for all the magic energy that is going to be routed to us through the chain of magicians and priests worldwide. You are the only magician who has the strength and ability to not be overwhelmed and consumed by it, Magnus. Even Ruffio, who is a prodigious talent, is years away from being able to manipulate those energies. I'm not sure even I could sustain it for very long. And in any event, I need to be in the rift, ensuring that the power you send me does as it is supposed to do."

"In the rift?" asked Magnus, his face a mask of disbelief. "You're going to pull everything in on top of yourself?"

"I have to be close to the rift to gauge how best to apply the inversion spell, then I have to back the Dread down into the pit."

"Why not simply ask the sun to reverse itself?" said Magnus bitterly. "How long do you expect you'll survive even trying to reach the rift?"

"I have the means to protect myself from the entities that have been flooding out of the dome," said Pug. "Long enough to reach the center of the city and then, after that . . ."

"Do you believe you can survive this, Father?"

Pug was silent for a moment. "Honestly no, but then I've felt that way before." He looked at Magnus. "When we went to the Dasati home world, I wasn't certain either of us would survive." He sighed. "And Nakor didn't, despite our thinking he somehow did."

"I know," said Magnus. "The longer we're around those two demons, the harder it is to remember they are not who they seem to be. But we've always considered risk."

"There is no risk," said Pug, suddenly impatient. "It's a certainty we'll all die if the Dread break through to this realm in strength. It will consume everything it touches, growing stronger by the minute while we weaken. We could flee to the Hall and find another world, and eventually we would succumb to old age, or some other mishap, but that thing in the pit would be swallowing worlds and ages after we were gone, everything in this realm would be gone!" He shook his head and lowered his voice. "And this is different," he said. "From what Macros showed us, this would be a tipping of a balance so profound that everything we imagine as real would return to the primal state. Nakor and I just discussed this a few minutes ago.

"It doesn't matter if it takes a day or a year or thousands of years, but eventually we'd all be inside that perfect, blissful ball of . . . whatever it is, was before creation. And none of this"—he waved his hand—"will have happened. Time will be as it was before. This . . . thing will not only obliterate everything that is, it will engulf everything that ever was."

Magnus was silent for a long moment. Then he said, "Was there ever so bleak a possible outcome?" He looked at his father and smiled. "May I offer a suggestion?"

"Certainly."

"When I was a boy, you told me more than once about your first experience within the Void, shutting down the Tsurani rift, and how you returned with Kulgan's staff as a guide. How it tethered you to him. I would like to be a tether if I may."

"I'm listening," said Pug.

"You know me as well as anyone can. If you can just reach out to me at the last moment, if possible, I will do everything in my power to pull you back to safety."

Pug smiled and said, "I will attempt to do that."

"Good," said Magnus softly, and both knew nothing more

need be said on the matter, because both knew the chances of their plan succeeding were virtually nonexistent.

Pug said, "Until that moment, you are the only one I can trust to shepherd the others, to take that energy I need and feed it to me. So, first and foremost, no matter what else happens, you must do that. Once I no longer need it, you must flee, for either I've failed and the Dread is among us, or that rift will be imploding, and most of what we're standing on will be sucked into a vortex of unimaginable power. Understood?"

"Understood." Magnus looked around. "What about the rest of them?"

Pug shook his head in regret. "Some things you can't think about, or bear the pain of doing so."

"Miranda?"

"She can get many free of here." He paused and thought for a moment, then said, "Thank you, son. You've given me an idea."

Pug hurried to find Miranda. "I've been speaking to Magnus and we've worked out a plan to shut down the rift without needing you to be part of it, so I have favors to ask."

"What?" said Miranda, and her suspicious look told Pug he'd have a difficult time convincing her that what they were planning had a modicum of hope of succeeding.

Pug said, "When I go inside the dome—"

"What?" interrupted Miranda. "*Inside?* When did that become part of your plan?"

"I have to get to the rift to ensure what I plan to do will work."

"And how is it supposed to work if that thing inside obliterates you before you get an opportunity to examine the rift?" she said, her voice rising until she was shouting.

Pug was silent for a moment, letting his mind wrestle with a flood of emotions. He was old enough and experienced enough that he could separate his feelings from his decision making. He had lost so many friends over the years, his first three children, and his two wives, but in this one moment, despite knowing that the being he was talking to wasn't really Miranda, he felt an almost overwhelming fear that he would never see that face again. He willed himself to push aside feelings and to concentrate on the task at hand.

"I know in many ways this is as difficult for you as it is for me," he began.

She grabbed him and kissed him passionately for a long moment, then whispered, "You have no idea." A tear ran down her cheek. "I can barely remember anything of my life as a demon. Every minute I spend in this form, those memories . . . my memories! They are mine!" She leaned forward and put her cheek against his. "I know this has hurt you and Magnus in ways I can only imagine, but here"—she struck her own chest with her fist—"I live and breathe as Miranda. I am your wife, Pug, and I am Magnus's mother." She looked up at the sky as if trying to compose herself. "I remember a day and more of labor and all that pain vanishing the moment he was born." She closed her eyes. "I miss Caleb every day."

Then she stepped back a half step and struck him on the chest with a halfhearted blow. "And now you're telling me to . . . pretend we don't both know you're going into that dome and you're never coming back." She took a deep breath and whispered, "I'm sorry. I'll do what you ask, of course. Just don't ask me not to care."

With a tear in his eye, he whispered, "I have not understood until now . . . just how painful this must be for you. I'm sorry." He kissed her. "I know you are not Miranda, but I want to tell you what I never got to say to her. When she . . . you died, part of me died with you. I have never for a moment in my life thought that love was limited, that there was a finite space in one's heart for people. I love Tomas like a brother, and still miss Prince Arutha and Martin Longbow, and Father Tully and Kulgan. I wish I could see Hochopepa and Shimone one last time, and watch Fantus frighten the serving staff in Krondor. I miss Carline and Laurie, and I miss Katala as much as I miss you. So different, the two of you, yet both of you made me better and kept me . . . from spending too much time inside myself. The things we've had to do, the places we've gone, the pain and loss we've endured . . ."

Now tears ran down his cheeks. "I miss Caleb every day, and Marie." Pug started to sob. "I miss the boys, Zane, and Tad, and Jommy, and their families. But I want them safely gone from here. I may not survive this. But I want you safe, too. When I tell you, promise me you'll leave and take as many of these as you can with you."

"Pug—" she whispered.

"Promise me!" he demanded, his voice thick with emotion. He knew he was cursed to watch everyone he loved die before him; it was why he had distanced himself from those he met after his encounter with Lims-Kragma after his battle with Jakan the demon. Of those he counted loved ones, he had only Tomas and Magnus left alive. With his foster grandchildren he had kept his distance, and with close associates like Ruffio he had not let personal bonds grow, as he refused to watch them die. But Miranda had already died, and unless the gods were cruel beyond understanding, what was left of her, her memories, her soul, and her heart, would live on within this body. "Promise," he repeated.

"I promise," she said, tears running down her face. "I have lived a short life, by mortal standards, yet I have centuries of memory. But most of all, I have known love beyond my ability to imagine in the realm of my birth."

"Just stay alive," he whispered.

She stepped back, wiping her eyes. "I will," she replied.

Pug looked around and said, "The time of reckoning is near." He pointed to where a fatigued Liallan stood, perspiration dripping from her face as she waited against another assault from the dome. "She must be saved."

"Why, of all of them?"

"She is the future of the dark elves," said Pug. "I know something of what occurs up there, and there is a dark elf named Narab . . . he must not take the Crown of the Moredhel. She can make them so much more than what they are now. Besides, we are in their debt." He indicated the pyre that was being lit. "They're here, giving their lives not just for themselves, but for even their most hated enemies on this world. We have a debt."

"I'll do what I can," she said.

Disentangling himself from her embrace, he looked to see if anyone was watching. It was amusing that with a cataclysmic event perhaps hours away, he was still concerned over their privacy. "We have very little time," he said. "Get ready."

She nodded. "What of our son?"

"I have told him what I need of him." He refused to share with her in this moment, in this form, what he had not shared with her when she was human: that Magnus was preordained to die before him.

"What happens next?" asked Miranda.

"We wait, and when the next upheaval occurs, I will use all my powers to get to the pit and examine the rift and begin the transformation. Magnus will act as a conduit for all the magic we are gathering, and if all goes according to plan, I'll be able to trap whatever is emerging through the rift in it, suspend it between the Void and here, then drop this entire mountain on top of it."

"The last time you did something like that, an entire world was destroyed, Pug," said Miranda.

Pain flickered across his face as he thought of the millions who had died to prevent the last incursion of the Dread into this space and time. "I know," he said softly. "I had less preparation and less understanding of the transit from that realm to this. I basically had no other idea how to close down that rift and destroy the link. But here we have an advantage. That red thing is its making, the Dread's, and by luck or genius, the original elf who tried to stem it created a perfect tool to manipulate it. I will use the spell to turn it back on itself, driving the Dread back into the Void, and the vortex it creates should pull most of this valley and some of the surrounding mountains after it, sealing the passage."

"There's a lot of conjecture there. If your calculations are off . . ." She left the end of her thought unfinished, for they both knew the possible consequences.

"I've been doing little but study this since I arrived," he said. "I know the risk, but we have no other choice. If I did have another course of action, I'd take it."

"How soon?"

"Soon. If there's not another major shift within the dome, or another breach in it, I'll order the dome opened from this side, and we'll try to achieve what we need."

"If you can do that, why wait?"

"It will take a great deal of energy to force the upheaval from this side. If we wait, we can let the Dread do half our work for us. But from what I'm seeing in that matrix, I suggest sooner rather than later." He looked up the hillside to where Nakor, Magnus, and Ruffio were in deep conversation with a pair of priests. "I need to speak with some others, so if we don't get the opportunity to speak again . . ."

"I know." She took his hand and squeezed it, then let it go.

Pug moved to where the three magicians were standing and nodded greeting. He was in time to hear Ruffio say, "All you need to ensure is that those back at your temples are ready. I judge we'll be ready soon." He glanced at Pug.

Pug said, "Very soon. In fact I was coming to ask you to start spreading the word." He glanced again at the dome and said, "Within hours."

The two priests bowed and moved off. Pug turned to Ruffio and Nakor and said, "I have something to ask of you both."

Ruffio said, "Anything."

"Magnus and I will be responsible for the assault on the rift. You, despite being magicians of prodigious power, will add little here by linking into the web of magic we will be using. Magnus will funnel the energy to me, which will allow me to form a protective barrier around myself and reach the pit and rift. I need you two to keep as many people alive as you can once the dome is reopened."

"And once it is closed again?" asked Ruffio.

"I need you to take as many of the Moredhel, the Sentinels, and any magician or priest too injured or weak to be part of the web, and get them as far from here as you can."

Nakor held up a small Tsurani orb. "I can do that."

"Where did you get that?" asked Pug. "I thought we'd allocated all of them."

"I've had it for years," said Nakor. "In my bag. I'm always traveling with someone else, so I've never had to use it."

"Good," said Pug. "Where's it calibrated to?"

"This one goes to Krondor, Rillanon, Stardock, the Isle, and somewhere else . . ." He toggled it and vanished. A moment later he returned. "Ah, to LaMut! That inn with the doorway into the Hall."

"How did you get back here?" asked Pug, pointing to the sphere.

"It's a trick," said Nakor with a grin.

"Then do you have a trick that can extend the field of that device to encompass more than just those holding on to you?"

Nakor's grin vanished. "I can do that. How many?"

"As many as you can manage," said Pug. "Take the Moredhel and Taredhel to LaMut, along with the Eledhel. From there they can make their way to the Northlands or Elvandar as they please. The wounded can be cared for there as well." He dropped his voice. "Make sure that the two elven princes are among the first. Calin has been trying to help, but he's just another warrior and we have more than we need. I'd trade a dozen warriors for another magic user. And Calis . . ." He lowered his voice. "I'll not chance his mother losing a husband and son on the same day."

Nakor said, "I understand, Pug."

To Ruffio he said, "Take as many as you can, as well. Once you've reached LaMut, I want you to return to the Villa."

"Very well," said Ruffio. "What then?"

"You wait, and if we survive all this, you will have the burden of rebuilding the Conclave and the Academy. Amirantha is there and he will do what he can to help you."

"But—" began the younger magician, but Pug held up his hand.

"Most of those here will probably not survive," said Pug. "If the damage to the dome is less than I anticipate, perhaps some will. No one here is ignorant of the risk. I've spoken to the leaders, and asked them to give permission to depart to those who wanted to leave."

"How many left?" asked Magnus.

"Three," said Pug. "A very old cleric of Sung who says his heart is weak and he can't be of help, but he can tend to the injured should we need to recall him. And two young magicians from the Academy who just admitted to being too frightened to risk not fleeing at the last moment, disrupting the web."

"They may be the intelligent ones," said Nakor with a grin.

"Anyway, I think we're ready," said Pug.

"What's this?" asked Ruffio, looking past Pug.

Pug turned and saw Calis and Arkan walking their way.

Calis said, "Pug, Arkan has a question."

"Yes?" said Pug.

The Moredhel chieftain paused for a moment, then said, "In a dream I was seen defending a human magician, clad in black." He pointed to Pug, then to Magnus. "I am unsure where I am destined to fight."

Pug didn't hesitate. He pointed to the large outcrop. "There. My son will be standing there and his concentration cannot be broken once he starts working his arts. If you will defend him, I will be in your debt."

"There is no debt," said the chieftain of the Ardanien. "It has been foretold and is ordained."

He turned and walked toward Liallan's pavilion.

Pug looked at Calis watching the Moredhel's retreating back. "He's an interesting fellow."

Calin was coming from where he saw to the wounded and

passed Arkan without a nod. When he reached Pug and the others, he said, "We are doing as well as we could hope. Some of the wounded will be crippled, but they will live." He saw his brother and Nakor watching Arkan and gave his brother a questioning look.

Calis nodded. "I've killed a fair number of his kin over the years." He looked down a moment, his expression one of regret. "Never enjoyed it, really."

Calin nodded and said nothing. There was nothing to say.

Calis glanced at Nakor. "He remembers a time when we soldiered for the King," he said.

"Indeed I do," said Nakor. "With Bobby de Longville and your band of desperate men." Then he said, "Sorry, I forget about naming the dead."

Calis shrugged. "I'm half human, remember?"

"I will leave you to reminisce, little brother," Calin said. He moved back uphill toward the clearing where the wounded were being tended and those resting could get a meal.

Then the younger Prince of Elvandar looked around as if drinking in every detail. "I've left some good men behind, Pug. Erik von Darkmoor, what a man he turned into. From the gallows to the palace. And men whose names maybe only Nakor and I remember, like Billy Goodwin and Jerome Handy."

Nakor nodded reflectively. "Remember Biggo?"

"He was someone you wanted on your side in a brawl," said Calis with a smile, "but at heart he was a gentle fellow. And Luis de Savona, and that little fellow Rupert."

"Avery," said Nakor. "He got very rich, I hear. Twice. And Sho Pi, who finally became a grand master in an order of monks who served Sung the Pure."

Calis said, "I've led good men and been honored to serve with better men." He glanced back at Arkan, then at Pug. "You couldn't ask for a better warrior to defend Magnus. He may have been taught to hate humans his entire life, but he will die defending your son."

"High praise," said Pug.

Calis merely said, "What do you need of me?"

"Stay close to Miranda, and when it is time to leave, don't argue, just go. Your mother will need you and your brother."

Something in the way Pug said that struck Calis, but he said nothing. He just nodded and went to where Miranda waited.

"Nakor," said Pug. "Once this is done, if you choose to stay, find Ruffio at the Villa, please?"

"Yes," said Nakor, knowing what Pug meant by "stay," for the demon part of him, Belog, understood that what they were attempting to do here would echo on the Fifth Circle, and that if Pug was successful, perhaps the Void would be halted there as well.

Pug waited. A drop of rain struck his cheek and he saw the storm forming above was getting darker. He sighed and began reviewing one more time what he planned to do.

29

OBLITERATION

The sentry shouted a warning.

"Dragons!" came the cry from one of the Moredhel guards, and Pug looked skyward. The dark sky and falling rain had shrouded them until the dragons dropped out of the cloud cover. Soon it was obvious that a massive flight of dragons was heading toward them.

Pug glanced first to Magnus, then to Miranda, Nakor, and Ruffio, and shouted, "Be wary! I have no idea what this portends."

The arrival of the dragons caused several magicians to lose concentration and suddenly the dome's surface began to waver. As the dome began to weaken, dragons descended to confront the Dread who escaped from the tears in its fabric. Magicians and priests fled as the massive dragons threatened to trample them.

Pug looked around frantically, trying to make sense of the chaotic spectacle before him, but was at a loss to understand what was happening until he saw an enormous golden dragon circling in to land nearby. On her back he could make out a figure in white and gold. "Tomas!" he shouted.

Calis hurried to Pug's side and they watched as the dragon bowed her neck and the warrior on her back effortlessly dismounted. Calis watched him take two strides and said, "That is not my father!"

Pug readied himself for another conflict, for if it was as Calis said, and this white-and-gold-clad warrior was no longer his father, it could only mean it was once again the Valheru, Ashen-Shugar.

Ashen-Shugar looked from face to face, and when his eyes came to rest on Calis, he slowed and an expression of curiosity replaced that of simmering rage. "What . . . ?" He stared at Calis. "You are of the race, but you are not. Who are you?"

"I am your son," said Calis evenly.

Ashen-Shugar's eyes closed for a moment, and he swayed.

Deep within a dark sea, a consciousness swam upward, seeking light, and when it broke the surface, it sprang upward, as if taking wing, and landed on a single rock above the black water. Within the mind of this combined being, Tomas again asserted himself and seized control.

The white-and-gold-clad warrior's eyes opened and focused, and a distant, hoarse voice whispered, "Pug, Calis, I have little time."

"Tomas?"

"Father?"

"I was hidden, deep within Ashen-Shugar, and I will soon be gone."

"What?" asked Calis, while Pug merely nodded understanding.

"I have no time to explain, but the dragons . . . Pug, the dragons are the power behind all this." He waved his hand, encompassing the battle unfolding between the dragons and the Dread. "Only they are linked to this world more profoundly than elven kind. Only they possess a magic older than man's."

Pug whispered. "Only they navigate the Void!"

Tomas said, "Only they can bend time."

"It's always been the dragons," said Pug.

Tomas said, "They serve a power more profound and ancient than we ever imagined. Whatever ultimate force opposes the Dread in this universe, the dragons are its servants." He looked at the stormy skies above and felt the splatter of rain on his face. "Even this," he said, "this last moment in my life, is a thing of beauty."

"Father?"

Calis saw his father look at him, gaze into his eyes, then turn back to Pug. "We must go. I do not know why, but I have been . . . Ashen-Shugar has been called to confront the Dread."

Blood drained from Pug's face, and he said, "I know why." He glanced around to see who could hear, and saw that Miranda, Nakor, Ruffio, and Magnus were all within earshot of the conversation. "It is the nature of the Dread that time does not exist as we think of it. For only a moment, as we see it, the Dread's entire attention must be turned to one thing, and that will echo across time and keep it from continuing to probe into our universe."

"But if it has happened . . ." began Miranda.

Pug held up his hand. "No time." He looked at Tomas. A brother since Pug could remember, the first person to take up his cause and be his champion, his protector when they were boys, Tomas nodded silently, showing that he understood what was coming. Tears welled up in Pug's eyes and he said, "Will you . . . will you be forced to endure this?"

Tears filled Tomas's eyes, too. "Thankfully, no. I shall soon be dead in every sense of the term. Whatever the gods have in store for me will be what it will be, but I will be spared that horror."

Pug felt the tears streak down his cheeks. "For that I am grateful, my oldest friend."

Tomas closed his eyes and his face contorted a moment, then he whispered, "It is time."

"Now?" asked Pug.

"Now!" said Tomas, and he looked at Calis. "Your mother knows how I feel. As do you. Always remember."

Pug threw a glance at Miranda, who took a step in his direction. He held up his hand and she faltered, then halted. They locked gazes for a lingering moment, then he and Tomas both moved toward the battle outside the rim of the dome.

Pug sent a signal to Magnus, who in turn began the process of linking the magicians and priests worldwide who would lend their power to shutting down the rift. Tomas drew his sword and cast aside his shield: any part of the Dread he approached would vanish in a single bright white flame and a small puff of smoke as soon as his sword touched it. Pug erected a protective shell around himself, and each Dread who touched it also exploded in a white flash.

Tomas's thoughts came to Pug. *At some point I will lose control, and Ashen-Shugar must be confronting the Dread or he will turn on you.*

Pug spoke aloud: "I understand." He looked at Magnus and there passed between them an unspoken good-bye.

Then Pug and Tomas entered the dome.

The Dread specters tried to swarm them, and Pug's protective bubble of energy exploded each smoky figure upon contact. "How this Dread can be one entity, yet manifest as many separate parts, is beyond my understanding."

Tomas nodded. "There are things we will never know, Pug. Who the dragons serve, and how they came to be the focus of all this, is my question. We must accept some mysteries are beyond understanding."

"Time is short," said Pug. They moved toward the center of the city, where they could see the red beam rising to fan out above to form the dome.

"Then hurry," said Tomas, and Pug could tell he was in a great deal of distress.

Pug jogged along beside him and could feel each contact with a Dread shape as if he were hitting something physically. The drain on his energy was trivial compared to what was beginning to come his way via Magnus. Still, managing the energy was more difficult than he had anticipated, and he tried to will himself to a calmer state of mind. He understood what was at stake, but giving in to panic or becoming unfocused was the fastest way to lose the day.

As they neared the center of the city, they came to the edge of the pit, a massive crater in the heart of the once-magnificent home of the Taredhel. Smoky black creatures of all sizes and a variety of shapes clambered up over the lip, and as soon as they came into sight of Pug and Tomas, they attacked.

Despite the two being perhaps the mightiest beings on this world at this moment, it was like swimming up a waterfall, so fast were the Dread rising up. Tomas was restricted by the simple limits of his physical reach, his ability to strike in only one direction at a time with his sword. Pug was fatigued by the need to keep his protective spell intact. He avoided physical damage, but the press of bodies was threatening to swarm him at the edge of the pit.

"We need to be down there!" he shouted to Tomas.

"I have no doubt you're right," the white-and-gold-clad warrior shouted back over the clamor. "I can barely maintain control. I need your help."

Pug siphoned some magic from the stream Magnus was sending and lifted himself and Tomas above the tallest

Dread climbing out of the pit. Some leaped to reach them but fell short, and a few tumbled back into the pit. The few that had wings flew up against the protective sphere and vanished in a shower of sparks, but didn't provide enough resistance to slow Pug down.

Pug and Tomas moved up and saw the pit was enormous, at least two hundred yards across. "What's that?" asked Tomas, indicating what appeared to be a dark shape rising from the center of the pit.

"I think that's the heart of the Dread, seeking a way out," replied his friend. "Hold on a moment longer."

Pug swooped down, and as they descended he watched dark gray vapor or smoke twisting and turning as it sped upward. "That is the Void itself," said Pug. "The actual stuff of the Void leaking into our universe."

"Hurry," said Tomas. "I can't control him much longer."

As they started a slow descent into the pit, Pug asked, "How did you come to let him regain control?"

Tomas laughed, and Pug heard a mix of the boy he had loved as a brother and a man resigned to his fate in that laugh. "I simply let go, Pug. Ashen-Shugar and I struggled during the early years of the war with the Tsurani, as I learned how to wield his powers, and I finally achieved dominance. He was made dormant all those years ago, and I found a perfect balance in my life with the magic the dragons gave me, made strong by the shielding enchantment of Elvandar. It was one of the reasons I so rarely left. But once I awoke him, returned him to control, I had to hide within his mind." There was an emotion that followed this statement that made Pug realize Tomas had endured something unspeakable while relinquishing control to the Dragon Lord. "I had to 'die' so that he could achieve the ferocity we need to defeat what is below us. While I controlled this body, I could only hold my own with Draken-Korin, but once I unleashed Ashen-Shugar, the fight was quickly over."

"Draken-Korin?" asked Pug.

"I can't explain," said Tomas. "Just be ready, for what I'm

about to do may bring as much danger as what we see below. But know this, Pug: you were like a brother to me."

"And you to me, Tomas."

"In a moment I will be gone. Good-bye, Pug."

Within the mind of the warrior in white, Tomas felt as if he was losing his control over the surging tide below his feet. He took a deep breath and closed his eyes, and black water suddenly rose up over the rock upon which he stood. It rose rapidly to his knees, then his waist, then his chest, and then he was underwater. Rather than struggle, he relaxed and let himself succumb to the downward tug of eternity, to a darkness so profound he could barely imagine light anymore. As he sank into nothingness he thanked whatever gods could hear him for the life he had lived. The entity that was Ashen-Shugar slowly came back into focus, reclaiming his dominion within the mind of the being that had shared his consciousnesses for more than a century.

I am Ashen-Shugar! he heard echoing as if from a vast distance.

As he felt his life finally slipping away, he said softly, *I am Tomas.*

Pug felt his friend slip away. *Good-bye, Tomas.*

He turned his attention downward and the pit of his stomach turned to ice. He stared down at a thing to frighten a god.

Below them, looking up, was an immense figure of black hate and smoky despair. Roughly man-shaped, it had no clearly determinable features. Rather than skin or hide, its shape was defined in a constantly rippling, writhing, flowing smokelike surface, tendrils of which rose up and spun off in different directions. Where the head and face should be was a contorted shape, sometimes oblong, moments later spherical. The only constants were two large, glowing orbs of red where eyes should be. A coronet of sparks like lightning and flames surrounded its head like a crown. It was massive: more than ten times the size of the creature Pug had seen battle the dragon Ryath under the city of Sethanon. If that manifestation had been a Dreadlord, this must be the Dreadking; no matter how the Dread managed to manifest in different locations in space and time, this was its fundamental heart, the core of its being. Of that Pug was certain.

It reached up as if seeking to grapple with Pug and Ashen-Shugar. And a distant sound of hollow anger reverberated from below, rising quickly and growing in volume until it shook the walls of the pit.

Pug looked at Ashen-Shugar and saw that his face was contorted in concentration and rage, with perspiration running from his brow and cheeks. Pug released his hold on what had been Tomas, as the fully empowered Valheru no longer needed Pug's protection from the attacking fragments of the Dread; indeed, his expression showed he considered him a trivial concern in the face of the monster attempting to climb out of the pit below.

Ashen-Shugar held tightly to his sword, its point downward, aligned with the creature below. Not a shred of humanity remained in the face Pug now beheld. It was a snarling mask of hatred and wrath unlike anything Pug had seen since confronting the Demon King, Maarg. And it was all the more chilling to see it displayed on features so well known and beloved.

Ashen-Shugar stared at the titanic figure of the Dread below him and screamed, "Into the Void again with you, monster!" The last Valheru threw himself into battle, leaping into the pit to grapple with the thing striving to enter Midkemia.

Pug pulled back slightly as the two titanic figures of power wrestled with each other, both ignoring the relatively insignificant magician hovering nearby.

Pug held his position a moment, gauging his next best course of action. He reached out mentally and examined the surroundings, his protective sphere destroying the few attacking flying Dread.

He still had difficulty realizing the Dread was a single entity, with all the embodiments of it in a variety of forms around him. He also had trouble mentally reconciling the notion that every manifestation of the Dread across space and time was happening "now" from the Dread's point of view, or why this manifestation, this "Dreadking," was the key to the struggle. Pug wasn't even sure after understanding that much that he knew what was happening to those parts of the Dread they defeated. Were they destroyed? Could any part of the Dread be destroyed? Or were they merely returned back to where they started, to work their way back to this plane and attack again?

For a brief instant Pug felt an overwhelming sense of hopelessness. How could his plan possibly work?

Magnus felt the net of magic stabilize, and knew everyone who would be providing Pug the magic needed to convolute the rift spell was now linked in. He used his own prodigious ability to quickly move from point to point along the lattice of magic, for a brief instant touching everyone to judge their endurance and ability to contribute. It took him only a minute, but when he finished he realized how much this was taxing everyone and how limited their opportunity was.

He took a moment to consider the fight before him, as the rate of attack from the dome seemed to be increasing dramatically. Mentally, he called out to Ruffio, *Any moment now, be ready.*

Before him, Arkan raised his bow and shot a smoky shape attempting to approach the black-clad magician.

Father, he sent to Pug, *we are ready. We have little time, mere minutes, I think.*

Pug heard Magnus and replied, *I'm going to begin. I will not have time to say anything until you hear me tell you to unleash all the energy at me. Then do what you can to get as many people as you can free of this area.*

He didn't wait for a reply but extended his senses to the boundaries of the rift spell and the place where it was transformed into the ruby energy that formed the dome. He wished for more time to further examine the lattice of energy and how it intersected the dome, but he knew time for study was passing and he had mere minutes in which to act.

Ashen-Shugar and the Dread were now fully engaged, with the Valheru striking furiously at the Void monster. Pug realized they seemed to recede, moving deeper into the pit. He wondered if the struggle was forcing the Dread downward, or if this was merely a trick of perception and perspective. He willed himself downward, following them.

A sudden burst of energy from below the combat took Pug by surprise and he felt himself lifted slightly upward. He saw that it was more of the floating wisps he had seen coming up from the pit. He focused on one of them and in a moment understood. He wasn't looking at anything, but rather through everything, into the Void itself. These wisps were really small tears in what Pug had thought of as reality until recently. The "smoke" or "wisps" were simply three-dimensional shreds of reality. Now he understood. The Void surrounded the Dread. The Void was the invisible glue that bound Mind and the Dread together. That was how the universe would end, the Void slipping through millions, billions, of tiny rifts like these to pull reality as Pug knew it back into that perfect, harmonious, blissful ball of everything.

Something called to Pug, something deeper in the pit. He watched as Ashen-Shugar and the Dread struggled, gripping each other like wrestlers in a clinch.

Pug felt a pull at him again, and quickly measured his

control of the energy Magnus was sending, then turned his attention to the source of what was pulling him. He hovered, relatively motionless, while it appeared the struggle continued to carry Ashen-Shugar and the Dread deeper into the pit.

Then a realization came to Pug: really, there could be no "deeper" to this pit, for it was an open doorway into the Void. While the shreds and wisps might be parts of the Void, and the smoky monsters part of the Dread, here was the clear threshold between the objective world and the Void. Once the threshold was crossed, one should either be in the Void or in this world.

Then Miranda's lesson as she had told it came to him: it was a matter of perception.

Pug tried to shift his perceptions, as he had at other times in dealing with beings living at different levels of energy, especially when he, Magnus, and Nakor had transitioned to the Dasati home world. Then he found the state he sought. His perceptions shifted.

Suddenly a complete change to the context around him struck Pug almost like a physical blow. There was no up nor down, no large or small, just energy flows, and the struggle was now a massive upheaval in competing states of being.

Lines of force both majestic and delicate, pulsing with energies in colors impossible for the human eye to comprehend, enveloped Pug. The beauty of them was heart-wrenching. Pug felt awe. His mind became a thing apart, able to reach out and touch fluctuating states of existence. He understood in part what Macros had sought to achieve when he was elevating his consciousness to that of a god.

Pug also understood the trap. The human intelligence, even one as prodigious as his own, wasn't equipped to deal with this level of apprehension and awareness. Like a moth to a flame, to linger too long in this state would result in being consumed by fire.

Pug forced himself back to his previous state and watched the struggle for a moment longer. He could now achieve awareness of these states, but he couldn't understand them, nor did he have the time to try.

Then it came to him: the Void existed without time. Time had left the Void with the creation of his reality, and what was left behind was able to perceive time because it was not caught up within time! Pug immediately shifted his perspective back to a different energy state and saw the tendrils not as empty spaces in his normal perception of reality, but as shreds of that which had been left behind, that longed to join with what had created the universe, to return it all to that fundamental blissful state.

Pug reached out and pulled himself deeper into the Void, and felt a sensation he had experienced for the first time when he had ventured into the Void to destroy the Tsurani rift into Midkemia. He used his tether to Magnus to communicate with him. *Can you still hear me?*

Yes, Father.

I think I have discovered something, Pug said. *I need you to measure the passing of time for me.*

My childhood counting trick?

Yes. Start now.

Pug found it almost impossible to negotiate the Void without falling into the habit of human perceptions demanding a frame of reference. He was "descending into" the Void and he understood abstractly that he wasn't moving at all and that time and space were both meaningless here. But he was trapped within his own human perceptions. He closed his eyes in acknowledgment of his physical limits, and discovered that it helped. His mind saw a play of images in oddly muted colors against black, like lingering afterimages, and they raced across his subjective field of vision. There was a feverlike quality to them and yet they were somehow familiar. The face of Princess Carline shifted into that of Katala, his first wife, then that of a student he had taught at the Academy a century before. Distorted landscapes and twisted images of places flowed around him: a street in the Holy City of Kentosani appeared upside down above his head, the white walls now black, the colors reversed, with red now green, blue now orange, and the people having the same distorted flowing shapes.

Suddenly he knew.

Magnus! How much time has passed?

None, Father. I just counted "one" and now you're back.

I understand, said Pug, and he entered time.

Nothing moved. Pug was fascinated by his new perception. Ashen-Shugar and the Dread were motionless, locked in a struggle, but frozen in the moment. Pug wondered if this was how the Dread saw time.

He was still limited by human perception, but as he exerted will, he found Ashen-Shugar moving in reverse, and he realized he was moving backward in time. He moved forward and returned to the second at which he became aware of his ability to move within time.

For a subjective moment he hesitated, wondering at the consequences of his actions. He studied the struggle around him and probed with his mind above, where his son and the others waited, and came away with an oddly dissatisfying realization: his ability to not move with time prevented him from interacting with any of those moving normally through time. Something about all of this seemed wrong, but he didn't know what it was. Then, Pug realized, he had all the time he would ever need to study the problem.

Beginning with the shreds of the Void fluttering around him, Pug began to examine . . . everything.

Magnus waited after his odd exchange with his father. The question about how much time had passed in the midst of a battle of colossal proportions was as strange as anything he could have imagined.

Magnus had prepared himself for his own death as well as for the death of his father, given the circumstances surrounding this conflict. Now he worried about others: Miranda,

Nakor, Calis, even the aloof Moredhel leader of the Snow Leopards. If he could contrive to get any or all of them away when his father had finished with whatever he was doing in the pit, Magnus would give his life finding a way. After all, he conceded, he was his father's son.

Pug found his consciousness expanding as he moved along the time lines, and found it an almost dizzying experience. He looked at Ashen-Shugar and the Dreadking locked in a frozen point in time and found he could negotiate around them, make them appear gigantic or tiny, move away and toward them from any angle. If he shifted his perception, he could see billions of strands of time and space moving away in every conceivable direction. He was able to follow them, too: he could see billions of branches of potential consequences to any action. It was an overwhelming sense of vision and power.

He felt euphoria rising up, despite the horrors of the war. Now he knew what it meant to have godlike powers, yet he understood that with that godhood came an absence of self. He also understood what Macros had sought to achieve on the banks of the lake many years ago. He realized the trap of power, knew he must not become indulgent in this examination of new knowledge, for to linger with the sense he had forever to learn, study, and contrive a better solution was also a trap. Somewhere he would realize he was lost in this new understanding, or worse, he would not care if he was lost.

He created a beacon of magic energy, freezing it in a state that anchored it in place, much as the Dread had created the Sven-ga'ri as markers, or the Taredhel had placed their portal flags, so that he could find his way back to this particular intersection of space and time and move along one strand of time. He saw Ashen-Shugar vanish above with himself at his side, and followed the Dread backward to the creation of the rift, the blinding explosion of energies that tore apart the barrier between the expanding universe of reality and that which was left behind: the Dread.

Suddenly Pug realized, *I can stop this before it starts!* Certainly he had enough power simply to destroy the Taredhel portal room before the Regent Lord betrayed his people.

That is forbidden, said a very familiar voice in Pug's mind.

The Oracle, said Pug.

Yes came the reply. *Now you understand the secret and the burden of my people. I have given you this perspective so that you can fully understand why what you are about to do is vital.*

But why not let me end this before it begins? I can prevent the deaths of thousands, tens of thousands!

Because as horrible as your current course is, it is the best of those available to you.

Suddenly Pug's mind filled with a kaleidoscope of images and feelings as countless possible time lines unfolded from each point at which he chose to take action. Each image, choice, and result flickered for the briefest instant, yet he understood fully what he saw. He was witness to horrific consequences, worlds going dark, suns being devoured, and in only one did he see his world emerging intact. The time line he was currently on, doing what he was fated to do.

But at a terrible price.

Why? he asked.

My race is the eldest in the universe, Pug. We were the first to achieve sentience when the first shreds of reality were formed. We witnessed the clashing forces of creation and destruction, what your lore calls the Two Blind Gods of the Beginning.

We saw the very structure of reality being woven for the first time as new beings of power arose, and we alone could see the earliest manifestations of time as it was unfolding from the core where all was born. We alone could take time and see down the pathways into a seemingly endless range of possible futures, and judge the most likely outcome.

It is why we are still here as the universe is moving into a new phase of existence, with the last vestiges of that creation, the Valheru, the elder gods, the First Born, the ancient races of a billion worlds are fading into the past.

You are here to do one thing, and lingering here and exploring, no matter how long you look, will not change the outcome, for when you finish your exploration, it will be precisely the same instant you left, and nothing will be changed. We have witnessed every conceivable choice, and there is only one outcome that doesn't reverse the expansion of reality, returning everything to as it once was, before creation.

Tomas had to die so that the full fury of Ashen-Shugar could be turned upon the Dreadking, a rage unhindered by human sensibilities.

Pug paused, his heart sinking, and he realized now the one piece of this he hadn't understood until now. Ashen-Shugar hadn't been needed as a distraction so Pug could come into the pit and explore the Void and its intersection with reality, freeing Pug of the Dreadking's attention; the Dragon Lord was the only entity on Midkemia powerful enough to become that one thing, that one moment of distraction, toward which all the Dreadking's attention would be turned, letting go of everything else across space and time, thereby robbing the Void of other opportunities to successfully achieve its goal. Ashen-Shugar and the Dreadking must remain locked in this moment for eternity.

Magnus! Pug sent to his son. *What is happening?*

Magnus saw the smoky tendrils and shadowy creatures pouring out of the fractured dome, and then suddenly they were motionless, frozen in place.

Father, the attacks have ceased!

Get as many away as you can, Pug sent.

The Oracle's voice came again to Pug. *You must now lock them into a struggle that will endure to the end of time. Only in that way can the mindless obsession of the Dread be for-*

ever focused into a single, fixed point in time, and then can the rest of creation grow.

I know, said Pug, and he realized with resignation that nothing had changed, except that more of those struggling above might survive.

When you are finished, I will awake in my cave beneath Sethanon, and from there I will see a new series of time lines, choices, and possibilities. But only if you finish this.

Pug was silent, then said, *I know.*

If it will comfort you, there is one thing you must understand above all, that one thing separates the realm in which you live, the moving and evolving world, and that which was left behind, from that which hungers for that perfect timeless bliss. You do what you do for love. You mortals make terrible mistakes for love, and you suffer for love, but you have love. The Dread only has longing, and longing drives frustration, and that drives anger, and in the end nothing is left but rage and hunger. Self-sacrifice is the highest form of love.

I understand, said Pug.

Magnus waited with the Moredhel warrior Arkan standing in front of him, his empty quiver and his bow lying on the ground as he stood with sword, ready to face the next wave of the Dread.

Now! came his father's voice in his mind, and Magnus took every bit of the energy in the matrix of magic and channeled it to his father.

For a long moment there was a pause, as if the universe held its breath.

Then chaos was unleashed.

The flood of magic Pug unleashed on the Dread and Ashen-Shugar was like a sledgehammer striking a nail, driving it through a board and out the other side. Both powerful beings were struck so hard they almost vanished as they were blown down into the pit, cast out of this universe, out into the Void.

The Dread was the Void. The Void was the Dread. It folded back in on itself, its sense of time and space contracted to the here and now as it faced a foe demanding its undivided attention.

Ashen-Shugar was suspended in time, in a bubble of reality, like a fly in amber, as he gripped the Dread.

The two of them spun down out of Pug's sight.

Then he felt the vortex.

The hole in the realms was sucking everything around him into the Void. Now came the end, for he had to plug that breach. Pug reached out with the power channeled to him and fed it directly into the Void, accelerating the collapse of all the matter surrounding it.

The world started to fall in on top of him.

Magnus felt the magic he was funneling ripped out of his hands, and started hearing screams of pain. The ruby dome imploded down into the ground, sucking every remaining Dread backward, as if they had been yanked with incredible speed by an invisible cord carrying them back whence they had emerged.

The sound was the sound of a thousand earthquakes, a rumbling so deep that it drowned out the thunder from the approaching storm clouds above. Rain came down in sheets and lightning flashed across the sky, and everywhere Magnus looked he saw magicians and priests fallen and writhing in pain, or lying still in death.

The dragons fled, launching themselves skyward on massive wings that cracked the air. The wind from their wings buffeted those still standing and knocked back even the most formidable Moredhel warrior or Taredhel Sentinel.

Magnus fell to the ground as it heaved under him like a thing alive. He rolled on his back and scrambled to get away from the terrible vortex storm that was building energy by the minute. He turned and saw that those who were able were fleeing up toward the higher meadow. Over his shoulder, he saw the Moredhel chieftain Arkan on the ground, unable to get his feet under him. Magnus reached out and Arkan found himself rising into the air, immune to the strong wind being created by the sucking energy of the vortex.

With a motion of his hand, Magnus moved the warrior to where Miranda stood, next to Liallan and a knot of her warriors. Nearby stood Calin and Calis, along with two stunned but still standing spellweavers. With a single wave of his hand, Magnus indicated it was time for her to take them to safety, and in a blink Miranda and more than a dozen Moredhel, Eledhel, and Taredhel were gone.

Magnus saw that Nakor and Ruffio were also missing, so he assumed they had followed instructions and were ferrying people away. He felt the energy field around him growing in intensity and he reached out mentally to see if he could contact his father, and encountered a strange emptiness, not as if his father was gone, but rather as if he was somewhere close but Magnus couldn't reach him.

Magnus realized that in all the planning his father had done for this moment, he hadn't anticipated how the lattice of magic would be severed, and how much damage this spell might cause. They had planned on utilizing the energy Magnus no longer controlled to plug the vortex, pulling down mountains if needed, but neither magician had anticipated the surge of magic and their inability to contain it once the Dread had been forced back into the Void. There had been a backlash neither Magnus nor his father had anticipated and its effects were devastating. Magicians and priests, spellweavers and shamans lay on the ground, their grotesque contortions and vacant eyes clearly marking them as dead. Magnus and Pug had known some magicians might be lost in this, but nothing on this scale. A terrible price had been paid by hundreds, if not thousands, around the world.

But it had been enough. The dome was now gone, and from

where Magnus stood he could see trees bending toward the pit in the ground, and knew that in only a few more minutes everything in this area would be sucked into the maw of the pit. The screaming of the wind in his ears deafened him to any other sound, but the vibration beneath his feet made him understand that the very soil and rock under his feet were being pulled toward the pit.

He used his magic to rise up, above the ground, and suddenly had to struggle against the pull from the vortex. Gauging his position and how much power it took to hold his place, he knew he was looking at mere minutes before he, too, would vanish into the maw of darkness opening up in the heart of the Grey Tower Mountains. Once more he reached out for Pug, and once more found an emptiness where his father should be. He felt a dark stab of uncertainty, for whatever he could do had been done. Now it only remained to see if their plan worked and if this sucking pit before him could be plugged and sealed.

Pug battled forces he had almost no experience with: walls of magic energy that swept over him, lines of enchantment that would warp reality if they were unleashed into the world, huge waves of rolling intersections between energy and matter, time unwinding and soaring spirals of thought. The crashing forces at play around him were overwhelming to the point that he could barely retain his own sense of identity, let alone remember his purpose.

From his perspective, Pug was witnessing the consumption of his world by the Void, an intaking of every shred of matter around the now-destroyed city of E'bar, from the mightiest tower or lofty tree to the tiniest strand of a spider's silk or a dust mote. With increasing volume and accelerating speed, rock, water, soil, plants, and animals were being pulled into the maw of the pit. He shifted his focus and moved along the time stream, back to his mystic marker, so he could return to being in sync with what was occurring on the surface. Fear rose in him as he realized he had grievously miscalculated how he was going to manipulate the power lent him by so many others. If he let things continue as they were going, far more damage would be done to this world than had already been inflicted. Pug assumed the alpine valley where E'bar had rested, the site of the original Tsurani rift, was now a gaping hole torn deep into the crust of the world, deepening by the minute as the spinning vortex he had created ripped apart the essential forces binding rock together, shredding granite into fine sand and powder in an instant, liquefying anything less stout, and even ripping apart the very air, causing sheets of flame and sprays of water to erupt as gases were torn asunder and recombined in seconds.

The deafening sound that filled the air, drowning out thought at times, was the dying cry of a world.

Magnus!

Here, Father! I thought I'd lost you.

Where are you?

North of the pit, on that large outcropping of rock. It's taken all my power to hold here. I can't endure this much longer.

Pug sensed the pain his son was experiencing. *You can do no more. It is time for you to cut any remaining tether between me and the world, then flee.*

I don't know if I can, Magnus replied.

You must.

Pug made one last calculation and knew he had to act before he lost any hope of sealing the tear between here and the Void.

Now!

Magnus closed his eyes, extended his consciousness for a moment, and saw that the energy that had been torn from his control had mostly been torn asunder, but a tiny tether of energy remained between what was left of the worldwide lattice of magic and Pug. *I understand, Father,* he said at last, and he severed what was left of Pug's connection with the world.

The entirety of the world shuddered.

Then, for a moment, everything was still.

Suddenly the totality of magic in Midkemia that had been confined and used by Pug recoiled, energies exploding out of the pit, and a massive bolt shot through Magnus as he attempted to disentangle himself from it, so that he was shaken like a rat by a terrier, his screams of agony filling the air, and deep below in the pit, Pug felt his son die.

Darkness crashed down on Pug.

Lightning shot down like a barrage of arrows as the clouds unleashed so much energy at the ground that the forests of the Grey Towers were set ablaze. Flaming trees moved toward the pit, cascading sheets of fire and embers ripped from their branches, all now sucked downward like a waterfall of fury around the entire rim of the pit, as a massive bubble of angry red magic shot upward from the center of the pit, shooting upward through the clouds as fast as the swiftest arrow until miles above the surface of Midkemia it reached its limit and lost momentum.

The last survivors not evacuated by Miranda, Nakor, Ruffio, and the others stared at the brilliant ruby pillar amid the chaos of this massive storm. Then the red magic slammed back into the surface and the world heaved and buckled inward.

Where the Grey Tower Mountains had risen since before the coming of man to Midkemia, a crumbling crater rim miles across now marked the limits of Pug's magic. An inconceivable inversion had forced geology to turn back upon itself and now a mile-deep caldera remained. At the bottom, millions of tons of rocks and detritus lay beneath a mile-deep cloud of dust.

Rivers now ran into what would come to be known as the Sunken Lands, and the planet seemed to groan as it began its transformation.

Then a wave of energy rose up from the mass of debris on

the crater floor and magic began to skip and shimmer along the surfaces of the rock. A second backlash of the magic Pug had harnessed now ran free. It gathered itself as if contracting, then shot up into the sky like a shimmering blue fountain. Energy spat upward as if from a volcano and raced around the world, landing at random.

The forest of the Green Reaches, marking the boundary between the Kingdom and Great Kesh, was awash in the blue light: trees began to twist and grow; once-small vines grew massive and thorny. As if becoming sentient, the forest pushed out from the center, and those who had gone to bed in Keshian Jonril the night before, surrounded by open farmland, would arise the next day to see trees towering twenty or thirty feet higher than before. Where pleasant woodlands had once stood, now an impenetrable forest choked every square mile between the mountain ranges known as the Peaks of Tranquillity and the Pillars of the Stars, reaching all the way to the shore of the Great Star Lake. Every caravan route and game trail, farmers' road and imperial highway was overgrown and vanished in one night.

To the west of the Far Coast a ripple of energy sped through the water and the Sunset Islands began to sink. At first few noticed, but within an hour ships at the docks were riding high and those in the bay off of Freeport were pulling up anchor. Within two hours, people were fleeing for whatever ship would take them, and by dawn the next day, only open ocean could be seen.

To the south of E'bar, in the mines of the Grey Towers, ancient passages that had once housed the chambers of the Lord of the Eagle's Reaches, the last of his kind, crumbled into dust and vanished into the crater. Dwarves who had heeded Pug's warning felt the earth cry out, and fled, many surviving eventually to reach kin in Dorgin or Stone Mountain. Many did not.

The last King of the Dwarves, Dolgan, died that day, and the legendary Hammer of Tholin was lost beneath the rock and soil.

As far to the south as the Isle of the Snake Men, and as far north as the Thunderhell Steppes, unnatural magic scarred the land. A herd of elk was suddenly turned to stone, and a field of poppies bloomed on the ice floes for a few moments before withering from the cold.

A caravan crossing the Jal-Pur from Ipithi to Durbin was struck by a massive wave of seawater that overturned wagons and nearly drowned camels and men before suddenly vanishing, leaving everyone soaked and disoriented, shaken but alive.

In Timons, an elderly man sat up and sang in a language no mortal had heard, bringing tears to the eyes of those who heard him, then he lay back and died peacefully.

In the Free City of Walinor, a massive wall of granite three hundred feet high thrust up from the earth and the town sank two feet, destroying foundations, felling walls, killing dozens of citizens. When the dust had settled, travel west became impossible, and from that day forward the sun would set in midafternoon as it dropped behind the western rim of the vast crater.

Around the globe the magic raced, arcing high into the air to turn clouds golden and pink for a moment, then diving into the ground to cause a spring to form or a marsh to dry up.

A ship in the Sea of Kingdoms saw a creature the size of a mountain rise up out of the water like a whale breaching, a thing of copper scales and golden fins, but instead of falling back into the water, it kept rising until it vanished into the clouds above.

On the other side of the world, the northern half of the escarpment of the continent of Wyñet rose an additional two hundred feet. The Saaur warriors and their families felt the upheaval and wondered what new threat had followed them to this world.

Where a mighty range of mountains had once stood, now only hills rose up from the Far Coast to the Free Cities, and those hills surrounded what would ever after be known as the Sunken Lands, a crater of immense size and depth that prevented travel between the two coasts.

At the heart of the rubble, as water sought out new levels, dust settled and strange and alien life fashioned by wild magic began to take root.

Beneath it all came a sound not unlike a sigh. And then there was silence.

30

AFTERMATH

Pug awoke.

At least that was how it felt as he became aware of having a body and an identity. He knew his name, and his history, and if he had held any doubt, he had a headache massive enough to remind him of the consequences of his first foray into Duke Borric's ale shed.

But he was surrounded by utter stillness and complete and utter darkness. He took a deep breath and was rewarded by the sensation of air entering his lungs, so he did not think he was trapped in the Void. Besides, the Void was a featureless gray, not this utter black.

Then he saw a pinpoint of light ahead and attempted to will himself toward it. Nothing happened. He tried a different approach and attempted to use the light as a reference and move toward it. Again, nothing happened. He held up his right hand before his face, blocking out the light for an instant, then tried to create light of his own.

Nothing happened.

Then he noticed the light seemed to be growing brighter. After a few minutes, he could see it was also growing larger, and he decided to wait. Not that he had any other option, he conceded ruefully.

He had questions, countless questions, but first and foremost, even more than where he now found himself, was how had he survived? He had pulled half the world of Midkemia down on himself, or at least that was how it had felt. The image that stayed with him was of the Valheru and Dread locked in time, struggling in an instant that would never change as a mountain fell on him, crushing him . . .

Pug felt remarkably fit for someone who had just been crushed under a mountain.

As the light grew larger, he realized it was approaching, and soon he heard the sound of footfalls: a hollow sound, leather slapping on a stone floor. Then he saw that in addition to coming closer, the light was swaying slightly, and he could see the shape of a man, or a manlike being.

A stocky man in a robe, holding a staff shaped roughly like a shepherd's crook from which hung a lantern, walked toward Pug at a steady pace, apparently in no hurry. As he neared, his features began to resolve themselves, but Pug failed to recognize him. He was stocky, rotund even, with an almost cherubic face. His hair was cut in a tonsure fringe and he wore a brown robe with a triple-wrapped brown leather belt. His feet were clad in cross-gartered sandals and his face bore a faint smile.

"There you are," he said. "Didn't quite end up where you should."

Pug was still unable to move and now he found he was

unable to speak. He was immobilized and none of his magic worked. All he could do was to watch and listen.

The monk motioned with his hand. "Come along," he said, then turned his back and started walking whence he came.

Pug floated along after him, though floating didn't really convey how he felt. It was more simply a case that he just was where he was, how he was, and apart from the monk, whom he could barely make out over the toes of his feet as he looked down the length of his body, there was nothing else to see.

Then, abruptly, the darkness vanished and Pug found himself floating above a white-tiled floor. The monk waved and Pug felt himself released from whatever paralysis had gripped him, and he started to fall. Reflexively, he tried to use a bit of magic to slow his fall; he couldn't, and landed on his backside.

"Sorry about that," said the monk.

Pug examined his surroundings as he stood. The whole large room was white and it contained a white table and two chairs of white wood bearing white satin cushions, a white sideboard, and a white canopied bed.

"You catch me in a white mood," said the monk, sitting in one of the two chairs. He indicated that Pug should sit. "This happens once in a while. I grow weary of colors and choices." He waved his hand and suddenly the floor was cerise and the walls a deep burgundy. The wood of the furniture was black lacquered and the canopy over the bed was rusty brown and there were suddenly golden fixtures on the walls, burning with light. "You see?" said the monk. "It's nice, but one grows bored quickly, and then there's the endless permutations and matches." He waved his hand and the black wood was now blond with a high gloss, the canopy and covers black, while the floor and walls were of a nicely contrasting honey-colored wood. At last he gave a wave of the hand and again everything turned white.

"Who are you?" asked Pug. "And where are we?"

"Where is something of a matter of conjecture. I have

wrestled with that concept for many years, and so far I have not achieved a reasonable answer. Just more conjecture and speculation." He sighed. "I think of this as my waiting room."

"Waiting room?" said Pug, as if the very concept of a room in which you wait was odd.

"Antechamber?"

"Ah," said Pug. "I have waited in antechambers before. I think I see." He studied the monk. "I assume you know who I am, as you came and got me."

"Yes," said the monk. "Pug, the magician. Known as Milamber on Kelewan before you blew up the planet." He shook his finger at Pug. "Forgive my presumption, but I thought that was a rather ham-fisted way to deal with the Dread incursion from the third realm."

Pug said evenly, "Best I could manage at short notice?"

"I suppose so," said the monk.

"Where was I a moment ago? When you came to fetch me?"

"I don't rightly know what to call it. It's not the Void, certainly, as that has distinct properties even if they are deuced hard to apprehend. I call where you were the Nether, as I think it's even below the Void. Or it might be the Neither, as its neither here nor there!" He seemed amused by that. "Forgive me. I have waited a very long time to use that jest."

"If we're waiting," said Pug, "what is it we are waiting for?"

"Ah, me, where are my manners?" said the monk. "I am waiting to be reborn, or rather I am in the process of being reborn, though it is very slow as such things go. I am Ishap."

Pug was speechless. Finally he said, "The Balancer?"

"The very one," said the monk, standing and taking a bow.

"I thought you . . . Controllers weren't personified."

"Well, that's usually the case, and sometime, when I finish returning, I'll have too much on my hands to bother interacting with mortals, or even the lesser gods on the majority of occasions for that matter. But at the moment I'm waiting."

"And what am I doing here?"

"That is a very good question," said Ishap. "And at the moment I have no really clear notion what you're doing in my waiting room."

"Midkemia is a strange world, in many ways," said Ishap.

"So I have discovered," agreed Pug.

They had been sitting for a while at the table, silently, each caught up in his own thoughts. Pug considered it very strange that he felt no significant emotions about what he had endured before arriving here. He had felt his son die, and seen his best friend die before that, had witnessed horrors and pain beyond imagining, yet he felt calm and without concern as he waited. Even his sense that this was strangely inappropriate as a response was distant and muted. He was content to sit in silence staring at the white walls, or to respond to Ishap's occasional remark, but he wasn't even sure if he would use the word "content" in this circumstance. Simply put, he was aware and unconcerned. Along with his other emotions, curiosity was blunted as well. Yet there was a certain desire for a logical conclusion.

"Would you care for something to eat?" asked Ishap. "We don't need to eat, but occasionally it serves to blunt the boredom."

"You get bored?"

The monk shrugged. "In a manner of speaking. I exist as you see me now because I am scarcely alive in terms of how gods are supposed to live. I'm little more than a mortal at this stage. On the other hand, I won't be needed until Arch-Indar is reborn. I can't balance until all the forces are in existence. There is only so much time that even a god can dedicate to reconstituting his being and gathering together his essence to become alive again. Occasionally, a break in the routine is welcome. I think some grapes."

A platter of grapes appeared and he plucked one, popped it into his mouth, and motioned that Pug should help himself. "Another advantage, the food is always perfect. These are delicious."

Pug declined. "I find it odd that I have little interest in any of this, which is hardly my nature. And perhaps even more unusual is that I merely find it odd and not profoundly disturbing."

"I suspect it's because you are now dead. The dead have little ambition."

"I'm dead?" Pug looked at the back of his right hand, then put it up to his face and touched his own cheek. "I don't feel dead."

"How would you know? Have you been dead before?"

"I believe so," said Pug. "I—"

Ishap waved his hand dismissively. "That business with the demon and your curse. Yes, I know about that, but you weren't dead. You merely hovered at the brink."

"If I'm now dead, then why am I not before Lims-Kragma?"

"I do not know," said Ishap. "Perhaps we should ask her."

He waved his hand and they were no longer in the little waiting room, but standing in a familiar setting, the Pavilion of the Gods. Pug looked around and said, "I don't understand."

Ishap actually grinned. "I do get lost in my rebirth at times, and your appearance is a wonderful excuse to break up the monotony; I don't know why I didn't think of this sooner. I was happy to find you once I became aware you were floating out there in the Nether. I thought a bit of a visit and a little conversation would be welcome, but this is far more entertaining." He glanced around, then shouted, "Lims-Kragma, if you would be so kind!"

Lims-Kragma appeared in all her majesty: black veils, a clinging gown with silver netting sewn into the hem and sleeves. "You've been granted a moment."

"A moment?" asked Pug. For the first time since his arrival, he felt a stir of feeling: irritation.

The other gods appeared and Kalkin said, "We felt you deserved to know you closed the rift. There was a great deal of destruction and much loss of life, but the world, and the larger universe, is safe for the time being."

"Time being?" muttered Pug.

Ishap smiled cheerily. "It's a matter of scale. The time being is several million years, so we can all catch our breath, in a manner of speaking."

Pug felt as if something profoundly important was missing within him. "I don't think I care, really. Should I?"

"The dead do not care," said the Goddess of Death.

"Then why am I here?" asked Pug. "Why are we not in your hall? Why am I not being judged and returned to the Wheel of Life or sent on to my reward?"

Kalkin, who now looked like Jimmy the Hand once more, smiled. "Well, there is this one thing, Pug. You're not entirely dead."

"I'm alive?"

"No, not that either," said Kalkin.

The ancient figure of Arch-Indar appeared and in a scolding tone said, "Tell him the truth, Trickster!"

"She's rapidly becoming a conscience," said Kalkin with a scowl. "When you manipulated the time stream—and by the way that was truly impressive—you contrived two unexpected things. First, you drove almost all the Dread back into the Void."

"Almost?"

"There's this . . . bit of the Dread that got trapped in the bottom of that crater you created. It's dormant, unaware, and buried under hundreds of feet of rock. Compared to the totality of what you faced, it was just a tiny bit. By the standards of what you've previously faced, you have a sleeping Dreadlord at the bottom of a vast crater."

"But it could awake?"

"It could," said Kalkin. He shrugged. "But that's not your concern."

Pug felt a stir of interest. "But it should be," he countered.

"There will be others who will concern themselves with that, in the future," said a proud-looking blond-haired goddess, who looked a great deal like Sandreena in her armor. "Protecting the weak is my province and I will ensure there are others."

"Who?" asked Pug. "There are few with any power and none still with power and experience left to protect this world."

"We are well aware of that," said Lims-Kragma.

"You said there were two unexpected things. What's the second?"

"You froze that Dread in time, which is why it's dormant, and until that time thread resolves itself, it will stay that way. And when you froze that thread of time, you froze yourself into it as well." He indicated Pug's left hand, which the magician raised to study. He realized it had been clenched since his awakening and within it something tiny but marvelous stirred. Pug felt a hint of satisfaction.

"And only the dragons can manipulate time," he said softly.

"So . . ." Kalkin shrugged.

"As long as I'm here, not quite dead, you have no power over me," said Pug to Lims-Kragma.

"No," she said. "You are neither in the realm of the living nor of the dead." She moved to stand before Pug and again he marveled at her cold beauty. "But before you count that as the means to cheat me, realize this: you are trapped between the realm of the living and the dead, and you must make a choice."

"To live or to die?" said Pug. "It would seem an easy choice."

"No," said Kalkin, "for you are not alive either. You can abide here, share a room with the other waiting gods, or drift as a spirit and observe the living, but you may not rejoin the living without our help."

"Are you offering that help?"

A god Pug recognized as Astalon the Just said, "If you wish it. We have considered your sacrifice and voted, six for life, six for death. So, the decision we have ruled must be yours. That is only just. If you choose death, this existence ends and you move on. You have earned much, Pug, and despite the feeling among some here that you've affronted their dignity in the past"—he glanced at Lims-Kragma—"your reward in your next life will be profound."

"I urge you to consider this," said Kalkin. "The Dread slumbers in the pit below the Sunken Lands as that crater will come to be known, and if it awakes, only you among mortals can face it. Choose life." He smiled as Jimmy had done years ago and said, "Besides, things are so much more interesting when you're around."

Pug considered, then said, "No."

"No?" asked Lims-Kragma. "Shall I take you to my hall now?"

"No," said Pug. "I will strike a bargain."

"What bargain?" asked Sung the Pure.

Looking around at the twelve lesser gods, Pug said, "There is another, one who is far more now than I was at his age and will be so much more than I am now when he reaches this age. Magnus must be saved to guard this world. He will rebuild the Academy and the Conclave, and in the end you'll have a more powerful guardian than I could ever be."

"You'd give up your life for your son's?" asked Lims-Kragma.

"Every time, without question," said Pug. "Have we a bargain?"

The twelve gods exchanged glances, and the shadow memory of Arch-Indar shimmered as if somehow becoming more vivid a memory than she had been a moment before. "He has earned it!"

A mature woman dressed in simple clothing, a faint scent of wheat accompanying her, stepped forward and looked at Pug, and she said, "Yes. So says Silban the Mother," and she vanished.

A young blond woman in white, her large blue eyes hinting at playful possibilities, nodded and said, "I, Ruthia, say yes, and luck will follow your son, Pug, at least for a while." She vanished.

A man with red-rimmed eyes, his gray clothing resembling nothing so much as one of the dreaded Nighthawks, stepped forward and said, "I, Ka-hooli, say yes," and the Howler After Fugitives vanished.

Astalon stepped forward. "I, the Just, say yes." He vanished.

Killian, clad in a gown of green leaves with a wreath of flowers in her earth-dark hair, said, "I say yes," and she was gone.

A slender woman also wearing white, but with none of the playful aspects of Ruthia, stepped forward next, her bearing aloof. "I, La-Timsa, say yes." Then she disappeared.

A warrior with massive shoulders, wearing red armor with a giant sword strapped to his back, came before Pug and put his hand on his shoulder. "War in and of itself is pointless; without serving a higher purpose, it is the most terrible thing; all true warriors know this. You have served me as well as any mortal living, but always for a higher good, and you mourn the loss of innocents and carry that burden. You are a good man. Tith-Onanka says yes." Then the God of War was gone.

The goddess who looked like Sandreena came before him and Pug felt a stirring of amusement. "Dala," he said.

She nodded and returned Sandreena's smile. "Of those not in my service, I treasure you most of all, protector of this world. I say yes," and she was gone.

A god in silver, slender and furtive-looking, said, "Guis-wa says yes," and he vanished.

The next god stepped forward and said, "Prandur says yes!" and vanished in a column of flame.

"He always loves his theatrics," said Kalkin. He turned and looked at Ishap and Arch-Indar and said, "You are no longer needed," and the two Controller gods vanished.

Kalkin, also known as Ban-ath, smiled. "Of all the mortals I have known, Pug, you are among my favorites. I will honor your request and say yes." Then he was gone.

Pug looked at Lims-Kragma and said, "You are the last, Goddess of Death."

She nodded. "It is not my nature to make bargains with humans, as my province is inexorable. All I need to do is wait. You, however, have created a unique situation, and I will confess I find rule-breaking irksome." She glanced to where Kalkin had stood a moment before. "But Arch-Indar is right; you have earned consideration. Moreover, you are right: your son will be a more powerful protector. He compelled me to his will before he truly understood what he was doing, a feat no other mortal, even you, has achieved. I count your choice the wisest choice. Death you shall have and Magnus will have life."

"What do I do?" asked Pug.

"You must let go of that tendril of time."

Pug looked down and realized that the thing he clenched in his left hand, the marvelous little energy that was confined in his fist, was time itself. "Really? That's all?"

"Yes," she replied.

Pug opened his hand and let go of the shred of time.

Suddenly he was again in the collapsing pit, with the screaming planet around him, crying out as if the very matter of its existence was being ripped away and sucked down the hole into the Void.

Pug realized this was the instant before his death. He reached out to where Magnus was seconds away from dying, and with every remaining shred of strength he had, he placed a protective sphere around his son and cast him as far away as he could.

Then came death.

Lims-Kragma turned and the Pavilion of the Gods was again occupied by the others. She looked around and said, "He won't be getting off as easily as he thinks."

The memory of Arch-Indar said, "He deserves much. He's sacrificed more than any other. He deserves to be happy."

The tiniest of smiles played on the lips of the Goddess of Death and she said, "That can be arranged."

Magnus had no idea what happened. He had felt the energy he had harnessed for his father yanked away from him, had tried his best to get everyone out, then felt the wave of energy that was about to obliterate him. One moment death was certain to claim him, then suddenly the next moment he was in a protective sphere of magic hurled across the sky like a rock thrown by a giant.

He arced through the storm clouds and could barely keep his senses about him as he tumbled and spun, and when he struck the surface, miles away, he was stunned to insensibility.

He lay motionless on the ground, trying to force himself to focus, but the huge tasks he had undertaken, the shock of the magic lattice ending, all overwhelmed him and he lost consciousness.

Hours later he stirred. He took a deep breath and the air tasted heavy with moisture, as if a storm had just passed. It took him a minute to gather his wits and he sat up, realizing he was covered in mud and his robe was soaked through to his skin.

He saw the sun was above the horizon to the east and realized he had slept through the balance of the night. It was a new day and he was alive.

Looking around for landmarks, he judged himself somewhere between the destruction of the valley containing E'bar and the northern boundary of the Kingdom, near the foothills of Stone Mountain.

He took a deep breath, and willed himself back to the peaks above the valley.

Materializing in midair, he caught himself before he plunged into the maelstrom below. The crater was vast, having consumed what had been a range of mountains more than a hundred miles across at its widest point, obliterating everything from the King's Road to Yabon down to the land of the dwarves.

Magnus stared down into roiling clouds of dust and

smoke, with flashes of lightning playing underneath, illuminating the dust from within. He could feel rampant magic, the lingering aftereffects of the unprecedented magic his father had used to destroy the Dread's incursion into this world. He willed himself lower.

Hovering above the dust and ash, Magnus sent his senses down and two things immediately were made known: first, there was a malevolent presence, a massive aspect of the Dread still there, miles below, but it was dormant and unmoving; second, magic was running amok, and already the changes being made were manifesting themselves. One day Magnus would return to investigate this new place, for he knew without a doubt that what he would find in that crater would be unique in Midkemia. Everything would be changed, from the very rocks and soil to all life, from the tiniest insect to the largest creatures.

He rose up and took another deep breath. There would be time.

He willed himself to move, and was suddenly in his father's study. He closed his eyes and sent out a mental question that was answered by a profound silence. Feeling an intense sadness, Magnus realized with certainty that this would now be *his* study.

A very fatigued Ruffio appeared a moment later. "I sensed you . . . I'm delighted to see you, Magnus."

They embraced like long-lost brothers, each relieved to see the other alive. "When you didn't appear yesterday, I feared the worst," said Ruffio.

"Yesterday?" said Magnus.

"The rift was closed two days ago, Magnus."

"I must have been unconscious for a full day more than I thought." He led Ruffio outside and stepped into the midday sun. He took a deep breath of fresh ocean air and said, "It is good to be alive."

"Indeed," said Ruffio.

"Tell me, how many . . . ?" He let the question go unfinished.

Ruffio didn't need to ask what he meant. "Most of our students here died, as they were the best and most committed. And many from Stardock died as well. I have only preliminary information, but the temples were hit hard as well. Many clerics died."

Magnus studied his friend's face. "What else?"

"Perhaps worse, a like number of those in the magic lattice we formed were driven mad. Some ramble or babble incoherently, others cower like children before unseen horrors, or rage like animals, or sit and stare out of vacant eyes. We are attempting to treat those as best we can." He looked as if he were fighting back tears. "We are less than one in three of what we were."

Magnus was shaken. They had known there would be risk, and had steeled themselves for losing the battle—and the world—but this he had not anticipated.

Ruffio said, "I thank the gods you're here. We will need your guidance and skills more than ever." He took a breath, then asked, "Your father?"

Magnus couldn't bring himself to speak. He merely shook his head.

Amirantha came into view and his face betrayed his delight at seeing Magnus. They exchanged greetings and Ruffio said, "Amirantha has proved to be a fine caretaker for this island while we were busy."

"It's not hard to manage an island with hardly anyone on it," quipped the warlock. "It's not as if you left that many here to care for."

"Still," said Ruffio, "I could really use your help in the years to come."

"Years?" said Amirantha, his bearded face turning to a scowl. "I've lingered here already longer than I intended."

"Where else have you to go?" asked Magnus bluntly.

"I thought once this was over I'd venture back to Novindus and check up on Brandos and his family."

"After that?" asked Ruffio. "We could use your experience."

"You have a home here if you wish," said Magnus.

"I'll consider it."

"Sandreena?" asked Magnus.

"She's inside," said Amirantha. "She's organizing the care for the . . . damaged."

Magnus was pleased to hear that, for he was asking if she had survived.

"She'll be here for a while," said Amirantha, "but eventually she'll want to get back to riding around protecting the weak. It's her calling."

"And you?" asked Magnus.

With a sigh of resignation, Amirantha, Warlock of the Satumbria, said, "Oh, I'll probably come back after I visit Brandos."

Magnus smiled. "Good."

"What of Miranda and Nakor?" asked Ruffio.

Magnus closed his eyes for a moment, then smiled. "They're both alive." He took in a deep breath, hiding his relief. "I'll return shortly."

Suddenly he was gone.

Ruffio and Amirantha nodded and turned their attention back to the work ahead. Both knew it would be years, decades even, before the Conclave and Stardock returned to what they had been before the last few days.

The inn was in a shambles. Miranda and Nakor were sitting in a corner when Magnus appeared. Without hesitation, Miranda leaped out of her chair and threw her arms around his neck.

He returned the embrace, content to let future dealings with her work themselves out and simply to enjoy the moment of shared intimacy with what was there of his mother.

"I was so worried," she whispered.

"I'm alive, though by what agency I have no idea."

Nakor grinned. "No doubt your father had a hand in it. It

was the sort of thing he always seemed to manage, no matter what the odds."

"I may never know," said Magnus. Looking around the room, he said, "What happened here?"

"A lot of very tired, wounded, sick, and otherwise impatient Moredhel warriors, with a sprinkling of those from Elvandar and E'bar tossed in, as well as a few of our boys and girls from the island," said Nakor.

Magnus weighed his knowledge of those involved, then looked at Nakor and said, "You offered to buy everyone a drink?"

Miranda could barely contain her amusement. "For a start."

"Are we at war with Liallan and the nations of the north now?"

"No, but we did have a few tense moments during the first night and into yesterday morning as everyone was leaving for their various destinations," said Miranda.

"The city watch, what's left of it, felt giving a few hundred dark elves a wide berth was their best choice," added Nakor.

"Calis and Calin?"

"They left immediately with the surviving spellweavers," said Miranda.

Magnus nodded. "Their mother will be relieved to see them." He said nothing about Tomas, for he was certain the majestic warrior had not survived. He wasn't even sure Tomas had been alive by the time the confrontation with the Dread began.

"What of you two?" said Magnus. "Are you returning to Sorcerer's Isle?"

Miranda's expression turned sad. "That's what we were discussing when you arrived. Please, sit down." She motioned him to the table. "No, we are not returning to Sorcerer's Isle."

"What are you going to do?" Magnus felt a mixture of regret and relief at her answer, for as much as he struggled with her true identity, the part of her that was his mother had been a comfort to have nearby.

"We must return to the Fifth Circle," said Nakor. "It will be in shambles, a far worse state than we left it in, but with the Dread vanquished, perhaps we can reverse the damage."

"We are unique in so many ways that we should have no trouble organizing things down there," said Miranda.

"Of that, I have no doubt," agreed Magnus.

"Dahun was something of a savant, in his own way," said Nakor. "He sought to ensure order that he knew was beneficial, to mimic what had existed in the innermost circle of the Fifth Realm."

"But he lacked perspective," said Miranda, with a wry smile. "He knew families and caring for one's young, and passing along knowledge, were good things; he just didn't know why they were good things." Her eyes held affection for the man who was never truly her son. "It's a matter of perspective."

"And you bring that perspective," said Magnus.

"Love," said Miranda. "No demon understands the . . . reality of love. It is something we must learn."

"It is a very worthy thing to do," said Magnus, not entirely certain how introducing such a concept into the fifth realm would change it. "I'm happy you have found a purpose beyond what we've already accomplished."

"Yes," said Miranda, taking his hand in her own and giving it one last squeeze. "I was unsure if you'd survived, and was waiting for some perfect moment to find out, and if you were on the island, to say good-bye there, but now that you're here . . ."

"There's no need to tarry," finished Nakor.

Magnus stood up. "I hardly know what to say. We could not have survived this without your knowledge and wisdom, and if there is anything I can do in the future to aid your . . . ambitions, I will willingly do it."

Miranda looked at the man who was not her son, but felt

as if he was, and tears gathered. "I think we shall never see one another again."

He let her hug him and then suddenly he was alone. The twist of magic he felt as other men feel a gust of wind told him they were now as far from Midkemia as one could possibly be. He looked around the inn one more time, then willed himself back to Sorcerer's Isle.

Alone for a moment beside his family's quarters, he looked as the afternoon sun sent sparkles shimmering across a sea driven to a light chop by a freshening breeze. Taking in a deep breath and luxuriating in this simple pleasure, Magnus knew it would take a long time to recover from the losses he had endured—his entire community had endured—yet he also felt good.

It was so good to be alive.

31

RENAISSANCE

Bells rang.

Rillanon was festive, for the threat of war was now behind it and the armies that had camped for months outside the city were gone. From the back of his horse, Hal resisted the urge to feel any joy over their victory. He still had a duchy that was controlled by foreigners and had watched too many good men die recently. He was in no mood for the politics of the Congress of Lords, which he was required to attend as a noble of the Kingdom of the Isles and as a potential claimant to the throne by dint of blood ties. He nodded in acknowledgment of the crowd's cheers, but his mind was miles away.

Jim Dasher had assured him that this particular ratification of the new King would be relatively short since the issue had already been decided and whatever politicking might occur in the Congress would merely amount to jockeying for the King's favor, rather than trading support for favors, which was a vastly different enterprise, according to Jim.

Hal glanced to his left and saw his brothers smiling and waving at the crowd lining the street from the docks to the palace. They rode behind the palanquin that carried Prince Edward. At last they would have a coronation ceremony, with Edward named King, and then try to return the Kingdom to some degree of normalcy.

As they entered the main gate of the palace, Hal wondered how that would be possible. Reports from the West indicated some monstrous upheaval, perhaps a volcanic eruption in the Grey Towers area. Details were still sketchy, but the destruction appeared enormous. Even without that additional disaster, he still had to deal with the matter of thousands of Keshian settlers in northern Crydee and parts of Yabon. He knew that he would have to leverage his newfound alliances with Yabon's Duke, and especially with LaMut's Earl, to regain any significant part of Crydee. And at this time another war was the last thing he wished to contemplate.

At least the civil war was over, Hal conceded with some relief as a lackey came to take his horse. Oliver was in chains, in a wagon that would soon roll into this courtyard, whence he would be escorted to a small but well-appointed apartment where he would reside under guard until his family bankrupted Maladon and Simrick to raise the ransom for his return. That ridiculous amount of wealth would help restore the damage done to the Kingdom, as well as ensure that Maladon and Simrick would have years of debt to repay before they considered financing another war.

Chadwick of Ran was being treated with a bit less deference, and there was one school of thought among Edward's advisers that considered a short trial and a long rope or the headsman's ax a fitting end to the question, while others took the position that Chadwick was only supporting the man he thought had the best claim to the Crown.

Hal was glad he didn't have to deal with those decisions. Edward was mending slowly, and he was still very weak, but he had Jim Dasher and his grandfather to advise him, as well as other committed nobles like the Dukes of Bas-Tyra and Silden.

Hal and his brothers were shown to quarters surprisingly close to the royal apartment and rested there before taking a quiet supper, just the three of them together. They spoke little, as the enormity of what they had endured since the Keshian invasion of Crydee was now finally settling in, and suddenly the question of what was next loomed.

"I don't think I've ever been this tired," said Hal.

Martin nodded, looking distracted.

Brendan grinned. "He's waiting for Bethany to arrive, along with our mothers."

Hal grinned. "Miss her?"

"Like my left arm," said Martin. "I still don't know how her mother took the news."

Hal laughed and leaned his chair back. "It doesn't matter. Your liege lord has given permission."

Martin winced. "She may be your vassal's wife, Hal, but she's going to be my mother-in-law."

Brendan laughed. "Have a baby soon. That always makes them happy, being a grandmother."

Martin grinned. "I'll keep that in mind."

"We've got a busy day tomorrow," said Hal. "You know we have to be there."

Neither brother looked happy with that fact. "We know," said Martin.

"It's just a formality," said Brendan.

"But an important one," said Hal. "This is the longest we've had without a king and our second civil war since the founding of the Kingdom. We need to show our support for Edward. Even shirttail cousins like us have to be clearly behind the new King."

"There are no other claimants for the Crown—unless Montgomery has developed ambitions?" said Martin.

Hal shook his head.

"Then at least the ceremony will be relatively short."

"Or so Jim Dasher assured me," replied Hal.

Brendan stood up, suppressing a yawn. "When did you see a temple ceremony that was short? I'm for bed."

"Me, too," said Martin.

Both brothers bade Hal a good night and left. He called for servants to clear away the plates and cups, and went to his bedchamber. He walked to the window, where a pale large moon was rising, the little moon already high in the sky, and saw the ships at anchor in the bay of Rillanon. He felt so different from when he had last seen that vista, as he prepared to play his part in the war.

He sighed and decided to turn in. The war might be over, but his service to the Crown would go on for years to come. Martin and Bethany would wed as soon as they could, perhaps in the next few weeks, given the chaos on the Far Coast and her father arriving for the meeting of the Congress. Brendan? Hal smiled. His youngest brother would probably become Ty Hawkins's comrade-in-arms, carousing in every tavern, inn, gaming house, and brothel in the Sea of Kingdoms before he settled down.

Hal stared out at the few lights aboard ships in the harbor and couldn't keep his thoughts from speeding across the sea to Roldem, where . . . He let the thought drift away. His future was to serve the nation, and being with the woman he loved would not be part of that, so he tried to turn his mind away from the most beautiful face he had ever beheld to a meeting of critical importance on the morrow.

Sleep was very slow in coming.

The Congress of Lords was subdued and there was simmering anger below the surface. Some of those within the chamber had been opposing one another on the battlefield just a short tinge earlier, or had been bitter political rivals before that. The leaders who supported Oliver were either dead or in prison, but many of their vassals had received a blanket pardon from Edward, as they were only obeying their lawful masters.

Yet all here bowed to the inevitable: they were here to see a king crowned. Three young men stood ready to advance their claim to the throne, by right of blood, though all three would defer to the man who reclined in a veritable sea of cushions nearby. Edward's color looked better to Hal, though he still appeared very weak. He sat back patiently in a sedan chair that had been carried in.

All four wore the red mantles of the Princes of the Kingdom, though Hal felt self-conscious in his. Martin seemed indifferent, only having eyes for Bethany, who stood in the gallery with other minor noble families; while Brendan positively preened in his. Hal whispered to his youngest brother, "No, you can't wear it to impress the tavern girls in the city."

Brendan's mouth opened and he said, "How did you—"

Gongs rang and Ishapian High Priests entered the hall. The ancient vaulted room was used only for formal meetings between the King and the Congress, and to crown a new monarch. It reeked of history. Following the Ishapians were sixteen priests, each from one of the four greater and twelve lesser orders. Hal noticed that some of them were very young and nervous, and began to wonder just how much truth there was in the rumors that a large number of priests had been killed by some as-yet-unrevealed cataclysm.

The sound of large bolts being thrown to lock up the side doors, as was traditional, echoed through the hall, and a sense of solemnity settled over the proceedings. An Ishapian closed the last door into the hall and affixed a wax seal to it, and Hal wondered whether it was a magic seal as the old tales told, meaning no one could break it save the priest until a king was crowned.

The most senior Ishapian came to stand before the throne,

facing the four claimants to the throne. He struck his staff on the floor, evenly sixteen times, one for each of the gods, and then intoned, "We come to crown the King!"

"Ishap bless the King," said the other priests.

"In the name of Ishap, the one god over all, and in the name of the four greater and twelve lesser gods, let all who have claim to the crown come forth!"

Four guards picked up Edward's sedan chair and carried him forward two steps, while the three brothers moved as one.

The Ishapian came to stand before Brendan. "Now is the hour and here is the place." He touched Brendan on the shoulder with his staff. "By what right do you come before us?"

Brendan felt a sudden compulsion and realized the staff possessed magic preventing him from speaking anything but the truth. As he had been coached, he answered, "By right of birth."

The priest repeated the question to the other three, then returned to stand before Brendan. "State your name and your claim," he said.

Brendan replied, "I am Brendan conDoin, son of Henry, of the royal blood," as he had been instructed.

Then the priest moved before Martin and repeated the question.

Martin answered, "I am Martin conDoin, son of Henry, of the royal blood."

Another step to the right and he stood before Hal. He repeated the question a third time.

Hal answered, "I am Henry conDoin, son of Henry, of the royal blood," and there was a slight murmur in the hall.

The priest came before Edward, who sat up as well as he could, placed the staff on his shoulder, and asked, "State your name and your claim."

Edward said, "I am Edward, Prince of Krondor, and I make no claim."

The room erupted.

The priest slammed the iron-shod staff on the floor several times to silence the crowd. "You make no claim?" he asked Edward.

"My mother was of the royal blood. I have a lesser claim."

The High Priest of Ishap seemed uncertain of what he was hearing. Tradition dictated that only men with claims come forward, and he had no idea what to say. He almost sputtered, then asked, "Do you not press that claim, Prince of Krondor?"

There was a momentary silence, and Prince Edward said, "No, I do not." He motioned to Charles of Bas-Tyra, who came forward and handed a scroll to the priest. "I had the Duke witness this before I was injured, in case I did not survive to see this day. I renounce my claim as heir. Moreover, as I have no male issue, I have named Henry conDoin, second of that name, as my heir. I could be no more certain of his worth as holder of the Crown if I had the honor to be his father and he my son."

Again the room was alive with low voices, questions and accusations, assertions and denials. The iron heel of the staff struck the stones. The priest looked from face to face and said, "As the heir has renounced his claim, and it was witnessed and here affirmed, so be it."

The High Priest of Ishap motioned for another priest to bring him the cushion upon which rested the ancient Crown of the Isles. "Now is the hour and here is the place. We are here to witness the coronation of His Majesty, Henry, fifth of that name, as our true King. Is there any here who challenge his right?" Several lords looked dour, but all those who would have been violently opposed were either dead or in chains. He spoke to Hal. "Will you, Henry, take up this burden and be our King?"

Hal stood speechless. For a long moment he tried to understand what was happening. The Duke of Bas-Tyra whispered, "Say yes, Hal, before we start another civil war!"

Hal looked at Martin, who was nodding encouragingly, then to Brendan, who seemed caught halfway between shock and elation; Hal then saw an emphatic "yes" mouthed by Lady Bethany. Behind them, almost in the shadows, stood Jim Dasher speaking quietly with Ty Hawkins, and both gave him a quick nod. Hal took a deep breath and swallowed hard, then said, "I will be your King."

There was a lull and then the room was filled with voices, a few at first, then rising quickly as even those who had been in opposition to Edward realized that a great danger had been averted and that peace was restored.

A priest of Sung approached and motioned to two others, who took Hal's red mantle from his shoulders, replacing it with the purple mantle of kingship. The simple, ancient gold circlet was placed on Hal's brow.

The priest intoned, "Now is the hour and here is the place. Do you, Henry conDoin, son of Henry, of the line of kings, swear to defend and protect the Kingdom of the Isles, faithfully serving her people, to provide for their welfare, weal, and prosperity?"

"I, Henry, do so swear and avow."

The High Priest led Henry to the throne, where he sat down. Then the priest knelt and took Henry's hand in his, kissing his ducal signet, which would be replaced with a king's, and then rose. An ancient sword, traditionally held to have once belonged to Dannis, the first conDoin King, was brought out and placed across Henry's knees.

"Now it is past, the hour of our choosing," said the old priest. "I hereby proclaim Henry, fifth of that name, our right, true, and undisputed king!"

The crowd responded with "Hail Henry! Long live the King!"

The priests of Ishap began a chant, the wax seal was broken, and all in the Congress came and bowed before their new monarch. Hal was so overcome he barely had enough wit to motion Martin and Brendan to come stand beside him. When, at last, Prince Edward was carried up, Hal left the throne and came to him, extending his ring hand so Edward wouldn't have to attempt to mount the dais to the throne.

"Why?" asked Hal.

Edward smiled. "As I said, I hope you forgive me. Why? Because it was the only choice, my king. An ancient and honorable line is again reborn and takes its rightful place ruling our land. I could never have sons, but if had, I could not be more proud nor love them more than you, my king." Tears ran down Edward's face as he said, "I am your most loyal servant."

"You will stay with me," said Hal, his own eyes welling with tears, "and for years to come, I will count on your wisdom."

The Duke of Bas-Tyra came to stand next to Hal. "Majesty, before the gala begins tonight, we have some less pleasant duties. There are some nobles residing in less hospitable quarters here in the palace, notably Chadwick of Ran."

Hal said, "Keep him comfortable, and when Oliver's ransom arrives, toss Chad in as a gift. He can go live with Oliver in Maladon. He's banished from the Kingdom on pain of death. The others we'll review tomorrow. I'll hear their pleas one at a time. Those who swear fealty may retain their rank and holdings. Those who will not are free to follow Oliver and Chadwick east."

Bas-Tyra nodded. "We'll talk on this more in the morning, Majesty. A few of them really need to be hanged." He bowed and departed.

Seemingly out of nowhere, servants appeared and old Duke James of Rillanon followed them. "That turned out better than I hoped," he said. Bowing, he said, "Majesty. Go rest and get ready. You will find tonight's gala is but the first of many to come over the years, and they can be as tedious as a high mass on a holy day."

Jim Dasher and the Lady Franciezka Sorboz were waiting in the King's private chambers when the three brothers arrived. Hal didn't wait for them to bow, but said, "Did you put this idea into Edward's head, Jim?"

Jim smiled. "On the contrary, Majesty. It was my idea to have Edward take the Crown, name you heir when no one was looking, then abdicate in a few years. His objection to that was health, obviously, but also that it would give the plotters time to reorganize and we might be looking at another war." Glancing at Lady Franciezka, he said, "In retrospect, his idea was better. Assuming you don't conspire to get yourself killed, Majesty, your political enemies will have to wait a very long time to try to seize the Crown."

Hal realized he was still wearing the traditional circlet and took it off, tossing it on a table, which almost caused a servant to faint in horror. The man scrambled to pick it up and put it back on its velvet cushion.

"Political enemies?" said Brendan in a dry tone. "You've come up in the world, brother."

"He gained them less than an hour ago," said Lady Franciezka. "And allies," she added. "Prince Albér of Roldem will act as his father's envoy to the Isles and will offer you Roldem's undying friendship before all at the gala tonight."

"Welcome news," said Martin. "From what I've seen and been told, we would have stood far less chance of victory without Roldem's aid."

Jim nodded. "I think we would have prevailed, but not as easily. Roldem's part in this gave us swifter victory and fewer dead."

Hal sat and realized everyone else was still standing. "Oh, sit down," he said with a wave of his hand. "This will take some getting used to."

Jim came over and put his hand on the new King's shoulder. "Sire, it will, but you have years ahead of you, and friends."

Lord James entered, walking slowly. He bowed as low as health permitted and gladly accepted a chair brought to him by a servant. "Now, before anything else, Majesty, we need to arrive at some decisions to be announced at the gala tonight." He smiled when he saw a tray of cups and a pitcher of wine arrive. He waited until Hal was offered the first and waved it off, then gladly took one. "You may wish to change your mind, Majesty."

"Lord James," said the newly crowned King. "When we're alone, call me Hal."

"That I will not do, Majesty," said the old noble. "From now on you are more than Henry conDoin of Crydee: you *are* the Kingdom of the Isles. When the Emperor of Great Kesh speaks to you, it is Kesh speaking to Isles." With a wag of his finger and a scolding tone, he added, "You cannot afford to forget you are no longer just one man, but the embodiment of a nation." The old Duke settled back in his chair. "Now, where was I? Oh, yes. The first order of business, sire, is that you need to accept my retirement. I'm abdicating my office. I'm too old for any more of this foolishness."

Hal realized that he was now the sole arbiter of some of the most critical matters of state. "I am sorry to hear that, my lord. Your counsel is most welcome."

James said, "Sire, I will not be dying for a few more weeks." He shrugged. "I may even manage to squeeze out a year or two more. But we need to make changes, and now, as the court is reeling from them already, a few more won't matter."

Hal looked at Jim Dasher.

The man of many titles and roles held up his hands. "I'm resigning too, Majesty, if you'll permit." He saw the look of confusion on Hal's face and said, "My role has not been compromised, but ended. I can no longer play the part of the minor Kingdom noble who holds office by dint of his grandfather's rank. After the disaster that was Sir William Alcorn and the like assaults on the royal houses in Kesh and Roldem, our entire intelligence apparatus needs rebuilding, from the top down."

Hal was silent for a moment, then said, "I assume you have a suitable replacement in mind?"

"Very much so, Majesty. We'll speak of this in private later, if you permit."

"What of you, then?" asked Hal.

"I intend to leave Rillanon and build a home on a tidy little island to the southwest of here." He looked at the Lady Franciezka.

She smiled. "My role is also at an end, Your Majesty. I will also be retiring and moving to . . . a new home."

Hal laughed. "Well, I expect if we lose your services—" He saw Duke James shake his head slightly and mouth the word "we."

Still laughing, Hal said, "We expect if we lose your services, it's a good thing you're both off on an island somewhere where you can do little damage." He looked at Lord James. "My lord, who then to replace you in Rillanon?"

"Earl Montgomery," said James. "He's an able administrator, one of your very distant cousins, and while he's no one's idea of a genius, he's very clever in his own way. Find someone to replace him as Earl of the city and you'll do well."

"I'll follow your advice . . . we'll follow your advice," said Hal. "Damn, that's going to take some getting used to."

"Krondor," said James. "You need a strong hand in Krondor."

Without hesitation Hal said, "Martin. There can be no other. He's as strong and smart and honorable a man as a brother could wish for, and he will be our rock in the West. He will also be next in line for the throne until I wed and have a son."

Brendan grinned as Martin looked surprised. "I expect this means Countess Marriann will get over Beth not marrying a duke." He turned and saw Hal staring at him. "What?" His grin faded. "I mean, what, Your Majesty?"

"You are my new Earl of Rillanon."

"Why, Majesty? There are many others . . ."

Hal held up his hand. "We need to keep you close. You were enough trouble being a duke's brat. The King's brother? I need you on a short leash. Besides, underneath that boyish manner and carefree attitude, you hide a practical mind and solid resolve. I'll need both."

Brendan didn't look pleased, but the others smiled. Jim Dasher said, "I have a list of names, Majesty, of people who deserve some special acknowledgment for their roles in the late war. We'll go over it later, but there are a few empty offices to fill and these names should be given special consideration." While others had rested after returning from the battle at the Fields of Albalyn, Jim had read reports long into the night and had made copious notes and a list of recommendations for Hal. A Captain du Gale of Silden, and a Sergeant Cribs from Salador, as well as others Jim had met in his travels during the war or read about in reports would discover that their names were on that list. Du Gale didn't know it yet but he was about to become the new Duke of Salador and Cribs the Knight-Marshal of the city. Both had been summoned to Rillanon and now waited in quarters in the city to be called to the palace.

Hal said, "Make sure the Earl of LaMut's name is there, as well. He's a unique man."

"It will be done, Majesty."

Lord James said, "Let us depart with His Majesty's permission, and let the lad rest."

Hal waved permission and pointed to his brothers. "Stay."

The others filed out, and at the last, Hal waved Jim Dasher over. "Another name: Tyrone Hawkins."

Martin said, "I haven't seen Ty since we got here, save for the ceremony when he was hiding in the corner with you."

Jim smiled. "His name is the first on the list, Majesty."

"Your replacement?" said Hal. Jim nodded. "Of course." He laughed. "I would never have guessed."

"That was the idea, Majesty," said Jim. "I've groomed him for years. If you had guessed, I didn't train him well enough."

"Does his father know?"

Jim shook his head. "I think Tal suspects, but he doesn't know. Both Hawkinses are good men, but they are servants of the Conclave as much as of the Kingdom of the Isles and Roldem. Ty will put the Crown's needs foremost. Tal's loyalties are more divided: the Conclave saved his life as a boy."

"So where is Ty now?"

"In my quarters, finishing some reports I couldn't get to,

and adding his own recommendations to that list, but he'll be dressed and ready in time for you to name him Baron of the King's Court at tonight's gala in reward for his services to the Crown. More rank than that will draw notice, but because he's not landed, he can move around easily at need."

"You've been planning this for a while?"

"It's the nature of the craft, Majesty." Jim Dasher grinned. "Ty is picking out his successor and will start the process of grooming him very soon. It's a necessity." He leaned over so that only Hal could hear. "When the time is right, Ty will tell you all you need to know. And there will be things that only you and he can know, Majesty."

Jim turned to Martin. "I don't envy you, Highness. Reports are starting to trickle in. The West is in shambles. Something on an unimaginable scale has occurred east of your old home. When I know more, I will of course make a full report. But you may discover Yabon and Crydee are not what they were before."

Brendan said, "We really should send someone home to look at what's going on, Hal."

"We will," said the King. "Now, is there anything else I need to know before I try to get some rest?"

"Just a hundred other appointments, a few state marriages to arrange, and some execution warrants to sign, but they can wait until later."

Jim bowed and as he turned to the door, Hal said, "Lady Franciezka? Are you to wed?"

Jim smiled and it was as genuine an expression of pleasure as Hal had ever seen from him. "I don't think I have a choice, do I?" He bowed and left the room.

A knock came at the door and Brendan looked from face to face, then said, "All right, I'll get it." Martin and Hal both laughed.

Brendan opened the door and his mother came into the room and embraced him. The Duchess Caralin could barely contain her tears of joy. Ignoring rank and formality, she hugged her boys as she found them, Martin after Brendan.

Hal embraced her and said, "Mother, why didn't you come straightaway?"

"I was told you were involved with matters of state . . . Your Majesty."

"You never wait for anyone when you need to see me, Mother."

Brendan stuck his head out the door and called, "More wine for the King!" not bothering to notice which servant hurried off. He closed it and smiled, saying, "This business of being the King's brother has some advantages."

The gala was festive, as the master of ceremonies had spent months planning it, due to the long delay in crowning a new king. Hal endured the obeisance of everyone who attended, spending hours watching people he barely knew kneel before him and pledge their love and devotion.

When at last the formal part of the evening was over, he rose and read from a proclamation prepared by Jim, pardoning a few nobles he barely knew, pronouncing an end to further enmity, and promising to be a wise and just ruler.

Prince Albér of Roldem had been presented earlier as envoy of his father, King Carole, and he spoke for a moment to Martin, who nodded and mounted the three steps of the dais and whispered, "Hal, Albér just said the oddest thing."

"What?" said King Henry, the fifth of that name.

"He said his mother said to tell you, 'Ask again.'"

Hal sat back, and tried his best to keep from grinning like a fool.

EPILOGUE

CRYDEE

The storm had passed.

The man in the black robes and slouch hat leaned on his staff and watched as the boy moved nimbly among the rocks, stopping to scoop up crabs, rock claws, and other shellfish that had been swept into the tide pools by the storm that had passed earlier in the day. He was a smallish boy with black hair and suntanned skin, dressed in homespun shorts and a tunic.

The man walked toward the boy slowly so as not to startle him by coming out of the trees unexpectedly. The boy popped a particularly large crab into his sack and looked up. Seeing the stranger, he smiled and nodded. He had dark eyes and ordinary features, though his manner made him appear engaging. "Hello!" he shouted brightly.

The man in black smiled in return, brushing his long white hair aside. "Fetching in dinner?"

"That I am, sir. The storm always drives an abundance into the pools, and today is my day to fetch out as much as I can carry so we can have a hot chowder tonight." The boy's manner was bright and easy and he seemed genuinely cheerful.

"I wandered in the woods during the storm," said the tall man as he leaned on his old walking stick. "Where exactly am I?"

The boy laughed, a joyous noise. "You are in Crydee, sir. How can you not know?"

The man smiled. "I expected I was in Crydee, but where in Crydee?"

"Oh," said the boy. "A few miles to the south of the town and the keep. I'll walk there with you."

"That would be welcome."

They started up the path leading to the road and the tall man said, "I am called Magnus."

The boy cocked his head for a moment. "That is an unusual name, sir, if you don't mind me saying. I am named Phillip."

"A pleasure, Phillip," said Magnus. As they walked to the road and turned north, he asked, "Who rules here?"

"Why King Henry and Queen Stephané, sir. King Henry was Duke of Crydee before he took the Crown in far-off Rillanon, as was his father before him. The reeve rules the castle for him, and the Baron of Carse is his Knight-Marshal in the West."

"So, no Duke of Crydee."

The boy shrugged. "The King still holds the title, sir, but

you can better ask the reeve." Then his expression brightened. "Or you can ask my father. He knows everything."

"Your father?"

"My father is the keep's cook," said the boy.

"So, you're an apprentice to the castle's cook?"

"Not really," said the boy. "I have another month before the Choosing. The truth is, I'm not a very good cook."

"What do you dream of, boy?"

The boy laughed aloud. "I dream of many things, sir. I dream of far-off lands, and places I will never see. I wonder what is beyond the stars, and I wish I knew more about . . . everything!" He laughed again.

"You do like to laugh," observed Magnus.

"Truth to tell, my mother claims I was born laughing. Everyone says that I enjoy things more than others." His face was alight. "And why wouldn't I? I have a family and a home and I eat well," he said, hefting the bag of crustaceans. "I would like to travel, but we can't have all we wish, can we?"

"You might be surprised," said Magnus as they crested a small rise in the road and the town and keep came into view. "Have you thought of apprenticing as something other than in the kitchen?"

"I have little aptitude for anything. I'm clumsy when it comes to working the boats, and have little gift for weapons. I'm too small to work the forge, and . . . well, the only thing I'm good at is reading."

"You read?"

"Everything! Father Ignatius taught me. There's a tower in the keep, full of books, and I've read them all."

Magnus paused. "Do you understand them?"

"Almost," said Phillip. "Some of the time I feel like I almost know what things mean. Some of the books are about other places, histories, and geography, but others are about how things work. I wish I understood those better."

"Perhaps if Father Ignatius doesn't object, I might look at those books and lend you a hand?"

"I think that would be all right, sir," said the boy as they trudged along the muddy road leading to Crydee town. "Have you been here before, sir?"

"Many years ago," said Magnus. "Many, many years ago."

"Crydee is hard to get to now," said Phillip, showing off his knowledge of things. "You have to come by ship now, through the Straits of Darkness. It used to be there was a highway from Crydee to Ylith, in the Duchy of Yabon, but that's no longer there."

"Why is that?" asked Magnus as they neared the edge of the town.

"No one is sure, but apparently something terrible happened there before I was born. A massive change, and . . . well, to be truthful, as strange as it sounds, to the east once rose mountains."

The forest blocked out any vista to the east, but no mountains rose up behind it. Magnus said, "What happened?"

"No one is certain. A great magic, they say." The boy shrugged. "Now there's only a giant pit, below a promontory. My father took me there once, and I got to stand on the rocks and look down into the crater. People call it the Sunken Lands, that crater."

"Interesting," said Magnus.

"The rocks have a very odd name, too."

"What would that be?"

"They call the rocks Magician's End."

Magnus closed his eyes for a moment. Then he said, "Indeed, that is an odd name." He paused, then asked, "Have you considered apprenticing as a magician?"

The boy laughed aloud, sounding delighted at the idea. "Can you do that?"

"We'll see," said Magnus as they reached the edge of the town. "I am something of a magician, or so others have claimed, and I am in need of an apprentice, Phillip."

"Oh, no one calls me Phillip," said the boy. "Though it is my name and my mother said it was important to introduce myself that way."

"Well, what do they call you, then?"

"Everyone in the town calls me Pug, sir."

Magnus stopped and put his hand on the boy's shoulder. "Why?"

"I don't know exactly, sir. It was just one of those things that happens. Someone called me that and it stuck." He seemed pleased to tell the story.

"You seem a happy lad," said Magnus.

"Mother says I am the happiest boy she has ever seen." He lost his grin and said, "Were you serious about being a magician, sir?"

Magnus nodded and they walked on in silence.

As they entered the town Magnus looked around and said, "So much has changed." Then he looked down at the boy beside him. "Yet some things are very familiar." He patted Pug's shoulder. "Let us go meet your father, and the reeve, and Father Ignatius, and when it's time, you and I will sit and discuss the subject of magic. You may have some knack for it."

Magnus knew for certain that would prove to be the case.